Also by Laurie Rawlinson Evans

The Mountain Shadows Series:

The Black Spirit

Beyond the Veil

LEGACY

OF THE

BOW

The Third Mountain Shadows Novel

LAURIE RAWLINSON EVANS

Published by:
Laurie E. Rawlinson

ISBN: 978-0-9993933-3-8 (sc)
ISBN: 978-0-9993933-4-5 (hc)
ISBN: 978-0-9993933-5-2 (e)

Lulu Publishing Services rev. date: 12/22/2020

Dedication

In appreciation for the warriors and the peace-keepers,

Those who serve and protect their country and people,

With Honor

Acknowledgments

I've come to the end of the Mountain Shadows trilogy, and Lulu Publishing Services has been a vital part of making my goal of publishing this fantasy saga a reality. My deepest appreciation to the people who have contributed to producing the three beautiful books I now call my own.

Thanks also to my friend and photographer, the talented and very patient Cathy Whitney. She traveled through snow and fire on *Legacy of the Bow* with smiles and laughter.

This epic journey has fulfilled a lifelong dream, but it gave me more than just the abiding thrill of seeing my own work in print. Along the way, I gained the quiet satisfaction of becoming a serious writer, learning and growing in ways I'd never anticipated. One of the most important lessons I learned was the pleasure found in the company of other writers, and as an active member of a writers group.

The Town Square Writers have shared years of fellowship and education across diverse genres. Many provided valuable input along the way, but I'd especially like to acknowledge the following members for their time and editorial support: Lauren Filarsky, Betty Lucke, Syl and Don Bestwick, Sierra Janisse, Kelly Hess, Peggy Lucke, and Scotti Butler.

Deepest thanks to those who agreed to Beta read the final manuscript, providing insightful comments and final polish: Sierra Janisse, Lauren Filarsky, Linda Brown Quimby, Syl Bestwick, Don Bestwick, and Linda Romine.

And, as always, my love and appreciation to my husband and sons, Terry, Colin, and Davis Evans for letting me be who I am without complaint. Thanks for the support, and maybe a little pride.

The Bow Brand: Design conceived by the author and computer designed by Colin Evans. The Custom Brand Shop made the branding iron.

Photographer: Catherine L. Whitney, Author and Cover photographs

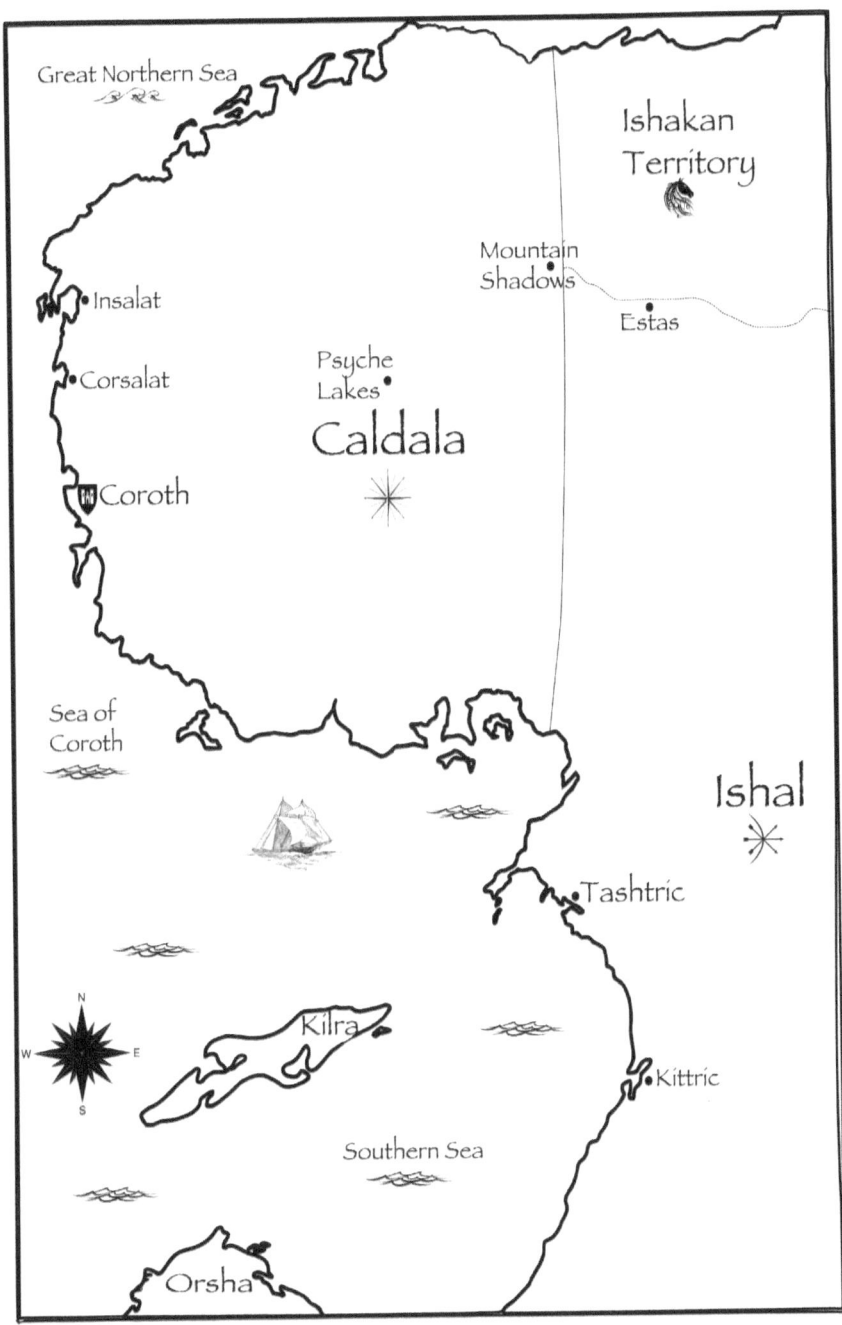

Great Northern Sea

Ishakan
Territory

Mountain
Shadows

Estas

Insalat

Corsalat

Psyche
Lakes

Caldala

Coroth

Sea of
Coroth

Ishal

Tashtric

Kilra

N
W   E
S

Kittric

Southern Sea

Orsha

The Prince's Agent

City of Coroth, Caldala, In the Year PA 4184

Logran, Prince of Coroth, looked up from his desk when his secretary came in.

"Captain Isfail is here, sir." She stepped aside for him to enter, shutting the door as she left.

Closing the distance with a broad smile of welcome, Logran clasped his cousin's outstretched arm. "It's good to see you!"

With a grin, Captain Ardan Isfail ran a hand through dark, wet hair. "Hell of a night to call me out. Couldn't you let me take a breath after we broke that pirate slaving operation for you?"

"Take off that wet cloak. I'll get you a whiskey." The prince poured two glasses. But when he turned back, Isfail still stood as he'd entered. "You did good work. Has Ambassador Muro returned to Ambassador Central?"

"No. Your princess needed her healing skills here, in the kitchens. One of the cooks seems to have burned themselves badly."

"I'd like to talk to both of you about the situation in Ishal."

Isfail shook his head, saying, "Another mission? So soon?"

"More in an advisory capacity," Logran assured him, handing him his drink. "While you were hunting pirates, I received a report from Akato Iro, Caldala's minister to Ishal, advising us that a group of rebels is gaining support in Ishal. Rumors of civil war are spreading through the trade routes." He shook his head, disturbed by this development. "I'll be meeting with the Caldalan

1

Parliament to discuss plans for fortifying our borders. We'll also need to be prepared should Ishal call for help."

Logran rang for his secretary, sending her to find Ambassador Muro. He leaned back against his desk, his brow furrowed in concentration. "It's rumored that Arthon Baronan is behind Ishal's rebellion. The Ambassador Core likely has useful information on him. I know they've sent people in to track him over the years."

Snorting in disgust, Isfail finally shrugged out of his damp cloak, tossing it over the back of a chair. "To what purpose? Ishal granted him sanctuary, despite his murderous crimes in our country."

"We're all frustrated by their decision, Dan."

"You didn't see firsthand what he left behind at Baronan Keep."

Hearing the old rage in his cousin's voice, the prince nodded, gripping Isfail's shoulder. "That's true. It doesn't mean we didn't do all we could to find Baronan and prosecute him. And that gave us more insight into Akira Muro."

Isfail turned to glance at the door. "I don't like going behind her back anymore. We've watched her long enough . . . far too long to my mind. She should be told," he insisted. "It's only her sense of honor that's kept her from finding out."

Logran frowned, looking away into the fire. "Can she be trusted?" Turning back to study the man who was not only family, but his most trusted covert agent, he picked up a decanter. "I need to know that Akira Muro will stand with the government. Even over the Ambassador Core. Karsh is testing her own strength, pressing the bounds of her position."

"Why do you allow her such power? It's obvious Most High Karsh cannot be trusted, yet you've placed Akira with me on several missions over the past eight years to determine her loyalties. The results speak for themselves. Akira Muro is beyond gifted, dedicated to Caldala, and loyal to the principality." Isfail held out his glass for the offered refill.

As he replaced the decanter and settled into a deep-cushioned chair, Logran gave a weary smile. "Karsh was elected by lawful vote. I can't subvert the laws and regulations without risking anarchy or civil war. You know that. Ana Karsh is a very powerful force caller and leads the Ambassador Core. Over time it has become clear that she's a potential problem for the House of Coroth. I can't afford to misjudge another ambassador."

"Akira is more powerful, and she serves Caldala and Coroth," Isfail insisted. He paced to the window and back again. "I don't like deceiving her. I'm asking your permission to tell her what I am."

Leaning back, Logran watched his restless movements with sudden humor. "Have you a more personal interest in the elusive ambassador, Cousin?"

Bracing his hands on the mantel, as if he'd find an answer in the flames he stared down into, Isfail seemed to consider his response. "And if I do?" He turned to face the surprise on Logran's face.

Bemused by this response to his teasing, Logran found himself at a loss for words. This was something he hadn't expected given his cousin's carefree enjoyment of women in general. And this woman was an ambassador!

Isfail chuckled, apparently amused at finding his royal cousin speechless.

"Damn it, Dan." Logran scowled. "You and your jokes."

"It's not a joke. Not to me," Isfail countered soberly. "I plan to court her when her contract's up. It doesn't change my loyalty to you."

Anger flashed in Logran's eyes. "I'd never think that." Then he sighed. "You're the best agent . . . the best friend I have, Dan. I depend on your counsel. I need you at my back."

Isfail walked over to lay his hands on his cousin's shoulders. "Always, my prince."

When both settled in chairs beside the fire, Isfail asked, impatiently now, "Why not tell her? How much more proof can you need? Damn it."

The low oath from his companion made Logran smile. He

nodded to the frustration in Isfail's glance. "We'll speak with her together."

*I*t didn't go as Isfail hoped.

He knew Akira Muro well enough to see beyond the cool, contained demeanor emanating from the silk-masked face the reticent ambassador showed the world. It was pure truth that he planned to court her and win her love once her twenty-year contract with the Ambassador Core was fulfilled. Isfail believed the friendship that had grown during the many missions they'd served together held hope of something richer, and more intimate.

He knew she'd been deeply hurt as a young girl, but over time they'd found a level of trust and companionship that he cherished. Isfail had believed Akira felt that too.

Until tonight—the night that Logran, Prince of Coroth, told Ambassador Akira Muro the deeper purpose of those missions, and explained his relationship to Militia Captain Ardan Isfail.

The consummate diplomat, the self-contained woman listened, then asked intelligent questions to ensure that she understood the details. She showed no sign of emotion upon learning of the underlying agenda—that Isfail had essentially been spying on her, testing her loyalties, in addition to using her unique abilities to resolve the varied missions assigned to them.

After the conversation concluded, the men stood when Akira nodded her understanding and asked to be excused, saying she needed to return to Ambassador Central.

"I'm pleased to have this delicate situation resolved," Logran said, taking her hands in both of his. "I hope you are not offended by the caution of the House of Coroth."

He glanced at Isfail's unreadable face. "My cousin is invaluable to me, both as independent agent and best friend. There's no one I trust more than Ardan." Logran turned his attention back to the masked woman. "He believed in your loyalty almost from the beginning."

Akira withdrew her hands and bowed—very stiffly. "Of

course, my prince. After so many years of . . . observation . . . may I assume that such missions are no longer necessary?"

Dipping his head briefly to the icily polite query, Logran replied, "I feel secure in your loyalties, Ambassador Muro, and appreciate the exemplary service you've given in helping resolve so many complex missions."

He accepted her wishes for a good evening and good health, giving a discreet signal for Isfail to escort her out.

The prince watched them leave, standing in the chill left behind that had nothing to do with the cold rain pattering against the window panes.

There was silence between them as the captain and the ambassador walked through the wide halls of the palace. Before they reached the doors to the outer courtyard, Isfail took her arm firmly and guided her into an empty sitting room.

"All right. We're going to talk this through," he ordered, turning her to face him and slipping off the black silk mask she wore.

Her eyes, guarded at the best of times, were closed to him now. The dark emerald gaze was devoid of feeling.

"Damn it, Akira. Talk to me!"

"What is there to say, Captain?"

He cursed at the emotionless response. Dragging a hand through his hair, Isfail stalked to a window and back again.

She stood very still, watching his agitated pacing. If she moved, Akira felt she might break. She'd forgotten how easily a heart could be betrayed. Everything she'd begun to believe about him, the trust, the hope that he could truly love her . . . It was all a lie.

Frozen in place, as cold as the sleet striking glass, Akira said nothing as he stalked back to her.

"What must I do to prove myself to you?" Isfail exclaimed, gripping her shoulders. "I love you!"

The words she wanted so badly only broke against the shields erected years before. Akira looked up into his stormy eyes. "You have nothing to prove, Captain Isfail. The situation is clear. The power of an ambassador can be a fearsome thing. I accept the caution of the House of Coroth in choosing to make me prove myself."

"But you don't accept *my* part in this, or forgive me for not revealing my role sooner."

Saying nothing, she turned to leave, pulling the mask back on. Akira felt him grab her once more. This time she sent a force jolt into his arm.

"Damn it!" Isfail swore, rubbing his forearm. "Will you just walk away from me now, away from my feelings for you?"

Pausing with a hand on the door latch, Akira tried to ignore the plea in his voice as she said quietly, "It was only an illusion, Captain. Now there is only reality. Goodbye."

Nine lunams after that stormy night, Isfail was back in the palace to discuss state concerns. He stood, silent, as he listened to Logran's news.

"We've just received word that rebels have taken over Ishal's Parliament. We don't know the status of the lawful government or of any foreign dignitaries based there."

"Minister Iro and his daughter?" Isfail asked in concern, knowing Caldala's representative to the neighboring country. And he knew Akira would worry over the fate of the minister's daughter, Alani, who had been a private student of Akira before accompanying her father on his assignment to Ishal.

"There's been no word yet. There are rumors that some of the ministers escaped." The prince shook his head, clearly annoyed by the lack of solid information. "Loyalists in Ishal have asked for help."

Isfail nodded, a hand fisted on the hilt of the short sword at his side.

"Commander Davon Gattes out of Corsalat will assemble a volunteer militia," Logran continued, missing the intent look from his cousin while he studied the mission reports on his desk. "I'd like you to apprise the Insalat Militia and spread word through your region for volunteers with experience."

"Aye, my prince."

Logran looked up with a frown at the terse response. "What?" He studied Isfail's lean face and finally noticed the difference in his cousin. There was no humor in the set of his mouth, no amusement in smoky gray eyes. The man looked honed down, fit to the extreme.

"Ambassador Muro?" Logran wondered as he straightened, leaning back in his chair.

Shrugging wide shoulders, Isfail only said, "You would know more than I. We haven't spoken since we all met together some lunams ago."

"I see." He did see, Logran thought, regretting the rift that he'd caused between his cousin and the woman Isfail cared for. But there was little he could do to bridge that gap now. "Dan—"

"If that's all, I'm going to get back to Insalat and start recruiting." At his cousin's nod, Isfail strode out, plans of his own already forming in his mind.

Kittric Harbor, Ishal, PA 4185

*T*he traitorous moons sailed in and out of clouds. Moonlight and shadows slid over blood-spattered walls, and the bodies of soldiers whose time in this world had ended. Still, there were those who continued to fight over cobbled dockyards slick with gore.

For the men and women of Gattes Militia, sent from their own country of Caldala to help neighboring Ishal put down violent insurrection, the lack of useful intelligence about the enemy had proven disastrous. Faced with far greater numbers of well-armed rebels than the Ishalian Parliament had reported, a hundred warriors under Militia Commander Davon Gattes engaged in a fierce battle to hold the vital shipping harbor of Kittric for the lawful government.

After two days battling the odds, Gattes and most of his command were dead. With no hope of relief, and no will to surrender, Captain Liden Amsha took command of the survivors behind the stone fortification of the harbormaster's tower. In the first hours of the third day, exhausted, barely able to stand, she fought back-to-back with fellow captain Ardan Isfail. Thick fog rolled in, bringing welcome cover to foil the enemy archers' aim. Giving in to injury and staggering fatigue, they slumped down.

Amsha felt her companion list to one side. "Isfail?"

There was no response.

She anticipated her own death as those few still alive huddled together to meet their fate. As they waited for a final assault, the night grew still. There was no sound of movement outside the battered walls. The voices that had called for them to surrender ceased abruptly. Now the night took on an unnatural silence that brought the militia survivors little relief.

Then a quiet voice sounded close by. "Ambassador Core Commander Muro here. Who is in charge?"

"Here," Amsha croaked, pushing to her feet. "Captain Amsha, Gattes Militia, out of Corsalat." She raised a hand against dim light when several dark lanterns flared as their side panels were lifted.

With moans and mutters of relief, those still conscious looked around at the ten black-masked ambassadors ranged in a protective perimeter around them.

One walked to the captain, taking the offered arm in a tight grip. "I'm Commander Muro. We'll get you out of here."

"Thank God," Amsha murmured, working up a weak smile that died quickly as she surveyed her battered troops. "Ah damn . . ." Stiffening her spine, she ordered, "Sound off."

Fourteen answered, some speaking for those who still breathed but were unconscious.

Signaling to her ambassador team, Muro left some on guard, sent others checking for the living among the too many dead, and the rest to triage the injured. Without a word, she knelt beside the man at her feet.

"Captain Isfail, from Insalat. Joined us just before we sailed," Amsha offered as another ambassador tended her more serious injuries. "Good man. Excellent swordsman." Her voice faltered as she saw the number of arrows piercing him.

Shaken by the shock of finding him here, Muro only nodded as she quickly scanned the damage—relieved when her trembling fingers found a weak pulse. He'd taken seven arrows and lost too much blood, but he was alive. Akira stroked back his blood-streaked hair, consoled by that fact.

"You are not going to die this way, Ardan," she whispered, working fast to stop the bleeding.

"Commander."

Muro glanced up at the masked man. "How many?"

"Twenty-seven living," Ambassador Garan replied and nodded toward the man she worked on. "Most serious. We'll need to carry them. The other healers are finishing what can be done here."

"Is the area secured?"

"We're clear for now. The moons are down, with dense fog for cover. There's a passage to the docks at the back. Vaneer is sending his boats."

Garan waited, wincing when Muro removed a broken arrow with a deft tug. Her bloodstained hand covered the wound and rippling green flames flowed up to her wrist as she healed torn flesh.

"Start moving the injured to the ship," Muro ordered quietly. "Take those who can walk first. Leave Arith and Coran on watch."

Crouching beside her, Amsha observed with some awe. "Will he live?"

"He's too stubborn to die," Muro muttered.

She continued to work while a group of burly seamen came in, led by the captain's son Micah. The young Vaneer consulted with Garan before directing his men to carry the injured to waiting boats.

"Ambassador Muro."

Looking up again a short time later, she stood, directing two waiting ambassadors to move Isfail out. "Mister Vaneer."

"This load will get the last of the wounded. We'd like to bring back the dead."

Grateful for his compassion, Muro looked around at her ambassadors. "Start with those here, in the stockade. Work in teams that include an ambassador. My people will detect danger sooner and help protect your men. Check with me before moving out to the streets."

She assigned Garan to work with Vaneer before going to confer with her lookouts.

*T*he first thing Isfail noticed as he regained consciousness was the familiar motion of a ship. In the hazy in-between, he wondered if this was what death felt like. Then he opened his tired eyes to worried emerald ones framed by black silk, and knew he'd woken to heaven.

"Akira," Isfail breathed, twining his fingers with hers when she reached for him.

"Why?" she whispered. "You weren't part of the Gattes militia. You shouldn't be here. Dan, you almost . . ." Her eyes closed as she gripped his hand.

His fingers tightened over hers. "Would it have mattered?"

Akira's eyes flew open, flashing green fire even as tears welled. "Yes! It would have mattered to me." But her fury died in an overwhelming flood of emotions that she could not reveal when she saw the look on Isfail's face. Despite the pallor and the lines of pain, there was such hope, even happiness there.

Before she could stop them, her tears spilled over, and Akira bent to press a kiss to his forehead. "You're going back to Caldala, and you're going to stay there. Ishal is not your fight."

Despite his weakness, Isfail refused to release the hand she started to pull away. He could see her drawing back, fighting to control the feelings that he wanted so desperately. "Akira . . . why are you here?"

"Fate," she said ruefully, then stroked gentle fingers over his cheek. "The prince commanded a reconnaissance mission to assess the situation in Ishal, and extract Minister Iro and his daughter Alani if possible."

Looking thoughtful, Akira studied Isfail's face. "He didn't tell me you were part of the Gattes troops, but he did direct us to land at Kittric." Her smile was pensive now. "He cares very much for his cousin."

Isfail gave a faint smile. "Logran was furious when I told him I'd signed up with Gattes. I guess he got over it." With some difficulty, he shifted his head to look at his surroundings. The captain's cabin of a merchant ship, he guessed as he struggled to see in the dim light.

"Why did you, Dan?"

He looked back into her melancholy gaze. "I won't put that burden on you, Kira. I'm responsible for my choices. But I needed something, some action, to burn out the emptiness losing you left in me." Isfail squeezed her hand when she shook her head. "I love you, Akira. Maybe you can't return that—just accept my feelings, and give me what you can. You care very much for me, as well." Isfail tried a weak grin when she just stared at him.

"You need to rest," Akira said after a moment. "Let me check your wounds now."

Releasing her hand, Isfail fought to keep his eyes open as she folded back the covers to examine him. Her small hands were warm, her touch light and soothing as she released her healing forces. Before he knew it, Isfail fell asleep with a smile on his lips.

Hours slipped by as Akira sat by his bunk, holding his hand and thinking about what he'd said. She did care . . . more than she'd wanted to accept. And it was an impossible situation. There was only one way for her with more than a decade left on her contract with the Ambassador Core. Ardan Isfail would survive, and he would forget her over time.

Leaving one last kiss on his lips, Akira rose and silently left the cabin, her heart aching with every step.

Captain Amsha was seated at the small table in the cabin when Isfail woke. Sunlight beamed through the square windowpanes, and the motion told him that the ship was moving through the water under full sail.

"Where are we?"

With a broad smile, Amsha got up and walked over, taking his hand in a firm grip. "So you're awake at last! Thought you were lost for sure, Isfail. Those ambassadors saved our skins, without a doubt."

"Akira—Ambassador Muro?" Isfail amended. "Where is she?"

Sliding a speculative look at him while she went to retrieve a water flask, Amsha told him, "She had Captain Vaneer put them off at a rough cove just west of the capital city. Her team's gone on to collect information on the rebellion and the current state of Ishal's government."

She supported him while he drank then adjusted the thin pillows beneath his head. "Ambassador Muro left specific directions for your care, Isfail. And I'm to see that you obey them, and make sure you're taken straight to Coroth after we land."

"She's gone," he murmured, watching the shafts of sunlight falter as storm clouds gathered over the sea. "Again."

One

Tash'tric, Ishal, Harvest Season, PA 4198

Misty rain swirled around the two men standing at the rail of the quarterdeck. They watched closely as their trading ship, *Maid of Kilra*, was pulled into her dock slip. Beyond the low stone and wood warehouses along the wharf, the men could barely make out the gilded domes of the government buildings that rose above the capital city of the country of Ishal. Captain Mattoc Vaneer exchanged quick looks with his son, Micah.

"I don't like it," the elder Vaneer muttered, fixing his gaze on the burly men standing with the harbormaster as thick hawser lines were made fast.

"Are those uniforms? They never wore uniforms before," Micah said, drawing attention to the rough brown attire on every dockworker in sight. "Isn't that Saldor from Kittric? What's he doing here?" Even the familiar harbormaster now wore the same, distinguished only by two darker brown armbands on both sleeves. Two of the men with him had a single armband on their right sleeves.

"Maybe Saldor was promoted." His father said quietly, "Follow my lead, Micah. I aim to steer clear of the trouble brewing here in Ishal, and get us out with men and ship intact."

Micah frowned. "What about Commander Isfail? You promised we'd look—"

His eyes fierce, the captain gripped Micah's wrist in warning. "I don't forget him." He glanced around at his crew milling about in uncomfortable silence. "You warned the men to say nothing about the *Royal Sea Eagle*?"

"As you ordered, Captain," Micah replied stiffly.

"Good. Only you and I know what was said when we rowed over to them in the night." The elder Vaneer sighed over the frustration on his son's face. "Isfail's a friend, I know, Micah, and betrothed to our Lady Akira Muro. But we can't help find him if we come to trouble ourselves."

He felt some of the tension leave the young man's stance. Micah was a good son, a fine man, with head enough to see the sense in his father's words.

They both turned to make their way to the main deck as the narrow gangplank was prepared, waiting for the captain's orders before it was lowered to meet the quay.

Once again, Captain Vaneer wondered why Ishal's Parliament had closed access to Kittric harbor. Tash'tric was smaller than the more protected harbor of Kittric to the south. It seemed self-defeating. With limited resources, Ishal relied on trade with neighboring countries to provide goods to meet the needs and desires of its burgeoning populace.

His own ship's holds were filled with bolts of fabric, casks of spices, and fine furnishings. In their turn, Ishalian merchants would exchange a variety of grains, hardwoods, fine pottery, and clothing made from some of the imported fabric. More rarely there would be one or more of the world-renowned Ishakan horses bound for some discerning horseman in another country.

Such goods were easier to load and unload at the larger, better-equipped docks of Kittric. But, for the past couple of months, Kittric harbor had been blocked to all ships not flying the standard of Ishal. All foreign ships were directed to the smaller port of Tash'tric.

Pointless to question why, Captain Vaneer thought. Still, he didn't like the surly looks directed their way or, even more troubling, the frightened faces of some of the laborers assembling to off-load cargo. Stroking his neat beard thoughtfully, he signaled his men to set the gangplank.

Micah waited while his father stepped down the narrow planks with a seaman's sure stride. Alert to every move of the Ishalian men below, he watched the harbormaster walk forward to meet the captain, but the broad smile of greeting seemed false for Saldor, who'd done business with the Vaneers for over a decade at Kittric.

Sliding a hand down to rest on the short sword at his side, Micah discreetly signaled Sam, the second mate, trusting him to make sure that all hands were prepared to defend their captain should it become necessary.

It was a relief when the harbormaster finished examining the ship's documents and said something Micah couldn't hear to the two men with single-banded jackets. Who were they? Micah wondered as they turned to the waiting laborers. He decided to think of them as foremen, for lack of a better title.

The subdued demeanor of the dockworkers was a far cry from the usual jostling and rough joviality encountered at most ports on their trade route, including Ishal's in the past. Now there were no good-natured curses from rough men doing a day's hard work. They came aboard in small groups under the sharp eyes and orders of the foremen, the thump and scrape of shuffling boots the only sounds to compete with the wind flapping canvas and waves slapping the hull.

Their silence was contagious, Micah saw, when his own crew handled their tasks without speaking to the Ishalians. It made for a tense and awkward off-loading, especially when one of the foremen came aboard, standing stiff and frowning as he supervised the men.

Every sailor on the *Maid of Kilra* seemed relieved when the long first day ended and the Ishalians left the ship. Even then, there was one last anomaly. The harbormaster appeared near dusk, insisting that the two gruff foremen be allowed to search the ship.

"Think they suspect some of the dockworkers might try to escape Ishal by stowing away?" Micah murmured to his father, who scowled over this new requirement and what he probably perceived as a direct insult to the integrity of his crew.

"Wouldn't blame them if they did," Captain Vaneer muttered angrily. "This might be our last call in Ishal until they end this farce." His weathered face creased in disgust before shifting to more worried lines. "I pity the people, Micah. What madness has taken hold here?"

Once the ship was free of intrusion, Captain Vaneer addressed his men. "You all know that our usual way is to release most of the crew, saving a security detail, to enjoy what's available in each port of call." He saw the uncertain glances toward the shore by some of the men.

"I'm altering those arrangements while the *Maid* is docked in Ishal. You'll organize yourselves into three groups. One group will be allowed off ship at a time. I'm open to suggestions on time allotments. The rest will stay aboard, with one group off-duty on ship, and the other on security. Each will rotate in turn." Vaneer was relieved to find no disappointment or dissent on the faces of the men.

Then a few arms raised in the gathering. The captain pointed to a veteran seaman.

"What if we don't want shore leave, Captain?" the man's deep voice sounded, bringing more than a few murmurs of agreement. "This here port is off, just waitin' for somethin' to happen. Somethin' bad."

Captain Vaneer stroked his beard, nodding as he saw the same thoughts on other faces. "Aye. I won't say you're wrong there, Grip. And no man need leave the ship if he's not of a mind. Those who do should stick together, and watch each others' backs."

Glancing toward the dock, Vaneer lowered his voice without conscious decision. "There's a sickness here and danger. I'll ask those who go ashore to keep your ears open and your mouths shut. Any who feel they've learned something of what's happening here, feel free to pass it to Micah or myself. It could help keep us from harm, even if it means weighing anchor without loading Ishalian goods."

At the dismay on many faces, Vaneer grimaced. The crew's

pay was enlarged by their cut of a successful venture. For some, it made all the difference when winters were harsh and the ship couldn't sail.

"If we do, I'll make good on an estimate of profit based on past trade records."

Micah glanced at him, a mixture of surprise and pride on his face.

The second mate looked about the crew, apparently seeing what he needed in the loyal men. "It's good of you, Captain, but the men stand behind you. If the *Maid* takes a loss over this dismal situation, we each bear the cut."

Vaneer struggled against rare emotion and was speechless for the moment. Standing straighter, he scanned the resolute faces before giving them a curt nod and turning to his cabin.

Grinning after him, Micah stepped down to walk among the men, grasping each arm in heartfelt appreciation, and giving an ear to their concerns and speculations.

*L*ater that evening, Micah sat with his father in the common room they shared between two narrow sleeping berths. Over bowls of fisherman's stew, they discussed their thoughts of the day and how they might glean information on Commander Isfail's whereabouts.

A single hard knock on the door announced the seaman who'd spoken earlier. No one remembered his real name; he'd earned the name Grip early on for his tenacious ability to hold onto any rope under any conditions. In his late middle years now, with most of his life spent aboard ship—the majority with Captain Vaneer's crew—he was a large man with heavily muscled arms from hoisting sail and climbing rigging. He pulled off a knit cap, nodding respectfully to Micah, who'd answered the knock, as he ducked in under the low door header. Thinning hair was tied back from a weathered brown face.

"Beg pardon, Captain. Could I have a word?" Grip asked.

The captain gestured to an empty chair as Micah resumed his seat. "What's on your mind?"

The seaman just braced his big hands on the back of the

offered chair, unused to the familiarity of sitting at the captain's table, though comfortable enough with the Vaneers. Grip eyed the two men, seeming uncertain now where to start. "Well, sirs." With a quick glance quayside, he cleared his throat.

"Out with it, man," Vaneer said impatiently.

"All right, then." Grip straightened, taking a firm grip on his cap. "We all know about the Caldalan ship, and that we're to say nothin' of it if any Ishalian asks." He paused while the Vaneers glanced at one another. "That's all to the good, as far as the crew goes. No one has a trust for these Ishals, not after what we saw today."

Micah spoke this time. "But you have some thoughts about it, is that right, Grip?"

"Aye, sir. I figure you learned somethin' from the Caldalans. I've sailed enough years to know that Coroth's *Royal Sea Eagle* doesn't fly without cause, and her Captain Wells doesn't sit idle off a hostile port without reason." When the two men just looked at him silently, Grip continued. "Well, I figure he passed some information to you, maybe needed somethin' from us."

Vaneer nodded and poured three glasses of whiskey. "Sit down, Grip. No one will hang you for impropriety, and I refuse to be hulked over any longer." He chuckled when the sailor sat gingerly on the edge of the chair. Grip took the offered glass.

"You've been on my crew long enough to earn my trust, so I'll tell you that your instincts and reasoning are sound," the captain began. "Captain Wells is concerned about Militia Commander Isfail, who has gone missing here. The commander was traveling under Caldala's royal seal to speak with the Ishalian Parliament. He never returned from that appointment. When Wells inquired after him, he and his ship were ordered from Tash'tric harbor under threat of seizure and imprisonment."

Grip's expression hardened. "That's evil news, Captain—an invitation to start a war, if I ever heard one. I have acquaintance of Commander Isfail from his early seafarin' days, and I knew his father before he was lost with his ship. Good men, both."

He took a deep swallow from his whiskey before leaning forward. "What can I do to help?"

At a nod from his father, Micah answered. "If any of the men hear anything about a foreigner being seized and held, tell us. You know sailors and dockworkers see much of what goes on with the ships. Someone noticed the confrontation with Wells and his ship. Someone might have seen Commander Isfail or heard news about him."

Nodding slowly, Grip gave a thin smile. "I've changed my mind about shore leave, Captain. I've a mind to lift a pint or two with the locals."

The shabby pub near the docks lived up to its name. *Tattered Sails* was a familiar haunt of sailors over the years, including Grip and his two companions on rare Tash'tric calls. They remembered it as a well-worn but lively place to swap tall tales and end a long day over many pints. It still smelled of ale, pipe smoke, and stale sweat. But the life seemed to have fled the dingy main room, and there were few locals seated at the tables this night.

Grip signaled the hopeful-looking barman for three ales as they settled at a table near the few already occupied. He gave a nod to some dockworkers he recognized from earlier in the day, but said nothing for the moment. Grip had already noticed the sour-faced foreman seated at the end of the long bar. There was little chance of striking up a useful conversation under that one's suspicious gaze, he decided.

His personal observation was confirmed when the barman brought the tall mugs to their table.

"Quiet here tonight," Grip said, watching the overly cheerful Ishalian while he laid out the drinks. "How's business?"

"Well enough," the barman replied, though he glanced at the foreman nervously. Then he bobbed his head and hurried back to the bar as a group of locals entered.

The three Kilran sailors exchanged looks, then Amon, the sail-maker on the *Maid of Kilra*, said, "Pub's as strange as the dock today. Might as well have stayed aboard ship, for there'll be no sport here tonight."

"Aye, the place is a tomb," agreed Eaton, their youngest companion with only three years sailing on the *Maid*. "There's not a lass in sight. How's a man supposed to find a little cuddle?"

With an amused snort, Grip slapped Eaton on the back. "Drink up, lad. The way this port feels, you're as like to disappear with a knife at your throat as up the stairs with an easy woman. I've heard rumors that good men have gone missing in Tash'tric of late, and we might be needin' to rescue your worthless hide." He smiled to take any sting from his words.

Then Grip caught the startled glance from one of the Ishalians at the nearest table. The man quickly looked away again.

Though they ordered another round, Grip and his friends found no opening to ask questions. The sharp-eyed man at the bar watched everything. And the Ishalian patrons were standoffish, with several leaving the pub early. Even the other foreign sailors did not linger in the oppressive atmosphere.

Tossing coins on the table, the Kilrans decided to return to their ship. Grip hunched in his heavy wool coat, disgruntled over the waste of the night and lack of leads about Commander Isfail's fate. Turning into a narrow street leading back to their dock, he walked just ahead of Amon and Eaton, slowing a bit when he saw a man step into the far end of the road.

"There's another behind us," Amon muttered as the sailors moved closer to one another, preparing to fight if necessary.

Eaton pulled a dagger from the sheath on his belt when a voice spoke from a dark doorway.

"No harm meant," the owner of the voice said quietly. "My friends only watch for the watchers."

When he eased into dim lamplight, Grip recognized the man from the pub, the one who'd reacted to his comment about people going missing. "Who're you then?"

"You don't need a name that will get my throat cut," the stranger replied. He stepped from the doorway, quickly checking for the men at each end of the dark road before looking at Grip. "You've seen for yourselves Ishal's not what it was."

"So why aren't you doing something about it?" Eaton scoffed with a young man's disdain.

"You think it's so easy, do you?" the Ishalian growled in rage. "They've taken the government and some of the militia, set their cutthroats and murderers on any who dare speak out. They threaten our families, and worse."

Laying a calloused hand on Eaton's stiff shoulder, Grip asked, "Who are they?"

"They call themselves The Bow." The man looked up and down the quiet street. "There's not much time to talk, watchers are everywhere. I was hardly more than a lad during the first rebellion, but this feels the same. They say a Caldalan, Baronan by name, started this, but he was killed years ago. There's been no word of who or what's behind it this time, but Ishal needs help." His voice was desperate now. "Can you get the word out?"

"Caldala's prince sent a man—Commander Isfail—to your Parliament," Grip stated gruffly. "He's disappeared. You'll not be gettin' help from Caldala unless he's safe home. What can you tell me about him?"

"Nothing." The stranger sounded sincere as he drew back into the shadows. "But I'll ask about, carefully. I know some of the loyal guard who might have heard something. Just get the word out beyond Ishal before there's no hope for us." He jerked his head toward the end of the road.

No one was there now.

"Go!"

Then the three sailors were alone in the street with mist off the bay winding wispy tendrils through the air. Grip led the way back toward their ship, his companions deliberately exchanging drunken slurs of insults as they approached two men standing in lamplight near the dock, observing them closely.

The Kilrans breathed easier when they were allowed to pass without comment.

Watchers, Grip decided, remembering the fear in the Ishalian's voice.

Two

*A*ric's mouth thinned with anger when he saw the Caldalan commander shackled to the cell wall. "Get him out of there," he growled.

His companions hurried to comply, narrowly avoiding the combative response from the abused man.

After a quick look down the dark hall, Aric moved into the rough stone cell. "Hold, Commander, we're here to help. But there's little time to get you away."

Commander Ardan Isfail's stormy gaze held Aric's resolute stare. With a curt nod, he quieted to let the others unlock his chains. He seemed determined to stand on his own feet when he shook off their assistance while rubbing abraded wrists.

"Why?" Isfail muttered.

While his men checked their escape route, Aric picked up the formal Caldalan Militia uniform jacket lying on the cell floor and handed it to Isfail, pointing to a campaign ribbon with its black bar. "Gattes Brigade. Some of us still remember our friends. Come. We must go."

With the other two men flanking Isfail, Aric led them deeper into the dungeons. After a short distance, he stopped. Feeling about in the dim light, Aric found the hidden mechanism that sent a section of the wall pivoting soundlessly.

"The sea tunnels?" Isfail whispered.

The others glanced at each other in concern, but Aric just looked at him. "Keep that to yourself."

With a nod, the prisoner moved with them into the black until hands gripped his shoulders. They waited for their leader to seal the door and light a torch.

*I*sfail took his first easy breath in days. "My thanks, sincerely." He offered his arm all around as the others relaxed with him.

"My apologies for your treatment, Commander," Aric said.

"Just Isfail, sir."

"Aric. Commander Caden Aric," the Ishalian countered with a brief smile. "But I'll not name my companions here—to protect them and their families should this get around."

"Understood."

As the group splashed through puddles in long, dark tunnels formed by ancient volcanism, Isfail remembered things Akira had told him while she was still an ambassador.

"We might have some acquaintances in common," he tested.

Glancing back, Aric lifted a brow in the flickering light. "It's possible."

"Someone close to me told me of these caves after a good friend escaped this way during the Baronan rebellion."

In the torchlight, Isfail saw grief cloud Aric's face.

"Aye." Aric's reply was gruff. "A good friend of mine, Garath Haill, got one of yours out this way then. I expect that's who you mean."

Isfail nodded to the curious look.

"So, you're close with the ambassadors, are you?"

"Aye," Isfail answered without hesitation.

Leading the way onto a higher bench of rock for a rest stop, Aric only gave a thin smile. "Don't let anyone hear that outside this group. You don't know who can be trusted these days." He grinned suddenly, leaning back against the rough black wall with a ration bar handed over by one of his men. "But, as I said, some of us remember our allies."

Aric eyed Isfail while he took a long drink from a water-skin. "So," he began, stoppering the leather spout, "High Ambassador Muro, you know of her?"

"Aye, though she's no longer in the Core." Isfail's voice was wary again.

"You'll want to warn her. The Bow's marked her for death, along with any other force callers they can take down."

"They've tried," Isfail stated coldly, taking the offered water. "What more can you tell me of them?"

"Don't underestimate them," Aric replied with a hard edge to his voice. "We don't have a firm handle on who's leading The Bow, but they're better organized than the ones started by Baronan years ago. And they've a dangerous intelligence network."

He scowled. "They'd infiltrated the government here before we knew what was happening."

Passing the water-skin to one of the other men, Isfail asked, "What about your militia?" He saw rage darken Aric's expression.

"Some here had already sided with the insurgents. You'd think we'd have seen the signs after what happened before," Aric growled, before sorrow etched deep lines in his face. "The rest of us were ordered to stand down by Parliament when things began to change. The ministry fools don't know what they're in for; they think they're still in control."

Meeting Isfail's eyes, Aric continued. "Did you see the younger, dark-haired lord before you were arrested?"

Isfail nodded, remembering the smirking visage while he'd been clapped in irons. And the sick pleasure in those dark eyes when the beatings began.

"Abron Dateh," Aric told him. "Titles himself *Lord* Dateh, but no one can confirm his lineage or where he's from. Even so, he became a regular presence in the assembly rooms about a year ago though he's not an elected parliamentarian. Since then, Dateh has had a voice in almost every decision. The militia was the first to see the cuts. Those who argued against were over-ruled or silenced, removed from service. The Bow took Tash'tric and other strategic cities about five lunams ago."

Hearing the bitterness in Aric's voice, Isfail wondered how Ishal's government had been so easily manipulated.

"So this Dateh is the leader of the cult?" Isfail asked.

"Likely, though no one really seems to know," Aric answered. "He keeps close to the Parliament halls for now, but most of us believe he'll make a decisive move to take over the government soon." Aric signaled his men, who quickly made ready to move on.

Getting to his feet again, Isfail found that the elated energy sparked by his rescue had faded, leaving fatigue behind. His ribs troubled him, and he felt every separate ache and pain caused by his ordeal. When he stumbled on the rough descent, Aric's hand caught him by the arm.

"Easy, Commander. We've time enough to make your ship."

Isfail glanced over. "How long has it been?"

"Since you were imprisoned? About six days." Aric glanced back at the two men following in the shifting torchlight. "We didn't know you were taken until one of my men got the word from his sister's husband."

At Isfail's questioning stare, Aric told him, "My guard unit was one of the first to be cut from Parliament service. I'd guess The Bow suspects where our loyalties stand. We've been reassigned to patrol duty in the outer districts. We know they keep us under surveillance."

"How were you able to get into the dungeons with all that?" Isfail asked as they made their way up and over a small ridge. His ribs had become a misery, but he was determined to keep up with the Ishalians.

Aric chuckled. "There are a few good men keeping a low profile, we'll say. When I got the word that a Caldalan commander had disappeared, I made some discreet inquiries." He jerked a thumb over his shoulder to the men following. "They're good men and volunteered to take the risk with me. One has a contact who's a dungeon guard."

Pausing, Isfail turned to them. "I am in your debt. What will happen to you now?" He included Aric in his question as he studied each face.

One of the others shrugged. "We knew we'd slip off someday. Now is the time." His companion nodded.

"Things are escalating," Aric said as he began to walk again.

"The Bow will come into full power soon. We know those who have spoken out against them are disappearing, or the bodies are left as warnings. Our people live in fear again. Some are already trying to make it over the borders, but most have homes here, family here. Some of us will go underground, build the resistance once more."

Isfail heard the ghosts of the past in Aric's summation.

They went on in silence for some time. The tunnel became narrower until only two could walk side by side. But Isfail heard the familiar sound of water moving, the distant slap of waves on rock. A damp wind stirred the air in the black tunnel, carrying the brine-heavy scent of the sea.

To his surprise, the way ended at a dark wall of uneven layers.

The others said nothing as one of the men squeezed by and scrambled nimbly up until he was standing above them. Glancing back at Aric, he moved sideways and seemed to disappear.

Aric chuckled at the look of confusion on Isfail's face. "Not to worry. That trick takes no force powers, as you'll soon see. He went ahead to be sure there are no unwelcome surprises where we're going." Aric signaled the other man to go up. He made the climb easily, crouching near the spot where his companion had vanished.

They waited in silence for several minutes before the man above them called the all clear. At their direction, Isfail began the short ascent, followed closely by Aric.

The mystery was revealed when torchlight showed that what had appeared to be a solid wall was, in reality, a tube forming two uneven walls offset by a few feet. The dim light and black rock created the illusion that a man was disappearing when he was just moving into the passage between the walls.

Isfail followed as they took a rising path until a sudden jog to the left opened into a large cavern. The man who'd gone through first was peering out a wide crevice in the wall to the right above them, where a faint hint of daylight seeped in. Giving them an all-clear sign, he climbed down to rejoin them.

After a short climb up another rough ridge, the small group

looked down on a dark tongue of rippling water. Isfail saw pale gray light beyond the tunnel mouth.

"Early morning and outgoing tide," Aric noted, settling on the ground. The others followed his example. "We've got a few hours until the way's clear, unless you'd like to take a cold swim."

"I'll wait," Isfail replied, smiling at the men's responding laughter. Rolling up his jacket, he used it to cushion his head while he stretched out on the hard rock. Despite a thumping headache added to his other discomforts, Isfail was asleep in minutes.

Three

Micah Vaneer watched the sun clear the eastern horizon on what promised to be a cloudless day. But the beauty did nothing to ease his worry or frustration. They'd been in port four days now, with no word on Isfail. Grip and other crewmen frequented the pubs in the evening, but took care to avoid suspicion from the ever-present watchers. The locals kept their distance, and there had been nothing more from the man who'd talked to Grip the first night in port.

His father counseled patience, and Micah knew they had to be careful. The feeling of something not right grew heavier with each day. Though there had been no trouble for ship or crew, they all seemed to feel the weight of uncertainty and oppression. The only relief came after work was finished for the day, and the gangplanks taken aboard for the night.

He saw dockworkers beginning to assemble near the warehouse assigned to their ship. The off-loading was completed and this would be the second day loading cargo. If all went as scheduled, they could take on fresh supplies within the next two days and sail with the outgoing tide three days from now.

It wasn't enough, Micah thought, his hands tightening on the rail.

"Mister Vaneer, sir."

Micah turned around to see Grip approaching. The sailor didn't look any easier than Micah felt. "Yes, Grip?"

"Have you heard anythin' at all, sir?"

"No."

Grip scowled—a ferocious expression on the weathered face.

"It doesn't sit well, Mister Vaneer, the idea of leavin' without Commander Isfail. 'Specially as 'twas the *Maid* that brought him home, more dead than alive, after the last bloody insurrection. It's not right these bastards have him again!"

This was one of the longest speeches Micah had ever heard from the normally taciturn man. And he felt the same in his own bones. "No, it's not right. There has to be a way to get to him."

"Not while our every move is watched," Captain Vaneer warned as he came over. "We still have a ship to protect. One man, no matter how valiant, is not worth risking the lives of my crew."

His mouth tight with anger, Micah fought for his temper. "That man risked everything to help the Ishalians over a decade ago, Captain. A royal heir, a proven soldier, and sailor. His blood spilled in Kittric, along with the many Caldalans who died there. Still he had the courage to return now, under royal seal for some purpose, possibly to investigate these recent events. And he's betrayed again."

Meeting his father's eyes, Micah stated, "I respect your duty to the crew, Father, but a good man, and a friend, deserves more from us."

Vaneer appeared to consider his son's words for a long moment before nodding. But as he began to speak, their attention was drawn to the unit of Ishalian guard marching onto the dock. The two foremen assigned to the *Maid of Kilra* hurried to meet them.

Both Vaneers moved to the top of the gangplank, waiting with impassive faces while the foremen answered abrupt-sounding questions from the officer in charge. Their answers did not seem to please him, and he gave an impatient gesture signaling them away before he strode up the gangplank to confront the Kilrans.

"You are the captain of this ship?" the officer asked of the elder Vaneer.

"Aye, I'm Captain Vaneer. You have business with my ship, sir?"

The officer handed over a sealed paper. "Commander Shanow, Captain. That is a warrant allowing me to have your ship searched."

*B*oth Vaneers frowned but the captain only read the paper carefully, noting the scrawled signature of the titular head of the Ishalian Parliament. He wondered who was really in charge there now and to what purpose his ship was targeted.

"This seems in order, Commander," he said, refolding the paper and slipping it into the inner pocket of his jacket. "I would like to know why this warrant has been issued." Vaneer met Shanow's cold stare as an equal.

"There has been a report that your ship might be used to smuggle out an enemy of the Ishalian government." Shanow glanced at Micah when the young man took a step toward him, anger on his face. He turned back to the captain. "This is not an accusation, Captain Vaneer, merely a precaution."

The Vaneers went to stand with the crewmen who had gathered close to see what was happening. Their captain spoke a few words explaining the situation and calming them. But most sent dark looks at the military men who boarded and proceeded to spread out over the ship.

"Commander Shanow," the captain called. "I would have some of my men stationed throughout the *Maid* while you search. Just to keep your men honest, we'll say." Vaneer gave a cool smile back to the dark insult on the Ishalian's face.

Shanow only made a sharp gesture of agreement.

"To the captain's cabin, Micah," Vaneer said quietly. "Grip, see to the cargo hold, and send some men to the separate compartments." He turned to his second mate. "Sam, take the deck and assign men throughout the crew's quarters. No one is to cause any trouble, or say anything that might bring it. They're to watch carefully and be prepared to report back."

They spread out to their assignments while Captain Vaneer joined Commander Shanow, who observed it all from the quarterdeck. Both men watched without speaking.

An hour later, the Ishalian soldiers formed up on the main deck with nothing to report. Shanow gave a nod and turned to Vaneer.

"Your ship is cleared, Captain. I appreciate your cooperation.

Should anyone approach you about taking on a passenger, report it to me at once. My unit will be stationed on the dock until this matter is resolved."

"Is mine the only ship under watch, Commander?" Vaneer asked with a testy note in his voice.

There was the briefest hint of a smile on Shanow's tense mouth. "No, Captain. But yours is my duty station." He nodded to Micah as the young man returned.

The crew of the *Maid* watched the soldiers disembark to take positions along the quay and near the dockside warehouse, where merchants and dockworkers waited to load crates and bales of goods.

Captain Vaneer signaled his son.

"The day's wasting, men!" Micah shouted to be heard over the grumblings of the crew. "Set the cargo gangplanks and move this along."

Joining his father at the rail of the quarterdeck, Micah said quietly, "Do you think this has anything to do with Commander Isfail?"

"Could be," Vaneer replied with his gaze on the soldiers who seemed to watch even more closely than the watchers. "But there could be others deemed enemies of this government. Whoever it is, they'll have the devil's own time getting past these soldiers."

The day moved into afternoon as outbound cargo continued to fill the hold. The Ishalians worked without speaking to the sailors, who had grown accustomed to the strained relations.

Each side went about their business with as little interaction as possible until a wooden crate toppled from the pallet being hoisted aboard, falling to the quay with the crash of splintering wood amid shouts of warning. Sailors rushed to the rail to see what this was about, soldiers and foremen pushed into the crowd of dockworkers shouting bitter accusations at one another.

Micah and his father strode down the gangplank to check the damage, arriving in time to see one of the soldiers thrusting a sword into the large, linen-wrapped bundles spilling from the shattered crate.

"What's this?" Captain Vaneer cried out. "What in hell are you doing, destroying my merchandise?" He pushed forward as Commander Shanow reached the scene. "You there, I demand payment for this!"

Shanow frowned as he studied the damage and looked at the soldier, who stood to attention now with a bright streamer of fabric fluttering from the sword in his hand. "Explain," he demanded.

"Sir." The soldier stared straight ahead with embarrassed color flooding his face. "The bundles looked as if they could conceal a person. Sir."

"So you decided to run them through with your blade?" Shanow asked dryly.

When the soldier just gulped, Commander Shanow indicated Captain Vaneer. "The captain has demanded payment for your destruction of valuable cargo. You will find out how much he is owed and present payment to him before the day is over."

The soldier's eyes grew wide. "But, Commander, I'm not responsible for the dropped crate."

"The clothing in the ruined crate could have been salvaged," Vaneer growled, lifting a handful of sliced fabric. "This cannot!"

Shanow raised a hand to silence his soldier's retort. "Payment will be made." He gestured to his lieutenant, who escorted the man away. At the militia commander's brisk orders, everyone else returned to work. Then he turned to the Vaneers.

"How soon will your ship be ready to sail, Captain?"

"I'm awaiting delivery from one more merchant. He says tomorrow. It can't be soon enough." Vaneer scowled, looking around the dock. "I'll be more than happy to leave this port, Commander, and hope to never do business here again with what your country has fallen to."

He jerked his head to Micah and turned back to his ship, but looked back when Shanow spoke with quiet menace.

"You would do well to be gone on tomorrow night's tide,

Captain Vaneer. I cannot guarantee the safety of your ship or crew beyond that. Tell your men to stay near the ship until you do."

With that, he turned sharply and walked away, leaving the Vaneers glancing at each other in concern.

It took some effort by Captain Vaneer to purchase and arrange delivery of food supplies sufficient to see the crew to their next port on such short notice. But local merchants appeared eager to supply what they could and secure the profit. Few would discuss the situation in Ishal in detail. Those who did kept their eyes on the doors and windows, speaking in hushed voices of curfews, threats, and restrictions on trade.

One widowed merchant named Lianna spoke bitterly of losing her husband to a mocked-up tribunal when he'd refused to cut the price of his meat for the strangers showing up in Tash'tric, those representing themselves as members of The Bow. The woman had watched when her man was hung in the central square just two lunams ago. Now Lianna feared for her son and daughter, and their families.

When Vaneer quietly offered to try and smuggle them onto his ship the next night, she shook her head with tears in her eyes.

"It's good of you, Captain," she whispered. "But sure death for us all if we're caught. Here . . . we might survive more bad times coming, as we did the last rebellion." She pressed an additional package of salt pork into his hands after they concluded their business. "Safe passage, sir."

"And you, Lianna." But the encounter left Vaneer disheartened as he walked back through strangely empty streets, accompanied only by the two burly sailors Micah had insisted he take with him. His son's words about it not being enough replayed in his head. It wasn't only Ardan Isfail who needed rescuing from this land of despair and injustice.

His mood only sharpened when they arrived at the dock to find Micah and several sailors confronting the belligerent foremen, while dockworkers stood back with expressions ranging from resentment to terror.

"What's going on here?" the captain bellowed, glaring at Shanow and his soldiers, who only stood at the perimeter without interfering.

When Vaneer gripped Micah's rigid shoulder, his son spat out, "These idiots want to open the crates!"

"We've a right to inspect anything suspicious," the older of the foremen shot back, raising a gnarled fist.

Pulling his son aside, Captain Vaneer faced the foremen. "And what makes these crates suspicious?"

For a moment, the foreman looked confused, then the younger one said, "They're big enough to conceal a man." The other nodded with a triumphant look at the sailors.

"What do you have to say about this, Commander?" Vaneer barked at the militia soldier.

Shanow's brow creased thoughtfully. "I say let them look, Captain. As long as no damage is done and the crate properly secured afterward." Now he moved forward with a few of his men.

"However," he said to the foremen. "You will not be opening any more of these crates without substantial cause. Is that understood?"

Begrudgingly, the two foremen agreed, as long as they were allowed to open one more crate at random.

Glancing at Micah, then Shanow, who waited with one hand on his sword hilt, Vaneer nodded.

The foremen proceeded to pry up the boards on the top of the crate. They called over two of the dockworkers to remove small bundles of straw packing until the contents were revealed—two large and tall pottery urns.

Obviously disappointed, the foremen had the workers replace the straw under the Vaneers' sharp supervision and then secure the top of the crate.

Satisfied by their failure to find stowaways, Captain Vaneer signaled his crew to hoist the large crate on board. Then he stalked up the gangplank, leaving Micah, Grip, and the two sturdy sailors to watch over the loading.

Four

The subtle difference in the ship's movement woke Grip in the small hours of the night. Weather's changing, he told himself, wide awake now and restless as he eased from his hammock and slipped on deck shoes. With silent tread, Grip made his way up, joining Amon on watch.

"Storm's brewing," Amon confirmed, looking out toward the harbor mouth.

"That it is," Grip agreed with a nod. "Exceptin' the failure to get news of the commander, it's good we're raisin' sail tomorrow. Today, that is," he corrected, remembering the early hour.

Amon shook his head, frowning. "Aye, it's a hard knowing, but I'm well ready to leave this accursed port. The captain surveyed the last of the cargo waiting in the warehouse. We should be finished with the load-on by mid-afternoon if that merchant delivers his goods before midday."

Clapping a big hand on his friend's back, Grip started back to the steep stairway leading down to the cargo holds. Taking one of the lanterns, he decided to make sure the crates on board were lashed in place securely. It would save time later today, and prevent cargo from shifting dangerously if they encountered heavy seas on the open ocean.

Walking down narrow rows, he tested the tension on binding ropes, giving them a hard pull to hear the satisfying *thwap* as they snapped taut against wood. What he didn't expect to hear after repeating the test against a large crate labeled *Fine Porcelain* was an infant's wailing cry.

*B*oth Vaneers sprang from their bunks, grabbing swords and daggers as the rapid, though muffled, knocking against the main cabin door demanded immediate attention. Reaching it first, Micah held his sword ready as he flung it open to a wide-eyed Amon.

"What's wrong?" Captain Vaneer demanded. He set his own blade aside to tuck his shirt into his trousers when a quick scan outside the open door showed no immediate danger. "Are we under attack?"

"No, Captain, sir," Amon answered quietly. "But there's a . . . situation in the cargo hold you need to see about."

When Micah started to light a lantern, Amon said, "I wouldn't do that as yet, Mister Micah. Best to avoid alerting the Ishalians, if we can, at least until you see what's below."

His brow furrowed in consternation, Captain Vaneer followed his sail-maker, keeping low and silent as he and Micah were led along the seaward side of the ship then down into the main hatch. Below decks, Amon handed each a lantern before continuing between rows of crates.

Down the aisle, Vaneer saw Grip standing in the glow of lantern light. He appeared to be examining a large crate before looking up as they approached.

"Well?" the captain said, meeting the curious look in Grip's eyes. "What is it?"

The sailor dipped his head to the crate. "You need to see this, Captain." He lifted the boards he'd already pried up.

The Vaneers looked in, both frowning back at Grip when they saw the straw packing surrounding small parcels, presumably containing porcelain ware. Micah dug a hand into the straw until he reached the wooden board that was often used to separate and protect the layers of fragile pottery.

Grip just gave them an odd smile and signaled Amon. "Help me with this." The two sailors found the loops of rope fastened to opposite sides of the inner tray and lifted. Micah helped them guide the wooden insert over the lip of the crate and onto the floor.

Then the four men peered into the crate again. The captain

swore softly at the sight of the young woman huddled among long canvas bundles. Obviously terrified, she held a small infant and a toddler close to her. The woman and child stared up at them with huge eyes.

"My God," Micah said, glancing at his father. "She's trying to get out of Ishal."

The captain just nodded, then smiled kindly down. "Don't be afraid, my dear. We'll see you safe."

Some of her fear seemed to ease, until they started to pry away the sides of the crate, intending to help her out.

"No!" she exclaimed, and the children started to cry. "Please, sirs. They'll search the ship before you sail. It could mean all our lives if they find us."

The men looked at each other in concern before Grip spoke to her. "Ma'am, I heard the baby cry—that's how I knew to look. What do you think will happen if the Ishals hear it when they search?"

If possible, her face was whiter than before, but she shook her head. "If they find us sealed in the crate, you can disavow knowledge. You and your ship should be safe." Looking back up with a plea in her eyes, she said, "Please, for pity's sake, my husband risks all to get us away. He'll be executed if we're discovered."

"He's one of the dockworkers?" Micah guessed.

"Yes."

Vaneer met his son's eyes and nodded before turning his attention back to the small family. "Does he have a way out of the country?"

Tears filled her eyes. "He plans to join the resistance as soon as your ship heads to sea. He knows others that have gone underground." The woman wiped her cheeks. "His father was one of those killed in the first rebellion."

"Are there other stowaways?" Micah asked.

She nodded. "I don't know how many, or in what crates. We'll make good on the loss of your goods, sir."

"That's no matter," Micah soothed, seeing his father shake his head.

It was an easy decision for Captain Mattoc Vaneer. Here was one good thing that could come of this port call. "We'll get you away for him. Grip here will stay with you for a couple more hours. Help with the little ones, or if you need to stretch your legs. We'll get you some food and fresh water," he offered, smiling when she held up a large leather bag. "Regardless, the fresher air and ability to stretch, relieve yourself, might make it easier when we need to crate you up again."

"God bless you, Captain," she whispered, burying her face into her toddler's curls to weep softly.

Leaving Grip to handle the rest, the Vaneers returned to their cabin after giving Amon orders to spread throughout the crew.

"If any of them are discovered later today," Micah began, "Shanow will demand to search every crate."

"Aye, that he will," the captain agreed gruffly. "So we'll pray that none are detected."

If the crew of the *Maid of Kilra* had any concerns about being caught with stowaways aboard, it did not show. Sailors went about their usual business of preparing the ship to sail that evening. Micah was one of the few who noticed that many had slipped belaying pins or extra knives into their belts. But even that didn't appear out of the ordinary with the level of tension throughout the port.

As he'd done the day before, Micah oversaw the loading of the final crates, keeping a sharp watch on dockworkers, the militia soldiers, and the ever-present foremen. Careful to keep his face expressionless, he scanned the men handling the crates, alert for any indication that anything was out of the ordinary. Though what was ordinary here anymore? Micah asked himself.

Knowing that it was unlikely, Micah still hoped that Isfail might have been secreted in one of the last of the crates. Once the *Maid* was safely away, he'd have the crew tap on each crate, checking for those with human cargo. Closing his eyes briefly, Micah prayed for a miracle.

A fitful wind grew stronger as midday came and went. Micah

looked up at the darkening clouds and felt the misty rain on his face as he walked down the wide cargo gangplank, passing the line of dockworkers hefting smaller crates and bundles. He saw Grip standing by the cargo net used to hoist larger crates aboard, his muscular arms crossed over his wide chest, a scowl on his face as he watched the foremen arguing over which crate they'd choose to open in their last random search.

Micah prayed their luck would hold as he approached the warehouse to see what was left to load. Commander Shanow was standing just outside the doors, his stern face unreadable as he scanned the long line of workers. Micah opened his mouth to offer a civil greeting, until he heard the sound of whimpering from the crate by his side.

Micah glanced back, praying that Shanow—only an arm-span away—had not heard it. But the commander's narrowed eyes were fixed on that very crate.

If Micah hadn't been focused on the man, he would not have seen Shanow's right hand lift slightly, fingers spread wide then clench into a tight fist before the hand returned to his sword hilt. At the evident signal Micah dropped a hand to his own sword as Shanow's lieutenant stepped quickly out of the unit.

A splintering crash nearby had Micah spinning around, swearing loudly. Two places up the line, a crate lay on its side with one corner splintered and crushed.

Commander Shanow called out to the foremen now pushing through the gathering crowd. Micah saw Grip bulling his way in with several sailors from the ship. Feeling his blood chill at the thought of what lay ahead, Micah steadied himself to fight.

The whimpering came again. There was no way those around him had failed to hear, but no one looked at it. Shanow strode to the damaged crate beyond without a glance at the suspicious one.

"What's this?" he exclaimed loudly, gesturing the foremen closer. "You there, get over here and open this crate. I heard something in here."

Hardly believing his ears, Micah inserted himself between the damaged crate and the one where the whimpering continued.

He almost missed the man who was allowed to slip unchallenged through soldiers and dockworkers alike, hunched over with his hands cupped close to his belly.

Shanow had stepped in front of the eager foremen, berating them for their failure to control the loading. Voices were raised in protest as ship's crew and the Ishalians began arguing over placing blame for damaging more cargo.

Dividing his attention between the overt drama just ahead and the subterfuge at his feet, Micah heard the creak of wood, glancing down in time to see the secretive man inserting something into the damaged crate as he pulled one of the broken boards out to widen the opening. Then he backed hurriedly away as people discreetly made way for him until he shifted to stand, unremarkable in the sea of brown garb. Micah marveled at the speed at which it had all been done.

Now he focused fully on the foremen, who appeared chastened and frustrated while the commander continued to berate them. Finally, Shanow gestured to the damaged crate.

"Open it up," he ordered, flicking a glance at the lieutenant who now stood to Micah's left.

Everyone watched, speculating loudly, as boards were pried loose from what had been the top. Canvas bags filled with grain spilled out onto the wet cobblestones, each too small to hold a person. The two foremen ordered the crowd back and began dragging out more of the bags.

Micah noticed his father, standing stiff and forbidding, his arms crossed tight over his chest, mouth grim. But the captain just stood, silent at this current assault on his cargo as rain fell over all.

More canvas bags were tossed out into the wet. As the crate emptied, Micah jolted as he now heard whimpering sounds from the damaged crate. This time, those standing around murmured questions and pressed closer to see the culprit. One of the crates dividing pieces was thrown carelessly aside in the foremen's zealous efforts to discover illicit contents.

Then one of the foremen swore while the other crawled in

and pulled out a wriggling puppy, then another, the man's face a study in disappointment. The men gathered around began to laugh, Micah among them. He looked at his father and saw the same amusement in his eyes as he stepped to Shanow.

"Are you satisfied, Commander?" Captain Vaneer asked with satisfaction. "Apparently your merchants can't keep their whelps out of my goods!"

Micah watched the commander's mouth tighten as irritation suffused his face.

"You're clear, Captain Vaneer. Finish your loading and prepare to sail." Shanow turned and barked orders to the flustered foremen to have the crate repacked properly. Stalking past Micah, he gave the crate behind him a sharp kick. That whimpering ceased.

When the sullen-faced foreman raised his arm, as if to hurl an offending puppy into the harbor, Micah stepped up quickly. "I believe that's our property." He grabbed the two skinny animals as the Ishalian made a rude comment, but Micah just grinned and followed his father onto the ship.

From the rail, the Vaneers watched the last of the crates loaded into the hold.

"I think the commander is in on the smuggling," Micah whispered, tucking the trembling puppies inside his coat.

His father's brow creased, but he said nothing in response.

Within an hour, the last of the cargo was secured and the loading ramp hauled aboard. The rain had ceased but the wind blew in stronger gusts, humming through the rigging. As they'd expected, the harbormaster came up the gangplank, followed by the two surly foremen. Commander Shanow and his lieutenant came onboard behind them. Captain Vaneer just nodded to their stated intention of searching for stowaways.

There was little he could do to stop it without inviting suspicion, and Grip had walked the cargo hold with Amon beforehand, in loud conversation about the Ishalians' plan to do a final search of the hold. Now the ship's fate rested in the stowaways maintaining absolute silence within their confines.

Micah watched as Shanow gestured his lieutenant to

accompany the search party then walked up to join the Vaneers on the quarterdeck.

"Commander," his father acknowledged in a stern voice.

"Captain Vaneer," Shanow replied, nodding to Micah as well. He unfastened his uniform jacket enough to withdraw an oilskin packet that he handed to the captain. "Your ship's paperwork, sir. The harbormaster asked me to return it while he led the search."

With a noncommittal grunt, the captain started to pull the papers out, but Shanow's hand closed over the flap.

"All the appropriate seals and stamps are in place, Captain," Shanow stated firmly. "You can review them after your ship has cleared the harbor."

Micah thought the soldier's emphasis on 'after' was significant, but he recognized that Shanow was reluctant to say more. When his father passed him the packet, Micah knew why. There was more than the usual port documents in there; a thicker pad was layered within the larger half folds. For a brief moment, Micah held Shanow's cool stare. Reading nothing in that impassive face, Micah said nothing, just inserted the packet inside his own coat, brushing over the sleeping animals.

At last, a relieved-looking harbormaster came on deck, though his two companions appeared disgruntled at best. The Vaneers and Commander Shanow went down to join them at the top of the gangplank.

"You're cleared to sail, Captain Vaneer, and I wish you a safe voyage," the harbormaster stated with genuine cheerfulness, in contrast to the forced greeting upon their arrival. With a last friendly salute, he made his way back to the quay.

The foremen said nothing, just stomped down the narrow planks.

Shanow surprised them with a quick grin and respectful dip of the head. "I wish you a successful journey, sirs. And hope to meet again in better times."

Micah and his father watched him as he joined his lieutenant, already on the quay. He led his militia unit away while the gangplank was raised, severing the final physical link to the port, saving the hawser lines that would be released when the tide was favorable.

*T*he moons appeared between tattered clouds that night—an auspicious sight, Micah decided as the *Maid of Kilra* unfurled her sails to catch wind and tide. But his smile faded as their ship cleared the harbor without Ardan Isfail.

His father nodded to their shared cabin. Micah wondered if his thoughts ran even with his. Did the captain share the acute disappointment of leaving a man behind?

Mattoc Vaneer was pouring two glasses of whiskey when Micah entered. He looked into the small box beside his berth where the puppies had been contained, and were now curled sound asleep after filling little stomachs with meat scraps from the galley.

"Let's have a look at those papers now," his father said.

Pulling out the oilcloth packet, Micah removed them. They bent over the table as his father unfolded the usual documents and found a small journal tucked within. Inside was written a set of coordinates—longitude and latitude—and a date.

There was a note on the facing page that Micah read aloud with growing excitement.

The man you seek will be waiting beyond a short point to the northwest. Follow these coordinates to find him around the date given.

Entrusted to your care and compassion are three families, hidden in five crates, each crate marked with a carved wave near the lid. Those of us loyal to our country beg you to give them sanctuary.

Say nothing of this subterfuge if you support our cause.
Godspeed.

An elegantly scripted capital *S* ended the message.

Five

While the crew of the *Maid of Kilra* dealt with their final days in Tash'tric port, the loyalist underground continued their schemes to get Commander Isfail out of Ishal. Within the cavern mouth, while the midday sun sent sparkles of light off the open water just beyond, Aric laid a hand on Isfail's shoulder.

Immediately awake, Isfail sat up, his breath catching as the sudden movement shot pain throughout his body. Rubbing his hands over his face, he asked, "What now?"

Then he noticed that it was just the two of them—the other men were gone.

Aric stood, pointing down to the narrow shelf of rock that had been previously submerged. "Tide's about to turn again. We need to move on, though we've got a solid hour before water's over the path."

Isfail followed him down the rugged slope, his movements stiff and cautious until the exercise loosened sore muscles. "Your men have gone ahead?"

"Yes. Another waits just outside with news we need to hear." Aric looked over his shoulder to study Isfail. "We'll soon know if we're sending you back by sea."

Hoping with everything in him for a ship home, Isfail still asked, "If not, is there another plan to get me out of Ishal alive?"

The broad shoulders ahead of him only shrugged.

Soon they paused just inside the cave, with bright sunlight reflecting off the small stretch of pale sand beyond. Aric grinned as he greeted the man who joined them in the shadows.

"Isfail, this is another good man," Aric stated by way of an introduction. "This would be our second rebellion served together."

The new man took the arm Isfail offered in a strong grip. "I'm Declan, Commander. It's a great pleasure to meet you. And an honor to assist your escape in any way possible."

As Isfail gave them a curious look, Aric slapped his companion on the back. "Your name and reputation precede you, Isfail. All who served during the first rebellion remember the fighters of the Gattes Brigade. It's our great shame that information was lacking in those days, and we could not come to your aid in Kittric."

Then Aric's face tightened. "You should know that we made it our mission to track down those who took part in that ambush." He seemed to pull his thoughts back from that time, and looked at Declan. "And what about now?"

"All was in order when our man reached the rendezvous point. I headed out after getting the news. If all continues as planned, the ship should be in sight within two days."

It sounded deliberately vague to Isfail as they walked out into the welcome warmth of sunshine. Maybe it needed to be, he thought, exhausted and in serious pain as he sat down on the sand and leaned back against a large driftwood trunk while the two men continued talking together.

God, he wanted to be home with Akira, to start their life together. For the first time since he'd joined the militia—almost thirty years of service—he just wanted to walk away from the intrigue and the fighting. *This* sure as hell wasn't his fight.

He was tired of Ishal's civil turmoil and the chaos that dragged other countries in. The wasted lives. What was wrong with these people that they followed like sheep to the slaughter whenever some fanatic like Arthon Baronan or this Abron Dateh incited a violent bid for power?

The Baronan rebellion had cost hundreds of Ishalian lives. How many would be lost to The Bow? And how many more Caldalan lives would be threatened?

Six

Village of Mountain Shadows, Caldala

Frost-coated grass crunched underfoot as Akira Muro led her mare, Kahshara, across the large meadow below Mountain Shadows. At the shrill cry above, Akira lifted a hand to shade her eyes from the sun cresting the eastern ridgeline as she searched the sky for the black falcon her lover, Ardan Isfail, had named Spirit.

Beside her, Arla pointed to the bird just beginning her swift stoop to target some prey across the field. "She's got something."

Akira nodded, watching the falcon strike with deadly accuracy. "I think she prefers her own kill to hand-fed meat. We're fortunate in the weather for now."

Riding security escort to Akira's other side, Cobon grunted in agreement. "Aye. The winter's slow in coming this year, unlike the last. Often follows that way, though, one hard winter then a soft one the next. This time last year, the road from Green River was close to impassable with snow and ice."

"It's unpredictable, at that," Arla added, glancing at Akira. "It's good that you and Team Kilronan got back from Coroth last week. The weather could close in any time, cutting us off from the lower territory."

Kahshara lowered her head to gently bump her master's shoulder, bringing a slight smile to Akira's somber face. Reaching up to stroke the horse's neck, Akira wondered if her pensive mood was as apparent to her human companions. Arla turned toward her, placing a strong hand on Akira's shoulder with a gentle squeeze that told her it was.

Never one to shy away from an awkward subject, Arla brought up the obvious issue as she asked, "Have you heard anything from Coroth?"

"Only family news from the princess, thoughts regarding the liaison position and other political information from Prince Logran," Akira replied, then looked up at Cobon when he cleared his throat.

"Not to worry, Lady Muro. If I know Isfail, he's handling himself just fine with those Ishalians."

The gruff heartiness brought a warmer smile to Akira's lips, even as she reminded him, "It's Akira, Cobon. Just Akira." She knew he'd taken a far more personal interest in her safety since he'd learned that she was betrothed to Isfail, his childhood companion.

Akira was grateful for the loyal friendships she'd found in Mountain Shadows since her final mission as an ambassador brought her to this village at the end of last winter. Her own childhood companions, Kilronan and Osharon, were senior protectorate masters here. Among many new friends throughout protectorate and village were their fellow masters, Arla and Cobon, who'd gone out of their way to provide companionship and cheer since she'd returned to the mountain stronghold.

But she'd returned without the most important person in her life. Just hours after Akira had accepted Isfail's proposal, duty had parted them. He'd left in search of the deadly Ana Karsh and information on The Bow, an organized group of assassins targeting Caldala's force callers.

That search had eventually led him to the neighboring country of Ishal, the base of the assassins. Three weeks later he had yet to return or send word.

Akira wished he could know that she had fought and defeated Karsh in a dramatic clash of extreme force abilities only days before leaving the capital city of Coroth to return to Mountain

Shadows. Perhaps then he could return to Caldala more quickly, knowing he needn't search for Karsh anymore.

Kahshara shook her head, sending her long, silky mane flying before snorting impatiently. Akira stopped, turning to stroke the mare's cheek with a gloved hand. "All right. We'll have a canter before we head back, but we have to be careful."

As Arla mounted her own horse beside her, she remarked, "The ground's not frozen yet, and the frost is already melting off."

Settling into her saddle, Akira let the mare have her head for the moment. "I'm probably over-cautious." Glancing at Arla, she gave a little shrug. "Kahshara's pregnant."

Cobon let out a loud guffaw, sending their horses' ears swiveling at the sound. "I thought that stallion of Isfail's was trying to have his way with her when he came to see you a couple of lunams ago."

"Very observant," Arla said dryly. "You have nothing better to do than follow the mating rituals of horses?"

Laughing quietly, Akira said, "Ardan and I talked it over when Kahshara came into season then. Tempest isn't from Ishakan stock but they're both of noble blood, so to speak." Shrugging again, she told them, "We'll see what comes of it."

"She's strong and healthy," Arla noted. "I don't think you need to pamper her, at least not this early."

As if in agreement, Akira signaled the mare into an easy canter, Arla and Cobon beside her. Even while welcoming their company, Akira was reminded that she was never allowed to be alone. But the exercise helped blow away the annoyance and restlessness it caused. They brought their horses back to a brisk walk when they approached the west gate.

Acknowledging the salutes of the guards, the trio made their way into the village.

"Heard you're sitting in on the promotion interviews this afternoon," Cobon began, amusement in his deep voice. "Better you than me."

Akira glanced at him. "I believe it's Lord Corcoran's latest ploy to keep me busy. I'd prefer to stay out of protectorate business, as he well knows."

Laughing, Arla said, "Good luck with that. He's going to take advantage of your experience and skills as long as he can."

More serious now, Cobon ran a hand down his mustache. "Got to say he could use it with the two petitioning for elevation to senior master rank. That's Vardon, as took over Telen's team, and Mika."

"Vardon's just expressing his goals for the future," Arla stated. "He knows he hasn't been in Mountain Shadows long enough for us to have his measure, despite his time in service. He'll be fine with not advancing this round."

Turning her head to look at Akira, Arla went on. "It's Mika that will be the interesting one. This is her third application for promotion in as many years."

With a thoughtful frown, Akira replied, "I've read through the protectorate records for her. Though she comes from Corsalat, she's been with Mountain Shadows seven years, five at master rank, with her own team. I felt she did well during the Mors defense, but I can't say that I know her very well personally."

"And that's part of it," Cobon said gruffly. "Mika's an asset as a warrior, but keeps to herself more than anyone in our service. Friendly enough, mind you, but makes no effort to socialize with the rest of us more than duty calls for."

"What about her team members?" Akira studied her companions' faces.

"They have no complaints," Arla answered. "She's fair, trains as hard as she expects them to. Has a good head on her shoulders, from what I know of her. Mika's held her own in some of the High Pass defenses over recent years. She fights well, seems a good leader to her warriors." With a shrug, Arla finished with, "Maybe it's just some indefinable thing that has Lord Corcoran delaying her promotion."

Cobon chuckled. "Maybe that's another reason for getting you into it, Akira. Sharing the burden of saying no." He grinned at Arla now. "Mika gets along well enough with your Assistant Master Halen."

With a shrug, Arla turned into the lane leading to the protectorate stables, lifting a hand in greeting to the gatekeeper. "Halen's free to get along with any woman he fancies, as long as he doesn't neglect his duties. But he needs to get serious about his own career. There's another one that's not going to advance this round."

"You don't approve of his application for a Master's position?" Akira asked in surprise as they dismounted at the stable.

"I don't disapprove," Arla replied, looking over as she began to remove her horse's saddle. "I had to sign off on his application. Halen's competent, but he hasn't exerted himself to be more than that."

Chuckling, Cobon teased, "Not many have your drive or dedication to the protectorate, lass. You'd run us all into the grave if we had to keep up with you."

Smiling at that, Akira led Kahshara to her box stall as Spirit flew gracefully through the big doors behind them to alight on the top rail.

*A*kira thought about Arla's, and Cobon's, insight later that evening. If anything was sufficient to distract her from her concerns for Isfail, it was the advancement interviews. Vardon's application and review went exactly as anticipated. His answers were good, well thought out, and his record was excellent. He'd brought up his short time in service here himself, and was cheerfully expecting to be put off until the next round.

Vardon's open, easy personality was a distinct contrast to Mika's reserve. It was clear to Akira that Master Mika was her own hurdle on the road to Senior Master rank. She'd been well prepared, had a good record of service, but expressed no clear goals for her future in Mountain Shadows Protectorate. Akira also felt an absence of community commitment in her attitude, though Mika didn't give any impression of being overly self-serving.

In contrast, Assistant Master Halen, petitioning to advance

to Master rank, came across as too carelessly confident, almost flippant in some of his answers to questions. Akira remembered him from her first days in Mountain Shadows, early in the spring. Halen had been a persistent flirt when Akira had been about the village in her disguise as a young woman named Lira. It had taken Kilronan's pointed presence to cool Halen's attentions.

Still, as Arla noted, Halen was competent and had a record of fulfilling his duties capably. What he lacked were the qualities that made a good team leader. Perhaps more experience under his own excellent team leader, and more maturity, would make his next application to advancement successful.

Well, Akira thought, she was glad it was Lord Corcoran's final call.

Cove West of Tash'tric, Ishal, Same Day

Isfail woke looking up at a cloud-laden evening sky. Apparently his companions had stretched him out on a pallet sometime during the day. He appreciated the consideration since last he remembered he'd been sitting against a log.

Aric and Declan sat beside a small fire where two skinned rabbits roasted on long wood spits propped over the flames. The smell wafting over had Isfail's stomach growling as he sat up.

Smiling over at him, Declan said, "You're back with the living then, Commander."

"Just Isfail will do." Rolling toward his good side, Isfail got stiffly to his feet and joined them.

"You look better for the rest," Aric noted. "I didn't see how rough you were back in the dark. Took a bad beating from the looks of those bruises."

Isfail swallowed a long drink of water and shrugged. "Some of the Parliament guards take pleasure in carrying out their duties. Though they might have been Dateh's men, the way he gave them orders." He saw Declan scowl at Aric, who frowned as he turned the spits.

"It's another shame on us," Aric finally said, then looked Isfail in the eyes. "We'll get you home. There's a trading ship preparing to leave Tash'tric harbor on this evening's tide. If all goes as planned, she'll round the point by tomorrow afternoon and be on the lookout for you."

"How?" Isfail asked in amazement.

Aric shook his head. "I won't give you the details. It's not likely you'll be taken again, but I won't risk my people. You can't reveal what you don't know." He pulled out a hunting knife to test one of the rabbits and then used it to slide the carcass onto a flat rock. As Aric repeated the procedure with the second rabbit, he gave Isfail a quick grin. "Eat up, Commander."

Declan pulled a small flask from his coat pocket and tossed it onto Isfail's lap. "That'll help it go down easier."

When Isfail took a cautious sip, he chuckled. "Aye, a little whiskey will help ease the aches as well."

The other men laughed, and the three of them made short work of the meat and the whiskey.

Sunset flared in spectacular color before fading to night, with clouds obscuring most of the stars. Despite the wind blowing cold off the ocean, they let the fire burn to embers. Isfail wondered if the Ishalians were as confident of their safety here as they seemed. Regardless, it was wise not to reveal their position with firelight.

"Well, Isfail," Aric began. "There are things your prince should know. We've spoken of how our lawful government is about to fall, but there's more. I'm not asking to risk Caldalan lives." He paused, poking at the embers.

"Ishal must fight for itself, as I see it," Declan joined in.

Isfail could make out their solemn faces by the embers' glow. "So what should Coroth know?"

Taking a deep breath then letting it go, Aric turned his face to him. "The Bow is targeting all force callers. You know that. Some here in Ishal have the blood, though they've been careful to keep any force ability discreet. They're the first at risk of elimination. And the Ishakans, of course."

Declan swore softly, causing Isfail to note the fierce frown on his shadowed face.

Aric nodded. "Our friend here has family in the tribes. He chafes to head north to fight for his people."

"I can understand his feelings," Isfail said. "My betrothed is a force caller, a powerful one. She's already been attacked by The Bow." He saw Aric's head tilt, and heard the man's quiet chuckle.

"You're to bind with Akira Muro?" Aric guessed, amusement in his voice. "I knew you to be a brave man, Isfail, but you've more courage than I've ever seen." Shaking his head, he laughed a little.

"No disrespect intended, sir," he said. "I've met the former ambassador, several years ago now. She was an impressive woman then, and struck me as dedicated to whatever cause she served."

"She is," Isfail agreed. "All I want is to get back to her."

"Well, I would wish you happiness," Aric said, his voice serious now. "But I fear you'll see little peace until The Bow is ended. The Ishakans are also in grave danger, Commander. Dateh is pushing the government to seize the northern territories and confiscate the land currently ceded to the indigenous horse tribes."

"They're already under attack," Declan said angrily. "The Mors drove them into the mountains, but any tribes who've tried to resettle the high meadows are targeted by rogue Ishalians. Families have been murdered. Some have been able to escape back into the high mountains, but Dateh is recruiting militia to hunt them down. We don't think an organized assault can be made this season. Our hope is that the tribes can hold out until winter prevents our enemies from entering their stronghold."

Isfail's hands fisted as he stiffened at the news. The Ishakans were peaceful, though they knew how to fight for themselves. How could this be stopped? How could Caldala respond to such atrocities? Once, help could have been sent directly into Ishakan territory through the High Pass, but that was impossible now.

He looked up from the dying embers when Aric spoke again.

"There's more. These rebels are staging something at Kittric.

We haven't been able to get accurate information out of that area yet. The Bow is controlling access." Aric took a long drink from a second flask of whiskey. "I'm telling you this because there are rumors that Dateh has greater ambitions than ruling Ishal, and Kittric will be the launching point."

Seven

The next morning, Isfail found Aric brooding by the fire. He sat across from him, accepting a chunk of bread from Declan to break his fast. Isfail drew his jacket closer, wincing as the cold and abused muscles shot pain from his ribs and caused spasms low in his back.

Aric looked up. "I've a favor to ask of you, Commander."

"Ask," Isfail replied.

Aric reached into an inner pocket to pull out a small package. After holding it in both hands, studying the simple wrapping for a long moment, he said, "I'll ask you to see that this gets to Alani Iro. Last I knew of her, she was entering the Ambassador service."

Isfail accepted the little package with a nod. "Aye, she's one of the ambassadors from Akira's former team. I know her."

"Good then," Aric said gruffly. He squinted—against the light of the sunrise bouncing off the sea, perhaps.

Isfail said nothing more, just tucked the package securely into his own jacket. Then Aric spoke again.

"My friend . . . like a brother to me, Garath Haill was." Now he looked at Isfail fully. "We served together in the militia, and in the underground during the first rebellion. We were on duty when the insurgents took the Parliament building and surrounds. Haill and I, our units, we were to see the foreign ministers and their people to safety.

"It went bad all too soon. The devils had a new weapon, something we'd never encountered before. Like hand-size cannon balls with fuses, but with the powder inside so they exploded

55

with devastating effect. The makings of them and those left were destroyed and forbidden after the rebellion."

Nodding, Isfail said, "Caldala heard about them. The prince has made the manufacturing and use of such devices punishable by imprisonment or death."

"They're evil, no doubt of it." His face taut with emotion, Aric continued. "Well, the short of it is, Haill was captured. He and Alani were put in the same cell, where a number of captives were held. There came an opportunity to escape with her and he took it. Eventually, Haill crossed paths with Ambassador Muro leading a reconnaissance team. They took Alani back home. He told me of it after we met up again shortly after they parted. He told me he loved her."

After a brief pause, he said, "Garath Haill gave his life in battle, protecting his men, just a few weeks after that. The only thing he ever asked of me was to see that Alani got his most important possessions if he should fall. So I did. When we'd overthrown the insurgents, and things were settled once more, I went to Caldala and found her. Told her of Haill's death. It was hard on both of us."

Isfail nodded, understanding too well.

"I'm wondering if you know . . ." Aric asked quietly, his eyes hopeful as they met Isfail's. "Would you know if there was a child?"

Surprised, Isfail stared at him then shook his head slowly, sorry to see that hope fade. "I don't know," he replied gravely. "But I've never heard that Alani had a child."

"Well, no matter, eh?" Aric's voice sounded forced now as his gaze dropped. "You'll see she gets that, and there's an end."

Isfail watched as Aric got up and wandered down to walk the narrow stretch of sand along their tiny shore.

"Garath Haill was a great soldier," Declan stated, his face uncharacteristically somber.

Nodding, Isfail said, "I know he's the one who managed to kill Arthon Baronan. That was the breaking point for the rebellion and gave you the opening to take down the rest."

"But not soon enough," Declan said bitterly. "We had another week of fierce and bloody fighting in the streets to rout the remaining rebels. Haill was killed the day before they surrendered." Dragging a stick through the sand, he added, "He threw himself on one of those accursed exploding balls—tossed into the middle of our platoon as we charged one of the last hold-outs." There was a pause as Declan stared out to sea, flinging the stick into the advancing waves.

"I was running right beside him, until he veered into me when that sparking devil's weapon landed to my right. He just rammed into me, sent me tumbling to the left, before he dove onto it. Haill saved my life."

Isfail blew out a long breath and saw Declan swipe a hand over his cheek. Some sacrifices caused lifelong heartache.

"Aric was there that day," Declan added. "I think it would be easier for him if Haill had another legacy. All these years, he's believed there was a child." Grieving blue eyes turned to Isfail. "I don't know why."

There was nothing he could say to comfort, so Isfail just laid his hand on the man's shoulder as they watched Aric continue his solitary walk.

*T*he hours seemed to crawl. The sun inched its path behind the cloud-laden sky while they waited for any sign of a ship. They talked of ideas to thwart the enemy, how to rally normally peaceful civilians, spread throughout Ishal, to fight. Other times, Aric and Declan answered more of Isfail's questions about The Bow, providing what information they had to help the Caldalans defend against them.

Isfail recalled Declan's ties to the Ishakans. Maybe he had some information that Isfail had been seeking for years on Akira's behalf.

Turning to him, he began, "Aric said you have Ishakan family. Do you know of a man named Kane Kalronan?" He watched the man's eyes go blank.

"There's no Ishakan by that name," Declan quickly answered.

Raising an eyebrow, Isfail looked into those shuttered eyes. "Kalronan's not of Ishakan blood. He's Caldalan, and a Psyche." He frowned now. "I have no desire to harm the man, and he's not in trouble." With some frustration, Isfail pressed, "I'm trying to get answers about family history for someone. Kane Kalronan is linked to that family."

Shaking his head, Isfail picked up a stone to fling it toward the waves. "Why the hell is every Ishakan I've asked so tight-lipped about him?"

He heard a snort of laughter and looked back at Declan.

"Kane wishes it," Declan finally admitted with a grin. "I'm only telling you because I believe you to be an honorable man, Commander, and because you will be bound to Akira Muro. The tribes know her well, respect her, as Kane does."

"So why is it so hard to meet with him?"

Declan's brow furrowed. "I really can't answer that. But he's a powerful *Nah'shalon*—keeper of power," he explained. "The partner of a powerful *Sha'ala* of our people. If he chooses it to be so, it is so. But if I get back to help my people fight, I'll try to find an opportunity to tell him that you'd like to speak with him." He sighed. "Though it might be some time before that happens, even if Kane chooses."

At the roll of thunder, the three men looked out to sea and the lightning that flickered in thick black clouds. White-capped waves roughened the surface of the water. Isfail felt his hopes of rescue fade knowing that the storm could prevent a sailing vessel from safely dropping anchor in this unprotected cove.

Then Declan gave an elated shout, punching his fist into the air as they watched a ship round the short point.

Isfail breathed a sigh of relief as he recognized the trading vessel flying the flag of Kilra. He stood up as the *Maid* tacked closer to shore, with her crew in a flurry of activity on deck. Soon a flagman appeared on the quarterdeck and Isfail grinned as the semaphore sequence hailed him while the ship dropped anchor.

Aric and Declan stood with him as a landing boat was lowered. Three men clambered down a rope ladder to take up oars and pull for the shore amid the restless waves.

"Looks like a fine day after all," Aric said, making Isfail laugh as the man glanced up at the ominous sky above them.

So close to leaving, Isfail was flooded with gratitude for what his companions had risked to see him this far. He would never know how many loyalists had worked to make this possible. Now he turned to the two men and offered his arm to each in turn.

"There are no words," Isfail said. "Nothing to adequately repay all of you for what you've done."

Aric glanced at Declan then said, "There's no matter of repayment, Isfail. You and your people came to our aid before, and paid a heavy price. We weren't going to allow it to happen again."

"My thanks anyway, Aric. And you, Declan, and all who did their part and risked the peril." Isfail turned his head and saw the landing boat surfing toward the little beach.

"What will you do now?" he asked.

"We've our own rebellion to set in motion," Aric said with a grin. He clapped Declan on the back. "Don't we, lad."

Isfail started to walk down to the wave line, then stopped and turned around. "I can make no promises or commitments for my country, but I will do whatever I can to help you in your fight."

Aric let out a long sigh as he turned his face to watch the boat slide onto the sand, and a man leap out to run toward them. Then his eyes met Isfail's once more. "It's appreciated, Commander. God willing, we'll meet again in happier times." He smiled as he said, "Give my respectful regards to your lady."

With a nod and a last salute to the two men, Isfail turned back into Micah Vaneer's joyful greeting and hearty grip. Then Micah was hustling him to the landing boat.

When he finally stood on the quarterdeck, with both Vaneers beside him and a deck full of cheerful sailors shouting their greetings, Isfail looked back to shore one more time. Aric and Declan had left the beach and now stood atop the high bluff of the point, arms raised in farewell against the cloud-heavy sky. Isfail raised his hand high in return, praying for their safety and success in the battle to come.

Eight

*T*he *Maid of Kilra* was safely out to sea when Isfail followed Micah into the captain's cabin. Welcoming the warmth after days outside without adequate outerwear, Isfail took a seat at the table at Micah's direction, listening as his friend told him about the Vaneers' experiences at Tash'tric. Head and body aching, he struggled to focus on the news.

"You'll have my berth," Micah said suddenly, the fatigue on Isfail's face apparently causing him to interrupt his recital. "I'll put up a hammock. There's ample room," he stated when Isfail started to object. Pulling a thick overcoat from a cabinet, Micah tossed it onto a wall hook. "You'll need that."

Isfail nodded, too tired to object. He'd spent his early years on naval ships and knew his own clothing unequal to even a few days aboard ship, especially with the storm now sending cold curtains of rain over all. When a quick knock on the door announced the ship's cook with biscuits and a bowl of thick soup, Isfail's thanks were heartfelt.

Taking the seat across from him, Micah folded his arms on the table and finished his news, telling of the Ishalians who'd been smuggled aboard. He showed Isfail the message written in the small journal.

"You say the commander, this Shanow, gave you this?" Isfail asked, looking at the scripted S closing the page. "He's aware of the people smuggled onto the *Maid*?"

"Pretty sure of that," Micah said with a grin, "as his wife and four children are among them."

At Isfail's surprised look, Micah continued. "Then there's the wife and daughters of the man who approached Grip the first night ashore, who promised to look for information on what happened to you. The last family is a widow and her two children; lost her husband in the Baronan rebellion. Says her brother's a militia commander on the side of the true soldiers."

Micah poured two cups of ale and pushed one across the table to Isfail. "Sam's given over his cabin to the women, daughters, and little ones. That's a crowd in there, but better than staying in packing cases. Though we've made use of some boxes as beds for the youngest." He took a swig of ale before going on. "The older lads, fifteen and twelve, we set up in hammocks in the crew's quarters under Amon's watch. Then the little one quarreled over why he couldn't be there with big brother."

That got a chuckle from Isfail. "So he's tucked into a hammock too?"

"So he is." Laughing, Micah tugged on his ear. "That's Shanow's younger boy. He's a gutsy one already."

"I look forward to meeting them," Isfail said as he stretched carefully. "In the morning, I think."

Within minutes he was sound asleep on the narrow bed, without a thought for the rolling pitch of the ship on the storm-tossed sea.

*T*he following day came with scattered white clouds drifting across a deep blue sky. With the ocean quiet enough to enjoy the sunshine, Isfail and Micah walked toward the group of women and children on the forward deck. One of the women stood as they approached, eyes as blue as the sky above, with dark red hair escaping the sedate knot at the nape of her neck to blow in the wind.

"Commander Isfail," she said, but when she began a curtsy, Isfail gestured it away.

As the older children scrambled up, leaving the younger ones collecting the two puppies they'd been playing with, the youngest woman got up from her place on the deck. Her arms were full of a very young baby, while a toddler hung onto her pants leg.

Isfail offered a hand to the woman who'd greeted him. "Yes, I'm Commander Ardan Isfail. It's my pleasure to meet such a courageous group."

At his questioning glance, she took a deep breath. "Mirastheny Shanow, my lord. My husband is Commander Gaios Shanow of the Ishalian First Militia. These are our children." She laid a hand on her sons' shoulders as she gave their names, then the daughter holding on to a wriggling puppy, and the youngest daughter gaping up at them from a blanket on the deck.

"It's my pleasure," Isfail repeated with a smile and an arm offered to the boys. The oldest flushed with a shy smile as he took it in a firm grip.

Isfail considered the younger boy's quick smile as he accepted a greeting. "How do you like bunking in the hold, young man?" Isfail laughed when a grin seemed to split the boy's face.

After a timid smile from the four-year-old girl, Isfail said, "You have a fine family, Madame Shanow. And the rest of your group?" Isfail asked, with a nod of his head to the older woman, who remained in a chair the captain had provided.

"Madame Ryska Olssen, Commander," Mirastheny introduced.

Isfail took the thin hand offered in both of his, thinking that the woman's pale blue eyes had seen too much as he met her strangely absent gaze. Although her lips tipped into a polite smile, Ryska said nothing.

At Isfail's glance back at her, Mirastheny said, "Ryska's husband was a militia captain. He died in the Baronan Rebellion, fighting for the true government." She looked at the woman and received a small nod before saying quietly, "Captain Olssen was tortured to death in front of her when he refused to name other loyalists. The villains broke her legs and raped her before that, and would have threatened the children but they'd been sent into hiding with her brother."

His face tightening as he listened, Isfail shot a concerned glance at Ryska's children.

"They know what happened to their parents, Commander,"

Mirastheny said in a cool voice. "One cannot protect the children, teach them to stand against evil, if they do not know the truth of their history."

Before he could respond, Ryska's son stepped forward. "I'm Garath," the young man said eagerly. "It is an honor to meet you, sir."

"And you, Garath. That's a fine name." Isfail held out his arm, pleased by the tight grip.

"Yes, Commander. I'm named for another hero of the First Rebellion."

Isfail nodded with a somber expression. "Captain Garath Haill, I'd wager."

The youth stood straight and proud, announcing, "Yes, sir. He was a great friend of my father and my uncle, and he was my godfather, and a brave soldier. Someday I will fight for my country too." Garath looked at his mother. "But now it is my duty to see my family to safety. I'm fifteen years old and the man of the family."

"Yes," Isfail said, laying a hand on Garath's shoulder. "It's the most important job you can do." He looked back to Ryska for a moment then asked Garath, "Is your uncle by chance a Commander Caden Aric?"

He saw the boy's quick glance at his mother, waiting for her nod before saying, "Yes, sir. He told me you are a great champion of the First Rebellion—you fought with the Gattes Brigade in Kittric!"

At a loss for an appropriate reply, Isfail sighed over the boy's misplaced admiration. "Some things in life are worth standing for. You already know that, because Garath Haill was a true hero." Isfail stroked a gentle hand over Garath's younger sister's golden hair, earning a bright smile from her even as he thought how hard a world it was that these children knew such darkness in their young lives.

"Your uncle is my hero," Isfail told them. "He and his friends saved me from a difficult situation. I'm grateful to them."

"Then you'll want to thank Darai's man, too, Commander,"

Mirastheny said with a smile, indicating the woman with the baby. "It was her husband who alerted Gaios to your disappearance, and he enlisted Commander Aric's assistance."

Isfail bowed to Darai, causing her to blush profusely. "I am in your husband's debt. Though I see it has brought hardship to your young family."

To his surprise, her response was resolute. "You did not bring the hardship, my lord. The Bow did that. If anything, helping you escape made the decision to leave easier for us." Darai kissed her infant's forehead while stroking the toddler's dark curls with her free hand. "Emmon, my man, and my brother, Declan, are now free to work with the resistance without worry for us."

Cocking his head, Isfail studied her, noting the dark hair and dusky features with new interest. "There was a Declan who joined us at the coast, a friend of Aric's."

Darai smiled, though it faded quickly. "Yes. Now he'll make his way to Ishaka, hoping to make a difference in the defense there."

There was a brief interruption when Micah reappeared with the ship's cook and a couple of sailors carrying tall pots of tea with plates of biscuits, sliced fruit, and cheeses. The sailors rolled barrels of varying sizes into place to act as seats for the adults before all but Micah returned to regular duty.

Isfail took the mug of hot tea Micah offered as he studied Mirastheny. "I could arrange for all of you to be given sanctuary in Caldala."

She gave him a tired smile. "Aren't you concerned that we might be spies for The Bow?"

Shaking his head, Isfail replied, "I don't believe you would risk your children, Madame Shanow. There was never any certainty that you'd be allowed into my country."

"No," she acknowledged, stroking a hand down her oldest son's back. "No, we risked everything to see our children safe, Commander. Gaios and I remember the last rebellion all too well." Mirastheny seemed to shake herself from those memories before saying, "Ryska and I both have family on Orsha. We plan to wait for our men there. Darai and her children will have a home with us for however long she wishes. Besides, there are people who have already infiltrated Caldala that might recognize us—hear about Ishalian refugees coming into your country. It would be too dangerous for both sides, Commander."

With a nod, Isfail looked around the group. "If you have a need, I will help you."

"Thank you, Commander." Ryska spoke for the first time. "We have gold with us, enough to pay for passage. Enough to see us through some lunams."

"It seems you have planned well, Madame."

"When you have lived through one disaster, you learn to prepare for the next," she told him calmly.

Later that afternoon, when the Ishalian group had returned to their assigned quarters, Isfail sat in the captain's cabin, writing notes in the journal that Shanow had given the Vaneers. He wanted to record all the details of the information that he'd learned.

At the knock on the door, Isfail called out, "Enter." Looking up as Micah came in carrying a long canvas bag, he lifted an eyebrow. "It's your cabin, Micah, no need to knock."

"Just wanted to see if you were presentable," Micah murmured with a quick grin, pointing his thumb back toward the door. "Madame Shanow would like a word."

Isfail got to his feet as Micah opened the door to admit the woman. "Madame," he greeted, lifting a hand to indicate the other chair.

"Thank you." Mirastheny included Micah in her thanks before she got straight to the purpose of her visit. "I have information that Gaios wanted you to have. I believe my husband would also entrust Captain Vaneer and his son with this news."

Micah left to find his father, and Isfail watched curiously as Mirastheny rose to open the canvas bag. She pulled out an oilskin-wrapped bundle and brought it to the table, setting it in front of the commander as the Vaneers returned.

"These are journals where Gaios recorded everything he's discovered about The Bow, and about Abron Dateh. He hopes they will be of use to Caldala but says that they're far from complete." She watched as Isfail removed the wrapping and opened one of the journals.

Brow furrowed, Isfail said, "This is a treasure of information, Madame. Surely these are more valuable to Ishal's resistance, though I welcome your husband's generosity in sharing with us."

Shaking her head, Mirastheny explained, "Our people must keep such knowledge in our memories, our minds. What you have there are the original journals. Gaios knew that his life would be forfeit if the wrong people found them. He started writing information down over two years ago, when rumors and misinformation began to discomfit him.

"Then Abron Dateh became a public presence, openly encouraging government dissent unless the ministers acknowledged The Bow as a legitimate following. As life began to deteriorate, those who had lived through the Baronan Rebellion began to see the same patterns, the same oppression of freedoms. Those who spoke up were initially laughed at and publically ridiculed, then they were publically shamed, attacked, even murdered." Her voice broke and her hands gripped the edge of the table.

Isfail waited for her to regain composure, seeing how difficult these revelations were for her.

"I'm sure you understand where this is going, Commander." Mirastheny retrieved a pair of capped wooden rods bracketing a tightly furled banner from the canvas bag. "This is what's coming. One of my husband's informants within Parliament got this to him two weeks ago. These will be posted throughout Ishal's cities on the Day of Ishalion—our country's celebration of Ishal's founding—less than three weeks from today."

She lifted one rod, allowing the weight of the other to unfurl the banner. Isfail's mouth tightened as he saw the sign of The Bow flanking the text, and read the call to action.

On this Great Day of Ishalion, Proud Citizens, Know the Enemy!
Defend Ishal from the Oppression of All Force Callers!
Take Back the Northern Territories from All Horse Tribes!
See Them. Report Them. Detain Them!
We are The Bow Whose Arrows Strike Down the Unnatural!

Nine

*P*repared for whatever might come, Gaios Shanow answered the summons from Ishal's Ministry of Defense. Though he gave silent thanks that his family was safely two days out to sea, he felt no fear for himself, only curiosity about the reason behind this directive. Every meeting, however unexpected, gave him more information that might be useful to the resistance.

"Commander Shanow, reporting as ordered." His face impassive, Shanow met the stern gaze of the official Minister of Defense.

Though he focused on the minister, he also noted the second man in the room—black hair and eyes, insolent in his richly garbed elegance as he lounged in a cushioned armchair. Abron Dateh, the self-titled Lord Dateh, with influence in all manner of parliamentary decisions.

An unknown less than three years ago, most in the government still considered Dateh a mystery, but Shanow had made it his mission to find what there was to know about Abron Dateh. It was that shocking information that had guided the difficult decision to send his family out of the country. He also knew that the knowledge put his life at risk if Dateh learned how much he'd discovered.

"Shanow," the defense minister began abruptly. "Your platoon was assigned to duty on the docks, overseeing a foreign trading ship."

"Yes, sir."

"There have been two complaints filed against you and your unit."

Shanow let a flicker of surprise show in his tawny eyes, but said nothing.

The minister lifted a paper from his desk. "One from a Captain Vaneer filed with the harbormaster, protesting the conduct of the Ishalian militia unit assigned to oversee his ship, the *Maid of Kilra*. The other from the dock supervisors stationed to oversee all activities at that berth."

Scowling, the minister continued. "Both complain of conduct overstepping the limits of your duty. What have you to say to these charges?"

"Only that I did my duty as ordered, sir. The Defense Ministry assigned my platoon to that ship, primarily to prevent an escaped prisoner from using it to flee Ishalian justice, with orders to use any means necessary. Our secondary duty was to ensure the orderly loading and dispatch of that ship." Shanow was aware of Dateh listening with close attention.

"So you believe that no one was smuggled out?" the minister asked, flicking a glance at Dateh.

"My men inspected the Kilran ship twice; when we first arrived at that dock and before she sailed. We had eyes on the ship around the clock." Shanow paused before saying, "As did the supervisors."

Looking down at the paper in his hand, the minister pressed, "Those supervisors say that you overstepped your authority and interfered with the loading on the last day."

Shanow met his hard look evenly. "I did, Minister, due to the incompetence of those supervisors. A crate was dropped during loading and sounds of crying or whimpering were heard coming from it. Instead of investigating the possibility of human cargo, those same supervisors spent their time arguing with the dock crew—an argument that spread to the ship's crew. I ordered the crate opened."

The man stared at him in surprise. "And what did you find?"

His face a model of composure, Shanow said, "Dogs, sir."

"Dogs?" Dateh interjected sharply, standing up.

Shanow glanced at him. "Yes, my lord, though they were actually pups."

The Minister of Defense set the papers aside, shaking his head. "Very well, Commander Shanow. I find no reason to continue an investigation. Dismissed."

*M*oving with a career soldier's straight-backed purpose, Shanow strode down the long, tile-paved halls of the building. Noting the rapping echo of his boot-steps in the emptiness, he glanced around, wondering at the absence of staff in the ornate edifice housing Ishal's Parliament. Had Dateh and his minions managed to purge those who actually worked for the legitimate government?

Shanow kept his expression neutral—spies could be anywhere—as he focused his attention on the gilded walls embellished with elaborate and over-bright mosaic designs, a monument to avarice, and greed for power. All traits that the government had displayed throughout his career, and none that served the citizenry of Ishal. The waste of money and resources displayed here had always made his skin crawl.

The glittering shell over a rotten hulk, Shanow thought, his mouth thinning in disgust. He could almost smell the stench of decay, the dissolution of a once proud people. Sold out once again to those who whispered of power and riches, tempting the bloated ranks of Ishal's Parliament.

Had they learned nothing from the first rebellion? When Arthon Baronan had spun his web of lies and promises to gain a foothold? All while building a private military of the cruel, the sadistic, and the disenfranchised, Baronan had skillfully masked his mad cunning as he courted the politicians of Ishal. Laws had been rewritten or willfully ignored, rights and freedoms had been taken from the citizenry when it appeared expedient to the new order. And the military had been stripped of authority and resources with such skillful guile that it was too late to reverse the damage when Baronan revealed his true ambition.

He could almost admire the man's devious tactics, Shanow

thought reluctantly. But he'd never forgive those who had sold out their country, then and now.

Deliberately relaxing hands that had clenched into fists, Shanow turned some of that disgust inward as he reached the large entry rotunda. Despite his own experience, he'd failed to see this current danger approaching until The Bow had gained a solid grip on the government. Now those loyal to the people of Ishal were scrambling to find a way to defend their country once more.

But those like himself, who'd lived through the first rebellion, had also learned to be secretive, to hide their true allegiances, and to quickly reestablish the loyalist underground. Even so, Shanow knew his own mask was thinning. As soon as someone noticed that Mirastheny and the children were gone, his freedom, his life, would be in peril. He had too much left to do to risk imprisonment. His steps quickened as he approached the large double doors.

"Commander!"

Pausing, Shanow fixed a polite, if somewhat impatient, expression on his face as he turned to face an enemy. "You wish to speak with me, Lord Dateh?"

Ten

I'm impressed by the way you handled the situation on the docks, Commander," Dateh began with a cordial smile as he led the way into the elegant suite of offices Shanow knew he'd talked his way into lunams ago. "I'm not a military man myself, so it's always interesting for me to observe how professional military men conduct themselves."

He offered Shanow a choice of brandy or ale.

"Thank you, my lord, but I don't drink spirits on duty," Shanow declined in a brusque voice.

"Of course." Dateh nodded with a thoughtful expression now. "I admire your dedication, sir. I've certainly not seen this quality of service with my own men. But then, personal guards only need to be competent and loyal, don't they? They're not trained to be self-disciplined, or in how to fight a war."

The commander stood quietly, offering no comment for the moment.

"I'm sure you're wondering why I've interrupted your duty." Dateh turned to face him fully. "I've been asked for my input on the Ishakan problem."

Now Shanow raised an eyebrow. "I am unaware of a problem, as you put it, with the Ishakan territories. I've heard nothing about this."

"Parliament has tried to keep the citizens from worrying about additional upheaval during this time of change."

Though he kept a hint of concern in his demeanor, Shanow saw that Dateh watched him closely. So he would see curiosity and that glimmer of concern, Shanow decided.

Apparently satisfied, Dateh continued. "As you know, Commander, Parliament has learned that outsiders are working to undermine the Ishalian government. There are rumors that the horse tribes are in league with force callers from Caldala."

His jaw hardening at this news, Shanow asked, "To what purpose?"

"It's thought that the successful defeat of the Mors by the Psyche Akira Muro has emboldened those with force ability. Many wish to expand into Ishal, seeking more land for their own communities and their own government, as Caldala becomes more restrictive. The Bow has been monitoring this threat for some time, until their leaders determined that it was time to come out publicly to defend the rightful citizens of Ishal."

So this is how they're playing it, Shanow thought, keeping his expression stern. Dateh is trying to manipulate historical fears of those with unusual abilities. The Bow is making the force-enabled citizens the aggressors. The resistance had already known that The Bow was holding up Akira Muro as a danger to Ishal, now Dateh was enlarging the threat to include the force-gifted Ishakan horse tribes.

"May I ask how the defense ministry plans to counter this threat?" Shanow asked in a terse voice, hoping to appear reluctant to gain this information from a lord outside that department.

"I will advise them to take military control of the Ishakan territories. At least to contain them and search for outside insurgents, cut off that avenue of attack," Dateh replied, sending a serious look to the commander as he added, "I feel that you are the right man to lead a military force against them."

Playing his part, Shanow straightened almost imperceptibly, pretending to consider his response.

"I'm sworn to protect my country, Lord Dateh, and to obey the orders of the Defense Ministry of Ishal. In that, I take pride in my service and my military record. I have always done what the government deems best for Ishal."

Studying the grim visage as if searching for any hint of weakness in Shanow's allegiance, a smile tipped Dateh's thin mouth. "Then I'm ready to give my opinion to the minister. I've kept you from your duty, Commander, but I value your time."

Shanow gave a curt nod of respect and left the room, wondering if he'd played his role convincingly.

"Well?" Abron Dateh didn't look back when Beros Felcan entered from the adjoining secretary's office where he'd been listening. Felcan was Dateh's closest confidant and most trusted companion, as far as he trusted anyone.

Taking a seat with the ease of that long association, Felcan made a grumbling sound. "I think you're playing with fire. Shanow's the top commander of the Ishalian militia. He's tough and he's loyal."

"I agree." Dateh settled across from him, slouching comfortably into a leather chair. "Those qualities could be just what we need to complete our objectives. Such absolute loyalty could make Shanow a very useful soldier, as long as the man believes any orders are given for the good of Ishal. He's exactly the kind of commander I need to eliminate the Ishakans. If Shanow is convinced that the Defense Ministry is behind the orders, he'll lead an effective campaign against the horse tribes and save us the trouble."

Felcan nodded slowly. "And that would divert loyalist sympathy for the Ishakans, if it appeared that Parliament was behind it. No connection to The Bow, so it would seem." He hefted his large frame and went to the small table holding a drink service.

Dateh inclined his head when his friend held up a decanter of deep red wine with a questioning look. As Felcan poured two glasses, Dateh echoed, "So it would seem. Meanwhile, militia units are removed from Tash'tric—the ones most likely to harbor loyalist sympathies. Our people can handle those left behind."

Sipping the excellent wine Felcan handed him, Dateh continued. "The defense minister will cooperate with my . . . suggestions. He has a long record of opposing the Ishakan territories and their independence."

"I'm sure those gold ore samples you showed him helped ensure his cooperation," Felcan added with a sly smile. He knew his friend's methods well.

"He does have a weakness." Dateh smirked. "As do others. Some will even do well in the new government. Promises of power and greater wealth are easy to give in exchange for their services now, cleaner and more efficient than threats and bloodshed. It has always been so."

Pressing a hand to Dateh's shoulder as he moved back to his own chair, Felcan chuckled. "We learned that early enough, didn't we? How old were we when we met? Thirteen? Fifteen? When my father sent me to live with his sister," Felcan mused. "I hated it there, until you came when Baronan bound my ridiculous aunt. Between us, we ruled that youth academy our fathers sent us to. Hardly any threats needed, despite your old lord's crazy vendettas."

For a moment, a frown drew Dateh's black eyebrows together. "Baronan could have succeeded all those years ago if he'd been sane enough to remember that. Instead, his taste for bloody revenge earned him an iron-willed resistance and a knife for his own throat. And it wasn't all good times for us."

Knowing when to remain silent, Felcan finished his wine. He watched while Dateh got to his feet, then said, "Shanow isn't one for bribery. We might need to use his family."

"No." Dateh had regained his calm. "That would only alienate him. We need his willing involvement, his uncompromised sense of duty."

"So you don't want them watched? No matter what, Shanow's not going to condone a slaughter of the Ishakans, especially women and children."

Dateh paused, turning back to meet Felcan's curious gaze as he stated, "Not yet. If Commander Shanow refuses to cooperate, his family will be useful in other ways. As far as the Ishakan problem, we can take care of it after the land is ours." His eyes narrowed as he turned to the map of Ishal mounted on a wall, stabbing a finger on the High Pass marked between Caldala and the Ishakan territories. "I want control of this."

"What's so important about taking over Ishaka, Abron? You've never explained why it's worth so much of our manpower and effort," Felcan asked impatiently. "From all we've heard, that old pass is blocked with more rock than can be moved. It's useless to any of our plans in Caldala."

"Because I want control over the only land access between what's rightfully *mine!*" Dateh shouted. "Soon, *I'll* control Ishal and Caldala! Explosives and men will clear the old pass."

Taking a deep breath, Dateh's face lost its sudden ferocity. "Let's get back to the operations in Caldala. The force callers remain the biggest obstacle to our plans. Ramort is in place, but we'll wait on that until the opportune time."

Breathing deep after Dateh's raging outburst, Felcan rubbed the back of his neck. "Ramort's unreliable. That's why we have—"

"It's an easy assignment," Dateh interrupted. "You have the more important one."

Felcan shrugged, relenting. "And I'll need to be on the road soon to meet your timeline. I could use more poison, and more arrows, at least the tips. We're running low."

Unease, a rare and unwelcome feeling, threw Abron Dateh off his confident stride, but this was Beros Felcan, the man who always made it work—who'd stood by him through the dark times. "I've been concentrating on our work in Parliament. Toxin production is off, and the volcanic glass needed to make the arrow heads hasn't been coming in." He saw the irritation on Felcan's face.

"There was a surplus of the poison. What happened to it?"

Waving that away, Dateh reminded him, "Remember that fool, Maron Illeri? It was a mistake to turn the poison production over to him."

"He was good at it," Felcan muttered.

"Maybe too good," Dateh shot back. "He decided to use those skills for his own gain, taking off with men we could use now, and some of the rare ingredients needed for the Black Arrows."

"Didn't get him far, did it?" Felcan sat back, apparently resigned to the lack of poisoned arrows. "Ishal asked Caldala to send the white witch, Muro, after him. Didn't she kill the brother too?" He seemed to ponder. "I heard something about it from our contact in Mountain Shadows. Coron Illeri tried to kill her in retaliation, but she drew him out. A protectorate warrior cut his throat."

"No loss," Dateh said, preferring to avoid any more questions about the Black Arrow poison. He didn't choose to reveal all his plans, and he had a purpose for the most important ingredients used in that poison. Felcan didn't need to know that Dateh hadn't turned *all* the poison production over to Illeri, or that he'd refined one of Arthon Baronan's most devastating formulas.

Turning back to the large table before him, Dateh pored over the map one of his spies had brought back from Caldala. Appreciating the detail inked onto the thin-shaved leather, he skimmed a hand over the supple surface. These maps were highly valued, being both laborious in execution and expensive. But—like politicians—gold or silver placed in the hands of a greedy Caldalan with dreams of power could buy much of value, including information.

Tonight, Dateh was looking for something specific, something that would strike at the heart of the Psyches. As his fingertip traced the main roads in Caldala, he suddenly laughed. The big man seated nearby looked over with interest then got up to join him.

"You have something?" Felcan asked with mild enthusiasm.

Dateh gave a nod. "My father told me that the force-enabled spread throughout his country from two settlements. He destroyed one, now The Bow will deal with the main nest."

Picking up a small dagger, Dateh drove it into the table, piercing the map at the location marked *Psyche Lakes*.

Shanow left the Parliament complex with the brisk strides of a man going about delayed business. He wanted to breathe open air, to feel the wind blow away the lingering sensation of being in the presence of something foul. Still, he thought he'd walked that fine line of hiding his true sentiments while presenting a believable façade to Dateh.

This unexpected interview had provided the resistance with some excellent insight into the enemy's next plan of attack. And might provide a way for him to openly leave Tash'tric, taking his men and as many loyal souls with them as they could manage. If Dateh moved forward quickly, Shanow and his soldiers could disrupt any intended assault against the Ishakans before The Bow could stop them.

Turning into the complex that housed the capital forces of the Ishalian Militia, Shanow checked in with the gate guard, a known informant for The Bow. Another time, it would be satisfying to watch the guard hang for treason, but better knowing the enemy in front of you. It was the ones you didn't know were there who stabbed you in the back.

He continued through courtyards that should be filled with militia soldiers going about the usual routine: platoons forming up to patrol the city, ones coming off rotation, those on base duty—servicing weapons, exercising horses, and more. Now it was too quiet, too sparsely populated. The defense ministry had ordered more than the usual number of soldiers out to patrol the city perimeters. Most of those commanders had some known link to the resistance during the Baronan Rebellion, though there had been no attempt by the new order to openly disband their units, so far. Perhaps Dateh and The Bow weren't yet secure in their control over Parliament.

Shanow had sent his own platoon out on normal duty under the leadership of his lieutenant, a man he trusted with his life. There were none among his men whose loyalty he'd question. There had been a couple of new soldiers among them when The Bow had first made their presence known, but Shanow had been able to shift them out of his unit and into other less-important ones without raising suspicion. He hoped they were good men, but he hadn't had a chance to fully vet their backgrounds during this critical time.

These thoughts were interrupted as he approached his small office, and Shanow went on alert. The door he'd closed and locked just this morning was open about a hand's width. Approaching with silent pace, he drew the dagger from the sheath at his side while he reached out and pushed the door fully open. Shanow eased back, looking through the narrow space between door edge and frame to see if anyone was hiding there, before scanning the room. There was no one there now.

Stepping in, Shanow frowned at what they'd left behind. Sloppy, he thought with a grim smile while he looked at the mess of papers pulled from records boxes, the drawers yanked out with their contents dumped carelessly; all the evidence of a hurried but thorough search.

"Amateurs," came a voice from behind him, but Shanow didn't flinch or look back. He'd recognized the careful approach, this time of an ally.

"Yes," Shanow replied, turning now to gesture Declan in before closing the door. It was thick wood and made it impossible for anyone to overhear a discreet conversation.

"What were they after?" asked Declan, cautiously opening the door to the single small closet. There was no one hiding there, just more signs of a search.

"There was nothing to find," Shanow told him, pouring two short glasses of whiskey while Declan leaned out the window that had been left open.

Looking both ways in the narrow alley it opened to, then craning his head to look up at the walls rising above, Declan shook his head as he pulled back, closing and locking the window. "No sign of anyone. They didn't force the window."

"No. They had a key and came in through the door." Shanow swallowed his first sip, letting the warm burn wash away the dregs of bitterness from his interview with Dateh. "Careless, I wonder? Or did Dateh want me to know he'd had my office searched?"

Scowling, Declan stared at him, listening closely as Shanow related the content of both of his meetings that morning. There were few surprises there; the resistance knew where the defense minister stood in this takeover. But Shanow knew the unexpected meeting with Dateh had Declan's full attention.

Then a worried look came into his companion's eyes. "Do you think they searched your home?"

Shanow shook his head. "No. I'd have received word if they had. And Mirastheny did a good job of making the house look lived in. I change things a bit when I'm there, to keep up the illusion. There's been no sign, so far, that watchers are on me or the house."

He leaned back in his desk chair while Declan slouched in the only other chair in the room. "I think Dateh has bigger plans for me. Let's keep him focused on that. Before we talk that over, how did the shipment go?"

Declan grinned, raising his glass in a toast.

Eleven

City of Coroth, Caldala

Captain, a carriage just turned in the entrance. No one is scheduled for an appointment at this time."

Royal Guard Captain Aroth looked up at the young soldier's words. He turned from the cramped desk where he'd been reviewing reports and peered through the small window in the gatehouse, trying to make out an insignia through the steady rainfall. A basic coach for hire pulled up.

The two guardsmen stepped out as it came to a stop just before the iron gates embellished with the medallion of the House of Coroth. Aroth nodded to the driver, who tipped his hat respectfully, then approached the coach as the near door opened. A canvas bag was tossed out onto the wet cobbles before a man wrapped in a long seaman's coat stepped down.

Aroth watched the stranger's careful movements, trying to see the face beneath a broad-brimmed hat. He placed a cautious hand on his sword hilt as the man picked up the bag and walked slowly toward him.

"No need for that sword, Captain."

The familiar voice brought a huge grin to Aroth's face as he opened the narrow pedestrian gate and gladly took the offered arm. "Commander Isfail! It's good to see you. Let's get you under shelter."

Signaling the now-smiling soldier to resume his post, Aroth quickly took the large bag from Isfail, walking with him down the curving lane to the main palace doors. "You've a tale to tell, haven't you, sir."

"That I have," Isfail replied in a weary voice. "What's the news here?"

"The biggest is that Ana Karsh is dead." Aroth dipped his head to Isfail's sharp look. "Aye, Commander. That was a night for the historians to tell about, but I'll leave it to the prince to give you the details. You'll want to know that Lady Muro returned to Mountain Shadows safely." He heard Isfail's murmur of thanks.

Aroth got a good look at him after they cleared the two guards at the large arched doors and stepped into the well-lit entry hall. "You'll forgive me, I hope, Commander, but you look like hell."

With a brief laugh, Isfail took back the canvas bag, waving away an attendant's attempt to carry it for him. "Just reflects the inner man, Aroth. Thanks."

As Commander Lord Ardan Isfail walked away, lifting a hand to acknowledge the greetings and bows from palace staff, Aroth watched his stiff movements and slumped shoulders with concern.

*A*t the half-open door to Logran's office, Isfail paused, watching as his cousin shifted in his chair, apparently reading the paper in his hand. God it was good to see him, to be back home again.

As Logran began to write, Isfail pushed the door wide and stepped in, hearing him ask, "What is it?"

"Working late?" He saw Logran's head jerk up.

"Dan!" Rushing around the desk, his cousin wrapped him in a strong—and painful—embrace. "Thank God."

"Careful, Lo. I'm filthy." But Isfail held tight another moment before drawing away to put the bag down.

Taking his arm, Logran guided him to a chair. "What the hell happened?"

Isfail sat, groaning thankfully into the comfort of soft, deep leather that cushioned unseen bruises. "Where shall I start?"

Giving Logran a painful grin, he accepted an offered glass of whiskey.

Princess Oona rushed in ahead of an attendant carrying a full tray.

"Dan!" she exclaimed pressing him back down when he began to rise. Taking his scruffy face in her hands, Oona pressed a kiss to both cheeks. "Thank God you're home."

It was easier for him to smile for her loving concern. "I do, my beauty. Now step back before my grime contaminates you."

"Nonsense." Oona took the tray, directing the girl in positioning a small table before dismissing her. Setting dishes and cups before him, she ordered, "Eat, Dan. You can answer Logran's questions after you tend to yourself."

Suddenly starving, Isfail ate greedily, less concerned with table etiquette than finally filling his belly with the generous servings of excellent food. He hardly noticed his worried cousins, though Isfail knew they waited for him to tell them everything about his troubles in Ishal.

With hunger and thirst appeased for the moment, Isfail sat back in the chair, trying to hide the grimace of pain as his ribs protested. He recognized the distress in Oona's eyes and refused to add to it. Then he saw Logran's eyes narrow in anger as his cousin stared at his wrist. Isfail looked down and saw that the ragged cuff of his right sleeve had slid back, exposing the scabbed abrasions left by the shackles. But the prince said nothing about it for the moment.

"Let's start with other news." Logran rose to pour three goblets of wine, handing one to Oona and setting another beside Isfail's plate. "You probably haven't heard that Karsh is dead."

"Aroth told me a few minutes ago, but I didn't stop to hear the whole story." He listened closely despite his desperate fatigue. There was only relief at hearing that Karsh and Jerrat, her assistant, were dead. He felt even greater relief that Akira had prevailed without coming to harm. "Have you found other accomplices?"

"Nothing definite, but something else turned up the morning

after," Logran told him. "Search teams were sent out all along the ridge to make sure nothing was missed again. The found a horse loose on the main road, saddled and bridled. No one has reported a horse missing."

At Isfail's inquiring glance, Logran added, "The two messengers sent to alert the Ambassador Core reported passing a lone rider that night, not far from the intersection with the lane to Central."

"Yet no one else, no body, was found after the battle?" Isfail wondered.

Logran shook his head. "Jerrat had been dead for several days, and all indications are that Karsh had been living in an underground chamber all that time."

"Another accomplice, perhaps."

"If so, they escaped without a horse."

Remembering the other reason for his disastrous trip, Isfail said with frustration, "I couldn't find a trace of The Bow before sailing from Insalat, not counting the evidence of squatters in Baronan's old keep, and that might not be a part of this. None of my sources could give me anything. It's as if they don't exist. I talked with every captain that logged out of a Caldalan port. I've sailors and soldiers out tracking runners and pirates down the coast and around our borders. Since I came straight here, I haven't checked to see if there's anything new, but my men were instructed to report anything significant to you."

Logran shook his head. "I've received nothing of import. We've been thankfully free from more attacks. Maybe their Caldalan accomplice fled to Ishal? We still haven't traced the man who threatened Akira in Mountain Shadows."

Easing back carefully, Isfail blew out a long breath. "I don't believe Ishal would knowingly harbor any Caldalan. We've bigger concerns there, Lo. Ishal's government is about to close their ports and borders to Caldala."

"What?" The prince bent forward in his seat. "That's impossible!"

"It's not," Isfail retorted grimly. "I was invited to a meeting with those officials still friendly to us. A secret meeting." He watched his cousin's face harden at the term. "They confirmed that The Bow was founded by Arthon Baronan, and has resurfaced in recent years. Investigation shows that someone's rebuilding Baronan's following. Somehow there's enough influence now to turn the government against Caldala and other countries."

Raking his fingers through tangled hair, Isfail stood up to pace.

"What's happened to set them against us?" Logran asked.

"The Mors' defeat." The cold irony in Isfail's reply had Logran staring in disbelief. "Instead of being grateful, they've twisted the fact that Akira was powerful enough to save their worthless lives into a fear that *all* force holders are as dangerous as the Black Death. They're buying the poisonous propaganda that anyone who has force abilities, along with any person or country who knowingly supports them, is the enemy."

"Fools," Logran spat out furiously. "After Caldalan blood was spilled to aid them in the Baronan insurrection. After they've used our ambassadors to carry out their judgments. Fools!"

"It's bad enough," Isfail went on wearily. "But they've turned on their own, too, Logran. I was told there's a public call to eliminate the Ishakans. To take over the northern territories."

His face aghast, the prince sank into a chair. "Genocide, Dan? How could they even consider it?"

"I don't have a clue." Isfail gave in to exhaustion, dropping back into his chair with his head in his hands. "It's madness, Lo. And if, when, they hear how Akira defeated Karsh, it will just be fuel for the bonfire."

Looking up now with bleak eyes, Isfail gave him the final blow. "They arrested me. Put me in prison on trumped-up charges that I was a spy."

Obviously livid, Logran stalked the room. "You were there under royal seal to speak with their Parliament. We will not stand for this."

Love threatened to overwhelm Isfail when Logran crouched down before him, concern heavy on his face. "Are you all right?"

Smiling slightly, Isfail nodded, lifting a hand gratefully to Logran's strong shoulder while Oona quietly sat on the arm of his chair to take his other hand. "It could have been worse. I spent less than a week in the dungeon. Friends got me out through the sea tunnels Akira once told us about. The loyalist underground network already in place got me to Vaneer's ship."

Scrubbing hands across his scruff-heavy face, with misery in a single moan, Isfail asked, "Akira?"

He felt Logran run a hand over his slumped head as his cousin stood up. "Safe. I received a letter from her just yesterday, asking after you. I was just writing to give her the latest news when you came. I'm glad to be able to send you back to her in one piece."

Isfail looked up in surprise and saw the regret in Logran's eyes.

"I was wrong to do this to you, Dan. Wrong to oppose you. Wrong to part you. I've given Akira my apologies. I beg you'll accept them."

Leaning back in the chair, Isfail drank deep. When he set down the empty glass, he considered his cousin's worried face. "You are my prince and my family. I owe you my loyalty. I give you my love, but I will bind my heart and life to Akira."

"So. I'm forgiven."

His eyelids heavy as stones, Isfail barely heard his cousin's teasing words before he surrendered to the need for sleep.

Waking on comfortable cushions in a room that didn't move beneath him was an experience that Isfail knew he'd failed to appreciate before now. After rubbing sleep-heavy eyes, he studied his surroundings. He was in Logran's office, stretched out on the leather couch. Looking toward the window, Isfail saw that it was still dark, though he had no idea of the time.

He moved to a sitting position, careful of his aching ribs and back. Now he could see the clock on the fireplace mantel—just past midnight. Isfail decided he could make it to his own rooms, smiling at the thought of the big bed there, a far cry from a stone cell, or a ship's berth.

But his vastly improved circumstances made him acutely aware of another need as he stood up. Isfail wondered how his royal cousins had withstood the stench as he realized that the foul smell emanated from him. Picking up the bag containing the banner and journals, he started for his rooms.

When he finally made it to his suite, Isfail stripped as fast as his abused body would allow, and swore to have that clothing burned. The warm shower was heaven, though the first incautious scrub with fine soap made him aware of the depth of the bruises. Isfail let the water carry away layers of filth then lowered himself gratefully into the steaming soaking tub.

"Dan?" Oona's worried call came from his bedroom.

"Don't come in here, my beauty," Isfail called back, eyes closed. "I don't wish to be called out to duel my cousin." He heard her laughter and the sound of cabinet doors being opened and closed.

"I believe I can control my passions, Dan. Do you need any help? I'd like you to see a master healer as soon as possible."

Isfail sighed. The only healer he wanted or needed was in Mountain Shadows. "I'll do, Oona. No need to worry."

There was no reply and he smiled, thinking she was plotting to see that he was taken care of. Oona was a blessing to them all.

She was looking out the large windows when he came from the bath wearing a thick robe, covering the worst of the damage to keep her from fussing. Isfail grinned at Logran, who was sitting by the fireplace where a fire warmed the room. "Are you both up late or very early?"

"Late. We wanted to let you sleep," Logran said as Isfail sat on the edge of his bed.

"And now that I won't wake myself with my own reek, I'd like to sleep some more," Isfail proclaimed cheerfully, laying a hand on the seldom-used sleep clothing Oona must have placed neatly on the bed.

But Oona was not to be denied, he saw, as she brought over a small basket filled with bandages and little pots of ointment. "You will at least allow me to tend to those wrists," she insisted.

Since he saw no reason to argue, Isfail submitted quietly to her ministrations as he looked at Logran. "There's more I need to tell you."

"I thought as much. We'll talk after you've had a chance to rest," Logran replied. "Who brought you back?"

"The Vaneers, on their *Maid of Kilra*." He saw a light come into his cousin's eyes.

"Captain Wells said he was able to talk to them."

Isfail nodded, watching Oona finish wrapping his right wrist. "So they said. I owe a life debt to the loyalists too. I don't know how many were involved in the operation to get me out."

Now Isfail met Logran's eyes seriously. "We've got to rout The Bow from Caldala. They're even more dangerous than we suspected."

Apparently satisfied at accomplishing this much, Oona secured the second bandage and set his left hand gently down. She touched Isfail's cheek. "Yes, I believe so, but you'll talk again after you sleep."

Brief minutes after Logran and his princess left, Isfail stretched out on clean, fragrant sheets stretched smooth over a thick mattress. All he needed to make it perfect would be Akira lying beside him. It was his last conscious thought before sliding into dreams of her.

Twelve

S un splashes off the sea rippled on his ceiling when Isfail woke the next day. For a moment he savored this rare opportunity to enjoy watching them. In the usual course of things, he was up and out long before the sun's angle over the water produced the lovely dance of light.

Taking stock of his aches, Isfail credited Oona for the fact that his wrists were greatly improved. The ribs still insisted on cautious movement as he got out of bed, and his lower back throbbed. Maybe he should allow Oona to bring in a healer. He'd think about it, Isfail decided as he finally rid himself of a stiff beard before indulging in another long soak.

A note in his front room accompanied the hot breakfast tray— How did Oona manage her timing? The brief message directed him to the smaller palace conference room to meet with the prince and some of the militia commanders stationed in Coroth. His royal cousin was wasting no time getting out the information Isfail brought back. That suited him, since he wanted to be on the road to Mountain Shadows as soon as he could arrange it.

W hen he walked into the meeting, Isfail nodded to High Minister Felpon, who looked out of place among the military men. But it made sense to advise Parliament of the latest news from Ishal at the earliest opportunity. When Logran beckoned to a seat beside him, Isfail sat down to relate his story and the information he'd gained regarding the status of the neighboring country.

Deliberately keeping allies' names out of his telling, Isfail outlined the current situation in Ishal, with emphasis on the dangers to Caldala's force-gifted population. He also made a point about the threat the Ishakan people and territories were under. To impress those present with the severity of the rebels' takeover, Isfail produced the banner, asking two of the attendants to hold it high so all could see the proclamation from The Bow.

Perhaps Logran recognized that Isfail was holding back, or maybe he thought that his cousin was still suffering from his ordeal, but he adjourned the meeting after allowing a brief time for questions from some of the military officers. Once Logran and Isfail were seated in the prince's private office, Logran gave him a long look.

"Now, Dan, what more did you learn?"

Isfail stood up, asking, "Key to the cabinet?"

Logran pressed a small carving on his desk, causing a tiny hidden compartment to open. The desk was an heirloom passed down through four generations of Caldala's ruling family and its secrets were known by only a few. Only the prince, Oona, and Isfail knew of its existence now. Taking out a small, ornate key, Logran handed it over, watching while Isfail used it to unlock the lowest drawer in a beautifully carved cabinet.

Isfail removed the wrapped bundle of journals that he'd placed there for safekeeping before joining the meeting. After removing the oilskin, he laid the journals in front of Logran and handed back the key.

"Commander Shanow directed his wife to get these to us, hoping the information he's recorded in them will help both Ishal and Caldala in defeating The Bow." Isfail returned to his chair while Logran opened one of the carefully compiled records.

"Valuable indeed," Logran murmured, looking up at Isfail after several minutes of reading. "You must have a reason for not mentioning them in the meeting. The commanders could make use of these details."

Sitting forward, Isfail related Mirastheny Shanow's fears about The Bow infiltrating Caldala, concluding with, "I'm more concerned than ever about the possibility of Caldala being compromised. You'll see in Shanow's journals how skillfully Dateh insinuated himself and his followers into the Ishalian government, into their military."

His eyes narrowing, Logran straightened. "You're thinking that we might have spies within our militia, perhaps even in Parliament?"

Seeing his cousin's anger brewing, Isfail replied, "I think you need to be aware of these facts. I think the House of Coroth should take extraordinary precautions to ensure that the royal family and Caldala's government are not weakened from within by foreign factions."

Isfail pushed up to pace, running both hands through his hair in agitation. "I looked into his eyes, Lo. Dateh had the power to order my arrest—I saw the *pleasure* in the bastard's eyes while he watched the beatings."

He didn't see the rage flare in Logran's eyes at this news.

"He has more control than his father. I don't think he's insane, but he enjoys the subjugation of those who might stand against his ambitions." Isfail paused when Logran placed a hand on his arm, his brows knit in confusion.

"You're speaking of this Dateh still?" Logran asked. "What do you mean by 'his father'?"

With an ironic chuckle, Isfail pointed a finger at the journals. "It's all there. Shanow dug out the fact that Dateh is, in reality, Abron Baronan—Arthon Baronan's son."

As Logran swore over this, Isfail said, "Like his father, Dateh has grand ambitions. But this Baronan doesn't just want to rule *one* country; there are rumors among the resistance that he has larger plans. Plans that have Kittric harbor closed to all foreign shipping, and all access to that region controlled by The Bow. So far, the resistance hasn't been able to ascertain what's happening there. But it's a good bet to say that it involves ships."

"You think he's putting together a battle fleet?" Logran took his seat again.

Isfail nodded. "I think you should consider mobilizing the

Royal Navy. I think Caldala needs all its military assets primed to fight."

Several minutes passed as Logran stared toward the window looking out into his private courtyard. Isfail knew his cousin was mulling over the implications of war with Ishal. Caldala had been peaceful for long years. Even the invasion attempt by the Mors had been dealt with before the enemy had breached Caldala's borders. Akira and Team Kilronan, through an extraordinary combination of courage and force ability, had closed the border and eliminated the invading forces.

If their speculation that Abron Baronan, as Lord Dateh now, was building an attack fleet was fact, it wouldn't be possible to slam the door, so to speak, as Akira had done at High Pass above Mountain Shadows. No, this defense would need ships and crews ready for battle on the open seas, and soldiers prepared to defend the coast.

Isfail brought himself from these thoughts when Logran turned back to him.

"You were planning to retire, Dan."

Taking a deep breath, Isfail grimaced, knowing what was coming. "Bad timing, eh?"

On a half-laugh, although there was no humor in his eyes now, the prince said, "I can't accept your papers, Commander, in light of the present danger to Caldala."

Silent, Isfail nodded as Logran continued, saying, "I can agree to active reserve, if you wish, but I'll need you available to command militia in the event of open war. You've been away from the navy too long, so I won't assign you to a ship, but even there your experience is useful in strategy."

"I've already recommended Captain Toth for promotion to my position in Insalat," Isfail said.

"I'll make sure that happens." Logran stared down at the journals. "How much time until they make a move, do you think?"

Isfail leaned against Logran's desk. "They can't organize any major assault this year. The Bow doesn't yet fully control Ishal, and their focus seems to be on eliminating the Ishakans first.

Unless we get new information soon, I think Coroth has time to strengthen Caldala's defensive assets."

"Another thing to add to the agenda for the conclave with the Protectorate Lords and Heads of Militias." Logran wrote out notes. "I'll make sure Most High Ambassador Garan is included too. And I want Akira here."

Knowing the moment he dreaded had come, Isfail reached into his pocket, producing the already much-read letter from Gaios Shanow included with the journals. He unfolded it, pausing to skim the respectful words before lingering over the final sentence. When he handed it to Logran, there was reluctance in the movement.

Silently, the prince read the Ishalian commander's words. When he got to the end he looked up into Isfail's hard eyes before reading aloud, "Any assistance Caldala can give us will be welcomed, but I believe the loyal citizens of Ishal would be best served by a military alliance with Lady Akira Muro."

Thirteen

Mountain Shadows, Three days later

Isfail leaned forward eagerly as his coach finally came in sight of the fortified village of Mountain Shadows. Every long, aching mile was worth it knowing he'd soon be with Akira again. Even the Royal Guard escort Logran had insisted upon couldn't dim his spirits as the protectorate soldiers at the gate stood to attention while the coach continued up the road without stopping.

But Isfail knew word would reach protectorate administration quickly and was not surprised to see Senior Master Arla and her team standing at formal attention with the admin guard when his coach rolled into the courtyard.

Where was Dan? Akira wondered yet again as she walked back from an urgent meeting with Mountain Shadows Protectorate's Lord Corcoran. It had been more than a lunam since she'd seen her lover. The jeweled band circling her life finger was the last tangible link to the man she'd trusted with her heart.

Now Coroth had called in the Council of Protectorate Lords and the Heads of the Militias. Something had happened, and Akira feared the worst. She would leave with Lord Corcoran early tomorrow for the capital, but every minute of uncertainty was an agony of waiting.

Unaware that Isfail's coach was passing through the west gate, lost in silent prayer for the safe return of the man she loved, Akira nearly walked straight into Aiden Kilronan.

His hands gripped her shoulders. "What's this?" he murmured, lifting her chin.

Leaning into him for a brief moment, she shook her head. "Nonsense, Aiden. Just that."

"I doubt that, Akira. You've never been the nonsensical type." He turned to walk with her to her residence. Squeezing her hand gently, he added, "I know you're worried about him. It's all right to admit that. Isfail can take care of himself. He'll return."

Akira looked into his green eyes, grateful for his understanding and compassion. He'd been her first love. Now, years of misunderstanding, separation, and turmoil later, Kilronan had accepted that she'd chosen another man. As he pressed his lips to her brow in comfort, Akira appreciated the sincere friendship he still offered.

"I hear we're going to Coroth," Kilronan said, taking the letter she handed him to read.

When his concerned eyes met hers, Akira shook her head. "I don't know why. Is it something new threatening Caldala?"

He leaned against the back of the sofa as she paced the spacious room.

"I've heard nothing from Elen or Garan, so this is unforeseen and urgent," she continued, thinking of her adopted brother, Elen Arith, and friend, Most High Ambassador Daas Garan, both based at Ambassador Central in Coroth. They would not hesitate to send her news of anything important.

"The Bow?" Kilronan speculated.

"Perhaps, but wouldn't Coroth have warned us? Their attacks have, so far, been against me specifically. The prince would want us to know before we traveled. How could they be a threat to an entire country?"

When he just looked thoughtful, Akira continued, saying, "Lord Corcoran will have Team Cobon riding with you. I believe he's leaving Osharon in the lead here."

"Good." Pushing off the sofa, Kilronan stopped her relentless pacing once more. "Go pack, Akira. There's no point in exhausting yourself. It looks like we'll travel hard and fast."

"Kahshara—" she began, thinking of her horse.

He stopped her with a look, pointing a finger at her from the door. "No. Same reasons as before. Behave."

She swore under her breath at his excess of caution even as he pulled the door closed behind him, then scowled when he stuck his head back in with a wide grin. "I heard that, Muro."

"Only in your mind, Kilronan," she retorted, fighting sudden amusement.

"True." Pushing the door wide, he tipped his head toward the courtyard. "Come out for a minute."

"You told me to pack," she grumbled.

"There's something you'll be interested in."

Giving up, Akira joined Kilronan at the door. Felt him steady her when she swayed with disbelief.

Isfail stood on the terrace.

*A*kira flew into the arms that opened wide. Everyone else ceased to exist as he lifted her, carrying her inside and booting the door closed behind him. His mouth was on hers— urgent, insistent—while he moved through the front room, refusing to set her down until they reached her bedroom.

Questions would wait, Akira realized as her mind hazed with the need to meet his desperate passion. Isfail sat down on the bed, cradling her on his lap, lifting a hand to her cheek where tears streamed. Akira linked her hand with his and welcomed the pulse of the power link that seemed to grow stronger every moment her love for him was returned. Even now, the force aura shimmered over their joined hands.

He kissed away the tears of joy and relief, murmuring her name as he shifted, freeing both hands to release the fastenings of the tunic she wore. Akira was already pushing off his sheepskin-lined coat then tugging up the sweater beneath. But as he lifted his arms to pull it over his head, Akira froze when she saw him.

"Oh God . . . Dan." Her fingers trembled as she brushed them over the bruises shadowing his skin.

"No, not now." His voice rough with desire, Isfail caught her searching hands and brought them to his lips. "I only need you, Kira. Need to be with you, be a part of you."

There was no denying him, Akira found, when he pulled her down with him, and no wanting to. His hands moved over her, eager to explore every familiar curve and hollow. His mouth followed, leaving Akira breathless and as desperate to rediscover all the secrets of his body, to give back exquisite sensations as they pleasured one another.

Lost in feelings made all the more intense by love shared, Akira pressed him down to the bed, her mouth meeting his to capture the moan that was both need and relief, rising over him to take him in as he gripped her hips.

Isfail met her luminous eyes as she began to move, sweeping his hands up her sides to cup those perfect breasts. He moved with her, always with her, as the ethereal flames rippled, enhancing the heat of their joining. Then he was flying, hurtling up in pleasure so intense it was almost pain. He felt Akira soar with him until that ecstasy burst, leaving him floating, sated, and finally home.

"My love, my only," he whispered. Wrapping his arms around Akira, Isfail pressed his face to her breast as he let newfound peace take him.

Fourteen

Rattling windowpanes as it whistled through the courtyard, the sound of the wind roused Akira from sleep. She glanced over when it rose to a scream, glad that Isfail had arrived before the storm broke over Mountain Shadows.

Akira looked back at the man in her bed. His arm was flung over her waist as he slept. He was beautifully made, with the build of a warrior, strong shoulders over a long torso tapering to narrow hips, long legs.

Tenderly brushing aside dark hair, she traced the features of the sharply angled face, thankful to be able to. It had been too many long weeks not knowing if he was safe.

Akira could see that he hadn't been.

Caught up in the intensity of their reunion, they'd shut the world out for a few hours. The overwhelming need as they'd loved had driven everything else from her thoughts. In the ensuing passion, he'd downplayed his injuries.

Now she studied the lean body sprawled facedown in exhausted slumber—frowned at the evidence of recent abuse. Long, layered bruises marked back and shoulders, and Akira recognized healing shackle abrasions banding his wrists.

Forcing down anger, she shifted carefully to avoid waking him. Akira gathered her hair, flipping the tangled length into a knot and out of her way. Kneeling on the bed, she ran light hands over his back, testing the depth of his injuries.

Her scan found bruised kidneys under clouds of purple, green, and yellow discoloration spreading low across his back. Hoping that was the worst of it, Akira continued her examination. When

98

Isfail rolled over, shadowed eyes blinking in sleepy confusion, she quickly scanned his chest and abdomen—finding more damage before his hands closed over hers.

"What are you doing?" he murmured, still working on waking fully.

Akira warmed with his slow smile.

"Taking care of *you*," she replied, spreading her fingers over fractured ribs.

The heat had Isfail glancing down, lifting his brow at the ripple of green flames flowing over her hands. It never ceased to amaze him, no matter how many times he'd seen it.

Within minutes he drew an easier breath. Isfail rolled to his stomach at her command, letting out a long sigh as Akira eased the throbbing pain in his back. When he turned over again, watching while she wrapped her hands around his wrist, he teased, "I think I'll keep you."

Though she smiled at that, he could see the worry in her eyes.

"Why didn't you see a healer before coming on?" Shaking her head, she murmured, "And the pain—I should have insisted on caring for you before we made love."

Isfail sat up, lifting her chin to meet her troubled eyes. "Being with you was what I needed. If I'd seen a healer in Coroth, Oona and Logran would have delayed my departure."

*H*e'd forgotten how small she was, Isfail realized, how delicate and fine-boned. Still, he always saw her as the strongest woman he'd ever known. She'd survived so much, physically and emotionally, but none of it had crushed her. Like the finest sword he carried into battle, Akira seemed tempered by the demands on her life, only growing stronger with each challenge.

But here, when she gave herself to him, she was tender, yielding, with all the passion he could ever wish for in a woman, and more. Akira loved him.

They would be bound as soon as she was ready, and they would find a place to settle, to build a life together. Somewhere beautiful, where she would be safe and could spend the rest of her life without the cares and demands she'd lived with for so long. Such were his dreams and deepest desires.

Would they ever see them come true?

Looking at the clock above the fireplace, Isfail knew they had to face today. Brushing back hair as fine as tangled white silk strands, he kissed Akira on the forehead before shifting to the edge of the bed.

"It's time to go back to the world," she murmured, rising with him.

"Yes. I need to tell you, all of you, about the situation in Ishal. We need to prepare for what's here, and what might be coming."

Rising on her toes to kiss him, Akira still slipped out of his arms too soon, saying, "Go ahead and shower first. I'll send for some food, then take mine while it's being arranged."

He'd rather share the shower and a lazy soak in the tub with her, but Isfail knew it was important to get his information to Corcoran and his warriors. He would have more private time with Akira with that detail out of the way. But as his mind began to organize what he needed to say, a worrisome detail surfaced.

"Akira."

She turned back at the concern in his voice, waiting as he came to place his hands on her shoulders.

"Could you get word to Lord Corcoran asking him to include *only* his senior masters in a private meeting this afternoon?"

Though she studied his serious gaze, Akira asked no questions, only nodded. "I'll see to it."

Fifteen

The faces were familiar now, Isfail thought, as he walked into the small conference room, his smile broadening for one in particular. Cobon was waiting just inside the door, his grin spreading as he gripped Isfail's outstretched arm tight while clapping him on the shoulder.

"About time you got here!" Cobon boomed, with both large hands squeezing his boyhood friend's arms, his eyes sharp and observant while he looked Isfail over.

"It was a long trip," Isfail replied. Pulling free, he slung an arm over Cobon's broad shoulders. "I won't thank you for filling my lady's head with slanderous tales of our youthful adventures."

Cobon gave a hearty laugh and those at the table joined in the mirth. "Aye, but she should know who she's binding with." He winked at Akira, who was taking a seat beside Lord Corcoran.

"Hmm," was all Isfail said to that before murmuring close to Cobon's ear, "My thanks for watching over her when I could not."

Shrugging that aside, Cobon simply said, "She's yours, my friend. We take care of our own."

Nodding, Isfail released him and they went to their seats. Before sitting down across from Akira, Isfail placed the small satchel he carried on the table, unstrapping it to remove the well-traveled journals of Commander Shanow. He greeted the other senior masters—Kilronan, Osharon, Arla, and Carelon—as he set the books down.

"Welcome back, Commander," Lord Corcoran began, as Isfail sat. "We all know each other here and time is short, so I'll ask you to handle this initial meeting. The details of this discussion will be kept confidential except as agreed upon by myself, Lady Muro, and Commander Isfail," Corcoran concluded with a stern look at each senior master. After their nods of understanding, he turned the meeting over to Isfail.

"Thank you, sir." With a quick glance at Akira, Isfail proceeded to give them a much-abbreviated account of his recent experiences in Ishal.

No one interrupted while he spoke of his ordeal, though faces tightened in anger, and Cobon thumped a hard fist on the table at one point. Akira sat silently, her eyes locked on Isfail's face, and he saw the ice-cold warrior in the woman he loved.

Moving directly to what he'd learned from the Vaneers and their experience in Tash'tric, Isfail added what he'd been told by Aric and his companions. The current situation in Ishal was made clear to everyone in the room.

He told them about the stowaways smuggled onto the *Maid of Kilra*, and the information Ishalian Commander Shanow had sent via his wife. Placing a hand on the stack of journals, Isfail said, "We have the Shanows to thank for these. His personal investigations and theories are recorded in them. I'll give a quick summation of the most important points, but the details are worth reading, if you have time. You'll find invaluable information relevant to the enemy that Ishal and Caldala are now facing. These journals must remain in my possession, but I will make them available as I can."

Osharon lifted a hand and, at Lord Corcoran's nod, asked, "What does this commander expect Caldala to do with these?"

"To use the details to understand the enemy. He wanted Caldala to have this information in order to plot a counter-offensive. To take the knowledge and help those loyal to Ishal and the elected government take back their country."

"Why the hell should we get involved in Ishal's problems?" Cobon grumbled irritably. "They've got themselves into this pretty mess. Caldala's spent enough lives on them in the past, and they got another shot at you, my friend. If you didn't have the luck of the devil, it sounds like they'd have put you in the ground this time."

When he would have interrupted Cobon's increasingly irate tirade, Lord Corcoran placed a firm hand on Isfail's arm to silence him, allowing Cobon to vent.

"And for what should we risk our lives, I'd like to know?" Cobon went on, his face darkening with rage. "People who follow the devils like sheep? We should fight for cowards that stand by and watch their own taken, abused, and murdered time and again? Bah!" He sat back in his chair, arms crossed over a broad chest.

The others turned their attention back to Isfail, who saw similar sentiments in their eyes, in the tight lines of strong faces.

"We should help," Isfail began resolutely, "because there are innocents suffering under this madness, because loyalists are already risking their lives to defend as many as they can. Because Dateh and his supporters have openly targeted the Ishakans, a peaceful people who also have force abilities, and they will not stop there." He went on to tell them about the attacks on the Ishakan families, and Shanow's request for help. For now, he did not bring up Shanow's personal appeal to Akira.

He looked around the attentive group. "We must fight what has already spread into Caldala and threatens our own. It's not just Akira anymore," Isfail stated as he turned his head to look pointedly at Kilronan. "She'll continue to be a prime target, no doubt. But every force caller is marked for death under The Bow's latest decree. *You* are their enemy. They've put all force-gifted in the same category as the Mors—deadly and not to be tolerated."

For some moments, the silence in the conference room was profound.

Then Akira spoke up. "That's Dateh's excuse, not the reason."

An appreciative smile lifted Isfail's serious mouth. "My lady sees through the smokescreen to the truth. I believe we'll find that Abron Dateh is concerned that the force-gifted are the greatest threat to his own ambitions. And a convenient diversion from his takeover of the government."

Pausing to wet his throat from the glass of water provided, Isfail moved on to the suspicions of a major plot being developed in Kittric. He repeated what little was passed on to him by the resistance, and read previously marked passages from the most recent of Shanow's journals. But even Shanow's diligence had only ascertained that Kittric Harbor and the surrounding city were kept tightly under the control of The Bow. There was evidence that resources needed for construction, such as wood and iron, were being diverted to the restricted area. And all of Ishal's limited fleet had been secured within Kittric harbor.

"It's a sure bet that Dateh and his troops are building a battle fleet," Lord Corcoran stated, taking the journal that Isfail offered.

"The prince and Coroth's admirals agree with you," Isfail said. "Even now, Caldala's Royal Navy is undergoing rigorous inspection, and will be fully outfitted for war."

Akira nodded. "All defense services should be prepared to defend our coast. I'll suggest that Most High Garan and the Ambassador Core be notified that their reconnaissance abilities will be needed."

"It's been done. And Garan will be included in the meetings that will begin as soon as we return to Coroth." Isfail looked at Corcoran now. "Will you be prepared to leave day after tomorrow, sir?"

The leader of Mountain Shadows Protectorate nodded. "I'll also be prepared to report on the progress of the new fortifications above High Pass. It's far from done, but we've completed a secure barracks building, making it easier to house and support two protectorate teams there. A watchtower is under construction to permit a wider view of the lower lake and altered cliff face, allowing us to detect anyone before they actually make it to the top."

Corcoran looked over with a smile as Gralla, his lady and administrator, came in, directing a crew from the kitchens carrying trays of refreshments. Everyone expressed appreciation for the break as most stood to stretch out the tension brought on by the news. But it was soon back to the task at hand as Isfail prepared to finish telling what he'd learned.

"I asked Lord Corcoran to confine this initial meeting to his senior masters, only his most trusted people. Through those I met, and Commander Shanow's wife and his writings, we've learned that The Bow, and their sympathizers, have dedicated the last few years to insinuating themselves into key positions." Studying the heightened concern on each face now, Isfail stated, "Not only in Ishal, but in Caldala as well, perhaps other countries."

"Our government and defense services may be compromised, in other words," Akira reinforced.

"We don't know, at this time, how serious this might be. I've given the prince my opinion that all reasonable suspicions be followed up on, all care be taken to only discuss sensitive information with those known to be loyal." Isfail drew in a deep breath, and let it out again with a shrug. "But nothing is foolproof. Caldala has been peaceful so long its citizens have had no reason to suspect neighbors or newcomers."

Opening the discussion at this point, Isfail recognized Arla's request to speak.

"Have you learned anything more substantial about this Bow cult? We need something that might make it easier to detect them. It's clear that they're a terrorist group, probably controlled by this Dateh. But weren't they started by Arthon Baronan?" Arla questioned.

"Yes. The only obvious indicator is seeing the mark on a follower—a brand or scar depicting a crescent bow with three arrowed lines. We've seen it on the shoulder, but it might be on other areas of the body. Otherwise, they're like average people, unless they're caught acting suspiciously."

"Regarding the mark or brand, it's usually hidden under clothing, but it's probably a mistake to count on a lack of it proving that someone is not part of Dateh's shadow army," Akira interjected. "I'd be surprised if all of his followers were willing to subject themselves to a branding, especially the higher officers. And we don't know when this—form of initiation, we'll say— was begun. I don't recall the men captured after the Baronan Rebellion having it."

Isfail pulled a couple of the journals out of the stack. "Shanow has discovered some interesting details on The Bow. More than we've ever known before. The original group was indeed assembled by Arthon Baronan." He saw Akira's eyes narrow at the slight emphasis he'd placed on the name.

"Most were killed in the first rebellion, in battle or executed by the loyalists when they regained control. However, The Bow has been rebuilt in the past several years." Isfail looked around at the intent faces. "By Baronan's son, the man now calling himself Abron Dateh."

Looking at Akira, he was surprised by the expression of intense concentration on her face. Her brows were furrowed together, lips pursed, as if she were struggling to reconcile this news with what they'd believed before.

Isfail turned his attention to Kilronan, who recalled the discoveries at Baronan Keep over a decade before as he said, "But you and Akira found the bodies of his lady and their son years ago."

"Another boy's body must have been planted to cover the fact that Baronan took his son with him when he escaped into Ishal." Again, Isfail indicated the journals spread on the large table. "Shanow and his investigators pieced together Arthon Baronan's activities and movements over the years. Though he was bound to an Ishalian noblewoman, he hid the boy's true identity, even from his new household. There were no children with his Ishalian wife, and none reported from unions with other women."

Looking at the clock, and the fading light of the rain-drizzled evening, Lord Corcoran obviously decided this was a good point to end this meeting. "You've given us a great deal to think about, Commander. Let's adjourn for today. I'd like to meet tomorrow morning to organize the trip to Coroth." He shifted his gaze to Kilronan and Osharon. "I want you two there. Cobon, you'll see to organizing teams, horses, and provisions."

"Aye, my lord."

Addressing all his senior masters, Corcoran said, "Before that, I want all of you here at second bell tomorrow morning to discuss protectorate security and administration while I'm gone. Dismissed."

Sixteen

Kilronan looked around as he left the meeting with the senior masters the next morning, curious as he sensed a silent pulse of power. He'd felt it before but hadn't really considered it significant—like a song just out of hearing.

"What's up?" Osharon asked, looking at Kilronan's puzzled face.

"Probably not important." Continuing to scan their surroundings, Kilronan saw Arla come out, deep in conversation with Carelon. Cobon followed, the only one of those three without force abilities, but nothing unusual there.

Turning back to his friend, he shook his head. "I've been picking up a unique force signature. I can't tell where it's coming from."

"Maronan?" Osharon offered, knowing the youth was approaching the usual age for the Psyche shift.

Shaking his head, Kilronan shrugged. "Not that strong. I've got a feeling Mar's shift will be more of a surge. And Akira's been working with him; she'd have told me if he was about to start the Psyche changes."

Continuing into the guest courtyard for a private discussion regarding the Coroth trip, they saw Akira and Isfail with Lord Corcoran.

"Looks like we can get started," Osharon noted, bounding up the steps with a growl to sweep Akira off her feet.

Isfail grinned as Osharon's antics broke Akira's somber mood and teased a laugh from her. He nodded to Kilronan, offering an arm as he joined them. "I didn't have a chance to greet you properly when I first arrived."

Taking the arm in a firm grip, Kilronan smiled. "You were distracted."

"That I was," Isfail murmured, taking Akira's hand to pull her close, releasing the now familiar surge of their power link.

"You're a Psyche!" Kilronan exclaimed in a shocked voice.

Corcoran and Osharon stared at Kilronan as if he'd grown two heads. But Isfail only glanced at Akira without comment.

"Shall we go in and get on with the meeting?" Isfail opened the door, guiding Akira in. He stiffened when Kilronan caught his arm. "I suggest you release me, Master. I'm in no mood to pull punches."

Though he dropped his hand, Kilronan pressed, "Who are you, damn it?"

"Kilronan," Lord Corcoran interjected firmly. "This is not the time. You and I will discuss this later."

With a curt nod, Kilronan backed off, bowing to his lord. "Yes, sir."

Osharon pressed him in. "Relax, Kil." But the shoulder under Osharon's hand remained rigid.

*I*nside, Akira assessed the tension in the group and went for the whiskey bottle. It was early in the day for it, but she thought it might be needed. Isfail followed as she poured glasses for all.

She saw the concern in his eyes. "How do you want to handle this?"

He lifted her hand to his lips. "What would I do without you, Kira?" When she smiled, he kissed her mouth, lingering for a moment.

"Can I trust them?" he wondered, leaning back against a counter.

"Yes," Akira answered without hesitation. "They'll keep your confidence if you ask."

Knocking back his whiskey, Isfail looked into her eyes as he held the glass out for a refill.

The protectorate men stood in awkward silence while Isfail passed around the libations. When Akira gestured toward the seating area, they moved to obey her unspoken directive.

Isfail remained standing for the moment, his eyes hard as they met Kilronan's.

"It appears we'll deal with this business first." He waved away Lord Corcoran's objection. "I accept that it's necessary to avoid larger problems." When Akira came to stand beside him, Isfail took her hand.

"As Akira discovered many years ago, I was born of Psyche blood."

Corcoran's brow twisted in consternation. "Forgive me for speaking bluntly, Commander, but I understood that the House of Coroth is blood pure. That is, hereditarily without Psyche ancestry."

Isfail nodded with an enigmatic smile. "And you would be correct, my lord. The official House of Coroth is blood pure, as you put it. But, little known to the public, my father's mother was a full Psyche. Bound to a man from Insalat, they raised two half-Psyche sons. My father was introduced to Danis of Coroth at a military ball. My sisters and I are the result of their binding."

Osharon, obviously fascinated by this turn of events, noted, "So you're a quarter Psyche. Have you force powers?"

"Unfortunately, no." Isfail chuckled at Akira's arch look. "My lady doesn't agree."

Kilronan nodded slowly. "Akira's right. You may not have full powers, but I'll wager you can sense force, and you're definitely faster than any warrior I've fought before."

Those present had witnessed the sword match lunams before, and Isfail's unheard of ability to intercept Kilronan's force bolt.

"Perhaps," Isfail conceded.

"Why do you feel the need to conceal your heritage?" Corcoran asked.

Isfail glanced once more at Akira, obviously unsettled by the lord's perception. When she slipped an arm around his waist, he took a deep breath. "We don't actively disavow the Psyche line, we just don't bring it up."

Lifting his chin to the disparaging look from Kilronan, Isfail continued defiantly, "We are as proud of that lineage as we are of Princess Danis, the ancestral line of Coroth. Yet, my mother's choice in binding challenged an unwritten tenet of the ruling line."

He took a drink of his whiskey. "Long ago, the House of Coroth decided to keep the reigning house apart from those who were force-gifted. As it was explained to me, this was meant as a way to ensure that the ruling house could not wield an unjust level of both political and physical control."

"Maybe," Kilronan countered. "We'll hope it was that altruistic and not a deliberate racial slur."

Isfail narrowed his eyes at him. "Over time, it became a tacit understanding that a union with a force-gifted would exclude any progeny thereof from ascending to the throne. Thus, though my sisters and I are hereditary heirs of the royal house, we are not approved heirs to the reigning House of Coroth."

"That's ridiculous," Osharon stated.

Akira smiled at his disgruntled pronouncement. "Perhaps."

"And that's why Coroth had no concerns about declaring Akira a princess," Kilronan stated in a cynical tone. "He didn't worry that she could ever take the throne through you. But it made him look good."

Isfail scowled, and Akira felt him stiffen at this implied insult to his cousin as he retorted, "Logran doesn't worry about Akira at all. He knows who she is and is secure in her loyalties."

Apparently deciding it was time to intervene, Lord Corcoran rose to fetch the bottle. "The prince is an intelligent man, a good man. We're fortunate to have him on the throne, especially now. Coroth, from all I know of him, will stand by the force-gifted, though some will advise him to reconsider that position." With that, he shifted the discussion back to planning the journey to Coroth.

*A*fter Corcoran and his masters left the residence, Isfail slouched in an armchair in Akira's bedroom, watching her move about selecting what she needed for the trip to Coroth.

Without appearing to, Akira studied him. She could see that he was still irritated by the confrontation with Kilronan, at being required to explain his own Psyche heritage. His jaw was tight, and the barometer of his gray eyes predicted stormy musings.

"I don't believe Kilronan meant to offend you, Dan," she said quietly. She smiled when his gaze flicked to hers.

"Perhaps not, my sweet," he replied, changing position to rest his forearms on his thighs, his fingers clenched. "Is he ever going to accept your choice? Accept me?"

"I think he does, for the most part." Akira turned to the new black trunk that had replaced the one damaged when Ana Karsh destroyed the guest quarters at the palace earlier in the year in an attempt to kill her. "Kilronan doesn't like surprises, especially those he feels fall in his area of expertise."

Isfail gave her a wry grin. "Like the intricacies of Psyche bloodlines?"

"Among other things." Akira carefully folded a favorite dress that he'd given her. "And maybe it's more sensitive when it involves you and me. He'll adjust."

"How have things been between you since our betrothal?"

Akira paused, turning to look at him. "Fine, and he's obviously worked on shifting those past feelings into a sincere friendship. There's been no animosity or ill will between us. I know he coordinated with Arla and Cobon to make sure one of them was available to offer companionship, even beyond the usual guard details."

"Good," Isfail said, appearing satisfied, and maybe a little more relaxed. "Kilronan and I might be able to be friends someday." He met her searching look. "I really would like that, Kira."

Stepping to him, Akira bent to kiss his mouth as he straightened. "I believe you, my love." She chuckled when he pulled her onto his lap, enjoying a longer play of lips before he settled her against him with a sigh.

Ishal had changed him, Akira realized now. She felt his need to be comforted, knowing he'd never ask aloud. There was a constant tension in his body, in his voice. Even their lovemaking had an edge of desperation in the way he held her, as if their time together was ephemeral and soon to be lost.

And though she'd seen him smile over small amusements, the easy humor, the lightness of spirit that was so much a part of him, were missing. Akira wanted to hear him laugh, really laugh, again. She refused to believe that their enemies had taken part of his soul in this latest assault. And she would be there for him this time, as he had been there for her through her dark times. That she could do.

Seventeen

hroughout dinner in the protectorate dining hall that evening, Akira saw the way Isfail studied everything, everyone. Was he right? Had Dateh managed to position one or more of his followers in Mountain Shadows?

This elite protectorate attracted warriors and support staff from around Caldala. Akira hadn't taken the time to learn the backgrounds and histories of most of them. Until now, it hadn't seemed necessary, even after a journeyman transfer had proven to be a member of The Bow when he attempted to kill her lunams ago. But the information from Commander Shanow made it clear that Baronan's cult had planted informants and assassins within Caldala for years.

Mountain Shadows was a small village, and many of its citizens were multi-generational local families. But there were those who had come from other regions, even other countries. Akira thought of Jor and Ala Kellan, who had emigrated from Orsha after losing most of their family at sea. The delightful protectorate chef, Juniro, had come from Ishal after the Baronan Rebellion, seeking a better life for his young daughter, Catonina, after her mother died in the plague that had further ravaged the war-torn country. These people had become important to Akira since she'd first come here at the end of last winter. She couldn't imagine any of them as agents of destruction.

Even now, the stout Juniro was making his way to their table with a platter of desserts. Akira's spirits lifted seeing the beatific good humor on his face as he placed the offering before her.

"For you, Lady Muro, and your fine man, yes?" He laughed

at the startled cough of breath from Isfail when he gave the commander a hearty clap on the back.

"You are fortunate man, yes, Lord Isfail?" Juniro went on, gentling his next pat of approval. "You must deserve this beautiful woman, cherish her, or I will slip something into your food."

But his jocularity faded as the couple looked concerned rather than amused. "I am apologizing. It was a poor joke."

Akira took the hand he offered, squeezing it tightly. "No need, Juniro. We're just distracted by the trip tomorrow. How is Nina?" she asked, using the little girl's nickname with sincere affection.

Regaining his good humor, Juniro lifted big hands. "Ah, my Nina! I can hardly keep up now. She has excitement for being in the village school. Before you healed my little one, she was too fragile to join the other children, yes? Now she is all eagerness."

Clasping his hands high, he looked skyward, saying, "May it continue, yes?" With a chuckle the chef began to clear tableware. "I have worries at first, because she is behind the other children in her studies, but I speak with Master Ramort, the schoolmaster, yes? He speaks well of her, and tells me she has a quick mind. He has no concerns, so I feel better. Enjoy."

As they watched him walk back toward the kitchen with plates balanced in his hands, Isfail asked, "What was wrong with his daughter?"

"Complications from the Gray Mist plague. Her mother died from it, in Ishal. After living through the first rebellion as a cook for the Tash'tric Militia, then losing his wife in the pestilence and poverty that crippled some of the ruined cities for years afterward, Juniro lost heart. He petitioned the House of Coroth and the appropriate division of Parliament to become a legal resident of Caldala."

She studied Isfail's thoughtful face. "You're wondering if he's a member of The Bow."

"I am, but I'll admit that he doesn't fit the profile I lean toward. He worked for the militia, and appears to have been thinking only of his daughter when he left Ishal." He took her hand in his. "Not everyone is an enemy, my sweet. I know that."

Akira picked up a delicate tart brimming with glossy fruit filling, waiting until Isfail had chosen an equally delectable pastry. "For tonight, we'll think of the good in people."

He reached for her hand as they bit into their dessert.

*T*he seasons are changing quickly," Akira remarked as they indulged in a long walk back to their quarters, arm in arm. The sky overhead was dense with stars in the dark of the moons, glorious as milky rivers and swirls of twinkling lights. She closed her eyes, drawing in the scents riding on brisk winds that sent the evergreens roaring. "The spices and ripe smells of harvest have given way to pine and spruce, and a cold freshness that hints at the coming snow. It makes me anticipate winter."

Isfail slipped his arm from hers to wrap it around her shoulders, snugging her closer. "It's a change from coastal storms," he said. "Fresh is a good way of describing it. There's no brine in the air, like the sea winds hold."

Akira knew he matched his long-legged pace to hers, and wanted to prolong this private amble. Tomorrow would begin another long journey, with the strain of waiting for an attack at any point along the way. And the capital city would bring no relief.

There would be seemingly endless strategy meetings with the military leaders, and the inevitable political maneuverings for positions of importance, as perceived by the politicians. To her, every position had importance, but Akira had too much experience in the diplomatic ranks to expect anything else.

Almost as if he could hear her thoughts, Isfail spoke. "We're facing bad times, my sweet. You and I, we've dealt with some of the worst in people, even in the role of peacekeepers," he mused, his arm tightening around her. "You as an ambassador, and I in the militia, together and apart. But usually within the scope of our authority."

Akira nodded, following his thoughts as her arm encircled his waist. "Now we're facing something larger, and potentially more deadly, with the terrible ambitions of this Abron Dateh and his control over the assassin cult."

"We don't even know how numerous The Bow is, Akira, or how many of them have already established themselves here in Caldala. They've come after you at least twice now, and that's bad enough, but they'll strike against other force-gifted soon. How can Caldala protect them all?"

She knew the worry in his voice, in his being, was not only for her safety, but also for his sisters and their families. It was not generally known that his bloodline held Psyche ancestry. Like herself, Ardan had lost his parents too early, and he'd taken on the responsibility for three younger sisters. Akira knew that this new danger to the force-gifted population weighed heavily on him for their sake. Today he'd been obliged to reveal their secret to a few more people.

She stopped at the door to her residence. Shifting away to cup his face in her hands, Akira looked deep into his eyes. "We'll see to it that your sisters and their families are protected, Dan. Whatever we need to do."

"Akira . . ."

There was more, she thought as they walked into the warmth and light of the front room. She heard the troubled voice, as if he were reluctant to move on with whatever he was going to say.

"Just say it, Dan. We'll deal with it." Akira watched the resignation come over him, the tightening of storm-shadowed eyes.

He reached into an inner pocket of his coat, withdrawing a much-creased paper. "This was given to me by Mirastheny Shanow, along with the journals. I've only shown this to Logran, until now. He agrees that any decision in response to this is yours alone."

Meeting his eyes, she held out her hand for the letter. Then she moved closer to a lamp, unfolding it, smoothing the creases as she glanced at the signature. Shanow had a bold, clear script, she thought absently, reading the brief appeal for help, lingering on the final words—'*I believe the loyal citizens of Ishal would be best served by a military alliance with Lady Akira Muro.*'

Would it ever end? Akira wondered. Would she ever *not* be seen as the ultimate weapon against the invasions, the wars and insurrections?

Then she looked at the man she loved, saw the pain and anger in his face, and knew it was for her, against those who asked this of her. If she said no, no she would not be drawn into another battle, would not be seen as the answer, he would stand for her, with her.

And he would stand beside her if she chose to fight for Ishal. He knew, as she did, that in order to defend innocents like the sisters he loved, they must fight for the innocents that good people like Gaios Shanow spoke for.

"We'll discuss how I can best serve the people of Caldala and Ishal once the strategy meetings begin." She handed the refolded letter back to him.

*I*sfail remembered her words, and the steadfast determination in Akira's eyes, as the entourage set out before dawn the next morning. Perhaps his recent adversity had shaken his confidence, just as the beatings had damaged his body.

He mulled it over as their carriage rolled through the gate behind Team Kilronan. Lord Corcoran's carriage came immediately behind, with Team Cobon guarding the rear. The pace picked up as they cleared the walls of the Mountain Shadows stronghold on the first leg of the journey to Coroth. Despite the lateness of the season, and the risk of early snowfall, they were all needed to strategize with the prince and other defense services leaders over this national threat.

Taking Akira's hand in his, he drew strength from this miraculous woman as the rising sun rimmed the mountain peaks, bright gold against the midnight blue sky. Her determination and faith fortified his own as surely as her skills healed his body.

Together they would fight for their right to live in peace.

Eighteen

City of Coroth, Three Days Later

T here was no time to rest from their journey before the travelers from Mountain Shadows were required at strategy meetings. Lord Corcoran met with his fellow Protectorate lords and ladies from across Caldala. Kilronan and Cobon joined him at this first meeting, the very afternoon they arrived at the palace, while their teams had a chance to settle in the guest quarters assigned to them.

That same afternoon, Isfail was occupied with the initial meeting of the heads of the militias based in cities and towns throughout the country. He'd requested that Captain Toth attend, as he would soon be taking command of the Insalat Militia.

The goal of each meeting was to bring together fellow leaders in their respective defense services. Some had not seen one another in years, and there were new people to meet and establish relationships with. Everyone understood that they had a common purpose; familiarity and trust would be critical in countering a major threat to their country and people.

Prince Logran spent some time with each group, making sure that every man and woman was introduced and acknowledged. He needed the loyalty and dedication of everyone, and wanted them to know that the House of Coroth would stand firm for its warriors in all divisions.

There was a third meeting taking place that afternoon. Logran had ordered Most High Garan to gather his high and senior ambassadors together at Central for the same purpose.

Tomorrow would see them all assembled in the great throne room of the palace to receive a first statement of what was currently known about the situation in Ishal. Details about this threat to Caldala would be provided, questions presented. Coroth's military advisors, including admirals and captains of the Royal Navy, would join in that general assembly.

Traders, ship captains, travelers of all kinds had been interviewed to add to the knowledge that Isfail had brought back. Court secretaries had worked night and day to compile the information to be disseminated to those who could put it to good use. Tonight, Logran would have Akira and Isfail go over the material in a final review before it was presented to the group.

*A*kira . . . Logran mused now, as he shared afternoon tea with her while the defense services meetings were concluding. He studied the petite woman, knowing she was assessing him in return. She had no active position in any of the defense services anymore. Officially, she was an honorary princess of the House of Coroth, Most Honorable Lady, and Retired High Ambassador.

Her mouth twitched as amusement flashed into her emerald eyes. Logran grinned, knowing she'd guessed his thoughts. Or tapped them.

"You're a dilemma, Akira."

"I suppose I am," she replied before taking a sip from her cup. "How are you going to bring me into this? Officially."

Laughing, Logran leaned back in his chair, enjoying her. When had trust and friendship become part of their relationship? He hardly knew. There'd been a time, brief lunams ago, when he'd tried to separate her from his beloved cousin, believing her to be too dangerous, too great a risk as a uniquely powerful force caller. Then she'd once again risked her life to defend the Caldalan people, engaging in a deadly duel with rogue ambassador Ana Karsh.

Had that been the turning point? Or had it been the sudden understanding that Akira loved Ardan as deeply his cousin loved her? Whatever the beginnings, Logran now cared for her, trusted her, and considered her one of his most important advisors on security concerns.

His voice was smug as he saw the questioning lift of a delicate eyebrow. "We'll just stick to the truth. You are an official advisor to the House of Coroth."

*A*kira wondered if she would ever become used to living in the grandeur of the palace. Oh, she was happy in Ardan's beautiful rooms, and almost at ease in the elegant comfort of the three-story family wing. But the idea of casual acceptance of life as a member of Caldala's ruling house was currently beyond her comprehension.

"You'll get used to it," Oona soothed as Akira's brow furrowed while she ran a light finger over an ornate, gilded statue. Prince Logran's life-partner had unusual sensitivity, and a remarkable ability to take care of those around her. Akira was grateful for Oona's warm friendship and mentoring.

Taking Akira's arm in hers as the two women toured the kitchens and service areas that occupied the lower floors, Oona met her doubtful look with a smile. "Besides," Oona said, "you won't need to manage or oversee any of this."

"Thank God," Akira stated with relief. "The idea of that is as challenging as the last two days of meetings." She laughed with her companion, secretly grateful for this respite from endless hours of evaluating defense strategies, and the posturing of some of the admiralty and militia commanders.

"I'm so glad the trip from the mountains was uneventful. I know it is a risk to travel back and forth, with the possibility of severe weather and all," Oona said as she guided them into an inner courtyard. Akira heard her sigh as the princess showed her through the paths. "The gardens certainly aren't at their best so late in the season."

Finding the woman's unusually scattershot conversation interesting, Akira decided that Oona had more on her mind than familiarizing her with the vast palace complex.

Though the day held a chill, the high walls around them

stopped the cold winds off the sea, and the midday sun warmed them as they settled on a carved bench.

Studying the tawny hues of the granite blocks that made up the walls of the palace, Akira realized she'd never appreciated the architectural beauty of the fortified castle before now. Where sunlight struck, glimmers of gold and silver reflected from minerals within the stone.

Despite its structural strength, there was a graceful beauty in the powerful architecture that pleased the eye. The four-story central structure that housed the throne room, reception halls, and other areas dedicated to royal business, reflected an appropriate level of grandeur without slipping into garish displays of overweening self-importance.

Three interior courtyards, including the one where they now sat, allowed natural light to penetrate many interior staterooms through windows overlooking gardens displaying fountains and small ponds. Akira now knew there were few rooms within the Palace of Coroth that did not allow some pleasing view— from the raw beauty of the ocean to the peaceful serenity of an expertly landscaped garden. Windows facing inland provided views of the city of Coroth, or the well-designed courts, drives, and outbuildings of the forward palace grounds; all surrounded by strong perimeter walls constructed of the same tawny granite.

"We'll save the north wing for this afternoon," Oona stated. "You know it holds the suites for visiting dignitaries and other guests. Ardan's sisters and their families stay there occasionally."

Akira gave a slight smile—they were now about to get into what had been distracting Oona. "He told me they are expected to arrive within a day or two. I'm anxious to meet them."

Taking her hand, Oona shifted to look at her. "I know they are eager to finally meet you. Respecting your former position in the Ambassador Core, and the need for circumspection, Ardan has told them little over the years, but they are perceptive women who love their only brother very much."

"It must have been difficult for them," Akira began quietly, "when he was missing in Ishal. Especially after what happened in the first rebellion." She felt the hand on hers grip tighter.

"I'm not sure what Ardan has said, but I believe he keeps a great deal from them to avoid the worry and heartache they're sure to feel. You know he took on the weight of the head of the family after his father, Armaran, was lost at sea?"

With a nod, Akira replied, "Yes, though he's never said so directly. It was easy to intuit from what he's told me over the years. Ardan takes on such responsibility easily for those he loves." Looking back to the sun-sparkled walls, she gave a wistful smile. "He's like this palace really, so strong and warm, with the ability to provide shelter and comfort to those in his care."

She turned and met Oona's gaze. "He's distracted by this new danger, worried that The Bow might target his family if they discover their Psyche heritage. I'm afraid they might be used to pressure the prince and Ardan politically, used as hostages, perhaps, to influence the House of Coroth's defenses or position on the rights of force-gifted."

Akira saw Oona draw herself up, her blue eyes hardening, revealing the fine steel core of Caldala's princess. "They will not have the chance. Ardan's family will reside at the palace until this is resolved. Logran and I will settle it when he returns from today's Parliament session."

In a rare spontaneous act, Akira threw her arms around her. "Thank you," she murmured, feeling Oona's arms wrap tightly in return. As they drew apart, Akira saw a tear spill down Oona's cheek, though the princess was smiling.

"We will be great friends, you and I," she said. "Ardan deserves a partner of your character and compassion, Akira. A woman whose strength is a match for his own. He would never be happy with less." She met Akira's blushing discomposure with a laugh.

"Come, my dear. We have more to explore."

Nineteen

*P*rince Logran leaned back in his carved chair in the formal meeting hall of Caldala's Parliament building, eyes narrowing. "What do you mean when you tell me that Parliament has concerns over the liaison position?" He knew they'd deliberately scheduled the liaison discussion as the last on the day's official agenda, and it rankled.

High Minister Felpon cleared his throat, obviously disconcerted by the prince's cold stare. "There is no disrespect intended, my prince. We feel that your idea has merit. Clearly, someone to unify the major defense forces and the government would benefit Caldala." He paused to look around at his peers, appearing to hope one would speak up to bolster his position.

When no one did, he cleared his throat again. "There is *concern* over the choice of the liaison, considering what we've recently learned of the current hostilities with our neighboring country of Ishal."

"Out with it, man," Logran said sharply, annoyed as he saw where this was heading. "Parliament is balking over Akira Muro—a Psyche. Is that it?"

Logran stood, forcing each minister to meet his eyes as he looked around the arc of occupied seats. "Just lunams ago, we all stood in this very chamber to recognize the services of the Honorable Lady Akira Muro in defending our country. We unanimously awarded her the highest honor a citizen can receive— The Star of the Sea medallion. Now Parliament is *concerned* that she might be untrustworthy, a possible danger to Caldala?"

The contempt in his voice had several ministers shifting

uneasily in their chairs. Some appeared embarrassed to have the words out in the open, while others were more guarded.

Minister Ominor spoke up. "Sir, is it wise to open Caldala's government to criticism and censure by appointing such a powerful force-gifted to an important position at this time?"

Logran studied him for a brief moment. Ominor represented Caldala's sparsely populated, most southern caldon.

"You have an objection to our force-gifted citizens, Minister?"

"I voice the concerns of my *caldon*, my prince," Ominor replied. "My people are afraid—"

"I believe that's *my* people," Logran interrupted deliberately to counter Ominor's insolent demeanor. For a moment he saw resentment in the minister's eyes, but it was quickly erased.

"As you say, my prince." Ominor dipped his head respectfully. "They are fearful of invasion, situated as we are, closest to Ishal."

Logran resumed his seat, tenting his fingers. "Actually, Green River Caldon is geographically closest to Ishal. With Mountain Shadows Protectorate and village practically on the border."

The prince pressed his point. "Akira Muro defended that border less than one year ago, with only a protectorate team of five warriors by her side."

He let the following silence carry the unstated rebuke.

High Minister Felpon cleared his throat. "Prince Logran, as the liaison position can be viewed as two distinct parts—that is, the recognition and funding of the position under the auspices of the Caldalan government, and the choice of a person suitable to fill such a position—perhaps Parliament can vote on each separately?"

With a regal nod, Logran only showed them his public face, serene if somewhat stern. He was tempted to reveal the contempt beneath it for their cowardice. Who would they run to, he wondered, if the force callers chose to relinquish their centuries-old commitment to defend the country that had given them sanctuary? Were their memories really so short that they'd forgotten the many times Akira had personally acted to ensure the peace?

Now, with the slightest hint of discomfiture at another country's challenge, these fools were ready to insult her, to look at Caldala's force-enabled countrymen with distrust.

Silently, he listened to the formal presentation defining the Defense Services Liaison position, its official title. Felpon droned on, then cleared his throat and called the vote. The position was approved by a majority of those present. Logran noted the two ministers who cast their votes against—Ominor, no surprise, and Wrax, of Southern Fork Caldon.

They represented the two southern caldons within the region bordered by a mountain range to their north-northwest, and the high mountains separating Caldala from Ishal to the east. Those hardy citizens were as isolated from the main population of their country as the ones in the far northern moors.

Both southern caldons, now wasn't that interesting. It seemed he had a need for some expert reconnaissance. He returned his attention to the proceedings as Felpon formally recorded the results before setting the agenda for a special session in the following week to hear testimonials, and decide on who would be appointed liaison.

The bell rang to end the session. Logran saw relief on several faces, suspecting that they were happy to delay the vote on the second part of this position. It gave him great pleasure to increase their discomposure by wishing each one a safe and peaceful evening before striding out of the hall with his royal guard.

It was then, as he fell easily into formal pace among the crisply uniformed guards, that the idea came to him.

Logran found Oona settled in their private sitting room with Isfail and Akira. The women were laughing, apparently at some tale Isfail had just related, judging by the cheerful teasing from his princess and Akira.

Excellent, Logran thought, everyone in high spirits. It *might* make this go down easier. As they turned to greet him, with Isfail getting up to fetch another bottle of wine and a fourth glass, Logran put on a broad grin and rubbed his hands briskly.

"Excellent! We're all here. Now, let's get on with plans for the royal binding ceremony."

The ensuing silence from the other three coincided with the sound of breaking glass as Akira's wine goblet hit the floor.

Twenty

Oona rang for an attendant as she motioned Isfail to Akira's side. Nothing more was said while she oversaw the cleanup as if it were nothing more than a minor accident, then ordered a tray of small finger foods and a tea service before closing the door behind the attendant.

Then she turned to her husband. "Logran, what do you mean by that impertinent remark?"

Before he could answer, Isfail said sharply, "I believe that's a subject to be decided by Akira and I first, cousin."

"Certainly, Dan," Logran replied with a quick bow to the apparently still dumbstruck Akira. "I meant no disrespect to either of you. However," he continued when Isfail was about to speak again, "You have made a public commitment to one another, and there are a number of reasons for conducting the ceremony sooner than later."

Oona looked at Akira, who had yet to say a word since Logran's startling statement. "Akira, my dear, what have you to say about this?"

It did not surprise anyone to see the woman abruptly get up from her seat beside Isfail and begin to pace the room. Oona's mouth quirked into an amused smile. Akira's habit of pacing under duress or intense thought was known by anyone close to her.

"Kira," Isfail said quietly. "There's no need to upset yourself over this. We'll go up and discuss it between ourselves before anything more is said."

Oona frowned at Logran when he started to speak, but he would not be thwarted.

"If I may just present a few considerations here," Logran began. "I realize this is sudden, but you're here. Dan's family will be arriving in a day or so. It would be easy enough to arrange a ceremony suited to both your positions."

He held up a hand as Isfail's eyes narrowed. "Hear me out. Dan, you *are* a hereditary heir to the House of Coroth and, as such, have a duty to conduct the more important of your personal affairs with appropriate ceremony. That includes your binding."

Oona sat down to hear him out. She knew there was truth in his statement.

"Akira." Logran turned to her. "You are recognized as a national hero, an honorary princess of Coroth, and you have accepted the hand of a member of the royal family. Whether it's to your personal liking or not, you are also obligated to submit to a public—"

"Spectacle," Akira snapped, throwing up her hands.

Logran grinned. "As you say. We can keep it to a minimum, but consider that the sooner it's arranged, the sooner it's over. You and Dan are here now, but you'll soon be returning to Mountain Shadows, where the winter season will likely prevent easy travel until next spring."

When Akira began twisting her hands together, Oona decided it was time to intervene. "Come, Akira. I'll walk with you back to your rooms and we'll have our tea there." She sent a cool look to her husband before glancing at Isfail, who stood watching Akira with worry in his eyes.

"Dan, I'll expect you in your suite within half an hour," Oona stated briskly as she ushered Akira out.

Isfail waited only until the door closed behind the women before turning on his cousin angrily. "What the hell, Lo! My ring has been on her hand for barely two lunams. I've scarcely had time with Akira through most of that! We haven't even had a chance to talk about this, and you have no business getting involved in our binding plans."

He watched Logran pour two glasses of whiskey, fuming over his cousin's silence. Isfail nearly tossed the glass aside when it was handed to him but managed to control his anger when he noticed the tension in Logran's face.

"This isn't really about us, is it," Isfail said quietly now, studying Logran's shadowed eyes. "What's happened?"

Logran indicated chairs before the fireplace. Once seated, he told him about the Parliament session and the resistance to Akira's appointment as the liaison.

Isfail's annoyance at Logran's interference became a simmering rage over the situation as he took in this news. "Parliament would reject Akira, after all she's done, all she's risked for this country's security? Because they don't have the courage to spit in Ishal's collective eye?" he ground out before swallowing his whiskey in one gulp. The string of invectives that followed was insufficient to calm his temper.

"They're a pack of fools, for the most part," Logran said, refilling the glasses. "Their lives and caldons have been peaceful and free of risk for too long. They've forgotten what it's like to fight for what they have, or stand up to keep it. The Mors invasion was barely noticed by the citizenry, resolved before most of the country had time to fear, and far from their daily lives."

Isfail took another long drink. "Akira told me that the one thing she'd failed to anticipate before the Mors defense . . . the thing that was the most difficult to understand, was the apathy and resistance of some of the warriors to use any means to fight the enemy. Some of the military had evidently been at peace too long to have the will for all out battle. And Kilronan told me, when Akira was first offered the liaison position in his protectorate, she warned Lord Corcoran that he could be opening his protectorate to a dark world of political machinations."

His eyes were bleak as he looked at his royal cousin. "You want us to be bound here, at the palace, as a political statement."

Logran nodded. "Yes. It's a public endorsement of Akira and shows that the House of Coroth will stand with all force-gifted."

"She won't take this well, Lo."

*A*bsently acknowledging the salutes of the guards who opened the doors to the family wing as he approached, Isfail entered the wide hall slowly, his head down as he pondered how to comfort Akira in this unexpected turn of events.

"Dan."

The quiet voice had him looking up to see Oona standing at the open door that bore the insignia of the royal house, the suite where their family resided. The staircase to his rooms split off further down the main hall, but she beckoned him into a private parlor.

"How's Akira?" he asked, moving to stare out a large window overlooking the sea.

"She asked for some time alone," Oona replied, bringing him a cup of tea. "I don't know if that included you."

Hearing the concern in her voice, Isfail leaned over to kiss her brow before they sat down in chairs in the scenic alcove. "I'll give her a little time."

"I worry for her, Dan," Oona murmured, meeting his eyes. "She's such an ancient soul for so young a woman. She's carried too much responsibility and had too little joy." She reached out to cover his hand with hers. "I want you both to find that joy in your life together."

Isfail smiled more easily and raised her hand to his lips. "We will, my beauty, if I have anything to say about it."

"Did Logran tell you why he started this?"

"Yes, but it won't make it any easier."

She nodded, looking out at a cloud-laden sky with a pensive expression on her elegant face. "Something happened at the Parliament meeting, and Logran feels that your binding ceremony will make a point about where Coroth stands."

Though it was an astute statement rather than a question, Isfail replied, "Yes. I know he'll talk with you about it."

"She's afraid, Dan." When he glanced over at her, Oona went on, "Afraid of what your binding means."

"Akira's feeling trapped. Caged because The Bow is targeting her, requiring her to be surrounded by guards. She can't even walk on the beach to settle her mind without a guard contingent." Setting aside his cup, Isfail got up, pushing his hands into the pockets of his trousers as he walked nearer to the window. "Once we're bound . . . I think it's just starting to hit her. I'm afraid, too, Oona. Afraid that I won't be worth all she'll be required to deal with. Afraid I'll lose her again."

A light touch on his arm had him turning to her serene smile.

"You won't. Akira loves you, Dan. As long as you're with her, you will be everything she needs."

"What would we do without you, my beauty? Without you looking after us all?"

"Just try and find out, you rogue." She walked over to open the door again. "Now go find your Akira and put a light in her heart. She needs you."

*A*kira wasn't in his suite of rooms when Isfail walked in just minutes after leaving Oona. He crushed the sudden fear that she had left it all behind. Akira wouldn't leave without telling him, not after all they'd been to one another.

Where would she go? Isfail mused, hands fisted on hips as he prowled from room to room until he stood at the large windows of the common room once more.

Watching the waves pound the narrow strip of sand, it came to him. Striding out again, he rushed down to a short hall, up a flight of stairs to the top floor, and the door leading to a private terrace, letting out a relieved breath when he went out and saw her.

Akira was standing at the balustrade, her hands braced on the top, her face turned to sea and sky. A blustering wind loosened tendrils of hair from the artfully upswept style she'd so carefully arranged before they'd gone down that day. For a moment Isfail just stood in the doorway, absorbing every detail of her exquisite profile.

She looks so sad, he thought, and so distant.

Then she turned her head to meet his gaze, and a slight smile appeared to ease that sorrow. "You found me. I knew you would."

Isfail came to stand behind her, wrapping his arms around to hold her tight. He placed a kiss just below her right ear. "I always will, my love."

She leaned back into his embrace, folding her hands over his. Isfail felt his fears dissolve like the wisps of clouds dissipating above the ocean. They stood like that, without needing words, as the sun spilled into the distant horizon, sending red and gold pooling over the sea.

When the velvet night overtook the last traces of day, Isfail took Akira's hand and led her back to their rooms.

"Would you like to talk about this?" he asked as he poured them both some wine.

Akira was pulling jeweled pins from her hair, letting the long mass of it fall free around her shoulders. "It was just such a surprise, Dan. It caught me off guard, that's all."

But she wasn't looking at him, he noticed, and those small, slim hands could not be still. He watched her put the hair pins on his desk then push them into a pile before sorting them into precise rows.

He brought her a glass of wine, setting it on the desk with his before catching her restless hands. When she met his gaze, Isfail said, "Tell me what you're afraid of, Akira. Is it the idea of a formal binding ceremony here, or the idea of binding with me at all?"

The shocked surprise on her face eased his worries, as did her fingers tightening around his.

"It's nothing to do with you!" Akira exclaimed, rising up to kiss him. She gave another long sigh while he pulled her to the couch. "I suppose I've avoided thinking of the formal service," she admitted as they sat.

Akira turned a bit to face him fully now, perhaps finding courage in his attentive silence. "You know I find public events . . . ceremonies difficult, Dan. I wish . . ."

When she trailed off and looked away, Isfail encouraged, "Wish what, my sweet?"

Now she looked at him with a rueful smile. "I wish we were ordinary people who could go before a Brother in a lovely little temple and recite the vows. I wish life could be that simple."

Isfail nodded as he got up to fetch their wine. "I understand that, Kira. Unfortunately, we both have very public status. I am what I am, an heir of Coroth, and you are—"

"The most feared woman in our world?"

Her bitter interjection had him frowning. "You know that's not what I was going to say."

Tears welled, shimmering in her eyes before Akira covered her face with her hands. "Forgive me, Dan," she murmured, her voice thick with emotion. "You would never think it, let alone say it."

"No," he whispered, pulling her into his arms as the tears flooded. "Kira, is it really so terrible to think of binding here that it darkens your indomitable spirit?"

"No," she whispered against his chest. "There's so much I want with you, Dan. To be yours, for you to be mine."

"I am yours, with or without the vows, my love."

Akira gathered her tangled emotions, ashamed of her bitter retort, but she understood—far too well—how this situation had come about. Would she never escape the consequences of her deadly reputation, one she seemed destined to face with every attempt at a normal life?

Stepping away from Isfail, Akira met his troubled gaze. "Logran wants us to be bound for political reasons. You and I both know it. Why don't you tell me what he said about the Parliament meeting?"

Twenty-One

Kilronan leaned back on the terrace railing the next morning, waiting for Akira to speak. He knew what was coming, knew the inevitability and finality of the choice she'd made less than two lunams ago, here on the beach below. And, to his surprise, Kilronan accepted her decision. If he had to lose the woman he'd loved his entire life, he would at least lose to a man he could admire and respect.

"Our binding date has been set," she told him, confirming his suspicions. "While I would prefer to have it privately, in Mountain Shadows, Ardan and I will be bound here."

"Very publically," Kilronan added with a grin, knowing how much Akira despised public ceremonies involving her.

He watched her grimace and reached out to take her hand, drawing her beside him. Kilronan wrapped an arm around her shoulders in comfort. "When?"

"In three days. We want to leave Coroth for the mountains as soon as we can." Akira glanced at him. "I know time is short for winter travel, and you're ready to go home."

"More than," he agreed. "It's already a big risk so late in the season."

She's avoiding the details of the ceremony, Kilronan decided. "Do you want us there?"

Obviously surprised, Akira turned to face him. "Of course I do." Then a hint of sorrow dimmed her eyes. "Unless you don't want to attend."

Smiling tenderly, Kilronan touched her face. "Akira . . . I'm resigned to the fact that Isfail is the winner here. I'll always stand by your side when you need me, and I'll give him my best as a friend. You don't need to worry about my feelings.

"It's too bad that Lord Corcoran and Cobon left yesterday," he added, wanting to lighten the mood. "They'd both want to witness this."

"Yes. Ardan said the same, and he'd wanted Cobon in his honor guard." She stared out over the ever-moving waves. "This didn't come up until last evening."

He listened closely while she told him about the Parliament debacle, and Prince Logran's idea of using their binding ceremony to very publically proclaim the House of Coroth's support for Akira, and the force community.

"It's not a bad idea," Kilronan said, grinning at her cynical look. "Politically, it's a great idea." When she muttered a low oath, he chuckled. "Look. There's no reason to delay your binding. Since we're all called to testify before Parliament on the liaison position the day after the ceremony, we could leave by the end of this week. You and Isfail might as well face the mountain winter with that behind you."

He kissed her temple. "Your life together is the important part, Akira. Just think of the public event as a spit in the face of Parliament."

When she laughed at that, he laughed with her.

"Now, what else is there?"

Her return smile was rueful now. "Are you tapping my thoughts?"

He tugged on the intricate braid she wore today. "You'd know if I were. So spill it, Muro."

"Ardan returned with more than Commander Shanow's journals and warnings. A personal letter was included." She met his sharpened gaze. "Shanow has asked for me."

Twenty-Two

*A*kira stood in the first full light of morning, gazing out a wide window overlooking the sea. The beauty of the day, the calm of blue waters that stretched to a clear horizon, matched the serenity that filled her so unexpectedly. It was as if the turmoil of her life could not touch this culmination of the love that had begun as a military partnership so many years ago.

Today, she—Akira Muro, a woman alternately celebrated, coveted, and feared—would bind her life with Ardan Isfail. The man who'd made her believe in love. A soft smile formed on her lips. Wonder filled her as she absorbed this miracle in her life.

Her dear friend—former ambassador, now celebrated designer—Isheill, tucked the final pearl-encrusted ornament into the elegant hairstyle she'd designed just for Akira, and stepped back with a smile. At last, she carefully slipped the delicate coronet on. For a moment, the two friends looked at the reflection in the mirror.

"Could you ever guess we'd be here, Isheill?" Akira asked quietly. "I've been a warrior or a diplomat all my life. Who is the woman in the glass now?"

"She is who she ever was, *asherka*. A great woman of character and ability." Sitting down on the padded bench, Isheill wrapped her arms around Akira, touching her forehead to hers. "Be happy, my friend, for I am happy for you. Your man is all I have wished for you. You have more than earned the honors bestowed on you by this royal house."

When Akira shook her head slightly, Isheill pulled back,

framing her face with long fingers. "This is truth. There will be dangers more to face, for you, for us all. We will meet them, and defeat them. And you will have love and happiness that are so deserved."

Covering Isheill's beautiful, tea-colored hands with her own, Akira smiled fully. "Then it is truth."

"*Sha!*" Isheill declared in her native tongue as she bounced up. "Now, the dress."

When Akira finally stood, gently stroking the soft sweep of silk, she was content. As always, Isheill had crafted a magnificent creation that suited her own unique appearance. With simple lines that somehow managed to look amazing, a faint blush hue reminiscent of the lining of a seashell, the formal gown beautifully enhanced her fair skin and pure-white hair.

"I couldn't imagine a more wonderful dress to be bound in." Akira turned to hug the first friend she'd made in her life with the Ambassador Core. "As always, Isheill, you've tamed me into a woman I can be proud to show the world."

For a moment, Isheill looked nonplused. "Someday, my Akira, I hope you will see your own beauty. For today, it is enough that my skills please you."

Stepping back, exotically gorgeous in a dress whose jeweled colors reflected her Ishakan heritage and culture, Isheill bowed deeply. "I go now to the temple, my love. It is my joy to observe your binding ceremony this day."

Tears welled in Akira's eyes at the sincerity in her friend's words and face. With last kisses on her cheeks, Isheill hugged her close, then left the room as Oona entered.

For a long moment, Logran's princess just stood, fingertips to her lips even as a smile bloomed there. "You are perfect, my dear."

Akira just shook her head again, though she was pleased with the compliment. "As long as I'm perfect for Dan." Oona laughed and kissed her cheeks in her affectionate way.

Taking Akira's arm, Oona drew her to the door. "I'll take you to the temple. The corridors have been cleared and everyone is on time."

*I*sfail waited impatiently in the antechamber near the right side entry of the palace temple. Once again, he stepped to the doorway to scan the airy, high-ceilinged hall filled with invited witnesses. It was an odd assembly, he considered, distracting himself with the thought. Ambassadors mixed with protectorate warriors, royal guards, and militiamen from his command in Insalat.

Then there were the requisite politicians: Parliament ministers, mayors, lords and ladies. He couldn't fault Logran's recommendation that it was wiser to include them as witnesses to this binding than to exclude them. There was no denying that Caldala would need all her government entities aligned to face the threat from Ishal.

He felt regret that political decisions had driven such an important event in their lives. Even more regret that many of the people important to Akira could not be here due to short notice and distance. Isfail swore to himself that he would arrange a proper reception for them once they returned to Mountain Shadows.

Looking for Kilronan and his team, he found them sharing a pew with former ambassador Isheill and High Ambassador Garan. At least Akira would have these friends to share this important ceremony with. It pleased him that Kilronan sat relaxed, with a smile on his face as he spoke with the animated Isheill.

Could he have accepted this binding as graciously if Akira had chosen the protectorate master?

Shaking himself from a thought that had no place here, Isfail quelled his impatience by appreciating the beauty of the day as he looked at the high, arched window behind the altar. Composed of multiple clear panes of glass, it had the added feature of tall wood-framed panels of stained glass bordering the sides. These could slide along interior wooden tracks along the base of the window to embellish the backdrop when desired, or distract from a view of inclement weather.

Today the sky was a pure blue, while a calm sea sparkled in

the sunlight. God's blessing on their union, he thought with a smile.

By now, Akira would be in the antechamber near the left side entry. His pulse quickened as he imagined her there, waiting impatiently, as he was.

The last of the guests had taken their seats. Isfail recognized the horn and drum fanfare that brought the assembly rising for the arrival of Prince Logran and Princess Oona. They were escorted to the two wide chairs in front of the central array of pews. Their children were already seated just behind, and his own family in the pews behind them. The congregation resumed their seats and the binding ceremony officially began.

He stood straighter as the Brother stepped up to bow to prince and princess, receiving the intricately braided length of gold and silver strands from Prince Logran—the binding rope that had been used to seal the pact for generations of the House of Coroth. A rush of familial pride filled Isfail, knowing that his name and Akira's would be added to the leather-bound tome recording all family events of significance.

Drums sounded the solemn march cadence announcing the honor guards. In unison, two columns—ten attendants each—marched into the temple from entry arches to the right and left of the main doors. Through the arch on the right came the men he'd chosen, including soon-to-be Commander Toth, Captain Aroth, his sisters' husbands, with friends and fellow soldiers completing his guard. They arranged themselves five to each side of the right aisle leading to the altar. As Isfail left the antechamber and stood in the arch, they lifted swords to form a shining arbor into the temple. Isfail grinned as Toth gave him a wink, even as his friend stood tall and immaculate in formal dress uniform at his station.

Simultaneously, the ambassadors of Reconnaissance Alpha took their positions in the left aisle, raising swords at the same moment as their counterparts in the right aisle. Akira had a fleeting moment to wonder whether the palace temple had ever hosted such an honor guard as she stepped up to the left arch, and the canopy of flashing blades held aloft by the black-uniformed ambassadors who were some of the most important, most loved people in her life. Then Elen glanced at her, his eyes crinkling above his formal uniform mask, and she knew he was smiling beneath finely embossed black leather.

There came a quiet building of drumbeats, then the traditional rhythm of horns sounded. Taking a deep breath, Akira prepared for the following cadence of drums. As the rolling staccato beats began, she started slowly between her former teammates—meeting each one's smiling eyes as she passed. They fell into formation behind her as she walked down the aisle angling from left to center. Akira was oblivious to the sea of faces in the pews to either side. She knew Ardan matched her steps with his own guard in the aisle angling from the right.

They met before the central altar, seeing only each other until a quiet word from the amused Brother had them turning to face him. Akira felt Ardan take her hand, holding it tight as the opening invocation filled the vaulted room.

It seemed but a brief moment until she faced Ardan once more, clasping his left wrist as he did hers.

"You, Akira," the Brother intoned solemnly, "and you, Ardan, come before God and these witnesses to bind your lives together. This is a commitment to each other and to God that you will honor each other for the rest of your days, celebrate and support each other in times of joy and times of sorrow, that you will be faithful in mind, body, and spirit to your chosen partner in life."

Looking into Ardan's brilliant gray eyes, seeing an eternity of love there, Akira felt the Brother wind the shimmering gold and silver rope around her wrist, then Ardan's. He pulled the knot snug, laying his hands over it as he prayed the blessing.

Power surged within her, unbidden, a wave of love so powerful, so *right*, that all things seemed possible. If she'd looked away from the joy in Ardan's eyes, Akira would have seen the golden glow pulsing around their joined wrists and hands.

The rope was slipped away and the Brother raised his arms

high with a beaming countenance. "Lord Isfail, you may kiss your lady."

Isfail's triumphant laughter was stilled as his mouth met hers, passionately sealing their binding pact. As he swept her into his arms, spinning joyfully in the thunder of enthusiastic applause from the standing congregation, Akira melded their thoughts and emotions. Her happiness and love swirled with his, binding their souls in this perfect moment.

In keeping with the newly bound couple's wishes, Oona had arranged a private reception in the smaller ballroom of the palace. Consulting with Isheill, the princess had ordered a suitable décor of seashell hues, natural and inviting. Tables of refreshments were garnished with ropes of pearls and arrangements of shells, complimenting bowls and urns of white flowers on cloths of aquamarine and dark blue-green.

Isfail had requested musicians for dancing, teasing Akira into her approval. Now, as he swept her around the floor in the opening dance, Akira decided the sensation of blissful flight was an appropriate beginning to this new life.

"We've done it," he whispered next to her ear. "You've survived your royal binding ceremony and still I see a smile in your beautiful eyes."

"I'm only doing this once," she teased, "despite all of Oona's talent and care in organizing a beautiful event in only three days. If you have any regrets, there's no going back."

"You said beautiful event!" He drew back with a grin. "Perhaps you *will* remember this unwanted spectacle without regret." Then his mouth caressed hers before he murmured, "I have you, truly mine now. There will never be regrets."

Akira saw the truth of it in Ardan's eyes, felt it in the way he held her in his arms, but it had been the sound of his laughter, full and unconstrained, before their first kiss as man and wife, that made the spectacle worthwhile.

*T*he threat of winter weather impeding their return to Mountain Shadows was reinforced by the arrival of a storm that roared in late that night. Sated with the pleasure of their private celebration, Akira paid little heed to the wind and rain that slapped against the windows of their palace suite. If anything, the tempest made her feel safe, cocooned behind strong walls and thick velvet curtains, as if the outside world and all its dangers could not reach them. No evil could fight its way through the roaring wind and pelting rain to shatter their happiness.

She knew it was an illusion, but with Ardan's arms around her, warm and sleepy from lovemaking, she would allow the dream to enfold her until the morning broke with all its demands.

Twenty-Three

*F*ortified to meet a day full of duties that promised to be less pleasing than the day before, Akira and Isfail joined Logran and Oona in their carriage for the ride to the Parliament building. Akira knew that Logran had pushed for the ministers to agree to listen to testimony from respected sources regarding her candidacy for the liaison position. He'd insisted that it be heard by Parliament before they returned to Mountain Shadows.

Admiring her new cousin-in-law's perseverance and conviction, Akira nevertheless felt that it was wasted time. Perhaps it was her years as a diplomat, the time spent studying the ways and workings of politicians, so much the same in the several countries she'd provided counsel in, which had cynical thoughts overshadowing any positive feelings that the Parliament vote would endorse her.

Maybe he sensed her resignation as she felt Isfail take her hand firmly in his. "What are you thinking, my sweet?"

Akira looked around at her companions' solemn faces. "That this decision is already set." Seeing their dismay, she worked up a smile. "We might as well have spent the day in more pleasant surroundings, visiting with Ardan's family."

Leaning forward, Oona took her free hand for a brief moment. "That may be, my dear, but we never admit defeat. We will hold our heads high and take our moment. If the ministers choose to display their cowardice, it is nothing to do with your qualifications."

"Thank you," Akira murmured, releasing her hand reluctantly.

"Don't worry," she said, looking at Logran's frowning visage. "How they vote may have already been decided, but it won't affect my life. Though you will have to decide who else is qualified as liaison, Logran."

He waved that away. "There is no one else anywhere near as qualified. They can go to hell as far as Coroth is concerned. We've managed without a formal liaison all this time."

Isfail's response was more troubling, but Akira was relieved to have it out in the open when he said, "I suspect we're all more concerned about how this shift within Parliament came about. We can all name those who will stand with Akira, and there are those ministers who aren't sure what to believe. Then there are ministers like Ominor and Wrax who've taken a strong stand against her. Why?"

"You suspect they've been compromised?" Logran asked, but Akira could see that the idea was not new for the prince.

"It's worth looking into," Isfail replied, glancing at Akira.

"Garan will send a reconnaissance team to investigate the southern caldons," Akira reminded them, pleased to see Logran's nod of agreement.

"He is to meet with me tomorrow." Logran's face held an anticipatory look about it, as if he were looking forward to the results. "He'll be here today, with the other ambassadors testifying on your behalf, along with Team Kilronan. Felpon should already have the written testimonials submitted by protectorate lords and ladies around Caldala. I know your Lord Corcoran had a few pithy remarks about the necessity of vouching for you, Akira."

She chuckled, and was sure that Evan Corcoran would have a great deal more to say if the vote went against her.

The guard escort and royal carriage turned into the wide, semi-circular court in front of the dignified stone edifice that housed Caldala's Parliament. "Here we go," the prince said with a wry smile. "Let's see how *this* spectacle turns out."

Akira took Isfail's hand for him to help her from the carriage before they followed Prince Logran and Princess Oona between stern rows of protective guardsmen. A crowd of spectators waved cheerfully on either side; calling out greetings and wishes for a happy union that warmed the chill. Isfail grinned down at her, and Akira held tighter to his arm with an easier smile.

It was the people of Caldala that mattered, she remembered, not the ones supposedly representing them here. The ministers could decide as they would, and she would do what she needed to do for her country—with or without their sanction or acknowledgement.

*I*t went as expected, despite the notable absence of testimonials *against* the liaison candidate, a fact the prince enjoyed pointing out with ice-clad disdain. Yet, even without justification on the nay side, the final vote denied Akira Muro the liaison position eleven to nine, splitting the ministers exactly as anticipated.

At least the ride back to the palace was free from the tension of uncertainty, Akira thought, as Isfail tried to cajole Logran out of his foul mood. Oona sided with Akira, taking a more pragmatic view of the whole event, though she had her own pithy comments about Felpon for Akira to add to her collection.

Since Most High Garan had to leave before the vote, plans had already been made for Akira and Isfail to go to Central that afternoon to pass on the news. There were other, more important, concerns to be discussed regarding the threat to force callers, including what the Ambassador Core's official role could be in tracking down The Bow within Caldala and defending against them.

Twenty-Four

wo ambassadors on duty at the entrance gate saluted as Isfail's coach rolled from the main road onto the packed sand lane, and into the large parkland surrounding the inner sanctum of Ambassador Central. Reconnaissance Alpha—commonly referred to as Recon Alpha—the team chosen and trained by Akira during her service to fill a need for accurate intelligence gathering, led the way on horseback. Protectorate Team Kilronan followed the coach, watchful for anything unusual.

The lane stretched before them, running through a cultivated landscape of native grasses edged by shrubs, flowing in curves and plantings that still pleased the eye in their late harvest season forms. The natural woodlands of mixed deciduous trees, nearly devoid of leaves, gave precedent to cypress and pine that crowded closer as the entry park narrowed. Shortly, it would begin the winding descent to the small coastal valley that contained the compound of Caldala's Ambassador Core known as Central.

With unseasonably fine weather, the Alpha members removed their concealing masks with relief now that they were within the privacy of their own grounds. But the enjoyment of a beautiful day was marred by the political maneuverings they'd just witnessed.

"Idiot bastards!" Sheara Korth exclaimed without warning. "What next?" At the surprised expressions on her companions' faces, she said, "Come on, you don't think those politicians are going to stop at insulting Akira, do you?"

Kalen Kalronan nodded, scowling. "Korth's right. The majority of those who voted against her are scared of losing their seats in

146

Parliament if war with Ishal breaks out, and a few might want to take advantage of the uncertainty."

"You're right." Evani Reva's voice was somber. "Coroth would be wise to keep an eye on Ominor."

"Yeah, and he is." Elen Arith spoke from the head of the formation. "It's one of the things we'll talk about today." But he just held up a hand when the instant appeals for more information came. "Akira will lay it out, and Isfail's authorized to represent the prince in any decisions."

"Does this have something to do with extending your contract, Arith?" Alon Coronan asked.

"No," Arith replied with well-feigned humor. "I just agreed that Reva needs more seasoning, more time to learn from the master before taking over as recon leader." Grinning at Reva's astonished face, he added, "Wasn't that you who asked Garan to extend my contract, Reva?"

"I don't know what you're talking about," she retorted. "My own contract ends next year, and I won't be extending. You can keep it until you're an old man for all I care."

"Oh thanks!" Alani Iro teased. "You can't really mean that I'm going to be responsible for Coronan when you're gone? Someone's always having to rescue him when we're on a mission, like that time he got kidnapped for a sex slave by that Kuldora Harak woman."

The others laughed, knowing Alon Coronan's awkward history well. Even shy little Aito Oti, riding with Isa Coran and Ivano Micharon at the back of their group, giggled over the remembered incident.

Reva smiled as she glanced at him. "He's not that bad, and he's learned a lot along the way. Anyway, I have plans to see the world without the black silk in front of my eyes."

"Come on, Reva. You could stick around one more year, couldn't you?" Coronan's voice sounded mournful.

"And do what? Cool my heels in Coroth?"

Aron Drinin chuckled, riding just behind the pair as he listened to their teasing remarks. He was one of the founding members of this first reconnaissance team, and he knew most of the secrets of Recon Alpha. "What's another year, Reva?"

"You can talk, Drinin. You're out with Kalronan and Iro soon." Reva lifted an eyebrow as she turned to grin at him. She looked back at Coronan as he laughed—only to see him jerk forward, then look down in confusion at the arrowhead protruding from his chest.

"Shields!" Reva yelled, grabbing Coronan as he slumped in his saddle. She heard Kilronan's identical order from behind the coach and was grateful for the immediate shimmer of an impenetrable force barrier around coach and riders.

*I*nside the coach, Akira and Isfail had been entertained by the banter from the recon team. Now Isfail grabbed his wife when she collapsed forward, all color draining from her face as her hands flew to her chest.

"No," Akira gasped as shouts rose around them. When Isfail dragged her hands away, searching for injury, she said in a shaky voice, "It's not me. It's Alon."

As battle erupted outside, Isfail pushed her to the floor, covering her with his own body. He held her tight when she struggled to get to her injured ambassador, gritting his teeth against the shock surge she sent into him. "Stay down!" he ordered, listening to the twang of bowstrings and the crack of force bolts around them.

Akira stilled beneath him before he felt one of her hands tugging at the cloak now twisted around her.

"Get off, Dan! I need to get something. Now!"

*A*lpha dropped from their horses, some raising their hands to reinforce the barrier around the group as others positioned to fire back at the attackers who ran from the cover of the encroaching trees.

Drinin pulled his wounded friend from his horse while Reva leaped down.

"Oti, Kalronan, warn Coroth!" she shouted, covering them

as they jumped back to their horses, lying flat to their saddles as they pounded back toward the gate. Then she knelt beside Coronan.

Reva blanched as she recognized the deadly Black Arrow tip. "Drinin, you've got to help me with this. We've got to get it out of him." While she struggled against fear, one part of her mind followed the battle. Time flowed now like thick syrup, though a part of her knew it was only seconds racing into brief minutes.

Alpha and Team Kilronan coordinated shield openings to send force bolts at the hooded, rough-clad archers as they emerged from the surrounding woodland. Now the deadly arrows were rebounding from the invisible force shielding to fall harmlessly to the ground.

Yet for Reva, the damage had been done. Her lover lay dying on the ground in front of her.

"Alon? Can you hear me?" she asked urgently, tearing his shirt away to see the damage. She scanned the wound as Drinin knelt, supporting Coronan against his thighs. Reva assessed a nicked artery against the immediate need to remove the poisoned arrow. "Alon, we're going to have to pull this out of you."

His bright blue eyes flickered open as he whispered, "See . . . you should have bound me . . . while you had the chance . . ." A pain-filled smile appeared before he coughed a spray of bright red blood.

"You're not getting out of it this easy," she retorted brusquely, her desperate eyes belying the sharp words. "Hold on." Taking a deep breath, Reva snapped off the barbed arrowhead.

"Pull the shaft from his back when I tell you," she ordered Drinin.

He nodded as she pressed her blood-covered hand over the chest wound.

Reva sent her healing force to stabilize the damaged artery then gave the order, bracing Coronan's shoulder as his body jerked again when the shaft was pulled from his back.

Pressing his mask tight against the gushing entry wound, Drinin watched Reva's pale face as she worked to save the man.

"Vani," Coronan whispered, fighting to breathe as the nerve-paralyzing toxin began to affect him. "I . . . love . . . you."

Tears welled in her eyes as they met his. "Don't you leave me, I've already signed that damned contract extension." She worked frantically to repair the artery and keep his rapidly failing heart beating.

But his muscles started to spasm as the fast-acting poison spread quickly. He tried to raise a hand to hers as she urged him to fight.

"Don't give up, Alon," Reva whispered as tears blurred her sight. "I need you." Bending to kiss his pale lips as he tried to smile, she turned her head to listen as he struggled now to speak.

"Be . . . strong . . ." he got out on an exhalation, his hand convulsing to squeeze hers before his eyes closed and the hand fell to his side.

"No, damn it. You can't leave me!" Reva shouted, forcing his heart to continue beating with her healing powers as the sounds of fighting died out around her.

"Vani," Drinin said quietly, reaching out to grasp her shoulder. "There's nothing more you can do."

"No!" she exclaimed, forcing the blood to keep circulating.

"Evani . . . he can't breathe anymore," he pleaded as she fought against death.

Reva refused to think about anything but keeping him alive. Her healing forces were almost spent now but her face set in determination, not even registering the woman who knelt beside them.

"Reva! We've got to get this into him," a familiar voice ordered.

Reva struggled as she was pulled away. "No!" she screamed in anguish. But she grew still as she saw Drinin tip Alon's head back, allowing Akira to pour liquid from a small vial down his throat. Akira's hand was coated with force flames as she stroked his neck to make him swallow before pouring a second vial of the antidote into his mouth.

She had them lay the still body flat on the ground. Placing her hands over his chest, Akira began a rhythmic series of compressions before forcing air into his lungs. "Come on, Alon. You can make it. Asura, take over here."

The healer from Kilronan's team moved immediately to the other side, smoothly taking over the compressions. Akira's slender hands glowed as she worked on the damage, carefully extracting several of the poison-laden barbs that were the trademark of the Ishalian Black Arrows.

Surrounded by Team Kilronan, who kept watch against further attack, Alpha stood silently as Arith held Reva's shaking body tight against him. It had taken both him and Isfail to pull her away. Long minutes passed as they all waited.

The thunder of hooves had both teams and the coachmen moving to defense posture before they recognized the platoon of Royal Guard arriving with Oti and Kalronan. Isfail stepped forward to speak with their captain while a second platoon rode in. After a brief discussion, Isfail returned to Akira's side while the captain sent the second platoon into the surrounding woods to look for any surviving assailants, and to collect evidence or clues to put together details of the assault. The first platoon continued to Ambassador Central to check the situation there.

Shortly after, Akira stood and took the grieving Reva into her arms, saying, "You did well." She pulled her down beside Coronan.

Reva's hands shook as she picked up one of Alon's, feeling the warmth in it, sobbing as his fingers closed weakly around hers. His eyelids fluttered before opening, causing her to work up a tremulous smile as he focused on her.

"Just . . . couldn't . . . let go . . . could you?" he asked in halting whispers.

"No," she choked out through her sobs of relief. "I couldn't let you go without telling you how much I love you."

Coronan's voice grew a little stronger. "Yeah?" His grip on her hand tightened as he asked, "So . . . you'll bind with me?"

"Yes," Reva replied softly, stroking his long black hair back. "What some people will go through to get their way." She watched his blurred eyes close, his hand still clutching hers as she turned to weep on Akira's shoulder.

Twenty-Five

*A*rith and Drinin lifted Coronan into the coach, placing him on one of the seats. Akira and Reva sat with him as they waited for news from Central, with the others surrounding the coach to counter any more ugly surprises. Isfail stood beside one of the doors, a crossbow in his hands as he watched the royal guards patrol the woods.

When a guard was sent back to give them the all clear they resumed their travel down the lane to the small fortification and compound that encompassed Ambassador Central. Seated beside Isfail, his hand tight around hers for comfort, Akira watched the narrow valley widen as it neared the coast, hearing the rumble of waves washing the shore of the small inlet grow louder.

It was a relief that there was no sign of an attack as they approached the exclusive community. The news brought by the royal guard had ambassadors running from every direction as the entourage came to a stop. But Akira decreed that Coronan be taken to the infirmary at once, leaving Arith, Isfail, and Kilronan to answer the questions shouted by the crowd that surrounded them. The Royal Guard captain mustered his men to continue searching the grounds and surrounding terrain for anything suspicious.

Isfail was impressed by the way Most High Ambassador Garan quickly took charge of his ambassadors, putting together scouting parties to work with the guardsmen, sending others to patrol the boundaries of their isolated valley, and more to guard each building. Order was soon restored and Garan had Recon

152

Alpha and the group from Coroth settled comfortably in his large office, where they waited for news.

Everyone looked up when Akira walked in within the hour, immediately reassuring those present. "He'll be all right now. Coronan's weak and it will probably be a few days before he can leave the infirmary. Reva's not ready to leave him yet so I left Asura with them to keep an eye on things with your most experienced healer."

Akira took a seat between Isfail and Arith on a leather couch. Besides Garan and the rest of Alpha, most of Team Kilronan was present, along with the Royal Guard captain.

Letting out a long breath, Garan began, asking, "What are we facing here? Ambassador Central has never been attacked before."

Kilronan glanced at Isfail and got his nod before saying, "We have to accept the fact that the whole force community has been targeted. It's not just individuals like Akira." He paused, looking into her weary eyes. "It's all of us," he continued, sweeping a hand to indicate those present.

"Perhaps we should have anticipated that The Bow would try an assault on Ambassador Central," Isfail joined in as he placed an arm around Akira's shoulders. "I am surprised by their boldness. And it might still be aimed at Akira, possibly Akira and Recon Alpha. If they'd been successful, it would have been a major strike on many of Caldala's strongest force callers."

He focused on Garan, who sat at one end of a long table, frowning as he tapped the fingers of one hand restlessly on the back of the other. "Would you agree, Most High?"

Folding his hands together to still their movement, Garan said quietly, "Just Garan will do, Commander, and yes, I agree. Especially since the attack appears specifically directed at your group today. So far, we have no sign that there was an attack planned here, at Central compound."

"It makes no sense," Drinin growled. "We'd just cleared the gate a few minutes before. There was no warning, just an arrow through Coronan! How did so many infiltrate the grounds without being detected?"

"What about your guards on the gate?" the captain asked. "No one was there when we checked."

Here Oti spoke up quickly. "They were gone when Kalronan and I rode out to warn Coroth."

"That's right," Kalronan agreed. "No one was on the gate when we returned. I was too distracted to notice when we rode out."

Garan frowned. "We need to locate them." Ringing a bell to summon his secretary, he asked, "Who had outer gate duty today?"

After consulting his duty roster, the man replied, "Ambassadors Gorth and Lunow, Most High. I'll see if they can be found."

"Send a scout squad with back-up to comb the woods near the gate if they haven't returned to the compound."

"I also have men going over that area, Most High," the captain added. "Your people might want to check with them to see what areas they've covered."

Garan nodded and dismissed the secretary. He looked toward Akira as she stood up to begin her habitual pacing.

"In retrospect, it's unfortunate that none of the assailants were taken alive. We could have extracted important information from them," she mused aloud.

The captain stepped forward. "It's interesting you should say that, my lady. I've never before seen an action where every one of the enemy was killed outright." When she nodded in agreement, he said, "I'm not convinced that all these men *were* killed by return fire. We located three bodies farther back in the woods, with footprints indicating that they had run from the battleground, yet all were dead."

He looked around at the attentive faces. "I had my men tag those bodies and note their position on the site map we drew up before any bodies or weaponry were removed. My men are finishing up there now. I'll have a copy brought to you, Most High."

"Thank you, Captain," Garan replied. "That's an admirable

practice, often used by Commander Muro when she was with us, as I recall." He glanced at Akira, who raised an eyebrow back at him while Arith chuckled over Garan's dry remark.

"Between the Royal Guard and the Ambassador Core, we can hope that all our questions will be resolved quickly," Isfail said. "Captain, I strongly suggest that all ships' crews arriving at our ports within the last week or so be interviewed—questions along the line of passenger manifests, information on crew defections, and the like. I'm sure Insalat Militia and Ocean Cliffs Protectorate will also want to be involved in that."

Akira sighed as she met Garan's eyes. "I suggest you also inquire into any unusual sightings of, or business transacted with anyone representing themselves as an ambassador."

Twenty-Six

Reva woke with a start, sitting up quickly as she checked the infirmary bed next to hers. She was relieved to see Coronan, sleeping quietly.

"Are you all right, Ambassador Reva?" Asura's soothing voice asked as she looked up from the book she was reading.

"Yes." Reva got up and stepped to Coronan's bed. Gently touching his face, she examined him carefully. His pulse rate and breathing were good, and she lifted the bandage to look at the angry red site of the chest wound. Akira had informed her that the poison would slow the healing of the damaged tissue for a few days. She'd made sure that there was a supply of the antidote to dose him with each day until the affected areas looked normal again.

Stroking her hand over a strong shoulder, Reva sat beside him.

"Can't keep your hands off me, woman?" his amused, if weak, voice murmured. Coronan's hand came up to hold Reva's against his chest as his eyes opened.

"Just keep telling yourself that," she replied before leaning over to kiss him.

His eyes grew serious. "Thanks, Vani. I wasn't ready to die yet."

"Guess I wasn't ready for you to die yet either. Don't scare me like that again." Reva ran a fingertip over his lips. "Anyway, thank Akira. She's been carrying the antidote to that Ishalian poison with her since the attacks began."

Coronan smiled a little. "She's Akira Muro."

"So I am." The low voice of the woman they'd been talking

156

about came from the door. "How are you feeling, Alon?" She walked over to them, a thoughtful look on her beautiful face.

"Great," he said with an effort at a grin. "I finally found the way to get Vani to agree to be bound with me."

Akira laughed as Reva looked flustered. "About time, I'd say. I was tired of you two sneaking around all the time." She squeezed Reva's shoulder when she came to check Coronan's wounds.

"Reva, help him up so I can see his back."

He breathed heavily with the effort to sit up, yet still found the strength to quip, "Man, am I lucky today . . . two gorgeous women coming to my bed to look at my body."

Reva just shook her head in resignation as Akira laughingly teased, "Coronan, just how *did* you end up in the Ambassador Core?"

"Really lucky," he whispered, grimacing as agony shot through him.

Akira felt the pain wracking his body. "It's a residual effect of the poison, my friend. Vani, let's give him another dose now." She finished examining the entry wound in his back while Reva poured the contents of a vial into a small glass of water. Coronan drank it down, his face white, beads of sweat appearing as the pain continued to run like fire through his nervous system.

"I can give you a pain block, Alon," Akira murmured.

"No," he whispered, closing his eyes. "I've got what I need." He reached for Reva's hand. "Thanks, Akira. I owe you forever."

Akira gently stroked his pale cheek. "Just make sure I get an invitation to the binding ceremony." She waited with Reva until he fell into an uneasy sleep.

"Akira?"

"He'll pull through," she replied to the worry in Reva's voice. "He's young, strong, and he has you to fight for. Your own healing skills will deal with the rest of the damage."

Akira stood up, saying, "We'll be returning to the palace now that he's out of danger. Arith will fill you both in on the meeting we had with Garan."

Chagrined, Reva recalled the reason for Akira's trip to Central today. "Akira, I'm sorry, I—"

Akira ran a hand down her arm, saying, "Vani, there's no shame in listening to your heart over your head sometimes. It's taken me too long to understand that. When we're blessed to find a partner worth committing our lives to, that's an important thing."

Shaken by the conviction in Akira's voice, Reva nodded, looking back at her lover. "Maybe I learned that today."

Turning her attention to the vials stored on the shelf nearby, Akira shifted the conversation back to necessities highlighted by the day's attack. "Tell Garan I have an assignment for the healers. The infirmary records contain the directions for making the antidote to the Black Arrow poison. I'll make sure you have access to the arrows collected today to make the distillate you'll need for the antidote preparation." She met Reva's intent gaze. "Prepare as much antidote as you can, and make sure all ambassadors carry some on them at all times. I'll be arranging for vials to be sent to the palace, and restocking my own supply before we leave."

Reva took a deep breath. "I'll make sure it happens. It would have been too late for Alon if you hadn't had the antidote with you."

"Yes." Akira went out, closing the door softly behind her, leaving Reva gripping a small vial in her fist while she watched over the man she loved.

Walking out into the shadowed light of dusk, Akira paused to watch ominous clouds boiling in on the evening wind. Isfail walked over, wrapping a cloak around her as he said, "The captain insists on escorting us back to the palace. The second platoon will patrol the grounds here with the ambassadors tonight, but I suspect a wider attack has been foiled."

Akira nodded, walking with him to the waiting coach. "I agree, but where will they strike next?"

Kilronan and his team were waiting with the royal guards. Akira met his eyes before Isfail handed her into the carriage.

"We'll all keep our senses open on the way back, Kil." With a nod and a quick smile, he gripped Isfail's offered arm before signaling his team to mount.

Within minutes they were leaving Ambassador Central and turning toward the city of Coroth.

*B*ehind them, watching the coach move up the narrow lane, Ambassador Aron Drinin sat in the encroaching shadows of night, turning the bloodstained shaft of the arrow that had nearly taken his closest friend's life. The secret Reva and Coronan had concealed for most of their time in the Core was out now. Whatever consequences they faced for breaking the ridiculous chastity vow were probably minor, and they were close to retirement anyway.

He looked down at the broken arrow, skimming a finger over the black feathers of its fletching, his mouth tightening. There were other secrets that would have more devastating consequences should they be discovered.

Looking up toward the road, Drinin watched the light from the carriage lamps disappear.

Twenty-Seven

It only took one look at the ominously silent rows of people occupying the wide steps leading to the grand entrance of the Parliament building to have High Minister Felpon banging on the carriage hatch. The concerned face of the coachman loomed overhead when it opened.

"Don't stop!" Felpon exclaimed, wiping his brow nervously. "Drive around to the service doors."

"Aye, sir." The small door closed quietly.

Felpon breathed easier as he felt the carriage sway gently with the turn onto the first street beyond the long block of civilian government buildings, then again as it turned into the service alley. But his relief was short-lived as they approached the humble entrance.

More people, standing silent and grim-faced, lined the narrow alleyway. They made no attempt to block or threaten the slowly moving carriage, but cold sweat beaded Felpon's brow at the thought of leaving the security of the box to face that intimidating gauntlet of disapproval.

Where were the guards? Where were the militiamen normally stationed here? He would have them replaced, Felpon decided with false bravado, and then shrank back as the door latch rattled.

The coachman opened the door, glancing around at the crowd. Still, no one moved, none of them said a word.

"All right, Minister?" he asked, lowering the steps and standing aside for Felpon to step down.

Drawing in a shaky breath, the high minister plastered a sickly smile on his face and faced the challenge. He tried a cheerful

160

salutation but the words died before leaving his fear-choked throat. Giving up, he gripped his satchel close and hurried between the bodies that parted slowly before him. Their unnervingly silent stares were more effective than a shouting mob.

Inside, Felpon rushed through halls empty of the normal bustle of staff. A few of the clerks had braved the odd workday; most appeared to be standing at windows to watch the scene outside. They returned to their desks when Felpon hurried by. None dared question him.

*A*ll the ministers were present when Felpon entered the assembly room. A hostile silence thickened the air, and ministers displayed clear divisions of opinion in the way they grouped around the large meeting table. Felpon cleared his throat, and the familiar sound had several looking his way.

The minister representing the High Falls caldon sprang to his feet, exclaiming, "Have you seen that crowd out there?" When Felpon only nodded, the minister continued, "And this is only the beginning, I tell you."

"They'll get bored with it after they think they've made their point," Ominor stated irritably. "We'll be back to our usual business by next week."

Wrax nodded agreement, but the look he gave Ominor didn't appear convinced.

Minister Adrani, representing Green River Caldon, disagreed. "You're underestimating them, Ominor. Parliament's official position on Akira Muro has stirred up a dormant volcano that was better left alone," she said firmly, watching Ominor scowl at her. Adrani had voted for Akira, and stood with the force callers, along with the other four women ministers, and four of the men. "Some of them are saying that Parliament ordered the attack on Ambassador Central the other day."

"That's ridiculous," Ominor scoffed, but even he appeared concerned by this news.

She studied the opposition group clustered together on the far side of the table. Those men represented southern or mid-nation caldons, eleven out of the twenty Caldalan local government divisions.

Adrani and her group of ministers covered a majority of the eastern borders, most of the coast, and all the northern territories. In her opinion, the others were soft and fat with their easy living and temperate climes. They didn't appreciate what others did to guard the borders.

She frowned as she glanced at Ominor and Wrax, huddled together in private conversation. Their southern caldons did have borders to watch over, and that section of coastline. Adrani wondered what they thought they would gain by publically standing against the force-gifted community.

Regardless, she acknowledged resentfully, the final vote had tainted the entire Parliament. Those who stood with the force-gifted could only inform their own caldons of their personal vote. For now, they would bear the same suspicion as the simple majority that had put them in this mess.

Parliament had taken an official position in refusing to approve Akira Muro for an important new position. They'd alienated the House of Coroth—and what good did these fools think would come of that? And what about the Ambassador Core and the Protectorate Defense Services—both major defense forces under the direct control of the prince? Every ambassador and protectorate warrior would now look at Parliament with distrust and disdain. Then there was the militia—most, if not all, units would side with the prince, and Commander Isfail and his new wife.

On top of that, there had been the well-orchestrated attack on Ambassador Central's grounds the very afternoon of Parliament's vote to deny Akira Muro the new liaison position.

The news was spreading throughout Caldala like wildfire. At least half the citizenry had force caller ancestry, from full bloods to mixed blood, with many in the rest of the population ready to support their force-gifted friends and neighbors.

Though the citizenry might not fully understand how the Ambassador Core functioned, most knew enough to value the role the ambassadors filled in diplomacy and peace-keeping, within their country and between nations. The Bow's attack on Central grounds had brought the current crisis to the majority's attention even more than the individual attacks had done.

And yet, the opposition ministers held to their decisions, even as they questioned the public outcry against Parliament.

No, she really didn't understand how this fiasco had come about.

*P*rince Logran was secretly delighted by the reports of the citizens' silent protest of Parliament when it was reported to him that day. Those fools needed to feel the disapproval of the people of Caldala. But his satisfaction had to be short-lived. There were good people representing their caldons, and he'd taken close note of which ones had voted for Akira. He'd even spoken with Minister Adrani when she'd come to the palace to speak with Akira directly and assure her of Green River Caldon's support.

Pacing to the windows of his study, hands clasped behind his back, Logran watched the heavy rain that sent water cascading over the central fountain, creating miniature rapids that filled the stone-lined creek beds designed as decorative gutters, leading excess water into drainage canals that channeled it to the sea. It served to calm his thoughts, allowing him to review the plans that must now be set in motion.

Many throughout Caldala would share Minister Adrani's concerns, but there would be those who would reject the need to stand by the force-gifted. It hadn't been so long ago that he'd had serious concerns about the risk of powerful force callers to the safety of the country he was required by birth to rule over. It was a duty he bore with pride and inherent responsibility.

It was Akira who had convinced him that they were really no more of a threat than a human without force abilities. All he had to do to reinforce that opinion was look at what Arthon Baronan had done and instigated—a man with no force ability, whose desire for power and thirst for violence had spawned the current crisis in Caldala and decades of civil war in Ishal, the country that had given him sanctuary. Now Baronan's son propagated that violent ambition long after his father's death.

Though the majority of public opinion supported defending the force-caller communities from The Bow's attacks, he knew trouble could come from both sides of the issue. The larger cities could find their local militias called out to deal with clashes between groups who'd decided that conflicting points of view should be decided with fists and knives.

He needed to head off those conflicts before they erupted into a crisis for his nation.

Akira and Isfail would leave for Insalat tomorrow, and on to the mountains after that. This afternoon they would all meet one last time, including his local commanders and Most High Garan. Logran wanted a consensus on which militia captains could be relied upon to look for common threads in these projected conflicts, hopefully before they became open fighting. He already had private letters out to the protectorate leaders to be on the lookout for malcontents trying to stir up trouble.

Finally, Logran wanted Akira's input and support in directing Garan to deploy Ambassador Reconnaissance Alpha to the south. His impression that Ominor, and possibly Wrax, had their own reasons for blocking Akira's installment in the liaison position had been reinforced by the observations Minister Adrani had relayed to him. Recon Alpha could be out and back with important information quickly. They were the best of the Ambassador Core, even with one of their team down.

Turning away from his view of the rain-drenched courtyard, Logran saw that it was time to meet Isfail and Akira. As he left his office for the small assembly room, he regretted that they would be leaving so soon. Mountain Shadows was more than the width of the nation distant from Coroth, and on the edge of Ishal. And there were the dangers of winter weather to negotiate, both on the journey there, and in living through the season.

He knew he and Oona would worry until they received what were sure to be rare communications.

*D*aas Garan glanced toward the seaward window of the palace sitting room he'd been shown to after the meeting with the prince. Linking his hands behind his back, he slowly walked over to watch the storm-tossed sea. Lighting flashed, swiftly followed by a crack of thunder.

His thoughts mirrored the restless confusion of the weather. The responsibilities of his recent appointment to Most High Ambassador hovered over him like the thick gray clouds. Every day felt as if it brought new challenges rushing at him like the waves pounding against the shore.

Garan caught a glimpse of his own face reflected in the glass and smiled ruefully. The prince's directives today were a relief, a welcome return to the purpose and usual duties of the Ambassador Core. Reconnaissance Alpha would be sent out to investigate the southern caldons for any indication of treasonous activities or infiltration by members of The Bow.

He turned at the sound of the door opening, welcoming the one person he knew could help him resolve any problem.

"Akira. Thank you for meeting with me privately." Though his pleasure was dimmed knowing she'd bound with another man, his smile was warm as she took his hand in both of hers.

"Of course, Garan," Akira said, releasing him to gesture to chairs in the window alcove. "You wanted to ask me about Coronan's injuries?"

Garan waited for her to sit before taking his own seat. "I think it's obvious that he won't be going on this mission with Recon Alpha, but I'd like to know what to expect, whether I need to consider medical retirement for him."

He watched her face grow thoughtful but she shook her head.

"No, I don't think so. He'll recover fully but it is a serious situation. The pain will be intense for a day or two, and I estimate at least a full lunam for him to regain full stamina. But you know Coronan, he still has his sense of humor." Akira's smile held humor. "And he has Reva."

"Yes . . . about that," Garan began, seeing Akira raise a

questioning eyebrow to him. "Well, what am I supposed to do about them? It's a major violation of Core rules."

"What is? Falling in love? I don't see how anyone can control their emotions, Garan."

He stiffened, trying to ignore his own experience with that fickle emotion. "That's not what I'm talking about."

"Then what are you talking about?"

Now he could see the amused mischief in her eyes. "You know exactly what I mean."

"Supposing I do, what evidence do you have that Reva and Coronan have violated any rule? The chastity vow for example?"

"Akira . . ." he growled in exasperation.

"Why are you so focused on this?" she chided, obviously tiring of this ridiculous discussion. "Don't you feel that an attack, a major infiltration of Central boundaries with obvious planning and deliberation, almost certainly involving complicity within the Ambassador Core, is more important to pursue than violations of the chastity vow?"

"Of course it is! But I'm also required to uphold the rules of the Ambassador Core," Garan responded angrily.

Akira scoffed, saying, "You didn't report the chastity violation when you knew about Ruton and Eleni Arith. When you were discreetly sharing Elen's room to allow them to spend nights together."

He looked away from her to the window, uncomfortable with her recollection.

"And how many others have we known about over the years? Did you feel obligated to report any of them?"

"I'm the Most High Ambassador now. I *am* obligated to enforce the founding principles of this service," Garan stated wearily, recalling his position and responsibilities.

"Then you'd better review the founding principles, Most High," Akira challenged, surprising him into meeting her eyes again. "Anaran never intended this society to be chaste, the chastity vow was not in the founding code. Anaran himself was not only bound, he fathered several children while building the

Ambassador Core. It was Karsh who introduced the chastity vow, pushing it to a vote the year she was promoted to High Ambassador."

Dumbfounded, Garan dropped into a chair in astonishment. "Are you sure?"

"You can check the historical records yourself. The archives contain complete records of the founding regulations and every change, including the date they went into effect," Akira informed him with confidence.

Garan stared at her. "Why haven't you ever said anything about this before? You, yourself, felt strongly about keeping the chastity vow."

"Yes, I did," she replied. "It was in place when I was sworn in. I believed in honoring my commitment as fully as I could. That doesn't mean I ever felt it should ruin other ambassadors' reputations or careers if they chose to ignore it. The quality of their service was more important than how they shared their bodies."

Garan continued to look at her incredulously. "You never mentioned any of this over all those years, Akira."

"Why would I discuss the chastity vow with you?" There was definitely amusement in her voice.

"Well, apparently you decided to investigate it at some point, checking all those archive records."

Akira considered his words and crestfallen expression. "My archive explorations began when I learned that Anaran was my great-grandfather. I wanted to know more about him."

After a long moment, Garan nodded his head as he looked toward the rain-lashed window again. "Maybe it's time to revisit the founding principles. And revoke some changes, for the well being of our serving ambassadors."

She moved to kiss his cheek affectionately. "I've always known you were a wise man, Daas."

Daas Garan took her slender hand to bring gently to his lips before saying, "I'll always wish that I'd achieved wisdom early enough to make a difference between us, Akira."

She drew back, feeling regret for not recognizing his feelings years ago. "My heart was broken then, Daas. That's why I accepted the chastity vow. Don't lock yours away anymore . . . let it be free to find another to love."

Akira squeezed his hand before releasing it to stand. "I'll come check on Coronan before we leave for Mountain Shadows."

Twenty-Eight

Insalat, Caldala, Two Days Later

With only a few days remaining before they would leave Insalat for the mountains, Kilronan accepted Isfail's invitation to join him at an inn an hour's ride south of their location. It amazed him that Akira expressed no desire to join the evening's expedition, but she was safe and well-guarded within the walls of Insalat's government and militia complex, and his team was with her.

Trusting Isfail's explanation that he'd often obtained useful information regarding Caldala's criminal elements there, Kilronan decided it could be worth the long, windy ride. But his confidence dipped at first sight of the rundown, two-story building clinging to a narrow strip of coastline just below the level of the main road.

"Tell me again why we're here?" Kilronan muttered as he took in the dingy public room, with its long bar black with age and questionable cleanliness. The patrons looked just as sketchy.

Isfail grinned and led him to an empty table, lifting a hand to the barkeep as they passed. "Information, my friend, and they serve a reasonable stout. But I don't recommend the food."

"I lost my appetite the minute we stepped in the door." Carefully settling in a rickety chair, Kilronan continued to scan the room. Some of the occupants were staring back at him with scowls drawing down their faces. "Not a friendly crowd."

"I noticed," Isfail replied. "I can't say it's ever been warm and welcoming, but there does seem to be more animosity tonight."

A curvaceous woman, obviously at home in the seedy pub, stepped up to their table, her hands planted on her hips. "Well, if it isn't himself. Haven't seen ye in a handful of years, Captain. Commander now, I hear." Then the hard mouth turned up in a cheerful smile.

Kilronan watched, stunned, as Isfail got to his feet to kiss her on the cheek.

"Hello, Rena. It's good to see you. Why are you still here, outshining this hell-hole?" Isfail asked.

Rather than take offense, Rena laughed. "It's that all right, but me and Jono, him there at the bar . . ." She paused to point out the tall, thin man pulling ale. "We got ourselves bound couple a years ago. Then the old owner decided to move on and sold us the place." Rena shrugged. "Hell, no one else wanted it, and we do a fair business most nights."

"Do you still have the stout on tap?" Isfail asked as he sat back down.

"We do. Same for ye?" Rena looked at Kilronan, and he saw her eyes flick to his hair.

"Yes, thanks." After watching her make her way back through the late afternoon crowd, Kilronan turned to Isfail. "How do you know her?"

"Pirates."

"Why do I hear that same answer so often from you?"

Isfail chuckled, sitting straighter to cross his arms on the table. "Akira and I crossed purposes here on an investigation. We didn't know the other was assigned from different directions. Anyway, a Kuldoran slaver was using this inn as his base. Rena ended up helping us capture him and his ship, freeing a number of young women along the way."

He leaned back as Rena returned with two tall mugs. "Thanks."

Kilronan nodded his appreciation as he took a drink. "It's good, thanks."

Settling a hip on a corner of the table, Rena studied him then turned to Isfail. "Yer friend's got yer manners, Captain."

She smirked at the old title, but her amusement was short-lived. Speaking more quietly now, she said, "Watch yerselves tonight, sirs. There're those here that don't like yer kind." Tipping her head at Kilronan, she stared pointedly at his white braid of hair.

"Can you tell us why?" Isfail murmured, though he looked relaxed as he took another drink.

Laying a friendly hand on his shoulder, Rena leaned in with a wicked smile, but her low-pitched words were serious. "We been gettin' a worse sort in the past year, off and on. Jono and me even alerted the militia. Corsalat, that is. They send couple of men from time to time, and things get better. But someun's been stirring up the rougher crowd against the forcers lately." She looked straight into Kilronan's eyes. "Don't walk out alone tonight."

With his mug at his lips, Isfail asked softly, "Have you heard anyone speak of The Bow?"

She gave slight dip of her head. "Rumors only. But I knows someun' who might be willin' to talk to ye."

With a laugh at odds with the worry in her dark eyes, Rena slapped Isfail on the shoulder. "It's good to see ya again. Tell yer lady I said hello, that is, if she's still keepin' company with yer sort."

Kilronan smiled at that, beating Isfail to the news. "They were bound last week."

Rena laughed even louder, but it was genuine this time. "I wish ye both well and happy." Leaning over, she planted a smacking kiss on Isfail's mouth. "Give her that for me."

"I certainly will." Isfail grabbed her hand as she started to turn away. "Take care of yourself, Rena, you and your Jono. If you need more help, ask for Commander Toth at Insalat. I'll be there for the next few days."

She nodded and walked back to the bar.

They sat for a time over their mugs, talking of inconsequential things whenever people crowded too near. But Kilronan knew Isfail was observing what went on as closely as he was. At a discreet sign from his companion, Kilronan swallowed the last of his drink as they pushed back from the table. Isfail went over to lay several coins in the barkeep's hand.

Five burly men separated from the crowd standing around the large hearth, blocking the way to the door. Some had short, thick batons in their meaty hands and others pulled knives from their belts. Kilronan channeled his power to build as he saw Isfail slide a long dagger from the sheath at his side.

A loud *thwack* had everyone looking at the bar. The barkeep—Jono, Kilronan assumed—held a large wooden bat over his head.

"No one's bringin' a fight inside my place!" he roared in a deep voice in contrast to his lanky build. "You want a fight, take it outside. You're not breakin' up my place!"

Kilronan noticed Rena standing behind him, a nasty looking butcher's knife in her hand, and her eyes focused on Isfail, who stood calmly amid the muttered imprecations around them.

"You heard the man," Isfail said with a wide smile. "Lead the way, boys." Kilronan lifted his brow to that, but followed as the commander trailed the malcontents into the twilight-shadowed yard of the inn.

Some of the rabble shrank back as Isfail twirled and spun the flashing dagger with the ease of a man confident in his ability to put it to use. Kilronan just shook his head with a grin, letting power flow down his arms, pooling in his hands.

"We hain't got no cause 'gainst you, Commander," someone called out from the pack of restless men now circling them. "Just move away from that forcer and be on yer way."

Isfail sent back a smile that brought a chill to Kilronan's bones; he saw its influence on the mob when several slithered back into the public house.

"You have a problem with my friend," Isfail stated clearly, looking around at the coarse faces in the dying light, "you have a problem with me."

Kilronan appreciated the support, slashing out a hand to send a force shield to deflect the barrage of knives and short bats that were hurled at them.

"Unnatural!" Enraged shouts rang out. "We don't want yer kind here."

"What have the force-gifted done to you?" Kilronan called out. "Name one harm that my people have caused you?"

Though the muttering continued, there was less confidence in it. A few more broke away and returned to their ale.

"My friend asks reasonable questions," Isfail shouted. "Who among you has an evil to lay on any of Caldala's citizens with force ability?"

"It ain't natural," someone called out with hesitation now. "Them forcers don't belong here."

"Come to that, ye don't look so natural, Boggy," Rena called from the open doorway, the butcher knife cradled in her crossed arms. "What with that funny eye and pig-nose." There were ripples of gruff laughter at this.

Kilronan watched three more men shrug and squeeze past Rena, avoiding her hard-eyed stare. They were down to the original five troublemakers now. He caught Isfail's glance and nodded, releasing the force shield.

"Come on then," Kilronan shouted, gesturing to the large man charging him. Too easy, Kilronan grinned, grabbing the upraised arm gripping a knife as he ducked under, coming up to throw the ruffian over his back. A hard stomp of his boot disarmed him and had the fool curling up with loud wails, cradling a broken arm.

Isfail had already taken down one man and was easily fending off another. Sensing the attack from behind, even as Rena shouted a warning, Kilronan fired a force bolt at the man at Isfail's back while whirling on the one rushing at him with a pike.

This one was more cautious, he noted, circling as the attacker skidded to a halt to jab at him out of striking distance. Kilronan could have taken him out with another force bolt, but decided to show the motley gathering that a real warrior didn't need to rely on special abilities.

At the next jab, his left hand whipped out, catching the pike just behind the head and jerking it past him. Caught by surprise, the attacker came with it, yelping in pain as his face connected with Kilronan's right fist. Snapping off the sharp tip, Kilronan tossed aside the broken pole before gripping the moaning, eye-rolling assailant.

"Now we can talk." Kilronan yanked aside the filthy tunic the semi-conscious foe wore. He wasn't surprised to find the brand of The Bow.

"This one too," Isfail called, standing over one of his.

Jono came out with a coil of rope, and handed it to Isfail. "Rena's sent for the militia. We don't want trouble here. Got no cause to worry about forcers." He tugged his forelock to Kilronan with a grin before pointing at the men on the ground. "But their sort's been trouble since they first come in."

"Do you know when they first came, and where they're from?"

Scratching his head, Jono seemed to think hard about it. "Seems like one of the girls said somethin' about customers with strange scars." He stared down at the distinctive mark as Kilronan pushed back clothing to allow him to see it more clearly in the dim light. "Aye, that's what she described, the bowed line crossed by three arrowed lines."

Kilronan looked at Rena when she spoke beside him. "Liza talked about 'em not long after I met the Captain here. I first saw that mark maybe three years back, fresher than this one, hadn't fully healed. I asked the man why he'd want such a thing branded on him."

"Did he answer?" Isfail asked.

"Said it made him special. His master marked those chosen to build a new world. He said a bit a' pain to start was worth bein' allowed to do whatever he wanted after." Rena scowled down at the man. "I just thought he was a witless fool."

Kilronan glanced at Isfail and saw the same concern on his face.

They stayed long enough to turn their tight-lipped prisoners over to a militia unit, with Isfail giving specific orders regarding their interrogation and detention. After quick goodbyes to Rena and Jono, Kilronan and Isfail mounted and rode up the rise to the main road, where they turned north toward Insalat to rejoin Akira and Kilronan's team.

They'd learned some interesting things on this excursion, Kilronan reflected as they rode in silence through the encroaching dark. He wondered if Isfail was as disturbed as he to know that the followers of The Bow had been a presence in Caldala years longer than they'd suspected.

Twenty-Nine

Insalat, Caldala

*A*kira was waiting in the elaborate guest quarters the mayor had insisted on assigning to the newly bound couple. Since Isfail was vacating his quarters for the recently installed Commander Toth, he considered their temporary accommodations entirely suitable. And it amused him to see Akira's discomfort with the somewhat gaudy décor.

She was ready to be distracted by the news of their adventures. Isfail began by fulfilling Rena's command and kissing his wife with a great deal more passion than Rena's hearty smack on the mouth was worth.

Laughing as he told her of their mutual acquaintance, Akira shook her head. "I'm glad to hear she's well and seems to be content. Rena's a courageous woman."

"So I hear," Kilronan said. "Pirates." He grinned with Akira and Isfail's responding laughter.

Then the talk became serious. Isfail watched Akira's face return to the quiet attentiveness of a born warrior as he and Kilronan took turns relating what had happened and what they'd learned.

"You say Rena alluded to someone who might tell you more," Akira recalled. "Were there specific plans to meet with them?"

"No," he answered, sitting beside her after handing Kilronan a far more palatable whiskey than Jono would ever serve. "Rena knows I'm here for a few days, or to contact Toth once we've gone. We'll see if anything comes of it."

"In the meantime, the prisoners might provide some useful information. If not," Kilronan added with a shrug, "there are five members of The Bow who won't be causing any more trouble."

Isfail, with Akira's help, spent most of the following day dealing with the belongings in his quarters in the militia barracks. Toth had asked if he'd be willing to sell him the ship's berth bed that his former commander had commissioned, and was delighted when Isfail gave it to him in appreciation of over fifteen years of service together, and friendship.

While this final packing and dispersing was happening, Kilronan and his team welcomed the hospitality of Toth and his soldiers. And, although he declined Fal Oshulta's discreet invitation to share her quarters and renew the affair begun in Coroth a few lunams before, Kilronan did enjoy her company and conversation over dinner in the dining hall while he was in Insalat.

It was during dinner that same day that a message was delivered to Isfail. Beside him, Akira examined the strangely literate scrawl. "Apparently Rena's contact is willing to talk."

Isfail nodded, reading through the words again. "He wants to meet at a pub I know on the docks."

"She," Akira corrected quietly, and chuckled at the confusion on Isfail's face.

"She?" When his wife nodded, he asked, "How do you know?"

"The script, it's not the sort a man would develop. It's practiced and feminine."

Well, Isfail considered, studying the loops and flourishes, who was he to question Akira's perception?

"I could be wrong," she said thoughtfully, "but you should be prepared for a woman."

"Hmm."

Since the sound was more perturbed than interested, Akira patted his hand. "It will be fine, my love. You did say that Rena and Jono gave you information from some of the working girls, didn't you?"

Isfail nodded. "I'd rather you and Kilronan came with me, but this sets a meeting two days from now. We were to leave for Mountain Shadows then." Catching Kilronan's eye, he gestured him over, smiling at Oshulta when she came with him.

When they sat across from them, Isfail passed Kilronan the message.

"Interesting that the contact is a woman," Oshulta commented, her eyes laughing into Akira's.

Ignoring them, Isfail waited for Kilronan's opinion.

"Two more days," Kilronan murmured, pinching the bridge of his nose. "And we don't know if there's more after that. Can't you just refer this to Toth?"

Before Isfail could reply, Akira asked, "What if I go on with Kilronan and his team, leaving tomorrow? We take greater risks with the weather and The Bow the longer we delay. You take Toth, and maybe Chief Oshulta with you. That way, the contact is familiar with those who will be here in Insalat."

Isfail saw the indecision in Kilronan's eyes, reflecting his own.

Akira continued. "You still have transitional paperwork and packing to do. The wagon is hired, and to be loaded early the day of this meeting. Now you'll be here to supervise that, rather than leaving it to someone else. You might only be two days behind us, no more than a week at most."

He could see the sense in it, and separating might confuse anyone who was trying to anticipate her travel plans in order to set an ambush. Still, he didn't like being apart from her. Isfail saw that Kilronan was waiting for his decision.

"No matter what, I won't be more than five days behind you." Even knowing it was Akira's suggestion, he glimpsed a quick moment of worry in her eyes before she smiled and took both his hands.

"We'll wait at Green River if the weather seems reasonable." Akira kissed him before murmuring, "And you'll stay there, if necessary, until it's safe for you to follow us."

Thirty

Southern Coast of Caldala, Somara Caldon

"Well look at that," Arith said thoughtfully, though his face tightened in anger. He crouched on a low ridge with Drinin, overlooking a large bay known as the Southern Crescent. And the two sailing ships there; one at anchor, while the other appeared to be preparing to sail, with crew on deck scrambling through the rigging and others turning a large capstan to weigh anchor.

"They're not Caldalan," Drinin noted, lowering the compact spyglass he'd used to scan for identifying markings or insignia. "I'll lay odds they're not officially registered to any country."

Arith frowned. "I'm not taking that wager." Holding out a hand for the spyglass, he brought it to his right eye to examine the ramshackle sheds bunched together, almost invisible in a small, rocky canyon opening to the narrow beach. "I count five men hanging about on the shore, two on the bluff above where the track starts to wind its way down to the shingle. All rough company."

Lowering the glass, he scanned the dark clouds bunched on the horizon. "Might be trying to beat that storm front coming in."

Taking back the glass, Drinin looked about. "We'll find out more when Reva and the others finish reconnoitering. We have a few hours before we need to meet up with them. Then we'll have to decide what to do about it. Looks like the one ship will be underway before that, though we'll be able to see whether it takes a north or south-bearing course."

"Coroth warranted us to make field decisions on his authority. I'd guess he had a strong suspicion about what we'd find." Arith settled back, feeling the last warmth from the setting sun giving way to the chill of evening. "Looks like Minister Ominor could be facing charges of treason."

*T*aking advantage of the darkness of an overcast night sky, Reva and her team rappelled quickly down a short cliff near the back of the canyon where the shacks had been thrown together. Communicating by mindsight, the five ambassadors moved stealthily toward the bay, checking every nook and crevice as they edged closer. No one wanted an alarm raised by an enemy alerted while relieving himself away from the pitiful encampment.

Silent black wraiths, they slipped through shadows, separating to check out each hut before coming together near the largest. Lantern light spread from narrow openings covered with oilcloth that snapped and flapped in the inconstant wind. Scents of cheap tobacco from smoking pipes mixed with a worse odor of unwashed bodies. Wafting through it all was the smell of fish and seaweed.

Reva discerned at least five voices among the irritable conversation, with no one taking the lead among the gripes and discontent expressed. It became obvious that these men had no authority, and were only useful for their strong backs, shallow minds, and willingness to take orders.

After listening for about half an hour to fitful comments about the living conditions, women, the need for a woman, the short supply of ale or whiskey, and whether they should be earning more silver for their services, the ambassador team had learned little of importance. Still, they did glean that these workmen were Caldalan. They'd been hired to support the ships that came in at irregular intervals, and would only be paid as long as they kept their mouths shut about the operation.

It seemed clear that the five had no interest in knowing anything about the ships, the men aboard them, or their reason for being here. As cold, fat raindrops started to fall, Reva finally signaled her team, retreating back the way they'd come and up the walls. With some frustration, she looked toward the ship remaining in the harbor. Would it be worth the risk to get out there?

Iro shook her head, as if Reva had spoken aloud. Nodding, Reva loped off, ignoring the strengthening rainfall as the storm came upon the shore. Her companions followed as they easily bypassed the sentries on the road, who huddled beneath sheets of oilcloth with little apparent concern for guard duty.

Less than half an hour later, Reva's group stationed themselves in a convenient, if dripping, stand of trees, through which ran the only road to the bay. A two-hour ride north would bring them to Lake Somara and a wide belt road around the city there. But here the track was rough and poorly defined, though it showed signs of recent use. With any luck, they might observe something useful in the time left before joining Arith and Drinin at a thicker stand of trees closer to Somara.

*A*mbassadors Isa Coran and Ivano Micharon were settled more comfortably in a tavern on the outskirts of Somara, the only major city in this southernmost caldon, built along the eastern shore of the large lake of the same name. Micharon—shifting uneasily without a mask and in civilian clothes—reached for Coran's hand.

She smiled and his anxiety eased.

"We are good, my love," Coran said. She lifted a hand to the dark scruff on his jawline. "It is exciting to be out this way. And we are well placed, tucked in this dark corner for lovers."

"Perhaps," Micharon mumbled, "but it makes me itch to be so exposed." Then he saw the men entering and his hand tightened on Coran's. He heard her hiss of anger as she recognized Gorth and Lunow, the ambassadors who'd been on gate duty the afternoon their team was attacked within Ambassador Central grounds, and who couldn't be found afterward. Now here they were, in civilian clothes, in the company of three men unknown to Micharon and Coran.

"We must not be seen," she whispered, tension in her voice as she tucked her face against his neck, the way a lover would. "Yet we need to learn more." He nodded agreement, turning into her while watching the men of interest from the corner of his eye.

They felt relief when the group took seats around a large table closer to the door. Since Gorth and Lunow had their backs to the corner where they sat, Micharon breathed more easily. With the noise level in the tavern, and the distance apart, he and Coran could not hear what was said, but the body language of the five men told a great deal.

The two suspect ambassadors showed no signs of duress as they talked with the strangers. Lunow actually laughed over something someone said. Gorth appeared to have his usual taciturn disposition, though he reached over, his face in profile showing a thin smile, when the largest of the strangers slid plump leather purses across the table to them. Tossing his in the air, Lunow gave a friendly looking punch to his neighbor's arm.

"Payment for looking the other way?" Coran speculated in an icy whisper.

Micharon said nothing, and watched everything. The big stranger had the air of one in charge, and his eyes were sharp, noting everyone who entered the tavern. That dark gaze had passed over the couple in the corner with no interest. A fortunate thing, Micharon decided.

There seemed to be some negotiation going on between the men. He saw Gorth shake his head, apparently in opposition to some scheme. Lunow gripped his arm, lifting his purse as if to tempt Gorth to agree to whatever was being discussed. Things became more animated as Micharon and Coran watched; only the big man sat relaxed, drinking from a tall glass of ale.

"We should go," Coran said, to Micharon's relief. "We will watch for them outside, where we have more cover."

Leaving coins on the table, Micharon held Coran's cloak, wrapping it securely around her small body and bringing up the hood. The night outside was cold and wet; no one would find his actions odd. After donning his own cloak and hood, he slipped his arm over Coran's shoulders, holding her close as they wound their way through crowded aisles without a glance at the group they'd been observing.

Both let out long breaths once outside, sending plumes of white into the air to be immediately washed away in the downpour. Without wasting a moment, they retrieved their horses, and walked them a short distance to some trees forming a dark grove, where they could see anyone who left the tavern.

Patience was rewarded when the five men came outside together. As the tavern door closed, shutting off the noise inside, Micharon heard Gorth exclaim, "You promised asylum, Felcan! What good's money if we're dead or worse? Lunow's a fool if he goes back and tries to make them think we had nothing to do with the attack."

The big man said gruffly, "Well then, there's a ship, as promised. Your talents will be useful elsewhere." Signaling the others, he led the way to the tavern stables.

*A*rith woke instantly, braced within a wide crotch of an old oak, though Reva and her team made no sound as they slipped into the small forest. From his lookout perch above, Drinin acknowledged his teammates with the shrill call of a night bird while Arith dropped out of the tree into their midst.

"One of these days you're going to land on top of me," Iro remarked, taking off the small pack she wore.

"Nope. That would be Coronan," Arith replied nonchalantly. "Wish he could have joined us on this little trip." He patted Reva's shoulder, and she shot him a quick smile.

"So did he, since he was already bored with the enforced time off."

But Arith heard the relief in Reva's voice. They all missed their teammate, but it could have been much worse.

With Drinin keeping watch above, they hunkered down to discuss what they'd seen. It was obvious that there was some illegal operation going on, but they had yet to find evidence tying it to Ishal or The Bow.

"Heads up," Drinin called down. "Five horsemen on the road, coming from the northwest."

"Five. Not Coran and Micharon then," Arith commented as they all stood, moving to hide among the trees. "Watch and listen, for now." With a leap, he caught a lower branch, swinging up to his former seat as his teammates blended expertly into the grove around the path.

Within minutes, Arith heard the steady clop and splash of horses' hooves on the puddle-marked road, noting that they were in no particular hurry. Then Drinin's mindsight to their group came.

"Well, well. Gorth and Lunow are with them, in civilian clothes. And don't they look pleased with themselves."

"The others?" Arith asked, his mindsight cool.

"I don't recognize them. Do you want a tap?"

"Not yet. Can't remember if either of them can sense a mind-tap." Arith eased around to try and get a better view of the riders as they left the rain-drenched open road and entered the dripping shadows within the trees. With the two rogue ambassadors, the risks in taking the group increased. The riders were within hearing range now, but said little. Was it worth revealing themselves? Arith wondered, or should they stay concealed and follow?

Then he observed as the biggest one reined his horse to a stop and dismounted. "This is the best cover before the bay," the man said. "See if you can get a fire going, but not big enough to attract attention." He handed his reins to one of the other men before wandering off into the trees.

"Nobody this far out to see," the man clearing a well-used fire circle muttered under his breath, not knowing that the ambassador in the tree nearest him could hear every word. "And wet wood beside." Despite his constant complaints, he proved adept at coaxing a fire into life.

Arith focused on Gorth and Lunow as they saw to their horses then sat on a log near the crackling fire. They pulled their cloaks around them but said nothing for the moment. The third stranger took a position by the road, crossbow in hand, though he slouched against a tree, watching the fire more than the road. But Arith noticed his posture straighten quickly when the big man returned.

"How far now, Felcan?" Lunow spoke up.

"About an hour," the big man replied. "Ship's sailing in three days."

"Three days!" Lunow exclaimed, obviously annoyed. "You never said it'd be that long."

Felcan shrugged, sounding unconcerned. "Just missed one today. You're lucky Dateh sent the second load of men, or you'd be waiting for the next to arrive."

Now it was getting interesting, Arith thought, knowing his teammates were alert to every word.

"Seems to me you're lucky too," Gorth grumbled. "With all the men you lost trying to take on Alpha and Kilronan's team, you could use reinforcements. They won that round handily, with only one injured man." He appeared to ignore the sinister looks sent his way by Felcan's men.

But the big man, this Felcan, chuckled as he prepared a pipe. "The point was made well enough, ambassador. I suppose that's former ambassador, eh? And you should consider that you and your mate there will likely hang for treason if we leave you behind."

Arith saw Gorth's fingertips spark as he lunged to his feet to stand face to face with Felcan, who only continued to puff on his pipe as his brow lifted.

"Not if Ominor has a care for his own neck," Gorth snapped, as hot as the flames cupped in his right hand now. "All the golden promises of power from your Bow will come to nothing for him, and Wrax, if I'm caught here. I won't be hanged alone."

"Heads up." Drinin's voice in his head distracted Arith from this interesting conversation. *"Two more riders approaching, off the road. Looks like Coran and Micharon, judging by height difference."*

"Wait for Coran's tap, then let them know about the group here. Have them circle to the west."

With half a mind on what was being said below, Arith knew he had a decision to make. Recon Alpha could take the suspects easily enough, bring them all in for interrogation and sentencing. But the news about another ship had him wondering if it would be better to send two of his team back to Coroth to report and bring back militia to lie in wait for the next delivery.

From what he'd already heard, Felcan, his men, even Gorth and Lunow would be on Caldalan soil for three more days; enough time to capture them, and less time for any undiscovered accomplices to sound an alarm. Right now, they had no way of knowing if there were other terrorists within Caldala making their way here to return to Ishal. They could disappear back into the populace if they learned that their secret access had been discovered.

There were advantages and disadvantages either way. Arith shared his thoughts with Reva and Drinin by mindsight.

"Storm season is already here," Reva noted. *"They won't be running many more ships, if any, after this lunam, and we're already aware of their base even if they are that crazy. My vote is to keep watch and see if any more traitors surface to be netted."*

"I agree," Drinin said. *"Send Oti and me back to report to Coroth and request reinforcements at the bay. We'll make sure the troops understand the need for stealth at this time. And we'll see about having Ominor and Wrax picked up from Parliament before they get word and disappear, or in case they have the ability to sound the alarm to anyone in The Bow. Let's make sure they have their day before the judgment court."*

Arith grinned at that. *"It's decided then."*

*T*he rain eased to a drizzle, then a light mist as Felcan's riders reached the coast. He noted the hunched forms of the guards, both of them more interested in sheltering against some rocks than watching the road. They were nearly upon them before one looked up and scrambled to his feet, waking the other.

"You're lucky we weren't soldiers, or thieves," Felcan said in a bored voice as he walked his horse past them. "That's a day's pay for failing your duty."

Looking out over the dark bay, he could make out the shadow of the ship at anchor there. It didn't mean anything to him that he'd lied to the stupid ambassadors. Men that would betray their own weren't worth the concern. Dateh had use for them, but wouldn't care if they needed to be eliminated before that.

He smiled to himself when he heard Lunow's eager exclamation.

"Look! There's a ship here after all. Maybe it came early."

"Look's like," Felcan drawled. He glanced back, noting Gorth's rigid form. That one wasn't as gullible or forgiving, which made him a dangerous recruit. But Dateh was right; having their own force callers could help tip things their way, Felcan considered, remembering Gorth's flaming hands.

They'd reached the rough shingle beach now and dismounted, turning the horses over to one of the men who hurried from the shanties.

"Message from ship's captain, sir," he said breathlessly, handing Felcan a folded paper. Then he led the horses away to a makeshift corral.

His frown deepening as he read, Felcan balled up the paper with a curse. "Looks like your desire to leave Caldala is granted, ambassadors." His voice held a verbal sneer on the titles. "The captain's barometer readings predict a major storm on the way. He wants to sail on the next favorable tide." Stuffing the wadded paper into a pocket, Felcan picked up his saddlebags and walked toward the sheds.

There were nearly thirty Bowmen traveling to this sailing point within the next two days, expecting to board a ship to take them back to Ishal. He'd have to leave orders for them to return to their Caldalan assignments until something else could be arranged. That didn't improve his mood. Dateh was expecting those troops to fortify their position when they openly took over the government.

Once again, it troubled and annoyed Felcan that Abron Dateh, as he liked to be called now, might have spread their resources too thin. But he wouldn't ignore the ship captain's concerns. The sea was unforgiving, and he valued his life too much to challenge an experienced seaman's decisions.

Dateh would have to accept the bad luck, and bad timing.

*F*rom their vantage point on the cliffs, Recon Alpha had to accept their own change of plans as they watched the ship make ready. A small landing boat was already being rowed out to the larger vessel, and it looked like Felcan, his men, and the ambassadors they'd recruited were on board.

Arith took it pragmatically while Reva let loose some creative language over their bad luck. They weren't close enough to the villains to change the outcome. For now, Arith decided, they'd hold fast, watch for any others who might converge here, and wait for reinforcements.

Frustration over losing their original quarry was assuaged when a large number of Bowman were successfully captured over the following days as they converged on the Southern Crescent. Working with the company of royal guards covertly sent to join them, Recon Alpha felt satisfied with their catch.

There was even greater satisfaction when Arith and Reva joined the Commander of the Royal Guard as they interrupted a Parliament session to arrest Minister Ominor and Minister Wrax on charges of treason and conspiracy to commit murder.

Thirty-One

Village of Green River, Caldala

Restless and edgy, Kilronan stood in the front courtyard of Green River Protectorate, assessing the thick clouds overhead. Mountain weather could change rapidly, especially this time of year. Nathon, a senior master here, and a friend since both men had begun their protectorate training in Mountain Shadows, studied the sky beside him.

"Could go any way, Kil," Nathon remarked. "But, whether easy snowfall or ice storm, you're looking at snow sometime today. I don't like the idea of your group taking the road to Mountain Shadows."

Kilronan nodded, still examining the cloud-layered sky. "I don't like it myself but, from what you told us last night, the odds will only get worse the longer we stay here."

"That's true enough," Nathon replied reluctantly. "We've already seen several feet of snow in the last two weeks." He looked at the snowdrifts lining the walls around them. "That means snow building on the ridges along the road." Nathon turned to look at Kilronan with concern. "You've got to pass The Chute, Kil. You know there's a chance of an avalanche there."

"The Chute?" Akira inquired from behind them.

The men turned to find her approaching from the door to the main hall. She was warmly covered in a fur-lined, hooded cloak.

Kilronan and Nathon bowed, grinning when she waved the respectful gesture away with an impatient sound.

"I take it you were discussing the travel conditions to

Mountain Shadows," Akira continued, looking at them for more information.

"Yes. We were discussing weather and potential hazards," Kilronan said. "The Chute is a section of the ridge along the narrowest part of the road. The terrain forms a steep canyon that funnels water or snow along a short section there. And that's also where the far side drops straight down into a deep valley."

Akira nodded. "Yes, I've noticed that section before. So you're saying there's a higher risk of encountering an avalanche there."

"Yes, my lady," Nathon agreed. "Snow accumulates, forming an overhang above The Chute. Some years, snow breaking from that shelf comes down and blocks the road to the pass for weeks, until a thaw or a work crew can clear it."

Kilronan met Akira's questioning gaze. "There's no doubt it's a risk. We've got to decide whether we're going to take it. If we stay, we could be in Green River indefinitely. If we can make the Wayfarer's Inn, about a mile beyond The Chute, we'll overnight there. From there, the road to Mountain Shadows switch-backs through heavy forest until we reach our valley, with fewer risks even if the weather closes in."

"You have the safety of your team to consider," Akira said.

His smile was confidant. "If it was just Team Kilronan, we'd already be on the road. The horses can travel more quickly than the coach. But we have a princess of Coroth whose safe passage is top priority."

Nathon barked a laugh at the elegant woman's rather inelegant verbal response to Kilronan's remark.

"Does Isfail know you swear like that?" Kilronan teased, gently tweaking her nose.

"I believe he's heard worse," Akira replied primly, brushing away his hand. "My vote is that we try the road today, and turn back if necessary. Let me know your decision," she told him, returning to the building.

Nathon studied his friend. "How long have you two known one another?"

"All our lives," Kilronan murmured. He shook off old longings that still clung to his heart as he watched her enter the protectorate hall, and turned to see the curiosity in Nathon's eyes. "And she's a cherished friend, recently bound to Commander Ardan Isfail, Insalat Militia."

"Isfail, eh?" Nathon shook his head as they walked to the stables to consult with the coachman. "You have powerful friends, Kil. You take the mountain road today, you might need them."

*A*n hour later, decision made then discussed again until Akira's patience was tested, they started up the road. Cobblestone paving eventually turned to crushed stone sections divided by thick timbers to maintain traction as the incline steepened. Overhead, clouds thickened, mottled grays dimming the light though the cloud-obscured sun was still climbing the sky.

Underlying slabs began to replace crushed stone until there was more slick, native rock than rough gravel. Wheels skidded from time to time, causing the coach to slide sideways or slip backward, dragging at the laboring team of horses.

Ice made travel even more treacherous as they climbed higher into the mountains. Kilronan slowed the pace, letting the horses pick their way carefully along the frozen patches. On one particularly bad stretch, the riders dismounted to lead their horses single file up the safest side of the road.

Akira walked beside Kilronan while Tomon, the coachman, led the team of horses up the dangerous road while the driver, Shan, kept a cautious hand on the brake lever. Everyone breathed easier when they topped the first rise and entered a sparse stand of trees. Akira returned to the coach while the others mounted their horses.

Here the road curved gently upward before emerging on a narrow bench that appeared to have been carved from the cliff face. One side overlooked a long valley that deepened as the road continued to rise along its narrow lip. Low, man-made walls edged straight drops where the long fall to the valley floor would mean the death of any unfortunate traveler.

Looking across the valley to the mountains, Akira saw snow

falling in great sweeps of white against snow-frosted forest. It was headed their way. Just a few minutes later, strong gusts buffeted the coach as they drove on.

Soon Kilronan rode up from his position behind them. When Akira lowered the side window, he shouted over the rising howl of the wind. "Weather's getting worse, Akira! The coach can't turn around here, not until the inn. We need to make better time."

She nodded her understanding. "Set the pace, Kil." Akira gripped the leather strap on the sidewall as the coach lurched forward. Then her eyes widened as she saw the snowstorm—opaque white waves pouring over the opposite ridge—rushing toward them as she heard Kilronan shout orders to his team to tighten up.

Within seconds, ice-laden winds slammed into them, slowing progress to a crawl. Akira used her telepathy to know that the others were surviving the brutal blizzard as they struggled to make some headway.

Shan had no trouble keeping his carriage close to the wall with the wind pushing from the drop side. Kilronan kept his team just ahead of the coach horses.

It was a miserable journey.

The storm reached full whiteout conditions in minutes. Akira could feel Kilronan and his team tiring, the horses struggling to continue on. Tomon had left his seat again to lead the coach horses. Travel became a hell of vicious wind and snow, with no visible landmarks to show where they were or how far they had to go to reach shelter.

Then the pitch of the wind changed. The swirling backwash that had buffeted the coach as the onrushing wind rebounded from the rock face ceased. Akira strained her eyes to see what had changed.

"We're crossing The Chute, Akira," Kilronan's mindsight informed her.

She could feel the tension in his communication.

"I'm sending Asura, Celina, and Maronan across the gap first.

They'll check road conditions. If it's clear, Eron and I will follow. We'll do our best to assess the situation before the slower coach crosses."

"How far do we have to go to get beyond avalanche danger if the road is clear?" Akira asked with her gloved hands clenched tight. He seemed to hesitate.

"It's almost half a length, normally about a five minute drive in a coach, less on horseback. We'll be lucky to get past the far edge of The Chute within a quarter of an hour with this weather."

"So, about half an hour for the coach to make it across with the poor man leading his team on foot," Akira said. She took a deep breath and tried to send some optimism through her mental communication. *"You'd better get your people moving."*

"I'll signal you if it's clear. Shan knows to expect your sign. Just send a force bump against the hatch loud enough for him to hear."

"All right."

A loud tap on one of the windows startled her, until she saw Kilronan leaning close from horseback. He pulled down the scarf covering his lower face to grin at her with a quick salute. She smiled back at him, knowing he needed her to, and pressed her hand to the glass. For a brief moment, his hand matched hers. Then he straightened, pulling the scarf back up to his eyes before disappearing into the white.

Time seemed to crawl though the pocket watch Akira consulted frequently showed the minutes passing. The first three riders should be clear by now. Kilronan and Eron would be crossing. With no message to advise her of new trouble she forced herself to relax.

Thirty-Two

*H*olding tight to the headstall of the lead horse, next to the cliff face, Tomon stamped booted feet, trying to keep them warm, as he stood exposed to the storm. His horses shifted, shivering and uneasy, and he wished they were all anywhere but here. The Wayfarer's Inn was still a good length from The Chute, but maybe they'd make better time once they passed this hazard.

The horse closest to the coach on this side stamped, neighing irritably and tossing his head. The coachman walked back to calm him, swearing into the ice-encrusted scarf covering his nose and mouth. The blizzard screamed eerily, like lost souls riding the frozen winds. Was that a shout, he wondered? He turned to look for a rider emerging from the white haze. Hearing things, Tomon thought with a shrug when no one appeared.

On the driver's bench, Shan huddled within his thick coat, listening for the signal from her ladyship. He peered to the right when he glimpsed movement. Just snow flurries, he decided, failing to notice the small clumps of snow shifting over the uneven stone shelf above them. When a large lump dropped onto the top of the coach behind him with a solid thump, he snapped the reins, urging the horses into motion with relief.

The horses struggled ahead and Tomon fought the wind back to the front of the team, grateful to be moving.

They were most of the way across when he felt the lead horse jerk his head up. Then his arm was wrenched as the animal leaped forward with the rest of the team following. Tomon ran with them but he knew the odds were long of winning this race.

Tumbling snow dragged at his feet. He heard the roar just as he saw the shadow of the cliff beyond The Chute. Tomon made one desperate leap toward that hope of safety before the first crush of snow bore him down.

*I*nside the coach, Akira had ceased to wonder why the driver had moved on without her signal. They were making progress, she decided, and there was little she could do about it at this point. The howling cacophony of the blizzard was deafening now, and the coach shook and swayed from side to side in the violent winds.

When it suddenly lurched forward, Akira gripped the seat to keep from pitching onto the floor. Then she felt the fear of the men, the panic of the horses, and closed her eyes to search the storm.

Too late, she realized, flinging her arms wide to surround herself with a force shield as a churning wall of snow slammed into the coach. Shattered glass struck the shield bubble as windows buckled and the coach flew sideways, propelled by the inexorable mass of tons of surging snow and ice. For a split-second, Akira thought she heard the horses scream. Then she only heard her own screams as she tumbled, fighting to keep up the shield as the box plummeted into the white abyss.

The fall seemed an eternity. Akira lost all sense of orientation as she focused on the force shield that kept her tenuous shelter from collapsing in on her. She felt like she was floating within it and realized the front of the coach was now below her.

Akira barely had time to register the impact with the valley floor before she flew backward and lost control of her shielding force. She was spared most of the final wild ride as the coach was rolled and tossed in the breaking surf of the avalanche flowing across the valley floor. Akira was unconscious before the last snowy wave slumped to a stop.

*W*aiting for the coach just beyond the most hazardous part of the road, Team Kilronan grouped close together on their mounts to help break the force of the storm. The horses sensed the danger first, suddenly straining against their riders' control as they fought to escape. Their frightened snorts muffled by the blizzard's roaring winds, they lunged away from the gap of The Chute.

Kilronan felt the new vibration in the air, the feeling that the mountain was about to fall on them. He had only time to bellow a warning as he shot up both hands to bend a force shield over his team, using his knees to control his terrified horse. Crowding Celina's and Maronan's mounts close to the rock wall, Asura and Eron threw their forces up to add to Kilronan's.

Snow and ice struck the invisible shield, shuddering impacts to challenge the warriors' shield strength. Team Kilronan stared at the white cascade bursting overhead with a roaring grind that blocked out the wailing storm.

Minutes later, the thundering river of snow ebbed to a thin ooze as the avalanche came to an end. Blizzard winds quickly scoured snow from the force shield above them.

Sending out a mindsight, Kilronan assured himself that his people were unharmed. Now he allowed himself to think of Akira's coach, praying that it had not entered The Chute. But there was no response to his telepathic calls, and no sense of Akira's presence anywhere within range.

Everyone's wide eyes were focused on him, peering above the woolen scarves and under the fur-lined hoods tied close around their faces. What could he do, Kilronan thought, frozen in place as he contemplated the unthinkable.

He released the shield, lowering his arms to take the reins once more. Windblown snow pelted them with stinging impact again.

"We've got to turn back, see if we can find the coach," Kilronan mindsighted, watching the others nod as they guided the horses that had calmed now that the danger had passed.

There was only a narrow corridor right next to the wall for them to travel single file—stone on one side, and a bank of snow on the other, where the protection of the force shield had ended.

Then the way was blocked by the high slope of churned-up snow that covered the road before spilling over into the canyon.

The team stared silently at the blockade. This would not be cleared easily, whether by force powers, or picks and shovels.

"Maronan?"

The youth took a moment before answering. *"I can't feel her, Master."*

Kilronan swung down then fired force bolt after bolt along the snow slide until he cleared a path to the edge of the drop-off. The others followed him to look over into white nothingness as the storm continued to obscure everything.

Then Asura dropped to her knees and began to dig frantically in the snow. As her companions joined her, the dark object she'd seen was uncovered.

A leather-gloved hand, fingers stretched as if reaching for help. They all recognized the thick, dark coat as the arm was revealed. Asura pulled off her own glove to check the wrist for a pulse then shook her head without a word.

Akira's coachman had lost his race against the killing snow.

The import of finding Tomon's body, and the implications for the coach, hit them all hard. For a long moment, there was no movement among the five people staring at the gloved hand.

Then chunks of snow began falling on them as the debris flow shifted toward the drop. Eron pulled Asura to her feet as Kilronan hustled them back to relative safety just before snow slumped over, burying the dead man once more.

Mind and heart numb, Kilronan still knew what he had to do. The coach was gone, over the cliff, and Akira with it. She was powerful, he told himself. She could have shielded herself, Kilronan fought to believe. But they could not reach the valley floor from here. Now he had to protect his team, get them to shelter.

"Mount up," he ordered, gripping the reins of his horse and settling onto the saddle.

The others obeyed without argument. Every one of them understood the situation. They followed as their master urged his horse up the road.

Thirty-Three

Consciousness returned with roaring snaps of snow-laden wind, and cold that pierced her bones. For a moment, Akira lay in the wreckage wondering what had happened. Then memory returned and she pushed up to sit, leaning against what remained of a once-plush seat.

The coach box lay on its side, the front wall splintered and crushed inward with snow spilling over the collapsed seat back. The windows on the side facing up were cracked, allowing windblown snow to sift in.

Using the broken frame to pull up, Akira struggled to her feet. The world outside was a dim blur when it wasn't an impenetrable wall of white. She thought she saw trees crowding close around, but the storm made it difficult to be sure. Snow covered much of the coach debris and she could see nothing to guide her back to her companions.

Akira refused to think that the avalanche might have taken Kilronan and his team. He would have had time to shield them, and they should have been beyond The Chute itself.

Her heart ached imagining the fate of the coachmen and the team of horses. They could hardly have survived the brute force of a full broadside of plummeting snow and ice. Whatever had befallen them, there wasn't any sign of them now.

Pulling the lap blanket from the mess at her feet, and huddling back into what little protection the damaged coach afforded, Akira arranged her winter cloak around her body and pulled up the fur-lined hood, snugging it close around her face before draping the lap blanket over her head and cloak. Within minutes, snow blanketed her tenuous shelter and built drifts that added an insulating layer against the ferocious wind chill.

She hoped she wouldn't have long to wait.

*L*ying awake in the Wayfarer's Inn, Kilronan listened as the storm blew itself out. His eyes stared into darkness as silence fell over the mountains.

It was too familiar, he thought, this feeling of unimaginable loss; the pain of not knowing if Akira had survived the fall.

The crushing drop of an avalanche this time instead of falling rock and the deadly force attack of a Mors. But the results were the same. Akira had disappeared. This time, even if she'd survived the impact with the valley floor, there was the winter weather to face, even more deadly if she lay injured and unable to protect herself.

This time he would need to leave her behind to get help. He had to go on to Mountain Shadows, get Team Carelon with their expertise with winter operations. Somehow a message must be sent to Green River Protectorate to get a rescue team moving up from that end of the valley.

Thinking through the steps he needed to take got Kilronan through the long night. His team members were ready as dawn broke with cold clear weather and blue skies. Alert to icy road conditions, they began the last stretch to Mountain Shadows, praying for miracles.

*W*hile Kilronan lay awake in the Wayfarer's Inn, agonizing over her fate, Akira awoke to the silence of the clear winter night and a luminous glow. She stood up and pushed the door above her outward, sending fresh snow sliding. The star-filled sky offered the welcome light of nearly full moons. It turned the snowfield and the snow-covered pines around her into a fantasy of surreal beauty.

She welcomed the quiet peace, but the end of the storm brought no relief from the cold. Though visibility was excellent, Akira could only see an unrelieved flow of bright snow in one direction, with a white and black perimeter of trees circling the rest. There was no sign of human habitation; no firelight or window shine, no dark plume of smoke or firefly flicker of escaping embers from a chimney or campfire rising in the still air.

Steep canyon walls appeared to rise beyond the trees, but a trick of light reflecting on snow could fool the eyes. Still, she knew she was in the deep and narrow canyon that the road to Mountain Shadows ran beside. Despite the bright moonlight, she had difficulty getting her bearings, and she wasn't familiar with the mountain topography in this area.

With no one to hear, Akira moaned from the pain of bruised and stiffened limbs as she forced herself to move. Nothing would be gained by waiting here in the wilderness. No rescue party could descend the precipitous fall that her coach had taken.

She had no doubt that someone would come looking for her, but for now she needed to find better shelter against the bitter cold. Even with her powers, Akira knew she must find a way to survive until help arrived or she could find her own way back to Green River village. Perhaps daylight would show her the most likely direction to take. If she could find a running stream, it should lead downhill and toward Green River.

Searching among the splintered wood and torn interior, Akira found a second lap blanket. Sweeping a hand through the snow intruding through the broken forward wall she gave a cry of elation as she touched a familiar leather case. Dropping to her knees, Akira used both gloved hands to shift the wreckage until she pulled free the large, flat case that held the crossbow Isfail had given her.

Tears of relief and sudden grief froze on her cheeks. Holding the case tight against her, Akira fought the first onslaught of fear that she might never see him again, and prayed he would be spared that same fear for her. Would someone be sent to tell him that she'd been lost, frozen in this inhospitable land? Would Dan grieve over her death a second time?

No!

Gripping the case, she scrabbled to her feet with even greater determination. She would not be the cause of more sorrow to those who loved her, those who had risked all to save her after the injuries from the Mors defense.

Pushing the case through the door first, Akira gripped the doorframe and lifted herself up to swing her legs out. She dropped lightly into snow that reached her knees.

Using one lap blanket as an extra cloak, Akira wrapped the other like a large shawl over head and shoulders, with a length pulled over the scarf covering her face so that only her eyes peered out below the hood. Lifting the strap of the crossbow case over her head to settle cross-body on the opposite shoulder, she turned away from the light breeze and began the slow trek through snow and forest.

Hope pushed back fatigue when Akira stumbled onto a shallow creek bed. It was frozen solid beneath a thick blanket of snow, but she recognized the dip in the land that revealed the watercourse. She considered using precious energy reserves to thaw a small portion of the creek to see if it would reveal its direction of flow but decided against it. It was dark beneath the trees and she couldn't waste what little power she had left after the shield drain.

Akira followed the shallow bed in the same general direction she'd been headed. Her mood brightened with the dawn when the creek joined a larger watercourse, one where a deeper stream ran beneath a thin coating of ice at the center. She smiled as the flow confirmed that she was headed downhill.

Canyon walls were now visible on her right, steep and unbroken. Akira adjusted the blanket shawl and continued on. The sky grew bright above, though the sun had yet to crest the top of the ridges. The stream widened, and the musical rush of water joined the soughing of the branches overhead as the wind strengthened in the warming day.

The sight of a cabin on the far bank rewarded Akira's efforts. Three tree trunks had been lashed together to form a narrow bridge from bank to bank, just downstream of the cabin. She picked up her pace, eager to reach this first sign that help might be available. Her hopes faltered when she noticed that the cabin had an empty look about it. No smoke drifted from the stone chimney, no footsteps marked the pristine snow coating the narrow porch.

Still, it was shelter, Akira thought, slogging through the snow and up two steps to the door. The cabin appeared in good repair, the door was straight and sturdy in its frame, one window covered by thick, well-hung shutters. Someone had a care for the isolated structure, perhaps a seasonal hunter or fisherman.

Reaching for the latched door, Akira opened her senses, searching for any presence within. A frown creased her brow as she found something . . . someone, but that life was weak, barely detectable.

Without further delay, Akira pressed the latch and the door opened easily. Scanning the gloom within, she cautiously entered. Nothing moved in the dark interior.

"Is anyone here?" she asked, leaving the door open to admit some light. There was no response.

Spotting an oil lamp on a square table, Akira set the wick ablaze, adjusting it until warm light spread into the sparsely furnished main room. Her attention turned to the narrow bed in a corner, and the long form huddled under woolen blankets. She set down the crossbow case before moving quickly to the bed. Akira stooped to check on the man.

Pale as death, closed eyes sunken in a gaunt face, he was barely breathing. Pulling off her gloves, Akira pressed her fingers to his cold throat and found a pulse, weak and slow. Then she noticed the three thin scars marking the left side of his face and slowly pulled her hand away.

The stranger who'd attacked her in the meadow at Mountain Shadows.

As if her shock was a shout in the funereal hush of the cabin, he awoke with a start, dark eyes burning with feverish delirium. Thin lips cracked from sickness and dehydration parted into a twisted smile.

"Come to finish the job, Lady Muro?"

Thirty-Four

He watched her arrange wood in the cold hearth. "There's no flint and steel . . . that I could find." The words were forced out through a ragged cough.

Then his eyes widened when she just lifted her hand toward carefully stacked logs. Flames ignited in the dry tinder, and soon a steady blaze was adding heat and light to their dismal shelter.

The woman had said little since he'd woken in shock at seeing the apparition before him. Barash found some semblance of amusement flickering in his muddled thoughts at the irony of his intended prey coming upon him in this forsaken wilderness. His body was wracked once more with a coughing fit. Groaning when this latest spasm was over, he hoped the end would come soon.

A gentle hand lifted his head while she held a cup of water to his lips. The liquid was warm, soothing his parched mouth and throat. When he started to gulp greedily, she pulled the cup back.

"Just sips for now," Akira cautioned before offering the drink again. She met his narrow gaze calmly. "There are some dried food stores here; a few basic supplies. I'll put together a soup as soon as I can."

She confused him. Why was she helping him? Barash wondered when she placed a damp cloth over his brow, and as he fell into fever-driven dreams of pain and longing.

Akira turned the cloth to draw out more heat. When she knew he'd fallen into a deep sleep, she folded back the blankets and eased aside clothing until she could read the condition of his body. Akira tried to ignore the evidence of old injuries and focus on what was critical now. She'd need to rest, rebuild her force energy to have enough strength to deal with his most immediate needs.

Several ribs had been broken within the last few lunams, she noted, and his right shoulder dislocated and set badly. It must cause him pain. With a slight frown, Akira brushed fingers over the smooth skin of his upper chest. Where she'd expected to see the mark of The Bow there was nothing. Who was he?

She refused to question whether it was wise to heal this man—one who seemed determined to cause her harm, or worse. Akira Muro was a healer. She would deal with what came after.

With a tired sigh, she did what little she could to ease his suffering. Without medicines and with little force energy to pull from, there was not much she could do at the moment. Akira rearranged his clothing and blankets then folded one of the lap blankets recovered from the coach into a pillow for his head.

Searching the cabin, she found some sleeping pallets folded in a small storeroom, along with a chest containing cotton and wool blankets. A smaller chest held a variety of men's clothing—thick trousers, sweaters, and a worn jacket. Fishing gear occupied one corner beside a pair of hunting bows. A quiver full of arrows hung off a peg beside them. Sealed jugs of lamp oil sat on a shelf.

Akira took a pallet to spread to one side of the hearth and retrieved some of the blankets for warmth and comfort. A more thorough search of the two small cabinets in the kitchen corner yielded a small box of dried tea and a bottle of whiskey. That brought a rueful smile as she poured a small amount of the liquor into a cup. She welcomed the warm burn as it flowed down her throat.

The sun was straight overhead when Akira ventured onto the porch again. What direction would a search party come from, she wondered? Should she wait here, where there was shelter against the weather? Or continue toward Green River once the man was able to survive on his own?

Fatigue overwhelmed her thoughts. The questions would

wait, Akira decided, stepping back in and securing the door. At least the cabin was warm and dry. She stretched out on the pallet and watched the flames until she drifted into much-needed sleep.

*I*t was twilight when Akira woke. The man was still asleep but his breathing sounded easier. His heartbeat was steady when she checked his pulse. He would need nourishment to fight the illness, so she moved to the tiny kitchen area.

Akira combined the beans and strips of dried meat she'd set to soak earlier in a heavy iron kettle. She covered them with water, added salt, and hung the kettle from a hook in the hearth. It amused her that she was in this situation since she was an inadequate cook at best. But, necessity required that she provide some sort of sustenance for the two of them.

Soon tea steeped in a rustic pot, the familiar aroma bringing a painful longing for home and an end to this dilemma.

The soup, such as it was, thickened and sent out its own appealing scent as the evening progressed. A rustle from the bed had her turning to her unexpected patient. He moved restlessly, muttering in delirium.

When Akira placed a hand on his forehead, his eyes flashed open. For a moment she saw fear in them.

"It's all right," she said with calm deliberation. "I'm here to help you. What is your name?" Akira wondered that she hadn't asked earlier.

"Barash," he croaked. "Just Barash."

"I'm Akira," she told him, not knowing how cognizant he was.

"Yes. I have to kill you."

Akira sat on the edge of the bed, meeting his confused gaze. "Why do you want to kill me?"

He moved his head slowly. "Orders. From Karsh."

Well. At least that was understandable, Akira decided. He was an assassin, set on her by her former superior. Yet Ana Karsh was now dead. Did he know that?

Barash accepted her help when she used rolled blankets to prop him up. Those dark eyes looked back at her with more clarity when she brought him a cup of tea. When she held the cup to his lips, he swallowed more easily than before. He remained silent when she spooned a small amount of soup broth into a shallow bowl.

If his intent perusal bothered her, Akira showed no sign as she sat on the edge of the bed once more.

Barash opened his mouth to take in the spoonful she offered. Then closed his eyes with pleasure, savoring the first food he'd had in days. When he opened his eyes again, he saw humor in hers.

"It's good," he rasped before swallowing a second spoonful.

"I think that's the first time anyone has praised my cooking." Akira chuckled. "I'll attribute it to your disability and starvation this time."

His brow furrowed. Once again, Barash felt the need to understand this woman. She was never what he expected in their brief encounters. He'd seen her at her most powerful, pulling death from a storm. Now she was gentle and soothing, caring as he'd once dreamed a mother might be. Yet she was younger than he by a couple of years. Still, there was wisdom and compassion in those strange eyes, on that beautiful face—caring, as a mother should care . . .

"You saved me the trouble of killing my dear old mother."

Akira spooned up more broth, refusing to show her surprise at this abrupt revelation. Her hand was steady as she lifted the spoon to his mouth.

"Ana Karsh was your mother?" As he swallowed, the full truth came to her in a rush as she remembered the odd feeling of familiarity when she'd first seen him in Mountain Shadows. He took his looks from his sire.

"And Arthon Baronan was your father."

Those dry lips cracked and bled as his mouth twisted in anger. "He planted the seed, but he was no father to me." Barash succumbed to another bout of coughing.

Setting the bowl aside, Akira picked up the dampened cloth

to carefully sponge his mouth. "I doubt that Baronan felt any more for his younger son."

Exhausted, Barash just looked into her eyes for a moment. "True enough, perhaps. But he found something of himself in the dark one, the one he took with him when he fled."

Akira sat back. There was far more here than she had anticipated. Could Barash be the key to finding out what had led to the massacre at Baronan's Keep so long ago? How much could he tell her of his father's crimes? How much would he tell her in his weakened state?

"Did you live with your father?" Akira fed him some more, waiting for him to swallow.

Rage and something dark moved in his eyes, but he shook his head, refusing to speak of it.

"You seem to know something about the last days at his keep," she prodded, hoping to keep him engaged.

"I know the one left behind was not who he was thought to be." Barash shook his head, now a brief smile touched his thin mouth. "But you know that." He rolled his head on the makeshift pillow to look at her.

"I know the dead child was not Arthon Baronan's son," Akira verified, deciding not to press for more details on this man's involvement, for the moment. "Who was he?"

Barash shrugged then paused as a coughing fit took him. When he regained breath to speak, he gave a desultory movement of a hand. "Nobody—a stable boy, maybe? The other escaped with a servant girl's help, through one of the outfall drains."

"How do you know?" Akira asked in a tight voice. His cavalier attitude about the dead child annoyed her.

"I followed them, saw where they hid."

"But you didn't give them away. Why?"

The softening of that hard face surprised her.

"That one was . . ." he murmured thoughtfully, "I liked that one." Immediately, he appeared embarrassed by his words.

"That's an odd way to express that," Akira said quietly. "What do you mean, *that one*?"

Now Barash gave a faint grin. "Ah, even the almighty Muro doesn't know that Baronan had two sons by his wife, Lady Arda. She birthed twin boys—the light and the dark." He appeared satisfied with the surprised look on Akira's face, though his eyelids drooped as fatigue overtook him.

Mulling this over, Akira took the bowl away, pleased that he'd kept the broth down. As she spooned up a bowl of soup for herself, she fit these new pieces of information into the puzzle that was the history of Lord Arthon Baronan—a deranged mass murderer, obsessed with ending the Psyche race. He'd fled Caldalan justice to find sanctuary in the country of Ishal, eventually fomenting a rebellion that took hundreds of Ishalian lives, and nearly toppled that country's lawful government before a loyalist assassinated him.

Arthon Baronan had founded the cult known as The Bow, which now infiltrated Caldala to continue his sworn cause of ending all force callers. Akira turned to meet Barash's dark eyes. All these lunams, since he'd attacked her at Mountain Shadows, she'd believed he must have a part in The Bow. Yet he did not carry the scar, the crescent with three lines, that other followers were marked with.

But she had learned one thing that solved the confusion she'd felt after learning that Abron Dateh was a son of Arthon Baronan. Was Barash in league with his half-brother? Did he even know who had revived their father's cult?

"Are you a leader in The Bow?" she asked, bringing a sturdy chair to sit next to the bed.

Barash somehow managed a scornful look from bleary eyes. "I've no wish to continue my dead, unlamented sire's vendetta."

"Yet you wish me dead," Akira pressed.

"Nothing to do with him," he muttered, his eyes closing. "Just Karsh . . . not me."

Akira sighed, her fingers pressed to his wrist to check his pulse as he slipped into sleep once more. Satisfied that he was stable for now, she used her healing forces to reduce the congestion in his lungs. She couldn't cure the pneumonia that weakened his body, but she could ease its effects until the illness ran its course.

When he was stronger, she would work on repairing the badly healed shoulder and ribs. For now, she would get some more rest before dealing with the next few days. And decide whether to tell him about Abron Dateh.

Thirty-Five

*A*rla and her team were on gate duty when Team Kilronan finally reached Mountain Shadows. One look at them as they approached had Arla sending a runner to alert protectorate administration.

"Kil." She met his strained look with concern. "What happened? Where's Akira?"

"Avalanche," Kilronan said, his voice emotionless. "It took the coach. I need Carelon."

With nothing more to say, Arla watched them urge their travel-weary horses up the road toward the fortress. How had this happened again? Arla thought, her heart aching for Akira, and Kilronan.

Lord Corcoran was in the courtyard when Kilronan and his team rode in. The grim set to their faces had him giving orders to the guard standing beside him. The woman hurried off to assemble the requested masters for an emergency meeting.

Kilronan dismounted, handing the reins of his gelding to a waiting stable boy. Then he met his lord's questioning eyes.

"Akira's coach was taken by an avalanche at The Chute. It's in the canyon." He spoke like a man in a dream, a nightmare. "The Alpine team—"

"Will go out as soon as possible," Corcoran interjected. "What about your team? Is anyone hurt?" He looked at the others while Kilronan shook his head.

"No. We'd gone ahead to check road conditions. We were able to take shelter against the far cliff face when we heard the avalanche coming down."

"Dismiss your team, Kilronan. They need to get warm and rest. We'll get a rescue party moving into the canyon at the earliest opportunity." But Corcoran looked toward the sun beginning its descent in the west and the clouds building over the northern mountains.

Within a quarter hour, Corcoran had the critical people seated in the small council chamber, listening closely while Kilronan related the disaster on the road. There were no questions to answer as he sat back down, Arla on one side of him and Osharon on the other.

Carelon, leader of the warriors known as the Alpine team for their mountaineering skills, broke the brief silence. "We know where the coach went down. That's an advantage." He looked over at the map that Gralla had fastened onto a stand, diagramming the canyon area and the course of the road above it.

Everyone watched as he got up and went to it, placing a finger at the location of The Chute then skimming it up the canyon profile to the rim closest to Mountain Shadows.

"It's an easy enough descent from our end, as long as the weather holds. Maybe a day to the avalanche debris." Carelon looked at Kilronan. "Could Akira have survived that fall?"

"Yes. If she had time to shield herself."

"Then we better get her home," Carelon said, returning to his seat with a nod to Lord Corcoran.

"As soon as possible," Corcoran stated. "This break in the weather allowed us to send a message to Green River using one of the carrier hawks. They'll no doubt send a rescue team up from the canyon mouth." He looked over as the afternoon light through the window dimmed while clouds once again covered the valley. "They may be able to send help before we can."

With regret, he looked at Kilronan. "The weather is closing in again."

Before Kilronan could speak, Carelon said, "Your pardon, Lord Corcoran, but I request that my team be allowed to set off as soon as we can make ready. You know we've been out in worse, and the incoming front shows no signs of being a blizzard like the one Kil's team just came through."

Nodding his head slowly, Lord Corcoran thought it over. Carelon was not a reckless warrior and his team had indeed taken missions in severe weather and uncertain mountain conditions. If any team could get to Akira quickly, it would be his.

Every minute counted if she was still alive. His eyes closed briefly as he willed it to be so. Surely Akira had not survived all that she'd faced in life to be lost in such a way.

Looking at Carelon, he said, "Get your team ready. Advise me when you're set to go."

With only Arla and Osharon remaining with them, Kilronan signaled to speak.

"Yes, Kil?" Corcoran said.

"You'll need to get a message to Isfail, sir. He was planning to follow us to Mountain Shadows within a week of our departure from Insalat." Kilronan rubbed a hand over his burning eyes. "Akira and Isfail were bound before we left Coroth."

*R*iding his stallion ahead of the wagon hired to carry his few trunks and the one of Akira's, Isfail arrived at Green River Protectorate in the mid-afternoon. Despite the cold, and the days of steady travel, Isfail was pleased to hear that Akira's group had left there just two days before. There was some concern expressed about the snowstorm that had reached Green River that same afternoon, but Akira's coach and Team Kilronan had not returned, so were assumed to have continued to Mountain Shadows.

Comfortable in the company of other warriors, Isfail enjoyed the hospitality of Green River Protectorate and the opportunity to begin building friendly relationships in his new home territory.

But the easy camaraderie shattered early that evening when Senior Master Nathon sought him out, his face grim as he asked Isfail to meet with the lord of the protectorate.

Isfail met the lord's respectful bow and greeting with a brief nod, hiding his impatience with the deference as he waited to hear what had brought him there.

With a brief cough, Lord Georen began, "Commander Isfail, Nathon here has informed me that you are the binding partner of Lady Akira, who left Green River under the escort of Mountain Shadows Team Kilronan."

"That's correct," Isfail said, feeling a sudden chill in his blood. "You have news of my wife?" He watched the lord exchange glances with Nathon.

"I truly regret to inform you, my lord, but Lady Akira's coach was lost in an avalanche on the road to Mountain Shadows. We just received word by messenger hawk." Lord Georen paused briefly as Isfail gripped the back of a chair. "Mountain Shadows requests that we send a search team up the mouth of the valley. Their team will descend into the far end of that canyon as soon as weather permits."

When Isfail continued to stare without saying a word, Georen said, "I must tell you honestly, sir, the odds of anyone surviving the fall into that canyon, with the avalanche and the weather, are not good."

Cold gray eyes met his, and Isfail stated, "Your team will be ready at first light. I'll be with them." He turned to the door, saying, "I want all the information you have available on that canyon. Now."

As the two protectorate men watched him stride away, Georen blew out a breath and looked at Nathon. "Well, an heir of Coroth outranks me, so we'll hope the coastal militia commander can handle himself in a mountain winter."

*D*aybreak found Isfail cursing the weather as he stood in the courtyard of Green River Protectorate with snow falling in heavy sweeps that obscured the buildings around him.

Master Nathon obviously sympathized, but could do nothing to change the weather. Still he noted, "It's no blizzard, sir, so we should be able to make a fast start when this clears."

"No chance of setting out in this?" Isfail asked, though he

was resigned to the answer Nathon gave him even before the man spoke.

"It won't help, my lord. We have good trackers and woodsmen here, but visibility is poor to none. Too easy to get off track and lose ourselves, and that would waste time and manpower."

Isfail nodded, seeing the sense of it though he was desperate to get to Akira. What if she lay injured in the wreckage of the coach? How could she survive exposed to the elements?

Stuffing clenched fists into the deep pockets of his coat, Isfail stalked the courtyard like a caged wolf.

At the eastern end, Team Carelon was making more headway. The narrow canyon that opened near Green River terminated in a deep curve of surrounding cliffs not far from Mountain Shadows. Carelon's Alpine team had reached the point of descent within an hour of setting out, and started the climb down just as the latest snowstorm swirled in.

When the night and the falling snow made it too difficult to see their way, Carelon called a halt on the first broad ledge. The team knew the terrain well and made a reasonable camp for the night in a natural alcove under overhanging rock. Sheltered from wind and snow, they huddled around a fire and planned the next day's travel.

They were ready to start again as soon as the day lightened enough to aid the descent. The heavy snowfall blurred and masked the surrounding features but there was little wind to add to the danger. All five team members reached the bottom without incident by midday.

Thirty-Six

That same morning, Akira pulled the cabin door closed behind her to keep the warmth from escaping. Crossing her arms, hands gripping her elbows, she stood on the narrow porch and faced the opaque wall of falling snow blanketing the land around the cabin. She gave a deep sigh, wondering how long this would last as she turned to go in.

Akira's brow furrowed when she saw Barash struggling from his coverings, and walked to him just as he managed to get one leg over the edge of the bed.

"I don't think that's a good idea," she said, studying the way he swayed even after he got the second foot onto the floor. Nearly as white as the falling snow, Barash lifted his head to stare at her. The defiance in his eyes warred with a look of embarrassment that puzzled her for a moment.

"No choice," he mumbled, trying to get to his feet.

And Akira suddenly understood, pursing her lips as she tried not to smile. "Just wait a moment. There's a chamber pot in the storage room."

But as she turned to get it, he growled, "There's an outbuilding. I'll use that."

Facing him, eyes stern, hands on hips, Akira countered, "It's snowing again, and you're in no shape to walk across this room, let alone plow through a new layer of snow in freezing weather."

"Not relieving myself . . . in front of a lady," he managed to say between harsh coughs.

She got a firm hold on his shoulder before he toppled forward. "This is unnecessary, Barash," she said quietly. "I'm a healer first, a lady much further down the list. I've dealt with everything that can happen with and to a person's body."

Her mouth quirked a little when he gave a stubborn shake of his head.

"I've not much of what little pride was left to me," he muttered as his shoulders drooped.

When he looked up again, the mortification in his eyes caused Akira's heart to ache for him. She ran a gentle hand down his scruff-laden cheek. "I'll give you what privacy I can, unless you need help. Then we'll see about cleaning you up some. You'd feel better and heal more quickly."

Barash stared into her eyes another moment, as if searching for something he needed to find. When he looked down at the floor, he nodded.

A blanket folded over a rope strung from hooks already set in the walls soothed his sensibilities. Akira heated water over the fire, discreetly alert for any sign Barash required assistance. She thought about this surprisingly self-conscious side of him, considering his acknowledged background as Ana Karsh's illegitimate son, the man she'd sent to kill Akira. How many more nefarious tasks had he done or been sent to do in his life?

What had his life been like as a child, and how had he been raised? Akira knew he had not lived at Ambassador Central. No one knew that Karsh had a child. Indeed, it was amazing to consider that the woman who had stringently enforced the Core's celibacy rule ever had a lover.

Arthon Baronan, Akira mused, the man who had set out to destroy all force-gifted. There couldn't be a less likely pairing, she thought, pouring hot water into the large wooden washtub she'd found in the storage room and set in front of the fireplace. While another pot of snowmelt heated, she retrieved a couple of buckets of snow from the ample supply outside the door and dumped them in to melt in the tub.

By the time she heard the shuffling and rustles that told her Barash had dealt with his more basic needs, Akira was pouring the second pot of boiling water in. She swirled her hand through the water, testing the temperature. Another pot of hot should do it, she decided.

"Barash?"

A muffled grunt was the only response.

Akira walked over and gave the blanket a tweak. "I have a bath almost ready for you."

"Don't think so," he muttered.

She pushed the blanket aside. He lay facing the wall. Akira said nothing more as she collected the chamber pot and took it to the door.

When that task was dealt with, Akira washed her hands, toweling them dry as she came to stand over him.

"We're cleaning you up, Barash."

She heard a reluctant chuckle.

"Taking one with me, my lady?" But the leer he tried to put in the words fell short.

"No. But I'll give you one if necessary."

Barash rolled to his back, looking up into her amused eyes. She wondered what he'd come up with next, but didn't expect his words, or the serious expression on his gaunt, scarred face.

"I hope your man knows his good fortune."

Akira's eyes softened. "I believe he does. He also knows what I am, and accepts all of me."

"That's good then," he said quietly before heaving out a long breath. "All right. I'll need some help, but I'll do what I can."

Later, blessedly clean, wrapped in a blanket in a chair before the fire, Barash blinked sleepily as he watched the flames. Even the pain from shoulder and ribs that he'd learned to live with couldn't spoil this rare feeling of contentment.

Akira pulled a comb carefully through his damp, tangled hair. It felt good, he decided. He couldn't remember anyone really tending to him like this.

"Why?" he asked, hardly aware that he'd spoken, until she responded while gently working through knotted strands.

"Why what?"

Barash turned his face a little. "Why are you doing this? You should have left me to die, or killed me for attacking you, wanting to kill you."

Akira was silent for several minutes, continuing to draw the comb smoothly now through his long black hair. When she set the comb aside, she walked around and sat, cross-legged, on the floor in front of him.

"I choose not to be an executioner, Barash. I have killed, and would again to defend myself or others, if I had to." She tipped her head to the side, studying him. "You needed help; I could give it."

"What do you want from me?" he asked, his voice weary. People always expected payment.

"You could help me understand you, understand Baronan, but I won't force that from you."

His mouth twisted as he retorted, "You can just pull it from my mind."

Nodding, she replied, "I can, but I won't unless you give me permission. I was taught and believe in a code of ethics, a code of justice. There are times when it's necessary to bend those rules, but this isn't one of them. Nothing you might tell me can change the past, it can only help me to know what happened, maybe why it happened. Perhaps some of your information can help me learn how to fight The Bow."

His brow tightened before he swayed with fatigue. Akira stood up, reaching for the clean clothes she'd brought from the storeroom. "Let's get you dressed. These will be large on you, but they smell better than what was left of your own."

Trying to make it as easy on her as he could in his disabled condition, Barash muttered as he struggled to pull up and fasten the wool trousers. "Burn those, will you?"

Akira laughed quietly before tossing his discarded clothing into the fire. He watched them make a satisfying blaze while Akira worked his hair into a long braid before helping him back into the freshly made bed.

Barash kept his eyes on her as she moved about the room,

cleaning up the bath things and preparing her own pallet. As his eyelids grew heavy, he silently offered up the only prayer of thanks he'd ever given in his life.

*T*eam Carelon reached the avalanche debris near the cliff face beneath the road. Those members with force abilities quickly ascertained that the only bodies there were the broken remains of the horse team.

They located the body of the coach driver as they followed the avalanche talus flowing out across the valley floor. Marking the location, they continued on as the snow fell thickly around them. It wasn't long before they came upon the shattered coach wreckage.

Carelon glanced at Leta, his assistant master, before hoisting himself up to search what remained of the box. "There's no one here," he called back, letting out his own blow of relief as he heard his team express some cheer at this news.

"Looks like she might have taken some things," Carelon told them as he dropped back down. "But it's hard to tell with the damage and the latest snowfall."

Leta, their best tracker, examined the snow around them, but the only discernable tracks belonged to their group. "We'll have a hard time following her trail with all the new snow, but she'll head down, back toward Green River. It's the logical thing to do."

Nodding, Carelon spread his team arms-length apart, following compass headings toward the canyon mouth until darkness had them setting up camp.

*I*n Green River, Isfail rechecked his saddlebags, frustrated as the snow continued its unrelenting fall. Though tempted to commandeer a small search team, he knew it was too great a risk. They could easily miss Akira in such weather, and it would only slow down a viable rescue attempt.

He reminded himself that she was smart and experienced in winter conditions as he paced the suite the protectorate had provided him. And she had abilities the average person would not have in such a situation.

Returning to one of the tall windows, Isfail cursed the opaque drift of snow outside the glass even as the light dimmed at the end of the long day.

Thirty-Seven

"W hat's it doing out there?" Barash mumbled sleepily as he awoke in time to see Akira closing the front door. "The snowfall is lighter. I could see as far as the stream and the trees closest to the cabin. The sun's going down."

She walked over to him, placing a cool hand on his forehead. "Your fever is gone. How are you feeling?"

Taking stock of the residual aches and pains, Barash grimaced. "Nothing I can't live with."

"I can help you with that bad shoulder and fix the broken ribs properly, but the healing treatment will be painful at the start."

Staring up at her, Barash scowled. Why would she do this? It was a question that continued to plague him. Though he'd never felt his misbegotten father's antipathy toward force callers, never even understood the man's obsession, he'd found little reason to trust them, either. His mother hadn't exemplified the best of their breed, he remembered.

Still, this woman had shown him nothing but kindness . . . so, what the hell.

Shrugging, he rolled to push himself to a sitting position, noticing with surprise that his energy was returning. "Can't hurt worse than some things I've dealt with." With a wry grin, Barash said, "Besides, you're responsible for the damage."

Her eyebrows winged up. "How so?"

"I was on the point when you battled Karsh. Whatever happened there sent me flying back into the trees." He rubbed his deformed shoulder. "Hit a tree. When I came to . . . well, it was quiet, and still dark. I managed to work my way back to where I'd

221

left a horse, but he was gone." Barash shrugged. "Managed to get out of Coroth, hiding in a wagon full of bags of grain."

"That must have been quite painful," Akira said in a solemn voice. "Maybe I should make up for that."

She was something, Barash thought, moving to the chair before the fire with Akira's help. He wished he knew what made her who she was.

*A*kira had Barash sit, facing the chair back, and directed him to grip the top rung securely. With one hand pressed against the damaged shoulder joint, she used her other to position that arm.

"All right, on the count of three." She felt him tense beneath her hands, and paused. "It will be easier on you if you're more relaxed. Take a few deep breaths then think of fishing."

"Fishing?" he exclaimed, sounding confused and distracted, but Akira had begun the count under her breath.

"Three," she said aloud, simultaneously sending hot healing force into his shoulder and manipulating the arm in a fast, twisting jerk that had Barash's face going white as bone, sweat beading his forehead.

His oath came out in a gasping wheeze as he slumped on the chair back.

Pressing a damp cloth to his face, Akira soothed, "That's the worst of it, and done."

Barash surfaced from the brief shock and considered throwing the chair across the room. "You're a sadist, my lady."

Just smiling at that, Akira wrapped a snow-filled pouch to his shoulder to keep any swelling down. "It's better now, isn't it?"

Gingerly testing arm and shoulder, Barash had to agree. "Yeah." But he considered her warily. "What about the ribs?"

"Not as bad, but it will be uncomfortable."

His dark eyebrows drew together into one long line for a moment as he thought about it. "Just get it done."

Then, looking discomfited, he glanced at her. "Please."

The ribs took longer, but weren't as bad. Though he felt a little sick and achy again by the time it was done, Barash found no reason to doubt her honesty. Propped up on his bed, sipping the tea she'd given him, he watched while she did something in the sparse kitchen area.

"Do you know why Baronan hated your kind?" he asked.

She didn't pause what she was doing. "No, at least not anything that makes sense. I know he wanted to bind a woman, a gifted force caller, but she turned him away and chose another." Akira looked over for a moment. "Men and women are often disappointed in such matters. So it doesn't seem reasonable for a man to persecute an entire race over that."

Shifting into a more comfortable position, Barash said, "He wasn't anywhere near reasonable. But he didn't seem to hate force callers early on. That came later."

"Really? Why do you say that?"

His brow furrowing in thought, Barash set aside his empty cup and rubbed his sore shoulder. "Well, he got on with Ana well enough, then married Lady Arda, who had some force ancestry. Looking back, I think old Baronan wanted those powers himself. Since he didn't, he used those women who did. Maybe he wanted offspring with the power."

"Do you have force abilities?" Akira asked calmly, continuing to dress out the rabbit she'd caught in a snare.

"No. I was a disappointment to both of them. Karsh wanted Baronan, but settled for me when I was old enough to be useful. Not useful enough without powers, but fit to send out to spy on people, strong-arm and intimidate, sometimes kill." He shrugged when he saw her steely glance.

"You can't fix everyone, Lady Muro, and I was born and raised a bastard, in every meaning of the word."

Akira brought over a bowl of dried apple slices. "We all have choices throughout our lives. You decide how you'll live the rest of yours." Tipping her head, she studied him. "What do you want, now that Karsh is gone?"

After puffing out a breath, Barash took a bite of apple, chewing thoughtfully before swallowing. "Good question. It's the first time in my life no one's told me what to do."

He gave her a fierce look. "Why do I tell you things?"

"It must be my charming personality," Akira said cheerfully, returning to her cooking.

"Hell no," he muttered, but couldn't hold back a slight smile when she burst out laughing. Feeling more settled, Barash stared at the ceiling and began to talk.

"He was wrong—you know what I mean? Baronan was wrong in the head, with a heart black as a moonless night without stars. He enjoyed using Ana Karsh as long as she put up with it, then thought nothing of it when she finally left him, although that's about the time he started his rants against force callers. Karsh had no use for me, so Baronan tossed me to the servants to care for."

Barash didn't see the grief on Akira's face for the little boy, so ill-used and unloved.

"I guess I looked enough like him to avoid being thrown out to starve." Barash thought back. "When Lady Arda had the two boys, Baronan was instantly drawn to the dark one."

"Dark one?" Akira interrupted.

"Yeah. He was long and thin, with hair and eyes black as his sire. But the firstborn had pale hair, eventually took his looks more from his mother's side."

Turning his head to Akira once more, Barash told her, "He was a fanatic, Baronan was, and from that first day, he took charge of the dark one. Seems like he got crazier every day. He swore there was just one son, his heir, and no one dared contradict him. Baronan would have killed the other, but he let him live to keep Lady Arda in line. She was useful, for her family connections and wealth."

His eyes grew sad. "She was a good woman—taught me to read, to write. He killed her in the end."

Akira had come to sit by the bed as he told the story. "Why?"

"He'd been gone a few days," Barash said. "Not unusual, but this time Lady Arda tried to escape with her boy. I could see from the loft of the stable, watching while she saddled one of the horses.

"But Baronan walked into the stable yard just as she was leading the horse and boy out." Barash looked down. "He was mad, crazy, and laughing. I was used to his mood changes, and this time I hid." His eyes seemed to see things beyond the insular world of the cabin in the woods. "I heard her screaming for Aron to run, run . . . then just screaming." He swiped at his eyes.

"It seemed forever. I don't remember how long I stayed buried in the hay, until the next day, though. I was just about to come out of my hole in the stables when more screams and shouts began—terrible sounds, women and men." Barash gulped, his voice shaking now.

"That did it. I got out and ran. Ran into the woods, wanting to get to a cave I knew on the other side of the ridge." Barash took the cup of water Akira handed him and drank it down. "I made it there, had just time enough to scurry into a tunnel when Baronan and his chosen son came out a hidden door. I saw his horse then, tied inside the cave mouth. He mounted, pulled the dark one up behind him, and rode away."

Barash shifted suddenly, shaking his head. "I found the door, followed the secret passages into the keep. Saw what waited there." He couldn't meet Akira's searching gaze. "I took a horse from the stable and eventually found a way to contact Karsh."

The grief he'd told himself he couldn't feel seemed to choke him now. Pressing the heels of his hands to damp eyes, he forced out a bitter laugh. "Now you know what I come from, why my heart's as cold as those that spawned me."

When her hands wrapped around his wrists, gently pulling his away from his face, he narrowed his reddened eyes to scowl at her pity. But there was only compassion in those glowing green eyes. Then she drew her fingertips lightly over the thin scars her falcon had left him with. The deep heat, just within tolerable limits, followed her touch, and quickly cooled.

Staring into her eyes as their luminous glow faded, Barash raised a hand to his face. The scars were gone. "Why?"

Akira said nothing as she got up to stir the rabbit stew. What was there to say? She lay awake long after he'd returned to sleep, trying to assemble her thoughts, find ways to get more information, more answers—and control her sympathy.

Thirty-Eight

It was later than he'd planned, Barash realized as he fumbled with his boots. The sun shone bright through the windows. Akira had opened the shutters to the clear morning before she left the cabin carrying a bow and full quiver a short time ago. If he could get out before she returned, he stood an even chance of getting away. He'd stayed here too long, revealed too much of himself to her.

With a grimace for his weakened state, Barash pushed to his feet—weak, yes, but a hell of lot stronger than he should have been.

"I can't allow you to go." Akira stood in the doorway.

He stared at her resolute face. No, she couldn't, he thought bitterly. She believed in a code of justice. "Will you kill me then, after saving me?"

"No."

Reaching for the thick coat he'd walked in with more than a week before, Barash shook his head. But he believed her, knowing that Akira Muro was the one person in this world he would believe. "Then you must stop me."

"Barash."

Her quiet tone had him dropping his head with a pained expression on his face. "You, of all people, should know that I'm not redeemable. But . . . a life for a life, my lady, and I won't attempt to take yours now," Barash said, his voice thick with emotion. "You gave me mine back. Such as it is. You'll have to take it now to stop me. I won't end in a prison, or with my head on an executioner's block."

"You don't have to continue the life you led before," Akira said firmly. "And I don't need to kill you to stop you."

He knew that too as he turned to the door.

"You need more time to regain your strength. You're not strong enough to face the winter wild this way," she continued with genuine concern.

Akira followed as he walked out, watching as he struggled to break a trail in the virgin snow. The sound of his gasping breath competed with the crunch of snow underfoot. She waited when he stopped, lifting his head to stare into the forest before him. Then he turned around to look at her.

"Your powers are amazing, Akira. Now remove the wall you've put before me."

She only held his gaze, her hands palm out, bringing the invisible force wall around him.

They both jerked as a loud shout broke the silence, looking over in surprise as several mounted men rode from the forest at the edge of the clearing.

Distracted by the sight of the familiar gray stallion and his rider plunging through drifts ahead of the others, Akira gave a cry of joy. Force-blasting a path through the snow, she ran to Isfail's arms as he launched himself from the saddle.

When Isfail released her to strip off his heavy coat, wrapping it around her shivering body, Akira remembered Barash.

She whipped her head around to look for him just as Carelon's warriors appeared, calling out to her from the far side of the stream.

But Barash was gone.

Thirty-Nine

"Who was that man?" Isfail asked, crouching before her as she sat by the fire in the little cabin, rubbing her shoulders.

"His name is Barash," Akira replied, meeting his concerned eyes. "I found him here, in the cabin when I came looking for shelter. He was injured, terribly ill. I couldn't leave him here to die, Dan."

He smiled, stroking her cheek. "Of course you couldn't."

"And another snowstorm began the same night I got here." Akira looked over as Carelon and Leta rushed in. She stood up to greet them.

"Are Kilronan and his team safe? How did you get to me so soon? Thank you!"

Grinning at the rush of words, Carelon nodded. "They're safe, my lady. Kil got them to Mountain Shadows in record time, considering the snow and all. Lord Corcoran sent a message to Green River in that short window of clear skies, and approved my team to set out immediately."

Glancing toward the door, Leta said, "That man we saw with you, he didn't look like he should be heading off alone. Should I track him before he gets too far to help?"

Taking a deep breath, Akira stared out the window. "Thank you, Leta. I found him here, very ill, and was able to heal the worst of his injuries and symptoms. But he was determined to leave today. I was trying to . . . talk him out of it when all of you arrived." She ignored Isfail's sharp glance at her hesitation.

"Maybe you could follow his trail, just far enough to be sure he didn't collapse close by."

While they waited for Leta and Carelon to report back, Akira thanked Master Nathon and his team as they helped her set the cabin to rights. They insisted that she sit with Isfail while she told them what had transpired since the avalanche.

She felt Ardan's arm tighten around her shoulders as she related how she'd survived the fall, and her decision to make her way back to Green River as her best hope of survival. Carelon's remaining team members praised that decision as they described how difficult both weather and terrain would have been if she'd chosen the opposite end of the canyon.

When Leta and Carelon came back in, Akira looked up quickly.

"He must have been more fit than I gave him credit for," Leta said, pulling off a thick wool cap. "And knows the area well enough to head straight for the road. It's only about a hundred paces to the southwest, and up a rocky slope maybe another hundred feet, rising or descending, depending on your direction of travel." She grinned at Nathon's chuckle. "We followed his tracks that far. Since he wasn't in sight, or laid out along the way, we decided he'd probably make it home."

Shaking her head, Akira sighed. "It was his decision to go. He'll survive, or he won't," she said, accepting that Barash's fate was in his hands alone now.

Carelon gave Akira a curious look. "I'm surprised he didn't stay to get you both to the road. It would be a faster way back to Green River than breaking your way through the snow alone."

"We hadn't gotten that far before you all arrived," she prevaricated. "I wasn't pleased that he wanted to push himself so soon. We were disagreeing about it, in fact."

While the protectorate warriors appeared to accept that, Akira knew Isfail was not as easily convinced. But he only kissed her temple and pulled her to her feet.

"We need to get you back to Green River," he stated, sending Nathon a sign before turning to Carelon. "Will you travel with us?"

"No. We need to report back to our protectorate. Everyone there will want to know that Lady Muro is safe." Carelon looked at Akira. "Will you stay at Green River, or return to the coast now?"

She looked at Isfail and saw indecision in his eyes. "We'll need to discuss it." She looked at Nathon, standing by the door. "Can the road up be cleared?"

"We'll send a work crew when the weather holds long enough," he replied, looking over to Carelon. "You're better at this than I am, Care. What do you think?"

The Mountain Shadows master ran a thumb along his jaw. "It's early in the season. As bad as it was, there probably wasn't a big buildup of snow yet. Get some force callers hitting in from both sides . . ." Then he winked at Akira. "Better yet, get the lady here on it."

Though Isfail laughed with the others, Akira felt the tension in the arm still around her.

"We'll send Lord Corcoran a message when a plan is decided on," Isfail stated. His brusque words were overlooked in his sincere gratitude as he thanked Carelon and his team for their fast response.

Within minutes, Akira was seated securely in front of him on Tempest, with Nathon and his team escorting them back to the safety of Green River. Her latest ordeal was over, but she wondered where the knowledge gained in a chance meeting would lead her, lead them all.

*W*as it fatigue, reaction, mixing with the security she felt when Ardan was with her? Akira only knew that the hours back to Green River passed in a blur. She dozed, safe in the arms around her. But she dreamed, shivering uncontrollably as she stood as if behind a shield, only able to watch as a little boy huddled, alone and terrified, between the raging madness of Arthon Baronan and the frozen indifference of a young Ana Karsh.

She jerked awake as Ardan wrapped his own coat around her, shifting her closer to his warm body. His smile was reassuring as he looked into her startled eyes. "Easy, my sweet. Just a dream, a bad one by the look of it, and no wonder after all you've been through."

Still groggy with exhaustion and distraught with the dregs of the nightmare, Akira tried to gain her bearings. "He was so lost, Dan, so pitiable. Poor child. How could they treat him so carelessly?"

"Who, Kira? A child in your dreams?" His voice soothed, but his eyes held concern as he studied her face.

"In his life," she murmured, closing her eyes once more. Grieving, Akira let the rhythm of the horse's gait rock her to sleep.

She woke in freezing dark while Isfail was shifting her to Nathon before swinging down from his horse. "I think I can walk," she told them, sounding hoarse and uncertain to her own ears. No wonder Ardan ignored her, taking her back into his arms, and carrying her through flickering torchlight where crowds of people pressed around in a jumble of anxious words that made little sense to her befuddled mind.

Now there was warmth all around, and light. She was lying on something soft as Ardan removed her outer clothing. Akira shuddered and he tucked a down-filled cover over her. She drifted, vaguely aware of strangers hovering about, healers, she thought hazily. Their voices mingled with Ardan's, worry and reassurance. She wanted to tell them there was nothing wrong, but her lips wouldn't form the words.

He lifted her against his arm, holding a cup of warm liquid to her mouth, encouraging her to swallow. An herbal tea, she recognized, and the sweetness of honey masking a bitter aftertaste.

Akira let sleep take her into dreams where familiar faces appeared in a mirror that held no reflection of herself, though she knew she was standing before it. One face became two, then three, though the third face was blurred and barely visible within swirling tendrils of smoke.

More mirrors appeared, reflected in the first, and all showed the faces that swam in and out of focus. Images bleeding back into the face of an old enemy, only to reform, reshaping that evil visage until it smoldered once more into one, then two, then three—while the sire drifted away in ashes and smoke.

*A*rdan was there when she awoke; sitting on the edge of the bed as he watched her eyes blink open. He stroked a tender hand over her cheek and smiled.

"Are you with me now?" he asked quietly.

"Thank God," Akira managed, love and relief flooding through her as she shifted to sit up against the pillows he arranged for her.

"I have been," he replied somberly, pushing strands of her hair away from her face. "You frightened me, Kira. I had you back, alive, after everything had frozen in me, then you just collapsed."

Taking his hand in both of hers, Akira tried to soothe him. "I think it all caught up with me once I felt safe—the stress of the blizzard, the absolute terror of being caught in the avalanche, then doing what needed doing to survive. I was so worried about Kilronan and his team, whether they were all right, and frantic thinking of you, what you'd go through if I wasn't found soon."

He grabbed her to him, his heart pounding against her. "I couldn't allow myself to feel, to think you'd been taken from me. Not again, Kira."

"I'm here, Dan. We're together," she whispered, pulling his face to hers for a long kiss. When she finally pulled away, she smiled ruefully. "But you probably would rather I bathe and find fresh clothing after all that."

Isfail chuckled, tweaking her nose gently. "You aren't anywhere near what I was when I got back from Ishal." He helped her from the bed, wrapping a thick robe around her against the room's early morning chill, despite the fire snapping in the hearth.

Akira walked to a window to see the overcast sky. Frost ferns swirled in icy beauty around the edges of the glass panes. She saw smoke billowing from chimneys, and recalled the phantom images of her dreams.

"Your dreams were uneasy, my sweet."

Startled by his perception, Akira only nodded.

"Does it have to do with what happened to you, or the man in the cabin?" When she glanced back at him in surprise, he met her eyes with questions in his. "I heard the way you shaded your answers, and it wasn't like you to allow a sick man to wander alone in such conditions. Who is he, Kira?"

Turning back to her own faint reflection in the window, Akira heard the strained patience in his voice and knew she had to trust him with all of it. Ardan had never failed her. It was wrong to hold the full story back from him.

She turned, clasping her hands in front of her. "I told you the truth, Dan. His name is Barash, I found him near death at that cabin and cared for him." As he gave her a long look, she continued wearily, "And I've encountered him once before, though I did not know his name then."

Akira walked slowly to a chair. "He was the man who attacked me in the meadow at Mountain Shadows before we came to Coroth for the Gala."

Raising her eyes, she met Isfail's astonished stare. Akira didn't think she'd ever seen him rendered speechless before. Then resisted the urge to apologize when, with one fast stride, he had her caged between his arms, bending over her with cold disbelief on his face, and fire kindled within those smoke-dark eyes. His voice sent icy chills through her as he spoke with hard-won calm.

"You spent days alone with a stranger who had previously tried to harm you . . . actually healed a known enemy." His voice rising now with every word, he went on, "Then let him walk away when rescue and reinforcements arrived. What the hell were you thinking, Akira!"

Pushing away from her with barely contained rage in every line of his body, Isfail stalked away. She watched him shake his head, running his fingers through his hair in obvious frustration.

"It's not that simple." Akira stood to face his wrath as he spun around to scowl at her. "Barash was acting on Ana Karsh's orders, both times." She flinched, seeing her mistake when Isfail paled.

"*Both* times?"

Holding up her hands, Akira knew she wasn't as prepared for this as she should be. Shaken, physically and emotionally, she wasn't handling this well.

"Please, Dan. I need you to listen."

"Oh, I'm listening!" he exclaimed. "I just can't believe what I'm hearing. What you've *finally* decided to tell me, *after* you prevented me from acting on it. After *you* chose to let a dangerous fugitive escape."

Isfail jerked away from her reaching hands and strode toward the door. Akira's heart trembled while she waited for him to walk out on her. But she saw him pause with a hand on the latch then lean his forehead against the thick wood panel.

"Kira," he said, with emotion reverberating in now quiet words. "You are my life, the beat of my heart. When I was told you'd been lost in that avalanche . . . I could not, would not, accept the possibility that I'd never hold you again."

"Dan," she whispered painfully.

Isfail turned to her. "I could not let myself feel, Akira. All I could think was I had to get out and find you. Do you understand that I could not survive believing you dead? That I could not face that again, after what happened in the Mors defense? And now to find that you deliberately placed your life in jeopardy, even denied me the chance to protect you from a proven enemy?"

His misery undid her. With tears burning her eyes, Akira ran to him, burying her face against his chest as his arms crushed her to him.

"I do know! I prayed you wouldn't hear of it until I was safe. It broke my heart to think of you grieving so once more. And it strengthened my own will to live, to fight for my life."

Akira leaned back, framing his beloved face with her hands. "Please believe me, Dan. I was never in any danger from Barash. Never. If I had even suspected he could harm me, he would be dead."

"Then why? Why, Akira?" Isfail slid his hands into the wild tangle of her hair. "We could have easily tracked him, taken him into custody, but you didn't tell us. You *let* him escape."

There was no denying it. She had deliberately given Barash a chance to escape once he'd slipped away. Now she sighed. "I'm not even sure why, Dan."

He took her hand, but when he tried to lead her back to the couch, Akira tugged him toward the bathing chamber. She had another reason to be grateful for his patience when he adjusted the shower temperature while she undressed, and filled the soaking tub while she cleaned up.

"Your bruises are looking better," he remarked as he disrobed and joined her under the shower to wash her back. "Green River's healers did a reasonable job."

"I heard them, and you, last night, though I was too groggy to really understand."

She took the time to formulate her thoughts until they were immersed in blissfully hot water with his arms folded around her. It wasn't his way to hold onto anger, she knew, and that was another thing to be grateful for.

So she told him everything she'd learned about Barash. Akira spared no details about the time in the cabin, or her perception of his conflicted emotions.

"And yours, Akira? You have your own thoughts and feelings about this man, this son of Baronan." Isfail turned her to face him, his face serious. "You sound like you pity him."

"I do," she admitted. "Perhaps it's hard to explain, or for you to understand. You're a strong man, an excellent man, who comes from a strong, loving family. You've made yourself into a powerful warrior and leader, and you've always known that base, that your family loved you and wanted the best for you. All your life," she said adamantly.

Isfail sat back, playing with her fingers as he studied her intense expression, and nodded. "And this Barash had the opposite, just as you lost the security of knowing your foundation, your family, at an early age. You feel empathy for his situation."

"Yes." Akira breathed a sigh of relief that he understood this much. "I know it's not the same, Dan. He never had anything, while I did have those I thought were my mother and father until

I was fourteen. It made a difference. I had friends, and Maran, even though my life tilted."

"Akira, he became an assassin for hire, someone who chose to harm in the service of an unstable, powerful force caller. Did he ever question that? Try to go another way?"

He watched her rise and step out of the tub, pulling the robe back on before turning to him with an empty expression on her very pale face. "What was I for all those years in the Ambassador Core? Following the orders and directions of those over me. I *chose* that career. I became their enforcer, their assassin. Was I different? I had more advantages, more choices than a boy unwanted from birth, abused by a psychopath and a madwoman, never shown love or compassion. Surviving by learning to fight and kill!"

Tears were pouring down her face as she ran from the bathing chamber. He caught her as she fumbled with the lid of her trunk, pulling her close when she tried to avoid his embrace.

"Hush," he murmured against her wet hair. "You've made your point, though I don't accept all your arguments. But I understand what you feel, my love. I think what you're trying to tell me is that this man might make the choice to be a better one. You needed to allow him that chance, just as you've given yourself that chance."

Burrowing into him with a sob, Akira nodded. There was more, and she would have to tell him. But she took the reprieve he offered when he encouraged her to come to the dining hall with him for breakfast.

Isfail knew there was more, just as he was beginning to accept that there was more to their shared Psyche heritage since they'd been formally bound. It went beyond the ability to mindsight with her that had strengthened over the years. It was more than being able to glean her thoughts from subtle body cues or a look in her eyes.

Did she know that he could almost *hear* her more intense thoughts? It required a deeper level of trust between them, didn't it? And it required a strong belief in each other, as well.

He believed in her, without any doubts, certainly more than she believed in herself. Her reasons for empathizing with this Barash had proven that once again. That she could compare herself with a criminal like that astounded him, even angered him. Yet, better than anyone, he knew that her career with the Ambassador Core under Most High Ana Karsh had left deep psychological scars.

Watching her now, as she discussed the possibility of getting up the road to Mountain Shadows with Nathon and some other Green River masters, it struck him. Maybe he should have more faith in her judgment about Barash's possibilities. Hadn't Ana Karsh been an evil destructive force in both their lives? Perhaps Akira needed to believe in Barash's ability to change in order to finally exorcise her own demons.

For one fierce moment, Isfail pondered over what he might do if Karsh's bastard son didn't step up to the challenge and somehow redeem himself.

Forty

Ishal, City of Tash'tric

It was too quiet, Aric decided. He rose from his bunk, dressing quickly, strapping on sheath and knives then sliding his sword into the back sheath. Before leaving his quarters, he scanned the shadowed grounds as far as he could see from his second-story window.

One of his men patrolled the perimeter wall of the old barracks on the northern outskirts of Tash'tric. The night was clear but the guard was barely visible in the flickering lights of torches bracketed to the inner walls. Aric guessed it was still a couple of hours before dawn. Still, some premonition of danger made his skin crawl, and he was a man who'd learned to listen to his instincts.

With only days before the national holiday, his unit felt the tension of anticipation. They'd learned that Dateh, using his private cult, The Bow, was planning to take over Ishal on the upcoming Day of Ishalion. Dateh had already cultivated his traitors within the Ishalian Parliament to support his coup, and his murderous supporters had been seeded throughout the larger cities.

Aric thought of friend and fellow commander, Gaios Shanow, who'd been able to move over twenty citizens out of immediate danger when his militia left for the north one week ago, ostensibly to subdue the Ishakans by order of the turncoat defense minister. But the minister and Dateh had miscalculated. Shanow was a loyalist, playing their game while smuggling innocents out as field camp support crew. By the time the rebels discovered the ploy, Shanow's troops would be in Ishakan territory, positioning themselves to defend the horse tribes, not attack them. Aric wished he could see Dateh's face when he found out that Shanow had foiled his plan to seize Ishakan lands.

Dateh's defense ministry was now openly investigating militia units suspected of loyalist leanings, including Aric's platoon, and the militia unit commanded by Rados Goden, based on the eastern edge of Tash'tric. They'd been reassigned from the central city barracks to the old perimeter installations. Probably to hinder their ability to defend the city, Aric decided.

Having lived through and fought against the first Baronan Rebellion, Aric had no illusions. Any soldiers suspected of loyalty to Ishal's true government would be arrested soon, and executed as examples to any citizens who might stand up to the usurpers.

Regardless, secret plans had been made before Shanow headed out. Aric and Goden would somehow lead their units out of Tash'tric before the holiday, and join Shanow's unit in Ishaka as soon as they could.

With the hairs on the back of his neck rising, Aric knew it was time. He had to get his men out before it was too late. Moving silently through cold dark passages, he opened the door to his captain's quarters. His mouth moved into a half-smile when he saw that Nolan was awake and already dressing.

"Get the men moving," Aric said quietly. "No lights, Nolan. Nothing that might alert the enemy."

"Yes, sir. We're mobilizing as planned?"

Nodding, Aric turned to the door. "Through the old orchards to the Westering Road. Regroup there. We'll take what we can. Full arms and the packs already prepared. You know where they're hidden."

Leaving Nolan already heading to the lieutenants' room, Aric ran lightly down the stairs. Within minutes, soldiers were saddling horses, preparing to leave Tash'tric. When his own mount was ready, Aric led the gelding to the smaller gates facing west, next to the stables. With the main gates facing a wide thoroughfare, where Dateh's watchers patrolled more openly in the past week, the idea was to leave as surreptitiously as possible, heading west into a rough stretch of abandoned orchards.

Inside the barracks, Nolan cleared the final ten-man bunkroom. He'd just started back out when one of the soldiers scrambling into gear said, "Where's Buret?"

Nolan and others looked toward the empty bunk.

"He probably went to the latrine," another soldier remarked while strapping on the sword sheath that crossed his back.

"Find him," Nolan said tersely. "Grab your packs and get to the horses. Now."

*A*ric gave the order and his lieutenants eased open the well-oiled gates. He nodded to the last guard on the wall, watching as the man continued his slow rounds for the benefit of anyone watching from outside the fortification. Signaling the go, Aric mounted his horse while Captain Nolan raised an arm to the hushed platoon forming up in the icy stable-yard.

The slap of boot steps had many looking toward the man running up the stone steps along the wall. He was carrying two lit torches.

"Stop him!" Aric barked.

The guard on the wall was already running to intercept. But the torchbearer had reached the top, raising the burning beacons high to cross and separate the flaming pitch in an obvious signal. Aric recognized the face in the torchlight.

It was Buret.

He swore as the guard fell to an arrow from beyond the wall, just as one of his bowmen took out the torch-waving traitor. But it was too late; flames lit the sky as burning arrows arced over the wall.

"Keep to the plan!" Aric called to Nolan as something battered the front gates with a resounding thump. "They'll try to cut us off. We go now."

He waited, crossbow cocked in his hand, focusing on the shuddering main portal while Nolan led the unit out and across a narrow road, into the old orchards beyond. Gesturing the two lieutenants to follow, Aric held his nervously prancing mount as a second volley of flaming arrows hissed through the air, streaking light through the darkness. Several struck the wood shingles, adding to the flames licking across the roofs. The hay stacked near the stables ignited as more arrows found a mark.

Hearing the sound of pounding hoof-beats, Aric saw that his lieutenants were galloping back to him across the road. "Go on!" he shouted, just as the main gates exploded inward.

Bowmen surged through the smoke and debris, arrows flying as if anticipating a yard full of newly roused soldiers.

Fighting to control his horse, Aric sent one then two bolts into the crowd before racing after his men. Hearing shouts behind him, Aric glanced back. In the light from the burning barracks he estimated twenty or more horsemen coming around the walls.

Damn! They'd almost made it away clean. Rage clouded his mind as he thought of the traitor in his unit. But an arrow whizzing past brought his attention back to the immediate danger.

Joining his lieutenants, Aric led them in a full-out race through the wizened trees. They caught up with the platoon and galloped through the darkness.

His jaw tightened as he saw what waited on the Westering Road just ahead. There would be no quarter given, Aric knew, from either direction. Drawing his sword with a ringing cry to arms, Commander Aric led his men into battle.

Forty-One

Ishakan Territories, Two Days Later

Commander!"

Shanow bolted up from a sound sleep, the first in weeks. He almost snapped at the soldier hovering next to his cot before he saw the alarm on his face. "What is it?"

"There's militia approaching, sir. Our scouts sent a runner. He says it looks like they've already seen battle, sir."

Buttoning his wool shirt before shrugging into a thick coat, Shanow reached for his sword belt. "Loyalists or enemy?"

"Not known, sir, but the scouts think they're loyalists." He followed Shanow out of the tent and into freezing darkness where more soldiers were mustering in the frozen slush of mud and snow.

Declan came toward them, leading two horses. "A second runner came in, Commander. He says they've identified Commander Aric and his men."

Stepping into his stirrup, Shanow swung into the saddle, signaling his men to follow.

They met up with the incoming loyalists about midway across the broad valley. Shanow could see that they'd indeed seen battle along the way, even in the predawn darkness. Some of the horses carried more than one man, other soldiers slumped in their saddles, from fatigue or injury, he couldn't yet discern. Some of the riders led horses with ominously still forms tied across their backs.

He saw his friend Aric at the front of the ragtag column,

243

leading a horse carrying a blanket-wrapped body draped across the saddle.

Calling orders and directions to his men to see to the newcomers, give aid to the wounded, Shanow trotted to Aric. "You had trouble, my friend." He was close enough now to see the blood on Aric's uniform; the sun edging up in the east showed the fury on his face.

"How many did you lose?" Shanow asked quietly.

Looking back at the body, Aric said in a rough voice, "Nineteen, including Nolan." He closed his eyes for a moment, his face tightening. "And one of my lieutenants. Good men all. They died fighting, died well in service to Ishal. I wasn't leaving them there for those—"

As Aric's voice broke, Shanow heard the grief every good commander feels at losing men, and he knew his friend was recalling the bodies impaled on spikes, or lashed to crosses, lining the streets in macabre display over ten years earlier.

Leaning out from his horse, he gripped Aric's shoulder tight for whatever comfort it might bring. "Let's get your men settled. We'll speak with the Ishakans about an appropriate burial ground." Shanow gestured toward the tribesmen who'd silently approached from the shadowed cliffs around them.

Declan brought one of them to Shanow. "Commander, this is Ton, a cousin of mine. He brings healers and men to help in whatever way the tribes can."

Shanow gripped the offered arm gratefully. "We thank the tribes for their compassion." After a brief discussion of needs and resources, Ton left to supervise his people, and send a message to the tribal leaders regarding a respectful burial for the dead.

The sun climbed higher as the camp accommodated Aric's militia, injuries were treated, and inventory taken of overall needs. With his men taken care of, Aric sat with Shanow, Declan, and Ton around a fire to give them the news. He spoke of the latest conditions in Tash'tric, and what little he'd seen as his militia had wound its way toward the Ishakan territories.

"We worried about getting across the river," Aric said wearily.

"But we found more true Ishalians away from the cities. They're preparing to make a stand against the usurpers. The bridge at Estas is still in their hands, and we were able to get some help there for the wounded."

He explained how they'd left the old garrison and why. "I had a traitor among us. Buret." Aric's voice was as unforgiving as the look on his face. "He got off a signal to the enemy just before we left."

"He's dead," Shanow said calmly, knowing Aric would have ordered it. "It sounds like your garrison had already been targeted for that night, morning, really. Your instincts saved the lives of your men," he noted, picking up a mug of tea, more to warm his hands than to drink. "You had them up and ready to evacuate, prepared to fight."

Nodding, Aric detailed their escape from the burning garrison, only to find an enemy roadblock waiting at the Westering Road. "Buret had apparently overheard the plans I'd only discussed with Nolan and my lieutenants, and he'd passed our escape route on. I don't know if Buret understood that we were joining you here, that we were going to defend Ishaka."

He shook his head. "I knew we couldn't pause a moment, with the enemy ahead and behind. We went straight into an offensive, caught them aback. They'd expected us to surrender, but we brought them a fight. My men outmatched Dateh's misbegotten Bow."

With a brief smile, Shanow raised his cup to him, took a long drink of lukewarm liquid. "Any word about Goden's unit?"

"No. I pray they weren't betrayed, had already left their garrison. Maybe they'll get here within a day or two."

"Yes," Shanow agreed, knowing it did no good to assume the worst before it was proven. Aric and Goden had planned to take different, circuitous routes out of Tash'tric, to avoid the enemy learning that they were joining Shanow in Ishaka. It could be two, even three more days before Goden and his men arrived, even if they avoided trouble.

"We brought what we could, but weren't able to pick up as

many supplies as I'd hoped, even in Estas. They were supportive, but also worried about looking out for their own needs if The Bow marches against us." Aric looked around at the well-ordered camp, despite the snow and mud. "We'll need enough to survive the winter, food for men and horses."

Shanow had reached that conclusion himself. They'd been lucky with the weather, so far. They'd only caught the edge of the latest storm, with the northern front blowing toward Caldala to spend its wrath. He already had Declan negotiating with the horse tribes, but they had little to spare even if they were willing. The Ishakans were going into their second winter holed up in the mountains, and they'd lost most of the grain and hay they traditionally cultivated in the broad valley. The Bow had set fire to the fields just before harvest, destroying precious food needed for their horses.

Though game was plentiful, hunting could become a risk if Dateh sent his men to harass them. Shanow had smuggled out as many winter supplies as he could without raising an alarm. Tents, blankets, dried foods, and so on, but he feared they would be woefully inadequate if the winter was a harsh one.

He looked at Declan and Ton. "Do the tribes have a good relationship with Caldala? You've told me that a Caldalan Psyche is a *Nah'Shalon*, Declan." Shanow saw Ton frown at Declan, who shrugged noncommittally. "Look, we're going to need supplies if we have to base here all winter. I would guess that the Ishakans might be running low after being driven out of their grazing grounds this year."

Ton said something in Ishakan to Declan, speaking low and urgently. Declan nodded and looked at his commander.

"Ton says his people are generous, but they are already carefully rationing what food they have to try and get their families and horses through the winter. They have plenty of blankets and warm clothing to share, and they can help us find better shelter in mountain caves around here."

"All right, thank you." Shanow nodded to Ton. "Tomorrow, we'll look into how we can contact Mountain Shadows Protectorate. It's the closest Caldalan fortification, if I'm remembering accurately."

Ton collected his people and went back toward the cliffs. Shifting closer to Shanow and Aric, Declan said quietly, "What about Commander Isfail? He offered to help if he could."

"And I believed him," Aric said tersely. "But Coroth is several days journey from here, and we'd need horses and wagons on that side. That's assuming we can convince the Caldalans to support us."

Shanow stared into the fire. "The first step is sending an envoy to Mountain Shadows to sound out the possibilities. We need to start now, before we're in a crisis." He stood up, emptying the dregs in his cup into the fire-pit.

"I want work details set up, alternate the men on watch duty, but don't relax the perimeter guards further out, in case The Bow does try something. I want men covering as much of our zone as possible, collecting dried grasses, grain, whatever is safe for horses to eat. And get hunting parties organized. Make sure to get approval from the tribes before anyone goes out, Declan."

As Aric and Declan walked away to get that started, Shanow turned to the west, looking down the narrowing valley that would end in a bowl rimmed by ancient granite cliffs demarking the border between Caldala and the Ishakan territory of Ishal. The lake there was called Lower Caldera Lake, he recalled, and had once been edged by a passable road leading into the neighboring country.

No more, he knew, but they had to find a way into Caldala.

Forty-Two

S tanding beside his horse on the edge of Lower Caldera Lake the next morning, Shanow looked across rippling water at a wall of jumbled slabs of stone. With sharp corners and edges too recently fractured to be smoothed by time and weather, or display the softening illusion of plants and lichen, it filled the ravine that had once been a land route into Caldala called High Pass. Ishal and Caldala had used it to move trade goods back and forth, and for land travel between the two countries.

Earlier this year, Akira Muro had—in a matter of minutes, by all accounts—shifted chunks of the granite ridge to block the pass. And breached the higher caldera wall of Lake Shisalla above to release the new waterfall that thundered into the lake, thereby defeating the deadly Mors invaders.

It was little wonder that some of his countrymen could be so easily led to believe that such a powerful force caller was a danger to them. He, however, knew that the biggest threat to Ishal came from ordinary people—people who craved power, control, and wealth.

His jaw clenched with anger knowing that the most dangerous enemies that had ever come from Caldala were Arthon Baronan, and now his son. The Ishalian Parliament had condemned its own citizens to two bloody insurrections by refusing to extradite Baronan when the Caldalan prince had formally requested Baronan's return to Caldala to face charges of mass murder.

No, it wasn't a force caller that had endangered the Ishalian people, or sought bloody dominion over Ishal.

Still, studying the evidence of one woman's ability, with the

248

impressive roar of two waterfalls filling the air, one feeding and one emptying the lake in front of him, Shanow could see how easily a skillful man with no conscience or honor could disseminate his propaganda of fear, and raise the shadow army known as The Bow to infiltrate two nations.

Torn from these reflections by the sounds of horses approaching, their hooves crunching through ice-crusted snow, Shanow turned to watch Commander Aric and Captain Declan riding out of the narrow canyon from their encampment. They looked around the snow-covered lakeshore filling the southeastern rim of the lake to the evergreens and granite bluffs that framed the bowl. He almost smiled when Declan hunched within his coat, swearing as a gust of wind sent icy droplets of mist from the upper falls swirling around them as they neared the bank.

"Mountain Shadows is the first village along the road from the old pass," Shanow noted by way of a greeting, his voice louder than usual to compete with the roaring water. "I expect their protectorate has warriors stationed on that ridge there. That's what I'd do. Can you make it up that, Declan?"

Declan's grin was cocky. "The wall's an easy climb."

"It's the walking on water that's tricky, eh?" Aric teased with wry humor.

"Not necessary." Declan pointed along the east side of the lake.

Shanow saw four men, dressed in the landscape-blending clothing favored by the horse tribes. Between them, they carried what looked to be a long, slender boat. It appeared the Ishakans had no objection to him contacting the Caldalans.

Leading their horses, the three soldiers strode quickly to meet them as they set the craft down at the edge of the lake. Shanow now recognized one as Ton, Declan's cousin. Declan gripped hands in the traditional greeting before introducing the two commanders to the other three men. Then he looked beyond the group, and immediately stood to attention with the tribesmen.

A woman was approaching on a powerful black stallion, her intense eyes focused on Shanow and Aric. As she came closer,

Shanow took in the details. Long black hair was pulled back into a high tail of ornate braids that draped the shoulders of a long-sleeved tunic of rich, sapphire blue. Over the tunic, she wore a vest of black wool embellished with intricate embroidery. Snug, black leather pants were tucked into black leather boots.

A formidable woman, Shanow thought, despite her fine-boned features and remarkable beauty. Those dark blue eyes held power in a face whose taut skin, the color of wild honey, was timeless. He couldn't even guess her age, though he knew something of her history. And knew she was young to hold her position of tribal leader of the Ishakan people.

When she reined her pure black stallion to a halt a few paces away, Declan dropped to one knee, his arms crossed over his chest, while the four Ishakans gave a deep bow.

She acknowledged their obeisance with a quick flick of her hand, but did not take her eyes off the two commanders. "You are Shanow and Aric." It wasn't a question.

The men bowed. Declan rose to his feet after a quiet word from the woman. He turned to his commander. "I am honored to present Syrai, *Sha'ala* of the horse tribes."

"It is indeed an honor to meet you, *Sha'ala Majera*." Shanow felt a flash of gratitude that Declan had carefully schooled them in Ishakan protocol as Aric gave his respectful greeting.

"Declan tells us that you and your soldiers have come to join forces with the Ishakan tribes. That you have chosen to stand with us against those Ishalians who would destroy the horse tribes and take our land for themselves." Syrai looked down on them with cool, curious eyes. "I have knowledge of you, Shanow, and you, Aric. You are worthy men who have reached positions of respect and power within your militia, and with your government. Why would you risk your freedom and your lives for the Ishakans, commanders?"

For a moment, Shanow just looked into those compelling eyes, seeing that this was a warrior who would only accept the truth. Well, he was a warrior who sought the truth and stood for justice.

He glanced at his fellow commander, receiving a nod from Aric to speak for both of them.

"We have served in the militia of Ishal's government our entire careers. In our early years, Aric and I believed that Parliament stood for just treatment and just laws for all the people in Ishal, including the Ishakan territories." He paused when Syrai lifted a finger.

"Yet my people have never had a representative, or a voice in your Parliament."

Shanow nodded. "That is true, and a serious misjudgment, looking back with the eyes of experience. Even so," he dared to emphasize, "the Ishakans were acknowledged as full citizens with equal rights back then."

Syrai nodded gravely, holding her silence.

"Unfortunately, we learned that many of those elected to serve in our Parliament were not immune to greed and flattery when Arthon Baronan was granted sanctuary in Ishal. Too late, we learned how insidious his control over Ishalian policies had become. We were blind to the building of his private army and the assassin cult he named The Bow."

Placing a hand on Aric's shoulder, Shanow continued. "We were captains when the first rebellion rose. We both lost family and friends in the battles to take back Ishal for its rightful citizens. We lived through those early atrocities, the torture and the crucifixions of innocent citizens in Tash'tric. It drove us to the loyalist underground to defeat the insurgents. And we vowed that it would never happen again."

"Yet here we are, Commander Shanow," Syrai noted grimly. "The Ishakans know that the government is ready to fall to this latest uprising, and Declan has reported that their leader is the son of the first Baronan. This Dateh appears to have built on his father's legacy. Perhaps he is more cunning and less driven by madness. A man who has planned thoroughly to manipulate the avaricious politicians to gain his ends."

She sat, still and upright, in her saddle, but her stallion tossed his head, as if sensing his master's mood.

"My people have been murdered, commanders. Families struck down as they returned to our rightful grazing territories after the evacuation to escape the Mors. This new enemy and his minions are attempting what the Black Death could not do, the annihilation of the horse tribes. Why?"

Shanow gestured for Aric to speak, stepping back as he began, "We've learned that some of the ministers have been compromised by the promise of gold, supposedly discovered here in the mountains of the Ishakan territories."

Now Syrai gave a bitter laugh. "Gold? I know of no substantial resources in our mountains, though there are gemstones of value." She shook her head. "Our true wealth is in our people and our horses."

"It doesn't matter if these rumors are true or not, my lady," Shanow interjected. "Dateh promises wealth and power. Whatever his personal goals are, he wants these lands."

"You may call me Syrai, commanders," she stated firmly, then looked at Shanow. "And what do you think his goals are?"

"I believe Dateh sees the strength of the tribes as a threat to his dominance over all of Ishal." He faced her calmly as her eyes blazed hot-blue fury. "I believe he targets the Caldalan force callers for the same reason. All of you who hold force ability are a threat to his ambitions. While he does not seem to have inherited his sire's insanity, he has retained the belief that force callers must be eliminated. We suspect that Dateh plans to extend his rule beyond our country."

Shifting in her saddle, she repeated, "Why do you risk yourselves to defend us? Why not spend your resources in the cities, fighting this Dateh and his Bow?"

Reluctantly, Shanow admitted, "The government and some of the militias are lost, too corrupted for the available loyalists to take back. Aric here barely made it out of Tash'tric, losing some of his men when Dateh's people ambushed them. Over the past few weeks, we've tried to remove as many innocents as possible, including our own families, from Ishal, at least from the areas that are now firmly in Dateh's control. He will publically take over leadership on the Day of Ishalion—tomorrow.

"We have one final reason for taking our stand here," Shanow stated with resolution. "The Ishakan people are part of our jurisdiction and we have a duty to protect the horse tribes, knowing that there has been an order put out for your destruction. My soldiers and I may die here, Syrai, but we will stand in front of the Ishakan people. Here, at least, we have a chance of winning."

For the first time, her serious mouth gave a slight smile. "Then my people will stand with you, Shanow."

Glancing at Declan, she spoke in quiet Ishakan, waiting for him to move closer before lifting an amulet hung on a black leather cord over her head. He bowed before reaching up take it from her as she offered it. Declan bowed once more, then stepped back to stand with the commanders.

Syrai touched the tips of the first two fingers of her right hand to her temple before sweeping the hand toward them, in what Shanow assumed to be a gesture of respect or farewell. Then she signaled the tribesmen who'd delivered the boat. To Shanow's surprise, the men each gave a piercing whistle as the *Sha'ala* dipped her head to the soldiers and guided her stallion back toward the east.

Four black horses cantered from the narrow belt of pines along the bluffs that formed part of the wall of surrounding hills. As they approached the Ishakans, the animals slowed to a trot. The men jogged to meet them, grabbing hanks of mane to leap into the saddles. Then they followed Syrai along the bank of the lake, and out of sight.

Aric let out a low whistle and said, "All right. That's a woman you don't cross." Turning to Declan, he asked, "Were those her bodyguards?"

Chuckling, Declan bent to examine the oars and ropes stashed in the boat. "Three of her sons and her daughter's man, Ton. They'd definitely defend her, but Syrai doesn't need their protection."

He straightened and showed them the amulet of polished

black obsidian held within a mounting where silver tracery formed the head of a horse, mane flying around it, encasing the volcanic glass. "Syrai said this was to show the Caldalans that the tribes support your request." Declan lifted it over his head reverently, tucking the amulet under his coat.

Taking a sealed pouch from an inner pocket, Shanow handed it to Declan. "You know what to do, what to tell the Caldalans, and this should give you the authority to negotiate for us. Their protectorates are honorable, so you shouldn't be in any danger of being detained before you have a chance to state your case. We'll have a lookout and runner here at all times. Try to signal from that ridge, near the old pass, once you've made contact. They must have warriors posted there. Then again once you've done what you can do and are ready to return."

"Yes, Commander." Declan readied the boat as he said, "Ton will be acting as liaison while I'm gone. The tribesmen will help however they can." Looking at Aric, Declan grinned. "Ready?"

"Well, if I can paddle a longboat, I should be able to bring this back." But Aric's expression wasn't as confident as his words. Shanow hid the smile that threatened.

"I'll be here with the horses," he noted calmly. "Just don't be all day about it."

Shanow watched them make their way against the currents stirred up by the waterfalls. So many uncertainties, he knew, in people, policies, in willingness to help strangers. He wished Declan well in this mission, one that could mean success or failure, even life or death, for countless Ishalians.

Forty-Three

Road Between Green River and Mountain Shadows, Caldala

*T*wo days after her rescue and return to Green River, Akira sat astride one of the protectorate's horses, looking at the slope of avalanche debris spreading over the road. Beside her, Isfail stood next to Tempest, discussing options for attacking the blockage with Master Nathon and the head of a work crew experienced in handling such problems.

Their voices mingled with the thoughts in her head and she recalled Carelon's teasing words about using her force ability. Shifting her gaze, she scanned the surrounding terrain. Overhead, a cold and cloudless blue sky contrasted with the blinding white of snow blanketing pale gray stone and sparkling on evergreen boughs.

"If this began to move," Akira said, interrupting the men's conversation. "What could happen around it?"

"My lady?" the elder crew foreman asked, seeking her meaning.

She looked at him with a half smile on her lips. "If I were to use force bolts on this, what could happen?"

She saw Isfail turn around, concern on his face. Nathon looked at her thoughtfully, apparently considering her words.

With sturdy arms crossed over a barrel chest, the foreman looked at the slide. Without looking back or saying a word, he held out a hand. One of his men hurried to him with a shovel and a pick. With just a brief glance at them, the foreman shook his head. Another man—no, Akira corrected herself, a woman—hustled forward with a long, heavy pole, sharpened to a wicked point at one end. Taking it, the older man stepped close to the mound of icy snow to give it several hard pokes at different points along its side.

"Not going to move easy," he muttered, giving it a few more thrusts, with mixed results in penetration depth. "Might not be able to shift this until a good thaw using my crew."

"What are potential hazards if I could get it started?" Akira asked.

Scratching stubby fingers along a stiff-bristled gray beard, the foreman said, "Wasn't that much build-up when this came down, and not a lot of snow since to rebuild the shelf." He walked over to the rim of the canyon to look back up the hillside. "Mostly kept to The Chute."

Now he looked straight into Akira's eyes. "I'd guess if you unplug this bottle, it'd just finish spilling over the edge. With luck, it'll take its tail with it. Best to move back, closer to the wall, in case we get some sideways slumping."

"What about other hazards in the debris, like boulders, trees?" Isfail cautioned.

The workman shook his grizzled head. "Not much of that here. The Chute empties near every year, so already swept anything like that clean. Might get some rock, I guess, breaking out over time."

"Where do you suggest I hit it first?" Akira asked.

Taking his sharp pole, he poked the snow near the drop-off. "Clear this, then see if the bulk starts to move. Try to take out her feet to make the weight shift down and forward."

She looked at Isfail and Nathon. Nathon had a look of anticipation in his dark eyes as he grinned. Isfail studied her a moment longer.

"I'll agree only if you promise to stop if you feel yourself weakening," he finally said.

"That's reasonable." She dismounted, handing her reins to Nathon, and waited while the others walked a little distance back down the road, closer to the cliff face. Isfail refused to leave her side and she only smiled at him.

Raising both arms, hands pointing at the target area, Akira felt the power that lived in her rise, hot and fast, to erupt as a narrow bolt of force energy from each hand. White chunks blew back while a large hunk of the avalanche lip hanging over the valley broke away.

She heard the crew raising excited voices behind them, moving closer as their desire to see what would happen outgrew caution.

Changing position to target more of the leading edge, Akira sent two more bolts cracking loudly into the still morning air. Another chunk toppled over the edge, followed by loud snaps and groans from the bulk of debris. Isfail placed a warning hand on her shoulder as the slide visibly shifted, sending small bits of ice rolling down the road.

Then the foreman was standing on Akira's other side, pointing a finger at a large crack that had appeared near the middle. "Put one there, milady. Maybe angle it so." He demonstrated with his own hand before stepping out of her way.

A single bolt snapped out, striking the crack and showering them with cold white particles. With a roaring whoosh, a good third of the pile broke away, its own weight aiding its slide into the canyon.

Cheers broke out close behind while the foreman pointed out another spot. "Can you hit that one hard, milady?"

He laughed with glee as the two bolts set off the main bulk. Grinding squeals and moans accompanied creaks and snaps as the remaining avalanche bulk began to move. It wasn't fast now, but it was steady.

They watched as tons of snow inched forward, gaining momentum as the weight behind pushed forward. Several minutes later, there was only a shallow tailing across the road, and they could see the far side.

"Wish Kilronan had known this was happening. Bet he'd

have been waiting right over there," Nathon commented with a chuckle. "I'd love to see his face over this one."

"Well, Lady Akira," the foreman began, grinning broadly. "I could surely use you on my crew, eh?" When she offered her arm, he took it in a firm grip before turning to his men.

"All right. Let's check above, make sure there's no surprises hanging up there. Then we'll clear the rest of this off the road."

The cheerful mood dimmed when they reached the body of the coachman, frozen in the remaining snow at the far side of the chute.

Isfail gathered Akira close, grateful it wasn't her body being carefully wrapped and loaded onto the work-wagon.

*T*he message sent by hawk from Green River had Mountain Shadows waiting for the first sign of them a day and a half later. The weather held clear and cold, and Osharon whooped loudly from his post at the gate when the first riders emerged from the trees.

In the time it took Akira and Isfail, escorted by Nathon's team, to arrive, villagers were lining the main road, braving the cold to greet them enthusiastically.

Though it slowed their progress, Akira was overwhelmed by the welcome. Isfail reached over to squeeze her hand, seeing her wipe away a few tears.

But it was Kilronan, pacing restlessly in front of the protectorate fortress while his team waited nearby that broke the shaky dam holding back Akira's emotions. Damning protocol, he ran to her horse, sweeping her down into a bone-crushing embrace as the others crowded around.

Nathon grinned, shaking his head.

Isfail laughed at the chaotic scene. His eyes sparkling as he watched Akira's tear-drenched face light up with joy as she touched each relieved face of Kilronan's team.

She was finally home.

Forty-Four

It took time to make it up the last stretch to protectorate administration. Kilronan finally had his team form a friendly blockade with Arla's, who'd run out to add to the welcome and laughingly encourage the villagers to allow Lady Muro to continue home now.

There were more embraces and welcoming shouts in the courtyard at administration, until a fiercely protective Gralla took command, bustling Akira and Isfail inside before any more disasters could befall them. Like a mother panther, she hissed when her husband, Lord Corcoran, bid her bring them into his private office.

"Evan, not now. She needs to rest!" But the patient determination on his face, and Akira's assurances, had her relenting. "Don't keep them long."

Corcoran kissed her forehead before enfolding Akira in a strong embrace. "You just cannot keep out of trouble, can you?"

Chuckling at that, Isfail sank gratefully onto the comfortable couch in the sitting area. Gralla stepped briskly out, coming back a short time later with a rolling cart holding a tea service, little treats, breads, and cheese. Taking a different approach, Corcoran pulled out glasses and his private reserve.

"I *won't* keep you long," he said, patting Isfail on the shoulder as he handed him a generous glass of whiskey. "Just long enough to set up a meeting or two tomorrow, after you've had a chance to get your bearings again."

Taking a seat beside Isfail, Akira smiled at Gralla as she

accepted a cup of tea. "It's good to be back. We can catch up on the news tomorrow."

"I'm sure there's a great deal to catch up on," Corcoran replied, settling into his favorite chair. "Fortunately, things have been quiet here, barring our anxiety over your situation, Akira." The brief tension that tightened his mouth over those recollections turned to a smile as Gralla laid a hand on his shoulder.

"But we hear congratulations are in order," he continued. "Once we learned you were safe, Kilronan finished telling us about your binding. We'd like to host a reception when you've had a chance to settle back in."

Isfail accepted for them, taking Akira's hand when she just sighed. "My lady is a bit weary, but I believe we'd both like to share our happiness." He winked at Akira when she squeezed his hand.

"We have other, less joyful, news to share," she reminded him.

"And I'm sure Kilronan has already talked about that too," Isfail said, meeting Corcoran's glance and slight nod. "But tonight is not for that. If it's all right with you, Lord and Lady Corcoran, we would retire until tomorrow."

Gralla sprang up. "Your residence is all ready for you. The fires have been lit, and I've made sure the kitchen is freshly stocked. Just ring in the morning when you're ready for breakfast."

"We can just go to the dining hall," Akira began, but Isfail brought her hand to his lips.

"Or we could enjoy a private breakfast to celebrate our first morning at home together." Isfail winked as Corcoran chuckled. "We would like to see Master Nathon and his team off, though," he amended.

"Yes," Akira agreed, taking his arm. "They were more than kind to me, and graciously insisted on escorting us all the way to Mountain Shadows. The wagon with our trunks should be here tomorrow."

"We'll see to that," Gralla promised, walking with them through the interior halls to open the back door to the guest quarters Akira had occupied since the early spring.

The scent of greenhouse flowers filled the room. Everything sparkled and Akira knew that Gralla and her staff had wanted to make their homecoming special. A bottle of sparkling wine was waiting in a silver bowl filled with snow. Two glasses stood ready next to a vase of exquisite flowers.

The older woman sniffed back tears when Akira wrapped her arms around her with a whispered, "Thank you, Gralla, so much."

When they were alone, and Isfail had gone to start the bath, Akira looked around the familiar living area, feeling residual tension slide away. Looking toward the bedroom, she tipped her head with a little smile.

Isfail was shrugging out of his heavy clothing with a sigh of relief when he saw Akira come into the bathing chamber holding two glasses of effervescent wine. Raising an eyebrow with a wicked grin, he took one, sipping as he watched her slowly undress.

*A*nother celebration was taking place in the protectorate recreation hall, with mugs of ale raised to anyone who'd had a part in bringing Akira and Isfail back to Mountain Shadows. Kilronan demurred, waving off the commendations with a smile, but enjoyed his teammates' laughter and cheer as they received their due. Carelon and his people weren't shy about accepting any accolades, while Nathon applauded his own team for their part in the rescue, and then made a grand show by stepping up onto a table to give a wildly embellished acceptance speech on behalf of Green River Protectorate.

Osharon appreciated it so much that he bought another round of drinks for all honored participants, clapping Nathon on the back when he stepped down from the table to cheers and applause.

"Good thing you're not based here, Nate," he proclaimed cheerfully. "I'd have too much competition."

Nathon laughed as Kilronan choked on the ale he'd just taken a drink of.

"See? Our good friend Kilronan agrees." Well into his cups, Osharon lifted his latest in toast.

Before Kilronan could form an appropriate answer, the double doors were shoved open and Cobon and his team entered.

"What's this then? Celebrating without us?" Cobon shouted. His team eagerly made their way into the crowded room while Cobon joined the table where Kilronan, Osharon, Nathon, and Arla sat.

"Glad to see us are ye then?" he rumbled with a wide grin, gripping Nathon's shoulder. "Haven't seen you in a while, Nate."

The Green River master just lifted his mug to him with a laugh. "They told me you were up at the pass."

"Just rotated out. Norli's team arrived a bit ahead of shift, lucky for us." Cobon took the mug of ale Arla handed him with a nod of thanks, then gave Kilronan's shoulder a punch. "Heard our lady and Isfail got in all right and fine after their adventures."

"Well enough," Kilronan replied. "We'll get caught up on news tomorrow afternoon at a senior masters meeting."

Grabbing a miraculously empty chair from a nearby table that overflowed with protectorate staff, Cobon winked at Mika there before spinning the seat next to Kilronan's. Straddling the chair as he eased his thirst, Cobon smacked his lips in pleasure before looking around the company. "I've got some news for you. We brought back a stranger with us tonight."

Osharon frowned at him. "What stranger? From the pass?"

Grinning, Cobon swiped the foam from his mustache. "Aye. Name's Declan, and he's come from a Commander Shanow, that one Isfail told us about." The grin moved to a scowl when Arla kicked him under the table. "What's that about then?"

Lifting her glass, she looked at him over the rim, nudging Kilronan who sat between them.

"I think Arla's remembering the details of that meeting more clearly than you seem to be," Kilronan said, also lifting his ale over his mouth.

"Oh, aye," Cobon said, finally getting the point. "Well, it's a boring duty, that, up on the ridge. And the winds are blowing cold. Who's up next?"

"Hey!" came Halen's voice behind him. "Where's my chair?" Arla's assistant master stood frowning, holding a pitcher of ale while his tablemates pointed.

Cobon let out a loud guffaw. "Forget it, lad. I'll buy the next round."

Forty-Five

When a message arrived early the next morning, Isfail found he would not enjoy a private morning with Akira after all. He handed her the note from Lord Corcoran, informing them of a new development.

"Captain Declan," she read aloud before looking into his eyes. "He was one of the men involved in getting you out of Ishal."

"Yes." Isfail sat down at the dining table, picking up the cup of tea she placed in front of him. "I cannot fathom why he's come to us over High Pass."

"It appears you won't have to wait long to find out since we're asked to join Lord Corcoran for breakfast."

Within the hour, they were walking into the private dining room within the administration complex. Gralla was showing Captain Declan the view of the miniature village out the large windows. Corcoran greeted Akira and Isfail before introducing the unexpected guest.

Declan surprised them all by going down on one knee. "It is a great honor, Lady Muro. My mother's people speak of you with the highest respect. If they had known I would have the privilege of meeting you, I know the *Sha'ala* and Commander Shanow would have sent personal greetings."

Uncomfortable with the veneration, Akira extended her hand to bring the man to his feet. "It is a privilege to meet one of the men who risked a great deal to save Commander Isfail," she replied gratefully. "It is truly my pleasure, Captain Declan."

Offering an arm with a welcoming smile, Isfail took Declan's

264

forearm in a tight grip. "It's good to see you again. Why the hell are you so far from Tash'tric?"

"Well," Declan replied with a wry smile. "That's the story and the point, I'd say." He glanced at Lord Corcoran. "We were just getting into some of that."

Over breakfast, which Declan wolfed down with obvious enjoyment, Lord Corcoran told Akira and Isfail that Cobon had reported in last night, relating how the protectorate teams on duty at the old pass had observed unusual activity in the lower caldera valley over the past few days. They'd watched as Declan and another man crossed the lake by boat, with Declan holding up a flag of peace.

"Cobon and the new man, Vardon, had their teams on alert," Corcoran informed them. "As senior master, Cobon made the call to let Declan climb the wall unimpeded. After some questioning, weapons check, and examining the letter Commander Shanow sent, Cobon decided to bring him to us."

Declan grinned. "Your master's thorough. He made me take off my clothes in your barracks up there, checking for any mark of The Bow. At least he's got a sense of humor I can get along with."

"Wait until Declan meets Osharon," Akira murmured to Isfail.

Though he chuckled at that, Isfail's thoughts took a darker turn considering the risk of Declan meeting infiltrators from Ishal. He waited through the man's explanation of what was happening just over the border, impressed by the alliance that had evidently formed between the horse tribes and Shanow's militia as he admired the workmanship of the pendant that the *sha'ala* had sent to support Declan's credibility as an envoy.

Handing the beautiful piece back to Akira for her to return to Declan, he caught her quizzical look.

"Something is bothering you," she said quietly. "You should share your thoughts if they concern Declan's mission."

Seeing everyone looking at him with silent expectation, Isfail leaned back in his chair. "First, I personally have no objection to helping Shanow, his cause, or the Ishakans. I'll support any feasible plan to provide them with supplies as soon as possible."

Meeting Declan's relieved look, Isfail went on. "My concern is that there's been no mention of potential risks in your mission, Declan. I'm not meaning the obvious logistical risks, which might be substantial, but the likely consequences if you were recognized by any of Dateh's infiltrators here in Caldala."

The shock on the soldier's face told Isfail that this had not been discussed before he'd been sent out.

"If there were spies here in Mountain Shadows, you mean?" Lord Corcoran's voice held acceptance of an unpleasant thought.

"Here, yes," Akira said, "and anywhere in Caldala. It would probably be best for Declan and his mission to be a closely kept secret." She held up a hand when Isfail and Corcoran began to speak. "If you're going to say that's impossible, I'll agree."

Settling back curiously, Isfail listened as she laid it out.

"Commander Shanow is playing a dangerous game at the moment; trying to hold up the charade that his unit is acting on Dateh's behalf against the Ishakans. It seems to me he could use as much time as possible to secure his position and consolidate reinforcements." Akira looked at Declan and got his nod.

"If Shanow's real plans can remain a secret until winter prevents an easy offensive by Dateh's followers, it gives the loyalists and the Ishakans more time to plan a defense for the spring of the following year," Isfail added.

"Yes," Akira agreed cautiously. "Assuming he can maintain his men in fighting condition over those lunams. That requires adequate shelter and food for men and horses."

Declan leaned forward eagerly. "And that's why I'm sent to you. The Ishakans are confidant that they can help us with shelter, clothing, and so forth. It's food, more for the horses, I think, that could be a problem. We can hunt and fish, although grain for bread and dried fruits would be welcome."

Lord Corcoran brought up other logistical concerns. "Assuming we can arrange the needed supplies, there's still the issue of delivering them. Akira knows better than anyone here how dangerous and unpredictable the road to this village can be in winter. We use sledges and sleighs to move goods if the weather is calm enough and there's little danger of avalanche. When the pass was open, there were winter traders who'd risk the weather."

"And then there's the issue of getting the supplies off the ridge and across the lower lake," Akira finished.

"I think we can work with the tribes to build some sturdy rafts," Declan announced eagerly. "What about lowering parcels with a system of ropes and pulleys?"

The group discussed ideas for a little while, until Akira returned to the security concerns. "I think it would be best to avoid any discussion of Commander Shanow's militia. Declan, if asked, you could use your Ishakan heritage to support a concern for the horse tribes and their very real predicament."

"But I've already spoken with Masters Cobon and Vardon," he replied anxiously. "Can they be trusted?"

"I believe so," Lord Corcoran said firmly. "I will speak with Cobon myself this morning." But he looked at Isfail and Akira with a grim expression on his face. "It may be too late, though. Three teams have heard of it, since Team Norli was certainly told of it when they relieved Cobon's team. Even if we're not compromised, people can't help but talk about anything that breaks the routine. And most of the protectorate celebrated Akira's safe return in the recreation hall last night. I'm sure Cobon and his team joined in."

"We'll just have to deal with what comes," Akira stated calmly.

That served to end their breakfast, with plans for Declan to share the midday meal in a few hours with Isfail and Akira. The afternoon would bring the meeting with the senior masters.

In the antechamber behind the dining room, used by serving staff to plate the food sent from the kitchens, Chef Juniro surreptitiously watched the diners move from the table and leave the room. Nerves jangled his usually jovial nature, upsetting his life as much as his daughter Nina's failing health once had before Lady Muro had cured her.

Juniro eased back from the door he'd deliberately left ajar when he'd heard that name, one that dragged him back to the misery of those final days in Ishal, when he'd been a cook for the Ishalian Militia. The life he'd worked so hard for here in Mountain Shadows, the contentment and community so important for his daughter, was it all about to be ruined?

He jumped as his staff hustled by, ready to clear the tables and clean the room. Taking a deep breath, Juniro pasted a smile on his round face, focusing on a normal routine.

There would be time enough to decide what must be done. But an image of a hard, solemn face flashed through his mind, with the memory of a woman's heartbroken weeping. Shame flashed through him as he remembered what he'd done.

It had only taken that mention of Shanow's name to remind him of the betrayal he'd tried to put behind him.

Forty-Six

Sometimes Isfail wished he didn't understand his wife so well. Maybe then he wouldn't feel this concern about what she might do. He watched her pace the living room of their quarters, obviously thinking through everything that had been said over breakfast and evaluating all possible solutions.

"Akira."

When she stopped pacing to look at him, Isfail took her hands in his. "I'm going to ask you for something. Understand that I'm asking as your partner, your husband, and the man who cannot live without you." He smiled at the way her brow furrowed in confusion. "I need you to promise me that you will not commit to joining the Ishakan defense at this time."

He saw the puzzlement in her eyes while he said, "We both have substantial financial resources to help support them over the winter, and can add our influence in soliciting aid for the loyalists and the Ishakans. Between us, we can do a great deal to help them, and we can do that without waiting for politicians to spend endless hours debating over it."

She studied him for a long moment, her face so serious he wished he had a solid ability to read her mind.

"I will agree to that, Dan. As long as you will agree to keep an open mind when there comes a time when I feel I can do what's needed by joining the defense."

He'd have to be content with that, Isfail knew.

She wrapped her arms around his neck, making him smile again. "I'm going to exercise Kahshara and let Spirit have some flight time. You could get Captain Declan and meet me at the big paddock."

"I can do that," he agreed more cheerfully.

Leaning against the paddock fence later that morning, Declan kept his eyes on the woman and the horse, moving as one unit while they went through the series of obstacles. "That's a fine pairing, though it still amazes me that the tribe let an outsider have that mare. She's the epitome of her breed. I suppose Lady Muro is the same."

Isfail met the young man's searching look. "Akira is everything you've heard and more." He stopped before expressing his own fears that his wife's abilities would draw her into another country's conflict again. "Did you happen to see Kane Kalronan, now that you're acting as liaison with the horse tribes?"

Declan shook his head. "My cousin Ton is bound to Kane's daughter. When I relayed your message to Ton, he told me Kane was leading a hunting party deep in the mountains, and looking for better range for the horses come springtime."

Perched beside Isfail on the paddock top rail, Spirit fluffed her feathers, making querulous twitters before tugging at her jesses with her beak.

"Annoyed that you're left out of the fun?" Isfail questioned, running a leather-gloved finger over her head. Relenting, he let her step onto his gauntlet and lifted his arm, sending her soaring into the sky.

The men watched as the falcon stroked up on strong wings before turning to stoop in a breathtaking rush toward horse and rider. They heard Akira's laughter as the bird spun about her with the swift dexterity of her species.

Later, enjoying a private meal in their quarters, Declan answered more specific questions about his militia unit and the situation with the Ishakans. For now, Isfail thought, they were in good enough condition to ease Akira's concerns and sense of duty.

He'd do all he could to keep it that way.

*L*ord Corcoran asked Isfail to lead off the senior masters' meeting that afternoon, giving any news from Coroth. After quick verifications of the information Kilronan had already reported, he told them of the latest development.

"I stayed behind Akira and Kilronan's team to keep a meeting with a potential informant," Isfail began before looking at Akira. "A woman, it turns out, as Akira had predicted. She prefers to keep her name secret at this time, so I'll just call her Captain, if I may."

Kilronan lifted a hand a few inches from the table. "Is she a captain?"

"The captain of a small trading ship," Isfail said with a brief nod. "I gathered that most of her trade is legitimate, but she's been making extra profit transporting people from Ishal over the past five years. In and out of Caldala, mostly, but some went to Kuldor, Mildrath, and the island nations."

"Sounds like Dateh's been seeding his ambitions," Cobon muttered.

"Possibly, but this captain told me her passengers have been traveling to and from Caldala exclusively for the past two years. Her impression is that they're well organized, but an odd assortment of characters. Some are well educated, while others seem barely literate, from different backgrounds and places. For the most part, they've been no trouble, but tight-mouthed about their mission or purpose."

Isfail paused, looking at Lord Corcoran. "I sent a full report on this to the prince by secure courier. I expect some response whenever the next courier run makes it here."

"How did you leave things with this captain, and why did she decide to talk about this now?" Akira asked.

"Commander Toth and Chief Oshulta accompanied me to the pub for the initial meeting. They sat apart until I made the contact and decided the captain was receptive to feeding us more information. She was willing to meet them, and will now contact Toth whenever she feels she has something of importance to pass on." Meeting Akira's eyes, Isfail said, "Rena convinced her to talk to us. As you'll hear shortly, the captain has developed some qualms about her questionable shipping in recent lunams."

He took a long drink from the glass of water before him. "She told me there have been troubling reports out of Kittric recently. A brother of hers is first mate aboard a pirate vessel that answered a call out of Ishal—for any ships and crews interested in guaranteed gold, and the chance at a grand sea battle against all who oppose them."

Osharon scoffed at that. "Come on. Even pirates aren't that stupid. Caldala's battle fleet alone could stand against them, and Orsha has one of the finest fleets in the island nations. There can't be that many pirate ships across the seas, and they're all for themselves, not a coordinated group of fighting men."

"A fact that is apparently coming to a head in Kittric, according to this informant. Her brother's captain and crew decided the promises of gold weren't secure enough to put up with the tyranny of The Bow running the operation there," Isfail told them.

"He actually said 'The Bow'?" Akira asked.

"She says he did, and evidently he's lucky to be able to say anything. The ship weighed anchor one night, on the dark of the moons, and sailed from the harbor, but not before taking a couple of balls from the cannons at the harbor mouth. Fortunately, the Kittric garrison was caught by surprise and damage wasn't crippling." Isfail looked around the intent faces. "The brother's ship was the first, and maybe last, ship to leave Kittric voluntarily. He got a message to his sister, warning her to steer clear of Kittric and anything to do with Ishal or The Bow."

Lord Corcoran looked thoughtful. "When did this happen?"

"About two lunams past."

Declan lifted a hand to be recognized. "Did she give you any details about what's happening in Kittric?"

"Only what I just told you. She did agree to try and find out more from her brother. They were to meet in their home village on Kilra later that lunam. Apparently her brother is rethinking his life as a mate aboard a pirate ship."

With no more questions forthcoming, Isfail ended by saying, "I sounded her out on the possibility she'd be willing to sail into Tash'tric as a legitimate trading vessel. We might be able to make use of that kind of access to real news sometime in the future."

Akira nodded. "What was her answer?"

"Not likely, but she'd keep her ears open for a captain who might be willing to work with us, if needed."

With that, he nodded to Lord Corcoran, who asked Declan to bring the masters up to date on his mission. As privately advised, he emphasized the need to support the Ishakan tribes, adding that this was the second winter they'd been forced into the mountains, and off their traditional over-wintering territory. Added to that, there was the loss of most of their crops to burning by the enemy.

Akira listened with half her attention to the ensuing ideas and logistical planning. Between Isfail's connections and Lord Corcoran's planning and organizational skills, she had confidence that resources would be supplied to their allies in need. Now she focused the rest of her thoughts on military strategy.

Between Isfail and Declan, she had some idea of Commander Shanow's skills, and knew they were impressive. Through her own dealings with the horse tribes, she believed they could and would mount a formidable defense against Dateh's Bow. How could she contribute to that defense from afar? Declan would be returning to his unit when Osharon's team left tomorrow to relieve Vardon's team at the pass. They'd all agreed that minimizing his time here reduced the possibility of any spies recognizing him.

Silently, she began to compose a response to Shanow's original request for Akira Muro to join the loyalists in defending the rightful citizens of Ishal.

Forty-Seven

*I*n the lunam that followed Akira and Isfail's return to Mountain Shadows the couple settled into winter in the high mountains. Neither one had actually spent a full winter season in such severe conditions, nor lived in a small village, so there were quite a few adjustments to challenge them.

There were times when Isfail enjoyed the remarkable scenery, the more relaxed pace of life, and the leisure to read a blizzard-howling day away in the comfort of the snug quarters the protectorate provided. Then there were others where he chafed at the inability to go out most anytime to ride his stallion, run beside the sea, or train with other soldiers.

Though Akira was better at concealing her frustration, he knew she was too active a soul to be content with a sedentary life for long. Fortunately, a pleasant afternoon with friends at *The Boar and Panther* provided a remedy for the problem of being housebound for several days at a time.

"So you're bored." Cobon chuckled before draining his first mug of ale. "I wondered how long it'd take for retirement to chaff at you." He lifted his chin to Arla, with a laugh in his eyes. "Who won the wager, then?"

"Kil," Arla replied easily, lifting a hand to Jor.

Cobon swore good-naturedly. "Should've been me, lass. I've known him a lot longer."

Arla grinned as she received a small pouch from Jor and handed it to Kilronan. "Then you should have picked today, not tomorrow."

Jor laughed with the rest as he put a full bottle of whiskey on the table, along with several short glasses to toast the winner, before returning to the bar.

"Is that what you do up here?" Isfail asked with good humor. "Wager over every little thing?"

Kilronan winked at Akira. "No, just the important ones. It's a small way to amuse ourselves in the slow season." He paused to lift his glass with the group. "Of course, we've got more to interest us this winter."

"Aye," Cobon joined in. "It's not just you, our resident royals." He guffawed when Akira choked over that. "No, we've got two new protectorate teams based here to help with border guard. Have to keep an eye on them, train them up to Mountain Shadows standards."

Pushing back her chair a little to stretch out long legs, Arla considered the last finger of whiskey in her glass. "At least they're all mountain bred. Some transfers from Cypress Springs and Three Falls in Marca's team, and we're lucky to get Nathon and his full team from Green River. Lord Georen was generous there, releasing a proven senior master and a strong team."

"Lord Corcoran did some impressive negotiating," Kilronan said, with a look at Isfail. "And I suspect there were some equally persuasive incentives offered by the House of Coroth."

Isfail grinned while Akira raised an eyebrow. "I heard Green River is also breaking in two new protectorate teams, of their choosing," Isfail informed them. "But it was Georen's and Nathon's choice in accepting the offered transfer, and Corcoran's of course."

"However it was done, Nathon's team is a welcome addition," Arla stated. "And Marca, out of Cypress Springs, is a strong master. It's good to have another senior who's a woman."

"Good thing Mika didn't make the cut again. You'll be outnumbering us men before we know it," Cobon teased, affecting a sorrowful manner before calling to Jor. "Could we get another bottle for the table, Master Kellen?"

Heavy snowfall had made for a slow afternoon, leaving Jor with little to do but take inventory and update his books. He brought over the bottle himself again, leaving his staff free to finish preparing the evening food offerings. "And it's glad I am to be seeing protectorate additions. You warriors aren't afraid of a little snow, doesn't keep you from heading to me pub of an afternoon."

Unsealing the new bottle, he proceeded to pour out. "How're the supply deliveries to the Ishakans going, then?"

Isfail took that one. "As smooth as the weather makes possible. Fortunately, Caldala had ample surpluses over the last two years, so it's no hardship to provide feed for the horses, and supplement the Ishakan people's needs." He took a drink, appreciating the quality of Kellen's stock. "Coordinators have been established at each stage of the process, ready to take the next step whenever the weather opens up enough to move goods on."

"Already made the first delivery," Cobon noted. "The tribes worked out some clever wide rafts to accept the bales and bags sent down by ropes. We'll get a better pulley system up as soon as we can. And it'll be easier once the lake freezes thick enough to pull sledges across."

"That's good then. Maybe you'll pass on that I've some kegs of ale I'm willing to donate." Jor glanced at Arla with a smile and returned to his ledgers.

"Thanks, Jor. We'll do that," she replied.

"I have an idea that might suit the two of you," Kilronan said, folding his arms on the table as Isfail and Akira looked at him. "Come work out with us. Akira's practiced on the protectorate grounds, and trained my team before the Mors defense. The whole protectorate could benefit from working with both of you, and give you something to occupy your time and keep sharp. I'm sure Lord Corcoran would approve it."

Arla and Cobon leaned forward with avid agreement.

"No doubt," Cobon said eagerly. "But even if he didn't, I'd volunteer for it on my own time."

"We all would," Arla seconded. "And there's the indoor arena where the horses are exercised; we could make use of that during really bad weather."

With enthusiastic approval all around, Isfail felt as if the long dark lunams ahead had just brightened.

*L*ater that night, after Jor had turned the shift over to one of his bartenders, Arla stood looking at the portrait that dominated the elegant little parlor in Jor's house behind the pub. She'd admired it many times over the years. The woman represented there was lovely, with humor and kindness captured in the painted eyes. The little girl, Jor's daughter at two years old, looked happy. Arla once again thought it was a shame that Jor hadn't allowed himself to be included in the portrait.

Within that very year, Lila Kellen was gone, lost with the ship carrying most of her family to a binding celebration on a nearby island. Jor had stayed behind to take care of their daughter. After the loss of his wife, a heartbroken Jor had emigrated to Caldala and Mountain Shadows, where his sister lived with her family.

"She was a bonny lass," he said from behind her.

Turning to him, Arla kissed him lightly on the mouth. "I know. It was a terrible loss for you, but you've been the best father, and you've made a good life here for the two of you."

"Aye," Jor replied, taking her hand in his as he continued to study the images in the gilt frame. "But sometimes I lie awake, imagining the life we would have had if the sea hadn't been so cruel."

As Arla stood silently, allowing him time with his thoughts, he seemed to shake away the sudden mood and turned to lead her to the small table where a tea service was set out. She glanced at him, perplexed, when he seated her with unusual courtliness. Jor was unfailingly kind and courteous, but usually with the casual cheer and ease he put to good use in his pub.

More comfortable with less elegance, Arla wondered what his serious demeanor portended. Taking the teacup he passed to her, she waited for him to speak. When he finally met her eyes, she tipped her head curiously.

"We're good friends, aren't we, darlin' Arla?" Jor began, reaching over to place a large hand over her free one. Without waiting for an answer, he said, "And we know where we stand with one another, don't we."

Nodding, Arla chuckled. "If you're leading up to ending our affair, my friend, all this state is unnecessary. We've enjoyed each other in bed—and out of it," she added with a sly glance that made him grin. "But there were never any commitments."

His hand tightened on hers. "Ah, lass, you've been the brightest joy in my life these past three years. I've been mightily tempted to ask you for that commitment, but it wouldn't be right. For either of us."

Now Jor's eyes were sad and serious. "We neither of us has an unclaimed heart. My Lila holds mine still, and yours yearns for Kilronan." When she just raised a skeptical eyebrow, Jor smiled. "No, you've never said a word, but a publican has a sharp eye and curious mind."

Patting her hand, Jor sat back and swallowed his tea, the delicate cup out of place in those workingman's hands, though he handled in with natural care. "Now, were I a selfish man, I could ask for your hand and, if you agreed, I'd be pleased and proud to have such a woman by my side through the rest of my years. But I've many more years behind me than in front of me, my darlin', and you deserve a young man with a full heart to give."

Her lips tipped up into a rueful smile. "Your age makes no difference, certainly not in your talents as a lover. Besides, Kilronan doesn't have a full heart to give me, even if he looked my way."

Jor linked his fingers with hers. "That may be so, for now, Arla. He's still grieving a bit for the loss of his first love. Akira chose another man, another good man. That's something of a blow to his ego, as well as his heart, but he handles it well enough."

"Most times."

He laughed as Arla's eyes danced, both remembering Kilronan's drunken debacle when Isfail first came to Mountain Shadows and claimed Akira's love.

"Well, as I said, I've a sharp eye and ears enough. It's clear to me that he's well on his way to a mended heart, and that's a sign I've been looking for."

Uncomfortable with this discussion, Arla shook her head. "Jor, if you want to end our relationship, just tell me. Don't try to push me at a man who's never really looked my way." She sighed when he took her hand in both of his, his eyes full of compassion when she finally met them.

"I'm not pushing you at him, darlin', just clearin' the path. And if he's not the man you want or need, there's plenty of young men, includin' the ones newly come." Jor tapped a finger against her down-turned lips. "No sulking there, lass."

That got a rise out her. "I'm hardly sulking." But she had to laugh when he gave her a cheerful wink. "All right, you've made up your stubborn mind. But you'll miss me in the long cold nights, old man."

Jor roared with laughter, standing up from the table to pull her close. "Ah, that I will, lass, and be cursin' the day I let good sense and a knowin' of what's right make decisions for me."

Forty-Eight

Winter Solstice

The opening door brought a gust of frigid air that had Akira pressing down the delicate strip of paper that wanted to take flight in that winter-crisp wind. She looked over as Isfail quickly closed the portal and turned to shed his thick, sheepskin-lined coat.

She straightened in her chair with a welcoming smile as he walked to her. Glancing at the small boughs of fragrant evergreen he carried, she asked, "Where did you get those?"

"Gralla," he answered, laying them on the table where she sat before leaning down to capture her warm lips with his cold ones.

Laughing when he pulled her up and into a close embrace, Akira shivered as Isfail pressed his chilled face against her neck. "Must you!" she exclaimed, though she wrapped her arms around him to share her warmth.

"Yes, I must," he replied with a wicked grin. "If I'm expected to spend our winters in this ice fortress, I expect some compensation." With that he swept her off her feet and headed for their bedroom.

Lounging in a comfortably hot soaking tub—after a satisfying interval enjoying the more sensual pleasures of his wife's company—Isfail watched Akira comb out her glorious hair. "Now this is the perfect way to spend the last day of the year," he drawled lazily.

Akira's lips quirked as she met his eyes in the mirror's reflection, saying, "And how would you spend the first day of the year?" His slow grin had a laugh bubbling up. Setting down the comb, she rose and faced him. "Exactly."

Isfail left the tub, taking the thick robe she had ready for him. "And there's to be a dance in two days, the first to enjoy in the New Year. Tell me more about this solstice celebration tonight." He followed her into their bedchamber, settling on the edge of the rumpled bed to watch her dress.

Sitting on the padded bench, Akira pulled on warm leggings and a thin, knit sweater that would provide warmth under the more elegant velvet gown she'd laid out for the service celebrating the turn of the year.

"I've been told it's a mountain tradition to bring in the year. Brother Timmel will give a short service in the temple an hour before midnight, ending with everyone forming a procession out to the meadow. We must remember to bring the evergreen boughs with our wishes tied to them."

"Ah," Isfail said. "So that's what that tower of wood is about. There will be a bonfire."

Akira nodded, wrapping herself in her own robe until it was time to dress for the midnight service. "People walk out and circle the bonfire in a spiraling single line. A child is usually chosen as the one to light the fire, then the people wind about, tossing in their evergreen bough holding a secret wish or desire they'd like fulfilled in the coming year."

He pulled her onto his lap as she started by him. "And what is your wish, my sweet?"

"If I told you, it might not come true," Akira stated primly before kissing him.

Chuckling, Isfail released her, setting her on her feet once more. "Well, I better see about my own wish. Of course . . ." He stood, cupping Akira's chin in his hand. "I was granted my dearest wish in the year passing. You."

Tears filled her eyes as Akira wrapped her arms around his neck, looking into those warm gray eyes. "Maybe that was why I had such a difficult time thinking of a wish, my love. I already have my heart's desire."

*T*here was nothing quite like a still winter's night, Arla decided, looking up at the black velvet sky adorned with countless stars. There to the east, a cloudlike river of stars created their own magical flow over the peaks of the mountains rimming the valley. It all seemed to hang just overhead, as if she could reach up and pluck one of those glittering ornaments from the sky. She found her hand stretching high and laughed to herself at the foolishness of the gesture.

Kilronan stood on the edge of the training field, bewitched by that moment of wonder and levity from a woman who seldom revealed such carefree frivolity. Then she became aware of him, though he hadn't moved or made a sound. He could see her body stiffen, feel the embarrassment at being caught in an unguarded moment.

"Kil." Arla hoped the night was dark enough to hide the blush that burned her face. Damn it, she thought, when he walked toward her. Damn it!

She felt a little better when she saw him stuff his hands into his coat pockets—something he always did when he felt awkward.

Now he stopped beside her, and looked up at the star-washed sky, his long white hair pulled back in a tail that seemed to glow in the dark. "Beautiful," he said, with a trace of . . . something she couldn't really define.

They stood for some moments in charged silence. Then Kilronan cleared his throat. "I was heading for the perimeter trail, taking the long way around to the temple." Tipping his head back down from scanning the night sky, he looked at her with a slight smile. "Could use some company to see out the year."

Arla laughed. "Been a hell of a year."

"Oh yes."

Matching each other's strides, they broke a new path through fresh snow, in easy conversation once more.

After the temple service, moving with the crowd toward the long meadow spreading out from the west gate, now joined by Cobon and Osharon, Arla bumped her shoulder against Kilronan's. "Where's your wish bough?"

Chuckling, he looked at her empty hands, a contrast to the evergreens their friends waved cheerfully above their heads. "Where's yours?"

"Couldn't come up with a particular wish, I guess."

He nodded. "Same here. The outgoing year was so intense, I think I'd just wish for less drama in the coming one."

Beside him, Osharon snorted in amusement. "Sure, that's going to happen. We've got poisoned arrows aimed at our backs, and a war in Ishal they're trying to drag us into. Sounds like plenty of drama to me."

"Always the optimist," Arla proclaimed. "Shut up, Shara. Let's see out the year without all the doom and gloom."

Kilronan laughed and threw his arm over his best friend's shoulders. "It's not your style anyway. Grab a pretty girl to go down the line with and enjoy it."

With laughter restored, they all took places in the stream of people crunching through snow in a wide spiral around the spectacular bonfire. The people of Mountain Shadows clapped and cheered as boughs were tossed to burst into flames, sending fragrant smoke wafting hundreds of hearts' desires into the velvet and diamonds sky.

Forty-Nine

High spirits prevailed over the first days of the new year, culminating with the annual dance called The First Turning of the Year. An event that almost everyone came out for, and looked forward to in the frozen days of winter. The town hall was decked out in bright banners and hanging decorations that turned in any breeze, catching the light of countless lanterns.

With so many people packed into the building, there was little need for the fires in the big stone hearths that bracketed the long gathering hall. Yet, somehow, the center of the room was kept free for the dancing inspired by a group of lively local musicians.

Kilronan laughed with Cobon when Osharon spun Arla into the whirling dance.

"I forget what a fine-looking lass our Master Arla is between festivals," Cobon said, sounding wistful, his chin resting on one large hand. "What's it about a woman in a fancy dress that makes a man forget the warrior inside her?"

That got another laugh out of Kilronan even as his brows drew together in amusement. "How many of those ales have you had, my friend?"

"Ah, you're a cool one then, Kil, if you don't appreciate what a pretty picture our Arla makes tonight." He sat back with a grin. "I suppose your eye's been blinded by our Lady Akira."

Against his will, Kilronan's eyes latched on the woman in question, who stood beside Isfail, the man she'd chosen over him. Her snowfall hair was caught up into a cascade that poured in curling luxuriance down the back of a high-necked gown of midnight-blue velvet, trimmed in sparkling silver embroidery, with delicate white lace at neck and wrists. The elegant dress was simple in cut yet stood out among the elaborate creations of the mayor's wife and her entourage, the wives of the few wealthy Mountain Shadows residents.

Most of the village women wore the colorful dresses whose patterns of embroidery and embellishment were handed down through mountain history. He waved a greeting to Ala Kellen, who flashed a smile as bright as her pretty traditional dress as she twirled by in Eron's company.

Continuing to scan the dancers, Kilronan chuckled as he saw Asura—and didn't his second-in-command look lovely—trying to coax new team master Vardon onto the dance floor. His friend Nathon, never a shy one, took advantage of Vardon's hesitation and swept Asura away in his own arms.

He heard the final strains of the folk song as the musicians finished the exuberant piece, and watched Osharon lead a laughing Arla back toward their table. Kilronan realized he had forgotten, maybe never seen, how beautiful she was with pleasure sparkling in her eyes. Her fiery hair was pinned up then allowed to tumble around her face with her milk-cream skin flushed the pink of rose petals.

The musicians began a ballad, slow and sweet. Kilronan started to his feet, intending to ask Arla for the dance, but settled again when Jor Kellen came up and offered her his hand. He saw Arla's warm smile as she stood and accepted Kellen's arm.

"Beat you to it," Osharon noted cheerfully.

"What?" Kilronan asked, reaching for his ale. He smiled. "Jor? I'll get at least one tonight. There are other dances."

"You might want to move faster," Osharon teased, winking at Cobon, who guffawed. "I think Jor's got the edge."

"Kellen?" With a shake of his head, Kilronan took a swallow of ale.

"They've been *dancing* for some time now."

Kilronan fought to keep from spewing the mouthful of

ale over the table, hearing Osharon's laughter when his friend thumped him on the back as he began to cough violently.

His eyes watering now, Kilronan waved off Cobon's offer of assistance. The master just grinned and wandered off in search of a dancing partner, apparently leaving Osharon to handle the situation.

Then a glass of water was set before him and Kilronan looked up to see Isfail giving him a sympathetic look. But it was the small hands laid on his shoulders that put an end to his spasm.

"Thanks, Akira," he said, slumping back in his seat.

Osharon winked at her before turning to say something to Isfail.

Kilronan looked back when Akira's fingers gripped hard. Her eyes were focused on the window across from them, then her hands shot up. "What—"

His question was cut off when doors crashed in and glass shattered from windows all around the hall. Women screamed as black-garbed intruders ran in the doorways and vaulted through the windows.

Akira's immediate force response had one down before the melee began, Kilronan saw as he finished one more with a force bolt. He swore as villagers stumbled into range, watching for a clear shot while Isfail turned into the charge of a dagger-wielding masked man, grasping that wrist as he spun and wrenched the man's shoulder out of its joint. The assailant's cry of agony was almost lost among the other noise. Isfail grabbed the fallen dagger and moved to Akira's side.

As he bent to retrieve the one weapon he'd brought with him, a knife in an ankle sheath, Kilronan quickly assessed the situation. Protectorate warriors and civilians alike didn't hesitate to engage the enemy. Fists, knives, anything that could be used as a weapon were brought to the fight. But the chaos of terrified villagers mixing with the assailants hampered those with force abilities.

As people scattered everywhere, Kilronan knew they could not use force bolts in an all-out defense without risking injury to the civilians. Force shields had limited effectiveness for the same reason, he realized as his fist connected with a masked face. Fast as a whip, Kilronan cut the man's throat before ducking under another one's sword.

He jerked his chin in appreciation when Isfail caught that man as Kilronan's move had the assailant overstepping. Isfail had an arm around his throat and a knee to his spine. Kilronan heard the man's neck snap then stepped back to form a protective triad with Akira and Isfail as they were surrounded.

"Kil!"

He heard Osharon's shout and shot up a hand to catch the short sword his friend tossed while fighting back to back with Akira and Isfail. The three of them had been set upon immediately after the assault began.

But the ploy proved deadly for the enemy as it opened a clear path for Akira to use the force skills honed since childhood. Kilronan passed the sword to Isfail, whose skill with the blade was unsurpassed, before finding his own opening to send a lethal bolt to eliminate one more. But even as their assailants fell, others took their place.

A shade faster than his own defensive move, Akira's arms flung wide when knives flew, only to bounce off the shield she'd curved around the three of them. Then Cobon, Osharon, and Arla challenged their attackers from behind.

"Try to take some alive!" Akira called, just as a large, masked man broke from the crowd, almost on top of her, dagger raised high. Kilronan grabbed her arm, heard her gasp as he yanked her behind him at the same time Isfail's sword flashed out and into the man's chest. From the corner of his eye, Kilronan saw the assailant fall at Isfail's feet.

A shrill whistle pierced the shouts and screams. As Kilronan spun toward the sound, he saw a couple of attackers running from the hall, closely followed by Carelon and several protectorate warriors.

After a quick check on Akira, Kilronan looked around the hall. Just minutes before, it had been a scene of joy and cheerful pleasure, dancers spinning about the room in colorful costume or fancy attire—laughter and easy conversation.

Now, the laughter had become sobs and weeping, conversation turned to an angry confusion of voices, many exclaiming "What the hell!" . . . or some variation of that sentiment.

As he scanned the room with disbelief replacing the cold purpose of combat, Kilronan saw blood on people's clothing, spattering the walls, and spreading in pools across the floor. Many were injured—wounded by the attackers, or hurt during the panic as they were knocked down, or into walls and furnishings.

Ominously still bodies were scattered about the room; most wore the black of the intruders, but there were some wearing festive clothing among them. Without conscious thought, he began to check the bodies nearest him for signs of life.

He saw Akira move through the milling confusion, joining Asura and Marga as they hurried to help the injured. Kilronan noticed that they went to Mountain Shadows residents first, leaving any wounded assailants to be rounded up by other warriors.

Signaling a couple of admin guards to help secure any living attackers still in the hall, Kilronan saw that Isfail had armed himself with a second sword and guarded the front doorway with Lord Corcoran, while Cobon and Osharon did the same with the other doors. Arla stalked the perimeter, directing warriors to defend each broken window. Relief penetrated the icy fog that seemed to numb Kilronan's every feeling when he saw Eron, Celina, and Maronan, unharmed, with them. And he saw the determination and rage on each face. Determination that there would be no more black surprises this night, and rage that such an attack had happened at all.

"Master Kilronan!"

He turned to find a white-faced Gralla approaching. Kilronan quickly laid his hands on her shoulders. "Are you all right, Gralla?" His eyes looked her up and down for signs of injury.

"I'm fine." But her voice trembled even as he watched her draw herself up.

"I'm fine," she repeated, taking a deep breath. "But Evan . . . Lord Corcoran, he needs you to join him. Outside."

Kilronan nodded, giving her another long appraisal before squeezing her shoulders gently. "I'll go. Sit down, Gralla."

But she shook her head. "Others need help."

He started to the door, seeing her reach out to a sobbing young woman.

Striding out into the night, Kilronan found Lord Corcoran standing with Carelon and his team. The lord's face was taut with rage even as he spoke with rigid calm. A black-masked man knelt in the trampled snow within their circle, arms tied behind his back. As Kilronan joined them, Carelon whipped off the mask, jerking the attacker's head back so all could see the face in the torchlight.

The blood seemed to drain from Corcoran's face as they all recognized one of the administration guards, Eson Haderon. For a moment, no one spoke, then there came a crack of sound as the back of Corcoran's hand struck hard against the traitor's face.

Without speaking, Carelon dragged the man back up from the snow where he'd fallen on his side.

"Why?" Lord Corcoran asked in a voice of bitter heat. When the man didn't answer, he signaled Kilronan, who set a booted foot on the back of the guard's leg, just above the ankle.

Haderon screamed when Kilronan shifted his weight with sudden deliberation. There was no sign of sympathy from those around him as bone snapped.

"Why?" Corcoran repeated, cold as ice now.

As he lifted a hand to Kilronan, who'd moved to the prisoner's other leg, the man shouted in agony, "No! I'll talk. I'll talk." His tear-filled eyes met Corcoran's hard stare briefly before hanging his head.

"We were to kill as many force callers as possible, with Lady Akira and Master Kilronan the primary targets," he sobbed. "Our leader decided this was an opportunity to strike, with the large crowd . . . and everyone focused on the festival tonight. There would be no major weapons on hand . . . and it would be harder for the force callers to use their powers with so many people in the hall." The guard's voice trailed off into wet, snuffling moans of pain.

"How long have you been a member of The Bow?" Corcoran demanded.

"Two years, about."

Closing his eyes briefly, Corcoran shook his head. Kilronan saw crushing disappointment on his lord's face, something he'd never seen before. But he watched Corcoran rally with a few more questions.

"How many of you are in this cell?"

"Ah . . . fourteen, sir. It should have been fifteen but one failed to show at the rendezvous tonight."

"Are you all from Mountain Shadows?"

The traitor cringed under the icy stare. "I think so, all but the leader. And I don't know names—we'd meet without revealing ourselves. But you'll not find our leader here now."

A second furious backhand rocked the man before Corcoran turned abruptly back to the light spilling through the open doors of the hall. "Take him away," he called back, sending Haderon off to the protectorate prison to await formal interrogation with no concern for his broken leg.

Kilronan followed, moving through the chaos with him to tally the cost.

When all were accounted for, nine assailants lay dead, four injured, with one missing, if the disgraced guard's count had been accurate. And those dead and captured traitors cut at the heart of Mountain Shadows and its close community. He recognized another admin guard among the dead—they'd shared a pint a time or two, Kilronan recalled with that feeling of disbelief, served by another of the dead assailants—the man who'd tended bar at the smallest pub in the village.

When he heard Cobon's voice cry out, Kilronan looked over to him. His friend knelt beside a body that Kilronan recognized as Cobon's youngest team member, twenty-two-year-old Niam, from Green River. Kilronan watched as Isfail strode over to lay consoling hands on his childhood friend's shoulders. But who could really comfort that grief, Kilronan wondered, temporarily frozen in place. He'd known fear and the grief of a master who'd lost one of his team.

Forcing himself to move, Kilronan made himself focus on the living. The room was emptying now as Osharon and Arla organized people into groups. He watched Arla wrap her arm around the shoulders of an elderly woman, tipping her head close to murmur words Kilronan couldn't hear before turning her over to Jor and Ala Kellen. Then Arla led the group out into the night, escorted by the rest of her team—to be sure they reached their homes safely, Kilronan knew.

Mouth tight, hands clenched in fists, Kilronan felt the fog begin to lift, burned away in the flames of rage. These people should have been safe! The words were a shout inside his head, a battle cry promising vengeance.

But that cry came out in a sound of despair when he saw Akira and Asura bent over Brother Avo Timmel, the friend who'd refused to give up on him through some of Kilronan's darkest hours. Moving as fast as he could around the traumatized people remaining, Kilronan finally knelt at Timmel's head.

He blanched at the sight of Akira's hands, coated to her wrists in blood, painstakingly restoring spilled loops of gut to Timmel's abdomen. A gaping wound spread, angling down from the man's right ribs to his left hipbone. Mercifully, the Brother lay unconscious.

Timmel's left arm was stretched out next to Kilronan. Taking that hand in his, Kilronan bowed his head in prayer as he willed the man to live. He was vaguely aware when a strong hand gripped his right shoulder before another settled firmly on his left.

It wasn't until Akira's skillful healing had closed the terrible wound that Kilronan looked up. She nodded to him, her deep eyes shadowed with exhaustion but hopeful. Kilronan glanced behind to thank those who'd stood vigil with him. He gripped

Osharon's hand for a moment then turned to see who stood to his left. His mouth tilted up slightly when he found Isfail there.

Eventually, the bloodstained hall emptied but for himself, Lord Corcoran, Akira, Isfail, Osharon, and Carelon. For long moments they all stood, surveying the destruction with exhausted eyes.

"It could have been worse," Osharon finally said. "At least there were no protectorate warriors among the traitors."

Carelon took a darker view. "That we know of—one of the bastards didn't show up for tonight's bloody work, remember? And there's the escaped leader."

"I've posted full teams at the gates and others patrolling the perimeter walls," Corcoran stated, his face grim. "I want all senior masters in conference by second bell tomorrow. I want you there too, Akira, and Isfail. We need to know what happened here, and how to keep it from happening again."

Kilronan met Akira's sorrowful gaze, standing there with drying blood covering her small hands, soaking the delicate lace at her wrists, ruining the lovely dress. He knew her thoughts as if he'd tapped them.

And felt the same heartbreak and grief at the knowledge that innocents had been harmed, had died, because The Bow had come after *them*.

W here were you?" he hissed, pausing in his hurried packing when his partner appeared in the bedroom doorway of the dark cottage.

"I told you I was on duty tonight," came the frustrated answer. "I don't control the roster. What happened? The protectorate and village are swarming with warriors, and security is locked down tight. I almost didn't make it here, even at this hour."

"The attack failed! I've got to get out of here," he snapped, grabbing up anything of value that could be stuffed in his bags. He shoved clothes into a valise with frantic haste; fear now overtaking anger before his arm was grabbed.

"What do you mean *failed*? The targets—"

"Muro and Kilronan live," he snarled in return, shaking free.

"I don't know how many of our men survived, but none made it to the rendezvous. The protectorate was on the hunt fast, I barely made it back here."

"You should have blended back into the crowd, learned more details. They wouldn't have suspected *you*."

Snatching up his baggage, he started toward the door. "I'm not waiting around for Muro to look into my head so Coroth can chop it off. Why didn't that damn woman die in that avalanche? Everything would have gone as planned here without *her*. Mountain Shadows is your problem now."

Hands clenched into fists, the uniformed figure followed, watching as the erstwhile leader made fast work of securing his bags onto the waiting horse, mounting, and disappearing into the blackness of the predawn forest.

Fifty

*T*he investigation continued through the night, with any evidence found brought to an emergency protectorate meeting at first light. Besides the two admin guards, the assailants included two stockmen, two farmers, a woodcutter, two sons of local shopkeepers, the son of the mayor's accountant, a teacher at the village school, a widower with three small children, and a man who tended bar at the smallest pub in the village. Of these, the shopkeepers' sons, the widower, and the guard questioned immediately after the attack had survived. They were now imprisoned and under rigorous interrogation.

The victims killed in the vicious attack included a young woman who worked at the protectorate stables, a village councilman, an admin guard who died defending his wife, and the youngest member of Cobon's team, who'd stood to shield a terrified group of children until a man twice his age—a guard he thought he knew—cut him down.

Survivors suffered a variety of wounds though most were healed before units of protectorate warriors escorted them home. The ones with more severe injuries were taken to the protectorate infirmary to recover. They included Brother Timmel, who'd stood with Cobon's fallen team member, defending the defenseless. He'd stepped into a slashing sword, but failed to end its deadly sweep before it took the young warrior's life. Although his were life-threatening injuries, Akira believed he would recover with round-the-clock care for the first critical week.

Now Corcoran studied his senior masters, seeing the grim lines of anger and fatigue on each face, reflecting his own feelings.

"There's little more to tell than what we learned last night. The prisoners have all given the same information, so far. None knew any others by name or face. They met in the dark, masked, seldom speaking except for the leader. There were no meetings planned in advance—a note would be left with only a coded location and time."

He sighed, rubbing a hand over his forehead. "We're working on finding the reason for their betrayal." He looked directly at Akira as he added, "I might ask for help with that if nothing is forthcoming today. Mind tapping might be the last recourse. Are you willing, Akira?"

She looked at Kilronan, then Isfail before answering. Corcoran could see her reluctance to cross that ethical line.

"I don't ask lightly. We don't have time to get approval from Coroth and Most High Garan."

Akira nodded slowly. "I agree, sir."

Corcoran turned the meeting's focus back to discovering any others who might be in league with The Bow, or know the leader who'd vanished like smoke in the night. Protectorate warriors had been posted at the residences of traitors. Family members and friends were being questioned, and their houses or quarters searched.

The mayor and town council had approved the measure within the village, and a census was being taken to account for every resident.

As he relayed this information to his protectorate masters, Corcoran said, "The only thing we have on our side in this is winter. With the pass closed to regular travel, there are only residents and protectorate personnel here. We're not having to track down visitors."

Isfail lifted a finger and Corcoran nodded to him. "What about the supply shipments to Ishaka? Are you able to account for everyone involved there, those not residents of Mountain Shadows?"

"That's a good point," Corcoran replied in a heavy voice. "We'll get on that immediately."

"It needs to be checked out," Akira agreed. "But I doubt you'll find your culprits there. The prisoners have admitted that all were in place two years ago, some as long as three. They say their leader is the same man, or has been the same man locally, since the beginning."

Kilronan nodded with a grim expression. "And the Ishakan mission was unexpected, only in place for two lunams now."

Corcoran's shoulders unbent a little. "Well, that's something, I suppose." He stood up. "I've assigned teams to cover usual duty, and others to continue tracking down how this atrocity came about. Check the posted roster as you leave. Everyone not on a specific task at the time should be at the town meeting at the temple this afternoon. Dismissed."

*A*kira felt the onslaught of memories as she took her seat beside Isfail, in chairs facing the congregation pews now filling up with unsmiling Mountain Shadows residents. The same ambiance of fear and confusion had filled this temple during the meetings in advance of the Mors invasion. Except for the addition of Isfail, and the heart-wrenching absence of Brother Timmel, the same group of speakers prepared to address the latest crisis.

Protectorate warriors lined the walls again, but this time their sharp eyes watched everyone filing in to take seats, on the alert for any suspicious behavior. Akira knew that more were posted outside to guard against another sneak attack. In this way, it was horribly different from the gatherings to defend against a foreign enemy. Despite the knowledge that Dateh and his infiltrators from Ishal were almost certainly behind last night's murderous attack, it had been Mountain Shadows residents who'd struck against their own.

Neighbor now looked at neighbor with suspicion. Family members didn't know if they could trust their own kin.

When she felt Isfail take her cold hand, warming it with his, Akira looked into her husband's eyes and knew he recognized her grief over the consequences to this community that had given her a home.

"We'll give it our best, my sweet," he murmured for her ears alone. "That's all we can do."

She squeezed his hand in acknowledgement before turning her attention to Lord Corcoran as he stood to open the meeting. Akira listened as he told those present what had been learned since the attack and answered some of the questions, deferring others when answers were not yet available.

"The most important thing all of us can do right now is to find the facts, search out anyone who has supported these traitors. Are there others here that worked with them, sympathized with their cause? These are things we need to know as soon as possible. To that end, the mayor and I are asking everyone to think back to anything that seemed odd or out of place."

When hands shot up around the room, he raised a hand. "I will ask you to censure anything that is obvious gossip or simply a more usual disagreement. Otherwise, we'll be bogged down in less critical disputes." That brought out a few relieved bursts of laughter, and a number of hands lowered.

Lord Corcoran gestured the mayor to his side, so that they took turns calling on those who felt they had something of note. Gralla wrote down information as it came to light, and Akira felt no doubt that the astute woman made her own notations about what might be salient commentary versus more petty or fantastical supposition.

As people finished expressing their thoughts, the mayor stepped forward. "It is of the utmost importance that we rout out this evil. But we must still remember our strength of community. Do not allow this terrible event to turn us against one another or the enemy wins."

A young man stood up from a back pew, hands clenched by his side, his face distorted by grief. "My sister is dead! Her throat cut by a man who was part of this *community*. Who's to pay for that? Where's justice for her?"

For a long moment, the assembly was silent. Then a woman jerked to her feet, face twisted, eyes red and streaming.

"You brought this on us!" the woman shrilled, jabbing a finger at Akira. "If you hadn't come, none of this would have happened!"

Akira felt Isfail stiffen beside her, and her glance saw his eyes narrowed, jaw set. She knew he was ready to defend her against any threat.

Lord Corcoran didn't give Akira or Isfail time to respond as he stood, his face hard as stone. "Lady Muro first came here, unannounced and unexpected, less than a year ago. We now have evidence—confirmed by your own man, Protectorate Guard Eson Haderon, a murdering traitor—that The Bow infiltrated Mountain Shadows more than two years ago."

His eyes were cold as he stared down the woman. "That being so, how can you blame Lady Muro for this? You've been bound to Eson Haderon for more than three years, yet you claim you had no prior knowledge of his murderous plans or allegiances. Why should we believe you, Madam Haderon, or your spurious accusations?"

Her face white as the snow now, she gaped at him before folding in on herself to sob out her denials. Around her, people shifted away, not one offered comfort.

Even so, there were those among the villagers that muttered angrily with suspicious glances toward those seated in front of the altar. Now there were angry calls accusing the protectorate of allowing the attack, for being the cause of the assault, others demanding that Lord Corcoran and his warriors leave Mountain Shadows.

Akira heard with resignation the inevitable denunciations of those with force ability.

Some of the villagers got up and started to walk out.

In another repeat of the past, Jor Kellen stood up with a loud order for everyone to "Shut up and sit down!"

He turned, glaring around the rest of those assembled. "What the hell are ya about?" he shouted at the crowd. "Turning on those who've kept your sorry lives safe and whole for all these years. This village would have been a smoking ruin last year—stacked with your worthless bodies—if not for Lady Muro and every other force caller and warrior in our protectorate! What would Mountain Shadows be without the warriors based here?"

He swung a strong arm wide. "Nothin', that's what—a poor village at the mercy of thieves and worse when the pass was open! Most of ya'd be scrabbling out a hard life tryin' to survive this high in the mountains. Instead, we live and prosper here, because the defense services protect us, providing jobs, needin' supplies and support that the village is paid well for."

The room was silent now except for Jor's contemptuous voice. "It wasn't the force callers that attacked innocent men and women. It was our own—those we thought were our own." Now he shook his head, mouth tightening in angry sorrow. "Vermin and traitors that lived among us, plotting ta do their neighbors harm. You'd do well to remember that, all of ya. Because turning on ourselves is feeding the enemy."

When Jor sat down, face tense, silence filled the room until one wavering voice spoke up.

"But these men said they meant to kill Lady Muro and Master Kilronan. What about that?"

Lord Corcoran lifted a hand to keep Jor in his seat. "They obviously want to eliminate our strongest fighters. Do you believe they would stop there, any of you? What is the purpose of eliminating a country's defense forces? It's to weaken it so that it's ready to be invaded, taken over."

There were reluctant but growing murmurs agreeing with his assessment. Now most of the gathering settled into an unhappy state of acceptance. Even those still not convinced waited for more information.

There was a loud clearing of a throat before Juniro stood up to speak. Like everyone else, his face was solemn. "I do not wish to cause anyone trouble, to speak badly of any who are innocent, but I would like to ask if anyone has looked for the schoolmaster today? Master Ramort?"

There was a rustle as people shifted, looking at one another and about the room as if to locate the man.

"We will check on him right now, Juniro," Corcoran said,

signaling Cobon, who immediately left with his team. "Why are you bringing this to our attention?"

Juniro sighed, swiping a meaty hand over his brow. "Because he is not here today, and was not at the dance last night. He is a favorite of my Nina, and she had looked for him to present him with a little cake she made. And he was often in the company of the teacher who participated in the attack."

*M*aster Ramort was not to be found; neither was the horse he boarded at the village stables. Corcoran and the mayor ordered his little cottage searched, but the results were mixed. The schoolmaster had kept a neat home, most of those interviewed reported. Now it displayed signs of a hurried retreat. Drawers were left open, clothing appeared to have been taken.

There was little of value left, but a thorough search found nothing to tie the schoolmaster to The Bow, or last night's destruction.

Still, the fact of his leaving immediately after made him a strong suspect. Unfortunately, Ramort may have had several hours lead time, and mild weather over the past week made the road from their valley to Green River passable.

Corcoran sent a messenger hawk as soon as the news reached him, following that by sending Team Nathon and Team Arla to search the road as far as the neighboring protectorate. With them, he sent a packet containing letters from himself and Isfail, detailing the situation in Mountain Shadows. With Isfail's royal seal marking it as urgent, it would be routed on to Coroth by fast courier from Green River.

Now they would do what they could to secure their territory, get life in Mountain Shadows back to some semblance of normalcy, and wait for directions from the prince.

Fifty-One

Baronan Keep, Caldala, Approximately Three Weeks Later

The trail was a mess of mud and slush as Barash let his mare make her way cautiously down a shallow slope ahead of the older gelding carrying the carcass of a small buck. Barash looked forward to the meat, even though the deer had just begun to fill out after winter's scarce fodder.

The long howl of a wolf told him that a pack had found the kill site, where he'd done a quick dressing out of the game. He'd kept the heart and liver, along with the carcass, leaving offal that had probably attracted the predators. Barash glanced back but didn't expect the wolves to be following yet.

As the cave mouth loomed ahead, the mare tipped her ears forward and broke into a trot as if anticipating the warmth and safety inside. Reining her in as they entered, Barash slid down with the gelding's lead rope in his hand and led the horses through a short passage. He felt for a heavy latch in the dark, lifting it to push a large, thick door inward, where torches illuminated a cavern outfitted as a rough stable and workspace.

Releasing reins and rope, Barash pushed the door closed again and settled a thick plank into brackets to prevent unwanted entry—wolf or man. The door and the laboriously constructed wall that closed off the original cave had taken him a full lunam to build. And that was after he'd regained enough strength to shift countless stones from the old cave-in into place.

Turning back to the horses already nosing about in the piles of dry hay, Barash released the ropes holding the deer and hauled the carcass to the far wall for further butchering. He took care of the horses, settling them in their stalls, before turning to the tedious and necessary task of dressing out the deer.

*B*arash wanted a roaring fire after washing off blood and grime in the shallow snowmelt pool a short ways into the old tube tunnel. But caution had him feeding a small fire in a fireplace at the back of the keep with very dry wood that would give off little to no visible smoke.

Huddling close to the warmth, he poured hot water from a small pot on the hearth into a mug with dried tea. As it steeped, he stirred another pot where small chunks of venison simmered with onion and other root vegetables. He really needed to get some salt and spices next time he risked a trip into a village or town.

Leaning back into the wing-backed tapestry chair he'd brought in from one of the larger rooms, he wrapped cold hands around the mug and sipped the hot tea. Barash welcomed the warmth spreading down his throat. The keep hadn't allowed many comforts over the cold winter but it had been a safe haven while he needed one.

He recalled the painful trip from that valley above Green River. Even now Barash marveled that he'd survived it. Weak, half-dead from exposure, he'd managed to steal a horse from a farm a day after slipping away from Akira and the protectorate soldiers.

Shaking his head as he stared into the flames, Barash gave a wry smile. He couldn't delude himself. She'd let him go. Those warriors could easily have tracked him, hunted him down in no time. Akira Muro had chosen to let him go.

Why? It was a question that haunted his thoughts over the long winter nights. Did she know he only had one place to return to? Barash turned his head to scan the darkness around this small pool of firelight and warmth.

The once grand and luxurious stronghold of his delusional father, Lord Arthon Baronan, and the only legacy the devil had provided his bastard son. A legacy that Barash would claim despite the legitimate sons Baronan had sired. The thin smile he turned toward the fire would have made the devil shiver.

Now what? Barash wondered yet again. He was a hunted criminal, living in an abandoned keep haunted by the ghosts of those his father had murdered. Unable to live openly there, or publically claim the estate, Barash knew he existed in a kind of limbo.

Had she foreseen this? Had Akira known that by allowing him his freedom, she was condemning him to finally look at his life full on and face the past that had damned him? Was there any place for him? Any way he could live that would escape the pattern set by his psychopath of a father and insane witch of a mother?

Setting down the mug, he dropped his face into his hands. God . . . for a moment he wanted Akira here so desperately, he despaired over the pain of loss. She had listened, talked with him, given him the tenderness he'd tried to convince himself he hadn't needed over the years. She'd offered friendship, caring that no one ever had.

He wasn't sure whether to thank her for it, or curse her for opening the door to that need. Rubbing his fingers over his brow, he released a bitter laugh.

The pot on the fire bubbled vigorously. Thankful for the distraction, Barash grabbed an iron hook to pull the bracket away from the flames. But as he lifted the pot off and lowered it to the stone hearth, he heard noises in the courtyard. Grabbing the hooked fire-poker, he pulled the damper closed to prevent any possibility of smoke or embers giving him away.

Barash shrugged his heavy coat on as he closed the door to the room behind him, striding silently through dark, familiar halls. Taking the servants stairway to the second floor, he made his way to a bedchamber overlooking the front courtyard. Standing to the side of a window, careful to avoid exposing himself, Barash looked down to see several horses standing near the old guardhouse.

He hurried to the adjacent room, where there was a better

vantage over that building. Torchlight flickered through the narrow windows before a brighter light flared, indicating a lantern had been lit in the common room of the guards' barracks.

When a man clothed in hooded wrappings came out, Barash edged closer to the window curtains in an excess of caution. But the intruder was obviously focused on unloading gear strapped to one of the two packhorses and never looked at the keep.

A second man joined him, his open cloak flapping in the wind, and Barash watched as they took the rest in. On the last trip, the two men led all the horses out of sight. Suspecting they were taking them to the stables beyond the keep, Barash jogged down the main hall to the rear chamber, confirming their destination as he saw them entering the strongly built stables.

It was another confirmation that he'd made the right decision in keeping his own horses in the cavern, Barash thought as he made his way up to the third floor. Positioning himself at a window over the narrow side court the men and horses had taken from the guardhouse, he waited to see them return.

These men had known about Baronan Keep. That was obvious, Barash mused. They knew their way around the grounds, knew about the guardhouse. He wondered why they hadn't come into the keep itself.

Barash looked down on the men returning from the stables, slouching along with their hands stuffed deep in their pockets while the long shadows of twilight spread. They didn't appear to speak to one another but he wouldn't have heard anything over the wind now thrashing the trees about. Barash went to the room closest to the guardhouse, carefully parting the window curtains to watch them enter.

He thought through the layout of that building. The ground level had a large common room, small armory, and kitchen. Upstairs were two long rooms with bunks where the guards had slept, and a smaller room for the guard captain. A narrow landing overlooked the common room below.

Finally, there was an attic space beneath the steep pitch of the slate-tiled roof, with doors at each end accessing a narrow parapet that edged the roof, with a stone railing notched with slit openings, through which bowmen could fire upon invaders if the keep were under attack. His paranoid sire had thought of everything, Barash remembered with a derisive snort.

But his dark eyes narrowed thoughtfully. He hadn't forgotten old skills.

Fifty-Two

It took less than a quarter of an hour to make his way to the parapet, with the early nightfall aiding his task. Silent and stealthy as a cat, Barash circled around the keep, careful to leave no tracks or trace. The strangers inside made it easy for him, showing no inclination to leave the fire that roared in the large fireplace now. He even considered going into the kitchen and up the narrow back stairs, but that risked leaving footprints in the dust of decades.

In the end, he quickly scaled the stone-block walls and lifted himself over the edge of the parapet. Barash knew he'd have to trust to luck, hoping that no one would check the attic. He could brush out prints with the evergreen branches he'd tucked under his coat, but even the brush stokes would disturb the thick layer of fine dirt.

Stepping silently around to the door nearest the great room, Barash held his breath as he tried the latch. There was a scrape of sound as it lifted, but the door moved without even a screech of disuse. Barash paused to slide his booted feet into the thin rope loops he'd secured to the short evergreen boughs. Sliding along cautiously, he heard the quiet swish of the needles as he traversed the floor to a small hatch just a few feet from the door he'd entered.

Lying down among long-forgotten trunks and baskets, Barash carefully lifted the hatch and peered down into the room two levels below. Slowly shifting his position, he was able to see the group lounging in front of the fireplace, and the supplies spread over the long table. A small ale cask had been tapped, sitting beside tankards evidently taken from those abandoned with the estate. Three men sat on benches near that end of the table.

From his vantage point above the great room, Barash observed the intruders. It was clear that some were familiar with the old keep. He wondered if they were the same ones who'd been here before. However it was, these men were at ease, and not expecting any opposition.

A tall, burly man was seated in the best chair in the room, with his booted feet resting on the raised hearth. He appeared to be the leader. His clothing was of excellent quality, and the other men seemed to defer to him.

All but one—thin, with the look of a scholar, his sand-colored hair pulled back in a short tail, this man leaned against a corner of the mantle, scowling at the seated man.

The other three wore the rough clothing of workmen, with the attitude of those who took orders without asking questions. They remained at the table, concentrating on their ale.

Barash guessed there was an argument going on as he heard the irritation in the larger man's voice.

"I'm not the one who failed in Mountain Shadows," the burly one was saying. "You think Dateh's going to hand you your silver and say, 'Too bad but thanks for trying?'"

One of the men at the table snickered into his cup.

His interest increased by the words 'Mountain Shadows,' Barash carefully shifted to try to hear more clearly.

The thin one's face darkened with anger. "Dateh underestimated those people! You think you could have done better against the all-powerful Muro and a hall full of protectorate warriors, including Kilronan? And let's not forget that cat-who-won't-die Isfail!"

Ignoring the warning look from the seated man, the light-haired one slammed his tankard down on the mantel, sloshing ale over the edge and splashing foam onto the hearth.

With a loud oath, the burly one jerked back his feet. "Watch yourself, Ramort! Remember who's in charge of operations here in Caldala."

"I remember, Felcan," Ramort snarled. "So why didn't the all-mighty Dateh put *you* in charge of executing the targets in Mountain Shadows, eh?"

Settling back again, the one called Felcan replied, "I've got my own target. If you want to keep your head, you'll keep your ears to the ground and wait for another opportunity to kill Muro. You finish her, Dateh will be more lenient."

"You think I can go back now? Just return as schoolmaster, as if nothing was wrong?" Ramort had gone pale, taking an awkward step back. "They're hunting for me!"

"You were a fool to run right after the botched attack." Felcan's voice held no sympathy. "It was a good set-up. Why should anyone look at the schoolmaster? You've marked your own grave. Maybe the others will do a better job. How many are still there? What about Pelom?"

"Who? Oh, right, still there, maybe more. I got out while the protectorate was searching for us."

Ramort's expression shifted to a remorseful one as he pleaded, "I've got to get out of Caldala. Get me on a ship, Felcan. I'll be of more use to The Bow in Tash'tric, anywhere in Ishal." As Felcan continued to stare into the fire, Ramort cursed. "I can't live here now. I have no job, no money."

"You're an insult to The Bow," Felcan announced with contempt. "You've been in Mountain Shadows for three years. What happened to your earnings?"

Barash could see Ramort's face glow red, even from his high perch.

"I invested it, in land," Ramort admitted. When Felcan gave him an amused look, he hissed. "I'll be rich when Lord Dateh rules Caldala."

"Well, you're poor now." Felcan chuckled.

"A ship," Ramort snarled. "There must be a ship you can get me on."

Rubbing a hand over his chin, Felcan looked thoughtful. "Better if you had tried to escape over the pass. You were right there."

"Are you joking? There are two protectorate teams on duty on the border, full-time now. And what about the Ishakans, and Shanow's soldiers?"

"That's just it. If you'd gotten to Shanow, he'd have seen you safely back to Tash'tric. Dateh posted his militia there to go after the Ishakans."

Looking stunned, then oddly elated, Ramort started laughing. "Then he's a fool and so are you! Word is Shanow and his men are defending the Ishakans. Not only that, but two more militias joined them over the last lunams."

His laughter grew louder when Felcan stood up suddenly, cursing as he grabbed Ramort's coat. "How long have you known about this? Why the hell didn't you pass that information on?"

Jerking free to fussily tug at his disheveled attire, Ramort sneered. "We were given a specific assignment, and I kept my ears open for anything that might affect that. No one told me I was supposed to relay information. What happened to Dateh's lauded spy network, all the people planted here in Caldala over the years, like Pelom? I assumed he was getting any news he needed."

Cursing loudly, Felcan circled the room, oblivious to the dull stares from the workmen, angry with Ramort—who now sat in the seat before the fire, grinning like an idiot.

Felcan slapped Ramort's tankard from the mantel as he returned, shaking his head like an angry bear as the ale flew. Damn it, he raged silently, he'd warned Dateh about Shanow. He'd been right to worry about the commander's loyalties, and too busy with the plots he'd been set to in Caldala to monitor what was happening in Ishal.

Damn it!

And what about the Kittric operations? In the brief time he'd been back in Ishal, Dateh had only said everything was going according to plan.

Everything was falling apart, Felcan decided, and Abron Dateh was a naïve fool when it came to making what were essentially military decisions. He needed to get back to Tash'tric before it was too late, before they lost the advantage there.

To his mind, Caldala was a lost cause. The people and the defense services were too strong, too loyal, guided by a solid government. That idiot Ominor had been arrested and imprisoned for treason, along with Wrax. The Bow had lost the Southern Crescent, and over thirty men. He still didn't know how they'd been discovered, but that port of entry was lost to them.

Ramort spoke up again. "A ship, Felcan?"

"Good luck with that," Felcan barked. "Our secondary entry isn't secure. We've lost touch with the ship captain that's been making the run for us there." He didn't tell the fool that he'd had the devil's own time getting back into Caldala to carry out Dateh's plot against Psyche Lakes.

For the first time, Felcan truly questioned whether he should do what Dateh wanted done. In his mind, he could hear the escape routes slamming shut around him. If something went wrong at Psyche Lakes, how would he make it back to Ishal? The old pass had been the back-up plan. Now it was a major risk, especially for a number of men.

Rubbing his hands hard over his face, he tried to think calmly. He'd take care of the attack on Psyche Lakes. That would shake up things in Caldala. Maybe distract attention from the coast long enough to get a ship to Orsha or Kuldor. He could get another to Ishal from Kuldor. But that would take at least three weeks to get back, maybe a lunam. Damn it!

Felcan turned to Ramort, who was brooding over a new mug of ale. "I suggest you get yourself a good disguise and book regular passage out of a major port, into Kuldor if you can. There'll be a trader back to Ishal from there." Pulling a fat pouch from his inner pocket, Felcan counted out a generous sum, and handed it to the eager man.

"You're to get back to Tash'tric as fast as you can and report directly to Abron Dateh. Tell him about Shanow, and anything else you've heard." As Ramort got up, Felcan grabbed his coat again and looked hard into his startled gaze. "If you don't do that, I swear *I'll* hunt you down."

"I will." Ramort gulped, his hand shaking as he transferred the coins to his own purse. "Should I start out tonight?" his voice quavered.

"First light tomorrow. Get some sleep." Felcan sat back down, but his earlier peace of mind was gone.

*I*n the attic above, Barash slipped away from the portal as a visibly shaken Ramort stumbled up the narrow stairs, but the man did not look up. Hearing the sound of a door opening and closing, Barash shifted back. Felcan was staring into the fire once more, but his posture was tense now. Two of the workmen were lying on benches, apparently sleeping despite the loud altercation that had just concluded. The third had his head on arms folded on the table. His snoring could be heard, filling the silence.

He didn't think he'd learn anything more tonight. Barash carefully closed the hatch before sitting up. For a while, he sat there, thinking about what he'd heard, and wondering what to do about it.

Why should he do anything about it?

He wasn't part of this—he was an outcast, a wanted man himself. He didn't owe Caldala anything, and what did he care about wars between countries? What did he care about the plots of Abron Dateh?

Abron . . .

Barash felt a cold clutch in his gut. Felcan had said Abron *Dateh*, but was the man now running The Bow and another bloody rebellion Abron *Baronan*? His half-brother? Who else could have told these interlopers about the abandoned Baronan Keep—it was an ideal place for them to safely meet and shelter while they plotted their attacks.

There were too many similarities to what had come before, he realized. The same signs of obsessive desire for power at any cost. Barash felt another chill go through him at what might happen if this *Dateh* actually got control of Caldala.

The keep would be lost to him! He would have nothing again.

Something else nagged at him, something he wanted to ignore. Blocking it from his mind, Barash eased up to a standing position and shuffled slowly to the door. Outside, he gently shut it, making sure the latch held before slipping off the tree boughs and walking silently around the parapet, climbing back down at the corner closest to the trees.

Returning to the main keep, he went around making sure all doors and windows were locked. He couldn't do anything about some of the broken windows, but he could secure the doors to those rooms. If anyone broke through, he'd hear it.

He decided to clear the room he'd used of personal items, taking time to eat some of the stew that had gone cold while he scouted the situation. Over the winter, he'd used those long hours to locate some of the hidden passageways old Baronan had designed into the keep. Now he pressed a cleverly hidden latch in a decorative wall panel, opening the access to a steep stairway leading down to a basement safe room. He'd store his things there, Barash decided, maybe sleep there. If necessary, he could go through another hidden door into the storage rooms below and the moving panel that accessed the cave.

It was colder in the underground room, but he had lanterns to light the small space, a pallet, and several thick blankets. As he lay there, replaying what he'd heard, that niggling ache returned, causing him to curse the fates.

These men wanted Akira dead. Could he ignore that knowledge after she'd given him his life, knowing they meant to try again? Could he get this information to her, warn her about this plot?

Or . . . could he seek out this half-brother who wanted to rule Caldala, and offer his bloody services and insider knowledge in exchange for ownership of Baronan Keep?

He didn't owe anybody anything. Barash scowled angrily. No one had ever given him anything worth having, even his miserable life. What right did Akira Muro have condemning him to this half-life of hiding in this hell-born keep? He had nothing and nowhere to call his own.

Twisting restlessly onto his side, he thought it over, and began to form a plan—one that was his alone.

Fifty-Three

Felcan listened for Ramort to leave before he stirred himself to get up. He refused to listen to the man's whining anymore. The schoolmaster had been one of Dateh's early recruits and, he had to admit, had seemed a good partner for their established mole in Mountain Shadows. But he knew the fastidious Ramort didn't have the guts when it came down to carrying out an assassination plot.

Three years ago, they'd only needed spies and infiltrators who could help weaken the High Pass access. There'd been no thought that someone like Akira Muro would not only destroy the pass, but also settle in such an isolated village. Ramort hadn't been the man for the job then, by a long shot.

He heard the front door open and then slam shut. Ramort obviously hadn't been pleased by the lack of send off. Felcan stretched and sat up, scratching his shoulder. He had to wait another full day before the rest of his men would get here, and he wanted a full strike team for the next step.

As he pulled on clothing, his thoughts skipped ahead again to how he was going to get out of Caldala after completing this mission. Dateh wanted him back to head up the takeover of the Ishakan territories. That wasn't going to go the way they'd planned if it was true that Shanow and three militias were holding ground there.

He picked up the small lantern he'd lit to push back the predawn darkness, and opened the door of the room he'd claimed for himself. With half a mind he registered the fact that there were no smells of food cooking. He'd peel the skin off those

314

useless workmen if they were still sprawled out, hung-over from the ale, rather than doing the tasks they were hired for.

Thumping down the steps, he prepared to bark out orders. But there were no laggards anywhere to be seen in the dark room beyond the lantern light. It was exactly as he'd left it last night, except no one was there. Felcan's brow furrowed as he turned toward the big stone hearth.

His hand flew to the dagger on his belt when he saw a man sitting in shadows at the edge of lamplight. Then he laughed, shoving the weapon back into its sheath.

"Damn it, Abron! What the hell are you doing here?" Felcan exclaimed with relief. "You could have warned me that you were joining us. I guess you wanted to see this one through yourself, eh?"

He was smiling as he crossed the room to the man who sat in silence. Then Felcan stopped short as light spread, his grin slowly fading as he stared. "You're not him. Who the hell are you?"

The slow, sinister curl of lips made Felcan shudder. The similarities were uncanny. This stranger could be Abron's twin—right down to the way the black eyes bore into a man, making him see his own death.

"I asked you a question. Who are you?" Felcan set the lantern on a side table and straightened, refusing to be intimidated by a specter. But when his hand moved to his dagger again, the man spoke with deadly calm in a low-pitched voice.

"I wouldn't, not if you want to live." Now he stood up, slowly drawing his own blade. "And I'll ask the questions. Who are you, all of you, and what are you doing trespassing on my land?"

"Your land," Felcan replied, sneering. "This is Baronan land, and we have permission from the owner."

The stranger's mouth formed that sinister smirk. "Baronan land, yes. My permission? No. I'm the Baronan here."

Felcan felt his mouth gape and quickly shut it. How could he dispute that when this man looked and sounded so much like Abron Baronan? But his friend had said he was the last of his family.

A darkly amused laugh had him refocusing on the man garbed in black.

"It seems Abron didn't think to mention his older brother." He slouched insolently back into the chair, tossing his dagger to spin in the air before catching it again with careless expertise. "As I said, I'm the Baronan here in Caldala, Barash by name, and *I* claim this keep that our mad father abandoned, along with lands belonging to it."

Anger stirred in Felcan that the man now calling himself Abron Dateh had not given him this information when he'd told them to use the old keep. What else had he kept secret over the years they'd known one another? Here he was, risking his life for Dateh's cause, only to find out there was an older brother still in Caldala. Was this Barash privy to the overall plan?

"What else are you laying claim to? What are you and Abron plotting together?" Felcan questioned sharply.

Barash raised a slashing eyebrow. "My brother's schemes are his own, as long as he doesn't interfere with mine. I haven't laid eyes on him since he ran off with old Baronan."

Felcan absorbed this information, his tension easing. "So he doesn't know you're here," he said slowly. "Still, why didn't he mention an older brother who could be his mirror image?"

With a careless shrug, Barash just looked at him. "He was always the one who wanted everything, maybe he didn't want any competition." He watched Felcan look around the room.

"Where are my men?" Felcan finally asked; sounding resigned to whatever answer he might hear.

"Stables," Barash replied easily, grinning as Felcan looked at him with suspicion. "They were easy enough to pick off, no need to kill them. Yet." He studied his dagger while he said, "That last one was annoying though. Couldn't keep his mouth shut, so he might have a sore head when he comes to."

But his eyes held a clear warning when he looked at Felcan again. "You have more coming?"

Though he was tempted to lie, Felcan nodded. "Four more, due here this afternoon. We'll head out near sunset tomorrow."

Rolling the handle of the dagger between his fingers, back and forth in practiced moves, Barash stared at Felcan. "Why should I let you stay here that long?"

"Look." Felcan bristled, tired of whatever game this Barash was playing. "You might look like Abron Baronan, but I only have your word that you're the legal owner of Baronan Keep. Maybe I should notify the local militia that you're here."

Barash laughed. "Go right ahead. I may or may not have legal claim, but I'm still a Baronan." When Felcan said nothing, Barash shook his head. "You and I both know you're here illegally. I have no allegiances to anyone, but you think I don't hear about what's happening in Ishal? You think I don't know about The Bow's attacks in Caldala? Who do you think the local militia will be more interested in? Maybe you are too stupid to live."

"All right." Felcan conceded the bluff, but he pounced on one thing buried in Barash's response. "Let's come to some agreement." He saw interest flicker in the man's dark eyes. "You said you have no allegiances. Why not work with your brother and The Bow? I can see you have abilities we can make use of, including your close appearance to Abron. That could be a great benefit to us. I believe Lord Dateh would be willing to reward his older brother with any properties you want if you work for our side."

Barash laughed derisively. "*Lord Dateh*, eh? He has fallen to delusions of grandeur. Why would I even consider working with such a fool?"

While Felcan struggled to quash his surge of anger over this usurper's insults, he saw Barash cross his arms over his chest with a thoughtful frown.

"But I'll hear you out. I'd consider a limited alliance for the deeds to old Baronan's properties." Barash gave Felcan a calculating look. "And enough silver to keep me living well for the rest of my days."

*I*t was nearly midday before the men in the stables were released and an uneasy semblance of order restored to the group in the barracks. One of the men prepared a barely edible meal of sausages and pan bread, his attention fearfully fixed on Barash more than his cooking.

Ramort had been terrified into silence—a condition that appealed to Felcan, more than making up for Barash's arrogance.

Well into the afternoon, four more men arrived. They were experienced Bowmen, there to do the work Felcan had for them. The presence of a stranger didn't appear to interest them one way or another.

But Barash watched everything and everyone as he leaned against the stair rail while drinking from a tall mug of ale.

Felcan sat on one of the benches at the table. He had the men haul in wooden boxes that had been stacked outside the door. After prying open the lids, he carefully lifted out several hollow clay balls, each made with one small opening, and set them on the table. Now he used a leather funnel to carefully fill the balls with black powder from a small cask on the bench beside him.

"We need to get back to Ishal after I finish a job," Felcan said, inserting a length of cannon fuse into one, then packing a strip of material into the hole to anchor the short bit of fuse dangling from the ball.

Barash shifted, stirring himself to take a seat on the stairs. Felcan wondered if he would ask about the little project here. He glanced at Barash, who said nothing. "The Bow made good use of these in the past," he said, holding up a finished explosive. "We developed them during the first rebellion."

"Didn't help you win that one, did they?" Barash remarked, leaning back with one elbow on the stair behind him. His mouth twisted into that insolent grin. "Myself, I like sharp steel, good rope, and my own hands."

"These get the job done in larger numbers," Felcan retorted irritably, feeling no doubt that this man was related to Abron. They were both arrogant and egotistical, with no concerns about killing, as long as it was done their way.

Barash gave a shrug. "No finesse. Just blood and pieces blasted everywhere in an unholy mess. It's a lazy man's way of killing without discrimination. That was old Baronan's way, all right. Apparently Abron learned from the master."

Giving up, Felcan changed the subject. "We have a contact at an inn along the coast, north of Corsalat. But we need to find the ship captain that's been making runs for us without raising suspicion."

A feeble snort came from Ramort's corner. "That sounds promising," he muttered scornfully.

Ignoring him, Felcan concentrated on pouring a small amount of melted candle wax into the hole. As it cooled it would create a plug, holding the contents inside. He set the ball back in the wooden case, fuse up.

"I have some contacts of my own," Barash said casually, finishing his ale. "I can get us on a ship, though we might end up on Kilra before Ishal."

"That would work," Felcan said, with his mood improving. "Take Ramort with you and make arrangements. We should get to the rendezvous at the inn within a week's time. The problem is the ports are heavily watched, especially since Ramort here botched an assassination attempt on some high-level targets." Picking up another clay ball, he repeated the process.

Barash turned amused eyes to the former schoolmaster. "This gets better and better. And who did you fail to kill?"

Shrinking back into the corner he'd settled in on a three-legged stool, Ramort said nothing, so Felcan answered for him.

"The one we wanted most was Akira Muro."

Now Barash eyed them with something like contempt. "You really are incompetent fools. Sending someone like him after Muro. He's lucky he's still in one piece."

Apparently Ramort had some pride left in him as he jerked to his feet with a shrill reply. "Let's see you take her on then!"

Chuckling, Barash lifted his empty mug to the pathetic specimen. "I wouldn't take her on." He laughed at Ramort's look of triumph. "Only an imbecile would try to take Akira Muro in an open fight. A smart man would kill her without direct confrontation."

He saw Felcan looking at him closely, his eyes tightening.

"You think you could kill her?" Felcan asked quietly.

"I know I could kill her, if I set my mind to it," Barash replied easily. "If someone made it worth my time."

Felcan stared at him for a long moment. "You kill Akira Muro, I guarantee you the deed to this keep and all properties once held by Arthon Baronan."

Fifty-Four

Mountain Shadows, Caldala

Akira bolted up, waking Isfail in the cold dark of a moonless night. He reached for her as she started to leave their bed.

"Hold on, love," he said, as her body trembled. "What's wrong?"

But she couldn't answer as she fought the panic, struggling to slow her breathing.

Isfail threw back the covers and pulled her to him. "Breathe, Kira." He cursed the lack of light, until she drew a deep breath and lifted a shaking hand to the lamp.

The flare of light settled to a warm glow and Isfail looked into eyes wide with fear and confusion. "Tell me what happened."

His calm voice lured her back, giving Akira a line to grab onto as the nightmare faded. She gripped the hand he laid over hers then wrapped her arms around him with a sob.

Holding her tight, Isfail murmured in her ear. "The old dreams, my sweet?"

"No," Akira replied with a shuddering sigh. "No." She held on, afraid to tell him. Afraid of what it might mean.

"Don't let me fall, Dan. Please, please don't let me lose myself!"

That familiar plea, one he hadn't heard in lunams, had Isfail drawing back, looking deep into eyes that now spilled hot tears. "Kira, I'll never let you fall, or let you go. Ever." He brought a gentle hand to her cheek. "You can tell me your fears, my love."

She could, Akira knew, her eyes closing briefly in relief as she began to calm. "I know." She laid her cheek against his bare chest, listening to the steady heartbeat. Knowing that heart beat for her.

"It's the voices," she began, letting him shift her back under the down-filled covers, wrapped close and safe in his strong arms. "I hear them in my dreams, but I don't see anyone."

"What do you see in the dreams?" he murmured, slowly stroking her back.

"Sometimes I'm in a valley. Lush green all around, wild, uninhabited." Akira stiffened and her voice dropped. "But it was. It was . . ."

The change in her voice threatened to unnerve him. It reminded Isfail of the way she'd sounded during past sleepwalking episodes. But she was awake now and, again, she hadn't had one of those spells in lunams—not since the terrible one at Ocean Cliffs Protectorate, before the ceremonies in Coroth.

Running gentle fingers through her hair, Isfail asked, "You said you're sometimes in a valley, what about the other times?"

Akira sighed, shifting to lay her head on his shoulder. "Sometimes it's misty white all around. It's cold."

"The avalanche?" he suggested, but she shook her head against him.

"No. Not that urgent, or desperate. I feel . . . tired, but determined."

"What are you doing in the dream?"

"Traveling. Riding a dark horse. It's white all around but I feel I know where I'm going." Akira pushed up to look into his eyes. "Yet it's not me."

Isfail's brow furrowed. "Do you think you're seeing it through someone else's thoughts?"

She was silent, staring down at him before pushing away to huddle beneath the blankets, her back to him. Akira felt her stomach clench with the fear that came without warning. When Isfail's arms pulled her back against him, his lips warm against her temple, she whispered, "Am I like my mother, Dan? Maran said Aira saw things no one else could see."

The last thing she expected was his quiet chuckle.

"We'll worry about that when you tell me about—What did he say? Ah, yes, *technologies* beyond imagining."

Akira turned back to him with a puzzled frown.

Kissing her softly, Isfail said, "The dreams you've described could mean something, or nothing, my sweet. Let's try not to worry until we see what more comes."

When she waved down the lamp to a dim glow, he held her close, hoping his love was enough to comfort and give her a peaceful night's sleep. But he knew she lay awake for a long time.

Her cheek resting against his chest, letting the beat of his heart steady her fears, Akira felt the first elusive touch of a consciousness not her own.

*T*hough Isfail tried to coax her to sleep, Akira was wakeful to the first light of dawn.

"I need to go out," Akira stated abruptly as they sat breaking their fast.

Isfail pushed his plate away, studying his wife as he picked up a cup of tea. He could see the fatigue and strain left from the dreams of the night. Then he looked toward the window and the opaque whiteness that hid the courtyard.

"It's hardly a morning for a walk, my sweet. Look at that ice fog."

She was already getting up to pace, her fingers rubbing her temples, with a distracted look on her face. "There's something . . . someone out there I need to find."

He was already on his feet, taking her shoulders to stop the restless movement. "Who, Akira? Who's out there?"

Akira heard the worry under his immediate alert for danger. But she didn't know how to answer. She shook her head, trying to rid herself of the sense that her thoughts were not her own, or not only her own. How could she explain that to him?

"Akira?" Isfail prodded. "Tell me what's happening."

Her eyes met his, the emerald green clouded by confusion. "I don't know. I just know I need to meet someone. He's close . . . but he won't come into the village before he talks to me."

"He?" Isfail felt anger stir for this unknown threat invading Akira's mind.

Again, she shook her head. "I don't know! I've never felt this before." Her head ached and she paled as her stomach roiled.

Isfail saw the sudden distress and caught her up, carrying her to their bed. Pulling a blanket over her, he laid a hand on her damp forehead but her skin was cold, not feverish.

"Can you call Asura, love?" he asked as he went to the bath chamber.

"It's nothing, Dan," Akira assured him, fighting the dizziness that had come over her. "Just reaction. There are too many thoughts in my head."

She tried to smile when he returned to stroke her face with a warm, damp cloth. Isfail sighed, setting aside the cloth to take her hands in his.

"Your color is returning." He examined her hands, watching warm color replace the blue under the neat nails. "I'd like Asura to come anyway."

"There's nothing physically wrong," Akira insisted, cautiously sitting up. "I know. I'm a healer, too, remember?"

Her teasing voice eased his worry and brought a smile as he kissed her lips. "How could I forget?"

Then he saw the determination on her face.

"We have to find out," she insisted.

Isfail stood, offering a hand to help her from the bed, his mind racing through anticipated challenges. "Of course we do."

But they wouldn't be finding out alone, he decided.

With no wind to disturb the fog, its cold surrounded them like an icy shroud. Though the morning sun infused a brighter glow, the frozen mist was thick enough to obscure their surroundings. There was little sound but the crunch of snow under hooves, the occasional blow of breath from the horses, and the subtle creak of leather as they rode, three abreast. Isfail and Kilronan flanked Akira as she guided them out the north gate to a broad trail into the woods beyond.

The thick walls surrounding Mountain Shadows were soon lost to sight. Winter-stripped trees appeared and fell behind as they held the horses to a walk through pristine snow. Silent and wary, all three strained to detect anyone as they traveled beyond Kilronan's preferred distance from the fortification. He was about to speak when Akira raised a hand, signaling a halt.

Isfail's grip tightened on the crossbow across his lap. Kilronan scanned the surroundings but didn't sense anything.

Then a horse and rider seemed to materialize from the icy air on the trail ahead. A faint shadow in the white mist, growing more distinct until a black horse and rider stood silently before them.

Akira felt a light touch in her mind though she'd blocked access.

"I mean no harm, Akira Muro. You know me, though we've never met."

"Kane," Akira said aloud, slipping back her hood.

"Sha, Kah'Shara." The stranger pulled down the black scarf covering his face then pushed back his own hood to reveal pure white hair. A weary smile joined the faint amusement in his deep green eyes. Then he straightened in his saddle before bending into a respectful bow.

"Le salen se vita longera, Sha'ala Majera."

"He greets her formally," Isfail said quietly when Kilronan glanced over. "I bring greetings for a long life, High Priestess."

"What?" Kilronan asked with a frown.

"It is an imperfect translation," the stranger responded. *"Sha'ala* is the title of a female leader of the Ishakan horse tribes, both a literal leader of the people and a spiritual leader."

"As is Syrai, your binding partner," Isfail noted. "You're Kane Kalronan. It's good to finally meet you."

That elusive smile returned. "And you, Commander Isfail. I understand you've been looking for me. I did not think to find you here."

"Akira and I were bound some lunams ago," Isfail informed him.

Kane gave him an appraising look before turning his attention back to Akira. "It is you I seek, little cousin. And it is to you that I bring my people's need."

Fifty-Five

Kane accepted the suspicion that underlay the polite interrogation from Lord Corcoran and his warriors in the hastily called masters council. With his own people in Ishaka essentially besieged by The Bow and under the death sentence of Lord Dateh and his Parliament cronies, he believed Mountain Shadows Protectorate had every right to view an unexpected visitor from Ishal as a potential threat.

So he sat, fighting fatigue and the feeling of despair at returning to the land that had taken everything that once mattered to him long years ago.

When Akira placed a hand over his, he managed a smile. This small, lovely woman who'd defeated monsters now sought to comfort him as the questions droned on and on. How like his Syrai she was in her compassion, brilliant mind, and strength of character.

He'd only ever seen her from afar, but he'd kept track of her all her life. Fulfilling a debt to a lost friend.

Some sign of that lifelong sorrow must have shown in his eyes, he thought when Akira's mind touched his.

"They will be finished soon and you can rest in our quarters."

"They do what they should do, little cousin. Do not worry about me."

Kane saw Isfail watching them, his eyes showing sympathy. He *hears*, Kane realized with some surprise. Was it only Akira's mindsight, or others as well?

A question from the man who'd been introduced in the woods, Kilronan, brought Kane from his inner wanderings.

"I'm sorry. Would you repeat your question?"

"How did you come into Caldala, sir?" Kilronan asked respectfully. "You've addressed all our questions with admirable candor. But you've appeared here in Mountain Shadows on your own horse, one of the Ishakan breed. It's highly unlikely that anyone from Ishaka would have made it to an Ishalian port or onto an outbound ship, based on what we've heard about the civil war there."

"You are correct, Master Kilronan. I took a more direct route from the Ishakan territory into the northernmost sector of Green River caldon."

For a long moment, everyone around the large table just stared at him.

Osharon broke the silence with a long, low whistle. "Considering the mountain range in that region, that's a journey I think we'd all like to hear about, but maybe you could just give us the short version for now. You look like you're ready to drop, sir."

"Indeed," Kane said evenly. "You've heard that my main purpose in coming is to petition your prince on behalf of my tribesmen. But another important reason is to advise Caldala that you have a new land access. We've discovered a passable rift between our countries. I'm sure you agree that this could be a security risk for your people and mine if left unguarded, as it is now. On Caldala's side, at least." He gave them an enigmatic look. "The horse tribes now watch the opening into our lands."

Lord Corcoran called the meeting back to order as questions shot out from all around the group. "I'm going to adjourn this meeting." His piercing look warned his warriors that he was not in a mood to accept dissent. "Master Kalronan deserves to rest, and this promises to be a lengthy discussion."

Inclining his head in a silent gesture of appreciation, Kane waited as the protectorate masters were dismissed in an orderly fashion. Their discipline spoke well of Lord Corcoran's leadership, he thought, while Akira and Isfail remained beside him.

Now Corcoran resumed his seat with a frown furrowing his brow. "I'd hoped this year would be less complicated than last. But we've already been sucker punched by enemies, we're dealing with Ishal's civil war and how Caldala might become embroiled in it, now this—a hole in our natural defenses."

"Better to know now, before we find ourselves facing an invasion from that direction," Isfail said quietly, though Kane could almost hear the thoughts racing through the commander's head: a new vulnerability in an isolated region, without a protectorate established there to defend, and nowhere near militia coverage. And any access was difficult in terms of roads—there were none—and terrain, advantage and disadvantage.

He had one last item to bring up now with only the relevant people present. Kane pulled a leather packet from the shoulder pack he'd brought in with him. "I promised Commander Shanow that I would deliver this, and he requested that it be revealed to only the three of you."

As Lord Corcoran accepted it and broke the seal, Kane went on, "He did say that bringing this information to your masters was at your discretion."

"It's a status report," Corcoran said, looking at Akira and Isfail. "We'll review it. But, for now, I'd prefer to keep this to the senior masters, at most." With a sigh, he stood, papers in hand.

"We can provide you with a suite here in the administration complex," he offered Kane, but smiled when Akira cleared her throat. "I see Lady Muro has another option."

It was Isfail, however, who voiced the alternative. "There is more than enough room in our quarters. I'm sure Kane and Akira would appreciate the chance to get to know one another under more relaxed circumstances."

"What you're politely not saying," Corcoran began ruefully, "is that he's probably safer with you."

Saying nothing about that cryptic statement, Kane just smiled as he accepted. He knew nothing about what was happening in this protectorate or village to warrant such caution, but he would certainly find out.

*T*here were luxuries he'd forgotten in his years of self-imposed exile, Kane decided as he lounged sleepily in the deep tub of hot water. While Ishakan life was not entirely primitive, it was traditionally nomadic. There were no architectural structures like the fortress around him, or the permanent living quarters of his hosts.

No esthetically designed bathing chamber to enjoy, and no indoor plumbing. He'd forgotten how much he missed indoor plumbing.

Still, he would never give up the life he had with Syrai and the horse tribes. He cherished the freedom and the responsibility Syrai's people had given him. Even the early years raising horses in strangely exotic Kuldor had led him to Syrai. She had given him Ishaka and a true family, like life-giving water to a man stumbling through the desert.

He would do what he needed to do for his tribe and return to her as soon as possible. Yawning, he left the tub, toweling off before putting on the thick robe Akira had left for him.

Instead of opening the door to the dim illumination and cold of winter caves, he stepped into the light and warmth of a large room. Akira was sitting on a sofa by the fire, while Isfail was up, already pouring a measure of whiskey to hand to their guest.

Kane sighed with pleasure after his first sip. "I must try to purchase some bottles of this to carry back. We don't often have the luxury of fine whiskey."

"I'll see to it," Isfail said as he took his seat by Akira's side, extending a hand to indicate a choice spot by the fire.

"I had forgotten people live this way," Kane told them with a slight smile as he settled into deep-cushioned comfort. "I was a youth when I left Caldala. Years later, in Kuldor, I had a house I built, but Kuldori furnishings were quite different. I've lived with the nomadic horse tribes for more than half of my life now, and it suits me."

He grinned, showing them a lighter side of his nature. "But I will enjoy the comforts of your world while I am here."

"There is so much I'd like to ask you, to talk with you about," Akira said. "But it can wait. Your room is ready for you whenever you'd like to settle in. We'll meet with Lord Corcoran after the midday meal tomorrow, so you can sleep or relax well into the morning."

Akira and Isfail stood up when he did, and Kane took her hand, bringing it to his lips. "I have waited a very long time to be with you, Akira. And even in these first brief hours, you give ease to my heart."

Turning to Isfail, he gave a slight bow before walking to the room they'd provided him and closing the door.

"What do you think he meant by that?" Akira mused as Isfail took the empty glasses to the kitchen.

Returning to take her hand while she waved down the lamps, Isfail smiled. "I think it will be fascinating to find out."

Fifty-Six

*I*t was fascinating, Isfail thought, watching Akira and Kane circle around one another the next morning. There was no doubt that each wanted to get to know the other, but they spent their conversations on what Isfail considered safe topics.

They talked about places they'd traveled to, people they'd met, and their impressions of other cultures. He never heard them approach the subject of family, at least not in his presence, and he believed Akira would include him in such personal discussions.

He decided to resist the urge to ask about that topic himself, and wondered if it would take another full Psyche to open that apparently sensitive subject. Maybe he'd ask Kilronan what he thought about it, if he had the chance. Or something of personal interest would be hinted at in the meeting with the senior masters this afternoon.

*T*he opening subject of the meeting was, as expected, the vulnerability in Caldala's mountainous border. Throughout anyone's memory, High Pass had been the only way to access their country by land, without risking lives trying to climb a dangerous range of mountains.

But, in searching for more secure locations for the Ishakans and better grazing options for their horses, Kane and his tribesmen had found a raw rift, a fresh tear in a region of basalt bluffs. Leaving some of his men to guard the opening, Kane had returned to inform his *sha'ala* partner and the tribal council. It had been decided that Kane would investigate the passage and, if it did access the neighboring country, he would petition Caldala on behalf of the tribes.

His cautious explorations had revealed a relatively clean shift, leaving a narrow passage easily traversed by a man on horseback. Kane estimated it to be as wide as the old pass had once been in most places, though only wide enough to comfortably admit a single horse and rider in some stretches.

He'd followed the new rift for most of a day before it opened into a narrow valley that was obviously older in origin. Kane had spent his first night camped beside an icy stream, surrounded by several campfires to dissuade an overly interested pack of wolves. A few force bolts had helped convince the predators that their hopes of an easy meal were in vain.

The next day had him following this valley in a winding configuration that matched the contour of a stream that gradually widened to a narrow river. A series of wide waterfalls had led into another canyon, but the banks had been passable on horseback.

"It took me three days to reach Mountain Shadows once I left the canyons," Kane finished. "With deep snow in places, and a brief snowstorm."

Kilronan studied him. "You originally left Caldala as a young man, so it might have taken longer now to travel unknown territory."

With one nod to note the point, Kane responded, "True. Though I traveled the northern part of Caldala extensively when I was a youth, including the moors, and this caldon, among others." He gave them his enigmatic smile. "And I'm quite good with a compass."

Carelon gave an appreciative laugh. "Got you there, Kil."

Chuckling himself, Kilronan acknowledged the jibe. "That helps our planning. So," he said, "We'll expect at least three days there, three days back, and however many needed to do the initial reconnoiter. Do you have suggestions for that?"

Kane appeared to think about it. "It took me a full two days once I entered the rift to come out in Caldala. I suggest we go in as far as the recent shift so that you can see for yourselves the magnitude of the movement."

"Did you get the impression that the rift might close again anytime soon?" Akira asked.

He looked at her solemnly. "It is not in my ability to predict that. But I saw no evidence of recent movement when I rode through, and my horse gave no sign of nervousness. We've learned to heed our horses' sensitivity to such matters, other animals too. They will usually react some moments before a human detects an earthquake, or major rock fall."

With some discussion on logistics, it was decided that Team Kilronan and Team Nathon would accompany Kane back to his point of access, investigate the situation and report back to both Mountain Shadows and Green River Protectorates. An official report would be written and immediately sent to the House of Coroth and Parliament.

It was all well reasoned and logically laid out.

And to almost everyone's surprise, Akira said nothing about wanting to go with the reconnaissance teams. If she noticed the questioning looks from Isfail and Kilronan, Akira declined to acknowledge them.

"Let's move on to the report from Commander Shanow," Lord Corcoran said, with his own brief look at Akira. "He says that the tribes have been generous in assisting the militia troops to endure the winter as comfortably as possible. Two more loyalist militia units were able to join them, though one had suffered heavy casualties in leaving Tash'tric, losing their own commander among them."

Turning a page, Corcoran continued his abbreviated report. "Shanow and his confidants have concerns that there might be spies among the third militia, but they'd had no problems from that quarter at the time he wrote this. They're keeping a close watch on the newest group.

"He expresses appreciation for the supplies from Caldala, saying that they've made their encampment tolerable, and kept morale high. With the winter beginning to break now, they're spending more time preparing the troops for battle and coordinating with the Ishakans in scouting parties to look for any sign of Dateh's troops."

Lord Corcoran sat back and looked around the group. "All good news. There's no mention of a need for military support from Caldala at this time." Now he gestured to Kane once more. "You've asked for time to present another matter, Master Kalronan."

"Yes." Kane stood up to address the masters. "My mission was two-fold—to warn our allies here in Caldala of a breach in their defenses, and to request an audience to discuss the plight of the tribes."

He walked to the map he'd asked for, and traced a finger around the perimeter of the acknowledged Ishakan territories. Then he ran that finger around the region that the tribes had had to fall back to, the current defensible zone. "The horse tribes retreated to the mountains about a year ago to avoid the Mors. We knew we could not defeat them with their massive force ability. But we had enough advance warning and were able to stock up on adequate feed and necessities for that winter, and we knew that terrain, the caves and canyons well."

Now he used his finger to show crossing out the wide, flat valley that was well within Ishakan land. "Most of our grain, hay, and crops are grown here. And the valleys around this region are our traditional winter grazing grounds. The Bow burned our fields just before harvest last year. They murdered Ishakan families who had returned to their summer settlements. Once we knew this was happening, the horse tribes sent our own people to defend those still out there, and we were able to drive the enemy out of our territory."

Kane frowned, anger in his eyes. "The council decided to pull back our people into the mountains. It was easier to defend, and we were getting news of Dateh's takeover in the cities. Then we learned that Ishal's Parliament had voted to claim the Ishakan territories, and there were rumors that Dateh's Bow was planning to eliminate the horse tribes.

"We were grateful when Commander Shanow arrived, proving that he would stand for us. Now other loyalists have come to join with him. The horse tribes will fight with them, for our lives and our lands. But we cannot last another winter in the mountains. Our treasure is in our horses, and they are weakening. We were fortunate that this winter was relatively mild, unlike the last. It's difficult to shelter our herds from severe weather."

He looked at Akira, and shook his head. "We had fewer foals born these past two seasons, and we lost a higher percentage of older animals. Without Caldala's generosity in providing feed, the losses would be much higher. But we cannot continue this way. If Dateh succeeds in taking over Ishal, we will be hard pressed to survive."

Lord Corcoran asked, "What can Caldala do to help you?"

Kane sat, looking tired again. "I am here to ask the House of Coroth if we could bring our horses into Caldala. The Northern Moors have good grazing, and are still mostly unsettled. We hope this would be a temporary accommodation, but we must negotiate a plan for both contingencies."

There was silence around the table while everyone thought about what Kane had said. Isfail was the first to speak.

"I will stand for the Ishakan people in this matter," Isfail said. "Akira and I will escort you to Coroth, and sponsor your petition." Beside him, Akira placed a hand over his and smiled.

Fifty-Seven

While the exploratory teams were out with Kane, Akira and Isfail made plans for the trip to Coroth. Along with what might be called business planning with Lord Corcoran, reports and letters to and from Coroth, there were more personal decisions to be made. And one was causing some concern.

Akira decided they should send the coach provided by Lord Corcoran out first, with most of their luggage. The coach would take the main road to Insalat, then the coast road to Coroth. Akira, Isfail, and Kane would leave before dawn the day after, on horseback, and follow the less-used Old River Road that ran beside the northern bank of Green River, eventually intersecting the coast road north of Corsalat.

"You're more exposed on horseback," Osharon said when the idea was brought to a limited senior masters' meeting.

Before Akira could respond, Arla spoke up. "True. But the coach has limitations too. Remember that one of the team of horses was brought down in last year's ambush. They would have more options and maneuverability on horseback."

She met Akira's eyes. "You're thinking the coach would be a decoy if The Bow hears you're traveling to Coroth. It'd be better to have a guard escort to maintain the illusion."

Shaking her head, Akira said, "Your protectorate needs all teams here, especially with things as they are just across the border. And you're already coordinating defense coverage for the new pass with Green River."

Isfail, who'd remained silent thus far, spoke up thoughtfully.

"The prince could send a contingent of Royal Guard to meet the coach in Green River. Mountain Shadows could provide an escort that far without taking too much time." He looked at Corcoran, who nodded agreement.

"You go along with this?" Osharon asked in amazement, staring at Isfail.

With a shrug, Isfail drummed his fingers on the table. "I don't like it, but the coach doesn't provide that much more cover. As Arla pointed out, it has its own vulnerabilities, and could be stranded in a well-planned ambush."

"The enemy won't be expecting us to take a slightly longer, less-traveled route, either," Akira explained. "Why would Commander Lord Isfail and his lady be riding and camping in the rough rather than traveling in appropriate style and comfort?"

"Only because they don't know *you*," Isfail stated, bringing her hand to his lips as the others chuckled.

Corcoran apparently decided it was an appropriate way to adjourn the meeting. He looked at Osharon as the master stood up. "Give my regards to your family."

Akira and Isfail walked out with him, the three continuing out into the high-walled lane leading to the guest quarters and a small gate above the protectorate fortress. "I'd forgotten," Akira said to Osharon, smiling up at him. "You're taking leave at Psyche Lakes. Please give them my regards as well, and blessings on your sister's coming-of-age celebration."

"She'll be insufferable," Osharon said, with a grin that showed his affection for his younger sister. "And she'll nag me about joining protectorate services. That's her latest ambition."

"Well," Akira said quietly, "It could be worse. Could you come by before you go? I have a gift for her, and perhaps you would take a small package to Maran for me?"

"No problem." Osharon tugged on her long braid playfully. "Kil's decided I'm his personal delivery service too. He gave me a pack full of stuff for his family before he left."

Laughing, Akira said, "Mine are small enough to tuck in wherever you have room."

A quick stop at Akira's quarters confirmed her description when she handed over a small cloth bag containing two small, labeled packets. She tipped up to kiss his cheek. "Thanks, Shara. Safe travels."

"You, too, sweetheart," he said cheerfully, and clapped Isfail's shoulder. "Take care of our princess, and yourself."

Nodding, Isfail stood with Akira, watching Osharon jog along the path to the fortification down the hill.

W hen the expedition to the new passage returned several days later, travel plans had been solidified.

With Kilronan in charge of reporting the results of the survey, he confirmed Kane's initial observations. After that meeting, Lord Corcoran called upon Kane, Akira, and Isfail to review a written version for the government heads. When the report had been fleshed out to everyone's satisfaction, Corcoran turned to specific details for their upcoming trip.

"Team Kilronan will escort you to Coroth." His statement was matter-of-fact as he pulled out a fresh sheet of paper and began to write.

Akira cleared her throat to gain Corcoran's attention once more. When he sat back, meeting her eyes, she said, "Sir, I don't think I've made this clear. This is a personal trip to Coroth and does not involve your protectorate. We are only informing you of our intentions, not requesting assistance or protectorate escort."

"Not entirely, Akira. Bringing specific details about the passage discovery to the prince concerns the security of the whole country." He continued to write as he spoke, but looked up when Akira went on.

"Regardless, I'm confidant that the three of us are capable of reaching Coroth without drawing on this protectorate's manpower."

A smile appeared in Corcoran's eyes before his quick look at Isfail. "Ahem . . . well, my dear." Shifting restlessly in his chair, Corcoran said, "Perhaps you haven't been informed of certain arrangements that were put in place once you became a member of Caldala's ruling family."

"Such as?" Akira questioned, frost touching her voice.

"The House of Coroth contracts with Mountain Shadows Protectorate to provide for your security. And Lord Isfail's, of course," Corcoran added hastily at a discreet sign from Isfail himself. "Team Kilronan has been specifically requested to escort you when you travel."

Appalled by this news, Akira took a moment to gather her thoughts before exclaiming, "Evan, this is ridiculous! Mountain Shadows needs every protectorate team here to defend the village. You can't have forgotten the attack against us just lunams ago."

She saw his eyes shift from amused to steely with remembered rage. "No, I haven't, so just cool your temper. I believe I've led this protectorate long enough to know what it takes to secure this region. And in case *you've* forgotten, that incident was specifically targeting you and Kilronan."

Isfail surged to his feet as Akira's face drained of color. "That's uncalled for, Corcoran!"

But Akira shook her head even as she leaned into him as a sudden wave of dizziness came over her.

But Corcoran was already moving around his desk, regret lining his face. "I'm sorry for that, my dear, and it wasn't what I really intended to say." Taking one of her hands, he lifted it to his lips before chafing her cold fingers.

None of them noticed Kane watching the whole scene intently, though he said nothing.

"My only point is that it's unlikely The Bow will mount an attack on Mountain Shadows when their main targets are not here. Perhaps that's a subtle distinction, at best," Corcoran continued, as Akira remained silent. "I'm far more concerned that the enemy might learn of your travels and lay a trap for you on the road. Between you and Kil, you have the best chance of detecting an enemy in time to defend yourselves."

Now Kane stood, crossing his arms over his chest as he studied the others. "I see that there's much I do not know regarding what's been happening here in Caldala, and in my cousin's life—dangers that I did not anticipate exposing her to. It would be better if I went on to Coroth alone. Perhaps Akira and Lord Isfail would provide me with letters of introduction so that I might be allowed to present my request to the prince."

Before Akira could protest, Isfail said firmly, "We're going with you. The plight of the Ishakan people is too urgent to risk any delays in Caldala's response. Akira and I can get you through the politics and make sure you receive a timely hearing."

Kane's dark green eyes met Akira's as she nodded with a slight smile.

"Your man speaks for you as well, little one?"

"He does."

Fifty-Eight

That evening, over a private dinner in Akira and Isfail's quarters, Kane broached the subject of family for the first time.

"I was saddened to hear of your father's death, Akira." He looked up from his study of his plate when a cold silence seemed to drop on the room.

With a sigh, Akira appeared to collect her thoughts, laying down her utensils and folding her hands in her lap. "Perhaps you are unaware that Hiro Muro was not actually my father."

Kane studied her with a slight frown between his eyes. "That bothers you a great deal, I see. But, yes, I knew he was bound to your mother when she carried another man's child."

The sudden grief in Akira's eyes dragged him in, making him question the choice he'd made to stay out of her life all the years. He'd thought it would be better for her to have a life free of the tragedy of her parents. Had he been wrong?

"What can you tell us?" Isfail asked, covering Akira's hands with one of his own.

Kane reevaluated what might be best for her. "Ask your questions, cousin. I will tell you what I can."

"You refer to me as your cousin. Is it only because we are Psyches?" Akira asked. "Or are we related?"

Hesitating briefly, Kane replied, "Maran is uncle to us both. I was born in Psyche Lakes."

Akira's brow furrowed over his obscure way of putting that, but another question was burning in her thoughts. "Did you know my natural father?"

"Yes."

When Isfail frowned at him, Kane realized he needed to move past his own reticence and answer Akira's questions more fully.

"Yes, I knew him. Kiran was my best friend, from childhood."

Kane watched her silently form the name with her lips. "You didn't know."

Her eyes brimmed with tears as she turned away, walking to the small kitchen to cover her grief preparing tea. "How could I know? My mother died when I was born, and no one ever told me any of this."

Hearing the bitterness and sorrow in her words, Kane looked at Isfail, who shook his head slightly, as if cautioning him to tread lightly.

"Don't do that!" Akira exclaimed, rounding on them. "Don't treat me like someone too fragile to be told the truth."

Isfail moved to her, pulling her into his arms as she resisted with tears flowing down her face. "Not fragile, love. I just want him to understand that you need to take this at your own pace."

Looking back at a visibly disconcerted Kane, Isfail said, "You two have been dancing around each other for days, never saying anything about your families, or your shared Psyche heritage."

Kissing Akira's forehead, he cupped her face now, lifting it so her wet gaze met his concerned one. "I didn't mean to upset you. Who knows better than I how strong you are? But you've chosen to keep your questions to yourself, until tonight."

"Yes," Akira murmured. "I don't know why I reacted that way. It was just so overwhelming—finally hearing my father's name."

"Come," Isfail encouraged gently, leading her to the couch. "I'll finish the tea while you and Kane talk."

Kane sat down on the hearth across from her, sad eyes studying, as if to measure her grief. "I wish to say something before we go on." He waited for her eyes to meet his. "Wherever I have traveled, whatever life I've led, I have thought of you, Akira. That may mean little to you, but it is true. I had ways of following your life and I used them. You were important to me, first as the only heart beating to keep Kiran and his Aira from being lost to memory. But, as you grew, and became who you are, I found I cared for you as much as those lost to me."

He looked down at his hands, clenched together between his thighs. "We have some bond, something that grew stronger over time, without us ever meeting in person. It is a deeper psychic connection than I have with any of my own children, and only matched by my link with Syrai."

"Is that how you are able to come into my mind, even when I try to block you?" Akira asked more calmly. When he sat back, looking at her in surprise, Akira told him, "Your thoughts were in my head, my dreams, before you came. Another consciousness inside me."

Isfail passed out cups of tea while Kane remained silent. "It frightened her. She had no idea what was happening."

"I do not know," Kane finally admitted. "You say you hear my thoughts?"

"Not really," Akira replied hesitantly. "It's more like seeing certain things through your eyes. And I don't know if all the . . . images have to do with you."

"What have you seen?"

Akira told him about the vivid dreams the night before he arrived. When she described the scenery, the sensations of cold and riding through the snow, feeling great fatigue, Kane nodded.

Then she described the verdant valley, the strong feelings associated with it, and watched Kane's eyes widen, the blood drain from his strong face. His eyes closed, and age seemed to weigh heavy upon him, despite the fact that he was only in middle years.

"What's wrong?" Akira asked with concern, while Isfail got up to pour a short glass of whiskey.

Kane took the glass, downing the contents in one long swallow. "I am well." But his brief response sounded false, even to his ears. Looking up at Isfail, he asked, "Do you have a map of the river road, one that includes what's known as the Dragon's Head of the Caldasian Chain?"

When the map was produced and spread over the table, now

cleared of dishes, the three of them stood around it while Kane traced the road they would travel on in two days. "Here," he said quietly, tapping the lonely Sentinel Peak before sliding his finger across the line denoting Green River, to the edge of the Dragon's Head.

His head bowed while he gave a long sigh. "Many of the answers to your past are here, Akira."

Fifty-Nine

Dragon's Head, Caldasian Range

kira and her companions wouldn't know if there had been a need for the decoy plan until they rejoined the coach at Coroth, but there had been no trouble for them so far. After a brief stay at Green River Protectorate, they'd left just after midnight, picking up the Old River Road between the village of Green River and the cypress swamps to the north.

Making good time with fair weather, their group spent one night camped in the foothills between the river and the town of Pallun before starting early the next morning. They reached the vicinity of Kane's requested detour before afternoon, stopping almost midway between Pallun and Corsalat.

Isfail studied a faint track bearing north, almost invisible amidst the overgrowth, then looked at Kane. "How long has it been since you've traveled here?"

Kane's face displayed an odd expression between pain and regret. "I was just seventeen that last trip." He lifted a hand and pointed to the solitary mountain, across the river to the southeast of their position, the one called Sentinel Peak. "You see that vertical ridge? We knew the way when we could look there and see the horizontal fault crossing it. The mountain cross, with both arms equal in length, as you see now."

Isfail glanced at Kilronan and got his quick nod before following Kane onto the overgrown track. Akira and the others followed. Bushes crowded in, their thin branches brushing at the riders. The horses lowered their heads as they pushed through, snorting as if the plants irritated them.

Eventually, the dense undergrowth thinned, giving way to a strange forest—thick trunks of old-growth trees with branches so long and heavy some dipped to the ground before rising toward the sky once more. Ferns replaced the shrubbery, and moss grew in thick cushions, making countless tiny streams that crossed one another until the way seemed to be more of a shallow watercourse rather than forest floor.

Kane led them up a slight rise where the woods opened to a small, sun-washed meadow of silver-green grasses sprinkled with tiny purple blossoms.

It was beautiful, Akira thought, peaceful. But this wild beauty wasn't enough to distract from the pressure in her head, the weight of watchfulness inside her.

"Lady Muro?" Asura signaled a stop, urging her horse forward even as Isfail brought his stallion around.

Akira wavered in the saddle, fighting the sudden onslaught of nausea. She barely felt her husband catch her as she began to slide off Kahshara. Then the darkness took her.

*A*kira. Come back, sweet."
His voice was gentle, calm, but the eyes Akira opened hers to were full of worry. She blinked, trying to squeeze the strong hand holding hers. "It's all right," she murmured, closing her eyes against the pain pounding in her head.

"It's not," Asura stated, placing a cool hand to Akira's forehead. "We need to make camp until you're fit to ride."

Akira shook her head in protest then struggled to sit up. She heard Asura giving quick instructions but Isfail was already supporting her as she vomited.

She didn't know how long the seizure lasted, but Akira became aware of lying with her head in Isfail's lap, with the others kneeling or crouched around her. Concern was evident on each face.

Surprisingly, it was Kane who shifted closer and placed a

soothing hand on her cheek. "We should turn back, little one, go on to Coroth. The ghosts of the past will always be waiting."

"They press on me, Kane. They reach out to me." Akira pressed a hand to the side of her head. "Inside me, always watching!" Her last words quavered as a tear slid down her face.

Placing his hand over hers, Kane looked deep into her eyes. "Is that what you believe?" When she nodded, he squeezed her hand lightly. "We'll see what happens next."

He looked at Isfail. "You fear that this might harm her."

"Yes," Isfail said sharply. "Can you tell me that she'll be safe if we go on?"

Kane seemed to listen to some inner voice for a moment before focusing on Isfail once more. "There is nothing here that will harm her now."

Isfail insisted that Akira ride with him if they were to go on with this expedition. She sat in front of him, grateful for his arms circling her as he held the reins. Though she felt somewhat better after emptying her system, the odd sensation of having more than one person's thoughts in her head grew stronger.

When Kane looked back at her with worry in his eyes, she fought the urge to ask him about it. Whatever it was, she wanted answers to her past.

They reached the edge of the forest, with everyone immediately reining in their mounts at the change in terrain. A spectacular cliff rose hundreds of feet before them, looking as if it was one great rock of ancient granite that stretched away on both sides until trees once more disguised its magnificence.

Breaking the awed silence, Kane said, "One of Caldala's wonders." He looked back with a smile when young Maronan spoke.

"Dragon's Mount," he said, his deepening voice breaking in his excitement.

"Yes," Akira said. "I thought about bringing Team Kilronan through this range, rather than Misosono, when we were training last year. But we ran out of time."

"We're here now," Kilronan said, his gaze still ranging over the amazing edifice.

But Isfail was assessing the cliff for other features. "Is that fold on our left significant?"

"The southern gate," Akira and Kane said in unison, staring at each other after they'd spoken.

Akira felt Isfail's arms tighten around her. She looked at Kane. "But it's no longer open."

"No." Kane murmured to his horse and led the group along the face to the left until he stopped on the far side of the rock feature. From here, they could see the outline of a narrow break in the rock, but it was filled by what appeared to be loose rock, packed tight enough to prevent passage.

His features set, devoid of feeling, Kane said, "I believe I'll need help with this." He dismounted, waiting as Isfail did the same before lifting Akira down while Team Kilronan walked over to stand with them.

"What do you want us to do, Kane?" Akira asked, lightly touching his arm.

He studied the fill for several minutes before indicating specific points. "We need strong force bolts there. How many of you have that ability?" He looked at Kilronan's people, lifting a brow in surprise when all raised a hand.

"Celina and Eron aren't at Psyche strength, but Asura has strong ability. Maronan—"

"Is full blood," Kane interrupted with a nod, studying the youth with interest. "One of our family line."

He glanced at Isfail with a slight smile. "It seems you're the only one who won't be able to contribute to this action. Still, you've a sharp eye and mind, so keep an eye out for better impact points."

Assigning positions, Kane reached out to take Akira's right hand, leaving her the left to fire from. He counted down and seven bolts hit the rock fill, creating a rumbling echo as the gap rippled with shifting rocks.

"Again," Kane said quietly. The second volley had holes

opening and rocks plunging down. The next set off a roaring clatter of noise and raised a thick cloud of dust and debris.

Shielding their eyes, they waited for the dust to settle. When it had, the gap was open. Leading their horses across the grass, around boulders and the rubble that now littered the ground, they traversed the narrow passage between solid rock walls.

Akira felt surprise that the distance from one side to the other was no more than five grown horses, lined nose to tail. Coming out behind Kane, that surprise was eclipsed by awe at what spread before her on the far side.

Sixty

*I*t was the valley of her dreams—wild and green, opening before them as they led their horses from the narrow crevice in the wall. Graceful trees were covered with new leaves, pale green to add to a multitude of colors and hues. Birds of many varieties winged through the air, their voices trilling and chattering in the mild breeze. Yet there were no sounds of civilization, no voices raised in song or greeting.

But there had been, Akira somehow knew. "Serenity Valley. There was once laughter here, joy." She didn't know she'd spoken aloud until she saw everyone looking at her. She met Kane's tormented eyes and felt his pain. "In the end . . . there were screams."

He said nothing as he stepped up into the saddle, guiding his mount down a narrow, winding path that led to the valley floor.

The rest of the group followed and found him watering his horse at a spring-fed pond. Kane's voice was calm when he asked Akira, "What do you feel here?"

She saw Isfail bring his horse next to Kahshara, felt his hand take hers. So she opened. At first, there was only the sense of peace, the pure impressions of life, of things that grew and thrived here. There was also curiosity, a wondering about their intrusion, and watchfulness toward the beings that had broken the isolation of the valley.

Then there was sorrow underlying the peacefulness of today. A memory of loss so deep, the very soil, the air, even the water seemed to hold that remembrance. Akira felt Kane's mind touch hers and knew that he had been a part of what was now gone.

"They called themselves the Lost Clan," she murmured, looking into the trees. "Now they truly are."

Kane led his horse away from the pond, deeper into the trees, following a path only he could see. Akira and the others followed. When small hillocks, mounds covered with flowering vines, began to appear along the way, Kane slowed his pace.

Akira thought he moved like a man carrying a burden too great to bear.

Then Isfail spoke beside her. "They're houses, Akira, what remains of them."

She realized that he meant the mounds of vines, her blood freezing as she looked at the one they were passing. A broken wall of stones was just visible, the corner of some forgotten building.

"There were ten along this lane," Kane said clearly, stopping to look around, his face a mask. "Most belonged to families. There were other residence lanes off the central square."

He lifted a hand to the south. "There were longhouses over there, where unbound men and women lived. A meeting hall to the north—all gone to rubble now."

Akira felt unbearable pain and sorrow as his head bowed.

"What happened here?" Kilronan asked as he dismounted.

"Arthon Baronan," Kane replied with fierce contempt.

"Baronan," Isfail echoed while they followed Kane to the overgrown ruins of what appeared to have been the village square. A wide, stone-encased well had been plumbed to feed a carved stone fountain. Now water burbled over a fractured lip, feeding a small stream flowing over and among flagstones made slippery with waterweed.

He watched while Kane removed the saddle and bridle from his Ishakan mare, sending her off to graze in the wild grasses that now filled what once had been gardens. While Kane continued his silence, the others saw to their own horses before Kilronan directed his team to set up camp.

Isfail took Akira's hand when she settled wearily on the remnants of the fountain surround. "How are you feeling, my sweet?" He worried over her pallor, and he'd seen the occasional distress in her eyes that told him she was fighting against the recurrent nausea.

But Akira took his hand in both of hers and smiled. "I'm fine, Dan." When he only raised an eyebrow, she sighed. "There's too much here, too many thoughts crowding my mind."

Placing a kiss on top of her head, Isfail said firmly, "We'll go on to Corsalat as soon as we finish here. If necessary I'll take you to Insalat and my quarters there. You'll get some rest and do whatever Asura tells you to do."

He caught Kilronan's concerned gaze and tipped his head to Asura. With a brief nod, Kilronan turned to his team's healer.

Akira looked up when Asura crouched beside her moments later. Smiling faintly, Akira just shook her head at Isfail, but she didn't protest when Asura insisted that she lie down in the shade.

Isfail walked over to Kilronan as the master signaled Maronan to them.

"What's wrong with her, Mar?" Kilronan asked quietly.

The youth's eyes grew dark when he looked inward. "Lady Muro is frightened by the other."

"The other?" Isfail and Kilronan said simultaneously then glanced at one another, frowning.

Maronan's face held a look of intense concentration. "It watches and waits. It's stronger in this place. She can't escape it here."

Raising a hand to halt Kilronan's next question, Isfail asked, "You say *It*, what do you mean? What is it saying to her?"

"Nothing. It doesn't speak, just watches her, waiting."

"Waiting for what?" Kilronan pressed.

Shaking his head slowly, Maronan replied, "I don't know. And that's what frightens her. She doesn't know."

"She doesn't?" Kane spoke close to them.

His voice surprised the three men and they all turned to see him leaning against a nearby tree. Kane studied them with a curious expression on his lean face.

"You said you're connected to her," Isfail said with a hint of temper. "Is this . . . illness something to do with that?"

"No." Kane looked over at Akira with that odd look on his face. "What she sees here, feels about the valley, those could be influenced by that connection. My own grief could be enhancing her feelings. But I don't believe that would make her physically ill."

He turned back to Isfail. "I agree that we should finish what we need to put behind us here as quickly as possible, for Akira's well-being."

They spent an hour after the midday meal with Kane giving them a brief tour of the valley around the original settlement. From a small hillock, he pointed out the far end, narrowing dramatically until it ended in a ridge of dark basalt. One of the most prominent and intriguing features there was the large tunnel mouth from a long-dead volcano, but other than its usefulness for storage, the clan hadn't been inspired to explore the long length of it. There'd been a partial cave-in about two hundred paces in, and it was generally thought that the long cave ended somewhere further along.

It was clear that the Psyches who'd once lived here had enjoyed a rich life. They'd farmed, raised livestock, and many had been talented crafters, working with textiles and precious metals, among other things. What architectural bits were left reflected a sense of beauty with their strength of purpose.

Later that evening, with everyone relaxed around a large fire, Kane started his tale.

"We can talk about the history of this valley and the lost clan another time." Kane looked directly at Akira. "I think what you need to know while we're here begins and ends with Baronan.

"Arthon Baronan first came through the tunnel in the harvest season, two years after I came from Psyche Lakes to live here with Kiran," Kane told them. "Although it was a surprise to find an outsider and one without Psyche heritage here among us, the clan gave Baronan an easy welcome. He expressed an avid interest in the colony, offering trade opportunities, and saying he wanted to learn more about us. But the mask of friendship quickly proved false."

Kane tossed another branch on the fire as twilight deepened around them. "The village elders had agreed to trade some breeding stock of the small cattle raised here against the promise of a breeding herd of a type of goat known for its silky coat. We had nothing like that for the production of clothing, blankets, or trade goods."

"How were you making blankets and warm clothing?" Asura wondered.

"The clan traded outside, in Pallun or other towns, for shorn wool." Kane sighed. "They thought this was a good trade that would benefit the village in the long run. But Baronan took the cattle agreed upon, saying the goats would be brought the next lunam."

Kilronan poked at the fire. "They never arrived," he speculated.

"No. Then there were other problems, little things at first," Kane continued. "Thefts from the village, animals missing, crops damaged. Kiran and other young men blamed Baronan and his men, but there was no evidence. The elders didn't want to confront such a powerful lord of Caldala. There was talk of sealing off the cave, making it look like an accident."

Isfail shrugged. "That could have made it less convenient for Baronan but he must have known about the other gateway."

"The way we came in is more easily defended and it was a much longer way for Baronan to go to harass the clan." Kane looked into the shadows under the trees. "We'd never know. The elders had just begun debating the matter when Baronan came with a woman. He called her Kara and said she was a force caller who wanted to learn about our force powers."

Kane met Akira's eyes. "She wielded dark powers, yet your Ambassador Core elected her as their highest leader."

"Ana Karsh," Akira said, refusing to look away. "Mistakes are always a part of life, Kane. I killed her some lunams ago."

"Some mistakes are more destructive than others. Mine was in failing to use what's in me to read her then, and end her." He shook his head, stabbing at the dirt with a stick. "Well, this time the village elders stood firm. They were courteous but asked them to leave and not return unless Baronan was willing to deal in good faith."

Kane looked around the group. "He just laughed and said the price for good faith would be our women. Then he pointed at Aira and said that she would be his tribute next time he came. It took three strong men to restrain Kiran from leaping at him in rage. Still, Baronan just smiled, one that would freeze the bones. The woman with him said nothing, just stared at Aira.

"The mood among the villagers present grew ugly, but the elders called for calm reason. They ordered Baronan and his woman away. They left, though Baronan promised to return before the next full moons. That was only six days away."

Akira shifted closer to Isfail as if seeking his comfort. "Is that when my father asked you to take my mother back to her family?"

He nodded. "The elders called a village meeting and laid out Baronan's threat. The clan was peace loving, but they had the ability to fight to defend their lives and they planned to. Several of those with strong force skills would go bring down the tunnel and seal the cave access the next day. Others would watch the crevice at the far end and defend it. It was agreed." But Kane shook his head.

"Early the next morning, Kiran came to me, insisting that I escort Aira to Psyche Lakes. He told me she was carrying their child and he wouldn't risk them." Kane gave a bitter laugh. "I was young, defiant. I told him that we'd fight and we'd win. But Kiran had the sight—he could dream future events. Sometimes even far past events. The visions weren't always clearly defined, but this time what he saw terrified him."

Looking at Akira once more, Kane said, "Your mother could see the past." Whatever he saw in her face evidently told him what he wanted to know. "Visions of things others cannot see create challenges for us. They can make us doubt ourselves, but we must accept them."

"They're part of who you are," Isfail said, holding Akira close.

"Yes." Silent for several moments, Kane seemed to look back in time. "But this time it wasn't enough. We, Kiran and I, were preparing the horses before sunup the next morning when the attack came. Baronan never intended to wait the six days."

Kane's voice was bitter. "The men sent to close the tunnel found an ambush, but two made it back to raise the alarm. Then we saw the signal from our people guarding the cleft. We were being attacked from both ends of the valley." With fierce eyes, Kane looked at the others. "But we weren't helpless, as Baronan and his men soon found out. The clan lost eight men in that first assault but we ended most of those who came into our valley; thirty-one by our count."

"But not Baronan," Isfail said. "He just sent his men that day?"

"We found him at the tunnel," Kane said with a thin smirk. "I guess he found it more to his liking to send others to kill for him."

Looking at the surprise on the faces around the fire, Kane shrugged. "He was brought to the village to face the tribunal of the clan elders. They . . . *we* should have seen that Baronan was unnatural. He was livid, enraged that we would dare imprison him, judge him. But his rage was cold and evil. He swore that he would have his revenge." Kane dragged his hands over his face. "We should have seen that fair justice would not end it."

"What did the clan do?" Kilronan asked from where he sat on the ground.

"He was held to account. The elders judged that he would be taken to Coroth and charged with murder and other crimes against the village. It would mean revealing more of ourselves to the outside world." Kane breathed deep. "No matter. *She* came that night. Ana Karsh. And she brought a storm of death."

"The black winds, that was her strongest ability," Akira said.

Nodding, Kane replied, "The clan had never seen anything like it. At first, people thought it was a freak storm. Kiran understood sooner than the rest. He ordered me to get Aira out. There was no time to argue. She was terrified, torn between wanting to stay with him and the need to protect the child she carried. I knew I had to do what Kiran wanted, so I took the pack he'd prepared days before. He lifted Aira onto the horse behind me while the winds stripped the trees, growing stronger by the minute. Slapping the horse, he ordered us to go."

When Celina made as if to speak, Kane nodded to her to continue, needing the respite before going on.

"I'm sorry, but I don't understand . . . Karsh was a strong force caller, but you said this was a colony of pure Psyches. How could she kill everyone? People fought back, right?" Celina asked.

Kane nodded slowly. "You ask a good question, but you might see the fighting ability of our race through your experience with Akira." He met the girl's curious stare. "No one, to my knowledge, no other Psyche has ever had Akira's power and range of force abilities. We were too naïve. We'd never been required to defend our valley. Though many of us had the ability to use force bolts and shields, we were untrained, unskilled in real fighting and defense tactics.

"Karsh and some of Baronan's men used stealth to approach the village. They were able to take out some of the guards we'd posted. That's when she called her demon winds."

"Kiran wouldn't go with you?" Kilronan asked.

"He wouldn't leave his clan. He loved Aira, but he stayed to fight for his people." Kane held Akira's grief-stricken gaze. "And he stayed to give us cover. I knew we'd never make the cleft with Karsh's winds tearing down the valley. There was only one way, a deer trail that Kiran and I had followed a few times. It meant going back through the village. People were running, some stood to fight, to use whatever they had to defend, to fight the unnatural storm.

"Riding full out beside us, Kiran set a shield wall, blocking the worst of the wind and debris." Kane could still see it all in his mind. "He turned back, waving me on when we began the climb up the southern slope. When my horse faltered we dismounted and continued up on foot. It was steep, rocky, and it was dark except for the moonlight. Dangerous if we'd stopped to think. But we made it to a narrow keyhole in the rock face, hardly big enough for Aira, let alone a man."

"You made it through," Isfail remarked when Kane fell silent for long minutes.

Kane breathed out. "I almost left her to go on alone. Aira hadn't spoken since her last touch from Kiran. She stood on the other side of that break in the rock, looking beyond me while I still stood on the valley side—her face bleak, white as the hair tangled around it. Then her eyes . . . your eyes." Kane stared at Akira. "You have her emerald green eyes, but yours are shaped long and a little tipped up, like Kiran's."

He shook himself from memories as he continued. "Aira looked at me, held out a hand while she laid the other on her belly. There was no choice. I pushed the pack to her and somehow worked myself through that damned hole."

No one said a word while Kane stared into the fire, his face a mask of grief. "When I returned less than a week later, it was too late."

Sixty-One

"Two hundred and sixty-three people lived peacefully here in Serenity Valley. They cared for themselves and harmed no one." Kane stared into the fire, lost in the past. "I found two hundred and sixty-one clan bodies when I returned after taking Aira away."

No one spoke and he continued in that haunted voice. "Everyone dead. At first . . . I just didn't know what to do. I spent that night sitting there." He pointed to the stone well in the overgrown square. "Just sat on the ground, leaning against the well, remembering all the faces, the friends whose bodies lay cold all around me. Even the farm animals, the horses . . . all killed. Death was a shroud over the valley, and I wanted to be one with it.

"I don't remember the night passing, but at sunrise I got up and did what I could to lay them to rest. One by one, I found them and carried each to their home . . . laid them on their beds."

Tears of grief rolled down Akira's face as she opened to his memories and the sight of the young man as pale, face as lifeless as the bodies he carried so tenderly.

"I felt the families should be together, so I placed the unbound men and women with their families when I could. Those who had none were returned to the longhouses where they'd lived."

Now he turned his ravaged face to Akira. "Kiran, my best friend, your father, I left him for last. I hated that he was alone in the house he'd built for Aira. But I had done what he asked of me."

Kane looked away again. "There have been times when I

hated him for sending me away. The next day, after I'd recovered the dead, it all erupted."

Akira saw it, understood what was in his anguished thoughts. "You destroyed the village. It was you who reduced these buildings to rubble."

"Tombs," Kane corrected bitterly. "The only graves I could give them to keep the carrion birds from picking their bones clean."

Isfail stood behind Akira with his hands warm on her shoulders. "It was the right thing to do."

Standing up restlessly, Kane stared into the darkness. "I would have done more. Baronan and his witch were gone. I followed the tracks to the west end of the valley. They'd climbed up the escarpment, gone through the old volcanic tunnel. Filled with hate and seeking revenge, I went into the cave. I drew up my hate, feeding my force powers on it, wanting to destroy Baronan and all who served him."

For one terrible moment, Akira understood that violent need to kill those who had ended these people, her father's people.

"But you didn't," she said quietly.

He gave a bitter laugh. "Don't look for any compassion there, little cousin. I stalked down that black hell-mouth, hungry for the kill. Over an hour in, I reached an opening at the other end." Kane stared off into the darkness once more. "As I stood there, planning my next move to locate Baronan in my unthinking rage, I heard Kiran's voice in my head, telling me not to be a fool."

Kicking a rock to strike against the stone well, Kane sighed. "He was always saying that."

"What did you do?" Kilronan asked.

"After some time, some thought, I turned back. About fifty paces in, I used the pent up forces within me to collapse the tunnel." Staring at the ground, Kane breathed deep. "It wouldn't have mattered if it had buried me under it. But . . . I returned to the valley, saddled my horse and rode away. I set off the rockslide to seal the crevice, hoping the dead could rest in peace. Then I left

Caldala, vowing never to return." Kane looked at Akira, gave her a mournful smile. "And I stayed away, until now."

Akira stood up and walked to him. "Can you find peace, Kane? Will you allow this part of you to heal?"

He let out a long breath. "Syrai asks me the same questions every year, on the anniversary of my leaving this valley." Kane touched Akira's cheek lightly. "She will be pleased to meet you. You are kindred souls."

"You love her," Isfail said, taking Akira's seat by the fire.

With a nod, Kane said, "Though we met under tragic circumstances for Syrai, she was my salvation."

The others had been listening quietly; now Maronan sat straighter just as Kilronan did. Isfail's eyes narrowed and he rose to move toward them when Akira and Kane shifted to stand back to back.

Where the night had held only normal sounds of wind whispering among the leaves and vegetation, the occasional hoot of an owl or squeak of a bat, now there was unnatural silence. The wind had stilled, but Akira felt a faint brush against her face, like tender fingers skimming by.

She met Isfail's eyes as he came to her. Kilronan and his team were already surrounding them, scanning the darkness around the old square for danger.

Kane stiffened as the faint trill of a flute filled the air like morning mist. "Do you hear that?" he whispered hoarsely, as if he were afraid it was only in his mind.

"A flute," Kilronan replied.

"Kiran played that melody," Kane told them.

Suddenly, silvery wisps filled the air around them, dancing on a breeze none could feel. They twined and slipped around the eight people who stared at the eerie spectacle in cautious wonder. Kilronan signaled his people closer around the three in the center, but the will-o-wisps spiraled and spun in a faster dance, flowing like water then bursting up in a shower of stars before winding around Akira and Kane in bright streams of iridescent light.

"They're happy," Maronan said, breaking the silence of the group. "Can you feel it, Lady Muro?"

"Yes," she whispered, lifting a hand, palm up to a silvery cloud that flowed between her lifted fingers. It pulsed there, shifting into soft blues and greens.

"It has sentience," Akira murmured. "Warmth and emotion. Maronan is right—they are happy that we're here." She looked at Kane. "Especially you."

Kane closed his eyes, lifting cupped palms up. The ethereal entities rushed to him, spinning like fairy dancers, their delicate colors sharpening and brightening around him. They bounced like joyful children in and out of his hands. They flowed gently around his arms, up to his face, where tears streamed. Some appeared to caress his face, his hair, in what could only be described as affection or love.

Akira's voice was charged with emotion while she gripped Isfail's hand tightly, saying, "They are the eternal spirits of those who lived here, the life energy of these Psyches. Kane protected them by sealing the valley from outsiders."

"Do they live here?" Asura asked breathlessly.

Shaking her head, Akira replied, "They do not have a corporeal existence anymore, but they are aware on another plane." She remembered her own near-death experience after defeating the Mors nearly a year ago. How she was able to see and converse with dead loved ones. "Their spirits, or souls, exist in a place beyond us, unless they choose to interact, as now."

"Do you know why they're here?" Isfail asked her, marveling at the miracle of this visitation.

"I think his grief and love brought them." Akira watched the wisps that stroked slowly over Kane's rapt face.

Then Kane spoke softly. "It is more, Akira. There are four living full Psyches here now." He opened his eyes and looked at Isfail. "And you. They feel the aura in you and the other."

Isfail gave a brief nod. "My father's mother was a full Psyche from the same village Akira comes from."

Kane's mouth lifted in a slight smile. "That is why they see you as one of them."

But Akira's eyebrows drew together. "The other?" But the sudden sprint of the spirits distracted her from Kane's amused expression. Sparkling streams and lights spun around her in a joyful whirling dance that defied Akira's mortal understanding. Warmth and feelings of delight suffused her.

Then, as suddenly as they'd appeared, the silvery wisps vanished. Before anyone could comment, the translucent form of a man seemed to coalesce from starlight.

Kane dropped to his knees as his head bowed, but raised his face when the apparition seemed to lift his chin with a ghostly hand.

There appeared to be some communion between man and spirit, but the others could hear no words. Even so, some of the grief seemed to lift from Kane's face as he got to his feet and held out a hand to Akira.

Without a word, she left Isfail's side to take Kane's hand. But it was the spirit who held her fascinated attention. This ephemeral man looked deep into her eyes. There was such love there, Akira realized with shock.

"This is—" Kane faltered for a moment, "Kiran. He is your father."

Akira felt the warm yet weightless touch to her cheek as the spirit reached out to her, as he used a transparent finger to wipe a tear from her face. And, finally, she could see that she had indeed inherited the shape of her father's eyes.

"I love you," she whispered.

For the briefest moment, there was regret and sorrow in those ghostly eyes before he smiled. Akira felt the kiss he pressed to her forehead before the spirit of her father faded.

Isfail's arms came around her as sobs shook her body. Akira felt Kane's hand touch her back.

"Kiran could not speak to you because you had no connection in life. I can tell you that it gave him peace to see his daughter, and to see Aira in you."

Gathering herself to speak clearly, Akira asked, "Is she with him? My mother?"

Kane shook his head. "She cannot come here because she died in Psyche Lakes. But they are together in another place. Someday, when it is your time, you will be with them."

Akira turned to Kane and saw the transformation in his eyes. "You needed this."

He sighed, looking out into the moonlit landscape. "I needed to know they *are* at peace, that they didn't blame me for abandoning them."

"As you blamed yourself," Isfail said with a soldier's compassion.

"Yes." Kane stroked Akira's hair. "Kiran reminded me that if I had stayed, he would have lost both wife and daughter. A soul can suffer, and he did when Aira appeared in the other world so soon after he died. Seeing you here gave him the love of his child, his legacy. Connecting with both of us gave him the closure Kiran needed to leave this place at last."

Sixty-Two

I sfail watched Akira sleep as dawn spread over the waking valley. He crouched beside her for a moment, concerned by how pale she was. As soon as he could, he was ending this journey into her past and taking her on to civilization. Asura had watch duty by the fire and nodded to him when he tipped his head toward his wife.

He stood up and walked into the trees to deal with bodily necessities before returning to the group at the square. Kilronan and Kane were standing atop a pile of rubble just west, so Isfail changed course to join them, nodding to their brief greetings as he worked his way up.

"We need to move on," Isfail stated without ceremony. "Akira needs proper accommodations to recover from whatever this illness is. She needs a master healer."

Kilronan nodded, obviously agreeing, but Kane just looked thoughtful.

"Is there something more you want from this place?" Isfail asked, meeting Kane's eyes with sympathy, despite his own need to take Akira away.

"Only to be sure that the valley is protected from intruders," Kane replied quietly. He looked around for a few minutes then he spoke to Kilronan. "I'd like to check out the tunnel but I think Isfail and I should go first, before risking the others."

Glancing at Isfail, Kilronan said, "I'll stay here and get things ready to go. You can send a message to us by mindsight and we'll join you later."

Since Kilronan was the only man other than himself that

Isfail trusted to keep Akira safe, he agreed and set off without objection.

It was beautiful land, Isfail thought, easily understanding why people had settled here. He and Kane left the valley floor and its wild remnants of crops that had once been cultivated there. Black and gray basalt rose above them, starting as a shallow slope that changed abruptly to sheer cliff.

Kane led the way on what Isfail could see had once been a foot-trail that led to the large black opening into the mountain face. Two tall men, one standing on the other's shoulders, could easily stand upright at the mouth and as far into the darkness as Isfail could see. Those tall men could stand side by side with both arms outstretched, fingertips to fingertips, and barely touch the other side of the walls.

There were remnants of wooden racks, some with barrels and casks still lying on them, or broken in the collapsed wreckage of others.

"We stored certain goods here," Kane told him, looking about the cave. "Some kept better in the cool cave conditions. There were also emergency supplies, should the clan need to shelter here." He lifted his shoulders. "I heard there were a few winters, and seasons with torrential rains, when that had been prudent."

He looked off into the blackness of the tunnel, silent for some minutes.

Righting one of the intact barrels to sit upon, Isfail said, "Was there a reason you wanted to talk with me alone?" He heard Kane let out a long breath before he spoke.

"I am concerned with the idea that Akira plans to act in Ishal's defense. I do not feel it is necessary to bring her into it, no matter how powerful an asset she would be. Shanow and his soldiers are dedicated, and he's kept them training physically and mentally over the winter. They are well prepared to counter any of The Bow." Kane turned to face Isfail. "And my people are cunning, expert scouts. We know our territory, and we have force abilities that we have been honing over the last year."

"This is all excellent news," Isfail said with relief. "I wish you would tell her this yourself." He stood up, crossing his arms over his chest as he wandered slowly about. "But I know her; she has strong feelings about justice and defense. If she feels she can prevent something, or tip the balance against an enemy, she can't be stopped."

"It is not her war," Kane insisted. "Why should she risk herself?"

With a droll smile, Isfail sat again. "That's not how she sees the world. If someone asks for help . . ."

"Then she is unique," Kane muttered. "Few of her kind would act so selflessly."

"I agree," Isfail said, studying the combination of anger and pain on Kane's face. "Do you feel that way because of your own people? Those you left in Psyche Lakes? I know Akira would like to understand her family, those she's descended from. You could help her with that, but you avoid talking about Psyche Lakes."

Kane frowned, though his voice held a hint of acceptance. "I haven't decided what to tell her. And, yes, I agree she has a right to know." But mixed with acceptance was concern. "I know she's mostly stayed away from Psyche Lakes from the time she entered the Ambassador Core. Does she go there now that she's in civilian life?"

Isfail shook his head. "She confronted Aino Muro in Mountain Shadows some lunams ago, and I think it's still uncomfortable for her. Akira has formed close relationships with Maronan and his grandfather, Maran, who is also Aira's brother." He recalled that the man was aware of this. "But she hasn't gone back to Psyche Lakes in a long time."

An expression of relief crossed Kane's face. "Let her stay away, Isfail. There's nothing she needs from that village."

"Why did you leave Caldala?" Isfail asked suddenly.

Something cold and bitter appeared in Kane's eyes, but he didn't answer as both men stood up.

Isfail persisted. "There's a great deal you didn't tell us last night. What happened when you took Aira to Psyche Lakes?" When the man started to turn away, Isfail placed a hand on his shoulder. He felt the tension in the Psyche's body, and heard the hard-won control in Kane's voice when he answered.

"Some things are better unsaid." Kane turned to Isfail. "Do you think Akira needs more grief, more weight on her heart right now?" His eyes blazed with emotion. "She is the only good to have come out of this tragedy, from the massacre of her father's people. I will not risk destroying Akira's faith in her legacy."

He gripped Isfail's jacket, surprising him with the effortless strength. "She is your life-partner, and you would do well to shield her from the sins of the past."

Releasing Isfail, Kane walked away then back again. Now his dark eyes held sorrow. "I know some of what she has faced in her life. I can feel her strength and her fragility. Akira will need all your love and support to get through the next lunams and beyond. Are you strong enough, my lord?"

He'd had enough of Kane's elusive and frustratingly vague words. "What the hell are you talking about? What do you know of what's coming?" Isfail snapped.

"Life." When Kane gave a rueful smile, looking at him with amused sympathy, Isfail snarled out an oath.

"Easy, Commander." Kane sighed and placed a hand on Isfail's shoulder. "I wanted to give Akira a chance to realize her own . . . condition. But I do understand your concerns, having been in this situation myself. And perhaps I am allowing too much weight from events in the past."

Even more confused, Isfail just stared at him. "You know what's wrong with her."

"Wrong's a . . . well, I'd say a wrong way to look at it." Now Kane cocked his head and studied Isfail curiously. "Do you really not have an idea? Have you never seen the signs in your own family?"

Staggered as understanding hit, Isfail said, "It's not possible. Akira said it wasn't."

It was Kane's turn to look surprised. "Did she?" He looked out over the valley. "I'd say it's time to find out."

*A*kira saw Isfail and Kane walking back to the ruined village square and went to meet them. "I thought we were all going to the tunnel? Or cave, I suppose, now that it's been sealed."

As Kilronan and his team started over, Isfail told them, "Kane was satisfied that it's still secure. But we can all go over in a little while. We needed to talk to you first," he said, looking into Akira's eyes.

"All right." Confused by the intensity in her husband's gaze, Akira allowed herself to be led to a little copse of trees nearby. "What's this about?"

"How are you feeling?" Isfail asked, taking both her hands in his.

Puzzled, she replied, "I'm fine this morning, Dan. I know you're worried, but I think I'm better."

"Kane might have the answer to what's been making you ill, my sweet. But it might come as a shock."

Rolling her eyes, Akira laughed a little. "You're making this a drama. Just tell me." She looked at Kane expectantly.

"The answer is within you, little cousin," Kane replied gently as he placed her hand low over her belly. "Look . . . and see." Then he walked away, leaving the couple alone beneath the greening new leaves.

Isfail laid a hand over her hand, tipping his forehead to hers as tears spilled from her eyes as their meaning struck her. Akira opened her mindsight, taking him with her as she risked the heartbreak. But joy overwhelmed her when she found the new life growing inside her body.

All fear of the nebulous presence evaporated when she felt the questing excitement from this tiny being. As yet unable to form thoughts, the infant could still sense Akira's mindtouch. The force of that first connection pulsed out, including Isfail in a burst of exquisite emotion.

*K*ilronan sat on the edge of the well, his forearms resting on his thighs, hands clasped loosely between his knees. He watched as light burned away the shadows on Akira's face, and joy replaced the strain. Shifting his gaze, he saw Isfail close his eyes as wonder overtook his worried expression.

For one brief moment, Kilronan felt an envy so deep he wanted to be anywhere but here. But when Isfail folded Akira into his arms, the love on the man's face before he turned it into her hair reminded Kilronan why he'd accepted Akira's choice, and jealousy dissipated as his mouth moved into a smile.

"You love her," Kane stated quietly, surprising Kilronan as he sat down beside him.

"That's not a question," Kilronan replied, straightening.

"What happened?"

Turning his head to meet serious eyes, Kilronan shrugged. "Poor decisions on my part." Looking back at Akira and Isfail, he sighed. "And a better man was there for her when I wasn't."

Kane studied him when Kilronan glanced back again. "It takes a good man to admit that." Shifting his own gaze to the couple now sitting beneath the trees, Kane said, "I witnessed what happened at High Pass, when she defeated the Mors. Syrai and I knew, as most of the Ishakan chieftains knew through the scouts, what was happening during that invasion. A few of us went to the cliffs just north of Lower Caldera Lake."

There was a short pause before Kane continued, saying, "I didn't believe anyone could survive what Akira called there, what she caused there. Yet here she is." His solemn face shifted into an expression of quiet love. "Blessed with new life."

Sixty-Three

O nce everyone had a chance to adjust to the news of Akira's pregnancy, spirits lifted all around. With everything packed up, horses ready, they rode the short distance to the point where the trail rose to the tube cave.

Akira insisted on following it back, using torches to illuminate the thick darkness. About half an hour in, the tunnel ended at a dense blockage of fallen rock. After looking it over and listening as rocks were thrown, to gain a sense of depth by the sounds the impacts made, Akira looked at Kane.

"You did a thorough job of it. It would take massive effort for anyone to get through this."

"The valley is secure then," he said. "At least from the direction Baronan entered by."

Kilronan, standing beside Isfail, asked, "What do you propose to do about the southern gate? The one we came in by?"

Looking back at him, Kane replied, "I think seven force callers can block a rift."

A short time later, Akira stood beside Kane just inside the southern gate, once more looking over Serenity Valley. She knew it now, knew its history, its people, and the tragedy of its downfall. But the ghosts were at peace now, and the man beside her had helped put them to rest.

One of last thing they'd done here was to kneel beside the rubble of the dwelling that had been her parents' home, where the bones of her father were entombed. There was sorrow, and there was peace in finally having the answers. Maronan, her amazing young cousin, had presented her with a large stone with her father's name deeply etched on it. Team Kilronan had helped him place it where Kane directed them.

At last, the southern rift was sealed, preserving Serenity Valley for its spirits.

*I*t was mid-afternoon when the group rode away from the Dragon's Head. Winding their way back through the meadows to the magical forest of ancient trees and winding streams, they mostly rode in thoughtful silence. Birds sang or chirruped around them, with only the occasional comment or short conversation among the riders.

Kane led the way back to the river road, holding there until all were gathered together.

Checking the sun's position, Isfail said, "We'll come off this road just north of Corsalat. We could overnight there. If Akira feels up to it, we could go on to Coroth tomorrow after a full night's rest."

"Ocean Cliffs Protectorate is only a couple of hours farther along," Akira added. "Lady Amsha would be happy to put us up there."

Seeing Isfail prepare to argue, Kilronan offered a compromise. "Why don't we wait until we reach Corsalat and decide then? Depending on the time, and how Akira's feeling, we can make the best decision on which option to take."

Kane chuckled over the protectorate warrior's masterful intervention. Smiling as Kilronan took the lead with Isfail and Akira, he found himself bringing up the rear of the group with Asura, Kilronan's assistant master.

"Do you mind if I ask you some questions?" she began, looking over at him with an easy smile.

"Not at all."

"As a healer, is there anything in particular I should be aware of with this pregnancy?"

He looked at her. "I would think you've known other pregnant women, assisted in births. I wouldn't expect any differences."

Asura looked uncertain. "She was terribly injured at the end of the Mors mission. Shattered bones, internal injuries, blood loss—I guess I'm concerned that she might have trouble carrying the baby to term."

They rode side by side in silence for a little while before Kane responded. "You're a caring woman, Asura. I don't have all the answers and I'm not gifted in healing arts. I can only tell you that Akira is very strong, physically and emotionally."

"I should have thought of the signs more," Asura said in a brooding voice. "I should have suspected she might be pregnant."

Kane chuckled at that. "Did she ever imply that she could not get pregnant? That's why her own man was caught by surprise."

Asura nodded. "You say that you don't have healing gifts, but you scanned her this morning."

"Akira needed to be assured that all was right with the infant. Having gone through this with Syrai, that was a way to give her some peace of mind."

"Do you know if it's a boy or girl?"

He only grinned without answering, then said, "I can tell you that their child is powerful."

"Even though Isfail isn't a full Psyche?" Asura was surprised by Kane's amused glance. "It doesn't worry you that your race is diminishing?"

"No." His dark green gaze looked far beyond the mountains they traveled through. "We are too few now. The strength of our race is lost without new blood. Isfail is a fine example of what can come of blending two strong bloodlines. The children he and Akira will bring into this world will have the best of both."

"How many children do you have?"

"Five." He glanced at her with humor in his eyes. "I believe you've met my youngest son, Kalen. He's the only one who sought adventure outside the tribes."

"Do the others have force abilities?"

"All do. Syrai and I have three more sons and a daughter." He relaxed the reins and let his mare pick her way over a rough stretch of road. "Our oldest son and his life-mate are awaiting their first child, due in the summer quarter."

Kane looked at Akira, riding ahead. "Kiran and I will both be blessed with the first of our children's children this year. I pray he knows that I will be here for them in this world, as he cannot."

Sixty-Four

They spent two days at Ocean Cliffs Protectorate. Lady Amsha, a longtime friend of Akira and Isfail, was delighted. Akira was miserable. Amsha commiserated on the mixed blessings of pregnancy, having two children of her own, but her effusive personality helped Akira make the best of it, and soothed Isfail's worries.

Ocean Cliff's lady was pleased to meet Kane, and peppered him with questions about his travels and his life among the Ishakans. It wasn't until they'd moved on that Kane realized that Lady Amsha had been astute enough not to question his purpose in Caldala. Perhaps Akira or Isfail had spoken with her, but it made for a few days of ease before facing the royal house.

Kane believed there would be no avoiding a thorough interrogation by the Prince of Caldala and his advisors. Perhaps Akira picked up his feelings while they enjoyed the view of the ocean from the guest quarters terrace.

"Prince Logran is a good man, a compassionate one," she told him, waving a farewell to Isfail when he hailed them as he rode out.

"That's good to hear," Kane replied. "Where's your man off to?"

"Insalat Militia was his last command. We agreed this was a good opportunity to check with his friend, new Commander Toth. They're investigating a point of access allowing the The Bow to infiltrate Caldala. The involved ship's captain is cooperating with Caldalan military through an acquaintance of ours, who owns an inn along this part of the coast."

Akira glanced at Kane with a quick smile. "If there's any news, particularly from Rena, the innkeeper, he can stop there on the return to Ocean Cliffs, to get the latest information."

"He trusts you're safe with us," Kane remarked, taking her hand in his.

"Yes, though he worries about me, even more with the baby."

"It is a man's prerogative," Kane said, squeezing her hand gently, "to want his family safe and well, more so when times are uncertain and dangerous. Sometimes there's little we can do to keep those we love safe."

Nodding slowly, Akira thought of Alani Iro, and the daughter she'd denied herself—to keep her safe—the child now on the brink of adulthood.

Village of Psyche Lakes

*L*ani Osharon was celebrating her coming of age with friends and family, especially thrilled to have her big brother, Osharon, home for the event. Despite more than two decades difference in years, sister and brother were close in affection, interests, and temper. Now Lani schemed to take advantage of all three—she wanted to join the protectorate forces.

All right, Lani thought, she still had three years before she could apply, but *Senior Master* Osharon of *Mountain Shadows Protectorate*—she giggled aloud at her own silent emphasis—could help her start training, and help persuade their parents that it was a good idea.

A tug on her recently cut hair broke into Lani's reverie.

"Ouch!"

"What's funny, kid?" Osharon asked, throwing an arm over her slim shoulders. "You know, this coming of age is supposed to be a serious business." His grin broadened when she spun around and punched him in a very solid gut, and chuckled when Lani winced, shaking her hand.

"Oh, sure," she replied. "As if you could take anything seriously."

"You're right," he agreed cheerfully. "It's supposed to be fun and full of great food."

"And fantastic frivolity!" Lani exclaimed, dashing off to execute a series of cartwheels on the grass that edged the village park, where people were already gathering.

She squealed with delight when Osharon scooped her up mid-wheel, spinning her around as he ended the alliteration.

"Fun frivolity for a fantastic fiend! Let's find it!" He set her down so that she staggered a little dizzily as they joined their laughing parents in the golden light of the setting sun that poured through the mountain gap to the west.

Torches were being lit around the wide pavilion where long tables were loaded with platters and bowls. As more cheerful villagers arrived, more edible offerings were added until it appeared the thick tables might collapse with the weight.

Colorful streamers and swags of bright cloth decorated the wooden beams, fluttering as the evening breeze wafted the scent of orchard blossoms through the air. Still cool enough in the early spring night for the celebrants to have brought sweaters, light coats, and shawls against the chill.

But the people of Psyche Lakes warmed up quickly when local musicians tuned up and began a light-hearted round of traditional melodies to set toes tapping and couples twirling over the dance floor. Joyful noise filled their little valley cupped within an ancient caldera.

The lights of the village reflected on the water of three narrow lakes that bordered the main village, and were the inspiration for its name. They were full now with the last of the snowmelt funneling down from the surrounding peaks.

Osharon stood, enjoying his ale as he watched Lani spin around the floor with a local boy. She's grown up so fast, he thought, knowing their parents felt the same. Had it really been twelve years since he'd gotten the news that she'd arrived?

He remembered the surprise, then his roar of laughter, when

a letter had reached him at Mountain Shadows, informing him that he was a big brother at twenty-five years old. As soon as he'd had a leave period, he'd rushed home to see the tiny upstart, and fallen in love at first sight. Her dark cap of newborn hair had lightened over the years to a smoked-honey gold. Where'd that come from? And baby blue eyes had quickly taken on a more hazel hue, until they settled on greenish amber.

Now she was on the cusp of womanhood, and not just the little sister he doted on.

Osharon scrubbed his fingers through his short black hair. Turning to his mother, he asked, "When did Lani decide to cut her hair off?"

She sighed, but it was more resigned than distressed. "Last week. I hated to see her beautiful long hair fall to the barber shears, but she was determined. I was able to talk her into a length that could still be tied back. And the shorter style does suit her."

When she turned her *look* on him, Osharon cringed inwardly. That look had followed him from the moment he'd been old enough to toddle. He knew what it meant. Nothing ever escaped his mother's sharp eyes or ears.

"She wants to be a protectorate warrior," she said coolly. "I wonder where Lani got that idea from?"

"I didn't start it." Osharon heard the hint of a whine in his voice, and cleared his throat.

"Did you try to stop it?" she asked, her foot tapping with frustration now, rather than the beat of the music.

"Mom." He heard her huff out a breath, and knew he wasn't in *big* trouble. Taking her hand, Osharon tugged her toward the dance floor, grinning as he heard her chuckle. As they took their places in the formation for the next set, he winked at Lani, lining up with their father across from them.

Felcan's men unlashed the wooden boxes from the packhorse in the dark. It had taken the better part of two days to travel cross-country, mostly after nightfall to avoid notice. He stood at the edge of the trees and looked across a narrow body of water to the pavilion, where lights and the sounds of music and celebration flowed into the night.

It was a perfect opportunity, he thought with a tight smile on his lips. Looked like most of the village was milling about. They just needed to get close enough to lob the explosives into the crowd and Dateh would have his bloody statement. The fact that entire families were enjoying the merriment had ceased to matter to Beros Felcan. His purpose was to help Abron Dateh win his war and claim Caldala.

Eliminating the forcers, especially this village—the home of the powerful Psyche race here in Caldala—was key to taking control. Tonight, they were making his job easy.

Signaling his men, Felcan waited for them to pick up the explosives boxes before leading them quietly to a point where they could slip across the strip of land between two lakes. Now they hunched behind short walls that circled the village proper.

When they came close to the open pavilion, and the villagers gathered there, Felcan held up a hand to halt his group. Moving carefully back, he made a hand sign to open the wooden crates. The lids had been loosened back in the trees so they lifted off with a barely audible squeak as the remaining nails pulled free.

Lifting a clay ball filled with black powder to place in his pack, Felcan stopped short, staring at it in the dim light. "What the hell?" he muttered. Setting it down on the grass beside him, he looked into the crate, then tipped it toward the light, his breath coming faster.

There were no fuses in any of them.

"None here either," one of his men said as they all shifted the balls about in a futile hope that the missing fuses would magically appear.

Teeth gritted tight as he resisted the urge to curse loudly, Felcan leaned back against the wall. How had this happened? He'd put all these together himself! They couldn't even do a last-minute fix, because he hadn't thought to bring the remaining fuse cord with him, so sure he'd been that they were all ready to light.

Knowing it was useless now, Felcan recalled that last night at Baronan Keep, with all his men there, finishing the bombs, and resealing the crates. He'd been with them all the way to the stables, where they'd been stacked, ready to be loaded onto the horse. And that's where they were when they were ready to leave, exactly as they'd left them. There'd been no reason to reopen the crates and check.

Who? Felcan wondered with a silent snarl. Who was the traitor? Everyone was with him now but Ramort and—

"Barash," Felcan hissed.

Sixty-Five

The object of Felcan's rage was, at that moment, settled comfortably in a rustic inn just north of Corsalat, ignoring the complaints from Ramort, his querulous traveling companion. Barash asked some careful questions of one of the barmaids, who remembered him fondly from earlier visits under another name. But Liza had little to tell him about a female sea captain who'd been known to carry strange cargo in the past few years.

When she came back with another round of drinks, Liza leaned on his shoulder to whisper in his ear. "Best to not ask those questions, Hadson," she warned him. "Rena's got an eye on you. She doesn't like the trouble some'a them that calls themselves The Bow have brought here. The ones that come on the ship ye're askin' about. He ain't got no brands on him, has he?" Liza looked pointedly at Ramort.

She didn't need Barash's negative shake of the head when Ramort looked back at her with such indignation and revulsion it made her laugh.

Barash glanced discreetly toward the mirror mounted on the end wall in front of him, where he could see the barman and his woman, Rena, working beside him. Sure enough, she looked over frequently.

"Thanks, Liza. We're not looking for trouble. Someone told us we could get a ship to Kuldor near Corsalat, with a lower passage rate. My friend here"—he elbowed Ramort—"has to get there on important business."

"Ah, yes," Ramort fumbled, his voice rising with anxiety. "Business, important I be there next week. Yes."

Looking down at the table, Barash hid his grimace. The fool was going to get them taken in for questioning before he could complete his mission. Now Liza was eyeing Ramort with a frown knitting her brow.

She straightened, saying, "Well, watch yerself, Hadson. Come back sometime when yer *friend* ain't with ya."

Watching her go while his mind circled around how he could find this ship captain, and track down her connection to The Bow, Barash took little notice when the big door opened, letting in the sound of the sea with the tall man who entered.

But the immediate quieting of noise had him taking a closer look as Rena moved from behind the bar with a welcoming grin. His table wasn't close enough to hear their words as she took his arm and led him to a seat at the corner of the bar, but he could see the man was no stranger to the owners.

Barash lifted his second glass, drinking slowly as he took the newcomer's measure—a soldier's bearing, early middle years, prosperous, self-confident. And somehow familiar, he thought.

When Rena lifted her chin in their direction, Barash said something casually absurd that had Ramort scowling at him while he grinned. He knew the man at the bar was looking their way, so he continued the inane flow of words while grinning foolishly at Ramort, whose face reddened as if he'd burst at any moment.

A sideways glance showed Barash that the man had turned back, watching Rena while she spoke with the barmaid. Whatever Liza said had the man giving an easy shrug.

"You mad idiot!" Ramort exclaimed, grabbing his coat and valise before stalking out the door.

Chuckling, Barash gulped down the last of his ale, leaving a generous amount of coin as Liza moved over to collect the glasses. He jerked her into a hard kiss that had her eyes smiling. "Thanks, darlin'. I've got to see him to a ship, but I'll be back. Who's your fancy friend there?"

Puzzled, she looked where he indicated. "Oh, some friend a' Rena's over the years. He is a fine one. Commander Isfail from Insalat, I hear. But he's bound to that forcer woman, that one they say killed all those invaders last year. That Lady Muro, I think her name is."

Showing no sign of his now acute interest, Barash said casually, "Living in Insalat, are they? Seems like I heard Lady Muro had settled way up in the mountains, near the old pass to Ishal."

"Funny, ain't it," she replied, filling her tray then swabbing the tabletop as he leaned against the wall. "I heard he's of the royal blood and there was a grand binding at the palace itself." She glanced toward the bar with round eyes. "Who'd think he'd be hanging out in a place like this, eh?"

Liza picked up the tray and shot Barash a flirty look over her shoulder. "Guess it's true about the royals, though. Him and his lady are on their way to Coroth. Look me up next time ye're passin' through."

Barash shrugged into his coat while she returned to the bar, then moved easily through the crowded common room. His thoughts raced knowing that Akira was somewhere in the same vicinity—opportunity or danger?

Outside, he saw Ramort huddled near their horses. He knew the schoolmaster was too much of a coward to leave without him, but he wondered what the man would say if he knew that the woman he'd failed to assassinate was within reach.

"Our mission just got easier," Barash said, swinging onto his gelding as Ramort scrambled awkwardly onto his horse. "As soon as we check out a seafarer's pub on the Insalat docks, we're headed south to Coroth."

"Is there a ship for us there?" Ramort asked eagerly.

"Don't worry, schoolmaster, you'll be taken care of."

Psyche Lakes

"ooks like it's winding down," one of his men said, peering cautiously over the wall. "People are starting to clean up. Musicians are packing it in."

Head tipped back to the wall where he sat, Felcan swore under his breath. They'd lost their best chance for multiple casualties. Without fuses, the hand bombs were just clay balls packed with black powder.

He had seven men, some crossbows, longbows, some short swords and knives. They didn't even have Black Arrows for this mission. They could attack, likely take out a number of villagers, but it could well be a suicide mission in this nest of force callers.

But he'd be damned if they'd come all this way for nothing. Moving to crouch on his haunches, he gestured the others closer.

"We'll divide up the bombs; each of you take your share." Felcan waited while they handed the balls around, quietly placing them in their packs and pockets, while he did the same.

"What now?" a veteran Bowman asked.

"There're torches bracketed all along the lanes and walkways. We're going to spread out, try to stay out of sight. People are still milling about here. Grab a torch and start lighting up the buildings, the houses, whatever will burn. Toss the balls in when you get a good blaze going. With luck, we'll get some explosions out of them so move on quickly. If you can hit occupied places, do it. Work fast and don't get caught. Remember these people are forcers, and powerful ones. If you can take some down with your bows, do it, but fighting close quarters is sure to get you killed."

Felcan took several deep breaths while others did the same, charging themselves up for the sprints. Looking around at taut faces in the night, he said, "Get it done fast. When you're out of bombs, head back to the horses. We'll meet there and get out of here. Good hunting, Bowmen."

Each man pulled a black mask over his head then Felcan slashed his hand in a move-out signal. Eight black-clad men ran quietly, keeping to shadows as they spread throughout the village.

*T*aking the cloth-wrapped bundle his mother handed him without breaking from his conversation with Master Maran, Osharon continued passing on news about Maran's niece. The old man obviously enjoyed catching up on Akira's life in Mountain Shadows.

"So she's off to Coroth again," Maran noted. "What's the point of all this back and forth? So much time on the road is too risky for her with all this nonsense from Ishal."

"I'm sure it'll all come out," Osharon said, having been advised by his protectorate lord not to speak of Kane Kalronan yet. "Besides, Akira saw far more travel as an ambassador, and probably more risk on some of her missions."

Maran started to respond, but broke off at the sound of a distant scream. Immediately people around them began shouting warnings.

"Fire!"

"Fire in the village!"

Grabbing his mother and sister to stop them from running after those already dashing off, Osharon ordered, "Stay here!" Then he leaped up on a table.

"Stop! This could be a terrorist attack!" As many looked back, halting their exodus, Osharon continued calling them back, aided now by others. He saw Kilronan's father and brother-in-law, and his own father urging their neighbors to stop and listen.

"This looks like The Bow!" Osharon shouted. "We need to defend our families and stop the attackers. Let's get everyone with military experience and force-fighting skills there." He pointed to the edge of the pavilion nearest the village. "And others to defend children and families here."

He jumped down, relieved as people quickly moved to follow his orders. He knew it was hard for them to hold back as more flames bloomed. Then shouts and screams rose as explosions rocked the night.

"Hell!" Osharon exclaimed. No doubt now that The Bow was behind this, and it was already much worse than the attack on

Mountain Shadows. With help from many local men, and a few women, Osharon had teams spreading out to locate their enemy.

He cursed while he ran with his father and Miden Kilronan as more desperate screams came from a row of blazing houses. Sprinting ahead, Osharon saw familiar black clothing as the man threw something into a burning house. As he started to run on, Osharon's force bolt ended him.

The three men continued, soon joined by more villagers prepared to fight for their homes and their lives.

Several more assailants were brought down, and fires were being put out once the risk of explosions diminished. Osharon and others reorganized to take account. They carried the enemy bodies to the steps of the meeting hall. Osharon left the village council to determine whether any were locals while he jogged back toward the pavilion. But he could see that it was empty now.

He turned to his parents' home, hoping they'd gone there. "Why would they listen to me and stay put?" he muttered to himself. "I'm just a protectorate warrior. Why should they hunker down and stay safe when I tell them to?"

But he felt relief when his mother and Lani met him at the door of their undamaged cottage. After soothing their fears, and putting them on guard against strangers, Osharon strode back to find his father and help subdue the last of the fires.

*F*elcan stumbled through the trees, breathless from that final dash. He'd seen one of his men go down, but hoped others would make it to the rendezvous point. Slowing now, he glanced back. No one was pursuing; he'd made it out of the village without being seen.

Stopping, he leaned over, bracing his hands on his knees as he took gasping breaths. When he straightened, he could see that fires were already being damped down. He hadn't heard as many explosions as he'd hoped.

They'd done some damage, but it could have been much more effective. He'd killed a couple of villagers that had been caught by surprise. Maybe his men had gotten more. But, damn! He hadn't expected the Psyches to organize so fast.

There should have been more panic, more chaos. But they'd had fighters out within minutes, tracking them down. There hadn't even been a chance to hit the people left at the pavilion. He'd planned to send every bolt in his quiver into those remaining there as he left, but there were too many people forming an obvious defensive perimeter.

A force shield, he'd recognized by the way they'd spaced themselves, holding out their hands and arms. Felcan hadn't been willing to reveal his position by trying an arrow shot. That's when he'd called the mission.

He staggered the rest of the distance to the horses tethered in a small clearing. Untying his own, he waited at a spot where he could view the village. Fires were down to a faint glow now. Felcan could see adults positioned around the low perimeter walls, guarding against further attack.

No one was getting out of Psyche Lakes, he knew now. His men were gone. Leaving the other horses, Felcan set about his own escape.

Sixty-Six

Coroth Palace, City of Coroth, Caldala

The riders from Mountain Shadows left Ocean Cliffs Protectorate on a morning bright with sunshine. Akira had refused to allow Isfail to send a message ahead requesting a carriage to meet them. Even his concern for her comfort wasn't enough to risk stirring her wrath when Kane advised him to be wary of irritable emotions.

"It will pass soon enough," Kane said calmly. "It's worse with the first. We men don't appreciate what a woman goes through when she's carrying new life." He grinned at Isfail. "You'll know by the time this child arrives, and be prepared for the next."

"I don't think she's ever frightened me before, with her temper, that is," Isfail told him, glancing back to where Akira rode with Asura and Maronan. "I thought I'd seen her in every possible mood, from joy to despair."

Laughing at that, Kane shook his head. "All I can say is flow with these new moods, as best you can."

"Well." Isfail turned back with a smug expression on his face. "At least it will deter her from becoming personally involved in the situation in Ishal."

Kane gave him a pitying look. "You think so? Commander, you have a great deal to learn about pregnant women and, I think, Akira Muro. A mother will fight like the most vicious beast when she feels her children are threatened. Somehow, I don't believe Akira will feel any different while this child is still a part of her."

Gazing ahead, Isfail said, "We'll see. I'll have help persuading her otherwise very soon." He pointed toward the flags flying on the highest tower of the palace of Coroth, now visible in the distance.

*T*he travelers were quickly escorted to the formal assembly room where the prince was meeting with another newly arrived delegation. Akira and Kilronan recognized the three elders from the Village of Psyche Lakes, Maran among them. But before Akira could greet her uncle, an accusatory shout rang out.

"Traitor!" Elder Cadon cried, his thin arm trembling with the force of his rage as he raised it to point a finger at Kane. "He's the one who brought this upon us!"

Prince Logran lifted a hand, sending his guard captain and the soldiers stationed around the chamber moving in. But Logran made a fist to hold their positions when Isfail stepped forward.

"My prince." Though he bowed respectfully, Isfail's eyes were direct when he met his royal cousin's questioning ones. "We know not what has occurred to incite this vigorous accusation, but this man has been in our company for almost a lunam. Kane Kalronan has come to Caldala to warn us of a weakness in our border security, and to request aid and asylum for the Ishakan people."

While Akira stood close beside Kane, whose hooded eyes and stoic countenance showed no response to this unexpected attack, Isfail continued. "We can and will vouch for his character, but I think he—*we* deserve to know what this is about."

Logran gave a sharp command to halt the ensuing rebukes before he answered, "These men have brought word that Psyche Lakes was attacked two days ago."

When Kilronan took a step forward in alarm, Akira sent a terse mindsight to him. *"Wait. Let's hear what they have to say."*

"Six villagers were killed, a few more injured, but the attackers misjudged the fighting strength of their intended victims," Logran told them. "Most of the assailants were killed, though not before torching several buildings."

"The Bow?" Akira asked, speaking for the first time.

The prince nodded as he stood, signaling his guard. When the men formed up, Logran stepped from his throne. "We will take this to a more private conference room and see if we can untangle the connections."

Seeing Akira's ashen face, Isfail exercised family privilege and moved through the guards to speak in his cousin's ear. "Akira needs to rest. Could Oona be sent for?"

Pausing at the entrance to a smaller room, Logran placed a hand on Isfail's shoulder even as he instructed a guard to notify the princess. "What's wrong?"

"I'd rather deal with that privately."

Though he nodded, Logran stepped over to offer his arm to Akira, leading her to a chair near him while Isfail brought her a glass of water, then seated himself between Akira and Logran. Kilronan and Asura positioned themselves behind her, with Kane taking the other seat by her side, his hand covering her cold one to push warming forces to ease her distress.

"You should let your man take you to your quarters, little cousin."

"No." Akira shifted to meet his eyes, wondering what Kane was shielding her from. She could feel the concern for her when she would have expected his emotions to be directed toward the hostility emanating from the Psyche Lakes group.

Maran distracted her as he came over, leaving the other two elders frowning after him. "Akira, my dear, you're very pale."

"Nothing to worry about, Uncle. I'm just tired. It's been a long trip from the mountains, and hearing about this attack is upsetting. We'll talk more after this is settled." Akira accepted his kiss on her cheek with a smile, but knew he'd keep close watch on her throughout the meeting.

With the elders on one side of the table, and the Mountain Shadows group on the other, Logran called them to order. Tipping a hand toward Maran, he asked, "Master Maran, would you summarize what happened in Psyche Lakes to inform our new arrivals?"

Akira took Isfail's hand below the table, grateful for Logran's discerning assessment of character. Maran was easily the better delegate. Calmly, he described the events of that night—the gathering of most of the villagers at the pavilion, the attack and firing of buildings, the random explosions.

He told them about the villagers' response, finding and killing seven men who were dressed and masked in black. One had been taken alive, but mortally wounded. He'd refused to answer questions before he died. Five of the assailants carried the brand of The Bow, while two older men had not been marked. They were all strangers to the villagers.

Maran gave a brief account of securing the village, putting out fires, and attending the wounded, then the dead. Akira was relieved that none of those dearest to her had been harmed, though Kilronan's sister's home had suffered minor damage when the cottage nearby had burned.

The morning after, search parties had discovered seven horses in full tack tethered in nearby woods. Hunters were able to discover the tracks of an eighth man and horse, following them out of the valley through the western gap. A team of volunteers had continued the pursuit.

"After some discussion, it was decided that the three of us would come to Coroth, report what happened, and request military support. We had already sent a rider to notify Cypress Springs Protectorate the night of the attack. Two of their teams arrived to help just as we were setting out," Maran ended.

"Thank you," Logran said, then paused a moment when Oona came in quietly. The men in the room immediately stood, waiting as she walked around the table.

Kane moved from his chair beside Akira and Oona sat down, nodding to Logran to continue when Akira gave her a wan smile. He sat, followed by the others. "Thank you for coming, my dear.

"Master Cadon has made a serious accusation against our visitor from Ishaka, Master Kane Kalronan, accusing him of being a traitor and somehow responsible for the attack against Psyche Lakes."

Akira felt Oona grip her hand more tightly, but she remained outwardly serene.

"This accusation has been denied by witnesses of unquestionable character and veracity," Logran went on, turning his attention to the accuser. "Have you evidence to support your outburst, Master Cadon?"

Red-faced now, the elder stood to speak. "No, my prince, and I regret speaking so rashly." He turned a frowning face to Kane. "I strongly disapprove of this man's past behavior, but that does not excuse my leveling such a claim without cause."

He gave a short bow to Logran before sitting down again, but Akira noted that he made no apology to Kane.

"I see," Logran said thoughtfully. "Perhaps you will guard your tongue more closely in the future, Master Cadon."

The old man huddled deeper in his chair, apparently feeling the reprimand in the words.

"And you, Masters?" Logran turned the question on the other two elders. "Is there anything you have to say about Master Kane Kalronan?"

"I have no grievance against Kane," Maran replied simply. "He chose a life beyond Caldala, but I see no harm in that. To my knowledge, he's never acted against or expressed a desire to harm his home village or anyone in Caldala. I think it obvious that he would not be involved with these assassins calling themselves The Bow since he's one of those the enemy professes to hate."

"Thank you, Master Maran." Logran looked at the third elder. "Would you care to comment, Elder Kalronan?"

"I have no reason to believe the accused would conspire against Psyche Lakes," Elder Kalronan stated brusquely.

Neither Kalronan looked at the other, Akira noticed. Until the name was spoken, she had not realized that this hard-looking man across the table was related to Kane. Was this the reason for his protective attitude?

Logran stood. "There are no grounds to suspect Master Kane Kalronan's involvement in the attack on Psyche Lakes, therefore this matter is done. I will meet with the delegation from Psyche Lakes, including military advisors and others deemed relevant, in two hours."

Signaling an attendant, he said, "Masters, you will be shown to your quarters and offered a luncheon during this recess."

The men expressed appreciation, and followed the attendant out. Akira saw the elder Kalronan give a quick, unsmiling glance back at Kane.

"Now," Logran said, leaning back in his chair with a sigh of relief. "That was quickly settled. Unless there's some urgency, I'd like to postpone hearing your news until I deal with this attack."

With a look to Akira and Kane for their agreement, Isfail said, "I think we can wait on that, but it is important."

"You said something about a security issue at the border," Logran remembered, straightening in his chair. "Give me some idea."

Isfail lifted a hand to Kilronan, nudging him to report.

"Kane brought us the information that there is a new passage through the mountains, my prince. Teams from Mountain Shadows were sent out to assess it. While we relied on Kane's specific information on the Ishakan side—which was undeniable since he came through on horseback—we did independently confirm the entrance into Caldala."

His eyes narrowing, Logran tapped his fingers on the table. "Damn it. This is the last thing we need right now." He looked at Kane. "Could this be used to advance an invasive force?"

Now Kane spoke quietly, "No, Prince Logran, at least not efficiently. Much of the new rift is narrow. It would take time to move men and horses through it. And it's a much longer route than High Pass was. The Ishakans have posted a guard at our end. Your protectorates have now established a guard in Caldala."

"All right, good." He offered Kane an arm to clasp. "I appreciate the effort you've taken to advise Coroth, sir. I'm sure you have more to tell us. For now, we'll provide you with accommodations in the guest wing. I gather that you'd be more comfortable on a floor separate from the Psyche Lakes delegation."

"You would be correct, sir," Kane replied without further enhancement.

Logran turned to Akira. "And what about you, Akira? You've

obviously caused some concern among your companions, as well I can see for myself." He looked at his wife when she let out an amused sound, raising an eyebrow to her.

"It seems Oona has a different perspective," he noted curiously.

Isfail cleared his throat. "Since our whole company learned of this during our travels, I see no reason to wait to inform you that Akira is expecting."

"Expecting what?" Logran replied with some confusion, until Oona burst out laughing. "A baby?"

"How soon they forget," Oona teased him.

A grin spread over his face as he stood quickly, grabbing Isfail in a hard hug before leaning over to kiss Akira lightly on the lips. "We will celebrate this news as soon as possible! Now, be off with you. Oona will see you to your suite. I'd like Dan for a little while." He gestured for Kilronan and his team to follow them.

"Akira," he called before they reached the door. "I'll be sure you're kept informed about the meeting this afternoon. I'd like to have your advice on all of this."

She gave him a brilliant smile, and was pleased she wasn't going to be required to connive her way in.

*K*ilronan joined them in their quarters late that afternoon, wanting to check on Akira. He thought she was holding up pretty well, but the combination of pregnancy sickness and the shock of a major attack against Psyche Lakes had been a double blow.

He was relieved to see her color returned when Isfail admitted him, ushering him into their comfortable living room where Akira sat, legs curled under her on the couch.

"Oona tells me this is all normal," Akira said when he gave her a close study.

"Rough," Kilronan replied, thanking Isfail as he was handed a glass of red wine. He noticed Akira was drinking what appeared to be milk. "Glad men can't get it."

As he'd hoped, she laughed, and Isfail slapped him on the back, grinning in solidarity.

Kilronan sat down, joining them in reviewing what had been said about the attack on Psyche Lakes. When they'd talked it over until there seemed nothing more to say for now, he finished his wine, declining another glass when Isfail offered.

"There's little we can do until the investigation is complete. Not much even then, unless any remaining culprits are apprehended," Isfail said, taking Akira's hand. "It doesn't appear that locals were involved in the attacks, unlike the one in Mountain Shadows. That's something positive."

Kilronan nodded, leaning forward. "It's an insular community. Everyone is of the blood, to one degree or another, with the older generations mostly pureblood. It's the founding colony here in Caldala, where the first force callers settled after Caldala granted them permanent asylum, several generations ago."

He looked at Akira. "I never knew there was a split three generations back that led to the Serenity Valley clan."

"Nor did I," she replied, but did not pursue the subject with him.

"Garan's already deployed ten ambassadors to Psyche Lakes, for protection and investigation, including several from Recon Alpha," she said. "Team Kilronan should go with the elder delegation tomorrow."

"They don't need protection," Kilronan argued, though part of him wanted to agree. "They're some of the toughest Psyches in the country." He rubbed the bridge of his nose, frowning over his conflicted emotions. Despite Maran's assurances that his family was unharmed, he wanted to check on them. But he knew Osharon was there and he'd make sure everyone was taken care of.

"You must go," Akira said to Kilronan, pulling him from his thoughts. "I release you and your team from your duty to me. Isfail and I are here at the palace, and surrounded by Royal Guard. Why would you need to stay?"

He knew her reasoning was sound; even Lord Corcoran would accept it, say the same. But still he felt divided between duty to Akira's safety and needing to be in Psyche Lakes with his family.

As if she knew his turmoil—and she probably did, he thought with a wry smile—Akira placed a hand on his cheek.

"Go, Aiden. I'll feel better if you do. Maronan should have a few days with Maran after all this. Don't make me ask Logran to order Team Kilronan to Psyche Lakes."

He laughed, reaching for her hand and bringing it to his lips. "Don't do anything foolish without me."

Akira chuckled, and Isfail put his arm around her. Giving them both a salute, Kilronan turned and strode from the room.

Sixty-Seven

*K*ane knew the man was there, though the beat of surf on sand covered any sound of approach. Without turning, he said, "I thought the Psyche Lakes group left early this morning."

"I asked for a delay. We have things to say, Kane."

"We have nothing to say." Turning to Elder Kalronan, Kane studied the face where age had settled in harsh lines scored deep in a hard and bitter visage. Just as hard and unyielding now as the day he'd stood before him and heard the decision that no help would be sent to Serenity Valley.

"You owe your clan respect," the elder warned, the words sharp verbal slaps to Kane's ears. But the time was long past since they could sting or instruct.

"I have no clan." Kane watched the angry color fade from his father's cheeks. But the retort was ice cold.

"You were my only child, yet you chose to leave Psyche Lakes for a feckless offshoot of Psyche blood, and a pack of malcontents. You scorned our clan then and now. It was your duty to be there to defend your people when we were attacked."

"It was Psyche Lakes' duty to defend Serenity Valley!" Kane lashed back. "And you did nothing. Not even to avenge them, because you and the others were cowards." He pointed back toward the palace. "Have you told Akira how the elders of Psyche Lakes chose to let her father die? Does she know the whole of your betrayal?"

As the elder pressed thin lips together, refusing to respond, Kane scoffed, "I'll wager none of you told Maran and Aira that I begged you to send help to Serenity Valley and you refused. You did nothing to hold Baronan and Karsh accountable."

Kane's hands were clenched at his sides, his determined composure shattered by his rage over those memories. "How much blood is on your hands? How many have died, will die, because you didn't have the spine to stand up all those years ago? My youngest son has more courage in him than all of you together. Everyday I pray that my children will not be the next victims of what you and your cronies allowed to breed."

Silence stretched between the two men, both refusing to stand down. Then the elder said flatly, "You have sons."

"I have sons and a daughter," Kane replied, pride filling his voice. "And I will see my first grandchild before harvest season."

The old man sighed, breaking eye contact as he folded his hands in front of him. "Your mother would wish to know them." When Kane remained silent, he looked up again, but it seemed his pride would not bend to ask more.

"Tell her what you will," Kane replied. "She always believed whatever you said about me anyway. For my part, I wish her well."

"Will you bring your children to Psyche Lakes?" Elder Kalronan asked as Kane turned to walk away.

"No."

Kane heard only the wind and waves as he strode out along the bluff. Perhaps he was as hard as his father in this matter, but the time for forgiveness had passed long years ago, and the family he'd made with Syrai would not be touched by the demons of his past.

Still, he smiled a little as he reached the cypress-crested ridge between Coroth and Ambassador Central. He embraced the petty satisfaction that Elder Kalronan didn't know that Kane's youngest son, Kalen, lived only a brief walk from the palace. And was, in fact, jogging up to meet him, waving with a huge grin on his face as Kane topped the ridge.

*A*nother anticipated reunion was happening on Central grounds. Isfail had acceded to Akira's desire to visit friends there. Garan, proposing that the couple join them for a late breakfast, immediately returned the message requesting the favor, assuring her that he would round up those she particularly wanted to see.

The heavily guarded coach made the trip without incident this time, and was greeted enthusiastically. Most High Garan pressed his status with a smile, stepping up to be the first to take Akira's hand after Isfail assisted her from the carriage.

"It was a less eventful trip than last time," Akira greeted him, kissing Garan's cheek with the privilege of long friendship in service.

"Yes," he said, turning to offer his arm to her husband for a firm grip. "It's been quiet here." Then his face grew serious. "We've heard about Psyche Lakes, of course."

They walked into the deep archway leading into the fortification with others following.

"We were told you'd sent several ambassadors to assist them, including some from Recon Alpha," Akira replied quietly. "That was a good decision."

Garan gave her a quick grin. "Glad you're not mad about that."

"You're the Most High, not me," she replied with a wicked smile. "But I'll be sure to express my displeasure if you take a wrong turn."

Isfail and Garan burst out laughing, along with those close enough to hear the exchange.

That included Arith, who was obviously waiting impatiently for his turn with her. "You've still got me, Drinin, Kalronan, Coran, and Oti here," he told her, taking the arm offered by Isfail as they walked along.

"Akira?" Garan asked when she faltered.

She felt Isfail's hand on her arm as she glanced at Arith. "Alani's in Psyche Lakes?"

"Yes," Garan answered in unison with Arith. "Is that a problem?"

"No," Akira said quickly, managing a smile. "No, of course not."

Isfail's brow lifted. "Let's take this inside. I'm sure Akira would like a chance to catch up with the news here, and maybe share some stories of our winter in the mountains."

Akira took the arm he offered, thankful he'd distracted them from her unintended lapse.

By the time they sat down to a celebratory meal, Akira had tried to greet as many ambassadors as she could, including a few of the latest recruits, who'd crowded in just for a chance to say hello to the legendary retired ambassador.

Now she was ready for a less chaotic visit with those closest to her, with Kane joining them with his son. She was pleased that most of the news was positive, and some full of humor. Then there were updates on more serious business.

There'd been no further attacks, and the mission to secure the southern coast and caldons had been successful. She'd already been informed that Ominor and Wrax had been replaced as Parliament ministers.

Wrax was now serving a life sentence in the prison tower outside of Coroth, having escaped execution by giving testimony against Ominor, along with everything he knew about those who'd been paying bribes to cross their lands unimpeded. Ominor had been executed for treason after admitting that he knew the illegals were Ishalian insurgents, members of a known terrorist group.

Unfortunately, rogue ambassadors Gorth and Lunow seemed to have escaped, along with the Bowman Felcan. It was the consensus that they'd managed to make it back to Ishal. That led to a discussion on what The Bow, or Dateh, would want with two ambassadors, beyond the obvious use of them in staging the past attack.

After that ran its course, Akira and Isfail answered questions about living in Mountain Shadows, with the others laughing at the humor Isfail managed to interject before talk turned to the attack there in late winter. That news had reached Ambassador Central shortly after Coroth received it, so it was easy to deal with that quickly.

Kane was brought directly into the conversation when asked to talk about the horse tribes' situation in Ishaka, how Shanow's troops had handled the winter, and the recently discovered mountain passage. This could have occupied them for days, but Kane declined to make it a major topic.

Instead, he looked at Akira, willing to sacrifice her to get the group's attention off himself. With a sly smile, he leaned back with a fresh cup of tea and said, "I would think your friends here would be interested in another big change in your life, little cousin."

Akira pursed her lips, deciding Isfail was no help when he just grinned back at her.

"Big changes, eh, Kira?" Arith leaned in with an encouraging wink. "What's bigger than living the royal life?" He laughed when she zinged him with a force shock under the table.

Isfail laid his hand over hers. "These people are family, my sweet."

Her lips curved as she looked back at him. "Yes, they are." She turned her hand under his to link fingers and looked around the table. "Ardan and I are expecting a new Isfail later this year."

Arith whooped as he sprang from his seat, grabbing her up from hers and spinning her around.

Isfail sat back, enjoying the scene as her recon ambassadors vied to congratulate her. He glanced at Kane, who smiled, shaking his head as Kalen took his turn spinning his former commander in his arms.

It was Garan who—though enjoying the moment—asked the question that might soon occur to other ambassadors. "This is truly joyful news, Akira, but your condition obviously flies against a long-standing belief, doesn't it?"

"The belief that powerful force callers, especially ambassadors, could not conceive," Akira replied. "It certainly does, which is why I did not consider pregnancy when all the signs were there. It was Kane who brought the possibility to my attention."

"*You* did, Father?" Kalen snorted out a laugh.

Kane kicked back in his chair. "I do have some experience in this area, Kal."

His dry retort had others laughing when Kalen turned red, but he grinned sheepishly as Kane gave him an affectionate punch on the shoulder.

"Now that we're leaving everyone in good humor," Isfail began, "We need to get back." He looked at Kane and got a nod. "Akira, Kane, and I are due at a meeting this afternoon."

Walking back to the coach with them, Drinin finally pried Arith's arm from Akira's shoulders as he said good-naturedly, "Give her over to someone else." Taking her arm in his, he drew her a little distance from the rest.

"I wish you joy, Akira," he murmured, leaning down to kiss her cheek. "I also would like a private appointment. There's something I need to talk with you about."

Akira searched his troubled gaze. "Of course, Aron. Could you come to the palace tomorrow morning? I can make it my first meeting of the day."

"I'll be there." He walked her back to Isfail, waiting with the others as they got into the carriage. Once again, Drinin watched her coach roll away with painful memories clouding his peace of mind.

*A*kira and Isfail had returned to their rooms in the family wing that evening, ready to end a long day with some private time, when a knock sounded on the door. It was Oona's secretary with a delivery. "A message arrived for you, my lord."

Taking the sealed missive with his thanks, Isfail closed the door and turned back. He studied the unusual script directing it to 'Lady Muro and Commander Isfail' before breaking the plain splat of hardened wax.

Akira looked up from the couch as he walked over to her.

"Do you know a Hadson Barok, Kira?"

"I don't recognize that name. Why?"

"He's requesting a meeting with us. A private meeting."

Taking the folded paper, Akira read the brief message. Then an odd smile came to her lips as she murmured, drawing out the name, "Hadson Barok . . . I'll need to reschedule my meeting with Drinin."

She met his curious gaze. "You wanted to meet the man I allowed to escape after the avalanche. Here's your opportunity, Dan."

His gaze sharpening, Isfail read the letter again. "Yes, it is," he agreed thoughtfully, wondering why this opportunity was being presented.

Sixty-Eight

To the south of the capital, beyond Ambassador Central, there was a peninsula jutting out into the Sea of Coroth. The headlands there were a favored spot for those seeking beautiful views and time away from the city. Whether fair weather, fog, or even milder coastal storms, there were those who sought out its untamed beauty.

Barash had discovered the allure of windy cliffs, the drama of waves breaking to high plumes of salt spray, after he'd come to work for Ana Karsh. It had been the first place where he'd ever felt at peace with the world, and with himself.

Today he sat on a wide, flat rock, dividing his attention between the beauty of the early morning light over the ocean and the rough trail leading out to the point. The sound of horses and harness jingling had him rising, turning to watch a carriage approach. He watched the Royal Guard escort come to a halt a short distance away, spacing themselves across the narrow jut of land.

He'd expected the soldiers. Should he need to get past them he knew other, less traveled, ways. Barash stood where he was when the carriage pulled up, recognizing Commander Isfail from the old inn near Corsalat. He caught the flash of recognition in the tall man's eyes before Isfail handed Akira down from the coach.

Taking a deep breath, Barash reminded himself he'd made this choice. Now the time had come to see it through. Moving slowly, arms held away from his sides, he stepped around the stone.

There was wariness and distrust in Isfail's eyes as he kept a protective step ahead of his lady. But Barash was surprised to see humor with the watchfulness in Akira's gaze.

They stopped some distance apart and Barash gave a respectful bow before speaking. "Thank you for meeting me here, Lady Muro. Commander Isfail."

"It's been some time, Barash . . . or do you prefer Hadson?" Akira asked.

He grinned a little. "It's sometimes useful. Barash is my only given name." He met the curiosity in her eyes. "It's . . . good to see you once more, my lady. To thank you for my life."

"Is that why we're here?" Isfail broke in, his voice hard.

Black eyes met dark gray. "My gratitude is real, but I have another reason. I've asked for this meeting to complete a mission."

Taking a step back, his hand reached slowly for his knife. His eyes widened at the speed at which Isfail's appeared in the soldier's hand. "I'm not the threat, Commander, and I know that Lady Muro could stop me faster than any blade could fly."

He waited for Isfail's curt nod before drawing his knife and walking carefully around the rock. Bending to the bound and gagged form he'd left there, Barash cut the rope around Ramort's ankles and dragged him to his feet.

Isfail and Akira glanced at one another in surprise before Akira took a sudden breath.

"It's the schoolmaster, the man Mountain Shadows has been searching for!" she exclaimed.

Isfail sheathed his knife and beckoned for two of the attending soldiers to collect the bound man, with a long look at Barash. "Perhaps you should tell us about this mission of yours."

*T*he sun was directly overhead, scattered clouds creating drifting shadows over land and sea. Barash had told them about encountering Felcan and his men at Baronan Keep. As he recounted what happened there, a signal from Isfail brought a coachman hurrying to spread out a large rug in the shade cast by the coach awning before producing two wicker hampers.

With Akira's quiet invitation, Barash joined the couple, sitting down at the edge of the rug to share a small feast of sliced meats, cheeses, breads, and a variety of fruit. There were bottles of ale, one of wine, and a jug containing water.

He told his story while enjoying this unexpected largesse. There were moments while he finished telling them how he'd decided to work against The Bow when he paused to answer a question from Akira or Isfail.

Barash fell silent as he tipped his head to examine some delectable offering. Then he looked up to find Akira's curious gaze on him and felt the back of his neck heat in embarrassment. "I . . . ah, wasn't expecting your hospitality."

For the first time, he heard amusement in Isfail's voice. "Why not enjoy the outing? And my lady is not to be denied." Then the commander's voice chilled. "You expect us to believe that you've changed, that a lifetime of criminal behavior should be forgiven? That we should trust you wholeheartedly now, after producing one of the murderers from Mountain Shadows? Because you had a change of heart after Akira healed you?"

His spine stiffening, Barash looked at them and said, "Lady Muro can look into my mind, verify the truth of what I've told you. I give you my consent."

"I could," she agreed, meeting Isfail's eyes for a long moment before turning back to him. "But I don't think either of us needs that to believe you."

Barash didn't expect the rush of feeling that staggered him. He had to look away, into the blinding reflection of sunlight off the waves. He squinted his eyes against the glare to hide the impact of being believed by decent people.

A soft touch on his shoulder had his head whipping back.

"Barash," Akira said quietly. "Will you come back to the palace? We'd like you to give your information about these people you met directly to Coroth and the military advisors. Isfail and I guarantee that no one will detain you." She gave him a curious smile. "And there's someone I think you should meet."

Taking a deep breath—another step along the road he'd laid out for himself—Barash agreed.

Sixty-Nine

High Ambassador Drinin was escorted to one of the garden courtyards designed within the palace structure itself. The afternoon light cast a warm glow over the serene landscaping. He might have marveled over the gardens there, if he hadn't been so distracted by what he was about to reveal. Even his belief in the woman he was willing to tell his darkest secret to wasn't enough to ease his anxiety.

She was there, smiling as she greeted him. But would he see that smile after she knew everything about him?

"Thanks for this, Akira," Drinin began as he slipped off his mask, quickly coming to the point before he lost his courage. "I am in need of your wisdom and counsel."

"Of course, Aron. Thank you for being flexible with your schedule." She waited for him to speak further, but he only looked about as they walked through the lovely palace garden.

"You are still unsure, aren't you?" Akira's quiet voice interrupted his thoughts, and he paused to lean against a large fountain. "Would you like to tell me why, my friend?"

Drinin composed himself before he looked into her serene eyes, his smile rueful. "I think there's a part of me that needs resolution, but it scares the hell out of me."

Akira waited while he pushed off the fountain rim. He knew he was unusually restive for the man she'd come to know so well over the years.

"Have I ever told you why I joined the Ambassador Core?" he asked abruptly. "You know more about those of us who've served under you than anyone." Breaking open the long-sealed door to a forsaken past, Drinin took a deep breath. "I was born to a completely different life, one of wealth and privilege—or so it appeared, on the surface. But this is the story of a monster. My father disowned me in favor of my brother."

How much could he tell her, he wondered. He should tell her all of it. He *would* tell her all of it. "My twin brother Abron. Abron Baronan, now calling himself Lord Abron Dateh."

He forced himself to turn and look at Akira. But there was no change in her expression, no horrified recognition, only a patient attentiveness in the slight quirk of an eyebrow.

"Twin sons of Lord Arthon Baronan, the man responsible for the murder of hundreds here in Caldala. Who fled to Ishal before the judgment of the House of Coroth could be levied. The man who instigated the first bloody insurrection in Ishal and would probably have been behind the current one if he hadn't been justifiably executed for his crimes by an Ishalian loyalist," Drinin said bitterly.

"My *father*." He spoke as if the word were poison on his tongue. "You can't know the atrocities I'd witnessed by my eleventh year, and I won't repeat them. But that year . . . two things happened that changed my life. Saved me, if you will."

Akira patted a place beside her on the bench as Drinin paused again with a pained expression on his face. "Sit down, Aron. I can see this is difficult for you. Tell me about the two events," she encouraged gently.

He sighed. "The first involved my mother, Lady Arda Drinin. He treated her despicably, using her for her connections and inheritance while flaunting his mistresses and debauchery. He once told me he only allowed me to live to keep her in line. My mother finally could take no more of the unspeakable acts of the man she'd been bound to. One day she woke me in the early morning and told me to come with her. I was old enough to understand, to at least sense that my father was a madman, and I was more than willing to go."

Drinin swallowed back tears over memories still as clear as that horrific day. "But Baronan had that mad cunning such monsters seem to possess. Somehow he knew or guessed what my mother intended. I don't know if someone betrayed her or if he was just diabolically canny. He was waiting when we came out of the stable." Drinin stood up abruptly, arms crossed tight across his chest.

"I can still hear her screams . . . in nightmares," he whispered. "She tried to gain me time to escape, but I couldn't leave her."

"Aron," Akira said with compassion. "Come, lean on me. You don't need to tell this alone."

Drinin turned, feeling as if he were seeing through the eyes of the shattered boy living within his scarred heart and soul. Hunched over now, he remembered his mother's face. So lined with fear that last year. Filled with terror when she saw the murderous psychopath blocking the gate to freedom. Still, she'd tried to protect him, tried to use untrained force skills to give her young son a chance to escape.

"She died . . . eventually," he murmured. "I . . . I couldn't save her. He threw us into a cell in the basement of the keep. My mother never regained consciousness, a true blessing. I don't know how long I sat beside her body. All I felt was relief that she wouldn't suffer anymore. I prayed to God to help me follow her."

Akira waited through another long pause before asking, "How did you escape?"

Shaking his head to release the living nightmare, he replied, "That was the second thing. A young woman came, my father's latest mistress, though not by her own choice. He did that, picked girls from the village, raped them into submission. She substituted a dead boy for me, another victim of the madness. I don't think there was anyone alive to notice by that time. Aron Baronan ceased to exist."

"What happened then?"

"We ran. Somehow she got us through the sewers. We got to the nearby river and disappeared." He began to feel more himself as he related the rest.

"I never knew why she helped me, or even how she knew we were in that cell," Drinin continued thoughtfully. "Her name was

Ketra. She was the only survivor of her own family. She didn't tell me about the massacre until two years later."

Akira slipped her arm around his. "You stayed together then?"

"She got us to the coast and found a job with a school in Corsalat. I learned that she had been a teacher before her own life was torn apart. Ketra took care of me, told people I was her younger brother." His voice expressed his sadness as he said, "I wish I knew why."

"Why what, my friend?"

"Why she saved the son of Arthon Baronan."

"I'd like to believe it was God's will, Aron. You were meant to do great good, as is evidenced by what you have already accomplished in your life."

Drinin considered this. Ketra had cared for and educated him until his fifteenth year. She was eight years older, but they had become as close as true brother and sister in those brief four years before she died; another victim of Arthon Baronan, whose corrupt body had infected hers with an incurable disease that took her life far too soon.

It was at her burial that he vowed to use the life she'd saved to serve others. That inspiration had seemed so clear on that overcast morning, somehow cleansing the grief from his heart, bringing peace and clarity to his mind. Maybe that was God's message to him, and Ketra had indeed been a divine messenger. He'd walked away with a new purpose and a new name to honor the mother who died defending him.

He smiled a little as he faced Akira again. "I met another miraculous woman within days of Ketra's death. Ambassador Akira Muro. It was as if you knew me, held all the answers to what to do with the rest of my life."

Studying her thoughtful face, it struck him again that Akira had shown no surprise as he'd unburdened himself. His mind floundered now in the shock of realizing that Akira had known his darkest secret all these years . . . and never said anything!

"How long have you known?" he whispered.

"I suspected your relationship with Arthon Baronan before I met you. You are not your father, Aron." Akira took his hand when he hung his head with a shamed expression.

"I investigated everyone's background when choosing people for Alpha. Yours was a little more complex than most. It took a bit more digging than usual, but the name Drinin eventually led me to your mother's family. One of your mother's sisters still lived then. She told me about her sister Arda."

Then Akira sighed. "That's true, but you deserve to know it all." While he stared at her, she said, "You've heard that I was part of the militia unit sent in to confront Arthon Baronan over the murders on Minister Iro's estate, that included his attack on Alani."

"Yes. It was one of your early missions with Commander Isfail. You were among the first to see the atrocities he'd left behind." Drinin shuddered. "I should have told you, but I couldn't let anyone know. I was ashamed and afraid," he said hoarsely. "Afraid that he would find out I was alive."

"There's no shame in being a terrified, abused child, Aron." Slipping an arm around his broad shoulders, she said, "I saw what you'd lived with, the horror of it. I was there when they found your mother. But I could see that the child's body was wrong. The fine clothing didn't fit properly, his hands and teeth showed him to be a child of hard work and little resources."

Straightening, Akira looked over and saw Isfail standing in his cousin's office. The two men were engaged in what appeared to be serious discussion over a map. Looking back into Drinin's questioning eyes, she said, "I asked Isfail to look for a young boy, giving him a very broad description. He located you in Corsalat within a lunam. One of us checked up on you on a regular basis."

Drinin nodded, accepting that Akira always had her own reasons for her actions, no matter how mysterious it might seem to others. "When Ketra died, I felt I had to balance my father's evil by giving my life in service to those in need. That's when I met you. When you told me about the Ambassador Core, I knew it was a direction from God. My road to atonement."

"What did *you* have to atone for, Aron? Not for the sins of your father. You have always been just what you are, a strong and compassionate person. That is why, even at so young an age, you could not leave your mother to face him alone."

"I've been afraid all my life, Akira," he murmured. "Afraid that the same evil waited in me." He saw her face set in stern lines.

"I don't believe that. If you were destined for such a path, it would have come out long ago. You have always been a good and courageous man. This is truth," she stated with conviction when he looked unconvinced. Now anger flashed in those emerald eyes. "Why would you doubt me?"

The sharp words surprised a laugh out of him. "Hell if I know." Drinin grinned when she shook her head with a smile now.

"Are you willing to talk about this with Isfail and the prince? There are things that have surfaced that we all need common ground on."

Blowing out a long breath, Drinin nodded.

Akira looked into his eyes. "You aren't the only one who suffered under Arthon Baronan, or who did what they needed to in order to survive. I'd like you to meet someone, another man I believe has made hard decisions to become a good and courageous man."

*I*t made him uneasy, Barash decided, after spending some time exploring the guest quarters they'd assigned to him. Aside from the decrepit grandeur that was moldering in Baronan Keep, he'd never had such luxurious accommodations, even temporarily. This warmly furnished apartment, with its big bedroom, a common room, and even its own privy chamber with shower, was unheard of in his world.

Amazed that the strength of Akira's endorsement was enough to vouchsafe one such as he, Barash felt a perverse sense of relief in the proximity of his quarters to the Royal Guard barracks. As if their presence would ensure his own good conduct if he proved unworthy of the trust Akira, especially, was granting him.

Taking an upholstered chair near the hearth, Barash sat down cautiously, still reflecting on the path he'd set for himself. They were making it easier for him than he'd expected. Being able to hand over Ramort, a key instigator of the deadly attack at Mountain Shadows, had been a good start.

He'd given them descriptions of Felcan and the other Bowmen he'd seen, as well as what he'd learned about them in that short encounter. And he'd repeated what Akira already knew about his relationship to Arthon Baronan, and his half-brother Abron.

Despite revealing a general outline of his own past indiscretions, Barash felt that the prince was keeping an open mind about his reformation, even though some of the military men were clear about their own skepticism.

He knew he would be closely watched and, for some reason, it soothed rather than offended.

A knock on the door broke into his thoughts, and Barash got up to answer. The relieved smile for Akira turned into cautious speculation when he saw the masked man with her, dressed in the uniform of the Ambassador Core.

"May we come in?" Akira asked. "I'd like you to meet someone."

"Of course, my lady." He stepped aside with an awkward bow. Straightening, Barash noticed that the man with her had stiffened, the eyes within the slit of the mask giving him a hard look.

Akira stood between them, glancing back and forth. "Aron, you may remove your mask."

Barash stared, feeling like he'd seen the man before, not yet placing him as he heard Akira give the introductions.

"Aron Drinin, I would like you to meet Barash. Barash, Aron Drinin." Now she stepped back to observe them without saying anything more.

Aron was the first to break the charged silence. "It's been a long time."

And it clicked in Barash's memory. "Aron . . . Aron Baronan." He grinned, studying the black uniform with more interest. "I'll be damned, an ambassador! Wouldn't old Baronan be turning in his grave?"

With that, the tension shattered. Akira smiled as the two men clasped arms, laughing.

Seventy

What defines a family? Akira wondered that evening. Her sense of self had suffered when she'd learned that the father and mother who'd raised her were not the ones to whom she was born. Then she'd learned of her true mother's death, and her true father's murder. Another crack in her heart, yet healed by the knowing that they had wanted her, loved her even before she was born. They had sacrificed one another to bring her safely into this world.

Lady Arda, Aron's mother, had loved him, enough to sacrifice herself to try and protect him. Before that, she'd had compassion for the illegitimate older son of Arthon Baronan, and given Barash a few years of nurturing. That may well have been the difference that sparked an essential core of decency in the man born to two terrible people. Her murder at the hands of their father had caused wounds that continued to give pain.

If the third Baronan son, Aron's twin, had been allowed his mother's love and nurturing, would he be a better man? Or would Abron, nonetheless, have followed his father's violent path?

Arthon Baronan had cut a swath of grief and destruction, directly and indirectly, through countless families. The proof of it followed Akira's life: her parents, herself, Alani Iro's family, Aron Drinin, Barash. It had nearly taken Ardan Isfail from her, and it continued a violent legacy in his son Abron. Now it spread its blood-soaked pall over Ishaka, and her cousin Kane's chosen people.

How much longer? Akira wondered. Would her child be touched by this madness across generations?

Pressing a hand to her belly, as if shielding the baby she carried, Akira fully understood the lengths a mother would go to protect her child.

And the memory of another woman's sacrifice continued to haunt her. Even the warmth of the family gathered over dinner fed that sorrow as she watched Logran and Oona with their beautiful children.

Perhaps the memories revived and lingered because she'd been a part of bringing two men together, linked by blood and carrying some elusive core of decency even though their origins were anything but. She'd left them sitting together in the guest quarters, deep in conversation about their lives since that last fateful day at Baronan Keep.

Akira doubted they'd really heard her when she'd said farewell. It was such an interesting meeting of the two half-brothers, she'd been tempted to stay, just to watch their interaction, hear their responses to each other's experiences—the ambassador and the assassin. Yet there was that immediate link, the recognition of brother for brother, somehow remembering that they'd once shared a tenuous caring for each other, even if it hadn't been openly acknowledged then.

If her father had survived, separated from his daughter, then they'd met in that forgotten valley, independent of Kane's introduction—would they have known each other? Recognized that essential blood tie?

Now, years later, would another mother see the child she'd given up out of love and grief? Neither knowing the other unless some elemental force brought them together.

Had she provided good counsel all those years ago when a grieving girl had come to her? How had she—naïve, innocent, hardly more than a girl herself then—presumed to advise on such a monumental decision?

Now, feeling the butterfly sensations of new life within her body, would she have given the same counsel?

Could she give up her child under similar circumstances?

"Kira?"

Startled by Isfail's quiet address, Akira brought her attention back to the present, giving him an apologetic smile. "Yes?"

Taking her hand, he tipped his head. "Are you feeling well? You were far away, my sweet."

In answer, she brought their joined hands to her lips. "Old thoughts, Dan, old memories." But her own words had her brow creasing slightly. "Ones I'd like to share with you. Maybe your perspective, especially now, would help me resolve my feelings about something."

Isfail brought his free hand to her cheek. "You can tell me anything, Kira."

Settled in their bedroom that night, Isfail watched while Akira removed pins, freeing her beautiful hair. It was one of his greatest pleasures, a sight that never failed to calm and arouse him at the same time. He grinned at the thought.

In the mirror, he saw her knowing smile and walked over to take the brush from her hand with a quiet laugh. "Vixen," he teased. "No mind tapping."

"I hardly need to read your mind, my love, when your thoughts are clear on your face, and . . ." Akira looked pointedly downward.

His grin just broadened as he began to brush her long, white hair in slow, smooth strokes. "So, what were you thinking about earlier?"

Meeting his eyes in the reflection, Akira sighed. "I suppose watching Aron and Barash reunite today left me considering how widespread Arthon Baronan's reach has been, how many people's lives and families were devastated, to one degree or another. It had me remembering something that happened several years ago. Yet the circumstances surrounding that event are disturbingly similar to what's happening now."

As her husband's easy brushstrokes comforted her, Akira released the secret she had held for so long.

"You know that I had more than one mission when my

reconnaissance team was sent into Ishal during the Baronan Rebellion years ago."

Their eyes met in the glass, tacitly agreeing not to reflect on Isfail's first skirmish with death in Ishal. As he bent to press a kiss to her temple, Akira reached up to grip his hand on her shoulder.

"After leaving the Gattes survivors on the ship, my team surreptitiously collected field information on the state of things in that country, including the success of the loyal resistance and the strength of the insurgent forces. Along with this, I was seeking information on the fate of Caldala's Minister Iro, his daughter Alani, and his staff. They were last known to be housed in official quarters within the Parliament complex, but had not been heard of since the coup." Restless now, Akira stood up as Isfail set the brush aside. "You've seen the reports of my team's reconnaissance findings, and know that the resistance finally reclaimed their country, so I won't go further on that."

As Isfail sat down, watching her pace the spacious bedroom, Akira recalled what followed.

"Minister Iro and his staff were killed in the first assault. Ishalian guard units had gone in to rescue the ministers and their people, with mixed success. One of the units took heavy losses and their captain was taken prisoner, along with Alani." Akira glanced at Isfail. "I've told you how they managed to escape through the sea tunnels, the same ones you were taken through."

For a moment, Akira shuddered, thinking how close she'd come to losing the man she loved. Then she felt Isfail's arms pull her close, warming her suddenly chilled body.

"Sit down, Kira," he coaxed, guiding her to the couch where he sat, pulling her onto his lap to wrap his arms around her.

"I won't go into everything Alani shared with me after we rescued her but, as such things go under extreme circumstances, she fell in love with the captain during their flight from Tash'tric."

"Extreme situations can bring on extreme emotions," Isfail noted. "You might be interested to know that I've heard some of this story from Commander Caden Aric. Captain Garath Haill was a close friend of his. He told me Haill confided his love for Alani before his death."

Akira nodded. "Yes. Aric, a captain then, brought Alani the news and some of Haill's possessions. I'd met Haill and Aric on an earlier diplomatic mission. They both impressed me as honorable men, and Haill certainly proved that with his dedication to keeping Alani safe until rescue arrived."

"He died for his men, and I'm sorry for Alani's loss. I can't say I know her well, but she's living a life in courageous service, and I know she's important to you." Isfail hugged her a little closer. "I can see why the current situation in Ishal brings those memories back."

Turning into him, Akira pressed her face to his throat. "It's become more personal for me, Dan. There's more to Alani's story, something only I know. Less than a lunam after she received news of Haill's death, Alani gave birth to their daughter."

She felt Isfail grow still against her and shifted back to look into his astonished face. "She came to me when she knew she was pregnant. Alani had been training with me as a private student while waiting for the conflict in Ishal to be resolved. I know she hoped Haill would send for her when it was safe, or come to her if the loyalists were defeated.

"I helped her conceal her condition. What she didn't know was that I was concerned that Haill might forget her." Akira gave her husband a wry smile. "My own experiences clouded my belief in a man's fidelity."

"Certainly reasonable at that time," he said gently. "And some men do forget, or go on to other women."

"Yes." Akira hugged him close. "Well, Alani was, and is, self-sufficient, being the only child and heir of her mother and father, but her emotional state was more vulnerable then. She saw her mother murdered by Arthon Baronan when she was a child and, at eighteen, her father was murdered in the attack on Ishal's Parliament complex. Haill was handsome and her protector while the world around her was falling apart. She was lost in a foreign country. It's no wonder her feelings for him were so strong."

Akira got up then, going to pour two glasses of wine before returning to hand him one and take a seat beside him.

"Haill's death was a terrible blow. I requested a leave of absence from the Core and took her to the mountains, to a lovely little town I'd come across on some mission. We had a little house there, and we spent hours talking. I encouraged her to talk, anyway."

Taking a long sip from her wine, Akira got up again and looked out over the sea. Without the moons, it rolled dark under a sky brilliant with countless stars. "Alani's inheritance would have made it possible for her to raise her child without hardship, but she feared that keeping the baby would risk the child's life. She'd already lost everyone she loved to Arthon Baronan and his violent schemes. I cannot even describe her terror at the thought of something happening to her daughter."

Isfail came to stand next to her, wrapping an arm around her shoulders. "What did happen?"

"Alani asked me to counsel her on finding a good family, and to arrange a completely anonymous adoption." Tears were trickling down Akira's face. "I did not try to dissuade her, even though I could see that it was breaking her heart. Who was I, Dan, to give advice to anyone on such a monumental decision? I was only a few years older, a young woman who had never known passion, or the depth of a mother's feelings for the baby she's nurtured inside her body, the child born of love between two people. How could I have encouraged her to give up that part of her to people she didn't even know?"

She found herself sobbing in Isfail's arms while he tried to ease her heartache.

"You were who she needed then, Akira. Alani was obviously stronger than you remember. Maybe you're looking back with years of experience behind you, but also with the new emotions and sensibilities of a mother-to-be."

He urged her to sit with him once more. "I've met Alani. She strikes me as a courageous woman, with humor and loyalty for her companions. She did what was right for her, to protect what she loved, and live a life that honored those she loved and lost. She chose to serve and to fight for what's right. Perhaps she sees that as a way to give her daughter a good and safe world to live in."

Wiping tears from her cheeks, Akira said, "I know that's true, and I shouldn't try to guess her feelings. But I also know Alani has never forgotten her child, or ceased to love her."

"Does she know where she is?"

"No." But, remembering where Alani was at that moment, Akira wondered if this was still true. "She felt it would be easier, and safer for the child. Her only stipulation was that I arrange the adoption, and that the child would never be told unless it was necessary, or she was grown."

"You know where Alani's daughter is, and I'll wager you've checked on her well-being all these years."

"She's the daughter of an excellent family, and she's just reached her coming-of-age. Yes, I keep track of her, but I've never gone back to see her. I'll admit it was too painful, thinking of Alani's sacrifice. There are people I trust who provide me with information."

Getting up to refill his wine glass and get a glass of water for Akira, Isfail frowned. "This presents me with an unexpected dilemma, my sweet. Though I'll begin by saying that I will abide by whatever decision you make on what I'm about to tell you."

"Oh?"

"I've told you about the talks I had with Aric and Declan while waiting for the ship. One thing I did not consider repeating, until now, was a question Aric asked about Alani."

Akira met his eyes with a wary look. "You did bring back a package for her."

"Yes. But he asked if there was a child." Isfail took a sip of wine, waiting for her reaction. "I told him I'd never heard of one. That was an obvious disappointment to him, and Declan later told me he thought Aric might feel less grief over Haill's death if there had been a child."

"You're asking me if you can give that information to him." Akira felt the added weight of Aric's grief now, but her loyalty to

Alani had to prevail. "I can't give you that permission, Dan. I can only say that, if an opportunity occurs, I'll let Alani know about Aric. She can decide."

Isfail framed her face with his hands, love warm in his eyes. "I'm honored that you've trusted me with such a vital confidence, Kira."

Lifting her face to his kiss, she murmured, "You're the only one is this world I can open my heart to, Dan. You would never betray my confidence."

Seventy-One

kira woke before dawn the next day, wondering if the vague nausea she felt was the continuing consequence of pregnancy, or due to an equally vague concern that she was beginning to contemplate a course of action that would certainly be met with strenuous objection by everyone around her.

Confiding Alani's deepest secret the night before had opened a mental chest full of Recon Alpha secrets, large and small, accumulated over the years. Some she felt no need to reveal, such as the knowledge that Isa Coran and Ivano Micharon had been bound together over three years before. The long-standing love affair between Evani Reva and Alon Coronan had been known or guessed by most of the team of ambassadors, but kept within Alpha until Coronan's brush with death made it common knowledge.

She smiled at that, and the problems it was creating for Garan. In fact, he'd requested a meeting with her over today's midday meal, and she expected the chastity vow to be one topic of discussion. Fortunately, she had an answer that she hoped he could live with as Most High Ambassador.

Lying safe and warm in bed, her thoughts sobered again. There had been more serious secrets and deceptions in her years as an ambassador. Many times in her long career she'd been required to act in covert ways. Her unique abilities had been refined and utilized to successfully meet military demands that the average Caldalan could never comprehend; many they would never willingly condone.

Turning to look at the man asleep beside her, a man who knew most of those secrets and still loved her, Akira knew she owed him the respect of involving him fully in these new thoughts and possible actions. There would be no secrets between the two of them.

Leaving Ardan sleeping, Akira dealt with morning necessities before going out to the living area and on to the little alcove outfitted for making tea. She smiled when she spotted the addition of an herbal blend that Oona had recommended.

Taking a chair beside the windows, she sipped her first cup and looked out at tendrils of fog that teased the observer with glimpses of sand, rocks, and restless sea as the day brightened.

Her thoughts were like that, she decided, showing her glimpses of what could be out there, realities and hazards once the mist of indecisions lifted. But only one decision was clear. She needed to bring Ardan in to help clarify a course of action.

A whisper of sound had her looking over to see him walking into the room. Dressed only in loose pants he had recently pulled on, dark hair tangled around his face, with eyes already sharp and focusing directly on her, he was a man to stir the senses of any woman.

Her face must have revealed that immediate sensual response since he walked over, bracing his hands on the arms of her chair as his mouth captured hers in a kiss meant for erotic nights.

"Why didn't I find you in bed when I woke up?" Isfail murmured against her lips.

"I was awake too early for you," Akira whispered back.

"Wake me next time." He grinned, straightening and picking up her teacup for a drink. The look on his face as he forced himself to swallow was priceless. Akira laughed as she rose to fix him a cup of his preferred blend.

She felt him give a last shudder of disgust as he wrapped his arms around her from behind.

"Is it that awful tasting to you?" Isfail inquired, taking the fresh cup of his regular blend that she handed him when she turned.

"No. It's just different, but Oona swears it helps with the morning nausea."

"Does it?"

Akira chuckled. "I think so, but that's not as bad anymore." She stilled, her hand automatically moving to the imperceptible rounding of her belly as her smile bloomed. Taking his hand, she pressed it under hers.

Isfail felt his world shift as she shared the fluttering of that new life with him. Dipping his forehead to hers, eyes closing, he opened to her mind, going deeper for the shadowy impression of the baby growing within her.

"I love you both," he said quietly.

"So do I," Akira replied.

They stood together for several more minutes, cherishing the time together before the day began with all its demands on their time, together and apart.

Village of Psyche Lakes

Cool rain cleared remaining smoke from the caldera valley but brought the pungent smell of wet ash. It also complicated the demolition and clean up of the dozen or so buildings that had burned in the attack.

Now villagers formed a team to set up barriers to keep the ash that was becoming a soggy, soupy mess from running into the lakes. Cleaning brigades worked hard to shovel, load, and cart debris out to designated disposal pits. Others continued salvaging what could still be used from the sites that had only been damaged.

Feeling a tap on his back as he hefted a charred timber into a waiting cart, Osharon looked back and grinned. He swiped his hands on his already filthy pants before taking his friend's arm. "When'd you get here?"

"Late last night," Kilronan replied, looking around the neighborhood where people were already hustling in the overcast morning. "We bunked at Maran's since my folks are full up with my sister's family."

"So you came back with the elder delegation?" Osharon reached for another timber with Kilronan picking up the other end. "What about Akira?"

"Yes, and no. Akira and Isfail stayed in Coroth, working on things there." Kilronan chuckled. "He's trying to keep her out of trouble."

Osharon laughed as they placed the timber in the cart, happy to have some humor added to the dismal morning. "Good luck to him. What's our Akira up to now?"

"She's pregnant."

Spinning around, Osharon grabbed his friend's shoulders with a wide grin. "We're having a baby?"

"She is. I'm pretty sure it's Isfail's, not yours."

Roaring with laughter, Osharon gave him a shake before returning to his task. "Can't argue with that. This is great news."

"A lot better than this," Kilronan replied. "My team's helping with Mara's house. I'll head over there soon. Just wanted to check in and see how you're doing."

Shrugging, Osharon straightened for a minute. "We're fine. No damage to my folks' place. But, to cap off the bigger picture, I'm angry about Lani's celebration. It was pretty much over when things heated up, but what do you think she's going to remember about her day?"

"It's a shame." Kilronan threw a chunk of debris into the cart. "We heard some of Akira's recon people were sent to help out, along with other ambassadors."

"Yeah. They're staying at the inn. They're out tracking, getting a better picture of how the bastards came in, how at least one escaped. Alpha looked at some of the incendiary balls that didn't burn." He raised his brow, twisting his mouth in a look of disbelief. "Reva and Micharon think the fuses had been pulled before use."

"Why would they do that? And how could the ambassadors tell?"

"Who knows how those Bow fanatics think? Seems Recon Alpha learned a lot about the use of explosives from the first Baronan Rebellion. Several bombs survived; I guess Reva and Micharon could see that none of them had fuses, but they appeared to have been prepared for them. We also gave them a detailed account of the explosions we heard. When you check out the damage, you can get a sense of the force involved, or whether the powder just burned."

Kilronan gave him a friendly punch on the shoulder. "I'll get back to you later. Catch you up on what happened on the trip, and in Coroth."

Osharon gave a grunt of acknowledgment and started back to work. An enthusiastic shout had him looking over. Lani was running up to Kilronan with a bright grin on her face. He watched them hug one another before Lani tagged along, chattering non-stop.

With a chuckle, Osharon went back to his job in a lighter mood. Shortly after, he stopped to wave when the ambassadors of Recon Alpha greeted him.

"Any luck?" he called to them.

Reva—at least, he thought it was Reva beneath the hood and mask—shook her head as the unit rode toward the council building. He swiped at his sweaty, dirt-streaked brow as he watched the riders pass Kilronan and Lani down the road. The ambassadors slowed, replying to something Kilronan was saying, then continued on their way.

As Osharon began to turn back to the ruins, he noticed one of the ambassadors twisting around to watch Kilronan and Lani turn down a side road.

The intermittent rain turned into a steady drench by nightfall, but it didn't deter Ambassador Alani Iro from seeking solitude and solace in the shadowed lanes of Psyche Lakes. Raindrops bounced in the yellow pools of lamplight, dancing to some secret rhythm of the weather. She tried to soothe her heart with that playful image.

Now that the smell of destruction had cleared the air, leaving only the homey scent of hearth fires, evergreens, and the occasional waft of honeysuckle from the vines twining over the short walls nearby, there was a peaceful feel to the village.

Breaking off a short length of fragrant blossoms, Iro brushed it against her wet cheek as she walked along deserted lanes. Despite her attempts to dismiss the girl she'd seen with Kilronan today, the child's face haunted her. The eyes . . .

Iro shook those thoughts away. But there were times when the memory of Garath Haill was so strong, she almost felt she could turn around and he'd be there. That was all this was, she told herself, those memories enhanced by the reminder of the last rebellion—the too-familiar smells of ash and black powder that lingered over the years, the burned homes, the ruin of people's lives.

Recon Alpha's ambassadors were returning to Coroth tomorrow. She'd try to forget the young girl the age her daughter would be—the child with her father's dark gold hair and amber eyes.

Iro circled back toward the inn, lifting her face to the sky to wash away hot tears with rivulets of cold rain.

Seventy-Two

Palace of Coroth

Another misty morning gave way to clouds building into a spring storm. As rain began to spatter against the windows of a small reception room, Akira and Kane pored over a map depicting the section of Green River Caldon where the new mountain access was located. One of Coroth's senior mapmakers had been working on it with Kane and Kilronan before the protectorate master left. Now Kane was reviewing the changes for accuracy, particularly in the new rift zone opening to Ishaka.

They all looked up when the door opened, and Isfail walked in with a man Akira knew well.

"Micah!" she exclaimed happily, walking to him with her hands outstretched for his. "At last, a chance to thank you personally for bringing Commander Isfail safely home." She stretched up to kiss his cheek. "Is your father here too?"

Leading him to a comfortable chair, Akira waited for Isfail and Kane to join them after the mapmaker nodded his goodbyes.

"No," Micah Vaneer answered cheerfully. "He's enjoying some well-deserved shore time. The *Maid* is taking a turn in dry dock."

Isfail wrapped an arm around Akira's shoulders. "Micah hasn't told you the big news."

Micah grinned. "So I will. The Captain decided I was ready for my own ship. She's a sassy little lady named *Spirit of the Sea*. My father released several of his crew to me while they're dry-docked, those that want to be back on the waves. They're sorting out some new sailors for me. We've been on our shakedown run for the past few lunams."

Micah's face grew serious as he met Isfail's curious look. "That's what brought me to Coroth, actually. We've brought news out of Ishal. I've been spreading it to every port we visit."

Seeing Kane lean forward, eyes intent, Akira said, "Tell us what you can."

"After our last port call with the *Maid*, when we were able to pick up Isfail, my father refused to take his ship there again, at least while there was danger and uncertainty." Micah accepted a cup of tea from the attendant who'd brought the tea service. "Once I took command of *Spirit*, we put in at ports around the islands before crossing over to Kuldor. We got news from other crews, some fresh from port calls in Tash'tric."

"They were allowed to dock there?" Isfail interrupted.

With a nod, Micah continued. "I've heard the situation is so bad, citizens are standing against the insurgents, and there are enough loyal militia left, they turned against those who'd switched sides, defying Dateh's defense ministry." Micah finished his tea. "They say there's fighting in the streets."

Akira's feelings were mixed. She was glad the people of Ishal were fighting back, but knew that many innocent lives would suffer and be lost.

"Remembering those we'd smuggled out," Micah said, "I put the matter to my crew, and we decided to put in at Tash'tric with food stuff and necessities. I was sweating it, I'll admit." His eyes met Isfail's. "Not knowing what we'd face. But luck was in, and the loyalist militia had taken over the docks. I don't know if they'll hold, but we managed to offload and get out. The harbormaster cleared the invoice with a note of credit, but we felt the food would get distributed fairly. That's what mattered."

Kane cleared his throat. "I'll honor your payment, Captain."

Micah shook his head. "Not necessary, sir, but I appreciate the offer."

"My cousin," Akira said quietly. "Kane Kalronan. He's an Ishakan by choice, Micah."

"Ah, I see." Micah offered his arm for Kane to grip. "I suppose it's a matter of honor to you, sir. Why don't we wait and see how things go."

Thinking about the fact that Micah Vaneer had been able to enter the harbor of Tash'tric without challenge, Akira saw possibilities opening up. "Micah, do you have any news about people going in or out of Tash'tric?"

"We did bring out a few families this time, with no trouble from any of Dateh's Watchers. In fact, we didn't see a one of them, not like our port call before that." Micah rubbed his forehead, looking thoughtful. "I didn't really notice whether other ships were carrying passengers, in either direction, though there were people milling about the wharf."

He grinned at Isfail. "I heard you met Captain Norsi."

"Did I?" Isfail replied, one brow lifting.

"Captain Endra Norsi of the *Black Squall*. Seems she's gotten herself in some trouble carrying Bowmen and illegals around the circuit, including Caldala."

Isfail's confusion cleared. "The anonymous captain who agreed to talk with us in Insalat. I was hoping she'd be willing to make up for bad faith by agreeing to help us in identifying members of The Bow and their travel plans. Do you know her?"

"Aye. She's from an old shipping family out of Kilra, mostly fallen on hard times, bad luck and bad blood. Her brother sails on a pirate cutter that recently cut ties with Dateh's hired mercenaries in Kittric."

"We heard that," Isfail said. "But there's no specific information coming out of Kittric."

"Only rumors that they're putting together a fleet that can defeat any other on the seas. From the little I've heard, The Bow keeps their plans close to the chest, and Kittric harbor is large enough that Ishal's shipbuilding is across the bay from where the pirate ships are docked.

"Dateh's men enjoy ordering the pirates about. With the

latest trouble, those miscreants are thinking about the possible long-term consequences of Dateh's terrorist fleet, and how their *trade* might suffer." He met Isfail's eyes. "I'm pretty sure those privateers not trapped in Kittric would be willing to join any action against The Bow's monster fleet."

Isfail sat back with a look of speculation. "That could be useful."

"Yes, it could." Something in Akira's voice had all eyes turning to her.

Logran sat in his private office that afternoon, elbows on his desk, hands pressed together with fingertips touching his unsmiling mouth. Earlier, he'd listened to Akira lay out her concerns before proposing some options. Now he watched Isfail stalk the room with a frown knitting his brow.

Shifting his arms to fold his hands over one another on the desktop, Logran said, "Akira makes a number of good points about the need for reconnaissance."

"Of course she does," Isfail snarled. "She always knows what needs to be done. It's what she decides *has* to be done that's the problem."

Akira's eyebrows rose at that. "I haven't decided anything. I'm telling you both what I've been thinking. The only thing I'm pressing for at this time is that we have a serious discussion about this with relevant parties as soon as possible. That would include Garan and Recon Alpha, when they're all back."

"They're due back tomorrow," Logran informed them. "And I'm going to take Akira's advice on this." He held up a hand when Isfail jerked about to stare at him. "We need to talk about this, Dan. I'm not saying I agree with everything that's been brought up."

He got up to pour two glasses of whiskey, ordering a tea service for Akira. Handing Isfail his whiskey, Logran went to look out at the sun-splashed courtyard. "Time's a factor now. Caldala's fleet is preparing to sail, taking a stand off the coast near the Southern Crescent. If Dateh's going to make an assault against Ishaka and the loyalists there, it should be soon. I must finalize decisions regarding the horse tribes."

When Akira caught his eyes with her hard emerald stare, Logran shrugged. "We've reached consensus on Kane's request. As I've already drafted the agreement and gone over it with him, there's no reason I can't give you the details. Caldala will grant the horse tribes temporary grazing and land rights in the Northern Territories. This will include raising food crops for their needs."

Logran refilled his glass. "They have not requested emigration status, and will not be granted citizenship, but will fall under Caldala's protection while they are within our borders. As long as there is no trouble caused by this agreement, it is granted for a term of three years, at which time it may be renegotiated, if necessary.

"In return, Caldala will receive ten percent of crop yield and tribesmen will support, and help with, the building of a new protectorate fortress near the Ishakan Rift Pass." He smiled at Akira. "As you and Kane have so aptly suggested naming it."

Isfail swallowed the last of his whiskey, feeling a bit mollified. "It's a good agreement."

"Yes. Parliament voted unanimously to approve it." Logran frowned a little, reminded of the liaison votes, but said nothing. "Kane will be leaving within the next two days to bring the contract to his council for ratification." He sat down, leaning back in his chair as he glanced between them. "What are you two planning to do? You know you can stay here."

Akira looked at her husband. "Perhaps we'll return with Kane. I'd like to see this pass for myself."

"Damn it," Isfail said with a sigh. "I knew it. You're going to insist on supporting the Ishakans."

She walked to him, wrapping her arms around his waist. "In some way, yes, but I haven't decided how. That's why we need the reconnaissance information, Dan. Coroth can't make a final decision on how much help to send unless we know the real situation in Ishal."

Seventy-Three

When the prince of Caldala requested someone's presence at an unscheduled meeting, it was understood that, barring severe illness or death, they *would* be there. If it meant rescheduling other business at the last minute, or dropping off your gear because you'd just returned from a mission, then riding immediately to the palace, that's what you did.

By the appointed time, the meeting room held the full count. This included Coroth's chief military advisor, along with High Ambassador Garan, the ten ambassadors of Reconnaissance Alpha, Kane Kalronan, and Barash—to the surprise of many.

Akira and Isfail sat at one end of the large table. Prince Logran headed the assembly at the other, with his wife, Princess Oona, who'd chosen to hear what was being discussed about security matters.

Logran opened the meeting by bringing everyone up to date on the news out of Ishal, as gathered from informants around the coast, and sea captains like Micah Vaneer.

Then Reva was asked to give a report on the situation in Psyche Lakes. Though it was a relief that casualties and damage were less than they might have been, it was a disappointment that the eighth assailant had yet to be found.

As Reva sat down, Akira lifted a hand. Logran nodded to her, saying, "I believe Lady Muro has a guest who can shed light on this."

Akira looked at Barash, who was obviously less than easy with his current situation as she introduced him. "Barash has unique inside information. He came to Coroth, asking to talk with Commander Isfail and myself regarding what he'd learned about The Bow's activities here in Caldala. While he did not know that Psyche Lakes was the intended target, he did sabotage the hand bombs he suspected were going to be used in a terrorist attack. And he captured the man who'd organized the attack on Mountain Shadows, and turned him over for trial." She lifted her hand for Barash to give a synopsis of his findings.

If Barash was surprised by the way everyone listened attentively, and asked pertinent questions without accusations, he didn't show it. But Akira noticed his look of relief when he finally returned to his seat.

"That was quick thinking, pulling the fuses," Reva said. "You saved a lot of lives."

Barash shrugged, but dipped his head respectfully.

Logran met Akira's eyes then turned the meeting over to her.

Hoping to keep things peaceful, Akira remained seated, only leaning forward with her arms crossed on the table. "The planned attack Barash was able to intercede in is a good example of our lack of intelligence. The Bow has been an organized presence in Caldala for more than three years. We've been fortunate in that many of their soldiers, if you can call them that, are poorly trained. But there are leaders, like this Felcan that Barash told us about, probably the man who escaped from Psyche Lakes, who have ability and dedication to their cause."

"Felcan's the one who got away from us in Somara Caldon," Arith reminded the group. "From what we saw of him, he's a strong leader, cunning and clever. It sounds like he's one of Dateh's head men."

Isfail agreed, but noted, "He'll have some trouble getting out of Caldala this time. Every port is being watched over by the militia, and ship captains are advised and required to check passenger manifests closely. They've also been given a description of Felcan since the latest attack. There are no ships sailing directly to Ishal." He gave a short sigh. "Of course, this Felcan has proven himself to be very clever, and he might find a way out, but we'll make him work for it." Now he tipped his head to Akira.

"We don't know if there are more terrorist groups in Caldala, but our soldiers captured a number of them trying to return to the ships that had been sailing in and out of the Southern Crescent. That route is now closed to them. High Pass is essentially closed to them with Mountain Shadows Protectorate keeping a tight watch there. And we don't have any evidence that they're aware of the new pass."

Taking a deep breath, Akira cut to the main purpose of this meeting. "But evidence, specific information on Dateh and The Bow, their plans, their resources . . . these are things we do not have. This is important information that's needed for Coroth and Caldala to plan a defense." She turned it back to Isfail.

"We know that there is much stronger loyalist sentiment this time around," Isfail said. "Ishal is experiencing a civil war, citizens against Bowmen. Loyal militia units are fighting back against the enemy, and others have positioned themselves to defend the Ishakan territories that have been targeted by Dateh. What we don't know is what's happening in Kittric, at least, not enough. They're building a fleet, yes, but how viable is it? What's their purpose in conscripting pirates? We know the pirates are beginning to cause trouble there. Our purpose today is finding a way to get more accurate information."

"This was a problem before," Akira continued ruthlessly. "The Kittric massacre would never have happened if we'd had good intelligence then. This was the reason I pushed for trained reconnaissance teams in the Core."

"You are not going into Kittric." Isfail's voice sounded calm, but everyone could hear the cold steel underlying the words.

Akira reached over to cover his clenched fist. "No. I promise you that's not what I'm proposing here." She looked around the group gathered at the table. "We will need to deal with Kittric directly at some point, unless the insurgents are defeated before that. But I will not be physically involved there."

"Damn right," Arith muttered, meeting her hard look with one of his own.

Akira straightened, resuming her cool demeanor. "What we

need is first-hand reconnaissance on the situation in Tash'tric, Dateh's seat of power. We've heard he has problems in Kittric as well, but what about the other cities? Land imports and shipping are nearly at a standstill; few countries or captains are willing to risk Ishal. With the turmoil, businesses must be shutting down, and food in short supply as farming is disrupted. We know there are loyalists willing to stand against another takeover. What's really happening in the civilian population?"

His bearing somewhat more relaxed, Isfail nodded. "If Ishalians are fighting back with some success, Caldala may only need to provide limited assistance, maybe supply loyalist forces and support their resistance."

"Exactly," Akira agreed.

Uncomfortable in the elegant meeting room—in a palace, of all places—Barash shifted, clearing his throat to gain Akira's attention. When she met his eyes, he said, "This could be a chance to cut off the head of The Bow. Could be we'd make that chance by sending the right people in."

"And the right people would be?" she asked, an eyebrow lifted.

He knew she expected what he was about to say. "Me."

"Not alone," Drinin spoke up, causing the others in Recon Alpha to stare at him.

"Of course not alone," Arith said, punching Drinin's shoulder lightly. "We're a team."

Akira watched them, and Barash watched her. He thought there was some plan already thought out behind that beautiful face. Glancing at Isfail, he saw that the commander's eyes were narrowed as he, too, studied his wife.

Then Akira lifted a hand slightly, and the room quieted. "We need two recon teams—one to Tash'tric, one to Kittric. And we'll need a team with us when we go to Ishaka."

Barash saw that Isfail had already known what she would say this time. The man's eyes had gone stormy-gray, but his expression was resigned as he met Akira's gaze.

She knew who would go to Tash'tric and Kittric too. Barash was now certain of that. But she had opened the discussion, offering the choice even while knowing who would be willing to risk the danger.

He sat silently, watching them all, listening to what followed, knowing he was ready for whatever came next—just another step on the road to redemption. Akira had shown him that road, and he'd chosen to take it.

Barash didn't know which was stronger, his gratitude—maybe a love he'd never known before Akira—or his hatred of Arthon Baronan. Either emotion was a good enough reason to stand for something decent, and against the evil his father had unleashed. Whether he lived or died, he'd have made his *own* mark on the world.

Seventy-Four

Everything was settled by mid-afternoon. Micah Vaneer, who'd expressed a willingness to sail on an ambassador mission, was sent for. He would transport both teams, calling first at Tash'tric where Drinin's team, including Barash, would disembark. Micah would go about regular business there for no more than two days. If the two men weren't back, he would sail the ship to a predetermined rendezvous along the coast.

Barash and Drinin, disguised as sailors on the *Spirit of the Sea*, would somehow blend into the crowds on the wharf and disappear into Tash'tric. The plan was to find an inn, change to more prosperous clothing, and get a message to Dateh, asking for a meeting.

It was extremely risky, and a lot would depend on what happened once they were there. They were counting on what they'd heard about Abron Dateh's ego and arrogance from Shanow's reports.

Regardless, Micah would sail from the area no more than one week later to drop the other ambassadors off at a cove closer to Kittric, with or without Drinin and Barash. If they missed the initial rendezvous, he would check back on his return to Caldala.

There was some ambiguity in reconnecting with Arith's team. A date was proposed to meet back at the same cove, but the ambassadors were confident that they could get themselves overland to Ishaka once they'd completed their reconnaissance. Akira gave the nod to their plan, leaving other options open.

Approximately two weeks after their teammates sailed, the rest of Recon Alpha would ride to Mountain Shadows, then on to the new pass with Akira, Isfail, and Kane, who'd chosen to delay his return.

That was the official plan.

With a great deal to take care of before Vaneer's ship would sail on tomorrow night's tide, Logran closed the meeting and released everyone to last-minute preparations.

When Isfail stayed behind to confer with Logran and the military advisor, Oona took Akira to the parlor overlooking the ocean.

"Why are you doing this, Akira?" she asked anxiously. "You don't even know whether you'll be needed in Ishaka. Send the others if you believe they're needed."

"Oona . . ." Akira sighed. "These are my people. It's hard enough to split Alpha team, with one group going without me to Kittric. Some of them were there during the Baronan Rebellion. This could be worse."

"Think of yourself for once," Oona begged, her hand gripping Akira's. "Think of your safety, and the baby's. These people are trying to kill you, to murder your entire race!"

Holding tight to her hand, Akira met Oona's worried gaze. "That's why I have to do this, to fight. What kind of life . . . what kind of world can I give this child if he will only be safe behind stone walls?"

"Think of Dan, then," Oona tried again. "How would he feel if something happened to you, to the baby?"

That argument had weight, Akira knew, feeling tears rise. She willed them back, knowing he understood her mind and heart. "Dan has endured a great deal for me, and I for him. I could not do what I must if I did not have him by my side." She sighed, thinking of all he'd agreed to, and all he would risk for her sake. Oona could never understand how deeply they understood one another.

Turning back to her, Akira wrapped both hands around hers. "We only have two choices, my friend. We fight for our right to live peacefully, or we find a new place, a new land, where our people will not be persecuted."

*I*n Coronan's room, in their barracks at Ambassador Central, Evani Reva thoroughly checked his pack. She'd have time, too much time, to prepare for the trip to Ishaka. But he would be leaving tomorrow evening.

Leaving Caldala for war-torn Ishal, leaving safety for danger. Leaving her.

"Vani," he said quietly, taking her trembling hands. "That's the third time you've done inventory. I've never forgotten anything, you know."

"No," she admitted, trying to stifle the tremor in her voice. "That's not where you get into trouble."

He kissed her lips lightly. "Hey, wasn't that you who said I've learned a lot?"

She wrapped her arms around his waist, tried a smile. "It was, so don't make a liar out of me." Pulling him close, Reva pressed her face to his shoulder. "We've never been apart on a real mission before. Who'll keep you out of trouble, lover?"

"Arith, Drinin, Iro, and Kalronan. It'll take four Alphas to take your place."

"Sure," she said, forcing humor into her reply. "And they'll have their hands full. Here, take these." Reva pulled her vials of Black Arrow antidote from her pocket.

"Vani, I've got my own." But she turned and slid them into a secure pocket in his pack. He let her. "Make sure you replace those," he ordered.

"I will." Grabbing his hand, she pulled him to her room. "I have something else for you. I was planning to give it to you when we retire in a few lunams, but it's for luck now."

She opened her wardrobe and pulled out a small leather box. Taking his left hand, she placed it on his palm, covering it with hers. "I love you, Alon." Reva kissed his mouth, then stepped back to watch him open the box.

He stared at the ring it held. A wide silver band set with an inlayed oval of black onyx. He removed it and saw the engraving inside—*High Ambassador Alon Coronan, With Love, Evani Reva.*

Smiling, Coronan handed it to her. "Aren't you going to put it on?"

She slid it on his life finger. "Looks right," she said with an easier smile.

"It looks perfect," he murmured, pulling her to her bed. "I'll get you one when I come back."

S eabirds called as they hovered on the winds overhead. Akira stood on the deck with Isfail, vaguely aware of the piercing cries, the flap of canvas, the hustle of deck hands preparing the ship for departure. She watched her ambassadors saying farewell to one another, saw the teasing smiles as they made fun of their Ishalian clothing, heard their laughter.

Kalronan had his hand on his father's shoulder, his head thrown back in laughter at some joke Korth was telling. Akira watched Kane's eyes crinkle in humor, and noticed for the first time how much father and son resembled one another, though Kalen had the black hair and blue eyes of his mother's ancestry. Still, there was so much of his father in him.

Her attention turned to Barash, another son who shared his father's looks, standing apart, but with a rare smile on his face as he watched Drinin kiss little Oti's cheek. She blushed but beamed with pleasure. Nearby, Micharon leaned down to kiss the top of Coran's head as she wrapped an arm around his waist in an unusual public display of their love for one another.

Reva and Coronan held hands. Akira recalled how he'd proudly shown off the ring that circled his life finger. She twisted the ring on her own finger, understanding that pride, and that love.

"Akira."

She turned to see Iro nearby, and stepped over to take her hand. "Alani. Are you sure you want to go to Kittric?"

"I need to do this—for Garath." She looked into Akira's worried gaze. "And for Lani."

Seeing the knowledge in Alani's dark blue eyes, Akira nodded. "You know where she is."

"I saw her, saw Garath in her. She's beautiful and happy." Iro glanced away with a heartbreaking smile. "She'll never know me, but I'll do everything I can to end these people who try to destroy us. To keep her safe and happy." Taking a deep breath, she added, "You can tell Aric about her."

Fumbling in a pocket of the Ishalian vest she wasn't used to yet, Iro pulled out the small velvet pouch that Aric had sent by Isfail, handing it to Akira. "I want you to keep these for her, just in case. My mother's and Garath's mother's rings."

Wrapping her arms around her friend, Akira held tight. "I will. Come back to me, Alani."

Iro managed a teasing smile. "I always do, Commander." Giving her a quick salute, she walked back to the rest of her team.

"You have time to call this off," Isfail said, placing an arm over Akira's shoulders.

He knows me so well, she thought. "I can't. This is what we're trained to do, what they're trained to do. There are too many lives at risk this time."

After a long moment of silence he said, "I know. It's the only reason we're doing this your way." Turning her to him, he looked deep into her eyes. "It's time to say goodbye, for now, my love."

Joining the others, they said those goodbyes, good-lucks, with hugs for those remaining behind. With Arith's arm around her waist, Akira stood for a moment with Drinin and Barash.

"Remember our plan. You'll be the first into a hostile situation, caught between the loyalists and Dateh's people. Barash has a strong resemblance to Dateh, advantage and disadvantage." She looked at Drinin, saying, "We don't know what happened to Gorth and Lunow. You could be recognized."

Both men nodded, then grinned at one another. "It's two Baronan brothers against one," said Drinin. "We'll get the job done, Commander."

"So will we," Arith said, giving her his cocky grin before

pulling her into a strong embrace. "Stay out of trouble, little sister."

"That's what you're supposed to do. I love you, Elen," she said shakily, her hand gripping the locket he'd given her the year before.

"We'll be back before you know it." He walked her to the gangplank for a final kiss.

When Akira and Isfail reached the dock, Akira spoke to Reva's group. "Be ready to head out to Mountain Shadows. Prince Logran will notify Garan when it's time. Isfail and I will join you and Kane then."

Looking back up to the deck, Akira saw Kane and his son embracing and couldn't help feeling the power of their connection. For a moment, it made her heart ache, knowing she was sending Kane's son into unfathomable danger.

All of them . . . every one a part of her mind and heart.

Isfail gently wiped a tear from her cheek while Reva's ambassadors went to their horses, leaving Akira and Isfail on the wharf. Kane jogged down the gangplank to follow them into the carriage.

Captain Vaneer called for the crew to make ready to sail. Several minutes later, as the carriage and its escort started back toward Coroth, the gangplank was hauled aboard as hawser lines were cast off, and the *Spirit of the Sea* unfurled her sails.

Seventy-Five

S tanding on the deck with Drinin days later, Barash had his first glimpse of Tash'tric harbor. Calm seas and favorable winds had allowed the ship to reach Ishal a day earlier than planned.

With Micah Vaneer beside them, the men studied the scene and the mostly empty docks.

"It's quieter than the last time my ship was here, with fewer ships," Micah observed. "But it appears the militia still controls this harbor." He glanced at the men beside him. "We'll see what news there is before you go ashore." He called for the remaining sails to be furled.

Then Micah's brow furrowed, and he indicated a Kilran cutter, flying a red flag with odd insignia—black clouds cut by a lightning bolt. It was tied up near the quay they were slowly approaching. "I'll be damned, that's Captain Norsi's ship. Wonder what she's doing here?"

Drinin and Barash followed orders, keeping with their disguise while the ship was made fast. As soon as the gangplank was set, Micah strode down with his first mate to speak with the harbormaster.

Barash watched it all, flicking a signal to Drinin when a hard-faced woman wearing the casual uniform of sailing captain approached Micah. He greeted her in an easy manner, taking the arm she offered.

The brothers watched discreetly while the two captains conversed with the harbormaster. He gestured a militia captain over. The group talked for several minutes before Micah and Norsi walked off together.

"Any ideas about that?" Barash asked Drinin.

"Too far away for me to tap. That's Akira's strength. I need to be closer." Drinin frowned. "Micah didn't look concerned, and the others went about their business without any sign of a problem. We'll just wait for now."

They finished their assigned tasks and went below, where Arith and the others listened to their observations. They were still speculating when Micah jogged down the steep stairway.

He didn't wait for questions. "Here's the lay, then. Dateh may be as cunning as reputed. He's managed to call a truce here in Tash'tric, calling off his men in exchange for an opportunity to negotiate the 'misconceptions' that have led to, in his words, 'the unfortunate conflict between neighbors.'"

Arith made a scoffing sound, but did not interrupt.

With a chuckle, Micah said, "Aye, the devil's trying to regroup, regain the high ground. I doubt he expected the citizens to fight back so fast."

"He's got to be stretched thin," Arith noted. "He's lost men in Caldala, and by all reports, he's got a lot in Kittric. How many are there to take on Ishaka, let alone keep control of Tash'tric?"

There was a brief mutter of speculation among those gathered in the second mate's tiny quarters.

"We may have a way to get you in and out of Kittric and, with luck, you'll find some of those answers," Micah told them, drawing attention back to him. "Captain Norsi's ship is sailing to Kittric in two days. Her brother has convinced her to take the risk to get information to some of the pirate brotherhood. Word's official that Caldala and Orsha have sealed an alliance of their fleets. They'll be sailing before the lunam is out, planning a blockade of Kittric and Tash'tric."

Arith grinned. "Coroth's intent was leaked, just like Akira and the others suggested."

"Aye, and it has the seafarers taking notice. The harbormaster claims the loyalists are keeping the rumors quiet, wanting The Bow to be taken by surprise."

"But Norsi wants to warn the pirates at Kittric," Drinin said with concern.

"Mostly that's her brother, the pirate, and his captain. In fact, Norsi's agreed to let *them* take her cutter into Kittric. No one there knows her *Black Squall*, except some of the pirates, and they're not likely to point her out to the Bowmen. They're hoping to get enough of them out before the pirate fleet is decimated along with Dateh's ships."

"It's probably good news," Arith mused, scratching his scruff-heavy jawline. "But how's this affect our mission?"

"Norsi is willing to make a deal, and she's certain her brother and his captain will honor it. They'll transport your people into Kittric and out again, as part of their crew, in exchange for amnesty for any misdeeds on behalf of The Bow."

"Is there honor among thieves?" Coronan asked on a laugh.

"It's a risk, to be sure," Micah replied. "But I'm convinced they're running scared, more concerned about the trouble Dateh and his kind will bring about if they succeed, than dealing with respectable, time-tested foes like the admiralty of Caldala."

Tipping his hat back on, he looked around the recon group. "You have two days to decide."

Micah gestured to Drinin and Barash as he led them to his cabin. "You have the same. We'll keep to the original plan for your separate mission. If you're back in time, you'll join the others in whatever they decide to do. If not, get to our rendezvous point." Turning his key in the lock to the captain's cabin, Micah glanced around before ushering them in. "Let's all finalize plans."

Seventy-Six

C uriosity outweighed caution by the time Abron Dateh finished reading a message delivered to his attention that morning. He settled back in the lavish leather chair that had once seated the Head Minister of the Ishalian Parliament. Now it was his.

Its former occupant had died suddenly, a victim of some strange, fast-onset sickness. By that point, Dateh had either co-opted willing ministers to his side, or arranged for those loyal to Ishal to meet with some unfortunate fate. A self-satisfied smirk showed as he reviewed his complete dominance of the government.

But it had all happened too easily, he sighed. Hardly any challenge, until the loyalists surprised him by fighting back. The organized resistance from some of the militia and civilians hadn't been expected so soon. It created problems for his soldiers, who should be preparing to move out to finish the takeover of Ishaka.

Dateh frowned then. He'd anticipated news from Shanow by this time. Felcan's warning teased his memory, making him uneasy. Still, Shanow's militia appeared to have over-wintered in the territories, and not returned to bolster the loyalist resistance.

And his offer to the locals had settled the street fighting for a time. Really, the people of Ishal were so easily maneuvered; it was hardly worth the effort. If he hadn't based so many of his people in Kittric, he would have razed the city out of sheer boredom.

Lifting the message once more, he smiled, knowing he

had nothing to fear. And here was something interesting and unexpected, ready made to entertain him.

A brief time later, two men were escorted in. Dateh studied the well-cut traveling clothes while a guard searched them for weapons. Two sheathed knives were relinquished, a common tool for self-defense that barely raised an eyebrow, Dateh decided. He would have been more suspicious if the men had come with no weapons on them, considering Ishal's state of unrest.

Remaining seated, in an attitude of power and control, Dateh indicated two chairs. "I was fascinated by your claims and, of course, skeptical. Yet here you are." He stared at Barash, amused by his resemblance to the man he saw in his own shaving mirror. "And my own eyes give credence that at least one of you was sired by Arthon Baronan."

He turned his perusal on Drinin. "While I barely remember you or my mother, I see that you have her fair hair and her eyes. No one would suspect we shared a womb. Now, the bastard there, we could be mistaken for the other, if one didn't look too closely. How did the two of you meet?"

"We reconnected at Baronan Keep," Drinin lied smoothly. "Barash has been living there, on and off." He looked at his half-brother. "You met Abron's man, Felcan, there didn't you?"

Dateh sat forward. "You saw Felcan? Where is he?"

Shrugging, Barash drawled carelessly, "No idea. Just found him and his men trespassing. He claimed you'd given him permission."

"Of course I did." Dateh scowled. "By rights, that property belongs to me, not some bastard sired on a witch." But he leaned back, pulling in his sudden temper. This half-brother who'd resurfaced could be an excellent double, so he'd be wise to draw him in.

"How long have you known each other?"

"Nearly five years now." Barash picked up the tale. "Aron here has a knack for trade. I have a knack for persuading people. It's been a successful joint venture."

Drinin sat back, stretched his legs out and crossed his ankles in a carefree pose. "Then Barash meets your man and hears how you're stirring trouble in Caldala. Trouble that's undermining our business. This was the first we'd heard that you were still alive, so we decided to come directly to the source. Felcan had some ideas on that, and told us how to find you."

Laughing, Dateh slouched back in the big chair. "Do you think I care about your business?"

"No," Drinin replied easily. "We all know you're after bigger things, just like old Baronan. We're just interested in keeping our own. You've never shown any interest in Caldala before, so we'd like to come to some agreement, should your power play in Ishal spill into our country."

He appreciated their bold approach, Dateh decided. It took guts to walk into his territory. And he was tired of being surrounded by witless, gutless fools. Felcan was the only one who'd ever challenged him before, and the only person he'd tolerated over the years.

"Why do you think I'm after the same as our father?"

Barash lifted a slashing black eyebrow. "You think we're fools? Aron and I keep our ears to the ground. We get news through our trade associates about civil war in Ishal, and we know you've crippled your own trade. There're few who will deal with your ports anymore. Well, port, since you've closed off Kittric, your largest." He met Dateh's black eyes directly. "You've stirred up the two largest admiralty fleets in these waters, so you better have something big to make it worth the risk."

Dateh just gave them a thin smile.

"You certainly inherited Baronan's lust for power," Drinin said. "And it sounds like you're aiming for Caldala as well as Ishal; maybe Kuldor next, or the island nations. Seems like you have greater ambitions than old Baronan."

"And why shouldn't I?" Dateh sneered. "Why shouldn't I want more than that mad old fool left for me?"

He struggled for calm, his words clipped now. "I could have been a lord in Caldala but for him. Instead, he drags me with him—into the wild with no thought of how we'd live." Abron gave his twin a bitter smile. "You were better off left for dead, brother."

Drinin's eyes hardened. "I was left with our mother, who was beaten to death trying to defend her son. She was his victim, or doesn't that matter to you? You cared nothing for her. You didn't even look at what he'd done to her when you walked out."

"What was she to me!" Dateh glared before turning to pour brandy with a shaking hand. "Baronan's brood mare, useless but for her family connections and money. She didn't have enough political standing to satisfy his ambitions." He whirled around, sending liquor flying as he swung the hand holding the glass toward Drinin. "You think I chose to be his heir, his favored one? And what did my *mother* do to fight for *me*? Nothing! *You* were her son."

Sending the glass crashing into the fireplace, he flipped a rude gesture at Barash. "Even our bastard older brother meant more to her than I did. I saw how she taught you to read, to write. While I was raised by Baronan's underlings!" Spittle flew from his lips as he raged. "You think those peasants *cared* about me? I survived because they were too terrified of what our insane father might do if anything happened to me."

Then he gave a laugh that chilled the bones. "And after all that, he slaughters the whole pack, bringing the wrath of justice down upon Baronan Keep so that we had to run like rats."

Drinin and Barash glanced at one another while Dateh breathed deep, struggling to control what had been unleashed. Smoothing his dark hair back, he began to speak in a more controlled voice.

"Somehow, Baronan got us near Coroth without being recognized. He stashed me in some miserable inn, ordered me to keep my mouth shut, and disappeared." Dateh rubbed the back of his hand across his downturned mouth as he picked up a fresh glass. "I really believed the cold bastard had abandoned me there. The innkeeper kept sending me suspicious looks and threatened to put me to work in the stables if my father didn't return soon."

When he fell silent for some minutes, Drinin said, "But he came back for you."

Dateh looked up. "A couple days later, he paid the innkeeper and hustled me off to the shipping harbor near Coroth." He sent another sneering look at Barash. "Ironically, *your* mother had arranged passage for him on a ship to Ishal. The idiot woman must have had a soft spot left for him. Too bad she didn't feel as much for you, eh?"

He chuckled when Barash refused to be baited. He had to admire the thick skin. "I was surprised to see him put on ambassador robes and mask considering his avowed hatred of force callers. But I guess he had enough cunning left to protect his own skin."

"Did she provide the same for you?" Drinin asked.

"No." Dateh's lips thinned as he poured another drink. "I don't think he told her anything about me, as there was only one passage booked. Baronan got around that by claiming I was an orphan being escorted to Ishal where my mother's parents lived." He shrugged. "And he had enough money to buy passage."

Dateh swirled the liquid in his glass. "When we finally made it to Ishal, he managed to insinuate himself into important political families." There was irony in his smile now. "The devil was always good at that, playing those fools, making them believe his lies. He convinced them that he'd been wrongfully accused, the victim of envy and prejudice, so Ishal denied extradition."

Getting up to lounge against a doorframe, Barash said coldly, "And you were back in the life you wanted."

Dateh just sneered, staring at both men. "You think so? Our dear father enjoyed debasing his sons, it seems." At their looks of confusion, Dateh grinned. "It was finally my turn to be disowned, at least in public. I was demoted to his personal valet, until educated enough to be his secretary."

Swallowing his drink, he continued. "Certainly, people could see the resemblance as I matured. I think it amused him that most believed I was his illegitimate offspring. His Ishalian lady refused to have me in the household once they were bound." He muttered the next in a vicious undertone. "She was a bitch and they deserved one another. But she didn't last as long as Lady Arda. She died in childbirth with Baronan's final whelp."

Stepping to a window, he added, "Our unlamented father often raved about how he'd raise an army and return to Caldala to avenge himself. But even his highborn Ishalian friends wouldn't support his petition to declare war on Caldala." Dateh poured yet another drink, lifting the decanter with a questioning look then shaking his head when both men declined. "Now he had one more group to seek revenge against for imagined wrongs. He was enlisting his first round of cutthroats to move against Ishal's Parliament when his last wife died."

As Dateh slumped into a chair across from him, Drinin asked, "What's the point of all this, Abron? It you despised him so much, why follow in his footsteps? You could return to Caldala."

Snorting into his glass, Dateh choked his swallow down. "Why would I? One thing I learned very well at Baronan's heels . . . Ishal is weak. Its government has always been more interested in lining pockets than overseeing a country. One man with a devoted following nearly toppled them in his time. I intend to succeed, and not just here.

"I'm smarter than he was. Caldala is strong, because it has the force callers."

Barash gave him a bored look. "So you've inherited that obsession too?"

Dateh narrowed his eyes. "Not an obsession. Reality. The force callers could stop my little army, and keep me from my goals. If I can turn normal people against them—take away their support in Caldala—forcers are occupied with their own problems, and less likely to watch me. And they could decide that the people they've chosen to defend aren't deserving of their efforts."

"There's an odd kind of sense in there," Drinin admitted. "Is that why you're stirring animosity against the Ishakans?"

"Just part of the plan," Dateh said carelessly. "Seeding the idea that the territories hold untapped wealth in gold helped me corrupt greedy parliamentarians, and some of the militia. I expected more distraction from the citizenry, but it doesn't appear that the loyalists bought into that ploy, not like the politicians. Now I'll have to send men to the territories when I could use them in Kittric."

"So you've taken what our father started and made it bigger, more vicious. Why not just campaign honorably, become the legitimate high minister? How long do you think your army of assassins will let you control them? Your Bowmen could easily turn against you."

"Ah, The Bow—an army of misfits, outcasts, men and women who live to destroy. The only thing that matters to them is regular payment in silver, the promise of gold, and an overlord who gives them the license to maim and kill." Dateh's face twisted into a look of contempt. "Why shouldn't they follow me? I was, after all, the first."

When his brothers just looked puzzled, Dateh laughed, but the sound held no humor.

"I'll share my little secret," he muttered as he pulled off his jacket, and tugged at shirt lacings until he could pull the garment over his head. Then he turned so they could see the faded scar over his right shoulder blade.

A ragged crescent bow crossed by three crooked arrows.

The quick shock on their faces was real, causing Dateh to laugh again. "The mad fool had an inspiration one drunken night. He was in some melancholy stupor, back in his mind to his life in Caldala." Dateh pulled on his shirt, and poured another drink. "Suddenly remembers his *legacy*, as he shouted it—his three sons. One of his few sentimental moments."

He raised his glass to them. "He had two of his servants hold me down, and carved this into me. And so, The Bow was born."

Setting down the half-full glass, he let his head loll back. "One of the only times he openly acknowledged me. He told me I would lead them to greatness after he gained control of Ishal." He closed his eyes and gave a fierce smile. "And I will."

"Why tell us all this?" Drinin asked.

"Why not?" Dateh shrugged, opening his eyes. "A word, a

signal from me, and the two of you are dead. Besides . . ." His smile was oddly self-deprecating now. "You are the only ones I *can* talk to—the only men in the world who might understand, so we'll talk more about your proposed agreement. That holds an unexpected appeal for me."

Then he smiled coolly. "It won't stop me from killing you, however, should I have the whim."

Seventy-Seven

*D*rinin wondered if his half-brother felt the same sense of relief as they walked out into warm sunshine; that feeling of an ax being lifted from their necks, for now at least. He was aware of the men following them—not so discreetly—but no one appeared to have orders to end them yet.

"Poorly trained," Barash muttered, causing Drinin to flash him a knowing smile.

"I don't think training has been a priority with either rogue Baronan, do you?"

Barash gave a low chuckle. "Probably to our advantage." He walked the two steps up into the inn where they'd taken rooms.

Following him as they climbed a dark stairway to the second floor, Drinin heard their footsteps echo in the unnatural silence of the mostly empty public house. Stopping to unlock the door to his room, he pushed it open, pausing a moment before gesturing for Barash to enter. Drinin followed, locking the portal from the inside. He walked directly to the single window and pulled the curtains tightly closed, preventing anyone from seeing into the room.

"An interesting encounter," a quiet voice spoke. The still air in the room seemed to sigh as Akira Muro shimmered into sight to one side of the window.

Grinning at the softening of Barash's hard face as the erstwhile assassin made a slight bow to Akira, Drinin moved to open a new bottle of wine. "Why couldn't you teach the rest of us that nice cloaking trick, Commander?"

"None of you worked hard enough on the mental discipline

required for cloaking, and it's former commander," Akira reminded him, running a light hand down his arm before turning to Barash with a warm smile as she took the glass Drinin offered. "You were both excellent. What are your thoughts about Abron Dateh?"

Barash stationed himself by the closed door, alert for sounds of anyone in the hall outside. Nodding to Drinin when the man held up the bottle of whiskey he'd just opened, Barash waited for his own glass then swallowed deep, letting the warm burn spread through him. Akira's presence did much to ease his tension; now the drink settled the last dregs. "He's a cool one, except when something sets him off. More dangerous than old Baronan, I think." He watched Akira nod, her delicate features thoughtful.

"Confident," Drinin agreed, sitting on the edge of the bed, leaving the single chair for Akira. "And even more ambitious, more calculating."

"Yes," she murmured, taking the seat. "He has big plans. We learned a little, but more about his motivations than specific plans. Dateh did not reveal much of use to us, though it pleased him to have an intimate audience to spill his grievances against his father to."

She focused on Barash for a long moment. "I didn't expect that you and he would look so much alike. You're a bit taller, and you have a leaner, more muscular build. But your coloring and facial features are remarkably similar." She glanced at Drinin, then back. "If I didn't know you, Barash, and the three of you were lined up before me, I'd think that you and he were the twins, not Aron and Abron."

"Could we use that somehow?" Drinin asked.

Her brow furrowed. "We'll see if something comes up."

"He and I have one more trait in common," Barash noted with a more sinister expression. "We both like to play with names." He met Akira's sharp eyes, waiting for her to work it out. It didn't take long.

"Not Dateh. *Death*," she murmured thoughtfully. "He, like his father, holds no value for life."

"We should have killed him," Barash said coldly. "Cut off the head of the rebellion. It worked before."

Akira looked at Drinin and saw the same thought in his eyes. "Maybe," she said. "We might take that option if we meet with him tomorrow. But it's a risk to assassinate him in the middle of his own stronghold, and we don't know if he's the only one The Bow follows. This Felcan is important, too, and might be able to use Dateh's assassination to stir increased animosity toward force callers or Caldala, if he ties it back to you. Martyrdom might accomplish more than a living Dateh showing himself for what he really is."

"If we decide on that, you're not going," Barash stated.

"He's right," Drinin said, when she started to speak. "You're getting out of here. We'll meet you at the rendezvous."

Crossing her arms across her chest, Akira lifted an eyebrow. "We all go, or no one goes. I'd rather not lose the two of you."

"And I'm not going to face Isfail after risking his wife and child any more than we already are," Drinin snarled.

As comprehension struck, Barash grabbed her shoulders. "You're pregnant? What the hell are you doing here?"

"Hush," Akira warned, glancing at the door. "You're both shouting. And I'm here because you need me here. I have the most experience in investigation and negotiation. And I'm the only one who can get us out of this mess if things take a bad turn."

Toward twilight, Drinin walked out into near-empty streets, following Micah's directions to a small shop specializing in farm goods and meat. Passing the shop, he checked the appearance of the elderly woman inside against the description given, taking care not to show any special interest in the place.

He continued down toward the wharf, entering the one open public house, where he was told that they no longer had a cook, so no food available. Only one of his watchers remained, Drinin saw as he wandered out, and that one looked bored.

By the time he reached the docks, deliberately strolling past the *Spirit of the Sea*, there was no longer anyone tailing him in the gloomy mists. Turning his head to check out Captain Norsi's ship, Drinin felt a hard jolt as a sailor knocked into him.

"Sorry, sur," the seaman slurred, letting out a belch redolent of cheap ale. He pushed off, staggering down the wharf as Drinin slid the cloth bag passed to him under his cloak.

As he made his way back to the inn, he noticed only one of Dateh's men, and that one was slouched on a barrel, apparently sleeping. He greeted the twitchy innkeeper politely as he continued up the stairs to deliver a cold, but safe, dinner to his two companions.

Outside, the fog thickened and the single watcher huddled deeper in his coat. He paid no attention to the man passing, wearing a dark, well-worn cloak with hood pulled close to protect the wearer from the cold damp.

Glancing back from the corner of the inn, the cloaked figure moved silently, disappearing into the thick shadows of an alleyway. Though Drinin and Barash scanned the alley at regular intervals from the windows of the rooms at the back of the inn, alert for danger, they never detected the one who kept watch through the night.

Growing restless with inactivity as the next morning passed, Barash felt relief when the hour came to meet with Dateh. He'd given up trying to convince Akira to return to the ship. She'd refused, though he figured she could have agreed and then followed them anyway with that trick of invisibility. Cloaking, he corrected himself, that's what they called it.

His lips turned up slightly. That would have been a great thing to have in his early years. Actually, he thought, it would be a great ability now. He could make his way to Dateh's office, invisible as air, slice his throat, and they could be on their way, no one the wiser. It would be a fitting end, the son ending as his crazy father had.

"It may come to that," Akira said softly.

Barash tipped his eyebrow. "Tapping?" he asked, using the word he'd heard from the ambassadors.

She smiled. "No need to, your face gave your thoughts away. And I understand the feeling. If it can be done without risking you and Aron, you'll get your chance." But her eyes grew sorrowful. "I don't like asking either of you to kill your brother."

He found his hand reaching out and pulled it back, thrusting it in his pocket. "He's worse than old Baronan, Lady Muro. We all saw that yesterday. I think he's falling into whatever madness our father carried with him. I don't see a brother when I look at him, not like I see Drinin."

With a ghost of a smile, Akira touched light fingertips to his face. "I'll remember that, should the time come."

Drinin came in, returning from his walk to the docks, demonstrating their continued wellbeing to those on Micah's ship. This time he'd carried the single pack that held the few possessions they'd brought to the inn, leaving it behind a stack of crates for one of Micah's sailors to retrieve. They hadn't wanted to leave any personal traces behind for Dateh's people to find and raise a warning.

"No one watching today. Either Dateh's too arrogant to think we're dangerous, or they're just lazy," he told them. "Or maybe they've been posted to the docks. There were two ships coming in, one already tying up."

Akira nodded, shrugging into a close-fitting leather jacket. Barash studied her slim form, dressed all in black. Her long white hair was braided and fastened up before she'd covered it with a black knit cap.

"She looks lethal, doesn't she," Drinin commented, punching Barash lightly on his shoulder. "Just stay on her good side. Trust me, I've had years of experience."

Barash chuckled, waiting for Akira to wink out of sight before opening the door.

*T*he men walked casually up the cobbled street toward the Parliament complex. It was a short walk and there was no hurry. They commented on the crowds that contrasted sharply with yesterday's empty streets. Then Drinin pointed out the market tents arranged around the square, beyond the far corner of the complex.

Barash acknowledged it, sweeping his gaze about in response to an itchy premonition of danger. He only saw strangers around them, and none of them seemed to be paying them any particular attention. Then he heard Akira's voice in his head.

"To the right of the fountain, it's Gorth and Lunow. Back to the ship," she ordered. *"Now."*

He wasn't about to argue with an invisible woman and risk drawing attention, so he turned back, with Drinin's hand pressing his shoulder. So Akira had spoken to both of them. Barash listened for shouts or sounds of pursuit, but there were none. Apparently, the traitors hadn't spotted Drinin.

Walking steadily among the people going in the same direction, Barash and Drinin drifted apart for a little ways then back together, changing up the pattern. Uneasily, Barash realized he had no way of knowing where Akira was. He wished she'd mindsight again, or brush her hand on his arm. Could she do that when she was cloaked? How did it work?

The descending throngs of people began to mingle with those coming into the city from the docks. Must be passengers from the ships Drinin had mentioned. Barash glanced around as the crowd thickened, looking for his brother.

Distracted for a moment, he didn't notice the man stepping into his path until they collided. Barash felt a hard punch to his stomach—and stared into Felcan's triumphant eyes. The man said nothing, just gave a sinister smile and stepped away.

Leaving his dagger planted in Barash's gut.

He wondered why there was no pain as he collapsed to his knees while people hurried past.

It was a dream, Barash thought, his mind distanced from reality. He should be falling, but something caught his shoulders. Ghost hands. Maybe they would take him to Hell. He stared blankly as the crowd parted around him, pretending not to see.

Someone pushed through from the side and Drinin crouched in front of him, his mouth tight, eyes piercing as he spoke.

"Can you stand?"

Barash looked down at his hands cupped around the knife hilt. Lots of blood, he noticed. He heard Drinin's quiet voice, and the fear in it.

"Go," Barash mumbled. "Get to the ship. Get *her* to the ship. I'm dead."

"You're not. Let's get him out of the street."

The spirit hands, Barash realized vaguely—Heaven, not Hell. He felt four real hands, strong hands, grip his arms, pulling him to his feet, supporting him. A dark cloak was thrown over him.

"This way," a new voice said. Barash wondered why it was familiar before he let go of the light.

Seventy-Eight

kira washed her bloody hands in a bowl of warm water, glancing up at the elderly woman who waited anxiously. "Thank you for sheltering us." She'd advised the woman not to ask for their names, or give her own.

"It's nothing," the woman whispered. "Will the young man be all right?"

"He's lost a lot of blood," Akira replied, taking the towel she offered. "But I think he will."

The old woman stared at her. "You're a force healer. I saw what you did." She looked at the smooth skin of the unconscious man's belly. "I saw the wound that's not there now."

Saying nothing, Akira drew a blanket over Barash, laying a hand on his forehead to check for fever.

"I won't be turning you in, my lady."

Akira looked up to meet faded blue eyes. "I believe you." She looked around the tiny attic room the woman had led them to. "But we don't want to bring you harm."

The elder shook her head. "You didn't bring it."

They turned to the sound of boot-steps. Drinin came in, his eyes immediately turning to Barash.

"He needs rest and liquids, but I believe he'll recover," Akira told him. She looked back to see Isfail standing in the narrow doorway. "Thank God you were close by."

She moved to him, needing his strong arms around her.

"Not close enough," Isfail murmured. "I saw the move, but couldn't prevent it. I didn't get a good enough look to recognize the man."

There was a slight rustle from the pallet on the floor as Barash moved his head, eyes still closed as his weak voice said, "Felcan."

Akira knelt beside him with Drinin. "So he did escape."

"One of the ships off-loading today was Kuldori," Isfail told them. "He must have gotten a trader out of Caldala." He met Akira's questioning look. "Vaneer's ship is preparing to sail, as planned. Norsi's ship is already gone. I don't know if Arith and his team were on it."

She looked at Drinin and saw the conflict in his eyes. "We'd never have gotten Barash to the ship alive. I'm glad that Arith and the others will be out of reach. You need to get to Micah before they sail. Dateh might include Gorth and Lunow in a search."

"I can't leave you here," Drinin argued and looked at his brother. "And he won't make it to the ship before it sails."

"Will he be able to leave the city tomorrow?" Isfail asked. "Akira and I will get him to the rendezvous."

"Yes," Barash whispered. "Go, Aron. Your friends need you more than I do." He made an obvious effort to open his eyes, focusing on Drinin's face. "Go. I'll stand the first round back in Caldala."

"There's your answer," Akira said, praying it would be true. She watched Drinin clutch his brother's raised hand, their eyes meeting for a long moment.

"I'll buy the second round," he said, then stood up and hurried out.

Barash looked at Akira then tipped his head toward the door. Akira and Isfail followed Drinin as he jogged down the steps. He paused to swirl his cloak on before wrapping his arms around Akira.

"I'll shield you to the ship," she said, concern in her voice now.

"No." He released her, turning to open the door. "Barash might need you."

Isfail already had his cloak on. "I'll see him safe." Ignoring Drinin's protest, he went through the door.

Akira stepped out into the narrow back alley, watching them until they were out of sight.

The old woman was stirring soup in her small kitchen. She began making tea when Akira came in, and said, "You mentioned a Captain Vaneer. He was here, purchasing supplies last year, when things were bad. He was very kind to me, offered to try and get us out on his ship."

"This is his son," Akira told her. "The elder captain is enjoying some time on land, but he told his son about you, and this Vaneer asked us to come by and see how you were faring. He wanted you to know that he's ready to assist you any time he's in port."

"Yes," she sniffled. "Yes, very kind men. I'll remember."

"Well, we're grateful now. Knowing about you is why we came here when our friend was attacked. We'll move on as soon as possible."

The elder brought their cups to the table, her eyes bright and a little fierce. "You're not to worry about me. I'm pleased to be able to do something, to stand against these monsters." She gripped the hand Akira placed on hers. "They've taken my man, but my children and their families were able to get a ship to Orsha when the truce began last lunam. I wouldn't go when there were younger people to fill the ships. There's little food available to stock my shop. There's nothing left to take from me. I'd rather fight in some way before my time comes."

"The one who attacked our friend, we know he's one of Lord Dateh's most important men. He'll tell him, which might set off a manhunt," Akira warned her. "They could search every building in this area, looking for the man upstairs."

"Fortunately, there's a confusion of blood trails," Isfail said, surprising the women as he came in. "That crowd tracked it up, down, and all directions. I made sure there was nothing to lead them here."

"I didn't expect you this quickly." Akira leaned into him.

"We agreed I'd stop by the first warehouse while Drinin ran to the ship. He was on deck when I left and the hawser lines were being cast off."

"Thank you, my love." Akira took his hand, relieved to have him back.

The old woman smiled at them. "He's your man, is he? You're a fine couple, good partners."

"Yes, we are." Akira agreed, looking into Isfail's eyes.

*D*ateh listened to Felcan's report with growing rage. His bastard brother had played him! And Drinin, his own twin, had been part of it! But Barash—he hoped he burned in hell after taking Felcan's dagger in the belly. No, he hoped he suffered for hours before he died. Though there would be more satisfaction in having him slowly tortured to death.

Psyche Lakes: hardly touched, seven Bowmen dead against only six of the force callers. And this, only lunams after the disaster at the Southern Crescent, with scores of Bowmen captured and their best access slammed shut! Dateh swept a table lamp to the floor.

All the captains and ships had distanced themselves, he'd been told. There were none willing to carry suspicious men or cargo to Caldala now. And the pirates he'd thought would be glad to join his fleet, to take their revenge on the admiralty, were defecting or causing trouble in Kittric, slowing progress while his Bowmen worked to keep control.

Cursing everyone as traitors and idiots, Dateh threw a cut glass decanter across the room to shatter against the hearth.

Felcan said, "The bastard's dead, Abron. Let's just concentrate on Ishal. We've got a bigger problem with—"

"What about Drinin?" Dateh snapped, interrupting him. "Where is he?"

Looking confused, Felcan shrugged. "Who's that?"

"Drinin! Aron Drinin!" Dateh shrieked, beyond reason in his apoplexy. "My traitor of a twin brother!"

Surging to his feet, Felcan said angrily. "How the hell should I know? We're in this mess because you never told me about a half-brother, one who looks enough alike I mistook him for you at first. Now you're saying there's yet *another* Baronan?" It was Felcan's turn to throw something and a glass joined the shards on the floor. "I can't work around things like your damn brothers when I'm not brought in on your family secrets, Abron!"

Refusing to see Felcan's argument as reasonable, Dateh threw out his arm to point to the door. "I want that body, and I want Drinin in chains before this day is done."

He watched Felcan stalk out, muttering to himself, and reached for a bottle.

Shouting for one of the senior Bowmen, Felcan sent lesser Parliament workers scattering out of his path with just a look. Damn Abron anyway! This was *his* fault, now he was supposed to clean up the mess. What the hell was happening in Kittric? The fleet should be nearly ready to launch by now. What about that?

But Abron *bloody* Dateh was more concerned with tracking down the damn *brothers* he'd let walk right in. "Serves him right," Felcan muttered, though he didn't really know what the two men had done to trigger Dateh's rage. He stalked on, sending an unwary minor politician into a wall. "He's losing his focus, just like his damn father."

"Sir?" the man he'd sent for queried cautiously as he matched his stride to Felcan's.

"Nothing," Felcan growled, pushing through the massive doors. "There's a dead man, name's Barash, lying in the street halfway to the docks. Get your men to collect the body and take it to the barracks until I say otherwise. Find out where he was staying, how he got here, everything you can about the man he was with. Aron Drinin. I want Drinin apprehended, and brought to me in restraints. Now."

"Yes, sir." Apparently no one's fool, he hurried off.

Standing on the grand front steps, Felcan focused on the city around him, struggling to regain his calm. He had to talk Dateh into some sense. They were too far into this to lose control now. They could still take Ishal, maybe pull back on this invasion fleet idea. And then there was Ishaka—

Felcan swore loudly, ignoring the frightened looks sent his way. This business with the brothers had distracted him from telling Dateh about Shanow's twist. He scrubbed his hands over his face. Dateh was going to call for heads when he found out.

"Felcan. We want to talk to you."

Turning to the imperious voice of former ambassador Gorth, he scowled at him and Lunow, standing just behind. "Unless you know where I can locate a man named Aron Drinin, you can make an appointment to talk to me when I have time."

Color drained from Gorth's face. "Drinin? Why?"

Seeing the reaction, Felcan gave the man his full attention. "He's here, in Ishal, causing trouble." He grabbed Gorth's arm when he started to leave. "What do you know?"

His voice hoarse with fear, Gorth jerked free, saying, "Aron Drinin is a high ambassador, one of Akira Muro's elite team. If he's in Ishal, he's probably not alone, and that's trouble for all of us!"

Felcan just closed his eyes. This was the final blow—Muro's ambassadors here in Tash'tric. Swearing under his breath now, Felcan reminded himself to stay calm and work it through. "Give me a description. You and Lunow are going to search the area with my men."

When Gorth started to protest, Felcan grabbed the front of his jacket, yanking him close, ignoring the man's force ability. "Don't cross me right now, Gorth, or I'll make you wish Drinin had found you first."

Seventy-Nine

The sun was on the horizon when Isfail slipped in the back of the shop after a quick reconnaissance. The elder had just put up the closed sign and locked the front door. He waited until she snuffed the lanterns and joined him in the small office before he said quietly, "They're searching, one group coming from the docks, one from the central city."

Taking the news in stride, she said, "I'll just go about my normal life, sir. They'll find nothing suspicious here."

He marveled at her serene expression and brought her age-knotted fingers to his lips. "We'll make sure there's nothing to find."

Isfail ran lightly up the narrow stairway and into the attic room. "Two search parties from opposite directions. Gorth's with one, Lunow the other."

Akira looked thoughtful. "It was always a risk," she murmured, laying a damp cloth on Barash's forehead. "They'll have told Felcan and Dateh that Drinin is with Recon Alpha, and they'll suspect that there's more of us here, in Tash'tric at least."

"Can they detect force ability?" Isfail asked, relieved when Akira shook her head.

"They're competent, but have no real psychic ability." She gave Barash—more alert now—an encouraging smile before standing. "Gorth's only ability is fire bending, but he's good. Lunow can bend wind and has some ability with water, though he's not as disciplined as he could be. He tends to be careless and lazy. They were both part of Ana Karsh's cadre when she was Most High Ambassador. I'm sure they didn't find Garan's leadership policies as conducive to their wants, which probably made them receptive to The Bow's offers. And Gorth's ego would celebrate being the only force callers accepted into Dateh's organization."

Isfail watched as she looked around the room then followed when she walked down to the second floor.

"It would be easier to create the illusion here," she told him, studying the single door closing off the attic stairs. "It will take more energy for me to cloak everyone in the attic, and we risk them walking in, possibly running into the shield. Gorth and Lunow would know what it was."

Akira's eyes intensified and Isfail blinked. The door was gone. A plain wall filled the space. Then the door reappeared.

"How does that feel?" he asked anxiously. "Are you taxing yourself?"

She smiled at him. "No. That's nothing to what I can do."

"Even with the baby?"

"Even with."

Lunow was with the group of four Bowmen who banged on the shop door an hour later. Twilight filled the street with shadows while lamplighters hurried about their duties. Carrying a lantern from the apartment attached to the shop, the old woman hurried to answer, hoping they wouldn't break down the door.

Letting some of the fear show on her face as she opened to the burly strangers, she asked in quavering voice, "Can I help you?" She backed away as they pushed into the dark shop.

"We're looking for a man," one of the Bowmen said in a loud voice, signaling another to give a description.

The man, dressed in Caldalan clothing, described the one they were looking for as he walked slowly around the shop with the others. "His name is Drinin, Aron Drinin," he ended.

She stood pensively by the open door. "There's no one here but me, sirs. Look all you like, but please don't damage anything."

Following behind them as they moved from the shop to her living quarters, she shuffled to a rocking chair and sat down. The men took no notice of her and, in fact, appeared bored with their task. When the four of them started up the stairs to the second floor, she began to silently pray.

Standing behind the closed and locked door, Akira kept her focus on casting the illusion that showed the hall door as an unbroken wall. She was aware of Isfail behind her, knew his sword was in his hand, ready to defend. The sound of footsteps grew louder.

Four men, she thought, knowing one was a traitor to his country and his service. Lunow. She wouldn't hesitate to take these men's lives if they were discovered, but didn't want to add to their own danger, or the old woman's, if there was a way to avoid a confrontation.

No one paused in the hall beyond the hidden door; the men said little, they just continued through the rooms of the second floor. She could hear doors open then close, furniture moved, and finally the sound of the searchers walking back down the stairs. A door slammed below.

Some time later, there came a soft tap, and the old woman called, "They've gone."

Akira released the cloaking shield with a relieved sigh.

*T*he hour was late, but Felcan knew that Dateh would still be in the office he'd commandeered. Taking a deep breath, he left Gorth and Lunow with two of his Bowmen in an outer office and walked in.

"Well?" Dateh snapped, staring out over the dark city from his window. "How long does it take to find a fugitive?"

Felcan could see that Dateh hadn't lost much of his earlier heat, and what he had to tell him wasn't likely to cool it. "I ordered the city cordoned off immediately after you and I spoke. I have men searching beyond the city. We've searched every building from the harbor to the Public Meeting Hall, but we haven't found either man."

"What do you mean *either* man?" Dateh seared him with a look. "You left a dead man in the street."

Straightening his stance, Felcan met the hard stare.

"Apparently not, or someone decided to hide the body. There was a lot of blood, but Barash wasn't there."

The last thing he expected was Dateh's laughter, becoming louder and shriller until it sounded almost manic as he collapsed into his seat behind the desk. Felcan waited, letting the mood run its course.

When Dateh finally quieted, leaning his head against the chair back with his eyes closed and a strange smile tilting his mouth, Felcan decided it was time to speak.

"I brought Gorth and Lunow, in case you'd like to question them yourself."

"Who?" Dateh asked quietly, his eyes still closed as if he had no crisis to worry about.

"The two Caldalan ambassadors who helped us attack Ambassador Central."

"Another failure," Dateh murmured. "Why would I need to question two traitors?"

Here it comes, Felcan thought, bracing for another storm. "They recognized the name Aron Drinin." He watched Dateh sit up abruptly, eyes flashing open as his mouth thinned. "Aron Drinin is an ambassador, one of Akira Muro's elite reconnaissance team. They expressed the opinion that there might be more of them in Ishal."

Rather than erupting in a violent rage as he had earlier in the day, Dateh's face seemed to lose all color, until his eyes stood out like black coals, burning into Felcan's.

"Muro's force callers?" Dateh spoke through clenched teeth. "Here in Tash'tric?"

"At least one." Felcan resisted the urge to flay Dateh about his twin brother being an ambassador. He obviously didn't know before now.

"Bring the turncoats to me," Dateh ordered, eerily regaining his composure.

Felcan stepped out, signaling two of his best men to escort Gorth and Lunow in, then posting the soldiers with crossbows ready behind them. He doubted these forcers would try anything;

they valued their lives more than heroics, but he wouldn't take any more chances.

They sat down in the chairs Dateh pointed to as he got up and walked to a tray where a new decanter had joined others, and fresh glasses gleamed in lamplight. Felcan watched, hiding his surprise when Dateh poured two fingers of amber liquid in two glasses, then walked over to hand each ambassador one. Gorth muttered his thanks, obviously cautious of the hospitality, while Lunow lifted his in a toast accompanied by a cheerful grin.

That one was a fool, Felcan thought, not for the first time.

"Tell me what you know about this Ambassador Drinin. Why is he here? What would be his purpose in coming here, and are more of his team with him?" Dateh poured himself a glass after seeing Felcan's shake of the head when he raised one to him.

Felcan listened attentively while the two men repeated what they'd already told him.

"You don't know if there are other reconnaissance ambassadors with him?" Dateh said in a silky interrogation. "What about their leader, Akira Muro?"

Lunow spoke up readily. "Definitely not. Muro retired last year. On top of that, she was bound into the royal family just before the attack on Central. Her man, that's Commander Lord Isfail, he's not going to allow his wife to lead a team into Ishal, is he?"

Seeing the ice in Dateh's eyes at the mention of Isfail, obviously still seething about that one escaping the Ishalian dungeons, Felcan's jaw tightened. This wasn't going to end well.

But Dateh remained coolly in control. Felcan saw him look at the silent Gorth.

"Your friend doesn't appear as sure of that," Dateh said. "What's your opinion?" He waited for Gorth to speak.

The man cleared his throat. "Well, Lord Dateh, I agree that Muro wouldn't lead a mission here, for a number of reasons. But she has a great deal of influence in the Ambassador Core, and in the House of Coroth. I, uh . . ." He cleared his throat once more, his usual arrogance effectively quashed. "I wouldn't underestimate her impact on any action against your rebellion, my lord."

"Well said," Dateh replied, coming to collect their glasses and moving to the small table near the wall that held the tray of decanters. He continued his questions as he poured the liquor.

"This Drinin was with a man presenting himself as a son of Arthon Baronan, calling himself Barash. What do you know of that?"

"Never heard of him, sir," Gorth replied solemnly.

"No one by that name in our service," Lunow answered quickly. "Lends more weight to Drinin being here on his own, though, doesn't it? No one like this Barash in Recon Alpha." He leaned back with a chummy smile as he took the glass from Dateh. "I think it's just someone impersonating Drinin, my lord. And him being with this Barash proves it. They just wanted something here, sir. Nothing to worry about."

Lunow took a large swallow of the liquid as Dateh sat back with a thoughtful smile. It grew bigger when Lunow gasped, dropping the glass as his hands flew to his throat. Dateh chuckled as the man pitched forward onto the floor, his eyes open and staring in death.

Felcan watched Gorth press back into his chair, hastily setting aside his own glass. But he made no move to go to his companion.

"Relax, Gorth." Dateh looked away from the body and met the terrified man's eyes. "I have use for a man who gives honest, thoughtful answers, and isn't an idiot. Remember that if you wish to stay alive."

Felcan lifted a hand and the soldiers hauled the body out before returning for a quivering Gorth. After they'd gone, Felcan started to tell Dateh about Shanow's deception, but Dateh said, "Enough, Beros."

"It's important, Abron." He saw the spark of rage in Dateh's eyes and backed down with a nod, turning to go. "I'll keep looking for them."

Eighty

Coast of Ishal, North of Kittric

T wo days after leaving Tash'tric harbor, Micah Vaneer held off shore until night was fully upon them. The moons had yet to rise as he guided his vessel to a shallow cove. At least the weather held clear. The spot he'd chosen had no protection for a ship during a strong gale.

Now he watched as a landing boat was lowered while Arith and his four teammates climbed nimbly down the boarding net. Micah called a farewell and wishes for a safe mission as they joined his men in the small craft. Two of his sailors unshipped the oars and the little boat pulled toward the shore.

He was uneasy with the number of changes in this plan, and now they were back to the original, with a hastily offered amendment. Someone she'd seen had spooked Captain Norsi at the wharf in Tash'tric. Micah had noticed the sudden activity on her ship, indicating she was preparing to sail, but the ambassadors of Recon Alpha were still on the *Spirit*.

Then a sailor had delivered a message from Norsi, stating she had her brother aboard and was going through with the plan to enter Kittric. She'd turn the *Black Squall* over to the pirate captain further down the coast. He'd given his oath that the ship would be at Kittric until the full moon, less than two weeks from today, and would honor their agreement to transport Arith's people out if they were on board by the deadline.

The ambassadors received the news with characteristic equanimity, something Micah had admired over the years. He'd never known a more confidant group of people. But he felt easier when Arith assured him that they could get themselves back to Caldala by way of the Ishakan territories if they needed to.

The landing boat had reached the rocky strand of beach. Micah watched the five ambassadors disappear into the short bluffs so quickly it was as if they'd never been. He waited until the returning landing boat cleared the wave break, then gave orders to weigh anchor.

By the time his sailors were back on board, the landing boat lifted to its davits, sails were unfurled, and the ship was beginning the turn back to a northwest heading.

He'd delivered the ambassadors of Recon Alpha. Now he could only wait off Kittric, ready to retrieve Arith's group from the *Black Squall*, and hope that the backup plan would be successful in extracting those left in Tash'tric.

Tash'tric, Ishal

*R*estless, Akira waited in the dark shop. Isfail was late returning from his most recent scouting pass. He'd hoped to find some horses tonight. Akira heard a soft step and turned her head to see Barash, a dark shadow in the office door. She turned to join him.

"He'll be back soon," Barash said quietly.

Akira nodded. "How do you feel?"

There was a long pause before he answered. "There's no pain, but I won't try lying to you. I'll only get us captured, or worse. I feel like an old man, no energy."

"Just wait 'til you are an old man, young sir," the shop owner said with a chuckle from the deepest shadows. She'd kept vigil with them in the small hours of the night.

Akira patted Barash's shoulder. "You lost a lot of blood. I can heal an insult to flesh, but I can't replace blood. Your body will take care of that."

They both turned at the same moment as Isfail entered with his cat-like stealth. He came to wrap an arm around Akira's shoulders, saying, "No luck with mounts, but we need to move tonight, if we can. There's something in the wind—Dateh's men are everywhere."

They all moved to the little kitchen, where the old woman busied herself putting supplies into their packs. She'd refused to take payment, and Akira feared that she was depleting her own sparse stock. But her next words came as a complete surprise.

"You'll take my horse cart." Her tone brooked no argument but she got three refusals. "The young man can't walk, let alone run."

"They'll have to go without me," Barash stated. "And I'll shift myself to new cover. I know how to do this, and I'll just keep hidden until I can make it back overland." He turned at Akira's dissent. "How do you think I made it back to the keep after we met last winter?"

The old woman ignored them. "You'll take the cart. No one will suspect anything, since I'm always on the roads before dawn when I'm foraging. I'll drive you out to the farms that I buy from. The soldiers won't stop an old woman, and this young lady will know how to keep you all hidden until we reach the Westering crossroads. I'll stock up with what I can, and return."

Isfail covered Akira's hand with his own, and she could feel his eyes on her in the dark. "It's a reasonable plan," he said quietly. She knew they waited for her to make the decision.

"All right," Akira said after a moment. "On two conditions. One, everyone does exactly what I say at all times, without arguing. Two, you come with us." She took one of the old woman's hands. "Put what you need the most in a small pack."

After a long silence, they heard the scrape of her chair and the woman said softly. "I will then."

"I'll help you," Barash offered, getting up to take her arm. They shuffled off to collect her things.

"It's hard on her," Akira said, holding tight to Isfail's hand. "Leaving her life here, all her possessions. Who knows if she'll be able to return? And if she does, will this still be here? I have a bad feeling about Tash'tric, Dan. We can't leave her here."

Isfail pulled her into his arms. "She'll live. She'll join her children and grandchildren in Orsha. We'll see to that, and they'll make a new life, whether they return or make that life somewhere else." He kissed the top of her head. "I'm going out to hitch up the cart."

Akira walked to the wall where she'd seen a small painting hung in a prominent location—one of the woman and her man when they were young. Taking it carefully down, she wrapped it in a cloth and slipped it into her own pack.

*D*awn was a thin streak on the horizon when the cart reached the first checkpoint. The old woman, wrapped in a thick shawl, hunched on the driver's seat beside a young girl with a long braid of muddy brown hair holding the reins. The girl's plain face drew no second looks from the soldiers.

"What's in the cart?" One of them asked in a bored voice, while a second soldier flipped back the canvas flap.

"Empty now, sirs, but for some bags and boxes to fill at the farms outside town," the old lady answered stiffly. "Have to go far afield these days to stock my shop. I'm an old woman. I shouldn't need to travel afar to put food in my shop."

"No, mistress," the bored one replied automatically when the other gave the all clear. "Who's the girl? You're usually alone."

"The eldest of my grandchildren," she replied with suspicion. "You keep your hands off her."

The soldier looked appalled by the idea as he stammered, "Go on. Good luck with your foraging."

When they were long out of earshot, Akira laughed. "You have dramatic talent, my friend."

"That young man is all right. He's always respectful, not like some. I was hoping he would be at the post today."

There was a shifting sound from behind the seat before Isfail asked, "Are you tiring, Akira? Holding a transformation summons and cloaking takes a lot of energy."

"We're fine." She smiled as her mind felt the curious seeking from the baby, and flicked the reins to urge a little more energy from the horse.

*I*sfail and Barash added a creative touch to abandoning the cart the following morning. One of the old woman's produce suppliers had been willing to sell two horses to her 'grandson' the previous afternoon. They'd traded the produce to a butcher for a horse he'd received in trade from another customer for some beef.

To keep up the cover, the old woman purchased a few newly killed rabbits from him, reputedly for her shop. With the scrawny gelding tied to the back of the cart, she left with her 'granddaughter' to return to Tash'tric.

At the first bend in the road, they retrieved Barash and the other two horses, and set the rest of the escape plans in motion. One of the dead rabbits was cut open and used to bloody Akira's clothing while Isfail and Barash did a credible job of faking an attack, including overturning the cart. Leaving bloodied and torn clothing scattered about, with a mess of hoof-prints in the muddy ground, the group deemed it good.

Isfail's concerns about the elder's ability to ride proved groundless when she handled her carthorse with competence as they rode into the scrub and woodlands until out of sight of the road. After spending the night camped at the base of a rocky escarpment in the wild, they followed the ridge northwest until they reached the gap that Akira remembered. They waited until nightfall to take the narrow lane leading west into the sparsely populated region beyond.

There they entered a narrow valley that lay behind the ridgeline they'd just followed, and before the staggered ranks of mountains that formed an impenetrable southern boundary between Ishal and Caldala. It ran from the sea in the south to the point some distance to the north where the ridge became mountains that curved west to meet the border range.

Following the ever-narrowing lane until it terminated at an abandoned farm, they settled in the old barn during the daylight hours to avoid the few residents of this hardy area. Late that night, Akira's group finally glimpsed the sea under a clear sky lit by starlight and the two moons.

Less than two hours ride brought them to the small beach that

Isfail remembered well. But this time, a ship waited for them. As they saw the flags signal from the *Royal Sea Eagle*, Isfail lifted his arms in acknowledgement. A landing boat was launched while Isfail and Barash removed saddles and bridles before setting the horses free.

Akira let Isfail lead her to the dark cave opening through which he'd escaped with Aric, as Alani Iro had once escaped here with Garath Haill. She said a silent prayer of thanks as they returned to join Barash and their elderly friend as they walked along the moonlit strip of beach to the landing boat sliding up on the sand.

Eighty-One

Coroth, Caldala

Within days of leaving Ishal, Akira and her companions returned to Coroth. With danger behind them, proper names were finally exchanged. Logran and Oona received their sheltering benefactress, Elder Lianna, with warm generosity. She was given accommodations in the guest wing until a ship was arranged to transport her to Orsha for a reunion with her family. Lianna wept with joy when Akira presented her with the rescued painting.

Akira felt grateful to have a couple of days in their own suite of rooms, time to recover from the mission before moving on to Mountain Shadows. Time to spend nights with Ardan in privacy and comfort, enjoying the movements of their baby together, and the ever more curious and contented, if still undefined, mental nudges the infant focused on Akira.

That nebulous contact soothed Akira's fears that some of the stress and strain of her activities could harm her child. She hoped that, as her body naturally protected the infant from physical harm, the strength of her mind would shield the baby's.

Sharing those beliefs with Ardan seemed to ease his worries, reminding Akira that he was as important as anyone else in this matter. She became more conscious of involving him in all her thoughts, concerns, and joys of the life growing within her.

They cherished this normalcy for the brief days they could. Then it was time to take the next step in the fight against The Bow.

The morning came when all the plans were finalized. Reva's

team had been notified. Kane was increasingly restless to head out, and Barash refused to be left behind. Isfail seemed to find his defiant stand amusing, even as Akira wondered why Barash was not content to return to Baronan Keep. He was no longer a wanted man, the prince had assured him of that, contingent on no more criminal behavior.

When she expressed that confusion to Isfail while their horses were made ready, Isfail kissed her brow and grinned. "Face it, my sweet. He's set himself up as your protector—another champion, if you will."

He chuckled at the look of shock on her face. "Akira, Barash is not going to leave your side, or at least the immediate company, until this is over."

It left her speechless, and Akira barely had her wits about her by the time their whole group was assembled and on the road.

Mountain Shadows

*T*hey took the fastest route for the season, traveling on main roads and spending nights at protectorates in Onshela, Three Falls, and finally Green River. Akira had to resist the urge to make a quick detour to Psyche Lakes and check on rebuilding progress.

An early start from Green River had them in Mountain Shadows before nightfall. And the enthusiastic welcome there brought smiles to the weary travelers' faces, though offers of refreshment, or rounds at the pub, were declined until the next day. With the Recon Alpha ambassadors and Barash settled in administration guest quarters, Akira and Isfail took Kane back to their own for a restful night's sleep.

*W*ith time so short, breakfast was arranged in Admin's private dining room, and included Lord Corcoran and his senior masters for a fast debriefing, and finalization of plans.

There was a quick round of introductions first, though the Mountain Shadows warriors already knew Reva's team and Kane

Kalronan. Barash was the only stranger in the gathering, and he nodded politely to each new face as names were given. Isfail enjoyed Akira's handling of the introduction, an adroit blending of fact with discreet avoidance of his criminal past.

Carelon unwittingly added credence to Akira's relating that Barash had traveled to Coroth to warn them of information he'd come upon.

"I remember you," Carelon spoke up. "You're the man Lady Muro found in that cabin, after she was caught in the avalanche."

"You have sharp eyes and a good memory," Barash replied smoothly. "Lady Muro saved my life. I owe her a great deal."

"And has already repaid any debt by the information he brought us," Akira said firmly. "He also captured the man he heard admit to planning the attack here at Mountain Shadows, the former schoolmaster. Ramort is now held in Coroth under interrogation for his involvement with our enemies."

As questions erupted from the protectorate people, Akira held up a hand. "I promise we'll cover this in more detail, as soon as we bring everyone here the more urgent news."

"As it turns out," Isfail added, knowing that Akira's ambassadors were aware of the relationship between Drinin and Barash. "Barash is related to Ambassador Drinin, and both men working together were instrumental in obtaining information needed for the Ishalian defense."

"Small world," Kilronan said, studying this new man intently before asking, "Where's the rest of Recon Alpha?"

That turned the discussion to everything that had happened after the Psyche Lakes attack. And required the revelation that Akira and Isfail had—with Kane's assistance in misdirection—secretly joined Drinin and Barash in Ishal.

Isfail could see that their covert mission shocked not only Kilronan and many of the Mountain Shadows people, but Reva's group as well. The only ones who'd known that Akira and Isfail were also on that mission were Kane, Drinin, Barash, and Micah. No one else in Recon Alpha had been advised.

Even Arith's group had been unaware. Akira had used her

cloaking skills when she'd come up the gangplank with Isfail just before it was lifted. Kane alone, knowing the plan, had been in the carriage when it left the docks. Micah had shared his cabin with the couple with none of the crew or other passengers the wiser.

Akira nodded quickly to Barash when he started to speak, welcoming the distraction.

"I, uh, have a question about that." He shifted, but held her gaze curiously. "I heard about your reputation years ago, about your abilities. I never heard about turning invisible—cloaking you called it. Is that different from shielding? Can all those with force skills do it? And why couldn't your ambassadors sense you on that ship? I've heard you can feel force abilities nearby."

"Those with force ancestry have their own set of skills," Akira replied. "Some have many force talents, others may only have a few, or just one. Practice will enhance skill sets if the innate ability is there."

She looked at Kilronan, gesturing to him. "Master Kilronan has the greatest shielding skill I've ever known, but he cannot cloak. Shielding uses natural forces to create an invisible physical barrier that can protect those behind it, but they're still visible. Cloaking is an unusual talent, where the wielder, and someone in contact with them, becomes invisible to those around them."

Though Barash stared at her, obviously hoping for a deeper explanation, none was forthcoming. Kilronan finished answering the questions.

"As far as we know, Akira is the only person who can do everything she can, and the only one who can detect others with, or using, forces around her." Kilronan gave her a disapproving look as he said, "That's why her recon team didn't detect her on that ship."

Before the commentary and expected admonitions could continue, Akira turned the meeting over to Lord Corcoran, who'd been included in plans through express couriers from Coroth.

"The Prince and Parliament have authorized military and ambassador support for the defense of the Ishakan people and territories," he began briskly. "Commander Isfail and Lady Muro, jointly, will oversee Caldala's involvement. This protectorate will be providing two full teams to go into Ishaka with them, joining Ambassador Reva's team."

Carelon lifted a hand to speak. "That leaves us two teams short, with two new teams still adjusting."

Nodding, Lord Corcoran announced, "Green River is taking over guard duty at Ishakan Rift. Osharon's team was relieved after Lady Muro's team came through Green River. His people should be back by tomorrow when this joint endeavor departs."

"Tomorrow?" Kilronan repeated somewhat incredulously, glancing at Akira.

Corcoran signaled Akira, who answered, "We need to move fast. Dateh and his men know Drinin and Barash were in Tash'tric, and the traitors Gorth and Lunow certainly would have suggested that it was a reconnaissance mission. They may suspect that other ambassadors have been sent to Kittric, an obvious target. Word was deliberately leaked that battle fleets are sailing from Caldala and Orsha."

She looked at the assembly. "The enemy is feeling the pressure. History indicates that The Bow and its leaders are not likely to back down, or surrender easily. And they don't fight using honorable tactics. We know the horse tribes and Commander Shanow's troops are primary targets, and the season is now favorable for Dateh to send his soldiers in. Time is a factor, especially with Dateh now aware that Caldala is committed to Ishal's defense."

At Akira's glance, Isfail outlined the military position and the discussion became more detailed.

Throughout the meeting, both Kane and Barash sat quietly and listened. When a break was called, they came to Akira.

"This will work," Kane said. "Your people are well-trained and disciplined. I believe they will work well with Commander Shanow's troops. I feel the same about Ambassador Reva's team. Between us, the force resistance alone could be enough, but my people will be grateful for the support of the military."

Turning to Barash, Akira murmured, "Are you still all right

with this?" When his brow furrowed, she said, "You don't have a specific allegiance, aren't part of one of these units."

His mouth tipped up in a half grin. "My allegiance is to you, Lady Muro. Caldala suits me well enough, but I take my orders from you and Isfail."

Kane chuckled over the disconcerted look on Akira's face as the meeting was called back to order.

Lord Corcoran finished up with his protectorate assignments. Team Kilronan and Team Arla would go to Ishal. Remaining teams would be on alert until further notice, with three teams based on the High Pass Ridge on a rotational basis. Besides defense duty, they would maintain support of needed supply shipments to Lower Caldala Lake, and critical communications.

With everything decided by midday, people went off to prepare or go about their duties.

Isfail opened the door to their residence an hour later, grinning at Kilronan. "It took you longer than I bet on."

"I needed to get my team packing first," Kilronan replied. "I don't know what you're thinking here, Isfail, taking Akira into all this in her condition."

"My condition?" Akira retorted from her chair in front of the fire, while Isfail just shook his head.

"You're in for it now, Kilronan," he muttered, moving to the kitchen for refreshments as the argument began.

"You're pregnant," Kilronan stated flatly, digging a deeper hole.

"I know that far better than you," Akira snapped. "And no one *takes* me anywhere! You should know that very well."

Ouch, Isfail thought with a wince, handing Kilronan a glass of ale. The man needed to stop right here, before he buried himself. Taking a deep breath, he stepped between them.

"All right," Isfail interjected. "We can't have the two of you at odds right now. We all know that Akira decides what she's capable of, and that she's the one best suited to oversee this operation."

When Kilronan started to speak, Isfail went on. "Your concern as a close friend, even as a warrior, is both understandable and commendable, Kil, but you have to ease back and respect her as a warrior in this." Now Isfail chuckled as he winked at his wife. "As I must."

She smiled back at him, reaching for his hand. "And I must appreciate having so many gallant warriors concerned for me. As long as none of you get in my way."

With the storm evidently averted, Isfail sat on the arm of her chair, raising his glass in salute to Kilronan. "What else do you want to talk about before this expedition gets underway?"

Swallowing his mouthful of ale, Kilronan asked, "Who's this Barash?" Now he gave Akira a long study. "You left out a lot there, my lady."

Meeting his uncompromising gaze, Akira replied, "He is what you were told, and considerably more. I'm not going to go into all of his background at this time. It's not relevant to what we're doing. Barash has proven his loyalty and courage in several ways since I've known him."

Nodding slowly, Kilronan took another drink. Isfail wondered how long it would take the man to find out all there was to know about their odd man out. But Isfail agreed with Akira, Barash had proven himself. More, Barash was one more layer of protection around Akira. If it became necessary in order to work together effectively, he'd push that point to Master Kilronan.

Eighty-Two

Kittric, Ishal

The port city wrapped like a ragged shawl around the gray harbor in the thin fog of early morning. From their vantage point on a hill just to the west, Arith's team assessed their mission target.

From here, the city appeared peaceful. Smoke curled from chimneys, giving the expectation that residents were preparing for the day. The ambassadors could see people, horses, and carts on the streets.

Then Drinin asked, "Does anyone else think that a lot of those houses look abandoned?" He pointed out the number of buildings whose chimneys rose above their roofs without any sign of smoke. Likewise, the roads or lanes in those areas showed little to no activity.

"The wharves are busy enough," Kalronan said. "Looks like things are focused there."

"Yeah," Arith added, "And it looks like shipping activity is divided into two camps. I wonder if that was deliberate. The pirates are clustered to the south. It looks like general shipping is along the docks in the north part of the bay."

Iro took out her own spyglass. "Fits what we've been told. And look, there's Norsi's *Black Squall* anchored with two other cutters."

"I guess the Ishalians didn't give them any trouble." Drinin continued to scan the area. "Looks calm all around from here."

Signaling them into a huddle, Arith went over the plan again. "We're going to enter the city in a group of three, that's me and the 'ronans. Drinin and Iro go as a couple. We'll take different routes in. Drinin and Iro, check out some of those abandoned areas, see what you can find out about that. We'll make our way down toward the docks."

He looked around his team. "Stay out of trouble. If anyone seems suspicious of you, takes too much interest, do what you need to do to blend into the background. We'll rendezvous at the main square around sunset. If there's trouble, try to get there earlier and stay hidden until you see one of us."

They moved down the far side of the hill and to the main road along the coast, where the two groups split to make their separate ways into enemy territory.

Tash'tric, Ishal

S triding through the ornate halls of the Parliament building, Felcan once again thought through what he intended to say to Abron Dateh. Days had gone by since he'd returned and had the unexpected confrontation with Barash. The search still continued for what he was convinced was a dead man, and this Aron Drinin. It was frustrating that the citywide search and closely watched checkpoints had failed to locate or find any sign of them. He'd dutifully tried to report to Dateh every day, but had to be satisfied with giving a short, written report to a nervous secretary outside Dateh's closed doors.

By now, Felcan was thoroughly fed up with his old friend's obsessive secrecy. Dateh would have no right to complain when he heard about Shanow, something Felcan had tried to warn him about many times. The sneer on Felcan's face at that thought had the secretary's nerves fraying as she opened the door to Dateh's inner sanctum.

When the door closed behind him, Felcan waited stubbornly for Dateh to speak first.

"What news?" Dateh said after a long interval, finally lifting his eyes from the paper on his desk. Felcan noted the puzzled brow with satisfaction.

"There's no sign of Drinin or Barash. Continuing the search for them is pointless and a waste of our men's time. There's also no indication that any of the ambassadors Gorth described are in Tash'tric." He stopped abruptly, putting further talk back on Dateh.

But the man just nodded with seeming unconcern. "I agree with you. The Bowmen have more important things to prepare for." He got up and poured two glasses, then frowned when Felcan refused. "Come now, Beros, I'd hardly poison my best friend."

"Wouldn't you, Abron?" Felcan took the glass but set it aside without drinking, a deliberate snub. "You've been treating me like an inferior since I returned from Caldala; refusing my advice, refusing to see me, sending me out like some lackey to do your bidding."

Dateh studied him as he drank, his dark eyes wary. "I regret giving that impression, Beros," he finally replied. "Perhaps my anger over that regrettable incident blinded me to your feelings. Still . . ."

Dateh gestured him over to the table where a map of Ishal was spread out. "It's time to plan the takeover of the Ishakan territories. You'll lead the Bowmen, of course. I don't foresee much opposition since Shanow and his militia have had several lunams now to break down any opposition."

"Abron—"

Felcan tried to speak, but Dateh rolled over him. "Even if Shanow was reluctant to eliminate the tribes, our soldiers will complete the eradication. The horses will be valuable, of course, but I want the territories under my absolute control. Caldala's weakest border point is there, which—"

"Abron, shut up!"

Felcan scowled back when Dateh swung around, obviously incensed.

"Be careful, Felcan," he warned.

"If you'd listen for half a minute, you'll find out that's what I'm trying to do for both of us." Felcan saw Dateh pull himself in with a curt nod.

"Continue then." Dateh went to his desk—putting him in his place as a subordinate, Felcan decided irritably.

"First, I don't want any stupidity from you over this. I tried to tell you right after I returned, but you wouldn't give me the time."

"All right." Dateh bit the words off. "Tell me."

"Ramort told me he'd learned that Shanow went to Ishaka to defend the horse tribes *against* invasion." Felcan watched Dateh's face turn to stone. "And at least two other militia units have joined him in the defense."

"Ramort is lying," Dateh retorted in an ominous voice.

"Ramort is dead or in a Caldalan prison by now," Felcan said, sure of his information. "Shanow negotiated with Mountain Shadows protectorate, just beyond the old pass, for the supplies they needed over the winter. We've got to expect that Caldala will provide warriors to support them, if they haven't already. We need to give up the Ishakan territories and solidify our hold on Ishal proper."

Felcan watched Dateh's eyes go blank and wondered if the man was actually stupefied by the news. Somehow this state was more frightening than his earlier rage. After several moments like this, Dateh appeared to shake himself back to attention. His demeanor was surprisingly business-like now, causing Felcan to wonder if he'd stepped out of reality himself.

"Even if Ramort was telling the truth, it makes no difference. We'll continue as planned, and Shanow will be dealt with." For a moment, rage seemed to tinge his eyes red, but Dateh recovered quickly and, pulling a blank sheet of paper to him, gave his attention to writing. "We should have investigated him more closely before sending him out."

That was the last he'd take. Felcan snapped.

"I told you," he snarled, stalking the room. "I said you were playing with fire trying to use Shanow!" He slammed his hands on Dateh's desk, incensed by his friend's lack of attention. "What are we to do now, Abron? The Ishakan territories are lost to us. They've got three full militias holding ground there. And the Caldalans!"

Dateh said nothing as he continued to scribble rapidly.

"Damn it!" Felcan shouted, hoping to break that icy calm. "Caldala's mobilized its navy. They're already sailing to blockade Kittric. We'll never get that motley fleet out in time."

"So what do you suggest, Beros?" Dateh finally said, sounding as unperturbed as if he were addressing one of those fools of ministers. "Let loose The Bow?"

Felcan barked a bitter laugh. "The Bow!" he exclaimed, derision filling the words. "We've lost the men placed in Caldala, and more than that will fall in Ishaka if you go through with this. What do you want? Will you just push on against all reason until what's left of your infamous fighting force is scattered, fumbling without direction or leadership?"

Now Dateh did look up, fury in those black eyes.

"They were never a well-trained, disciplined army like the militias, Abron," Felcan said, tempering his voice in hopes of making his friend see reason. "They're a rabble of malcontents who want the freedom to do as they please. They thrive on the abuses, the torture, and the kill. As long as they believe your promises, you can control them. But we've lost the advantage of stealth and ambush in Ishaka and Caldala. Superior fighting forces have the field. Your men will scatter like rabbits when they come up against real warriors, and they'll lose all belief in you and your plans."

"All I need is an obedient killing machine," Dateh hissed so fiercely that Felcan took a step back from the dark fury. "Obedience!" he snapped again, snatching up the paper. "The fools in Kittric will learn the price of their betrayal."

"What betrayal?" Felcan pressed, thrown off by the shift in focus. "Our men in Kittric aren't shipbuilders or sailors, that's why you thought the pirates would provide the backbone to put together a fighting fleet. But they're all the same under the skin! A bunch of ignorant, unskilled peasants looking for an easy, lawless life, and none of them wanted to take orders from their own kind. It's not too late to pull our Bowmen out of Kittric, use them to squash any loyalist resurgence. Forget about this fleet, for now."

He walked to the door and back. "We should have posted more of our senior men as overseers there, instead of sending so many to Caldala, or basing them here in Tash'tric."

"They're here to train the men for Ishaka," Dateh replied coldly, flipping back again. "And you're very wrong, Felcan. We will win the territories, and Caldala. I'm going to remind them all what happens when a Baronan is crossed."

Feeling as if ice suddenly packed his spine, Felcan froze in place. "What are you talking about?"

Dateh ignored the question as he held up the paper, now folded and sealed with the mark of The Bow. "Send for one of the senior Bowmen, and Gorth. I learned more than just rebellion from my father."

Eighty-Three

Ishakan Territories

With the narrow rift behind them at last, Akira breathed more easily. They still rode through tight canyons, with steep peaks rising above them, but the diminishing shriek of the wind through the passages was welcome, despite its continued chill. Snow and ice mantled the ledges, formed drifts along north-facing walls. They were all fortunate that the winter had been milder than the previous year.

Ahead, Kane lifted his hand to signal a halt. Tilting her head, Akira heard a sound blending with the rush of wind. No, she realized, the wind was not the source of the whistle, so skillfully played to replicate a natural sound. She saw Kane raise his hands, cupping them over his mouth before she heard a distinct warbling call, reminiscent of mountain grouse.

Kane urged his horse into a fast walk, then a trot, looking back briefly to meet Akira's eyes. But he said nothing as he led them out of the narrow defile. Beyond the opening, a small meadow spread, its ground cover and grasses beginning to green with the warming weather.

But Akira's attention was all for the horsemen forming an imposing arc in the middle of the field, at least twenty, all mounted on distinctive black horses. At their center, a horse length ahead of the others, sat a woman on a spectacular stallion.

Syrai, Akira knew, slowing to a walk with the rest of her group as Kane closed the distance quickly. Her heart warmed watching them greet one another. Syrai lifted her left forearm, her fingers pointed to the sky. Kane reined in next to her, wrapping his forearm with hers so their hands clasped. The force aura bloomed around them as they leaned toward one another.

Feeling unexpectedly sentimental, Akira was pleased to see that the Ishakan *Sha'ala* was not so bound in ceremony that she would forego a long, sensual kiss with the mate who'd been absent for lunams. Judging by the smiles on the faces of the other horsemen, such a display of affection was approved of.

Beside her now, Isfail reached over to stroke her arm. "That's a good start."

"It's love and unity. I hope we can use that to unify our disparate forces."

"Akira—"

"Please don't ask again, Dan." She turned to look into his worried eyes. "I have to do this. We have to do this, together." Akira laid a gloved hand on the wool cloak wrapped over her belly. "This child deserves a chance to live in peace. The Baronan legacy of death must end."

But she knew, despite his words to Kilronan as they'd begun this mission, and his sincere belief in her ability as a warrior, Isfail would rather she were safe back in Caldala. What she hadn't told him was that she wished he were too.

She wondered if Syrai sensed her mood as the woman looked from Akira to Isfail and back again with a pensive smile. Akira gave the Ishakan greeting of respect, words and gestures, including a slight bow where she sat in the saddle.

"You are welcome here, *Sha'ala Majera*," Syrai responded with the same gestures, and an even deeper bow. "You honor the horse tribes, and my people are grateful."

"Our people stand together, Syrai. We of the blood are one."

Syrai's smile was warm now. "We are one, Akira." She turned her head to Isfail with a welcoming gesture. "This is your man, another great warrior."

Isfail gave a perfect rendition of the appropriate greeting in Ishakan.

"I am honored, Commander Isfail—now we will all speak in the common tongue."

Syrai offered her arm in the Caldalan gesture of amity as the rest of the Caldalan group was introduced.

But her eyes lingered on Barash a moment longer than the rest before she gripped his forearm. Akira felt relief when she saw the briefly clouded gaze clear when Syrai met her eyes.

"My people have outfitted one of the larger caves for your comfort. If you wish to pass any personal packs to these tribesmen"—she swept a hand to her escort—"they will see that they are delivered safely. We will ride directly to Commander Shanow's encampment."

Once that was dealt with, and the packhorses turned over, Syrai and Kane led the way out of the little meadow, guiding the group along a mountain stream that wound its way through a series of small canyons. When the stream joined a lake the color of sapphires—the same blue as the eyes of an Ishakan—Kane called a halt.

More tribesmen had prepared food and drink, and were waiting to assist them.

Tired and unusually hungry, Akira was thankful for their foresight and consideration. At Kane's urging, she settled onto a thick cushion with a sigh, and a smile for Syrai who came to sit beside her.

"It is a brave, or foolish, woman who goes to war when she carries new life."

Akira chuckled as she let the overwarm cloak slide from her shoulders. "So I've been told in other words. But then, it took your *Nah'shalon* to inform me that I was pregnant. Though I might eventually have figured it out on my own."

Syrai laughed up at Kane who stood beside her. "You did not share that story with me, *asherke*."

"I did not want to embarrass my little cousin with her lack of knowledge."

Akira saw the twinkle in his eyes, welcoming this change in

him. He was at home here, and his personality shift reflected it. "I see where Kalen's humor comes from."

And she saw a mother's pride and longing in Syrai's gaze. "He is missed, but he will return before the snows fall again. We will laugh together, and he will share his life apart with his tribe."

"Then he will be missed among my people," Akira said sincerely, laying her hand over Syrai's. "Our lives have been enriched in knowing him."

Alerted by scouts, Shanow and Declan rode out to meet them as they left the last of the narrow mountain passages and came out into the valley where Lower Caldera Lake shimmered golden in the setting sunlight.

With obvious enthusiasm, Declan greeted Isfail after his more formal greetings to his tribal leaders. Syrai told him to handle the introductions from there and approved the solemnity of his introduction of Lady Muro. He hadn't forgotten her exalted status among the tribes.

Shanow gave a deep bow of respect, remembering what he'd heard of her power and experience. "I had hoped to have the honor of meeting you one day, Lady Muro. I only regret that it takes place in a time of war."

"The situation is regrettable, Commander Shanow, but the honor is mine." Akira held out an arm, gripping his firmly. "I am in your debt for the part you and your soldiers played in saving Commander Isfail. Perhaps we can dispense with the formalities now."

He gave her a slight smile. "It would be a pleasure, but there is no debt owed."

With Declan, they moved on through the ambassadors and the protectorate teams until Barash was the last to be introduced. Both Shanow and Declan stiffened, staring at him in disbelief.

Akira swore under her breath and, with Isfail, strode forward to forestall an incident. Placing a hand on Barash's rigid arm, Akira took up introductions. "This is our friend, Barash. Perhaps you've noticed his resemblance to the man calling himself Lord Dateh."

Shanow met her eyes with a curt nod, but seemed willing to withhold judgment.

"Barash is indeed a half-brother to Abron Baronan, Dateh's real name. They were not raised together, and Arthon Baronan abandoned Barash at a very early age. The two men are decidedly not the same in any way."

"Why is he with you?" Shanow asked.

"He brought important information to us about Dateh's operations in Caldala, and he joined us in a reconnaissance mission to Tash'tric earlier this lunam. He has my complete confidence and trust, Commander."

"And mine," Isfail added, stepping to the other side of Barash.

"Lady Syrai or Kane can look into my head, sir," Barash invited stiffly. "I would not dishonor Lady Muro's faith in me. I owe her my life and my allegiance."

Shanow studied him for a moment longer then offered his arm. "I will not doubt her judgment, sir. While I admit that your resemblance to the man I loathe with everything in me caused me a moment's pause, it is wrong for me to assume that you share his evil."

Akira saw Barash's throat work with some emotion as he gripped Shanow's arm in return. "I will not betray you, Commander."

Now Shanow gave a crooked grin. "I believe you, Barash." As he turned back to speak with Isfail, Barash looked at Akira.

"I'm sorry, my lady. You were right, I should have stayed in Caldala." He ran a hand over his head. "I didn't even think how my likeness to their worst enemy could compromise your mission."

"It won't, Barash, and I believe you'll prove just how strong your allegiance is here." Akira put her hand on his shoulder, giving it a gentle squeeze. "I believe in you, my friend."

He smiled briefly then turned when Kane asked him a question.

Akira walked away, going to her horse for her water flask. "Baronan's son?"

She looked over her saddle into Kilronan's hard stare. "And that tone of voice is why I chose not to get into it earlier. Are we defined by our relations?"

"You told us he was related to Drinin, one of your Alpha ambassadors," he retorted angrily.

She enjoyed the shock on his irritated face when she replied, "He is. Aron Drinin is Abron Baronan's twin brother. Now tell me how untrustworthy my ambassador is, a man who has dedicated his life to honorable service in the Ambassador Core."

"Back off, Kil," Arla ordered as she walked to them. "You should know better than to question a superior."

She winked at Akira, who fought to suppress a smile.

"Damn it," Kilronan muttered before stalking off to soothe his pride.

"He'll get over it," Arla said, watching him join his team. "You know he has to know everything about anyone hanging around you."

"And he needs to get over that habit too," Akira stated. The baby shifted suddenly, and she placed a hand over the spot.

Arla looked at her with concern. "Everything all right?"

"She's just restless."

"She?" Arla asked with a grin.

"Could be he. It's easier to use one pronoun." Akira stretched. "I've chosen not to try to find that out. But it might be unavoidable as the baby grows."

They walked together toward the group assembling around a welcome fire where Commander Aric joined them. After stating his appreciation to the Caldalans for their support, Aric came to greet Akira and Isfail.

"It's good to see you both," Aric said with a warm smile.

Akira took his hand in both of hers. "Thank you for making that possible, Commander. I can never repay you for what you did in saving Isfail."

Shaking his head, Aric replied, "No thanks needed, my lady.

You both have done more for my country over the years than our own government. Now you're here once more."

Sitting beside them, Aric turned the conversation to the current situation, with others joining in around the fire.

The wind blew colder as night came on. There were hot beverages and thick soup with bread provided by the tribe. As they ate together, plans were made for everyone to tour the potential battleground the next day. With scouts keeping a close lookout on their perimeter, they would be alerted before Dateh's men arrived.

When the group broke up, some to rest, some to duty, Akira asked Aric to linger a moment. When his eyes met hers curiously, she hoped the news she'd received permission to share would indeed give this honorable man some solace. With Isfail's hand firmly holding hers, Akira said softly, "Isfail gave me the package you sent for Alani and I delivered it to her."

Taking a folded and sealed paper from her pocket, Akira handed it to Aric. "She wanted me to thank you, and give you this if we met."

Aric nodded, smiling slightly as he opened and read the note within.

With a sigh, Akira reached out and took Aric's hand. "Alani also wanted you to know that she and Garath have a daughter." She felt his hand grip hers tightly. "When this is over, we'll take you to see her, if that's what you want."

He said nothing for a moment, seeming to fight some fierce emotion as his eyes looked away into the night. Then Aric took a deep breath, letting it out slowly. Bringing Akira's hand to his lips for a long moment, he looked deep into her eyes.

"I would like that." Aric's voice was low and hoarse, but there was a light in his eyes that hadn't been there earlier.

He released her hand, offering an arm to Isfail with a firm grip. "I am grateful to you both." Then Aric turned and strode quickly into the darkness.

"You didn't tell him that the child was raised by others," Isfail noted quietly as he slipped an arm around Akira.

"He doesn't need to know that now," she murmured. "Let his heart be at peace."

Later that night, remarkably comfortable on a bed made of a stack of quilted and cushioned mats, with soft, woven blankets to cover them, Akira lay in Isfail's arms, listening to his even breathing as he slept. She couldn't help but smile when a warm feeling of contentment spread through her as their child reflected her feelings.

Eighty-Four

Kittric, Ishal

S trangest situation I've ever seen," Arith said from his chair in the front room of the abandoned home they were using as a base. "How does The Bow think they can defeat Orsha's fleet, let alone Caldala's? And Orsha only has five ships outfitted for battle."

"Smoke and mirrors," Drinin replied from his place near a window as he watched for signs of trouble. "Block your main shipping harbor, put out the word that you're assembling a secret fleet capable of conquering the world." He shrugged. "Who's to know different when you're talking about a crazy man who's already proven himself capable of taking control of a whole country?"

Legs stretched out as he sat in a tipped-back chair, Coronan still managed to look serious—an unusual look for him. "Iro says another pirate ship slipped out last night."

"As long as our pirate ship's still there, it's a good sign. The Bow's losing its hold on Kittric." Arith poured himself another cup of tea.

Kalronan came in from the back, shrugging out of a seaman's coat before tossing his cap onto the table. "Any more of that?" he asked, picking up the pot. "Yes!"

Shifting to give him room at the table, Arith asked, "Did you get to the *Black Squall*?"

Swallowing his first sip with a satisfied sound, Kalronan

replied, "They're preparing to leave tomorrow night, as planned. The captain said to be on board as soon as we can."

"Good." Arith nodded to a heavy-eyed Iro as she walked in, yawning. "We've got what we came for. Still don't understand what this is all about, but The Bow's fleet isn't a threat to anyone."

Getting her own cup of tea, Iro settled near the window, looking out with Drinin. "Do you think that really was Gorth last night? Riding around in that ale delivery wagon?"

"Sure looked like him," Kalronan replied. "I guess he's been demoted."

Glancing back at them, Drinin offered another possibility. "I'd guess that he's here on orders from Felcan and Dateh, looking for us, any of us from Recon Alpha. They're not fools, despite this weirdness in Kittric. Once they knew I was here, they'd suspect there were more recon ambassadors in Ishal. Kittric is a logical target."

"Good thing we saw him first," Coronan said, bringing his chair upright with a soft thump. "There's no way he can flush us out."

At the window, Iro stiffened then stood up, staring out intently. "Maybe there is." She turned back with a look of warning. "Gorth's a fire bender, isn't he?"

"Yes." Arith stood up quickly, the others following.

"The city is on fire."

Within minutes, they'd collected their packs and were crouched on the roof terrace, scanning the scene around them. There could be no doubt that numerous fires had been deliberately set. Smoke and flames were spreading out from strategic points around Kittric—rapidly cutting off retreat routes inland, as if designed to funnel people toward the harbor.

"How could anyone do this?" Kalronan asked as screams and shouts for help rose throughout the narrow streets.

"He's his father's son," Iro whispered in a haunted voice. "This is just like the first rebellion."

"We're getting out of here," Arith told them, pointing toward a clear run of alleyways. "That way, then however we can get to the docks."

They made it more than halfway before the fires weren't their most immediate concern. Turning into the trade district with its numerous public houses, they pulled up at the sight of crowds of people battering one another, fighting viciously in the streets, oblivious to the approaching flames.

"Oh my God," Iro said in horror. "What's wrong with them?"

"Look out!" Drinin shouted before anyone could attempt to answer. Jerking his teammate back, he shot a force bolt at the man covered in blood, cackling with mad laughter as he ran at them brandishing a long butcher's knife. The man fell even as others took his place.

The team shifted to protect each other, holding nothing back as they fought for their lives against people too crazed to back down.

"Out of here!" Arith shouted, leading them through a gap in a wall. With the fires pushing them into bigger crowds—some obviously under some mad affliction, others seemingly normal people fleeing for their lives—Recon Alpha used all their skills to make their way toward the harbor.

An empty shop, its windows smashed out, provided a temporary resting place. Crouched behind a short counter at the back, near a point of exit, the ambassadors watched people rush by in the street. Some were screaming in fear, others laughing with homicidal glee.

"What's gotten into them?" Coronan wondered before taking a drink from his water pouch. "It's like they've been drugged."

"They have," Drinin said in an enraged voice. "Remember the Illeri brothers? Akira ended up killing both of them, but it was the older one, Maron, who used poison in the village water source to kill an entire village. They were Ishalian. Anyone want to put money on it that they were part of The Bow?"

"Could have distributed it through the public houses," Arith said with cold certainty. "We saw Gorth going the rounds with that ale delivery. Now we've got fires and mayhem. But this is more like the massacre at Baronan Keep years ago. Akira told us people had gone mad, attacking one another."

"But why? Why would anyone order this?" Kalronan asked again, his young face anguished.

"Because he can," Drinin murmured.

*D*amn!" Arith exclaimed in a whisper some time later, as he huddled beside a ruined wall with his team. Everywhere they turned, Kittric was burning, impeding their progress as they continued toward the docks.

Coronan's most laconic voice came from behind him. "Just like old times. Ow!" he exclaimed quietly, chuckling as Iro smacked him again. "Cut it out, or I'll tell Reva."

Arith turned to him with a grin, thankful that Coronan still had his sense of humor. "Lay off him, Iro."

She turned to him, saying, "How's Drinin doing?"

Arith sent out a mindsight then quickly rose to a crouch, signaling the others to follow. Moving silently through the shadows, they joined Drinin in an abandoned warehouse, where thick coils of smoke were beginning to haze the air.

"Stay close." Drinin's voice was terse as he led the way through the dim interior, lit only by flickering firelight through high windows. They all seemed to breathe a sigh of relief as they emerged at the waterfront.

"Good," Arith said. "The cutter should be at quay number five. If we get separated, keep going until you're on board. Got it?" He waited for each nod before leading them into the shifting shadows of the harbor warehouses.

Panicked Ishalians filled the docks, overwhelming even the pirate crews in their desperate flight from the city. The air was thick with smoke and wails of despair. All around them, more warehouses began to burn as the fires spread. Those already fully engulfed were collapsing, sending firebrands and debris showering over the masses.

The burning of once-proud Kittric was a scene from Hell as the conflagration forced more people toward the harbor. But they were met with the reality of ships overflowing with refugees that tried to move away from the wharf, or left burning at the piers.

Drinin and Coronan grabbed Iro's arms when she tripped, almost going down in the pressing crowds. Arith glanced back, signaling Kalronan to go ahead while the others fought to keep moving forward.

More screams pierced the night as an explosion sounded farther down the wharf. People surged back toward them, fleeing the flames that now engulfed docks to the east. Arith felt himself grabbed from behind as he was forced back.

"Get to the walls!" Coronan shouted near his ear, and the four locked arms to try to stay together.

A brief struggle got them to the stacks of shipping goods lining the fronts of the remaining warehouses. They scrambled up to run as best they could over the uneven piles, Arith leading and Coronan bringing up the rear.

"There's the flag!" Arith yelled, pointing to the mast standard waving the blood-red colors of the *Black Squall*, looking like a whipping flame in the firelight. But an inferno blazed ahead of them, cutting them off from the ship. As refugees fled, the ambassadors searched for a way to get to their ship.

"Follow me!" Coronan shouted, leaping down. The others followed as he pushed across the crowded timbers to a narrow ladder. Looking down to verify that it led to a maintenance catwalk below the main wharf, Coronan slid down the hand railing and scanned ahead. Embers fell from the burning topside, but the catwalk appeared sound for the moment. Signaling to his teammates, he waited until Drinin joined him, then sent him on, with Arith and Iro close behind.

They ran under the burning section until Drinin climbed rapidly up an access ladder on the other side of the flaming blockade. When all were standing on the dock again, they tried to find the ship amid the chaos.

"There!" Iro cried.

"Hurry!" Kalronan's mindsight rang through their minds. *"The captain's ordered to cast off!"*

"Go! Go! Go!" Arith yelled, urging his companions forward as flames continued to devour the tar-soaked timbers behind them. Surprisingly, the pirate crew held the gangplank when they saw them racing toward the ship.

Coronan reached it first, waving Iro and Drinin up as he saw Arith stumble while the lines were cast off. "Keep going!" he shouted as he ran back to help Arith to his feet.

Finally on board, the others leaned anxiously over the railing as they waited helplessly. Iro begged the deck hands to hold the gangplank a moment longer. The first mate gave a grim-faced nod, watching as warehouses crashed and imploded. Then the two men bolted up the gangplank, just as a rending cacophony of sound announced the failure of the longest-burning section of the dock itself. The captain shouted orders to clear the moorings as a shudder rippled down weakened timbers.

The sails flapped in the shifting gusts of hot air spiraling around the inferno. Pirates struggled aloft to set canvas to catch a steady wind.

Near the top of the gangplank, Arith grabbed Coronan's right hand and leaped for the ship as the plank slipped, grabbing a rail as hands reached to catch him. Coronan held tight as he slammed against the side of the ship while Arith was hauled aboard, twisting to keep his grip on his friend's hand.

Kalronan gripped Drinin's belt when he dropped to the gangplank opening in the rails to reach for Coronan's free hand.

The men pulled, trying to lift Coronan high enough to drag him to safety. Another explosion shook the docks, the blast spewing flaming debris forcefully against the slowly moving ship. Drinin lost his grip as he slid back on the tilting deck. Iro leaped over him, reaching for Coronan. Her eyes widened with horror as she saw the terrible shard of wood impaling his body, leaving his left arm dangling uselessly.

Arith's face twisting with sheer determination, he held on tight to the injured man swinging below him as the others reached down. Then Coronan looked up, his intense blue eyes burning into the faces above him.

"Tell Evani . . . I will always love her," he said with fatalistic calm, his hand inexorably slipping from Arith's desperate grasp.

"Alon!" Kalronan and Iro screamed as he fell, disappearing into the dark waters where flames reflected the horror around them.

Drinin leaped up, grabbing a throw rope as Arith and Kalronan gripped the rails to dive into the water after their friend, but urgent shouts around them had them looking toward the bow of the cutter.

Even pirates could pray, Arith discovered amid the oaths and shouts of despair.

A burning Ishalian galleon, flying a flag displaying the mark of The Bow, bore down on their ship. Its mad crew raised arms in defiant victory even as the holds full of gunpowder ignited while the figurehead impaled the *Black Squall*.

The nightmare erupted with a deafening roar of flames.

Eighty-Five

Ishakan Territories

With the thundering roar of the waterfall known as Cloud Maker masking any attempt at speech, Akira stood with Reva and Kilronan, looking out across the wide valley below. She wondered if Kilronan was remembering it as they'd last seen it, with the rough and ragged tents of the Mors—the Black Death—flapping like carrion birds over a carcass.

Did he feel a trace of the fear again, the same cold sickness she could now admit to at the memory of young Maronan, badly injured, a captive of the malevolent Vrorg, the leader of the Mors? It was hard to believe that was only a year ago. Now Maronan matched his older teammate Eron in height and was more young man than youth with the Psyche shift upon him.

Today, the broad grasslands were quiet, with no sign yet of another enemy—men this time. Most of them Ishalian men, striking against their Ishakan countrymen in greed or fear stoked by Abron Baronan in his guise of Lord Dateh. They'd already burned this vital grazing ground of the horse tribes last harvest season, in an attempt to drive the Ishakans out, or force them to surrender their lands.

She watched several people start across the valley on horseback. Akira recognized Micharon and Coran from Reva's team, Arla and her team, and Barash riding next to Declan. It pleased her to see Declan's animated gesturing as he evidently pointed out landmarks to the newcomers. Even from a distance, she could see the grin on his face. There was no sign that he held any grudge against Barash.

Now she saw Isfail cantering after them with Shanow beside him. The morning's plan had included familiarizing the Caldalans with the most likely places for an attack. On the far side of the valley there was a wide strand of thick forest that ran for miles along the Mounastra River.

With only one intact bridge into Ishaka, any army of Dateh's would have to take the roads to the river town of Estas to cross the bridge there. Once on Ishakan land, the forest provided cover for offense and defense for both sides.

Kane and Syrai had reviewed the scouting perimeters and how the scouts reported back. The sleek little falcons trained by the horse tribes, and used as efficient message carriers, had Akira longing for her black falcon, Spirit. But her bird was not familiar with this landscape and was safer back in Mountain Shadows.

The tribal scouts discussed their circuits with them, and offered to start making their rounds with partners from the ambassador and protectorate teams so they'd learn the area. That's when Barash forwarded an idea. Alluding to skills obtained in covert matters, he volunteered to go farther afield, even beyond the bridge to gather advance recon on the movements of Dateh's men.

Mercilessly pushing down an instant of fear for his safety, Akira just listened as the discussion played out. There was no question that early warning would benefit everyone involved in the defense. Shanow and Aric had approved the plan immediately, another vote of confidence for Barash's integrity.

With no dissenting opinion, no votes against, Barash was started on a fast course in Ishalian geography. Akira knew he was planning to discreetly investigate the Estas Bridge during today's recon.

She scanned the valley once again, understanding there was no turning back. During a private conversation with Syrai that morning, both women had admitted to the same *knowing* that the enemy would come soon. It was both a comfort and an uneasy validation that Syrai reinforced her own feelings. In fact, they appeared to have shared the same nightmare last night, a terrible dream of flames reflected in dark water, leaving both waking with a heartbreaking sense of loss.

Trying to shake off the dregs of the nightmare, Akira focused on what was before her. For a moment she enjoyed the view from their lofty vantage point. Ishal dropped off just beyond the river, so they couldn't really see what was beyond Estas. It was a long three days ride, taken at an easy canter, to Tash'tric from here.

Akira looked to the south, trying to bring Kittric's location to mind. She started to turn when Kilronan spoke to her, but froze when that dark echo of death swept over her once more.

"We're agreed that this is an ideal spot to coordinate force defenses from," Kilronan said again, giving her a concerned study when she still didn't respond.

Reva stepped up, putting her hand on Akira's shoulder. "Akira, what is it?" But the luminous eyes that turned to her spilled tears of grief.

*A*kira recovered enough to let Reva and Kilronan help her back to camp, where Syrai was already waiting. But the look on the *Sha'ala's* face did not bring comfort. Reva left them alone after determining that Akira and her baby were physically healthy.

"Something is wrong," Syrai began, sitting cross-legged beside the cot Akira rested on in Shanow's tent. "I cannot see it clearly."

"Only impressions, emotions," Akira confirmed, making herself calm enough to send reassuring images to the baby making anxious mental impressions. That alone was enough to force Akira to deal with this less emotionally. "I just know that it is beyond my ability to change now."

Syrai nodded and stood up, taking a deep breath herself as she glanced around the commander's neat tent. "Yes. It is done. We will know more soon enough. But it is not here, in the territories." She bent to press Akira's hand. "Cherish your child, let her know she is loved. It will help you as well."

"Syrai?" Akira called after her, "A daughter?"

Smiling, Syrai tipped her head. "Do you want to know?"

"No."

"I thought not."

*B*y the time Isfail and the others returned, Akira had recovered her equanimity enough for Reva to stop hovering over her, to her great relief. She told Isfail what had happened, how it had affected Syrai as well. Fortunately, there was more relevant news to be shared by the field party, and the evening meeting centered on what they'd learned.

Shanow laid out positions, discussing strategy with Aric and Isfail, and turning to Akira and Syrai for their approval when plans solidified. Once things began to wrap up, Akira asked for their attention, signaling Barash to bring the strongbox she'd had him retrieve for her.

"We all know that the Baronans are infamous for many things, one being the Ishalian Black Arrow. The use of terrible poisons was Arthon Baronan's trademark. Some kill quickly, like the Black Arrow poison, others initiate a kind of psychotic madness, causing their victims to attack others with extreme violence before death." Akira opened the case and took out a small vial.

"Caldala's Ambassador Core developed an antidote to the Black Arrow poison after the First Rebellion. I asked them to increase production as much as they could after The Bow's attack on Ambassador Central's own grounds. Before we left Coroth on this mission, I was given one hundred and twenty vials of antidote, all that the Core could spare. After leaving twenty vials with Lord Corcoran at Mountain Shadows Protectorate, to distribute at his discretion, I have one hundred here."

She looked around the attentive faces. "Not enough for every person, but enough for those at greatest risk. I will take responsibility for distribution, but I propose that each of the leadership have one on them at all times, the same with front line scouts, both protectorate teams, and the ambassador team.

A number of vials will be in Syrai's care, and I will have vials for care of the wounded that get to us. I suggest that all leaders carry at least three extra vials for use on the battlefield if needed."

"What about the other poisons?" Aric asked tersely. "Are they used on weapons too?"

Akira shook her head. "Those are ingested. The times we've encountered their use, they were introduced to water supplies like wells or cisterns, casks of ale, that kind of portal." She looked around the enraged faces. "It doesn't look like a feasible attack here because the horse tribes use fresh water sources where such poisons are quickly diluted and washed away. But you should consider carrying your own water supplies while scouting close to Ishal, and don't accept or drink from water containers or sources you're not sure of. We have no antidote for that type of poison."

There were no more questions, and everyone appeared to understand the importance of her plan. The vials were distributed, with a small number remaining in the box. Barash was the last to come to her, but shook his head when she held out his ration.

"Save it for someone important."

Akira frowned. "You don't want to make me angry, Barash."

He shrugged stiffly. "Give it to someone you really need, is all. I can fend for myself."

"Why did you insist on coming if you don't believe you're needed?" she asked, watching his face flush. Akira took his hand, pressing two vials into it. "I need you, Barash, for your courage and your willingness to scout out our enemy. Don't discount your importance to us all."

His fingers closed around the vials as he met her eyes. Akira saw his struggle to accept her words, and knew he doubted himself more than anyone here doubted him. But his head jerked in a nod and he carefully slid the vials into an inner pocket before lifting the box and returning it to the cave.

Eighty-Six

The Island Nation of Kilra

*K*alen Kalronan struggled to open his eyes against the pain that possessed him as he regained consciousness. A dim mist obscured his vision as his eyelids parted. Gray shapes appeared in the mist and a roaring sound seemed to be directed at him. He gave up trying to make sense of it all and returned to the peace of oblivion.

Another day passed before he opened his eyes with more clarity of vision. He was in a white-walled infirmary. A few other patients occupied beds at the far end of the long room. It was so quiet, Kalronan thought. Windows were open and bright sunlight filled the room. White curtains fluttered in a silent breeze.

A white-veiled Sister noticed he was awake and came quickly over. She gently picked up the hand not covered in bandaging. Her lips were moving as he struggled to make sense of the soft roar. The Sister's eyes looked puzzled as her lips grew still. She lightly touched his ear and pointed to her mouth.

Kalronan finally understood and tried to shake his aching head, but his neck protested in an agony of pain. The Sister took his face between her hands and shook her head to indicate that he should not move. She gave him a comforting smile before walking quickly away.

When he woke again, another dawn brightened the windows. The same Sister sat reading by his bed. She looked up with an encouraging smile as he stirred.

"Where am I?" he managed to whisper hoarsely. His words sounded distant to him, but the Sister's smile widened.

"You are on Kilra, sir, in the port town of Duorn," she answered in a faraway voice. "Captain Vaneer was able to rescue some from the tragedy at Kittric harbor. We were the nearest safe port."

She carefully restrained him as he struggled to sit up. "No, young man. Your injuries are severe, you must lie still."

Tears ran down his face with the pain, body and soul. Still, he asked with desperate hope, "My friends?"

He closed his eyes against her sad face and the slow shake of her head.

A cool hand came to rest on his forehead as she said from that odd distance, "I will have the captain come. He may be able to answer your questions more completely."

The next day, Kalronan opened his eyes to the sight of a sea captain, standing with hands clasped behind his back as he looked out the window opposite his bed. At the rustle of the bed sheets, the man turned to him. His tanned face was familiar, though lined with fatigue, heavy with regret as he came to stand next to the bed.

"It's good to see you awake, Ambassador Kalronan." He must have seen the lack of recognition on Kalronan's face. "I'm Captain Micah Vaneer," he said before carefully clasping the arm slowly lifted to him. "I'm glad to see one more saved from the madness at Kittric."

Vaneer's voice was clear and sharp, Kalronan noted thankfully. "I guess I owe you my life," he whispered in reply. "You know me?"

"We've sailed together in the past, and my ship carried you and your team on this mission. I wish there'd been a better outcome." Vaneer sat back. "I'm told you asked about friends." His voice was sympathetic in its direct approach.

"Yes. Four of them, also ambassadors, but dressed in Ishalian clothing . . . like me. Three men, one woman."

Captain Vaneer turned his face toward the window, looking

away for several moments. "We pulled as many from the water as we could find, alive and dead. Mostly ship's crew judging by their clothing and appearance; the first mate and a few seamen also survived."

Vaneer paused before reaching into a pocket. "We did recover two others . . . Ambassador Iro and an unknown man. I'm sorry, but it was too late," he said quietly. "Their bodies were laid to rest at the Temple grounds here."

He waited a moment before continuing. "As to the man, I could not identify the body." He gently placed a small object in Kalronan's uninjured hand. "We took that from his finger for his people. Maybe they'll find some comfort in knowing he rests well."

Clearing his throat, he looked away from the despair that came across Kalronan's face. Then Vaneer stood up slowly, saying, "I'll come back tomorrow. The Sisters know how to reach me if I can help in any way." He didn't wait for an answer.

Kalronan clutched the ring in his hand, remembering how Alon Coronan could make them all laugh.

Vaneer found him lying back in a well-cushioned chair the next afternoon. Kalronan's pale face was turned to the grass-covered hills outside.

"It's good to see you up, Ambassador Kalronan," he remarked quietly as he took a chair next to him.

Pain-filled blue eyes turned to him as a stronger voice replied, "It's Kalen. Thank you, Captain. I appreciate all you've done. Is this your home port?"

Vaneer nodded, reminded that Kalronan's memory had been damaged. "Aye. I've been plying the trade route for several years, many of them with my father, from Kuldor to Caldala mostly, and the islands. Met lots of people over the years." He glanced at Kalronan as he said, "Known you and your Ambassador Core team over the years too. One, in particular, became a good friend." He waited until the man looked at him again.

"Ambassador Elen Arith, he was on this mission," Vaneer

said. He looked down sadly, away from the pain in the survivor's eyes. "Aye, when I recognized you, I knew Arith was among the missing."

"Yes," Kalronan said in a slightly stronger voice. "And Aron Drinin. They were on board the cutter when she blew up, along with the rest of us."

"Arith has a sister he'd talk about a lot," Vaneer continued quietly. "She meant the world to him. Akira Muro. I've known her longest, and she's now bound to another friend, Commander Ardan Isfail. I don't know how to tell her."

Kalronan turned back to look out the window again. "Captain Vaneer . . . is there any chance they might have been picked up by another ship?"

A long pause preceded the end of his hopes as the captain told him, "My ship was the only one nearby. We were anchored outside the bay, hoping to retrieve your team from the *Black Squall*. When the fires began, then spread to the harbor, I had my men ready to take on refugees. Then the insanity began. Only God knows why, but the terrorists got control of a number of vessels, setting them afire before steering them into other ships. They knew what they were about all right," he said bitterly. "It wasn't long before the harbor near the wharfs was nearly impassable.

"I'd been watching the *Black Squall* as she came about, wondering if she'd make it out. Saw her set sails and turn from the dock. But there was a devil ship waiting for her. My ship carries no guns, so we could only watch," Vaneer said with regret. "I put my shore boats in the water as soon as I could, looking for survivors. We couldn't do much though. My ship was the last to leave Kittric that night."

He leaned forward to place a comforting hand on Kalronan's shoulder. "She waits to take you home. Just give me a date to sail." Squeezing the shoulder gently, he stood up and left.

Kalronan listened to the slow steps walk away.

Kittric, Ishal

*A*rith remembered flying through the air before hitting the water. Surfacing, he'd grabbed ahold of one friend, towing his unconscious body the short distance to the muddy bank under the wharf. They'd hidden under the docks while Arith scanned the water for any sign of the other three. Eventually, he'd had to abandon the search as the burning structures above made it too dangerous to stay there.

Avoiding the gangs roaming the streets of this Ishalian hell, the two ambassadors had struggled from shadow to shadow, looking for somewhere to hide. They were grossly outnumbered among the insane people celebrating as they ran through smoke and ashes, brutalizing anyone who tried to flee the madness. Or falling to the ground, tearing at their faces, gouging their own flesh as they screamed in agony before the final death spasms contorted their bodies into the grotesque.

Near dawn, Arith found a stone garden shed nearly buried under the smoldering ruins of the adjacent house. He half carried his barely conscious teammate in before concealing the access with more rubble. With emergency supplies from the packs that had miraculously stayed on their backs throughout the ordeal, he did his best in the light of a carefully shielded dark-lantern to treat wounds from flying wood and metal, burns from exploding gunpowder and the burning oil and debris on the water.

They'd made it this far, but the supplies in their field packs wouldn't last long. Arith thought he could probably scavenge food and clothing from some of the surviving houses. Maybe some sheets or other cloth to use for makeshift bandages. He'd do what he needed to do to get them out of here alive.

Two days later, Arith crouched protectively beside Alon Coronan, scanning the ruins around them and hoping for some sign of help. But the wind moaned through scorched and skeletal buildings, whistled along abandoned streets. Ravens were the only other living creatures, drawn to the bodies all around.

Despair threatened to overwhelm him as he prayed for guidance and his three missing friends.

"I'm not giving up, Elen," Coronan's hoarse voice reproached him. "And you're not either."

"Who says I'm giving up, you idiot?" Arith turned to him with a grin. Careful to keep the anguish from his face as he saw his partner's burns and bandages, he teased, "I might have to leave you at a temple if I can find one. You're slowing me down, friend."

"Not happening," came the determined reply as Coronan struggled to his feet. "Come on." He grimaced painfully. "You're slowing *me* down."

Arith slid an arm under his good shoulder, and they made their slow way through blackened Kittric. For now, they were the only people living in this city of the dead.

Eighty-Seven

Tash'tric, Ishal

How it had it gone so wrong? Felcan wondered bitterly. Had he really been so blind to Abron's fall into madness? It had been so enticing when they'd started talking about taking Ishal for themselves, so many years ago. Abron had laughed away any concerns, teased away his reluctance to recruit malcontents to rebuild his father's cult so they'd have their own army to convince Ishal to follow them.

And it had been exciting, the ease of taking whatever they wanted. The thrill of cultivating a mix of flattery, promises, and subtle threats to manipulate people had been addictive. Somehow Abron had convinced him that Ishal would be better off with them in charge, protecting the people from themselves.

Felcan had never felt any particular altruism toward his fellow man, but he'd recognized that a country had to have a proper government for everyone to prosper. And Dateh had ideas on how that government should be run. They'd seemed like good ideas then, and better than the way Parliament's ministers were running things. They'd been a greedy, corrupt bunch of politicians, just like those ministers seduced by the gilded tongue of old Arthon Baronan.

Surely he and Abron could do a better job, and reap the benefits.

He'd seen the wisdom of instilling distrust against force callers, since they were the only ones who could really defeat them. It was always a mistake to have people stronger than you around, who could turn against you, he'd agreed, even as he privately recognized the irony in that philosophy. And it was another kind of game to see how it could be done. Felcan had enjoyed the deception and the subterfuge. He'd discovered an aptitude for placing agents, planning movements, and organizing attacks by their men in Caldala. There was pride in the skill needed in arranging transportation, and training the more intelligent of their Bowmen for more refined solutions; his own cousin Pelom among them, the earliest one placed in Mountain Shadows.

Kittric had never been a plan he could willingly support. The idea of building a fleet capable of fulfilling Abron's grandiose plans of empire building had sounded ridiculous from the start. So ridiculous that he'd considered it something Abron would play at then toss out. But he'd never imagined it would end up like this.

Felcan tugged at his hair in frustration. He'd just received word about Kittric from the Bowman Dateh had sent out with Gorth. It staggered him—the mental image of Kittric burning, hundreds of people dead in the streets, ships burning at docks, in the harbor. Felcan groaned, pressing the heels of his hands to his eyes, sick in mind and heart.

Not again. But it *was* happening again, just like it had when he was a youth. Only worse. It was madness on a much larger scale.

"Excuse me, sir."

Felcan lowered his hands and looked at Dateh's secretary. "What is it?"

"Lord Dateh is looking for you."

He wanted to shout that Dateh could keep looking for all he cared, but the woman's terrified face kept him silent. Felcan just nodded and took the hall to Dateh's office.

"There you are," Dateh said irritably when he came in. He never bothered with civilities anymore, Felcan noticed with a frown. They were all just tools for him to use, to send out to do his bidding with abject obedience.

"What do you want?"

Dateh glanced up. "I've called in The Bow, and I've received reports that over a thousand have gathered from around the country. They're ready for you to lead them against the traitors in Ishaka. The wagons are already loaded with the explosives, and I've ordered a runner chain along the way so you can keep me informed."

Was he joking? Felcan thought. "A thousand untrained men, men who've never fought together in an organized action? You really think they're ready to move out?"

When Dateh gave him a look of ice-cold disdain, Felcan threw up his hands. "You have no idea what you're doing, Abron! I just heard about Kittric. You killed hundreds of your men, thousands of civilians, and that's not counting the pirates."

"What does that matter?" Dateh replied. "Kittric was a disappointment. I made an example of them. No one will dare fail me now."

Felcan closed his eyes, rubbing his aching temples. "Abron, the way you're going, there won't be anybody left to follow or fail you. What you've done in Kittric will bring down the wrath of neighboring countries. Can't you see you're turning into your father?"

There was silence, and he opened his eyes to see Dateh studying him as if he were something that needed to be stepped on. For the first time, Felcan really believed the man he'd grown up with, the friend he'd done unspeakable things for, would kill him without a second thought.

"I am greater than my father," Dateh hissed. "And all the world will know it. *All* of Ishal is mine. Caldala will be mine. I will surpass my pathetic lord. I will be king!" His voice rising from a low murmur to a high-pitched shriek as he ended, "I will show them all, those *brothers* who think they're more clever, who mock me!"

His eyes focused on Felcan again. "Do *you* mock me, Beros? We swore a blood oath to forever stand by the other. Do you abandon me on the brink of victory?"

Felcan met those black eyes and saw hell-smoke and madness.

For a moment he smelled blood and burning flesh, heard the screams of the damned once more.

He saw his own death.

"Who do we have left to lead the units I'll need to organize?" Felcan asked, in defeated capitulation.

After all, it was a three-day march to the Mounastra River, and the bridge at Estas to the Ishakan territories beyond. A long road, and time enough for a man to disappear along the way.

Ostra River

*A*rith and Coronan found desperately needed shelter at a temple in a small village on the Ostra River a couple days after escaping Kittric. The kindly Brother there concealed them in a hidden room beneath the altar.

"You'll be safe here," Brother Ashan said quietly as he hovered over them with herbal remedies and fresh bandages.

Both men were in poor condition after their hazardous flight from Kittric. But Arith felt his heart sink as he saw their benefactor shake his head sadly over Coronan, praying to a higher power to help heal him.

Over the next days, the man of God nursed them in secret. A strong storm front helped discourage anyone who might take an unwanted interest in activities at the temple.

Brother Ashan was a careful collector of news. One morning he brought word that Dateh's men had been called in to join rebellion forces gathering to attack Ishaka. They were expected to be moving out on the Estas Road within days.

This was bad news for the ambassadors, who'd planned to continue north along the river to the Tasdoras, the major roadway between Tash'tric and the border crossing into neighboring Kuldor. They could travel the Tasdoras until it crossed the Mounastra, the great river whose headwaters spilled from Lower Caldera Lake. Then make their way northwest along the river to the town of Estas, and the bridge there. The Ishakan territories began on the other side of the river. They'd get help and support from Shanow's troops, if they could get to them. But it looked like they'd be heading into a battle zone now.

"We have to find another way out," Arith said with a dispirited sigh.

"We'll continue along the river, cross before the falls."

Arith turned his shaggy head to Coronan. "How are *you* going to make that trip? Your leg won't hold up over that distance."

"Watch me."

Several days passed as they waited for a dark night. Late that night, Brother Ashan led them cautiously through the quiet lanes to a bridge on the other side of the village.

"Good luck, my friends," he whispered, grasping each man's arm in turn.

"Thank you," they replied in unison, then hurried as fast as injuries would allow across the bridge, disappearing into the shadows of the orchards on the far side.

The next night, in a windy rainstorm, they huddled among trees above a farm. They'd only made half the distance they'd hoped to that day.

"Come on. It's too cold to stop here." Coronan's voice trembled.

Arith nodded, his eyes searching the farmyard below. "Yeah, well, we need food, cloaks, and horses. I'm going to see if they're willing to sell."

Silence met this plan, until there was a reluctant, "All right. I've got your back." He huddled on the ground with his bad leg stretched out at an awkward angle, watching his friend make his way stealthily down the low hill to approach the farmhouse. A sudden outbreak of barking was quickly silenced before the door opened. Warm light spilled over Arith as the man on the hill watched.

Half an hour later, the two men rode away; well worn but adequate cloaks fastened around them, and sacks of provisions tied behind the second-hand saddles. The horses were strong farm stock, and they put some distance between them and the rural settlement before the sun rose and it was time to hide.

This set the pattern of their flight as they traveled through Ishal. Hide and rest during the daylight hours, make their way carefully during the dark.

Eighty-Eight

*D*ateh's army began to arrive in Estas a few days after setting out from Tash'tric. Stationed in a tree with a convenient view of the Estas road and the center of the town, Barash watched through the small spyglass Isfail had provided him. First platoon, he thought, or whatever the loose-knit horde called it. He observed long enough to get an initial count, then climbed stealthily down and back along the predetermined route, notifying scouts and Arla's team along the way before mounting the horse they had ready for him to ride to Shanow's encampment.

The news brought an odd sense of relief from the stress of waiting. The enemy was here, the next stage would begin, that much closer to the end of this psychological siege.

As the appointed commander of all military operations, Shanow began rotating militia units out to the valley where they would make their stand. Akira did the same with the ambassadors, coordinating with Isfail and Kilronan on the protectorate teams. For now, there was no sign that the enemy was ready to attack. But messenger falcons were a common sight now as scouts sent regular reports.

Over the next few days, more of Dateh's soldiers arrived, overrunning the town. Barash risked a nighttime solo mission across the river, using the bridge's understructure to make the crossing unseen.

The challenge and the risk thrilled him, as much for the rush of energy and excitement as the unexpected pleasure of using his covert skills in the service of an honorable cause.

That exhilaration faded when he saw Felcan, giving orders to a group of men who appeared more disciplined and savvy than most of Dateh's troops. Creeping silently, keeping to deep shadows, Barash made his way closer.

He hadn't forgotten the dagger in his gut, but he'd save personal revenge for later, after he'd done his job and returned information to his side. But his skin crawled as he heard Felcan talk about laying down explosives.

When he'd learned what he could about their strategy, Barash did a quick search to see if he could locate their weapons, especially the black powder balls. Felcan seemed to have learned his lesson, though. Nothing was stored on the perimeter of the camps. He saw wagons near the center, but couldn't risk checking their contents. If he were caught, this important information wouldn't get to Akira and Shanow.

Furtively making his way to a public house that had been taken over by The Bow's rough soldiers, he climbed to the upper floor and slid his knife under a window frame to work the latch. In seconds, Barash was in the room, quiet as a cat, cautiously opening the door enough to hear the crowd below. A careful hour spent filtering the raucous conversation provided more information from Bowmen talking of the attack plans, and revealed the surprising information that those assembled were the final number.

Barash would have laughed if he'd known Dateh's count of boots on the ground. Instead of the thousand men Felcan had been told about, there were barely half that here. The Ishakan forces equaled that and were far better prepared.

Satisfied with what he'd learned, Barash used the dark after moons-set to get to the bridge, and the beams and rafters of its understructure.

The sun was just a glow between the mountaintops, with a cloud ceiling that once more threatened rain while leadership gathered around a morning fire to review Barash's information again. No one seemed surprised by the news of explosives. It had been another trademark of The Bow's offensive weapons since the first rebellion. But the estimated number of troops was welcomed as a good sign that Dateh's forces were not as numerous or as deadly as reputed.

"It's too bad Barash couldn't get his hands on those bombs," Kilronan said, warming his hands around a cup of hot tea. "His fast thinking, pulling the fuses without Felcan knowing, kept the attack at Psyche Lakes to minimal losses."

Akira looked around the group sitting or standing around the fire. "Where is Barash?"

"He went out before dawn," Isfail replied, settling beside her with his breakfast of smoked ham wrapped in a soft flatbread favored by the Ishakans. "He was planning to scout along the riverbank on this side." He gave Akira a curious look. "You believe I have some latent Psyche ability, my sweet. I'm beginning to think Barash might have something more from his ancestry. He told me he had an itch, something about the river being more accessible than it appeared."

Kilronan crouched beside Akira. "I never heard that old Baronan had force ancestry?"

"He didn't," she remarked coolly. "Barash's mother did. Ana Karsh."

When Kilronan nearly toppled backward, Isfail said nothing, just watched the shock fade on the protectorate warrior's face as he stared at Akira.

"Ana Karsh . . . of course. I should have guessed that, the son of Baronan and Karsh—Barash. Clear as day. Who wouldn't have figured that out?" Shaking his head, Kilronan stood up and walked away.

Akira winked at Isfail, who struggled to suppress his laughter.

As silent and wary as the deer he sometimes came upon among the dripping trees, Barash made his way along the Mounastra. He'd started just below the lower falls of the headwaters, heading down the riverbank in an easterly direction— passing the bridge at Estas without being seen.

He planned to reconnoiter the river to the sharp ridgeline where the forest ended and rapids turned the generally placid flow into a swirling, foaming rush of white water crashing around rocks. No one would hazard a crossing there.

Rain made it wet progress and Barash took care to leave as little trace of his passage as possible, keeping to ways carpeted by thickly fallen leaves or evergreen needles. He'd passed several scouting parties of Ishakans, and been impressed by their superior skills. Not once had he come upon them unaware; they'd always appeared beside him without warning, some giving him a companionable slap on the shoulder when they saw the surprise on his face.

They were a friendly people, Barash mused, thinking he would like to spend time with them after this was over. Maybe, if he proved himself, he would ask Kane to petition the tribal council, see if they would allow him to learn from them.

Despite his thoughtful musings, Barash's eyes were sharp and constantly alert for anything suspicious. Now he stopped, conscious that something wasn't right. He only heard normal sounds—birds with their subdued rainy day fluttering, and the irritated chatter of two squirrels squabbling over territory. But he held still and stretched all his senses.

Scanning the ground, he noticed that leaves were displaced, as if they'd been kicked aside by careless footfalls. Slowly, he followed the signs. Two of them, he thought, moving hurriedly. They'd come from somewhere in front of him, then turned back at the point he'd picked up the trail.

It was fresh—the rain that was now falling in fast, fat drops had not had time to flatten the disturbed leaves again. Now there was only the patter of rain through the foliage, the drip and splat of water on the ground. The wildlife had gone silent.

Keeping close to wet tree trunks, Barash slithered between them like an eel among waterweeds until he heard the sounds people made. He knew they weren't any of his people. They made an attempt to keep quiet, but obviously had no skill in it.

Sliding down to hands and knees, Barash crept along until

he saw three men standing on the riverbank. A flat-bottomed rowboat was tied to a tree, and he could make out their intentions. They were winding a much thicker rope around the large trunk of an old mountain oak.

They were setting up a ferry crossing. Barash shifted until he could see across the river, nodding to himself as he saw the solid-looking raft being hefted down the shallow slope of the opposite bank. He estimated it would probably carry twenty troops at a time.

Felcan was probably planning to flank the defenders, distracting them with what looked like a frontal assault while secretly sending in soldiers downriver. Crouching lower, he peered through the undergrowth. Three men here now, but were there others? He didn't think Felcan would underestimate Shanow; he'd expect there would be scouting parties. Had he sent more men ahead of this work team to clear the way?

The familiar cry of a messenger falcon told him that someone else had discovered the Bow's intrusion and was alerting leadership. None of the men working on the ferry mooring paid any attention to the bird.

More men had appeared on the far bank. He needed to work fast, Barash realized. It looked like they were about to launch their raft. The men here seemed to be satisfied with their work; one raised an arm to the group across the river, while the other two untied the boat and began to row back.

Without a sound, the two in the boat were struck by arrows, slumping lifeless as the boat turned with the river's current and floated toward the rapids. Shouts rose from the opposite bank as the remaining man looked frantically about him as he edged into the trees.

"Bad decision," Barash whispered close to his ear before slitting his throat.

"Quiet work," Ton commended, appearing silently behind him, and pulling a larger blade from its sheath. "We need to cut the rope." He gestured briefly toward the laden raft being pulled hand over hand across the river.

"Both of us can't be shielded by that tree," Barash muttered, holding out his hand for the knife. "Cover me." He glanced at the bow slung over Ton's shoulder. "You have the range with that."

Ton nodded, and in one smooth sequence had an arrow nocked and the bowstring pulled taut. "Go."

Sprinting low, Barash reached the oak. Using the trunk for protection, he began sawing through the rope. Ton's knife sliced deep with each pass and soon the twisted strands were parting in audible snaps. Risking a glance at the river, Barash saw that the raft had reached the midpoint, putting their archers within range.

Ton's bow twanged and one of the men pulling the raft along dropped. Two more arrows flew from the forest, taking down two more. But arrows flew at them now as the enemy retaliated.

"Don't let them nick you," Barash reminded Ton, sweat streaming into his eyes as he sawed faster, then flinched as an arrow sliced the tree trunk, barely missing his shoulder. He heard Ton chuckle just ahead of another snap of his bow.

Barash watched as the weakened rope seemed to stretch, and ducked just in time to avoid a nasty lash from a flying end as it parted violently. Pressed against the tree, he listened to the enraged curses of the thwarted Ishalians.

Dashing back to Ton's position, he watched with satisfaction as the raft spun out of control. Arrows from this side continued to pick off Bowmen, until those remaining chose the river over the deadly accuracy of Ishaka's archers.

Ton grinned at Barash, and started to speak until a shrill bird cry came from the east. "Trouble," Ton said, dashing off with Barash close behind. Another tribesman silently joined them in their race through the trees.

Barash and Ton split left and right when an archer burst through the trees ahead of them, his Black Arrow piercing the air between them to imbed itself in a tree. Slamming his body into the Bowman, Barash took him to the ground in a headlock that broke the attacker's neck. Ton and his fellow scout had run ahead, toward the sounds of fighting.

Arriving in time to see Arla thrust a Black Arrow into the last standing Bowman, Barash flashed her a grin that immediately died as he saw the arrow piercing her thigh. Ton grabbed her as she fell and Barash rushed over, already pulling one of the antidote vials from his pocket while she began to gasp.

"Drink it!" he ordered, his hand supporting her neck as he saw fear in the protectorate master's eyes. He looked into them as he emptied the vial into her mouth. "Swallow. You'll live."

From the corner of his eye, he saw Ton jerk the arrow out. Blood gushed with it and Arla's assistant master, Halen, immediately clamped both hands around her thigh, shouting for a tourniquet. Still looking into Arla's pain-filled eyes, Barash yanked a length of wide leather from around his waist, flipping it to Ton.

Arla was breathing in rapid pants now, but in response to the pain; the antidote was working. Barash eased her head onto the lap of one of her teammates. Looking around the scene of the fight, he suddenly felt light-headed, with sweat running down his face.

As he swiped a forearm across his brow, he knew how close it had been. A minute later, Arla would have died of poison or bled out.

"Thanks," a hoarse but amazingly unruffled voice said.

Barash looked back at her. "Any time."

Arla gave the slightest smile. "Thanks again, but I'd rather have a strong drink."

Her teammates laughed in relief, and Barash's grin returned. "Yeah. Me too."

He stood up and left her to the care of her people while a horse was retrieved to get her back to camp.

Five bodies lay around them, six counting the one he'd killed a few feet away. Now he was concerned about how many others had boated over before that crossing point was discovered.

As if he knew his thoughts, Ton walked up, saying, "My scouts are sweeping the area. The one who stayed at the river to make sure no one from the raft made it to our bank has reported to me."

Nodding, Barash looked over while Arla was helped onto

a horse. She wobbled a little in the saddle but quickly steadied herself. That was one tough woman, he thought as he turned back to Ton.

"I'll help sweep."

"My scouts are many and we won't be caught by surprise again. Take Master Arla back now. She needs Syrai and Akira as soon as possible to save that leg. They will be ready for her."

Barash looked up as a messenger falcon took to the sky with rapid wing strokes.

*I*n Estas, Felcan listened, grim faced, as one of his lieutenants reported on the defeat at the attempted ferry crossing. That had been the easiest point on the river for such an operation, yet it was a complete failure. They hadn't even been able to save the raft, which had broken up in the rapids just downriver.

"How many soldiers were lost?" he asked again.

"Twenty-six, sir," the lieutenant repeated, adding, "Likely another six, with the men who'd gone into the woods to reconnoiter. The Ishakans were on us so fast I can't see any of those men making it back. They're dead or captured by now."

Felcan rubbed the back of his neck. "No use trying that again. We know they're scouting the riverbanks and they're well organized."

"Yes, sir."

Seeing the relief on the man's face, Felcan nearly laughed. He was probably thankful that he wasn't reporting to Dateh, at risk of having his head taken off—literally.

"What do you think our chances are of winning this battle, Lieutenant?"

Now there was surprise on his face, Felcan thought, meeting the man's cautious look.

"Sir?"

Lifting his shoulders in a shrug, Felcan sat back on one of the crates of black powder bombs stacked in the commandeered barn to keep dry. "I'm asking for your opinion. You're one of the few here who has militia experience, a good head on his shoulders, and some guts, enough to report to me as soon as you returned."

The man took a few minutes to think about it. "Well, sir, I think our chances of winning are no more than even, but personally, I'd bet on the Ishakans with the men we've got to work with."

Felcan smiled, relaxing. "And if I told you we're also facing three units of Ishalian militia who have planted themselves across the river to defend the people and the territories?"

The man actually paled, but he still spoke his mind. "Then, sir, I'd say this is a suicide mission."

Felcan stood and clapped a hand on his shoulder. "Yes, it is—unless we can cook up something they're not expecting. If I were you, I'd be finding out how long it takes to get to the capital of Kuldor, Lieutenant."

He walked toward the bridge in the rain, leaving the soldier staring after him, and wondered why he wasn't taking his own advice.

Eighty-Nine

Returning from their own scouting mission, one to find optimal positions for Team Kilronan to provide flanking support, Kilronan noticed the increased activity in camp. He wondered if the Ishakan scouts had brought back news that had stirred things up while they'd been out.

Those suspicions grew when he saw Akira striding toward them as they reached the horse paddock.

"What's the news?" he asked as he dismounted quickly, handing his reins to Asura.

"There was an incident in the forest earlier," she told him, including the others in her telling. "Some of Dateh's men came across the river by boat, and there was a skirmish with one of our scout teams. The Bowmen were all killed. We'll talk about in more detail in a little while." She met Kilronan's eyes. "Let your team get something to eat while there's time."

Turning over the horses to the militiamen on support duty, Kilronan's team headed toward the large tent used as a dining hall.

Akira took Kilronan's arm, deliberately steering him in another direction. He saw that they were headed toward the tent set up as an infirmary and frowned.

"Some of our people were hurt in that skirmish?"

She nodded, walking faster as the rain intensified. "Only one major injury when the team was ambushed, and that's been seen to." She paused under the vestibule. "But there was a lot of blood loss so she'll be laid up for a while."

"She?"

"Aiden," Akira said quietly, laying a hand on his arm. "It was Arla's team that was attacked. She took a Black Arrow in the left thigh."

For a moment, he searched her sympathetic eyes then Kilronan pushed through the tent flaps and rushed inside.

He didn't see Akira step in after him, a smile in her eyes now as she watched him drop to one knee beside Arla's cot.

*H*er face was too white against the bright braid of hair lying over her shoulder, Kilronan thought, his heart pounding as he saw her closed eyes and still form. Akira's words echoed in his mind—*blood loss, Black Arrow*—and he gripped the slender hand lying so still on the sheet. Warm, he breathed out in relief, and strong as her long fingers wrapped around his.

"What are you doing here?" Her voice sounded sleepy, and a little annoyed. It made him smile.

"What the hell are *you* doing here?" Kilronan retorted. "We could use every warrior we've got and you're lying down on the job?"

Scowling now, Arla released his hand, pushing it aside before rising up on her elbows. "I'll do my job, Kilronan. Now get your fine a—"

He cut off the insult by grabbing her to him and into a fierce kiss, relief and passion boiling out in equal measures until he felt her mouth respond to his, her arms locking tight around his neck.

When they eventually moved back from one another, Kilronan wasn't sure who was the most surprised. But he'd started it, and he knew now he wasn't about to end it.

Arla sat up on her cot, wrapping her arms around one bent knee as she studied him with a cautious smile. "Maybe I should get shot more often."

He heard the question underlying the amusement. "Seems like a hard way to get a kiss." Kilronan cleared his throat, suddenly unsure how to go on.

"Not really, as long as I have a master healer to make it all go away." Stretching out both long limbs under the blanket, she patted the injured thigh in an evident attempt to make light of all this. "I've always thought my legs were my best attraction."

Kilronan coughed, feeling heat rise up the back of his neck. "You've got great legs, all right, but the rest of you makes a man look every time."

Tipping her head, Arla gave him a cynical look. "You're in a fine mood, Kilronan. Now why don't you get out and do something useful. It's been entertaining," she began and saw his expression shift. She sighed, glancing away. "Sorry, I know you were worried for me. If you want the truth, I was scared, really scared I was going to die." She linked fingers with him when she felt him take her hand again.

"The arrow strike was the least of it. They just kind of ran into my patrol, neither group expecting the other." Arla frowned.

"Stupid," he heard her mutter.

"I should have been on alert, but . . ." She shrugged. "We engaged immediately, faster than they did. Knives and hand-to-hand took three down fast. Then one of them gets off an arrow, hitting the ground right next to me. I'm too damn cocky to pay attention to the other one at the edge of the clearing, because I'm grabbing for the arrow to use on them."

She rubbed the wounded leg through the covers. "I feel the strike and the force of it nearly takes me down just as one of them rushes me." She smiled a little now. "He got a Black Arrow in his gut. But I'm no better off, already feeling my lungs shutting down. Then there's a crowd around me, Ton's scouts and Barash all coming to the rescue."

Looking up, she met Kilronan's serious eyes. "If they hadn't, I'd be dead, Kil. Barash already had the antidote in his hand, ordering me to swallow it. I never even thought of going for mine."

She took a deep breath. "So lay off the guy."

"Friend for life," Kilronan assured her, squeezing her hand. "As long as he knows you're mine." He watched her eyebrows shoot up and laughed. "We'll talk about it when this is done."

"Oh, we'll definitely talk about it, you idiot," Arla replied, yanking her hand free to grab his jacket. Nearly unbalancing him as she jerked him to her, she met his mouth with hers.

Near Estas

*A*rith decided they needed to give up the horses. They were close to the large town of Estas, where the only surviving bridge to the northern territories crossed the Mounastra. There was little hope of riding across unnoticed. As they'd feared, Dateh's Bowmen had reached it before them and taken control of this important crossing point between Ishal and the Ishakan territories.

Garbed in the rough clothing of an Ishakan farm hand, with shaggy hair tied back in the local way and unshaven face, Arith risked the farmer's market to barter the horses for heavier clothing and goods to restock their packs. He'd left Coronan well hidden, knowing his injuries would attract too much attention.

Arith wandered the market, carefully gleaning important information from the local chatter. He strolled with apparently idle interest along the river to survey the bridge before making his way back to his companion.

As Coronan hungrily wolfed down the meat pie Arith had procured, he asked between bites, "What did you find out?"

"Tough. It's going to be tough," Arith said in frustration. "They've got the bridge heavily guarded. It's a long span here, remember?"

"Yeah."

They ate silently for a while.

"What about a boat?"

"Doubtful," Arith replied. "Lots of attention along the moorings. It would be hard to get at one with the villagers threatened by the Bowmen. I don't think it's a good risk to approach someone about taking us across."

There was more silence, broken only by the congested cough that now shook Coronan's emaciated body.

"Then we swim."

"You're crazy." Arith shook his head, leaning back and biting into an apple. "The river's fast and wide here."

"Not here. Let's go west. It narrows as it comes down the mountains."

Arith stared in disbelief at what he was hearing. "That fever is affecting your brain. How are you going to get that far in the shape you're in? And that's white water coming off the mountains. You can't get across that."

He watched the determined set to Coronan's mouth as sunken eyes stared into his.

"*I'm* going back to Evani and Caldala. And you're going to get me there, Commander."

Ninety

S hanow surveyed his troops, hundreds of loyal men and women, Ishalians and Ishakans gathered in fields below. Behind the foothills where he sat on his horse, and safely beyond the battlefield, clusters of tents edged small meadows where black horses grazed, foals romping in the sun—a pastoral vision of peace, if one ignored the signs of war.

He let himself visualize the faces of his wife, his children, and prayed that he would be a part of returning their country to them. To finally rid Ishal of the blight of Baronan's poisonous legacy of greed and death. To ensure a strong government that would stand for all rightful citizens of Ishal.

When Isfail rode to the top of the rise, Shanow turned with a solemn greeting. "We have fair weather, Commander."

"Perhaps I wouldn't mind a few thunderstorms," Isfail reminded him as he reined his horse in.

Shanow smiled. "And how is your remarkable wife?"

"Optimistic," Isfail replied, returning a smile. But Shanow saw the shadow in his eyes.

He'd feel worry, too, if it was his Mirastheny here, lunams pregnant with their first child, preparing to wage force battle against the enemy. What was it like, Shanow wondered, to share life with a woman like Akira Muro? How did you live that life knowing that an army built by a madman sought her death and the elimination of her people?

But then, maybe it explained why these Caldalans would risk their lives for the Ishakan people. All force-gifted stood together against those who would end them. And the House of Coroth had chosen to stand with them. Shanow admired Prince Logran's courage in taking that position. The man risked a great deal politically.

Gaios Shanow could only wish that Ishal had had such strong leadership. Maybe they would not now be fighting this evil that had infected too many in his country. That need to rebuild Ishal into a strong and honorable country had led him to deploy his militia to the wide valley where they would make their stand.

Dateh's army was expected to cross the Mounastra any day now.

"Was I right in validating the plans we made? Should we have taken the fight to Estas?" he asked aloud, surprised by his own question. But Isfail's answer was calm and succinct.

"You made the right decision," Isfail replied. "This has to end now. We all agreed that attacking Estas would only scatter them. Most of the Bowmen have little real fortitude or allegiance, but they could reform and cause trouble again another time, just as they did for Dateh. Making them come to us puts the offense squarely on them and brings them into a battle they can't win." He looked at Shanow with storm-dark gray eyes. "Don't regret the decision to take no prisoners. They have no such compassion, I promise you."

Shanow returned a grim smile as he sat straighter in the saddle. "No, they don't, and no honor." His gaze returned to the soldiers drilling in the field. "Barash confirmed the presence of Ishalian militia soldiers in Dateh's army. At least fifty, judging by those in uniform."

He looked at Isfail, saying, "I can only be sure of my own unit. Are there traitors embedded in the two platoons that joined us here? Waiting for a vulnerable moment to strike from within?"

"I guess we'll find out," Isfail replied after a long moment. "We'll just have to be ready for anything. Personally, I don't think Dateh's Bowmen stand a chance."

Shanow knew his troops were ready. The combined militia units had trained throughout the winter and they were a superb fighting force, joined by two elite protectorate teams from

Caldala. With force callers and archers from the horse tribes surrounding the fighting grounds on the ridges and cliffs rising above Shanow's troops, they were even more formidable.

And then there was Akira Muro.

No, Shanow thought with an easier mind, Dateh's army didn't stand a chance in the Battle for Ishaka.

S itting on his horse in the middle of the Estas Bridge, Beros Felcan was reminded of the foothills and forests of his family estates east of Lake Takal—beauty and despair.

He'd met Abron Baronan there. They'd become friends, hunted together, been schooled together. And they'd comforted one another in the dark times, the shame-filled times, when there was no one else who cared.

What had happened to the boy he'd spent his youth with, as close as brothers as they shared secrets and dreams? The secrets had bound them to one another. The dreams had led to this nightmare.

Powerless in their youth, they'd watched Lord Baronan reel Lord Felcan into his plot to become Master of Ishal. The failed rebellion had taken both their lives. Hiding in the desolate hunting cabins to escape the aftermath, Abron had determined that they would succeed where his father had not. And Beros had warmed his cold misery in the fires of his only friend's obsession, believing they would triumph and life would be all they hoped for. He'd helped raise a new army of Bowmen by selling his inheritance, his lands; even drawing his only cousin in as their first soldier of the new Bow.

He'd even accepted the brand in a drunken moment—a pledge of fidelity and shared pain. Now Abron would order his death without any feeling of remorse.

He wondered again why he was here. He could turn around and ride on to Kuldor. Why not? What did he owe an old friend who'd become his father's son in every way?

Taking up the reins, he urged his horse around and back to where his army—a ridiculous term for this rabble of fools—was making final preparations to attack. Felcan saw the lieutenant he'd spoken with the day before, giving orders to the men in charge of a wagon carrying half of their explosives.

Why hadn't he left in the night, taken the road to Kuldor himself, as Felcan had suggested? Was he a fool or a martyr? Did he believe in The Bow, in Dateh's right to rule? Or was he just a resolute soldier, who would stand with those he'd signed on with, right or wrong? Seizing the only honor he could ever claim in this doomed venture.

With a sardonic twist of the mouth, Felcan decided that was as good an answer as he was ever going to get. After all, he really had nothing left to live for. Lifting his right arm high, he gave the signal to form up, listening to a horn sound for all to hear and obey.

*A*kira stood on a low outcropping, letting the waterfall's roar fade into the background. Shanow's militia was arrayed in crisp formation below her, with Aric's unit in flanking positions closer to the road through the trees. Dateh's army would have to take that road to move quickly.

She didn't think they'd try to burn the forests, though fire was a favorite weapon of The Bow. In this case, it wouldn't do anything to benefit their assault, and could actually work against them if it hemmed them in between a forest fire and the Ishakan defense. And even if they were so inclined, Kilronan's water benders, Maronan and Asura, were prepared to utilize the river to quench the flames.

She smiled to herself, remembering Kilronan's protective hovering over Arla last night until his fellow master tired of it and yanked him down to sit beside her. Akira hoped they would soon resolve the feelings each had been dancing around for lunams and enjoy one another.

A flurry of cotton-ball kicks brought soft laughter. She was beginning to understand how her own emotions often had her child responding in some fashion. Whether it was little bursts of movement or impressions translated into mental nudges, the baby was increasing its deliberate interaction with her. Whenever possible, Akira shared some of those moments with Isfail.

Sighing, Akira wished for this to move on, to be over. She was ready to go home, whether Mountain Shadows or Coroth. Ready to enjoy this miracle of pregnancy, and leisurely prepare for the birth of her baby. She enjoyed sharing these thoughts and feelings with Syrai, who not only had her own experience to share, but was eagerly awaiting her first grandchild.

Having her good friend, Evani Reva, here was also a comfort, and it added an amusing element when Reva took a proprietary stance and declared that she was going to be the one to help deliver Akira's baby, so Akira and Isfail better plan to set up their household back in Coroth.

All these personal musings vanished when she saw several falcons erupt from the trees, winging rapidly back to the command base.

Looking down the ridge to her left, Akira met Syrai's gaze. Dateh's army had begun their march.

Ninety-One

They didn't fire the trees—they blasted them with explosives. Prepared for the Ishakans to ambush his troops as they passed between thick stands of concealing forest, Felcan ordered a demolition crew to precede the main ranks.

With the wagon horses and men outfitted with bulky leather coverings designed to deflect arrows, the munitions wagon charged from the bridge. The Bowmen immediately began lighting fuses and flinging their black powder bombs. The resulting explosions splintered and toppled trees, sending wildlife running or flapping away.

The defenders had anticipated something like this once the enemy learned there were scouts watching the river. Patrols had been withdrawn to more defensible grounds.

This included a narrow ridge tapering down from the mountain range, and edging the riverbank from the falls. As the wagon passed below them, Ton, Arla, Declan, and Barash shot flaming arrows into the crates it carried, and any of the men they could hit.

Dateh's leaders might have prepared armor for men and horses, but they hadn't thought about the possibility of fire in the munitions crates. Bowmen scrambled to yank out arrows and put out fires, but the warriors on the ridge continued their assault. Soon there were too many flaming arrows for the surviving men to deal with. The frightened horses snorted and thrashed until they broke the wagon tongue in their panic, dragging it with them when they pulled free and galloped away down the road. The men threw themselves out of the wagon just before it exploded in a whooshing roar.

The final rumbling booms of noise and smoke had Shanow's soldiers yelling a battle cry while they rushed toward the trees.

G ritting his teeth as he stared at the wreckage smoldering in the road and scattered in flaming debris amid the splintered trees around them, Felcan cursed the pitfalls of what had seemed like a damn good plan. Shouting to the forward ranks to fall back across the bridge, he reassessed his approach amid the smoke and stink of burnt powder.

With some of his best archers beside him, Felcan scanned the rocks above, where he'd seen the flaming arrows fly from. The next time one of those archers appeared, his men would end their resistance. But no targets showed themselves before the sound of advancing soldiers sent Felcan and his men retreating to Estas.

It might have warned him about what was in store, but Felcan was too enraged by this failure and the loss of so many bombs to think about it. Shadows were lengthening in the late afternoon, and he wasn't going to follow this failure with an ill-advised night campaign against a superior militia.

Ninety-Two

ith soldiers providing cover and scouts watching the bridge and riverbanks, tribesmen put out the fires. There was discussion between the military leaders about clearing the road. In the end, it was the general consensus that anything that hindered their enemy's movements was best left alone.

However, the discovery of several unexploded bombs among the wagon debris was a different matter. There was talk of using one to destroy the others, but some of the officers suggested that they could be gathered up, perhaps used against The Bow, if needed. Though Shanow and Isfail shared a strong distaste for these indiscriminate tools of war, they agreed. Cautiously, a couple of Aric's more experienced soldiers took great care in raking them away from any hot spots to cool thoroughly before being collected.

Commander Aric assigned his men to watch duty at the road and bridge, coordinating with Ishakan scouts to cover night duty. The captain from the late Commander Goden's unit volunteered his soldiers to rotate watches with them. Satisfied that they'd be forewarned if Dateh's army tried again, Shanow returned to the command base with Isfail by his side.

When they reached the main camp, the commanders found a small celebration taking place, not all to do with their success at repelling the first attack on Ishaka. A new shipment of supplies had arrived, including several barrels of ale, courtesy of Jor Kellen, the owner of the *Boar and Panther* pub in Mountain Shadows.

Isfail grinned at Shanow. "Should we count this timely largess as a sign of things to come?"

After looking around at the hopeful faces of his soldiers, Shanow eyed the barrels, calculating their potential for inebriation. "Looks like enough for everyone to raise a toast and wet their throats while keeping a clear head for battle." He raised a hand to still the cheers. "Captain Declan will oversee an orderly distribution. Remember, the real fight is still to come, so keep sharp. Keep to your duty schedules or you'll answer to me."

Shanow and Isfail went on to the mess tent where Kilronan, Arla, and Halen were sitting with unexpected visitors—Master Mika and her team from Mountain Shadows. Introductions were made for Shanow's sake then Isfail said, "I hadn't heard that Lord Corcoran was sending us a third team."

Looking uncomfortable, Mika explained, "No. We were on border watch with Team Cobon and Team Vardon when supplies arrived from the valley without prior notification. There weren't enough people from your side to handle it, especially the extra barrels. I volunteered my team to help bring them on."

She glanced at Kilronan and Arla. "We heard an explosion when we were off-loading the raft. I thought you might need more warriors."

Halen grinned at her. "Looks like The Bow needed the help, but thanks for coming."

Seeing Arla's brow furrow, Isfail wondered if Halen was heading for a reprimand.

"Where's Akira?" he asked Kilronan.

"With Syrai, in the infirmary tent." Kilronan stood up, stretching out his back. "I think they're reviewing today's action and response."

Shanow uncrossed his arms. "I'll join them."

Turning back to the protectorate group, Isfail found Mika watching Shanow as he left the tent. "Will your team be returning soon, Mika?" He thought he saw a glimmer of resentment in her dark eyes when they shifted to him. But it was gone in a flash as she gave him a brief nod.

"Yes. I thought we'd get what news we can to take back to Lord Corcoran."

"Give him my regards," Isfail replied in an easy manner. "And thanks for the assist." Walking from the tent, he listened as the retelling of today's attack begin again, and tried to resolve the feeling of something not quite right.

"Wait up," Kilronan called, coming out behind him. Isfail saw him look over toward the fires where several soldiers were laughing and joking together, enjoying mugs of ale.

"Good of Master Kellan," Isfail said.

"It is," Kilronan agreed. "Want to go commandeer a cask?"

Isfail chuckled but shook his head. "I'll wait until this is finished, thanks."

They joined Shanow, Akira, Kane, and Syrai in the infirmary tent, currently empty of patients. Taking a seat next to his wife, Isfail glanced around the group, and saw that Barash was seated on a cot in the shadows. Lifting a hand in greeting, Isfail guessed the man was keeping a closer eye on Akira now that the enemy had made their first move.

"Seems a little tame for a first assault," Kilronan said.

"We were just talking that over," Shanow agreed, nodding to Declan as the captain came in. "What's the mood of the troops?"

Declan grinned. "Between the early rout of the enemy and the ale, they're in a fine mood. I sent an untapped keg to Commander Aric's patrol in the forest. No reason they shouldn't share a toast. It should be enough for all the men rotating through there tonight."

Looking around the small group, Isfail noticed that the mood was more solemn than the soldiers' outside. Akira met his gaze, saying, "I don't know what to believe at this point. Barash says Felcan was leading that advance. I doubt he'll give up so soon."

"As long as we keep discipline and eyes sharp, we have the advantage," Shanow replied. "From Barash's and our scouts' observations, most of their fighters aren't trained men."

Shanow stood up, signaling Declan. "Still best not to lower

our guard. There are some militia traitors among them. We'll take a last turn around the sentry posts, and make sure the troops are ready for whatever comes next."

As the others rose and separated—Syrai and Kane to talk to Ton and check with the tribesmen posted here, and Kilronan to do the same with the protectorate teams—Isfail and Akira left the tent with Barash, making their way toward the large cave that served as living quarters for the Caldalan contingent.

Barash paused before they started up the rocky path, looking back at the people leaving the dining tent. Mika and her team split off, waving their farewells as they jogged off in the direction of the old pass. Arla and her team walked toward the men handing out the ale.

"Problem?" Isfail asked, feeling Akira's hand tighten on his arm.

"That new protectorate team," Barash said stiffly. "Seems strange they're just going back to Caldala, not staying to fight."

Akira ran a hand down his back. "They're not here officially, as I heard it. Just helping deliver the supplies."

"So they say," Barash muttered. "I think I'll scout around some. Not tired yet."

They watched him slip off into the shadows before Akira turned to Isfail. "What do you think?"

"I don't know, but I had my own itch earlier tonight, while I was talking to them. Nothing I can put a reason to. Did Kilronan say anything?" Isfail asked.

Akira shook her head. "I didn't speak with Mika's team myself, so I didn't catch anything out of the ordinary." She looked toward the fires and the people gathered around them, the quiet tents where others slept, the platoons standing ready near the perimeter. Everything seemed to be as it should be.

"Let's get some sleep. Dawn will come soon enough, and I don't believe Dateh's army will be far behind." Isfail took Akira's hand to lead her up the stony path. "We'll post a double watch on the cave tonight."

But Reva had already set Micharon on first watch with one of

Shanow's soldiers when they approached the narrow cave mouth. He greeted them quietly, passing on the watch rotation for the night. Satisfied, Akira and Isfail found their own sleeping nook by the dim light of multiple lanterns placed around the wide interior.

With a tired sigh, Akira welcomed Isfail's arms around her.

*B*y the time Barash reached the lake, Master Mika's protectorate team was already aboard the raft, dark figures in the night shadows of the cliff face. He watched from his own cover as the Ishakan tribesman on duty pulled them across using the improvised ferry rope, until they reached the rough landing on the far side. Shortly after, he could make out climbers, shades of black on black, moving up the cliff.

When he saw the lone ferryman returning, Barash turned back, ready to make his final patrol of their perimeter. Silently, he jogged down the little valley until he could slip into the forest to check on Aric's men.

Ninety-Three

*I*nside the fortified outpost on the ridge, Cobon looked up from his chair by the warm hearth when Vardon came in. "Ready to change shifts, lad?"

"Ready for some sleep," Vardon said, dragging off a wool cap. "Mika's men just returned, so we're nearly at full count."

Cobon rose and stretched, nodding as his own team came into the common room, ready for duty. Then he turned back to Vardon. "What do you mean, nearly?"

Yawning, Vardon lifted his shoulders. "Mika's not back yet. Her assistant master said she wanted to get more details on Dateh's army. They made an unsuccessful first assault this morning." Then Vardon winked at Cobon. "Her second says they're betting she wanted some one on one time with Halen."

Frowning at that, Cobon signaled his team to take their posts. "She'll be looking at a disciplinary action if that's the case, no matter her years in rank. I think I'll go have a few questions answered by her team."

*T*hose years of protectorate training served Mika well as she surveyed the camp, quickly assessing the layout and militia positions. She gave Shanow credit for the tight security. It was going to be difficult to undermine them in a way that wouldn't sound an alarm. If Muro and her force callers were alerted, they'd locate her within minutes.

Once again, she wished for some Black Arrows. Dropping one or two in each keg of ale before they were delivered might have introduced enough poison to kill or incapacitate a large number of soldiers before the ale was suspected.

Mika slipped further back into her hiding place when she saw Kilronan striding her way with his team. She watched as they went past, then turned toward a trail leading up the short ridge behind the main camp. Earlier, she'd heard some comments about the primitive living conditions, something about camping in a cave.

She looked around, searching for Arla's team. There was another she needed to avoid. Arla was sharp and a fierce warrior. The slightest hint of something out of place could draw her attention.

There they were, riding toward the trees. Mika breathed a sigh of relief. She had some time to finish searching out possibilities. Now she saw Commander Shanow, lifting a hand in greeting to Arla's riders as he returned to base camp with another Ishalian commander and a small group of soldiers. They must have a patrol watching the road across the Estas bridge, Mika speculated. Change of duty time.

Could she do something there? Somehow take out that sentry station? Halen had told her that they'd seized several unexploded hand bombs from the morning attack. If she could locate that stash, she could cause some real damage and make it across the bridge to her people, alerting the army of Bowmen to attack while the loyalists were in turmoil.

Searching for her best path across the fields, Mika set off, avoiding the light cast by the moons. She didn't notice the Ishakan scouts in the forest, who watched her jog through faint patches of moonlight along the edge of the empty road. And they, in turn, had no cause for concern over a woman in Caldalan Protectorate uniform following after the team that had ridden by not long before.

Arla nodded to Barash when he walked from the murky forest. "I thought you'd be getting some sleep," she said, offering him a mug of hot tea from the pot by a small fire.

"Soon," he replied, taking the cup but remaining on his feet as he drank, his eyes scanning the soldiers standing alert and watchful about them. "Anything happening across the bridge?"

"Not that we've heard from Aric's men. It's been quiet."

Barash looked at her. "Should I slip over and see what I can find out?"

"No. We'll need you with us whenever they get serious about an attack." She grinned up at him. "And I'm not having my head taken off by Akira if I let you risk yourself needlessly." She chuckled when she saw him stuff his hands in his jacket pockets, ducking his head in his rare tell of discomfiture.

She decided not to tease him more. "Have you had any experience with those explosives, besides removing fuses?"

He shook his head, crouching down to pick up a curved shard of hardened clay. "Ugly business," Barash said. "A blade, an arrow, even your hands, they're more . . . honorable, I guess. At least you know who you're aiming to kill."

"Yes," Arla agreed, glancing over at him. "But now we've got some of them. Personally, I'd rather blow up the lot rather than use them, even against The Bow."

"What about the bridge?" Barash asked. "I haven't heard anyone talk about blowing that apart."

Arla studied him. "It's been brought up, but it's not that simple. When the Mors invaded, people learned they wouldn't cross water. Ishal chose to destroy all their bridges, except the Estas, which was part of the main trade route to Caldala through High Pass."

"There's no open pass now," Barash said.

"But it's the only way for the Ishakans to move freely through Ishal to the coast, for trade and supplies. It takes time and manpower to build a solid bridge across a major river." Arla saw his brow furrow as he considered her words. "We all hope this war will be resolved quickly. One bridge is reasonably defensible."

Arla stood up, looking toward Estas. "You have to weigh the costs versus the value of cutting off access. Besides, I'd rather let the enemy come at me and fight on my ground than end up in a prolonged siege, with endless skirmishes." Kicking at broken pieces of fired clay and shards of wood, Arla murmured. "Better those bombs have been taken back to base."

*M*ika listened from her hiding place nearby, appreciating the pragmatic decision against destroying the bridge. But that could change if this went on too long; she had to get word to Dateh's leadership across the river. Hunkering closer to the ground within a deadfall of trees, Mika waited for a patrolling soldier to walk on. She hadn't seen any sign of the bombs Halen had spoken of, and the warriors here were taking their duty seriously. Even if she was willing to forego an effort to impact Shanow's resistance, she couldn't get across the bridge unseen, if at all.

So close . . . Mika pressed her face into her hands to stifle a moan. All the years, the loneliness, crashed down on her now that she was so close to home. Was Felcan leading the army just across the bridge? Did he even remember her? It had been years since they'd spoken; when he'd encouraged her to join the Caldalan Protectorate services.

It had been Abron's devious cunning that had come up with the idea of seeding Bowmen in the exodus after the failed rebellion, when Ishalians were leaving the war-torn cities seeking a better life in other countries. But it had been her cousin Beros who'd convinced her to go to Caldala.

Mika sank closer to the forest floor, letting the suppressed memories come. She'd been Pelom Felcan then, a devoted acolyte to their dreams of avenging their fathers and building the new order under The Bow. Though Abron Baronan had no use for women warriors, Beros Felcan had convinced him that women would be unexpected spies. And Pelom, with her loyalty to their cause, and skills as a fighter, was the perfect infiltrator.

Beros had even impressed *her* with his zeal, convincing her she was critical to undermining Caldala's border security—it would just take time to rebuild The Bow. So she'd left everything she'd known; Pelom Felcan had become Pelom Mika. Over time, she'd become a respected Protectorate warrior, and earned a place in Mountain Shadows.

And waited for the call to action.

She'd lived among the Caldalans, served the defense service well—all the while a secret outsider, a spy, still waiting to be recalled by her own. Pelom Mika had put up with Ramort when he'd been sent to Mountain Shadows, and the humiliation of being assigned as his assistant. That had been Abron's doing, she knew. Well, that had backfired, hadn't it?

Now it was up to her alone to make the exiled years count.

Cautiously rising up, Mika saw that Arla had moved to speak with a militia captain. Barash was alone by the fire, refilling his cup from the pot there. Time to leave before he returned to the main camp. She'd look around one more time. If nothing better presented itself, she'd try to kill Shanow and other militia officers. That disruption could be enough to give The Bow the advantage.

The moons were lower in the sky when she reached the guarded perimeter. Though clouds covered them intermittently, they still cast enough light to make her even more cautious in her approach. Mika studied the tents from a vantage point behind a boulder. She recognized the dining tent, and the kitchen tent where they'd left the ale barrels. No one had offered to show her team around the camp earlier so she'd have to rely on her own training and experience to guess the rest of the layout.

The large tent closer to the low cliff face was probably the infirmary. The officers were likely set up in the cluster of tents to the west of the small tent city that sheltered the soldiers. Mika shook her head in frustration at the number of soldiers patrolling the entire camp. Then she noticed a number of them gathered close to the ridge to the east.

An ideal location for munitions storage.

It took nearly half an hour to make her way around, avoiding sentry stations. Then she stumbled over the rough ground, wincing as the resulting rattle of stones had a sharp-eared sentry calling out. Before she could run, he was upon her, sword drawn.

To her stunned surprise, he just pulled back, saying, "Sorry,

Master. I didn't realize any of the protectorate people were still about. Thought the frontline warriors were taking the chance to rest." He sheathed his sword while Mika searched for some appropriate reply.

"I'm glad to know you Ishalians are fast to respond," Mika rasped, hoping her voice sounded natural. I'm just taking a last walk around before joining my team." The soldier nodded and stepped back to his post, leaving her to control her pounding heart. But the encounter taught her that most of the Ishalian militia only saw her uniform. Could she use it to her advantage? Continue the long charade of being an ally? Suppressing a baleful sneer, Mika drew on years of pretense as she walked openly toward a shallow cavity in the cliff face.

Her luck held when she saw the small stack of familiar clay balls. They'd been cached on the far side of a thick abutment of stone, well apart from the weapons storage. Shanow and company had evidently not been willing to risk an explosion there, Mika thought while she continued her confident stroll past the soldiers who paid little to no attention to her.

A distraction was needed to liberate the bombs, as many as she could easily carry. She thought that through while she continued in an unhurried manner toward the trail on the west side of camp.

"Mika!"

Ninety-Four

The familiar voice had her freezing in place. Not now, Mika thought, her eyes squeezing shut. Forcing a smile, she blinked them open as Halen rushed toward her. Confusion vied with the pleasure on his face as he reached her.

"I thought you'd gone back," he said, taking her hands in his.

"I did," she replied, a little too forcefully as her mind spun, trying to come up with a convincing story, and found inspiration. "Umm . . . Cobon sent me back. He wanted to know if I could get a couple of those bombs. So our people could see how they're made."

Mika shrugged when Halen stared at her and hurried on, "Look, I said I'd try. If it's not possible, I'll just go back and tell him."

"Seems odd, him asking," Halen said thoughtfully. "Let's check with Arla—"

"No," Mika interrupted, willing a smile onto her face. "Don't bother her. I know you all need to get some sleep. Why are you up?"

"We're just coming off sentry duty on the bridge road. Arla sent me back early to tell Kilronan his team wasn't needed since Commander Shanow sent an extra platoon out. I just finished delivering the message and came down to see if there was any ale left." Halen laughed as he pulled her close. "This is better."

Mika threw herself into the kiss, wrapping her arms around him, wondering if this could be the distraction she needed. She'd never been comfortable with calculated seduction, but Halen had been interested, and an easy conquest. Unfortunately, he hadn't shared, or hadn't had, as much information from the closed seniors' meetings as she'd hoped.

Obviously pleased by her eager response, Halen drew her to a more private spot behind the vacant infirmary tent.

"We could make use of one of the cots inside," he whispered near her ear.

She drew away. "And if someone comes in we'll both be in big trouble. I don't think Senior Master Arla would look the other way, do you? Besides, Cobon expected me to come back quickly. If I'm not getting those bombs, I need to go."

Wincing, Halen shook his head. "You're right." Rubbing the back of his neck, his disappointed expression brightened. "I'll get the bombs and meet you back here. We won't have to waste time answering questions about who you are. Then I'll walk to the lake with you, spend more time together."

Could it really be that simple after all her hours of clandestine wanderings this night? Mika watched him jog away, pondering what would happen if any of the guards mentioned seeing another protectorate warrior recently. And what if the rest of Team Arla returned? She edged around the tent until she could watch the road.

The anxious watch filled the long minutes until she saw Halen coming toward her, his stride relaxed, with a bulging leather pouch slung over his shoulder. He grinned when he reached her.

"Got three. That should satisfy Cobon." He took her hand and led her across the field.

"How'd you do it?" Mika asked, relieved and elated.

"I've gotten to know a couple of the guards who had duty tonight. Just told them the truth—that Caldalan Protectorate Services was interested in studying how they were made." He winked at her. "I think they were relieved to get that many out of camp. Most of these soldiers hate the things."

They entered a thin copse of young trees as they came to the little valley. Mika's thoughts were racing. She needed to get away from Halen and use the explosives. The night felt like it was racing toward morning now, leaving her little time to cripple the resistance here. Sooner or later her luck would run out.

Only three bombs—she'd have to pick the most effective targets for the time she had. Once the first went off, the camp would come alive. She'd have to strike the most important at the start. Maybe she'd have a chance to do more damage in the ensuing commotion.

Should she save one of her bombs to take out the others, to prevent them from being used against The Bow? No. She'd try to kill as many warriors as possible. If she made it to the munitions, she'd use those bombs to inflict as much damage as she could.

The roar of the waterfalls was louder now, reminding her time *was* running out. None left to somehow detach herself peacefully from Halen. Mika strengthened her will—she was a Bowman, he was the enemy—overruling the feeling of abhorrence for what she was about to do.

Steeling herself, Mika carefully released the narrow blade from her right wrist gauntlet. "Halen?"

He turned to her with a smile on his lips that died when her blade slid high between his ribs. Already reaching for the pouch as his knees buckled, Mika gasped at the speed of his reaction. Halen jerked the knife from his chest and struck out, slashing her forearm to the bone even as his rage-filled eyes emptied in death.

Sobbing in shock and pain, Mika knelt to work the leather pouch off the dead man's arm. Her right hand and forearm were covered in blood and nearly useless. She grabbed at a clay ball that rolled from the pouch with her left. Putting it back with the other two, Mika lifted the strap over her head with shaking hands.

Fighting down her panic, she grabbed the knife from the ground and sliced off a strip of Halen's shirt, using it to wrap around her wounded arm to stanch the flow of blood. Without another look at the lover she'd murdered, Mika stumbled back toward the camp.

*A*rla noticed the couple entering the little valley as she led her team back into camp. She thought the taller one was Halen, with moonlight reflecting off his sand-colored hair. Was that Mika with him? What the hell was she doing back here? Swearing under her breath, Arla began devising ways to discipline her wayward assistant master. He'd be lucky to maintain his rank, or his position on her team. And she'd be filing a formal complaint against Master Mika when all this was over.

Sliding from the saddle, she waved off the tribesman who offered to see to her horse before seeing to the mount herself. Tending to the gelding should burn off some of her annoyance. Arla sent the rest of her team on to get some rest while she stripped the saddle off.

She'd just finished brushing the horse down when Kilronan spoke behind her. "What's got you steamed up?"

Arla looked back over her shoulder. "Did Halen deliver my message?"

"Less than a hour ago," Kilronan answered, watching her curiously. "I haven't seen him since then. What's the matter?"

Turning her gelding into the paddock, Arla huffed as she slipped the latch rope over the gatepost. "I think he went off with Mika."

"Mika?" Kilronan repeated in surprise, walking with her toward the ridge trail. "Didn't Mika's team go back to the pass hours ago?"

Her eyes hard, Arla looked in the direction of the lake. "That's what I thought, but Halen was walking with someone in dark clothing, tall but not as tall as Barash."

"Barash joined us in the cave over an hour ago. He appeared to be sleeping when I came out," Kilronan said.

They started up the rise as Arla continued, watching the uneven path as they climbed. "Who else would— Kil," she said abruptly, pointing at the ground.

They both crouched to get a better look at the dark blotches marking the trail. Running a finger through the viscous substance, Arla met Kilronan's intent eyes. "Still wet."

Like matched runners off a mark, they sprinted up the trail.

*A*bove them, Mika heard the pounding footfalls and shouts of warning. Time's up, she thought, fumbling with the torch taken from those set to light the way to the cave. She'd managed to reach a place just above the cave entrance before being spotted. Now she crouched, lighting one fuse, then another as two militia guards scrambled up toward her.

Hearing voices from the cave, Mika stood up, a sputtering bomb in each hand.

Kilronan and Arla skidded to a halt as they saw her—a blood-streaked demon in the shifting torchlight, her face twisted in defiance as Mika tossed a hissing ball of death. Shooting up his hands, Kilronan sent a shield at the cave mouth, deflecting the first bomb back up the rise behind Mika. Simultaneously, Arla threw her knife with deadly accuracy.

Mika staggered with the blade buried in her chest before deliberately falling onto the bomb still clutched in her hand.

The night lit up when the two bombs exploded, setting off the third still in the leather pouch. Shock waves blasted Kilronan and Arla down the sloping ridge. The explosions killed one militia guard outright before the second was crushed in the rock fall that followed.

*I*nside the cave, awakened by the shouts outside, Isfail bolted up at the same time Reva's team ran to cover the cave entrance. In the dim light, he saw the protectorate warriors grabbing up weapons. One of the militia guards ran past the opening, yelling for them to stay put. Barash leaped over, positioning himself near Isfail, knives ready to defend.

Akira was scrambling from the bedding when Reva suddenly turned from the cave mouth, calling for shields and shouting for everyone to take cover. Isfail spun back, throwing himself over Akira just before the booms of multiple explosions. The cave shook, rock falling in chunks. The air filled with dust and dirt as their world shuddered, sending lanterns toppling. Absolute dark filled the cave as Isfail listened to the rumble and crash, as if the ridge was disintegrating around them.

Ninety-Five

Alerted by shouts of warning, Shanow was already running from his tent, the entire camp coming to high alert around him. When explosions filled the air with terrible sound and shards of rock started to rain down, Shanow feared the worst. He called orders to his lieutenants to muster all troops and prepare for battle.

Declan ran to him, his face taut with anger. Shanow halted his words with a raised hand. "Likely sabotage, but take reinforcements to the bridge detail. Fall back if Dateh's army is on the move and stay out of explosives range. Remember our strategy." When his captain's expression cleared with a quick nod, Shanow placed a hand briefly on his shoulder. "Watch yourself, Declan."

The captain saluted and rushed to comply.

Shanow looked around as he signaled other men to him, satisfied that his soldiers were maintaining discipline and covering their duty stations. More torches flared to life to press back the predawn shadows. Aric was organizing search parties to hunt down whoever had attacked them. Declan had his men mounting their horses now. Looking up at movement above, Shanow saw Ishakans swarming the cliff against the gray light of dawn.

Strapping on his sword, Shanow took the men now gathered around him and jogged toward the cave housing the Caldalans, dreading what he'd find there. To his surprise, Syrai was kneeling at the base of the trail with Kane standing beside her. Shanow ran faster as he saw the man lying prone in front of her.

Kilronan, bloody and battered, moved under the hand Syrai placed over his forehead. He groaned as his eyes flickered open, then cursed when he started to sit up.

"Your left arm is broken," Syrai said quietly, her face showing no emotion. But when she glanced up, Shanow saw grief and strain in the vivid blue depths.

"Can you tell us what happened?" he asked Kilronan as Syrai and Kane worked together to quickly heal the man's injuries.

"It was Mika," Kilronan told them in a disbelieving voice. "She had bombs, at the cave!" Jerking from Syrai, Kilronan staggered to his feet. "Akira . . . my team . . ." His eyes were frantic as he looked up the trail where Kane was already running up ahead of Shanow and his men. "Arla."

"Here," a thick voice answered. Arla, leaning on one of Aric's men, walked to them. She was bruised, pressing one hand to a bad gash on her forehead, and unsteady on her feet.

Leaving Kilronan, Syrai went to her and laid a hand over the wound. Seconds later, the bleeding stopped and there was only an ugly scrape remaining.

"We will do more when we can," Syrai told them. "We must focus on what is above." She looked at the soldier. "See to them," she ordered, before dashing up the rubble-strewn trail.

*H*er face pressed into Isfail's shoulder, arms tight around him with her hands palms out, Akira listened. There was only the whispering trickle of sand falling, the indistinct clatter of a rock rolling overhead. Turning her head, she tried to peer through the blackness, reaching out with her mindsight.

Isfail shifted slightly over her. "Are you all right?" he asked quickly. "The baby?"

"We're both unharmed," Akira reassured him, and their child. "You?"

He coughed, lifting himself off her as he tried to assess the situation. "I'm good. You got your shield up just in time."

There was a sliding sound next to them and Akira reached

out to Barash as she sensed him sitting up. Her hand was gripped tightly. "Are you hurt?"

"No. Just shaken up," he replied. "The others?"

Reva's voice came, strong and steady. "Sound off!"

One by one, people spoke their names in the blackness; some sounded more frayed than others. Akira detected minor injuries among them, but nothing life threatening. Some had gotten force shields up in time, covering as many around them as they could. But all the ambassadors were accounted for, and all members of Kilronan and Arla's teams except the masters.

"They weren't here," Barash announced, coughing again. "Arla wasn't back and Kilronan went out several minutes before . . . this."

There was more coughing and rustles of movement in the dark. Then Celina spoke up. "I've got one of the lanterns." There was a snap and a small flame flickered, growing stronger as the wick caught. By its light, more lanterns were found and lit, until a foggy glow revealed the dust-laden survivors spread about the cave.

Asura had her teammates tear up some bedding, handing wide strips of cloth out for people to cover noses and mouths, filtering out the worst of the airborne particles.

Like the occupants, the space showed the effects of the explosions above. Despite Isfail's protests, Akira began searching the rock surfaces around them, pressing her hands to cold stone at frequent intervals. With Isfail and Barash following close behind, she continued her survey while Reva organized the rest to evaluate the blockage at the cave mouth.

After an assist from Isfail to raise her high enough to sense the integrity of the ceiling, Akira said, "We're safe enough for now. It's fortunate that the geology here is relatively fissure free and stable."

"So let's get out of here," Maronan said eagerly, lifting a lantern to better inspect the barrier.

*A*cross the river, Felcan was mustering his army, cursing the slow response of untrained men. Several, including Felcan, had heard the explosions echoing from Ishaka. A short time after, the scouts he'd posted near the bridge reported that the number of resistance sentries on the opposite embankment had increased.

It appeared that someone had attacked Shanow's camp. Felcan saw a faint glimmer of hope. If they could rush them while they were still reeling, maybe incapacitated by a surprise attack, The Bow would have its victory. Rallying his lieutenants, Felcan shouted orders to assemble for battle.

Within the hour, they were organized to march against Ishaka. Preparing to cross the bridge into the forest, Felcan issued final directives to the first two ranks. One unit was tasked with using the explosives distributed among them, and the others were archers charged with laying down a suppressing volley of arrows over the ridges.

Despite the earlier failure, he'd elected to use half their hand bombs in preemptive destruction to clear the way, accepting that the noise would announce their coming, but Shanow's scouts would have warned them anyway. His own men had already reported that the soldiers across the bridge had disappeared.

Lifting an arm, Felcan flung it forward, signaling the army to move into Ishaka.

*T*ribesmen were already at work shifting debris from the slide over the cave mouth when Kane and Shanow arrived. A broad fall of rock and soil flowed over most of the flat ledge in front of the cave.

"How long to remove this?" Shanow asked, turning to Kane.

"With men? Some hours." Kane's eyes looked distant as he turned to stare at the cave. "They are alive," he murmured, taking Syrai's hand to draw more energy.

Syrai looked over when Kilronan and Arla joined them, pale and seeming to hold on to each other for support. "Kane has connected with Akira. They are all alive, only minor injuries."

"Are they safe in there? Could the cave collapse on them?" Kilronan's voice was harsh with worry and pain.

Shaking his head, Kane continued to focus on his mental contact with Akira. "She says the rock is firm, but there is much dust in the air. It is difficult to breath."

Turning to Ton, who had joined them with more tribesmen, Syrai said something in fast Ishakan. Immediately, Ton took his men and women carefully up the surrounding terrain.

"They will see if the air shafts to that cave are still open. Otherwise, there is more to worry about than the dust in the air," Syrai explained.

"We must get them out," Arla said, reaching out for Kilronan's hand.

He straightened, ignoring the pain in his arm. "Force bolts. Clear your men."

Shanow started to nod before they all jerked around at the sounds of explosions from the direction of the river. Falcons were already winging toward the base. Aric was directing the troops into their formations.

With a brief oath, Shanow said, "The Bow is attacking. They've taken out our force protection and the protectorate warriors, and they're moving on it while we're distracted."

"We are strong," Syrai said with admirable calm and conviction. "Go to your troops, Commander. The Horse Tribes will stand with you."

With one glance back at the blocked cave, Shanow ordered his soldiers to return to camp. Kilronan met Kane's eyes as Syrai ran down the path with them, Ton leaping down to follow her.

"I've got to help them," Kilronan said to Kane. "You've got to get our people out of there." He turned to Arla and saw the acceptance in her eyes. "Stay here, do what you can."

She jerked him into a hard, fast kiss before stepping back. "Guard your back, Kil."

Ninety-Six

The idea to rush the defenders did not give Felcan all the advantage he'd hoped for. Shanow's troops were ready for them, arrayed in disciplined ranks across the valley as Dateh's army charged out of the trees.

This time, though, Felcan was alert to the fact that none of the defenders attempted to bar their way. No arrows flew as his men rode from the dubious cover of the forest. Raising his hand, Felcan signaled the men behind him to a stop. Mortifyingly conscious of how his disorderly ranks compared to Shanow's soldiers, Felcan actively wished Dateh were here so he could prove the point he'd tried to make weeks ago.

He looked back at the rhythmic sound of horses approaching behind his milling army, and saw another militia unit emerge from the trees, led by the man he recognized as Shanow's Captain Declan. Somehow, they'd been waiting in the forest to come behind them and cut off that escape route.

Hearing the voices raised in alarm alternating with mindless bravado among the Bowmen, Felcan gave a brief thought to surrendering. But a sudden tumult had him spinning his horse around. Some of his men jeered when two bombs, fuses lit, arced toward Declan's unit.

"Hold!" Felcan roared, hoping to prevent an engagement none of them would survive.

They all fell silent when the clay balls appeared to strike an invisible wall, exploding as they dropped to the ground.

"Forcers."

Felcan heard the mutters and hoarse whispers from the men.

"Witchcraft."

"Dateh was right!" some shouted. "Kill them all!"

Trying to signal his few lieutenants to help calm the men, Felcan saw that Shanow's militia units were on the move, their horses trotting forward in ominous cadence.

"Kill them all!" was taken up by a number of Dateh's Bowmen. Felcan watched several bombs fly toward Shanow himself, only to be blocked again by something that could not be seen.

Well done," Syrai mindsighted Kilronan as she watched Dateh's army slow, drawing closer together. She saw the protectorate master lift a hand in salute from his position on horseback near Shanow. But she also felt his weakness from the earlier injuries. Kilronan had little force energy left to pull on. Could he outlast The Bow's stock of explosives?

Syrai saw that Felcan was rallying his men, giving them orders she couldn't hear. Taking slow, deep breaths, she watched the two armies advance. Now she understood Felcan's strategy as a forward line of horsemen raised their arms, prepared to throw their deadly bombs in a broad attack against the front line of defenders.

As the bombs flew, fuses trailing wisps of smoke through the air, Syrai prayed. It was impossible for Kilronan to shield the whole breadth of Shanow's advance. As the bombs reached the pinnacles of their arcs and began to descend, she heard Dateh's soldiers start to cheer.

Then a rapid series of explosions filled the air with sound and smoke as every bomb went off in mid-flight.

Felcan pulled on his horse's reins, slowing in disbelief while groans and oaths rose around him even as they charged on. He'd just witnessed the complete destruction of the final salvo of bombs in his arsenal. It was impossible! How had it been done?

Then his attention was drawn to the small woman with wild white hair, alone on the ridge behind the advancing militia, seeing the way her arms spread, hands palm out. Akira Muro, the name whispered in his brain—eliminate her and take back the fight.

Smoothly, the bow was in his hands, his last Black Arrow nocked. Felcan released the bowstring, watched the arrow fly true.

Until *it* stopped in mid-flight and burst into flames, showering the air with sparkling embers.

Mouth gaping with incredulity, Felcan saw that the white witch was staring straight at him across the distance. There was the clash of swords and cries of fury and pain around him now. Somewhere in his mind he knew Shanow's militia was upon them, but he just sat on his horse, uncaring.

He heard the drum of hoof-beats coming fast but couldn't take his eyes from the woman.

Felcan was still staring up at her when Barash's sword took off his head.

Ninety-Seven

T he sun had yet to reach its zenith, but the battle was over. Hundreds of Dateh's men lay dead in the trampled grass of the wide valley. Most had fallen to the militiamen. The rest, trying to flee, met the arrows of the horse tribes. None of the army sent by a madman had survived.

Dateh's dead Bowmen did not merit a gracious burial; in fact, the Ishakans refused to have those remains pollute their tribal territories. Soldiers and tribesmen collected the bodies in wagons borrowed from Estas, where the townspeople, under some persuasive pressure from Commander Shanow, agreed to handle their disposal by collective funeral pyres.

There were casualties in the militia as well. Some perished when one of the Bowmen blew himself up with the bomb he carried, laughing before spreading death around him.

One of the five defenders lost in the suicide bombing was Commander Caden Aric.

Early the next day, the thirty-seven men and women who'd died defending Ishaka were buried in ground sanctified by the Council of the Horse Tribes, joining those already interred there from Aric's original unit.

Commander Shanow and Captain Declan took part in the solemnly beautiful ceremony. With Isfail, Ton, and two men from Aric's command, they carried Caden Aric's body, wrapped in an exquisitely embroidered funerary blanket gifted by Syrai, to his final resting place.

One by one, with gentle dignity, the remaining thirty-six dead were carried to their graves, their names spoken, their courage sung.

*E*xhausted in the aftermath, and with the healing of battle injuries, Akira tried to deal with the horror of the battle she'd witnessed. It had been necessary to wage this war, but only because Abron Baronan, the despotic Lord Dateh, had decreed it.

She knew without a doubt that they'd done the right thing.

There must be warriors who would stand between the innocent and those who would willfully cause harm and destruction. But it was never easy for those with honor to take up the sword—only necessary.

And there was always a cost—in lives, health, peace of mind, property. Among those taken this time was a man she'd met long ago, one she'd admired. Caden Aric had been a good friend of Garath Haill, another victim of the Baronan legacy. Akira dreaded telling Alani Iro of his death, and there was regret knowing that Aric would never see Haill's daughter. But that could not be changed now.

She knew Isfail was with Shanow and Declan as they stood in honor guard at the graves of the dead, a time-honored military tradition.

Lying down on a mat in the large tent set up near Shanow's, Akira let go and wept for them all. Eventually, taking comfort from the gentle movements and mental brushes of her child, she gave in to fatigue and slept.

*S*itting in silence in the shadows, Barash held his own vigil while she slept, refusing to leave her alone and vulnerable after the carnage and loss. He'd never fought this way. When he'd killed before, it had been on Karsh's orders, or as part of whatever task she'd set for him. Or he'd killed in self-defense.

Now he'd killed in defense of others. He was cold-blooded enough that striking down this kind of enemy brought no self-searching, no moral questioning. But in the past lunams, he'd come to understand the feelings of grief and sorrow with the loss of companions and friends. To feel a true sense of gratitude and relief that others survived.

Leaning his head back against the canvas wall, Barash remembered that moment when he'd seen Felcan aim his Black Arrow at Akira, and the hot rage that the bastard would dare try to harm her.

He was already kicking his horse into a gallop, looking over his shoulder to see the arrow burst into flames. Then his focus was all on Felcan as he drew the sword from the sheath on his back, continuing in one sweep of motion to slice through Felcan's neck. He hadn't looked back as he drove into the melee, taking on the enemy until he pulled up beside Isfail to look out over the blood-soaked field.

Now he touched his shoulder where one of Dateh's soldiers had landed a gashing blow. Akira had healed it, closing the wound until no one would know it had ever been. Her hands had been gentle, but her eyes had been full of grief.

So he watched over her, and waited to return to Caldala.

*I*t was full dark when Isfail stepped into the tent. In the dim light of candle lanterns, he scanned the sleeping occupants. Both protectorate teams—since he'd just spoken briefly with one of Arla's journeymen, on night watch just outside—and the five ambassadors, lying on mats on the opposite side of the tent.

Isfail didn't bother searching for Barash. Walking carefully over to the foot of the double mat where Akira slept, he crouched down next to the silent sentinel, placing a hand on his shoulder as he met the dark eyes. "You're relieved from duty, soldier." He saw Barash's mouth quirk slightly as they both stood up.

Watching the man walk, silent as any cat, past the protectorate group to his own mat, Isfail smiled in the dark. As always, Akira had been right about him.

Removing his outerwear, Isfail lifted the covers and slipped in behind her, wrapping an arm over to rest his hand over the slight rounding of her belly. As if the baby was aware of his presence, Isfail sensed the faintest flutter. Drifting to sleep, he told himself it was far too early for him to be able to feel the tiny being's movements this way.

Secure within his embrace, Akira just smiled.

Ninety-Eight

The sun shone its light in intermittent shafts through building clouds as the camp slowly came to life the day after the battle. There were those who'd risen early to join the Ishakan scouts as they systematically walked the wide valley, collecting anything remaining from the day before.

Others loaded the last of the enemy bodies into two wagons to take them to Estas. Everything found by the end of the scout sweeps was thrown in with the corpses. Despite the light rain that began to fall, the day seemed to brighten when the wagons carrying the dead disappeared into the trees on their final trip across the bridge.

In the smaller dining tent, the resistance leaders gathered over hot tea and warm bread. Akira and Isfail finished telling how they'd all escaped the cave. Once Kane and some of the tribesmen had assessed the risk of further slippage, Kane had coordinated with the ambassadors and Kilronan's team to use force bolts to clear the debris from the mouth. Sending Akira out first, at her insistence, to join the force defense against Dateh's army, Isfail and the others had followed to fight with those on the valley floor.

Now they talked about what came next.

"You have a long road ahead," Akira began, sitting beside Isfail with Shanow, Syrai, and Kane across from them. "Ishal is in upheaval, with no legitimate governing body."

"It will be work to rebuild trust, but many stood up as loyalists. We'll start from there." Shanow turned to Syrai and Kane. "I think the Ishakan people need to have a strong voice, not only in their territories, but in rebuilding the whole of Ishal. We've had talks over the winter about the possibility of Ishaka becoming an independent nation."

Kane gave a wry smile, but left the *Sha'ala* with the response.

"It will be put to the people of the horse tribes," Syrai said firmly. "This is not an easy decision, to consider becoming a nation of our own. Some will see it as an answer, not realizing there is more to fully governing ourselves than convening our own councils. There are practical matters of the responsibility for making laws, broader ones than we now have, setting up our own militia, matters of formal trade agreements. It goes on and on."

Shanow gave her one of his rare smiles. "The tribes are fortunate to have the benefit of your wisdom. Perhaps you and Kane will share that wisdom and experience with the rest of us as we rebuild, however your people decide."

He turned back to Akira and Isfail. "We are in your debt, personally and as a nation, and grateful for Caldala's support. I hope that you, your Prince, and your Parliament will allow Ishal to look to you for inspiration."

"I know Prince Logran would support anything that can be done to ensure that our neighboring country, or countries," Isfail said, winking at Syrai, "can build a stable and hopeful government that serves all the people. I think you'll find that Caldala will welcome Ishal and Ishaka as allies."

"We still have Dateh and his sham Parliament to deal with," Shanow reminded them. "And we'll need to track down any remaining members of The Bow."

Akira looked at Isfail. "As we will in our country."

*T*alk turned to details of breaking camp. Akira wondered if the others felt the same melancholy over the knowledge that they would soon part. The intensity of these days, weeks, and even lunams created fast bonds of trust and friendship. She knew she would miss these people deeply once they went their separate ways.

Then there came a stir of activity outside the tent, voices

calling out in curious greeting. Akira met Isfail's glance with surprise when she heard Osharon's voice answer Kilronan's hail. A runner had been sent to inform Mountain Shadows Protectorate of Mika's betrayal immediately after the battle. Akira wondered if they wanted more details so soon.

As they looked toward the opening, beginning to stand up, Kilronan came in, his face grave as he focused on Akira.

"Osharon's brought news." Now he looked around the group. "You all need to hear it."

He pushed back the flap and Osharon came in; again, eyes went first to Akira. But he took a moment for proper greetings as he was introduced to those gathered.

Syrai caught Akira's eye and gave a slight nod.

"You have something to tell us, Osharon," Akira began, "urgent enough to come here."

Osharon set the cup he'd been handed down and ran a hand through his hair. "I do, my lady. It's hard news, but the prince directed Lord Corcoran to arrange to get it to you." Reaching into his coat, he withdrew a flat courier pouch, walking around the table to hand it to Akira.

She looked up at him when he laid a hand on her shoulder for a moment. Akira felt icy apprehension at she looked into his eyes. She looked at Kilronan, who stood stiff and unsmiling across the tent.

Taking a deep breath, she broke the seal and took out two letters—one from Prince Logran, and a rumpled and water-stained paper addressed to the House of Coroth from Captain Wells of the *Royal Sea Eagle*.

Her hands shook a little as she handed Logran's letter to Isfail and unfolded the letter from the captain. With eyes scanning rapidly, she began to read aloud.

"'*But upon reaching Port Kittric, the armada discovered that the harbor held only burned out hulls. The docks, wharf . . . indeed, it appeared that the entire city had been destroyed. Fires still smoldered in places, and a number of bodies could be seen washed upon the shore.*

It was agreed that landing boats with armed sailors would go ashore to try to discover the cause of such terrible destruction, hoping to find people who could inform us of what had happened. They reported back, telling us they found only the dead as far as they searched.

With the disheartening scope of this disaster, the admiralty fleet reports that there is no longer a danger from any attack fleet rumored to be assembling in Kittric Harbor. We regretfully leave the investigation of this human tragedy to the Ishalian government.'"

There was silence in the tent, broken only by the sound of rain pattering on canvas.

Isfail gripped Akira's hand tight, searching her blank eyes for a moment before saying, "Prince Logran writes that he received the letter from Wells the day before another message arrived from Captain Micah Vaneer. He doesn't give all the details, but Vaneer and his crew witnessed the final hours of the disaster at Kittric from the harbor mouth. It was beyond his ship's ability to provide help."

Pausing, he touched Akira's wet cheek before he went on. "He sent landing boats in as soon as he could to look for the people he'd originally come for, to transport them back to Caldala—five ambassadors sent in for reconnaissance."

Looking across to the pale, set faces of Syrai and Kane, Isfail gave the only good news. "Kalen Kalronan was found alive and will be transported back as soon as he is able to travel." He watched Syrai bow her head, leaning into Kane with a tearful murmur of gratitude.

Now the hardest news, Isfail knew. "The bodies of ambassadors Alani Iro and Alon Coronan were recovered, and given honorable burial in Duorn, Kilra." He felt Akira falter, her fingers ice-cold within his grasp. "Ambassadors Elen Arith and Aron Drinin remain missing . . . and are presumed dead."

Tash'tric

*D*ateh looked over at the filthy runner as he toyed with a whiskey decanter. The man was satisfyingly terrified, he thought, as he picked up another glass.

"You're actually reporting that my army failed in Ishaka?" The question was made in a dark yet silky voice.

"Y-yes, my l-lord," the man stammered as he backed closer to the door.

"And how do you know this? Did you observe their defeat?"

"N-no, m-my lord." Gasping in a great breath, he blurted out, "The bodies. They sent the bodies back to Estas. Lots of bodies piled in wagons. The town was building big bonfires, pyres to burn the bodies."

Dateh turned, one brow lifted. "These were *my* army's dead?"

Giving one bob of the head, the man swallowed. "I knew some of them, my lord, sir. And . . ." He gulped.

"And?" Dateh encouraged, turning to hold out a glass.

The man's eyes darted to it and his face blanched. "Well, sir. It was a gruesome sight, sir, but Commander Felcan's head rolled right out of one of the wagons."

The hand holding out the glass jerked, spilling amber liquid onto the rug.

Dateh's mind seemed to go blank; for a moment he could not think. Then it all flowed back like an ice-cold wind.

It was simple really, Dateh considered, putting down the glass as he turned to his desk. Fools and cowards surrounded him, he decided, his thoughts spinning with dark purpose. But there were useful fools, and no point in killing the bearer of bad news when he was still useful.

"Find the local militia commander and send him to me. And tell that idiot Gorth to come."

"Now, my lord?" He flinched back at the look when Dateh turned to him, picking up the abandoned glass and flinging it at the wall.

"Of course now!"

Ninety-Nine

The base camp was once more a scene of purposeful activity. Shanow strode among his men, supervising preparations for departure, making sure each of the militia units understood their assignments. With one commander short—his jaw clenched, thinking of his friend's death—he placed Declan in charge of the platoon that would start sweeping the countryside, tracking down remaining Bowmen. Goden's captain would lead another unit directly to Kittric to try and locate survivors, and assess the situation there.

Shanow had decided to leave his own unit here in Ishaka under his most trusted lieutenant, now field-elevated to the rank of captain. Without knowing what had befallen Kittric, he couldn't feel easy leaving the Horse Tribes without military support.

When he was confident that everyone would move out as ordered, he returned to his tent to get ready for his own mission. His new captain would coordinate with Syrai to secure the Ishakan territories until he returned.

It had to be brutal, Barash thought from where he sat on the ground, watching the two women across the width of the tent. Akira held Evani Reva close to her as the other ambassadors stood around them with stunned faces. It was the only time he'd seen the leader of the recon ambassadors fall apart. It was about the news from Caldala, he knew, remembering the big, black-haired protectorate master who'd appeared in camp this morning. The one who'd taken a long second look at him, as if he were trying to remember where he'd seen him before?

580

Now things were moving in a different direction. He'd seen Shanow muster his men, watched the protectorate teams talking quickly among themselves as they saddled horses and packed up gear.

Some frisson of fear had kept him from asking questions. Some premonition that his life was about to change again had Barash refusing that inevitability as long as possible. But Akira was walking toward him now. As much as he wanted to leap up and run, to put off the words he was about to hear, Barash got to his feet and waited. He saw the desolation in her beautiful, haunted eyes and ached to drive it away, so he let her take his hands in her small ones.

He listened to the words—the words he could see were even harder for her to accept, than his to hear. Things had gone bad in Kittric. Her ambassador team had suffered losses.

Aron Drinin—the brother lost, then found—now lost again, maybe forever.

Barash didn't know how to feel when Akira wrapped her arms around him. But he held her tight, feeling her tears against his neck. He didn't know how to accept the comfort she offered, so he gave instead, never feeling his own hot tears as he pressed his face into her soft hair.

S tanding just inside the tent, Isfail watched them, as he'd watched while Akira brought the news to her ambassadors. For one of the few times in all the years, he did not know how to help her, how to console this bitter loss. Words were weak, and had little power to give solace to this heartbreak.

From terrible experience he knew nothing could assuage the pain. He'd felt that empty, hopeless grief. Then he'd lived again when he'd found that Akira had survived the Mors defense. A miracle, but miracles were few. They couldn't bring Alani Iro and Alon Coronan from the grave.

So he waited, watching, hoping that those left behind could sustain each other through this first crippling blow.

Akira stepped back from Barash. Isfail smiled a little when

the man kissed her forehead as she touched his cheek. Then she turned to look at him, knowing he'd been there, Isfail knew. When she came to him, he enfolded her in his arms, just holding on to keep her from falling.

*T*he valley felt too empty in the late afternoon. The rain clouds had dispersed, leaving the fading daylight gilding the remaining tents.

The militia units had headed out hours before. Next to leave were Arla and her team, with one of the packhorses laden with the protectorate dead—Halen, and Mika's remains. Halen's murder had been one more terrible act of betrayal by Mika, and a hard blow for Arla and her team to begin to come to terms with as tribesmen guided them back to the Ishakan rift.

Osharon followed the faster route back, taking the boat across the lake then climbing the low cliff. With him, he carried letters to Coroth, along with hastily assembled reports of the battle.

Those remaining gathered in the larger dining tent, engaged in an occasionally heated debate on one more mission. But Akira was refusing to give ground.

"I'm going," she stated, with a determination that would not be swayed. "I will be there when we end this."

Sitting beside her, Isfail knew better than to argue. She needed to see this through, and he wasn't going to risk watching her lose herself again because she wasn't able to see it done. So he smiled a little when Kilronan scowled at her.

"There is no reason for you to risk yourself, Akira!" he shouted, not for the first time.

Shanow finally stepped between them. "This is pointless, Kilronan. We need to move on and move out."

Kilronan clenched his jaw, folding his arms over his chest as he sat back with his teammates.

"We're agreed that Abron Dateh must be stopped, and our best chance is now, as soon as possible, before he decides to disappear and start again another day." Shanow glanced around at the affirmatives. "This is going to be a fast, tight action led by Lady

Muro, Commander Isfail, and myself." He ignored Kilronan's muffled curse as he said, "We'll be supported by Recon Alpha and Team Kilronan."

"And me," Barash interjected coolly.

"I don't forget you," Shanow said sharply. "Or Kane. You're going to need to accept the chain of command." He straightened, his voice quieting. "We've all lost people to this madness. If this is going to succeed, we need to work together and put aside personal revenge."

Barash nodded. "My apologies."

"Mine too," Kilronan said gruffly. "Let's get it done."

One Hundred ❧

*A*rith sat cross-legged beside Alon Coronan, listening to the rasping wheeze as his friend slipped closer to death. Sickness and the injuries received during the explosions were taking their toll. Despite his partner's valiant struggle from the moment he'd pulled him from the burning water, Arith feared it had been futile. Here they were, less than a day from their home country, and he prayed to keep his last man alive.

He stoked the fire, gazing into these life-giving flames as he remembered the hell-born fires that had taken lives. But they'd made it this far, and now sheltered in a familiar cave within a day's easy jog of Lower Caldera Lake. A day for an able warrior, he thought, feeding the fire in the old fire pit as he listened uneasily to the harsh cough wracking the barely recognizable man with him.

Infection from the Kittric injuries, everything made worse by the long immersion in the icy waters of the river crossing, had taken such a toll that Arith despaired again of being able to get Coronan any further. How was he ever going to climb the cliff that was the old pass into Caldala?

"I'll make it," a frail voice choked out between coughs.

"Why do you always think you can read my mind?" Arith tried to tease.

"Because I can," Coronan replied, attempting a smile.

Arith handed him a hot mug of water. "Serves me right for traveling with ambassadors. Here, pretend that's a strong cup of tea laced with whiskey."

They sat, silently drinking the soothing warmth until Arith

noted, "Strange, isn't it? We haven't heard or seen any sign of fighting. You think it's over? We've been in the rough for weeks. Maybe we could try a signal fire? But with the luck we've been having, we'd just bring the enemy."

"I'd be happy for an Ishakan scouting party," came the slow reply.

Arith nodded. "We'll have to raft across the lake or see if we can make it over the rim of the lower falls, then climb up onto the southern plateau. Akira said there's a protectorate outpost there now."

There was a long silence, broken only by the terrible sound of coughing, before he heard a reluctant reply.

"I can't make it across the rim. My balance isn't near good enough anymore."

"Then we raft and climb the cliff face. Can you head out tomorrow? Looks like rain's on the way again."

"I can do anything," came Coronan's suddenly fierce reply.

"Yeah," Arith said with another attempt at humor. "Except balance." He choked out a laugh at the weak force push sent his way as he tried not to worry.

But Arith woke the next morning to find Coronan unresponsive, burning up with fever. Injury, rough travel in inclement weather, and the resulting infections had finally taken the courageous warrior down. Arith had no way to help him, and he wouldn't leave Coronan to die alone. He'd never survive long enough for him to go for help, and Arith was heartsick that he would die just hours from their own country.

Taking a hot, dry hand in both of his, Arith closed his eyes and prayed. Overwhelmed by emotions he'd been able to keep at bay with the need to take care of his last man, the only one of his team left to him after the disaster in Kittric, Arith suddenly felt he couldn't go on if Coronan died.

Then he swore at himself. His friend deserved more—a good friend who deserved better than this hell, ending his life in a dank cave far from those who loved him.

"Damn the risk!" Arith cursed as he pushed up and left the

cave. Within minutes he had a small bonfire ablaze on the rocky ledge outside the cave, sending smoke into the overcast day. If it brought The Bow, so be it.

Hours passed as Arith spread wet shirts over Coronan's burning chest and forehead. He dribbled water into his mouth and down his throat. There was nothing he could really do but try to get the fever down, and feed the fire outside the cave.

A thin rain was falling now, but the bonfire was stoked hot enough to send out a thick, dark plume into the drizzle.

Coronan had begun to shiver violently, and Arith covered him with both their blankets before lying down beside him to share his body heat.

"Elen."

Arith jolted at the barely audible whisper and rose on his elbow. "Hey, glad you're awake!"

"Elen," he rasped again. "Promise you'll take me home. I want to go home to Vani."

Gripping a hand that was more bone than flesh, Arith nodded, fighting back tears. "I promise, Alon. No matter what it takes, I'll get you home."

There was a quavering smile as Alon Coronan closed his eyes again.

Arith sat with him for some time, hoping that those hadn't been his final words. But his breathing seemed a little easier, and his skin felt cooler.

Fatigue pressed down on Arith as he struggled to his feet to go feed the bonfire. Movement caught his eye, and his hands flew up in attack stance. A man stood in shadows at the cave entrance, then another, until five people blocked the cave mouth.

Arith stood in front of Coronan's unconscious body, prepared to defend as silence dragged on.

One of the men stepped into the dim firelight inside the cave. Arith breathed a sigh of relief. He was Ishakan, one of the horse tribesmen.

"Our people saw the smoke. Who are you?" the stranger asked curiously. Before Arith could answer, the Ishakan gestured to his companions, pointing a long staff at the man lying on the floor. "See to him," he directed quietly.

The others walked in, making no sound. It was then that Arith saw two of the scouts were women. One knelt beside Coronan, her competent hand movements marking her as an experienced healer.

The leader studied Arith, who still hadn't gathered the wits to speak. "You should sit, or you will fall." The deep voice held a trace of amusement. He spoke the common tongue well, but Arith could hear the Ishakan speech cadence.

Arith moved to a short log and sat. "My name's Arith, I'm a Caldalan . . . *we* are," he amended, looking at Coronan. "We're ambassadors sent to collect information on the situation in Ishal, but . . ."

The Ishakan nodded. "It went wrong for you. You were in Kittric?"

"How did you know?"

"We were given news of the madness there, and the fires." For a moment, Arith saw rage in his dark eyes. "I am Ton, of the horse tribes. Your *sha'ala*, Akira, and other Caldalans fought with us, with Shanow's warriors nearly a week ago."

"You defeated Dateh's men," Arith said with certainty, his hands clenched into fists.

"We were great with power, with friends." The Ishakan gave him a fierce look. "No one could defeat us in our vengeance. The blood of The Bow watered the land they burned. Now there are few left to challenge us."

Arith rubbed his tired eyes. "So Akira and the others have returned to Caldala? And Shanow's militia?"

"Many have gone on to track down what remain of Dateh's soldiers in Ishal, and to Kittric to investigate. Our *Nah'shalon* Kane, *Sha'ala* Akira, and Commander Isfail, have gone to Tash'tric with Commander Shanow and others." He met Arith's eyes. "What of the others who were with you?"

When Arith just shook his head, the man turned away,

murmuring something in Ishakan to one of his scouts. He nodded to Ton and left the cave.

"He will carry the news and return with help." Ton looked out into the rainy day.

Arith noticed the tears on the healer's face. "Your *nah'shalon*, he's Kane Kalronan. His son was one of my team. Our ship was destroyed and I couldn't find him after, or two others. I don't know if they survived."

Ton turned back. "Kalen is the brother of my woman. We have news that he survived. We wait to bring him home from Kilra." His dark eyes seemed to assess Arith. "It brings me sorrow to tell you that the other two ambassadors lie buried with honor. Now we will care for you and your friend, and we will get you back to your people."

Arith held out an arm with a curt nod, returning a strong grip though his heart felt too heavy with grief. "There are no thanks great enough."

The Ishakan gave him an understanding look. "Your people came to fight for my people. There is no need for thanks. We are one, we are tribe."

One Hundred-One

*T*hey smelled the fires and death even before they saw the shifting orange glow over the low rise ahead of them. The first bodies appeared on the road at the checkpoint Shanow had warned them about. Some had died at the hands of others, judging by their wounds and the weapons lying about.

Others had died in a contorted agony that immediately assailed Akira's mind with long-ago images from the massacre at Baronan Keep.

"He used the poison," she said in bleak disbelief. As she began a hurried dismount, Isfail jumped from his own horse to catch her. Akira stumbled away to lose what was in her stomach.

Isfail supported her during the sickness, and Kane offered a clean square of linen with a water pouch as Reva stepped in to care for her.

Standing by, holding the horses' reins, Shanow said, "I should not have allowed you to come. This horror falls on my people's failure to stand for our country. You've done more than enough." He looked at Isfail. "Go back. We had no trouble on the roads. Take your lady back to Ishaka and home."

"We're not going back," Akira said clearly. "This is going to end here."

"Akira—"

"This will end," she repeated sharply, interrupting Kilronan. "I *will* end this curse, this madness—whatever it is!"

Kane laid a hand on her cheek. "It will end here, little cousin. Shanow and I can do this without risking you and your child."

Tears filled her eyes as she gripped his hand. "I must be part of this. I sent my people into Kittric. There must be justice."

"Justice or vengeance, little one?"

"I don't care what you call it," Akira said, stiffening her spine with sudden steel in her reply. She stepped back, swiping away tears. "I spent my life doing what they told me to do. I backed away because diplomacy demanded it. I could have assassinated Arthon Baronan when he first settled in Ishal, long before he assembled The Bow, before the first rebellion, before the Gattes massacre!"

They all listened to her impassioned tirade in silence.

"I could have stopped *this* Baronan when he was first identified as Abron Dateh. But civilized people make civilized laws. So *innocent* people have to die, to suffer in cruel ways because those who could protect them are told *they* must follow the laws! But murderers and criminals scorn those laws while the heads of government debate."

Akira swept an arm toward the glowing horizon. "This is the result of those who are allowed to flout the laws of decent people. The people who died here!" She pushed back when Isfail tried to take her in his arms.

"Akira, this isn't your fault," he said gently. "You know the justice systems prevail most of the time. This is the work of people too warped, too far beyond civilized humanity for usual justice. You can't take on the burden of the world's evil."

"Usual justice," she repeated bitterly. "Exactly. The *usual* justice of Caldala and Ishal failed, over and over. The Baronans here, and the mindless criminals who followed them, those who did their bidding for gain or perverse pleasure, counted on that."

"The blame for all of this lies with Ishal's government, Akira," Shanow stated. "Both Baronans were able to use a long-corrupt Parliament to pursue their ambition. It was our ministers who refused to extradite Baronan and his son from the beginning, and they gave him the power and resources to continue his evil.

All for the wealth and power he promised them. And his son grew up learning the same weaknesses and how they can be manipulated."

He paused when Reva and her team moved to back Akira. "All that's true," Reva said in an empty voice. "And we will stop it here. With all respect, Commander Shanow, Recon Alpha only follows one commander."

Shanow sighed as he met Akira's eyes. "Caldala would never have allowed this to happen once Baronan revealed his true face with the massacre at his keep. I know that, now that I've met you and your warriors, now that I've stood with you against them. Your Prince and Parliament took swift action against the ministers who would sell the security of your nation for personal gain. Not here. Most looked away, either for their own gain, or because they did not have the fortitude to stand up against it."

He looked toward the burning city. "It took the courage and selflessness of one man to end the first uprising. No matter what it takes—you're right, Akira—it ends here."

Maybe his country *had* ended here, Shanow thought with some dread while they rode down the wide avenue leading to the heart of Tash'tric. The large townhouses of the wealthy they now passed by were gutted by fire or intentionally damaged, just like the smaller homes of everyday people had been in the outer limits of the city. His home was certainly gone too.

Shanow felt a touch on his arm and looked over at Akira, riding next to him. The sympathy in her eyes had him briefly covering her hand with his.

They both stiffened when screams and strange cackling sounds arose from a side street. But they'd seen no living people yet, just the occasional cries of anguish or the mad laughter of the damned. For the most part, their group rode without speaking through smoke and ash. The crackle and roar of the fires, and the crashing of buildings falling in ruin, muffled the sound of their passage.

It appeared that the city center had been the first to feel Dateh's revenge. Bodies were a common sight now, though not as many as they'd anticipated. Kilronan's team and Reva's ambassadors kept close, weapons ready, vigilantly scanning for any sign of hostiles or the insane.

They came to the large square near the walls of the Parliament complex. From the looks of it, this atrocity had begun on a market day. Colorful stalls were smashed, goods shattered and trampled underfoot. People lay dead in pools of dried blood.

"Should we check for survivors?" Asura asked from Kilronan's team, her compassionate eyes dimmed by the soul-sucking horror around them.

"No." The answer came from several of their company simultaneously.

"We can't risk a confrontation by stopping," Akira explained in a dull voice. "There are too many, and most are beyond help."

Pottery shards crunched under their horses' hooves as they continued on through the stench of char and decay.

Isfail gave a low order to halt as they approached the wide steps leading up to the massive doors of Ishal's Parliament building. Over twenty men stood there, brandishing swords and long knives, though their faces displayed varying expressions of fear and horror.

Then Akira looked up at the man stepping out through the wide, open doors.

"Gorth," Reva said aloud, hate permeating the single word. All the ambassadors stared at the traitor, all raising their hands to attack, to kill.

"He's mine," Akira murmured.

Kilronan signaled his team forward, challenging the men on the steps. He glanced at Shanow, waiting for his nod before dismounting. Several men ran at them with loud shouts and upraised blades, others turned to run away. Team Kilronan killed them all in a barrage of force bolts.

Akira held Gorth's stare as she started up the steps, followed by Isfail and Shanow, flanked by Recon Alpha, Barash, and Team Kilronan.

"Can't you face me one on one?" Gorth called, but the waver in his mocking voice betrayed his fear. "You need all these warriors?"

Seeing his fingers tremble as they sparked, Akira reached the top with a deadly smile shaping her lips, one hand rising to signal her companions to hold where they were. "Any one of them could deal with you. You sold your services to the devil, murdered innocents, and betrayed your country. Why?"

Flames shivered around his shaking hands, his face contorted, hate mixed with fear now. "I deserved more! The Bow offered it. Dateh wants his own force army. *I* will lead them."

Akira tipped her head, never breaking eye contact. "And Lunow? What part does he have in this new force army?"

Gorth's eyes shifted away for a moment. "He's dead." Looking back at her, he said, "Lunow thought Lord Dateh was a fool, and he paid the price for his stupidity."

"And you learned the lesson well," Akira said with a nod. "Did you start the fires in Kittric, Gorth?"

Terror filled the man's eyes as he took a step back. "Dateh . . ."

"The hundreds in Kittric had no chance to fight, to defend themselves against your treachery. Now Tash'tric. You sneak in the shadows, strike without warning against people caught unaware, unsuspecting. You are beneath contempt," Akira said, her voice condemning.

"Can you take *me* on, Gorth?" Fire rose in spiraling majesty from Akira's upturned hands, a vivid contrast to Gorth's wavering flames.

Sweat poured down his ashen face as he tried vainly to speak.

"Die," Akira said quietly, sending a mindsight.

A single force bolt shot from Reva's hand in execution.

No one spoke as they followed Shanow into the tomb-like halls of Ishal's Parliament complex.

One Hundred-Two

S tanding at the wide window in an elaborate bedchamber once occupied by the former high minister, Dateh looked out, watching flames ripple outside the stone walls of the Parliament complex. Tash'tric would be purged by fire.

Lifting a glass to his mouth, his eyes crinkled in pleasure as he recalled seeing the gout of flames that had ignited the last ship to dock in Tash'tric harbor, over an hour ago. Gorth was very good at his arson, and obedient. Perhaps he'd be useful in the new government, Dateh reflected, refilling his glass.

He could build a stable of force callers who had Gorth's mercenary sensibilities. Dateh had never shared his sire's antipathy toward the breed; the force callers had just been potential obstacles to his own ambitions. But Gorth had shown him how useful they could be.

Looking out again, Dateh thought it was too bad that these windows could not be opened. He wasn't able to relish the screams of those he'd sentenced to death. He'd ordered heads to roll . . .

Abron Dateh's insane thoughts blanked, deposed momentarily by the mental image of Beros Felcan's severed head rolling from a wagon—dead eyes staring at him in accusation. Then the moment passed.

Tomorrow he'd enjoy the balcony where public announcements were made. He wondered if there would still be citizens mutilating one another in the streets? It occurred to him, as he walked out to the living room, he'd need to find new citizens to rule over. That was an inconvenient consequence when one poisoned the water supply serving an entire city.

Dateh stopped with his glass nearly to his lips, puzzled by the sight of six people standing before the hearth. Five stood in a line behind the central figure—a small, white-haired woman. He struggled to clear his head.

"Who the hell are you? How dare you enter without my permission?" Dateh asked, an imperious pitch to his voice.

The woman in the center spoke first. "We are your judgment, Abron Baronan."

He lifted a corner of his mouth in a sneer that faded as he recognized the man who stepped up next. "You're dead, damn you! You bastard."

"We are vengeance," Barash said, ignoring the outburst.

"We are justice for the dead." A tall, gray-eyed man and dark-haired woman said together.

Dateh swore while Kane and Shanow stepped up beside the others.

"We are retribution for our people." The men's voices were resolute.

"For Ishal," Shanow said coldly while lifting a crossbow.

"For Ishaka," Kane said quietly, raising his hand.

"For Aron," Barash said, his voice the chill of death, a throwing knife poised to fly.

"For Recon Alpha," Reva said clearly, raising a hand.

"For Gattes," Isfail finished, crossbow ready.

With a howl of triumph, Dateh released the knives at his wrists, sending them streaking toward the central figure, the white witch. Then gawked when they stopped in mid-flight. He watched in horror as the knives flipped around and flew back, screaming as the blades sliced across both his cheeks, scoring red furrows of pain.

None of the others seemed to have moved.

His eyes locked with the luminous green eyes of Akira Muro. "Witch!" he snarled, frozen in his rage.

"Death," she amended calmly with hands raised. The snap of force bolts and crossbows coincided with the silent flight of Barash's knife.

One Hundred-Three

Outside the complex, scanning bloody streets strewn with the dead, Reva's ambassadors waited with Kilronan's team. Akira saw relief on their faces when they came out the massive doorway.

"It's done," she said without inflection, meeting Kilronan's eyes.

"Not quite," Shanow said, surprising the others as he looked back at the elaborate façade, the gilded architectural ornaments.

Turning to Akira, he asked, "Can you take it down?"

For a moment, she looked deep into his eyes. "If that is what you want."

He nodded, lifting his face to the stars, dimly seen through a thin fog of mist and smoke. "I take personal responsibility. Maybe it's wrong," he said bitterly. "But our people deserve a new start."

Kane put a hand on Shanow's shoulder, linking them as he met Akira's searching gaze. "Yes."

Isfail sat on his horse, watching from parkland above the central district of Tash'tric. Shanow sat to his right, his hands clenched tight around his reins as he witnessed the final fall of the old Parliament.

To the left of Isfail, Barash stood on a short wall, staring down at the waterspouts rising from the harbor. Isfail reached out to grip his shoulder for a moment before looking back at the twisting winds—black with smoke, glittering with embers—rising just beyond the Parliament complex.

Fires were already burning inside the assembly rooms, the

resident wings, and the offices—courtesy of Akira and Celina, the fire-caller from Kilronan's team. Force bolts and the telekinetic powers of protectorate warriors and ambassadors had begun the destruction.

Now the three men on the hill watched, awestruck, as waterspouts and tornadoes converged, sending walls toppling with their combined energies. Debris spewed into the sky lightening with the dawn. The crash and rumble of falling stone echoed throughout the dead streets of Tash'tric.

As the sounds faded, Akira rode into the park, followed by the other force callers. Isfail saw the fatigue on all their faces.

He took the hand Akira held out to him as they all looked down on ravaged Tash'tric, capital city of Ishal. Where the huge government complex had once towered above the surrounding city, there were only heaps of shattered rubble to mark the broken faith and empty follies of the past.

Ishakan Territories, Three Days Later

*T*he tribesmen had been busy, Akira thought as they entered the forest on the last stretch of road. Where explosives had blown down trees and gouged the land, there now stood neat stacks of logs around clearings of raked-out soil. The restoration helped soothe her emotions and prove that life went on for those strong enough to rebuild.

She listened to her companions talking around her, too weary to join in, but glad to hear them after the hours of silence since they'd left ruined Tash'tric.

Isfail and Shanow shared ideas for gathering the surviving citizens together to begin again. Kilronan occasionally added his thoughts on building stronger national defense services.

The younger members of Team Kilronan had finally begun light-hearted conversations, and their brief outbursts of laughter revived her own spirit.

Her ambassadors hadn't yet found their balance and the quiet voices spoke as often of how to go on as any anticipation of returning home.

The loss was too deep, Akira knew. Now that her need for revenge, or justice, was spent, her grief dragged at her. She couldn't open that door yet, afraid of the pain and how it might affect her baby.

As long as she didn't think of the finality, Elen lived in hope. She would once again hear Aron laugh with Barash. As long as she didn't *know* . . .

Light grew brighter as they approached the edge of the forest and Akira blinked at the intensity of the sunlit meadow. Like the forest, there had been progress in erasing the evidence of war. Though the battlefield had been fenced off, the upper valley held small herds of the beautiful Ishakan horses.

Akira didn't know that tears streaked her face at the glorious sight, but she heard pleasure spike in the voices around her, and felt the baby give a series of little kicks, responding to that surge of happiness.

Syrai cantered out to meet them, slowing to match her horse's pace to Kane's. Touching his cheek, she listened to his solemn voice for a moment, then Akira saw her lean closer to him, murmuring in Ishakan too soft for others to hear.

Kane straightened, a smile finally lifting his expression.

They continued to the corral where tribesmen took their horses. There Syrai told them, "We have refreshment waiting at the tents. Rest, for we will feast tonight."

With the rest of their group walking slowly behind, Akira and Isfail entered their large tent, going from bright sunshine to warmly diffused light. Akira had no time to take in her surroundings before she was grabbed up in a hard embrace and spun in a familiar gesture.

Locking her arms around Elen, Akira sobbed with joy.

Reva smiled tearfully, watching the reunion while the others crowded around. She knew that someday she'd laugh again, call teasing remarks and exchange jokes. For now, she turned away to shed her tears in private.

"Vani."

She closed her eyes—listening to ghosts would break her.

"Vani."

Tears leaked, and she shook her head in the sudden silence around her. Then she heard Akira's gentle voice say, "He can't come to you. Open your eyes and go to him."

Reva looked through the tears. Alon Coronan lifted a bandaged hand from a thickly padded bed. With a keening cry, she stumbled to him.

One Hundred-Four

Caldala and Beyond

Time could and did heal, though it took longer for some wounds than others. The remaining ambassadors of Recon Alpha waited for Coronan to get back on his feet before sailing to Kilra on the *Spirit of the Sea*, to honor their fallen friends. Barash went with them at Akira's urging, and a new headstone was set for Aron Drinin.

The mystery of Coronan's ring, that had led to the misidentification of the body, was finally resolved. Coronan believed it had come off in Drinin's hand when he'd lost his grip on Coronan's hand during the big warehouse explosion. Arith guessed that Drinin had put the ring on his own finger to secure it.

Later that first evening on the island, Akira walked alone to sit beside Alani's grave. Akira spoke her thoughts aloud— talking of Lani Osharon, of Aric's death, and of the monument already raised in a new park in Tash'tric. The memorial was being inscribed with the names of the honorable dead, and how Akira had arranged, with Shanow's willing assistance, to have the names of Garath Haill, Alani Iro, and Caden Aric placed together. The sun was on the horizon when Akira kissed her fingers and touched the stone.

"Your daughter will know you one day," she whispered. Standing up, she paused by Drinin's grave with a heart too heavy for more than essential words.

"You left him too soon, Aron. I pray I won't lose him. Be at peace, my dear friend." Leaving the flowers she'd brought on each grave, Akira walked slowly down the hill.

Two days later, Micah Vaneer welcomed them back on board. The brief trip to Kilra added the final closure to their tragedy.

There were kinder partings for Recon Alpha in the lunam after. Reva and Coronan retired and were bound soon after. Micharon and Coran retired as well, and publically announced that they'd been bound years before.

Arith chose to extend his contract extension another year, staying to train the next generation of reconnaissance teams with Oti and Korth. There would never be another Ambassador Reconnaissance Alpha, but there would always be the service for Core and Coroth.

Though content to be alive and continue with his surviving friends, Kalronan was retired early on Garan's recommendation. Some wounds might never heal, and Kalronan couldn't yet escape the night terrors of fire and water. He was ready to go home.

Shortly after the various ceremonies, Akira and Isfail prepared to escort him back to his people. Shanow had learned they would be in the Ishakan territories and sent a letter via Lord Corcoran, asking to visit with them there.

In the dining hall of Mountain Shadows Protectorate the night before they would leave for the Ishakan Rift, Juniro approached the table they shared with Kilronan and Arla. His face was troubled but his voice determined as the spoke to Akira.

"Lady Muro, I have heard that you will be seeing Commander Gaios Shanow in Ishaka in a few days' time. Will you do me the honor of delivering this to him?" He handed her a sealed letter.

"Of course, Juniro." She looked at it in puzzlement as the portly chef slowly returned to his kitchen.

Ishakan Territories, Three Lunams After the Battle for Ishaka

Isfail watched the mix of pride and sorrow on Akira's face as former ambassador Kalen Kalronan slid from his horse to join his mother and father. There was pride there, too, as Syrai and Kane welcomed their youngest son back to the tribes after twelve years away.

Caldala and the Ambassador Core's loss, Isfail thought, but with a smile as he took the arm the newly retired ambassador offered. But he saw the cost of friends lost in Kalen's eyes, even as a grin flashed briefly on the young man's face. Now Kalen gave a deep sigh, turning to Akira, and a war raged on his taut features.

"This isn't easy, Commander," he finally said, his voice breaking. "I'm ready to come home, but—"

Akira pulled him into her arms, their tears mingling as she pressed her cheek to his. "This is the right decision, the right time, Kalen. You have served with courage and distinction, something you will be proud of throughout your life." She pulled away, struggling for a smile as she said, "Or you *will* be hearing from me."

They all laughed at that, though there was emotion in the humor.

Running a hand down his arm, Akira took his forearm in a hard clasp. "I will always be proud of you, and be grateful for the times we served together. Bring that experience and your strengths back to the Ishakans." Rising to her toes, she kissed him lightly. "We will not lose the friendship we have, all of us. You will see us again."

Kalen nodded, unable to speak, folding his arms around her one more time before breaking away. He crossed a fisted hand to his shoulder in an ambassador salute to Akira, then Isfail, before stepping back. Kane wrapped an arm around his shoulders as they walked to their horses.

As her men prepared to go, Syrai stepped close to Akira, taking both her hands and bringing them to her heart. "My son left me as a boy, looking for adventure in his father's land. You return to me a man, whole, full of wisdom and strength. I pray that he still has a heart for adventure to temper the lifetime of knowledge and duty to come. And I will forever be grateful to the woman who mentored him, trained him, and cared for him."

Syrai released her hands then placed one of her own lightly over the baby growing within Akira, speaking softly in Ishakan before translating, "May this child have the strength and wisdom of her mother and her father, for this child is fortunate in both."

With a warm smile for Akira and Isfail, she moved to her horse, taking the reins from Kane to mount. Giving them a nod and the Ishakan salute of respect, the reunited family set their horses to a canter and rode away.

They're a remarkable people," Shanow said later that day, sitting with Akira and Isfail inside a large tent near the familiar meadow. "I would like to see the horse tribes remain a part of Ishal, with a more active role in our government." He shook his head with a rueful smile. "Whatever that will be."

Isfail looked at the view between the tied-back flaps, the peacefully grazing horses and fields of waving grain. "When will you bring your own family back?"

Shanow took a moment to answer. "I'm in two minds about it. Ishal is in worse shape than after the first rebellion, and I remember how bad that was—not enough food, the bodies of the dead breeding pestilence before burial, and the hard work of rebuilding. I'm sure Mirastheny recalls it too. She lost her sister in the plague that followed."

When he paused, Akira said quietly, "But part of you needs them here."

"Yes." He looked at her. "But I could not have had her here during this, sharing the hardship and the battle." Shanow met Isfail's eyes. "I don't know if that makes me weak, or you a fool."

"Neither." Isfail chuckled, without taking offense. "If you think I command Akira, think again." Taking his wife's hand, he said more soberly, "We know each other, to our peril. Sometimes the risks she's willing to take shake me to the bone, but I'll stand beside her, and I know she'll stand beside me, wherever life takes us."

Akira decided it was a good time to keep her promise to Juniro.

"Commander," she said, claiming his attention. "I was asked to bring you this letter from Mountain Shadows."

She watched as he opened the sealed paper, saw his eyes widen as he read. A few moments later, he refolded it, carefully tucking the letter inside his jacket.

"You know the man who sent this?" he asked, his tawny eyes direct.

"Yes, I know Juniro."

"He writes to me about a child." For the first time, Akira saw regret on this strong man's face.

"Catonina?"

"She is well?"

Akira took his hand and saw surprise, then gratitude in his eyes. "She is beautiful, and well, full of life." When he nodded once, looking toward the High Pass cliff, she said, "You know her."

His lips twitched into an odd smile. "Catonina is my niece. My sister died within the same week as Mirastheny's, both of the plague. We wanted to take the child into our home—she was ill, Juniro devastated by his loss, and he didn't have our resources."

Akira waited for him to continue, and he looked down at her with a hint of humor now. "Does anyone evade you, Lady Muro? You have a way of drawing out things that most of us want to forget."

"Juniro and Nina are dear to me," Akira replied. "As you have become important to me. If I can help ease the pain that I feel between you, I would like to try."

"There's not much more to say. Juniro and Nina disappeared. We went over with food and a healer shortly after burying my sister, but they were gone. I looked for them, had men searching, asking at the ports, but there was no trace. Ishal was in turmoil, and I had a duty to my country. I had to let go."

The sorrow was still there, Akira realized, for his sister and her child. "I'm sorry, Gaios. It was a cruel but desperate path for Juniro to take."

He patted the jacket, where the letter was tucked away. "This explains it all, and asks for forgiveness. More, it asks if we would visit them in Mountain Shadows when we can, and if he could bring Catonina to visit us once Ishal stabilizes."

"Will you have an answer for him?"

Shanow was silent for some time before he said, "Those years, from the start of the first rebellion, through the bad times afterward, they'd taken a toll. We had no children of our own then. Mirastheny was pregnant with our oldest, and we were grieving for the loss of family. Perhaps we were blind to Juniro's grief. Fearing for my own children this time, choosing to send them away to protect them—I can understand, and forgive Juniro for his choices."

He squeezed Akira's hand, and leaned in to kiss her cheek. "Would you pass that to Nina for me, and tell Juniro . . . give him my gratitude for saving her life. Someday I'll tell him that myself."

Isfail offered his arm in a firm grasp and stood with Akira to retire to their tent.

*T*hey were guests of the horse tribes during that brief visit so the pleasure of the trip, and the conversations with Syrai, Kane, and Shanow about Ishal's future, made the time pass too quickly. There came the morning when Shanow mounted his horse, nodding his head to them before trotting back toward the forest road.

Akira tipped her head to Isfail's shoulder as they walked to their own horses, once more saying goodbye to Syrai, Kane, and Kalen. Parting from their Ishakan family halfway through the Ishakan Rift, Akira felt divided between pleasure and sadness, and more than ready to be home.

Three more days of travel saw them back in Mountain Shadows in time to witness the binding ceremony of Kilronan and Arla, sanctioned and joined together by Brother Avo Timmel. It brought joy to Akira, seeing two people she cared for so much finally start their lives together.

A week later, acceding to Isfail's request that they spend the final weeks of her pregnancy in Coroth, Akira hugged Gralla one more time before being assisted into the luxurious coach sent by the royal house to bring them home. For once, Akira didn't complain. While Isfail climbed in to sit beside her, she lifted a hand to those gathered to see them off. Evan and Gralla Corcoran, with Gralla wiping tears away as she smiled back. Asura, Eron, Celina, and Maronan—tall and straight, and still beaming his boyish grin—Cobon giving them a smiling salute, Carelon and Leta, with Osharon beside them, blowing a kiss at Akira with a wink that held back her tears as she chuckled.

And standing beside the coach, Kilronan and Arla. They'd spent the last evening together, enjoying each other's company, finally laughing over past misadventures—before Ishal. Now it was time to leave. When they met again, life would have changed them all, but the love and friendships would last.

Akira glanced over when Isfail took her hand, managing a watery smile when he gently wiped a tear from her cheek. A tap on the window had her looking back. Kilronan spread his hand on the glass. For a moment Akira saw the boy she'd first loved . . . then the man's warm smile reminded her that love never dies. She matched her free hand to his.

Nodding, Kilronan stepped back, sending them a formal salute before signaling the coachman. Akira leaned her head on Isfail's shoulder while his arm slid around her as the coach began to roll. She drew his hand to the small mound of her belly, where their baby shifted, drumming tiny feet or fists enthusiastically.

Epilogue

Kirdan Isfail came into the world in the bed her father had been born in over four decades earlier. The newest addition to the royal family was officially welcomed with fireworks and celebration throughout the palace and city of Coroth, and the news would spread to all of Caldala from there.

None of that mattered within Isfail and Akira's private suite in the family wing. The day after the birth, their tiny daughter cradled in one arm and Akira's hand in his, Isfail's smile reflected his elation as he stared at his child.

"She won't disappear, you know," Akira murmured, squeezing his hand, but her eyes shone with her own joy, and the fingers of her free hand gently brushed over down-soft copper curls.

"Neither of you will."

She heard the remnants of fear in his quiet words, and knew the past lunam had been terrifying for him. From the moment she'd collapsed shortly after they arrived at Coroth, through the anxious uncertainty that their baby would be born too soon. Finally, the days of erratic labor until Kirdan's birth, almost a full moon cycle premature.

But the newborn lungs proved strong enough in Kirdan's enraged cries as she expressed her feelings about being forced into independence. Evani Reva had soothed the infant with loving coos, her skillful hands steady as she patted her dry before placing Kirdan in her mother's arms for the first time.

Ardan had eased onto the bed beside them, emotion strangling all the words he wanted to say as he stroked a fingertip over a miniscule fist before pressing his face into Akira's damp, tousled

607

hair. An all-consuming love had filled her then, for the child and the man. So much love that the force glow had pulsed around the three of them.

"I believe she wants you, my sweet," he said now, passing the fussing baby back with a chuckle. He kissed Akira's forehead. "As do I, but Logran asked me to see him about a consult request from Commander Shanow."

Akira caressed his cheek, smiling at his hesitation. "We'll be fine, and I'll be waiting for news of our friends. I hope they're finding some success in rebuilding their country and their lives." As he straightened and began to move to the door, she called out, "Dan, would you see if there's any response from Barash?"

"Of course, my sweet." He smiled back at her. "Don't worry, Kira. I don't think he'll ignore your request. You changed his life."

With Kirdan peacefully nursing, Akira thought of his words about changing a life. With the child she'd wanted so deeply and never expected to have kneading her breast with tiny fists, one dark green eye looking up at her with all the secrets a newborn holds, Akira stroked a petal-soft cheek. Would she have this exquisite blessing if her life had taken the path she'd wanted at fourteen, if Aiden Kilronan had shared his heart and his life with her then? Would she cherish this moment as much if she had not been who and what she'd become in the Ambassador Core?

Akira let the memories come, reflections of the often-unsettled life that had brought her here, to this most unexpected fulfillment.

As a young girl, there was the unraveling of security, of family, of first love, that had sent her into the Ambassador Core. The early years of self-loathing that had driven her to embrace her power in an effort to escape those feelings of worthlessness.

But there were also friends who'd persevered, breaking through the walls she'd raised around her heart—Elen Arith and Isheill, who had refused to give up on her, and all the ambassadors of Recon Alpha.

Then Ardan Isfail had come into her work and her life—the militia warrior who'd engaged her mind, challenged her skills, and refused to be ignored. He'd been there through the times she'd believed there was nothing but deception and destruction in her service, when she'd despised herself, her spirit broken. There were all the long years she hadn't been able to trust the love he offered, but still she'd longed to have that love.

Even her feelings for Kilronan, her first love, hadn't been enough for her to forget Isfail. And when he'd come for her after she'd shattered in the aftermath of the Mors defeat, Akira had known that Ardan Isfail was the love of her life.

Together they'd followed the strange legacy of Arthon Baronan, inexplicably woven through their lives. From the first scenes of horrific massacre at Baronan Keep, until the final confrontation with psychotic Abron Dateh in the Parliament complex of war-torn Ishal, the Baronan legacy had been a black cloud threatening to veil all in darkness.

Even Baronan's family legacy—the three sons so different from one another—had played a role throughout her life and career. Aron Drinin had been the first, the dearest. Now Barash was the only one left.

He'd begun his life in shadows, unwanted, and unloved, and become an assassin for his mother's benefit. Then he'd crossed paths with Akira. Maybe she'd never really know what it was that led him to a better path, but it was Barash who'd chosen to track Abron down, to risk his life to help Caldala, and Akira.

He'd disappeared after they'd returned from Aron's grave in Kilra, though she thought she'd caught a glimpse of him at the memorial service for Aron and Alani in Coroth. Did he mourn the brother he'd felt some connection with, even as a lost boy himself?

Akira knew she would always grieve for what had been lost in that senseless legacy of hate, madness, and violence—the loved ones, the friends old and new, even the countless civilians who had died so cruelly. Tears welled with the pain that would never completely heal over the loss of Alani and Aron. The final shattering of lives another strike against the peace that had always seemed to elude her.

A soft, drowsy warmth comforting her mind brought Akira's

thoughts back, her smile infinitely joyful as she watched Kirdan's eyes crinkle before drooping into sleep. Looking down at the sleeping perfection of her daughter, feeling Ardan's love as surely as if his arms were still around her, both of them holding the child they'd created against all odds, Akira found her own peace at last.

Isfail slipped back into the room, meeting her smile with one of his own until he placed his lips on hers. Drawing back slightly, he whispered, "You've received Barash's response."

*H*e stared at the official papers, hardly knowing what to think. Then he read them again. A proclamation of pardon from the House of Coroth: *'for services rendered to the principality and nation of Caldala. All past crimes are held to be redeemed, any culpability assumed as the son of Arthon Baronan for crimes committed by Arthon Baronan, or Abron Baronan, stand as refuted.'*

Then there was the packet containing full and clear deeds to properties legitimately owned by Arthon Baronan within the country of Caldala, including those seized by lawful act of Parliament while his father was a fugitive. Now assigned to Barash as sole owner.

They included Baronan Keep.

Barash could hardly believe it. The only thing he'd wanted, ever, was now his—his because he'd finally stood for himself, for what *he* decided was right.

He looked out over the sea, feeling a burning sensation in his eyes. But the cost had been high. He'd give it all up if it would bring Aron back. Maybe that was the price of past sins.

Then he looked at the woman sitting on the bench nearby. Barash knew she'd lost more than he had, suffered more. Still, her eyes were warm when she looked at him—as if she could see into him, see something worth saving. Because she *had* saved him, physically and in every way that mattered, from the moment he'd first seen her.

They thought he'd fought for freedom, for brotherhood, for redemption of his name. But he knew he'd fought for Akira, for what she believed in, because he could never repay her for what she'd given him. Because she'd found something in him that was worth trusting, and she'd believed in him.

Taking a deep breath, he sat carefully beside her. "Thank you." He lifted the packet of papers.

"You earned that yourself."

He laughed ruefully. "They'd never have done this without you and Isfail standing for me."

Akira's smile turned mischievous. "Maybe." He looked down when her hand closed over his. "You have a chance, Barash. Make the most of it. I believe in you."

Turning his hand, he gripped hers tight. "That's why I have a new start."

For a moment they sat together on the palace terrace, looking toward the sunset colors beginning to spread above the horizon and spill onto the sea.

When Isfail approached with the baby bundled against the ocean breezes, Barash jerked to his feet.

"No need to disturb yourself," Isfail said with amusement, settling Kirdan in Akira's arms. "Sit back down, man," he ordered as he moved to stand behind his wife.

Gingerly resuming his seat, Barash studied the baby whose serious eyes studied him back. He smiled when her tiny hand brushed across her face and she found a finger to suckle, still watching him with those wide green eyes.

"She looks like you, your eyes," he said wonderingly, glancing up into Akira's remarkable eyes. "Part of your legacy. I have to make my own now."

When Isfail placed gentle hands on her shoulders, Akira included him in her smile. "We've both found a better life, Barash. Let's make the most of it."

The End

Legacy of the Bow

Cast of Characters

Adrani—Caldalan Parliament Minister, Green River Caldon
Aira—Sister of Maran, Mother of Akira
Amon—Sail-Maker on *Maid of Kilra*
Amsha, Liden—High Lady of Ocean Cliffs Protectorate
    Former Captain in Gattes Militia
Anaran—Founder of Caldala's Ambassador Core
Aric, Caden—Commander, Ishalian Militia
Arith, Elen—High Ambassador, Reconnaissance Alpha
Arla, Jessa—Senior Master, Mountain Shadows Team Arla
Aroth—Captain, Royal Guard Militia
Ashan—Brother of a Temple on the Ostra River
Asura—Assistant Master, Mountain Shadows Team Kilronan

Barash—Spy, Assassin
Barok, Hadson—Alias of Barash
Baronan, Arda Drinin—Lady, Wife of Arthon
Baronan, Aron—Son of Arthon
Baronan, Arthon—Lord, Exiled Caldalan
Buret—Soldier in Aric's Ishalian Militia Unit

Cadon—Village Elder, Psyche Lakes
Carelon—Senior Master, Mountain Shadows
    Team Carelon   [Care]
Catonina—Chef Juniro's Daughter, Mountain Shadows   [Nina]
Celina—Journeyman, Mountain Shadows Team Kilronan   [Cee]

Cobon—Senior Master, Mountain Shadows Team Cobon
Coran, Isa—High Ambassador, Reconnaissance Alpha
Corcoran, Evan—High Lord of Mountain Shadows Protectorate
Corcoran, Gralla—Lady of Lord Corcoran,
    Mountain Shadows Protectorate
Coronan, Alon—High Ambassador, Reconnaissance Alpha

Danis—Princess, Aunt to Logran, Mother of Ardan Isfail
Darai—Wife of Emmon, Sister of Declan
Dateh, Abron—Leader of The Bow
Declan—Captain, Shanow's Ishalian Militia Unit
Drinin, Aron—High Ambassador, Reconnaissance Alpha

Eaton—Seaman on the *Maid of Kilra*
Emmon—Dock Worker, Tash'tric Harbor, Husband of Darai
Eron—Journeyman, Mountain Shadows Team Kilronan

Felpon—High Minister of Caldala's Parliament
Felcan, Beros—Confidant and Enabler to Abron Dateh

Garan, Daas—Most High Ambassador of Caldala's
    Ambassador Core
Gattes, Davon—Commander, Corsalat Militia
Georen—Lord of Green River Protectorate
Goden, Rados—Commander, Ishalian Militia
Gorth—Senior Ambassador
Grip—Seaman on the *Maid of Kilra*

Haderon, Eson—Administration Guard, Mountain
    Shadows Protectorate
Haill, Garath—Captain, Ishalian Militia
Halen—Assistant Master, Mountain Shadows Team Arla

Illeri, Coron—Ishalian Assassin
Illeri, Maron—Ishalian Assassin
Iro, Akato—Lord Minister, International Services,
    Caldalan Parliament

Iro, Alani—High Ambassador, Reconnaissance Alpha   [Lani]
Isfail, Ardan—Commander, Insalat Militia   [Dan]
Isfail, Armaran—Admiral, Caldalan Royal Navy,
    Father of Ardan
Isheill—Retired Ambassador, Now Celebrated
    Designer in Coroth

Jono—Owner of Inn Near Corsalat, Husband of Rena
Juniro—Head Chef for Mountain Shadows Protectorate

Kalronan—Village Elder, Psyche Lakes
Kalronan, Kalen—High Ambassador,
    Reconnaissance Alpha   [Kal]
Kalronan, Kane—Caldalan Ex-Patriot, Husband
    of Syrai, Father of Kalen
Karsh, Ana—Former Most High Ambassador,
    Stripped of her rank for treason
Kellen, Ala—Jor's Daughter and Barmaid, Mountain Shadows
Kellen, Jor—Pub-master of *The Boar and Panther*,
    Mountain Shadows
Kellan, Lila—Wife of Jor, Mother of Ala
Ketra—Schoolteacher, Corsalat
Kilronan, Aiden—Senior Master, Mountain
    Shadows Team Kilronan   [Kil]
Kilronan, Miden—Retired Militia Commander,
    Father of Aiden and Mara
Kiran—Cousin of Kane, Serenity Valley
Korth, Sheara—Ambassador, Reconnaissance Alpha

Leta—Assistant Master, Mountain Shadows Team Carelon
Lianna—Shopkeeper in Tash'tric
Liza—Barmaid at Inn Near Corsalat
Logran—Prince of Coroth, Also Titled Coroth   [Lo]
Lunow—Senior Ambassador

Maran—Retired Ambassador and Retired Militia Commander
Marca—Senior Master, Mountain Shadows Team Marca
Maronan—Journeyman, Mountain Shadows
    Team Kilronan [Mar]
Micharon, Ivano—High Ambassador, Reconnaissance Alpha
Mika—Master, Mountain Shadows Team Mika
Muro, Aino—Wife of Hiro, Mother to Akira
Muro, Akira—Retired High Ambassador [Kira]
Muro, Hiro—Husband of Aino, Father to Akira

Nathon—Senior Master, Mountain Shadows
    Team Nathon [Nate]
Formerly at Green River Protectorate
Niam—Journeyman, Mountain Shadows Team Cobon
Nolan—Captain in Aric's Ishalian Militia Unit
Norsi, Endra—Captain of the Kilran Cutter, *Black Squall*

Olssen, Garath—Eldest Son of Ryska
Olssen, Ryska—Widow, Sister of Aric, Mother of Garath
Ominor, Minister—Caldalan Parliament, Somara Caldon
Oona—Princess of Coroth, Wife of Logran
Osharon, Daan—Senior Master, Mountain
    Shadows Team Osharon [Shara]
Osharon, Lani—Sister to Osharon of Mountain
    Shadows Protectorate
Oshulta, Fal—Chief-of-Staff, Insalat
Oti, Aito—Ambassador, Reconnaissance Alpha

Pelom—Ishalian Spy in Caldala

Ramort—Schoolmaster, Mountain Shadows
Rena—Barmaid at Inn Near Corsalat, Wife of Jono
Reva, Evani—High Ambassador, Reconnaissance Alpha [Vani]

Saldor—Harbormaster, Tash'tric
Sam—Second Mate of *Maid of Kilra*
Shan—Coach Driver

Shanow, Gaios—Commander, Ishalian Militia
Shanow—Mirastheny, Wife of Gaios
Syrai—Ishakan *Sha'ala*, Leader of the Horse Tribes

Timmel, Avo—Brother of the Temple of Mountain Shadows
Tomon—Coachman
Ton—Son-in-Law of Kane and Syrai, Cousin of Declan
Toth—Commander, Insalat Militia

Vaneer, Sr., Mattoc—Captain of the *Maid of Kilra*,
    Father of Micah
Vaneer, Micah—First Mate on *Maid of Kilra*, Captain
    of *Spirit of the Sea*
Vardon, Master—Mountain Shadows Team Vardon

Wells—Captain of the *Royal Sea Eagle,* the royal
    flagship of the House of Coroth
Wrax—Caldalan Parliament Minister, Southern Fork Caldon

Mors: An invading race of beings with massive telekinetic force powers, from a distant country. The Mors swept the continent in the first book, *The Black Spirit*. They were defeated by then High Ambassador Akira Muro with the help of Team Kilronan, at High Pass before they were able to enter Caldala.

The Bow: The army of rebels originally organized by Arthon Baronan in Ishal to help him take over the country of Ishal. It was revived and expanded by Baronan's son Abron and Beros Felcan to use against Ishal and Caldala. The army consisted of mercenaries, malcontents, and soldiers who'd turned against their country.

Glossary

Lunam: The average number of days of the cycle between a new moon to the next new moon of the larger planetary moon.

Ishakan Words and Meanings

Asherka: My love, feminine form
Asherke: My love, masculine form
Kah'shara: Black Spirit
Le salen se vita longera, Sha'ala Majera: I bring you greetings for a long life, High Priestess.
Na: No
Nah'shalon: A male leader of great power
Sha: True
Sha'ala: The female leader of the Horse Tribes—practically and spiritually

OTHER BOOKS BY THE BLUESTOCKING BELLES

Find buy links and story blurbs for all the following books on our website at https://bluestockingbelles.net/belles-joint-projects/

The Bluestocking Belles donate a portion of the proceeds to benefit the Malala Fund.

A Christmas Quintet (2024)

Five charming stories for your holiday season:

• Friends to Lovers—The farmer's daughter, the viscount's son, and the estate manager reunite as adults. Della is starry-eyed for the viscount's son, but is he really the one for her? (Regency, Christmas)

• Fake Relationship—When the pressure to marry is overwhelming, can a plan put in place at a Christmas house party turn into a love that will last forever? (Regency, Christmas)

• Second-Chance Love—An accident leaves the modiste burned, blinded and in despair until the physician offers hope and stirs memories. (Regency, Christmas)

• Country Mouse and Marriage-Shy Duke—Invited at the last minute to make up the numbers, she expects to be an interested observer. The duke has other ideas. (Georgian, Twelfth Night)

• Two Spies, One Secret—Trapped in a deserted wilderness, will they set aside secrets and past betrayals to rekindle their love and ring in the New Year together? (Medieval, Hogmanay)

Christmastide Kisses (2023)

Six gentlemen and the ladies with whom they discover the power of a Christmastide Kiss.

Under the Harvest Moon (2023)

As the village of Reabridge in Cheshire prepares for the first Harvest Festival following Waterloo, families are overjoyed to welcome back their loved ones from the war.

But excitement quickly turns to mystery when mere weeks before the festival, an orphaned child turns up in the town—a toddler born near Toulouse to an English mother who left clues that tie her to Reabridge.

With two prominent families feuding for generations and the central event of the Harvest Moon festival looming, tensions rise, and secrets begin to surface.

Belles & Beaux (2022)

Just in time for Christmas 2022 comes this boxed set of eight charming stories of love, family, and miracles. Each Belle has contributed a tale set in the festive season—one just long enough to fit in between tasks at this busy time of the year. The tales are unrelated, except by the festive season.

Desperate Daughters (2022)

The Earl of Seahaven desperately wanted a son and heir but died leaving nine daughters and a fifth wife. Cruelly turned out by the new earl, they live hand-to-mouth in a small cottage.

The young dowager Countess's one regret is that she cannot give Seahaven's dear girls a chance at happiness.

When a cousin offers the use of her townhouse in York during the season, the Countess rallies her stepdaughters.

They will pool their resources so that the youngest marriageable daughters might make successful matches, thereby saving them all.

So start their adventures in York, amid a whirl of balls, lectures, and alfresco picnics. Is it possible each of them might find love by the time the York horse races bring the Season to a close?

Belles & Beaux (2022)

Just in time for Christmas 2022 comes this boxed set of eight charming stories of love, family, and miracles. Each Belle has contributed a tale set in the festive season—one just long enough to fit in between tasks at this busy time of the year. The tales are unrelated, except by the festive season.

Some have been written for this collection, some are made-to-order stories never before published, some have been used as fan giveaways. All are delightful.

Storm & Shelter (2021)

OTHER BOOKS BY THE BLUESTOCKING BELLES

Find buy links and story blurbs for all the following books on our website at
https://bluestockingbelles.net/belles-joint-projects/

The Bluestocking Belles donate a portion of the proceeds to benefit the Malala Fund.

A Christmas Quintet (2024)

Five charming stories for your holiday season:

• Friends to Lovers—The farmer's daughter, the viscount's son, and the estate manager reunite as adults. Della is starry-eyed for the viscount's son, but is he really the one for her? (Regency, Christmas)

• Fake Relationship—When the pressure to marry is overwhelming, can a plan put in place at a Christmas house party turn into a love that will last forever? (Regency, Christmas)

• Second-Chance Love—An accident leaves the modiste burned, blinded and in despair until the physician offers hope and stirs memories. (Regency, Christmas)

• Country Mouse and Marriage-Shy Duke—Invited at the last minute to make up the numbers, she expects to be an interested observer. The duke has other ideas. (Georgian, Twelfth Night)

• Two Spies, One Secret—Trapped in a deserted wilderness, will they set aside secrets and past betrayals to rekindle their love and ring in the New Year together? (Medieval, Hogmanay)

Christmastide Kisses (2023)

Six gentlemen and the ladies with whom they discover the power of a Christmastide Kiss.

Under the Harvest Moon (2023)

As the village of Reabridge in Cheshire prepares for the first Harvest Festival following Waterloo, families are overjoyed to welcome back their loved ones from the war.

But excitement quickly turns to mystery when mere weeks before the festival, an orphaned child turns up in the town—a toddler born near Toulouse to an English mother who left clues that tie her to Reabridge.

With two prominent families feuding for generations and the central event of the Harvest Moon festival looming, tensions rise, and secrets begin to surface.

Belles & Beaux (2022)

Just in time for Christmas 2022 comes this boxed set of eight charming stories of love, family, and miracles. Each Belle has contributed a tale set in the festive season—one just long enough to fit in between tasks at this busy time of the year. The tales are unrelated, except by the festive season.

Desperate Daughters (2022)

The Earl of Seahaven desperately wanted a son and heir but died leaving nine daughters and a fifth wife. Cruelly turned out by the new earl, they live hand-to-mouth in a small cottage.

The young dowager Countess's one regret is that she cannot give Seahaven's dear girls a chance at happiness.

When a cousin offers the use of her townhouse in York during the season, the Countess rallies her stepdaughters.

They will pool their resources so that the youngest marriageable daughters might make successful matches, thereby saving them all.

So start their adventures in York, amid a whirl of balls, lectures, and alfresco picnics. Is it possible each of them might find love by the time the York horse races bring the Season to a close?

Belles & Beaux (2022)

Just in time for Christmas 2022 comes this boxed set of eight charming stories of love, family, and miracles. Each Belle has contributed a tale set in the festive season—one just long enough to fit in between tasks at this busy time of the year. The tales are unrelated, except by the festive season.

Some have been written for this collection, some are made-to-order stories never before published, some have been used as fan giveaways. All are delightful.

Storm & Shelter (2021)